WEREWOLVES

AND
SHAPESHIFTERS

ENCOUNTERS WITH THE BEAST WITHIN

EDITED WITH COMMENTARY BY

JOHN SKIPP

BLACK DOG
& LEVENTHAL
PUBLISHERS
NEW YORK

Library of Congress Cataloging-in-Publication Data available upon request.

Published by Black Dog & Leventhal Publishers, Inc.
151 West 19th Street, New York, NY 10011

Distributed by Workman Publishing Company
225 Varick Street, New York, NY 10014

Design by Red Herring Design
Art by Tom Singer, Barn Door Studios
Printed in the United States
ISBN: 978-1-57912-852-4

h g f e d c b a

For Scooby Hamilton
(a.k.a. "Scampers McFadden")
and every love-beast on this Earth.

CONTENTS
1855

TABLE OF CONTENTS

TO WALK ON FOUR LEGS
BREAKS THE LAW
(AND THAT'S ALL RIGHT WITH ME)

AN UNCIVILIZED INTRODUCTION BY JOHN SKIPP

This is a book of astounding stories.

That's really all you need to know.

But since the subject is, of course, this whole werewolf/shapeshifter situation we're in—what with everybody and his cousin transforming willy-nilly, whether the full moon is up or not—it probably behooves me to set the mood, if not spill the beans entirely.

Secrets are part of the thrill of this ride, after all. Secrets and surprises, of which there will be many, I sincerely guarantee you.

Please feel free to slip into something a little more comfortable, while we're at it. Shed your skin, or grow a new one.

Around these parts—and within these pages—it's okay to let it all hang out.

It's also okay to be afraid. In fact, you'd have to be crazy not to. It's a scary-ass world out here.

But this is how we learn.

In the great pantheon of miracles and monsterdom, werewolves and other shape-shiftery types hold a special fascination, as shown by their enduring popularity: from ancient folklore and fairy tale to modern fantasy, paranormal romance, science fiction, horror, magical realism, black comic satire, and the freakiest Bizarro hinterlands known to man or beast.

Because they are both us and something profoundly other—something primal, just waiting to erupt and disrupt us from within—there's an amazing complexity and complicity in their stories that you don't get much of anywhere else.

Werecreatures are largely monsters of impulse and instinct. They are us, forced by forces beyond our control to do the things we either fear we might or wish we could, depending on how crazy and/or grounded we are at the time.

As such, they specifically pinpoint the schism between our natural selves and our socialized selves.

Who we'd like to think we are.

And what we suspect we might actually be.

In the process of probing that schism, and assembling this book, I've been thinking a lot about animals. The ones we're okay with. The ones we are not. The ones that we're friends with. The ones that we eat.

And the ones that would more-than-happily devour us instead, given half a chance.

In an awful lot of ways, civilization has evolved specifically to narrow the odds on getting eaten alive by any other species. It certainly started out that way: lonely, too-smart, all-but-hairless hominids, huddling together in the terrifying dark and desperately dreaming of fire, of spear, of safety from the bottomless tyranny of terror. Dreaming our way out of the nightmare that God had seemingly abandoned us inside: a monstrous world of tooth and claw, in which we were more often than not the prey.

You gotta know, this is where our deepest cellular memories of horror are rooted: in the creatures that shredded our earliest ancestors. The sights and sounds and smells of them are forever etched upon our DNA.

That ancestral dread resonates through us still, in both our bodies and in the stories we tell—and have always told—to ourselves, and each other.

Depending on where we lived, our natural predators were our monsters. In the jungle, you had your panthers and pythons. In the veldt, lions reigned. Bears ruled the tundra. If you lived on the water, it could be sharks or piranha.

In the forest, it was the wolf that you feared most.

But because we're such clever mammals, we learned from the creatures that surrounded us. Modeled useful behaviors. Came to recognize the unique advantages presented by our thumbs and brains. Differentiated ourselves from all other life forms. Shoved the Us vs. Them wedge in place.

But we always knew that we were animals, too. Vibrantly animal. Disgustingly animal.

This was the beginning of the schism, and the law.

As time went on, and we pulled our act together, humanity proceeded to seize the reins. Fire was a neat trick. Electricity worked, too. Horticulture. Agriculture. Science, science, science. Eventually leading to the harnessing of all our natural resources. Domestication of the previously random and wild.

These are the things in which we, as a species, have utterly excelled.

And the weapons. Oh, the weapons. We've gotten reeeeeally good at that. Once we figured out how to take down creatures far larger and more physically imposing than ourselves—once the ruthless elimination of our natural predators commenced in earnest—the world became our own little oyster: a glistening thing that we ripped from a shell, deliciously going down with little to no resistance.

At this point, on this Earth, humanity's the uncontested champ. WE'RE NUMBER ONE! The number one predator. Western civilization, in particular, has long and largely defined itself as a war on nature's dominance, if not on nature itself. And who can argue with success?

So these days, we're only allowed to eat one another. And only in a figurative sense. We do it through business. We do it through family. We do it through government, through armies, through crime. We do it through love, that great crime of passion. We abstract it as much as we possibly can.

But if we do it straight up—if we actually tear one another limb from limb, and feast on the entrails—there's a word for that.

Monster.

The good news—here in the twenty-first century—is that it's pretty much a dog-eat-dog food world. The bulk of us have turned out to be fairly well-behaved, or at least have the veneer down pat. Violence is news because it bursts the normative bubble, rips a hole in the social fabric that we use to cover our nakedness.

So unless you're a soldier in midconflagration, an insurgent/terrorist with a bomb strapped to your back, a serial killer in full psychotic spree, a renegade cop on their winner-take-all trail, or one of the weird things displayed proudly within the pages of this book, I'd say the odds are good that you probably didn't kill nearly half the people that you met today!

That math pretty well speaks for itself.

HOORAY FOR SOCIETY!

But civilization is a mighty long crawl, through the tangled roots of history and our own conflicted nature. It's not a coincidence that we call our cities jungles, and also refer to those who break the rules in monstrous ways as "animals".

And this, my friends, is the heart of the werething's allure.

The animal within us—the so-called monster within us—that harkens back to our core, in oh-so-many beautiful and terrifying ways.

Because that's the thing: it's not all bad. Yes, for some, it's a curse. But for others, it's a total liberation.

There's a genuine longing that many of us feel to reconnect with the nature our technocracy has spurned. To dive deep into our senses, shut down the backseat driver of our endlessly-yammering rational minds, and just for God's sake *be*.

It's the thing that makes us envy our pets, watch in awestruck silence as a hawk soars overhead. It's also the secret behind our love of sports, of watching two boxers beat each other to pulp.

At root, it's a hunger for simplicity, for connectedness. A purer sense of self, society be damned.

And therein lies the blood-red schism at the core of our malaise. And maybe—just maybe—the key to our transcendence.

It's a scary-ass world out here.

But this is how we learn.

We'll further discuss the roots of all this, and catalog some of the seminal works, in the nifty-yet-informative appendices you'll find at the back of the book. And I'll be sprinkling context and observations throughout the text that follows.

But the heart of this book—and its sprawling soul—is contained in the thirty-odd stories that follow. Astounding stories that wrestle both playfully and savagely with the shape-shifting subject at hand.

This is a full-spectrum showcase of excellent strangeness, drawing on the full strengths of every type of imaginative literature at play in the culture today. There are heartbreakers here, and genuine shockers. There are sweet-hearted charmers and raucous laugh-out-loud subversions. Inarguable art, and unapologetic entertainment.

Roughly half of them are original to this collection, here blowing minds for the very first time. The rest are split between time-honored classics and little-known wonders you may have missed.

Guaranteed, there is something here to offend and delight every reader, sometimes in the course of a single sentence.

What they all have in common is a penetrating glimpse of the animal we are, the jungle we inhabit, and the civilized species we'd like to hope we have become.

Which is why I so thoroughly love this book, jam-packed as it is with brilliant writers both old and new, all of them vividly tackling the mysteries of nature and identity, society and self.

And mutating our perceptions like a sonofabitch, in the process.

This is how we learn to become ourselves, at last.

Enjoy your transformation.

THE COMPANY OF WOLVES

BY ANGELA CARTER

Our journey begins in the woods, as well it should: a ravishing sensorial fairy-tale forest—profoundly alive, overflowing with myth and magic and meaning—where the stories we tell are as real as the eyes that watch us from the shadows.

It is here that the brilliant Angela Carter sought to "extract the latent content" from traditional folktales (as, in this case, Little Red Riding Hood). At this she wildly succeeded, with exhilarating wordplay and pierced layer-upon-layer of penetrating insight, breaking the rules of language and lore wherever it suited her purposes.

I was stunned upon first reading this story, having only seen the film of the same name, which she coauthored with the director Neil Jordan. Stunned not just by its greatness, its singular vision, but by how much of that astonishing film was contained in these few short pages.

One beast, and only one, howls in the woods by night.

The wolf is carnivore incarnate and he's as cunning as he is ferocious; once he's had a taste of flesh then nothing else will do.

At night, the eyes of wolves shine like candle flames, yellowish, reddish, but that is because the pupils of their eyes fatten on darkness and catch the light from your lantern to flash it back to you—red for danger; if a wolf's eyes reflect only moonlight, then they gleam a cold and unnatural green, a mineral, a piercing color. If the benighted traveler spies those luminous, terrible sequins stitched suddenly on the black thickets, then he knows he must run, if fear has not struck him stock-still.

But those eyes are all you will be able to glimpse of the forest assassins as they cluster invisibly round your smell of meat as you go through the wood unwisely late. They will be like shadows, they will be like wraiths, grey members of a congregation of nightmare; hark! his long, wavering howl. . .an aria of fear made audible.

The wolfsong is the sound of the rending you will suffer, in itself a murdering.

It is winter and cold weather. In this region of mountain and forest, there is now nothing for the wolves to eat. Goats and sheep are locked up in the byre, the deer departed for the remaining pasturage on the southern slopes—wolves grow lean and famished. There is so little flesh on them that you could count the starveling ribs through their pelts, if they gave you to me before they pounced. Those slavering jaws; the lolling tongue; the rim of saliva on the grizzled chops— of all the teeming perils of the night and the forest, ghosts, hobgoblins, ogres that grill babies upon gridirons, witches that fatten their captives in cages for cannibal tables, the wolf is worst for he cannot listen to reason.

You are always in danger in the forest, where no people are. Step between the portals of the great pines where the shaggy branches tangle about you, trapping the unwary traveler in nets as if the vegetation itself were in a plot with the wolves who live there, as though the wicked trees go fishing on behalf of their friends— step between the gateposts of the forest with the greatest trepidation and infinite precautions, for if you stray from the path for one instant, the wolves will eat you. They are grey as famine, they are as unkind as plague.

The grave-eyed children of the sparse villages always carry knives with them when they go to tend the little flocks of goats that provide the homesteads with acrid milk and rank, maggoty cheese. Their knives are half as big as they are, the blades are sharpened daily.

But the wolves have ways of arriving at your own hearthside. We try and try but sometimes we cannot keep them out. There is no winter's night the cottager does not fear to see a lean, grey, famished snout questing under the door, and there was a woman once bitten in her own kitchen as she was straining the macaroni.

Fear and flee the wolf; for, worst of all, the wolf may be more than he seems.

There was a hunter once, near here, who trapped a wolf in a pit. This wolf had massacred the sheep and goats; eaten up a mad old man who used to live by himself in a hut halfway up the mountain and sang to Jesus all day; pounced on a girl looking after the sheep, but she made such a commotion that men came with rifles and scared him away and tried to track him to the forest but he was cunning and easily gave them the slip. So this hunter dug a pit and put a duck in it, for bait, all alive-oh; and he covered the pit with straw smeared with wolf-dung. Quack, quack! went the duck and a wolf came slinking out of the forest, a big one, a heavy one; he weighed as much as a grown man and the straw gave way beneath him—into the pit he tumbled. The hunter jumped down after him, slit his throat, cut off all his paws for a trophy.

And then no wolf at all lay in front of the hunter but the bloody trunk of a man, headless, footless, dying, dead.

A witch from up the valley once turned an entire wedding party into wolves because the groom had settled on another girl. She used to order them to visit her, at night, from spite, and they would sit and howl around her cottage for her, serenading her with their misery.

Not so very long ago, a young woman in our village married a man who vanished clean away on her wedding night. The bed was made with new sheets and the bride lay down in it; the groom said, he was going out to relieve himself, insisted on it, for the sake of decency, and she drew the coverlet up to her chin and lay there. And she waited and she waited and then she waited again—surely he's been gone a long time? Until she jumps up in bed and shrieks to hear a howling, coming on the wind from the forest.

That long-drawn, wavering howl has, for all its fearful resonance, some inherent sadness in it, as if the beasts would love to be less beastly if only they knew how and never cease to mourn their own condition. There is a vast melancholy in the canticles of the wolves, melancholy infinite as the forest, endless as these long nights of winter and yet that ghastly sadness, that mourning for their own, irremediable appetites, can never move the heart for not one phrase in it hints at the possibility of redemption; grace could not come to the wolf from its own despair, only through some external mediator, so that, sometimes, the beast will look as if he half welcomes the knife that dispatches him.

The young woman's brothers searched the outhouses and the haystacks but never found any remains so the sensible girl dried her eyes and found herself another husband not too shy to piss into a pot who spent the night indoors. She gave him a pair of bonny babies and all went right as a trivet until, one freezing night, the night of the solstice, the hinge of the year when things do not fit together as well as they should, the longest night, her first good man came home again.

A great thump on the door announced him as she was stirring the soup for the father of her children and she knew him the moment she lifted the latch to him although it was years since she'd worn black for him and now he was in rags and his hair hung down his back and never saw a comb, alive with lice.

"Here I am again, missus," he said. "Get me my bowl of cabbage and be quick about it."

Then her second husband came in with wood for the fire and when the first one saw she'd slept with another man and, worse, clapped his red eyes on her little children who'd crept into the kitchen to see what all the din was about, he shouted: 'I wish I were a wolf again, to teach this whore a lesson!' So a wolf he instantly became and tore off the eldest boy's left foot before he was chopped by the hatchet they used for chopping logs. But when the wolf lay bleeding and gasping its last, the pelt peeled off again and he was just as he had been, years ago, when he ran away from his marriage bed, so that she wept and her second husband beat her.

They say there's an ointment the Devil gives you that turns you into a wolf the minute you rub it on. Or, that he was born feet first and had a wolf for his father and his torso is a man's but his legs and genitals are a wolf's. And he has a wolf's heart.

Seven years is a werewolf's natural span but if you burn his human clothes, you condemn him to wolfishness for the rest of his life; so old wives hereabouts think it some protection to throw a hat or an apron at the werewolf, as if clothes made the man. Yet by the eyes, those phosphorescent eyes, you know him in all his shapes; the eyes alone unchanged by metamorphosis.

Before he can become a wolf, the lycanthrope strips stark naked. If you spy a naked man among the pines, you must run as if the Devil were after you.

It is midwinter and the robin, the friend of man, sits on the handle of the gardener's spade and sings. It is the worst time in all the year for wolves but this strong-minded child insists she will go off through the wood. She is quite sure the wild beasts cannot harm her although, well-warned, she lays a carving knife in the basket her mother has packed with cheeses. There is a bottle of harsh liquor distilled from brambles; a batch of flat oatcakes baked on the heathstone; a pot or two of jam. The girl will take these delicious gifts to a reclusive grandmother so old the burden of her years is crushing her to death. Granny lives two hours' trudge through the winter woods; the child wraps herself up in her thick shawl, draws it over her head. She steps into her stout wooden shoes; she is dressed and ready and it is Christmas Eve. The malign door of the solstice still swings upon its hinges but she has been too much loved ever to feel scared.

Children do not stay young for long in this savage country. There are no toys for them to play with so they work hard and grow wise, but this one, so pretty and the youngest of her family, a little late-comer, had been indulged by her mother and the grandmother who'd knitted her the red shawl that, today, has the ominous if brilliant look of blood on snow. Her breasts have just begun to swell; her hair is like lint, so fair it hardly makes a shadow on her pale forehead; her cheeks are an emblematic scarlet and white and she has just started her woman's bleeding, the clock inside her that will strike, henceforward, once a month.

She stands and moves within the invisible pentacle of her own virginity. She is an unbroken egg; she is a sealed vessel; she has inside her a magic space the entrance to which is shut tight with a plug of membrane; she is a closed system; she does not know how to shiver. She has her knife and she is afraid of nothing.

Her father might forbid her, if he were home, but he is away in the forest, gathering wood, and her mother cannot deny her.

The forest closed upon her like a pair of jaws.

There is always something to look at in the forest, even in the middle of winter—the huddled mounds of birds, succumbed to the lethargy of the season, heaped on the creaking boughs and too forlorn to sing; the bright frills of the winter fungi on the blotched trunks of the trees; the cuneiform slots of rabbits and deer, the herringbone tracks of the birds, a hare as lean as a rasher of bacon streaking across the path where the thin sunlight dapples the russet brakes of last year's bracken.

When she heard the freezing howl of a distant wolf, her practiced hand sprang to the handle of her knife, but she saw no sign of a wolf at all, nor of a naked man, neither, but then she heard a clattering among the brushwood and there sprang on to the path a fully clothed one, a very handsome young one, in the green coat and wide awake hat of a hunter, laden with carcasses of game birds. She had her hand on her knife at the first rustle of twigs but he laughed with a flash of white teeth when he saw her and made her a comic yet flattering little bow; she'd never seen such a fine fellow before, not among the rustic clowns of her native village. So on they went, through the thickening light of the afternoon.

Soon they were laughing and joking like old friends. When he offered to carry her basket, she gave it to him although her knife was in it because he told her his rifle would protect them. As the day darkened, it began to snow again; she felt the first flakes settle on her eyelashes but now there was only half a mile to go and there would be a fire, and hot tea, and a welcome, a warm one surely, for the dashing huntsman as well as for herself.

This young man had a remarkable object in his pocket. It was a compass. She looked at the little round glassface in the palm of his hand and watched the wavering needle with a vague wonder. He assured her this compass had taken him safely through the wood on his hunting trip because the needle always told him with perfect accuracy where the north was. She did not believe it; she knew she should never leave the path on the way through the wood or else she would be lost instantly. He laughed at her again; gleaming trails of spittle clung to his teeth. He said, if he plunged off the path into the forest that surrounded them, he would guarantee to arrive at her grandmother's house a good quarter of an hour before she did, plotting his way through the undergrowth with his compass, while she trudged the long way, along the winding path.

I don't believe you. Besides, aren't you afraid of the wolves?

He only tapped the gleaming butt of his rifle and grinned.

Is it a bet? he asked her. Shall we make a game of it? What will you give me if I get to your grandmother's house before you?

What would you like? she asked disingenuously.

A kiss.

Commonplaces of a rustic seduction; she lowered her eyes and blushed.

He went through the undergrowth and took her basket with him but she forgot to be afraid of the beasts, although now the moon was rising, for she wanted to dawdle on her way to make sure the handsome gentleman would win his wager.

Grandmother's house stood by itself a little way out of the village. The freshly falling snow blew in eddies about the kitchen garden and the Youngman stepped delicately up the snowy path to the door as if he were reluctant to get his feet wet, swinging his bundle of game and the girl's basket and humming a little tune to himself.

There is a faint trace of blood on his chin; he has been snacking on his catch.

He rapped upon the panels with his knuckles.

Aged and frail, granny is three-quarters succumbed to the mortality the ache in her bones promises her and almost ready to give in entirely. A boy came out from the village to build up her hearth for the night an hour ago and the kitchen crackles with busy firelight. She has her Bible for company, she is a pious old woman. She is propped up on several pillows in the bed set into the wall peasant-fashion. Wrapped up in the patchwork quilt she made before she was married, more years ago than she cares to remember. Two china spaniels with liver-colored blotches on their coats and black noses sit on either side of the fireplace. There is a bright rug of woven rags on the pantiles. The grandfather clock ticks away her eroding time.

We keep the wolves outside by living well.

He rapped upon the panels with his hairy knuckles.

It is your granddaughter, he mimicked in a high soprano.

Lift up the latch and walk in, my darling.

You can tell them by their eyes, eyes of a beast of prey, nocturnal, devastating eyes as red as a wound; you can hurl your Bible at him and your apron after, granny, you thought that was a sure prophylactic against these infernal vermin. . . now call on Christ and his mother and all the angels in heaven to protect you but it won't do you any good.

His feral muzzle is sharp as a knife; he drops his golden burden of gnawed pheasant on the table and puts down your dear girl's basket, too. Oh, my God, what have you done with her?

Off with his disguise, that coat of forest-colored cloth, the hat with the feather tucked into the ribbon; his matted hair streams down his white shirt and she can see the lice moving in it. The sticks in the hearth shift and hiss; night and the forest has come into the kitchen with darkness tangled in its hair.

He strips off his shirt. His skin is the color and texture of vellum. A crisp stripe of hair runs down his belly, his nipples are ripe and dark as poison fruit but he's so thin you could count the ribs under his skin if only he gave you the time. He strips off his trousers and she can see how hairy his legs are. His genitals, huge. Ah! huge.

The last thing the old lady saw in all this world was a young man, eyes like cinders, naked as a stone, approaching her bed.

The wolf is carnivore incarnate.

When he had finished with her, he licked his chops and quickly dressed himself again, until he was just as he had been when he came through her door. He burned the inedible hair in the fireplace and wrapped the bones up in a napkin that he hid away under the bed in the wooden chest in which he found a clean pair of sheets. These he carefully put on the bed instead of the tell-tale stained ones he had stowed away in the laundry basket. He plumped up the pillows and shook out the patchwork quilt, he picked up the Bible from the floor, closed it and laid it on the table. All was as it had been before except that grandmother was gone. The sticks twitched in the grate, the clock ticked and the young man sat patiently, deceitfully beside the bed in granny's nightcap.

Rat-a-tap-tap.

Who's there, he quavers in granny's antique falsetto.

Only your granddaughter.

So she came in, bringing with her a flurry of snow that melted in tears on the tiles, and perhaps she was a little disappointed to see only her grandmother sitting beside the fire. But then he flung off the blanket and sprang to the door, pressing his back against it so that she could not get out again.

The girl looked round the room and saw there was not even the indentation of a head on the smooth cheek of the pillow and how, for the first time she'd seen it so, the Bible lay closed on the table. The tick of the clock cracked like a whip. She wanted her knife from her basket but she did not dare to reach for it because his eyes were fixed upon her—huge eyes that now seemed to shine with a unique, interior light, eyes the size of saucers, saucers full of Greek fire, diabolic phosphorescence.

What big eyes you have.

All the better to see you with.

No trace at all of the old woman except for a tuft of white hair that had caught in the bark of an unburned log. When the girl saw that, she knew she was in danger of death.

Where is my grandmother?

There's nobody here but we two, my darling.

Now a great howling rose up all around them, near, very near, as close as the kitchen garden, the howling of a multitude of wolves; she knew the worst wolves are hairy on the inside and she shivered, in spite of the scarlet shawl she pulled more closely round herself as if it could protect her although it was as red as the blood she must spill.

Who has come to sing us carols, she said.

Those are the voices of my brothers, darling; I love the company of wolves. Look out of the window and you'll see them.

Snow half-caked the lattice and she opened it to look into the garden. It was a white night of moon and snow; the blizzard whirled round the gaunt, grey beasts who squatted on their haunches among the rows of winter cabbage, pointing their sharp snouts to the moon and howling as if their hearts would break. Ten wolves; twenty wolves—so many wolves she could not count them, howling in concert as if demented or deranged. Their eyes reflected the light from the kitchen and shone like a hundred candles.

It is very cold, poor things, she said; no wonder they howl so.

She closed the window on the wolves' threnody and took off her scarlet shawl, the color of poppies, the color of sacrifices, the color of her menses, and, since her fear did her no good, she ceased to be afraid.

What shall I do with my shawl?

Throw it on the fire, dear one. You won't need it again.

She bundled up her shawl and threw it on the blaze, which instantly consumed it. Then she drew her blouse over her head; her small breasts gleamed as if the snow had invaded the room.

What shall I do with my blouse?

Into the fire with it, too, my pet.

The thin muslin went flaring up the chimney like a magic bird and now off came her skirt, her woolen stockings, her shoes, and on to the fire they went, too, and were gone for good. The firelight shone through the edges of her skin; now she was clothed only in her untouched integument of flesh. Thus dazzling, naked she combed out her hair with her fingers; her hair looked white as the snow outside. Then went directly to the man with red eyes in whose unkempt mane the lice moved; she stood up on tiptoe and unbuttoned the collar of his shirt.

What big arms you have.

All the better to hug you with.

Every wolf in the world now howled a prothalamion outside the window as she freely gave him the kiss she owed him.

What big teeth you have!

She saw how his jaw began to slaver and the room was full of the clamor of the forest's *Liebestod* but the wise child never flinched, even as he answered: All the better to eat you with.

The girl burst out laughing; she knew she was nobody's meat. She laughed at him full in the face, she ripped off his shirt for him and flung it into the fire, in the fiery wake of her own discarded clothing. The flames danced like dead souls on

Walpursignacht and the old bones under the bed set up a terrible clattering but she did not pay them any heed.

Carnivore incarnate, only immaculate flesh appeases him.

She will lay his fearful head on her lap and she will pick out the lice from his pelt and perhaps she will put the lice into her mouth and eat them, as he will bid her, as she would do in a savage marriage ceremony.

The blizzard will die down.

The blizzard died down, leaving the mountains as randomly covered with snow as if a blind woman had thrown a sheet over them, the upper branches of the forest pines limed, creaking, swollen with the fall.

Snowlight, moonlight, a confusion of paw-prints.

All silent, all silent.

Midnight; and the clock strikes. It is Christmas day, the werewolves' birthday, the door of the solstice stands wide open; let them all sink through.

See! sweet and sound she sleeps in granny's bed, between the paws of the tender wolf.

THE OTHER SIDE: A BRETON LEGEND

BY COUNT ERIC STANISLAUS STENBOCK

"The Other Side" is the oldest tale unveiled in this collection, and one of the weirdest and wildest: a vintage mushroom slice of psychedelic subversion circa 1893.

It was written by Count Stenbock, a fascinating trust-fund aristocrat, decadent poet, and all-around free thinker whose deep well of talent went largely untapped throughout the course of his all-too-brief adventure on Earth.

This little stunner, published two years before his passing, catches the Count at his most fantastic in every sense of the word: juxtaposing the young Church against a primal delirium one can still taste across the ages.

"Not that I like it, but one does feel so much better after it—oh, thank you, Mère Yvonne, yes, just a little drop more." So the old crones fell to drinking their hot brandy and water (although of course they only took it medicinally, as a remedy for their rheumatics), all seated round the big fire and Mère Pinquèle continued her story.

"Oh, yes, then when they get to the top of the hill, there is an altar with six candles quite black and a sort of something in between, that nobody sees quite clearly, and the old black ram with the man's face and long horns begins to say Mass in a sort of gibberish nobody understands, and two black strange things like monkeys glide about with the book and the cruets—and there's music too, such music. There are things the top-half like black cats, and the bottom-part like men only their legs are all covered with close black hair, and they play on the bag-pipes, and when they come to the elevation, then ——" Amid the old crones there was lying on the hearth-rug, before the fire, a boy whose large lovely eyes dilated and whose limbs quivered in the very ecstasy of terror.

"Is that all true, Mère Pinquèle?" he said.

"Oh, quite true, and not only that, the best part is yet to come; for they take a child and ——." Here Mère Pinquèle showed her fang-like teeth.

"Oh! Mère Pinquèle, are you a witch too?"

"Silence, Gabriel," said Mère Yvonne, "how can you say anything so wicked? Why, bless me, the boy ought to have been in bed ages ago."

Just then all shuddered, and all made the sign of the cross except Mère Pinquèle, for they heard that most dreadful of dreadful sounds—the howl of a wolf, which begins with three sharp barks and then lifts itself up in a long protracted wail of commingled cruelty and despair, and at last subsides into a whispered growl fraught with eternal malice.

There was a forest and a village and a brook; the village was on one side of the brook, none had dared to cross to the other side. Where the village was, all was green and glad and fertile and fruitful; on the other side the trees never put forth green leaves, and a dark shadow hung over it even at noon-day, and in the night-time one could hear the wolves howling—the were-wolves and the wolf-men and the men-wolves, and those very wicked men who for nine days in every year are turned into wolves; but on the green side no wolf was ever seen, and only one little running brook like a silver streak flowed between.

It was spring now and the old crones sat no longer by the fire but before their cottages sunning themselves, and everyone felt so happy that they ceased to tell stories of the "other side." But Gabriel wandered by the brook as he was wont to wander, drawn thither by some strange attraction mingled with intense horror.

His schoolfellows did not like Gabriel; all laughed and jeered at him, because he was less cruel and more gentle of nature than the rest, and even as a rare and beautiful bird escaped from a cage is hacked to death by the common sparrows, so was Gabriel among his fellows. Everyone wondered how Mère Yvonne, that buxom and worthy matron, could have produced a son like this, with strange dreamy eyes, who was as they said *"pas comme les autres gamins."* His only friends were the Abbé Félicien whose Mass he served each morning, and one little girl called Carmeille, who loved him, no one could make out why.

The sun had already set. Gabriel still wandered by the brook, filled with vague terror and irresistible fascination. The sun set and the moon rose, the full moon, very large and very clear, and the moonlight flooded the forest both this side and "the other side," and just on the "other side" of the brook, hanging over, Gabriel saw a large deep blue flower, whose strange intoxicating perfume reached him and fascinated him even where he stood.

"If I could only make one step across," he thought, "nothing could harm me if I only plucked that one flower, and nobody would know I had been over at all," for the villagers looked with hatred and suspicion on anyone who was said to have crossed to the "other side," so summing up courage he leapt lightly to the other side of the brook. Then the moon breaking from a cloud shone with unusual brilliance, and he saw, stretching before him, long reaches of the same strange blue flowers, each one lovelier than the last, til, not being able to make up his mind which one flower to take or whether to take several, he went on and on, and the moon shone very brightly and a strange unseen bird, somewhat like a nightingale, but louder and lovelier, sang, and his heart was filled with longing for he knew not what, and the moon shone and the nightingale sang. But all of a sudden a black cloud covered the moon entirely, and all was black, utter darkness, and through the darkness he heard wolves howling and shrieking in the hideous ardour of the chase, and there passed before him a horrible procession of wolves (black wolves with red fiery eyes), and with them men that had the heads of wolves and wolves that had the heads of men, and above them flew owls (black owls with red fiery eyes), and bats and long serpentine black things, and last of all seated on an enormous black ram with hideous human face the wolf-keeper on whose face was eternal shadow; but they continued their horrid chase and passed him by, and when they had passed the moon shone out more beautiful than ever, and the strange nightingale sang again, and the strange intense blue flowers were in long reaches in front to the right and to the left. But one thing was there that had not been before, among the deep blue flowers walked one with long gleaming golden hair, and she turned once round and her eyes were of the same colour as the strange blue flowers, and she walked on and Gabriel could not choose but follow. But when a cloud passed over the moon he saw no beautiful woman but a wolf, so in utter terror he turned and fled, plucking one of the strange blue flowers on the way, and leapt again over the brook and ran home.

When he got home Gabriel could not resist showing his treasure to his mother, though he knew she would not appreciate it; but when she saw the strange blue flower, Mère Yvonne turned pale and said, "Why child, where hast thou been? Sure it is the witch flower"; and so saying she snatched it from him and cast it into the corner, and immediately all its beauty and strange fragrance faded from it and it looked charred as though it had been burnt. So Gabriel sat down silently and rather sulkily, and having eaten no supper went up to bed, but he did not sleep but waited and waited till all was quiet within the house. Then he crept downstairs in his long white night-shirt and bare feet on the square cold stones and picked hurriedly up the charred and faded flower and put it in his warm bosom next to his heart, and immediately the flower bloomed again lovelier than ever, and he fell into a deep sleep, but through his sleep he seemed to hear a soft low voice singing underneath his window in a strange language (in which the subtle sounds melted into one another), but he could distinguish no word except his own name.

When he went forth in the morning to serve Mass, he still kept the flower with him next to his heart. Now when the priest began Mass and said "*Intriobo ad altare Dei*," then said Gabriel "*Qui nequiquam laetificavit juventutem meam*." And the Abbé Félicien turned round on hearing this strange response, and he saw the boy's face deadly pale, his eyes fixed and his limbs rigid, and as the priest looked on him Gabriel fell fainting to the floor, so the sacristan had to carry him home and seek another acolyte for the Abbé Félicien.

Now when the Abbé Félicien came to see after him, Gabriel felt strangely reluctant to say anything about the blue flower and for the first time he deceived the priest.

In the afternoon as sunset drew nigh he felt better and Carmeille came to see him and begged him to go out with her into the fresh air. So they went out hand in hand, the dark haired, gazelle-eyed boy, and the fair wavy-haired girl, and something, he knew not what, led his steps (half knowingly and yet not so, for he could not but walk thither) to the brook, and they sat down together on the bank.

Gabriel thought at least he might tell his secret to Carmeille, so he took out the flower from his bosom and said, "Look here, Carmeille, hast thou seen ever so lovely a flower as this?" but Carmeille turned pale and faint and said, "Oh, Gabriel what is this flower? I but touched it and I felt something strange come over me. No, no, I don't like its perfume, no there's something not quite right about it, oh, dear Gabriel, do let me throw it away," and before he had time to answer, she cast it from her, and again all its beauty and fragrance went from it and it looked charred as though it had been burnt. But suddenly where the flower had been thrown on this side of the brook, there appeared a wolf, which stood and looked at the children.

Carmeille said, "What shall we do," and clung to Gabriel, but the wolf looked at them very steadfastly and Gabriel recognized in the eyes of the wolf the strange deep intense blue eyes of the wolf-woman he had seen on the "other side," so he said, "Stay here, dear Carmeille, see she is looking gently at us and will not hurt us."

"But it is a wolf," said Carmeille, and quivered all over with fear, but again Gabriel said languidly, "She will not hurt us." Then Carmeille seized Gabriel's hand in an agony of terror and dragged him along with her till they reached the village, where she gave the alarm and all the lads of the village gathered together.

They had never seen a wolf on this side of the brook, so they excited themselves greatly and arranged a grand wolf hunt for the morrow, but Gabriel sat silently apart and said no word.

That night Gabriel could not sleep at all nor could he bring himself to say his prayers; but he sat in his little room by the window with his shirt open at the throat and the strange blue flower at his heart and again this night he heard a voice singing beneath his window in the same soft, subtle, liquid language as before —

> *"Ma zála liral va jé*
> *Cwamûlo zhajéla je*
> *Cárma urádi el javé*
> *Járma, symai,- carmé—*
> *Zhála javály thra je*
> *al vú al vlaûle va azré*
> *Safralje vairálje va já?*
> *Cárma serâja*
> *Lâja*
> *lâja Luzhà!"*

and as he looked he could see the silvern shadows slide on the limmering light of golden hair, and the strange eyes gleaming dark blue through the night and it seemed to him that he could not but follow; so he walked half clad and bare foot as he was with eyes fixed as in a dream silently down the stairs and out into the night.

And ever and again she turned to look on him with her strange blue eyes full of tenderness and passion and sadness beyond the sadness of things human—and as he foreknew his steps led him to the brink of the brook. Then she, taking his hand, familiarly said, "Won't you help me over, Gabriel?"

Then it seemed to him as though he had known her all his life—so he went with her to the "other side" but he saw no one by him; and looking again beside him there were two wolves. In a frenzy of terror, he (who had never thought to kill any living thing before) seized a log of wood lying by and smote one of the wolves on the head.

Immediately he saw the wolf-woman again at his side with blood streaming from her forehead, staining her wonderful golden hair, and with eyes looking at him with infinite reproach, she said—"Who did this?"

Then she whispered a few words to the other wolf, which leapt over the brook and made its way towards the village, and turning again towards him she said, "Oh Gabriel, how could you strike me, who would have loved you so long and so well." Then it seemed to him again as though he had known her all his life but he felt dazed and said nothing—but she gathered a dark green strangely shaped leaf and holding it to her forehead, she said—"Gabriel, kiss the place, all will be well again." So he kissed as she had bidden him and he felt the salt taste of blood in his mouth and then he knew no more.

Again he saw the wolf-keeper with his horrible troupe around him, but this time not engaged in the chase but sitting in strange conclave in a circle and the black owls sat in the trees and the black bats hung downwards from the branches. Gabriel stood alone in the middle with a hundred wicked eyes fixed on him. They seemed to deliberate about what should be done with him, speaking in that same strange tongue which he had heard in the songs beneath his window. Suddenly he felt a hand pressing in his and saw the mysterious wolf-woman by his side. Then began what seemed a kind of incantation where human or half-human creatures seemed to howl, and beasts to speak with human speech but in the unknown tongue. Then the wolf-keeper whose face was ever veiled in shadow spake some words in a voice that seemed to come from afar off, but all he could distinguish was his own name Gabriel and her name Lilith. Then he felt arms enlacing him.

Gabriel awoke—in his own room—so it was a dream after all—but what a dreadful dream. Yes, but was it his own room? Of course there was his coat hanging over the chair—yes but—the Crucifix—where was the Crucifix and the *benetier* and the consecrated palm branch and the antique image of Our Lady *perpetuae salutis*, with the little ever-burning lamp before it, before which he placed every day the flowers he had gathered, yet had not dared to place the blue flower.

Every morning he lifted his still dream-laden eyes to it and said Ave Maria and made the sign of the cross, which bringeth peace to the soul—but how horrible, how maddening, it was not there, not at all. No surely he could not be awake, at least not *quite* awake, he would make the benedictive sign and he would be freed from this fearful illusion—yes but the sign, he would make the sign—oh, but what was the sign? Had he forgotten? or was his arm paralyzed? No he could not move. Then he had forgotten—and the prayer—he must remember that. *A—vae—nunc—mortis—fructus.* No surely it did not run thus—but something like it surely—yes, he was awake he could move at any rate—he would reassure himself—he would get up-he would see the grey old church with the exquisitely pointed gables bathed in the light of dawn, and presently the deep solemn bell would toll and he would run down and don his red cassock and lace-worked cotta and light the tall candles on the altar and wait reverently to vest the good and gracious Abbé Félicien, kissing each vestment as he lifted it with reverent hands.

But surely this was not the light of dawn; it was like sunset! He leapt from his small white bed, and a vague terror came over him, he trembled and had to hold on to the chair before he reached the window. No, the solemn spires of the grey church were not to be seen- he was in the depths of the forest; but in a part he had never seen before—but surely he had explored every part, it must be the "other side." To terror succeeded a languor and lassitude not without charm—passivity, acquiescence, indulgence—he felt, as it were, the strong caress of another will flowing over him like water and clothing him with invisible hands in an impalpable garment; so he dressed himself almost mechanically and walked downstairs, the same stairs it seemed to him down which it was his wont to run and spring. The broad square stones seemed singularly beautiful and irridescent with many strange colours—how was it he had never noticed this before—but he was gradually losing the power of wondering—he entered the room below—the wonted coffee and bread-rolls were on the table.

"Why Gabriel, how late you are to-day" The voice was very sweet but the intonation strange—and there sat Lilith, the mysterious wolf-woman, her glittering gold hair tied in a loose knot and an embroidery whereon she was tracing strange serpentine patterns, lay over the lap of her maize coloured garment—and she looked at Gabriel steadfastly with her wonderful dark blue eyes and said, "Why, Gabriel, you are late to-day" and Gabriel answered, "I was tired yesterday, give me some coffee."

A dream within a dream—yes, he had known her all his life, and they dwelt together; had they not always done so? And she would take him through the glades of the forest and gather for him flowers, such as he had never seen before, and tell him stories in her strange, low deep voice, which seemed ever to be accompanied by the faint vibration of strings, looking at him fixedly the while with her marvellous blue eyes.

Little by little the flame of vitality which burned within him seemed to grow fainter and fainter, and his lithe lissom limbs waxed languorous and luxurious—yet was he ever filled with a languid content and a will not his own perpetually overshadowed him.

One day in their wanderings he saw a strange dark blue flower like unto the eyes of Lilith, and a sudden half remembrance flashed through his mind.

"What is this blue flower?" he said, and Lilith shuddered and said nothing; but as they went a little further there was a brook—*the* brook he thought, and felt his fetters falling off him, and he prepared to spring over the brook; but Lilith seized him by the arm and held him back with all her strength, and trembling all over she said, "Promise me Gabriel that you will not cross over." But he said, "Tell me what is this blue flower, and why you will not tell me?" And she said, "Look Gabriel at the brook." And he looked and saw that though it was just like the brook of separation it was not the same, the waters did not flow.

As Gabriel looked steadfastly into the still waters it seemed to him as though he saw voices—some impression of the Vespers for the Dead. "*Hei mihi quia incolatus sum,*" and again "*De profundis clamavi ad te*"—oh, that veil, that overshadowing veil! Why could he not hear properly and see, and why did he only remember as one looking through a threefold semi-transparent curtain. Yes they were praying for him—but who were they? He heard again the voice of Lilith in whispered anguish, "Come away!"

Then he said, this time in monotone, "What is this blue flower, and what is its use?"

And the low thrilling voice answered, "it is called 'lûli uzhûri,' two drops pressed upon the face of the sleeper and he will *sleep*."

He was as a child in her hands and suffered himself to be led from thence, nevertheless he plucked listlessly one of the blue flowers, holding it downwards in his hand. What did she mean? Would the sleeper wake? Would the blue flower leave any stain? Could that stain be wiped off?

But as he lay asleep at early dawn he heard voices from afar off praying for him—the Abbé Félicien, Carmeille, his mother too, then some familiar words struck his ear: "*Libera mea porta inferi.*" Mass was being said for the repose of his soul, he knew this. No, he could not stay, he would leap over the brook, he knew the way—he had forgotten that the brook did not flow. Ah, but Lilith would know—what should he do? The blue flower—there it lay close by his bedside—he understood now; so he crept very silently to where Lilith lay asleep, her long hair glistening gold, shining like a glory round about her. He pressed two drops on her forehead, she sighed once, and a shade of præternatural anguish passed over her beautiful face. He fled—terror, remorse, and hope tearing his soul and making fleet his feet. He came to the brook—he did not see that the water did not flow— of course it was the brook for separation; one bound, he should be with things human again. He leapt over and—

A change had come over him—what was it? He could not tell—did he walk on all fours? Yes surely. He looked into the brook, whose still waters were fixed as a mirror, and there, horror, he beheld himself; or was it himself? His head and face, yes; but his body transformed to that of a wolf. Even as he looked he heard a sound of hideous mocking laughter behind him. He turned round—there, in a gleam of red lurid light, he saw one whose body was human, but whose head was that of a wolf, with eyes of infinite malice; and, while this hideous being laughed with a loud human laugh, he, essaying to speak, could only utter the prolonged howl of a wolf.

But we will transfer our thoughts from the alien things on the "other side" to the simple human village where Gabriel used to dwell. Mère Yvonne was not much surprised when Gabriel did not turn up to breakfast—he often did not, so absent-minded was he; this time she said, "I suppose he has gone with the others to the wolf hunt." Not that Gabriel was given to hunting, but, as she sagely said, "there was no knowing what he might do next." The boys said, "Of course that muff

Gabriel is skulking and hiding himself, he's afraid to join the wolf hunt; why, he wouldn't even kill a cat," for their one notion of excellence was slaughter—so the greater the game the greater the glory. They were chiefly now confined to cats and sparrows, but they all hoped in after time to become generals of armies.

Yet these children had been taught all their life through with the gentle words of Christ—but alas, nearly all the seed falls by the wayside, where it could not bear flower or fruit; how little these know the suffering and bitter anguish or realize the full meaning of the words to those, of whom it is written "Some fell among thorns."

The wolf hunt was so far a success that they did actually see a wolf, but not a success, as they did not kill it before it leapt over the brook to the "other side," where, of course, they were afraid to pursue it. No emotion is more inrooted and intense in the minds of common people than hatred and fear of anything "strange."

Days passed by but Gabriel was nowhere seen—and Mère Yvonne began to see clearly at last how deeply she loved her only son, who was so unlike her that she had thought herself an object of pity to other mothers—the goose and the swan's egg. People searched and pretended to search, they even went to the length of dragging the ponds, which the boys thought very amusing, as it enabled them to kill a great number of water rats, and Carmeille sat in a corner and cried all day long. Mère Pinquèle also sat in a corner and chuckled and said that she had always said Gabriel would come to no good. The Abbé Félicien looked pale and anxious, but said very little, save to God and those that dwelt with God.

At last, as Gabriel was not there, they supposed he must be nowhere—that is *dead*. (Their knowledge of other localities being so limited, that it did not even occur to them to suppose he might be living elsewhere than in the village.) So it was agreed that an empty catafalque should be put up in the church with tall candles round it, and Mère Yvonne said all the prayers that were in her prayer book, beginning at the beginning and ending at the end, regardless of their appropriateness—not even omitting the instructions of the rubrics. And Carmeille sat in the corner of the little side chapel and cried, and cried. And the Abbé Félicien caused the boys to sing the Vespers for the Dead (this did not amuse them so much as dragging the pond), and on the following morning, in the silence of early dawn, said the Dirge and the Requiem—*and this Gabriel heard.*

Then the Abbé Félicien received a message to bring the Holy Viaticum to one sick. So they set forth in solemn procession with great torches, and their way lay along the brook of separation.

Essaying to speak he could only utter the prolonged howl of a wolf—the most fearful of all bestial sounds. He howled and howled again—perhaps Lilith would hear him! Perhaps she could rescue him? Then he remembered the blue flower— the beginning and end of all his woe. His cries aroused all the denizens of the forest—the wolves, the wolf-men, and the men-wolves. He fled before them in an agony of terror—behind him, seated on the black ram with human face, was the wolf-keeper, whose face was veiled in eternal shadow. Only once he turned to look behind—for among the shrieks and howls of bestial chase he heard one thrilling voice moan with pain. And there among them he beheld Lilith, her body too was that of a wolf, almost hidden in the masses of her glittering golden hair, on her forehead was a stain of blue, like in colour to her mysterious eyes, now veiled with tears she could not shed.

The way of the Most Holy Viaticum lay along the brook of separation. They heard the fearful howlings afar off, the torch bearers turned pale and trembled— but the Abbé Félicien, holding aloft the Ciborium, said "They cannot harm us."

Suddenly the whole horrid chase came in sight. Gabriel sprang over the brook, the Abbé Félicien held the most Blessed Sacrament before him, and his shape was restored to him and he fell down prostrate in adoration. But the Abbé Félicien still held aloft the Sacred Ciborium, and the people fell on their knees in the agony of fear, but the face of the priest seemed to shine with divine effulgence. Then the wolf-keeper held up in his hands the shape of something horrible and inconceivable—a monstrance to the Sacrament of Hell, and three times he raised it, in mockery of the blessed rite of Benediction. And on the third time streams of fire went forth from his fingers, and all the "other side" of the forest took fire, and great darkness was over all.

All who were there and saw and heard it have kept the impress thereof for the rest of their lives—nor til in their death hour was the remembrance thereof absent from their minds. Shrieks, horrible beyond conception, were heard til nightfall—then the rain rained.

The "other side" is harmless now—charred ashes only; but none dare to cross but Gabriel alone—for once a year for nine days a strange madness comes over him.

THE LADY ON THE GREY

BY JOHN COLLIER

I first encountered this story in the classic Alfred Hitchcock anthology
Stories They Wouldn't Let Me Do on TV, *back in 1968. I was eleven at
the time, and thoroughly sucked in by the then mind-boggling concept that
there were some things even Alfred Hitchcock could get in trouble for saying.*

*This is where I first encountered the writings of H. H. Munro (a.k.a.
Saki), M. R. James, Roald Dahl, William Hope Hodgson, Ray Bradbury, and
Robert Bloch, among others. A priceless primer of the greats I would proceed to
seek out through the rest of my formative years.*

*John Collier was another name I'd never heard before. But "The Lady on the
Grey" was such a pitch-perfect little beauty—so lovely, so playful, so simultaneously
creepy and just in its implications—that it remains a lifelong favorite.*

The little kid I used to be is delighted to share it with you now.

Ringwood was the last of an Anglo-Irish family that had played the devil in County Clare for a matter of three centuries. At last, all their big houses were sold up, or burned down by the long-suffering Irish, and of their thousands of acres not a single foot remained. Ringwood, however, had a few hundred a year of his own, and if the family estates had vanished, he had at least inherited a family instinct that prompted him to regard all Ireland as his domain and to rejoice in its abundance of horses, foxes, salmon, game, and girls.

In pursuit of these delights, Ringwood ranged and roved from Donegal to Wexford through all the seasons of the year. There were not many hunts he had not led at some time or other on a borrowed mount, or many bridges he had not leaned over through half a May morning, or many inn parlors where he had not snored away a wet winter afternoon in front of the fire.

He had an intimate by the name of Bates, who was another of the same breed and the same kidney. Bates was equally long and lean, and equally hard up, and he had the same wind-flushed, bony face, the same shabby arrogance, and the same seigniorial approach to the little girls in the cottages and cowsheds.

Neither of these blades ever wrote a letter, but each generally knew where the other was to be found. The ticket collector, respectfully blind as he snipped Ringwood's third-class ticket in a first-class compartment, would mention that Mr. Bates had traveled that way only last Tuesday, stopping off at Killorglin for a week or two after the snipe. The chambermaid, coy in the clammy bedroom of a fishing inn, would find time to tell Bates that Ringwood had gone on up to Lough Corrib for a go at the pike. Policemen, priests, bagmen, gamekeepers, even the tinkers on the roads, would pass on this verbal patrin. Then, if it seemed to one that his friend was on to a good thing, the other would pack up his battered kit bag, put rods and guns into their cases, and drift off to join in the sport.

So it happened that one winter afternoon, when Ringwood was strolling back from a singularly blank day on the bog of Ballyneary, he was hailed by a one-eyed horse dealer of his acquaintance, who came trotting by in a gig, as people still do in Ireland. This worthy told our friend that he had just come down from Galway, where he had seen Mr. Bates, who was on his way to a village called Knockderry and had told him very particularly to mention it to Mr. Ringwood if he came across him.

Ringwood turned this message over in his mind and noted that it was a very particular one, and that no mention was made as to whether it was fishing or shooting his friend was engaged in, or whether he had met with some Croesus who had a string of hunters that he was prepared to lend. He certainly would have put a name to it if it were anything of that sort, he thought. I'll bet my life it's a pair of sisters he's got on the track of. It must be!

At this thought, he grinned from the tip of his long nose, like a fox, and he lost no time in packing his bag and setting off for this place Knockderry, which he had never visited before in all his roving up and down the country in pursuit of fur, feather, and girls.

He found it was a long way off the beaten track, and a very quiet place when he got to it. There were the usual low, bleak hills all around, and a river running along the valley, and the usual ruined tower up on a slight rise, girdled with a straggly wood and approached by the remains of an avenue.

The village itself was like many another: a few groups of shabby cottages, a decaying mill, half a dozen beer shops, and one inn, at which a gentleman hardened to rural cookery might conceivably put up.

Ringwood strode in and found the landlady in the kitchen and asked for his friend Mr. Bates.

"Why, sure, Your Honor," said the landlady, "the gentleman's staying here. At least, he is, so to speak, and then, now, he isn't."

"How's that?" asked Ringwood.

"His bag's here," said the landlady, "and his things are here, and my grandest room taken up with them, though I've another every bit as good, and himself staying in the house best part of a week. But the day before yesterday he went out for a bit of a constitutional, and—would you believe it, sir?—we've seen neither hide nor hair of him since."

"Oh, he'll be back," said Ringwood. "Meanwhile, show me a room. I'll stay here and wait for him."

Accordingly, he settled in, and waited all the evening, but Bates failed to appear. However, that sort of thing bothers no one in Ireland, and Ringwood's only impatience was in connection with the pair of sisters, whose acquaintance he was extremely anxious to make.

During the next day or two, Ringwood employed his time in strolling up and down all the lanes and bypaths in the neighborhood, in the hope of discovering these beauties, or else some other. He was not particular as to which it should be, but on the whole he would have preferred a cottage girl, because he had no wish to waste time on elaborate approaches.

On the second afternoon, just as the early dusk was falling, he was about a mile outside the village and he met a straggle of muddy cows coming along the road, and a girl driving them. Our friend took a look at the girl and stopped dead in his tracks, grinning more like a fox than ever.

This girl was still a child in her teens, and her bare legs were spattered with mud and scratched by brambles, but she was so pretty that the seigniorial blood of all the Ringwoods boiled in the veins of their last descendant and he felt an overmastering desire for a cup of milk. He therefore waited a minute or two and then followed leisurely along the lane, meaning to turn in as soon as he saw the byre and beg the favor of this innocent refreshment, and perhaps a little conversation into the bargain.

They say, though, that blessings never come singly, any more than misfortunes. As Ringwood followed his charmer, swearing to himself that there couldn't be such another in the whole country, he heard the fall of a horse's hoofs and looked up, and there, approaching him at a walking pace, was a gray horse, which must have turned in from some bypath or other, because there certainly had been no horse in sight a moment before.

A gray horse is no great matter, especially when one is so urgently in pursuit of a cup of milk, but this gray horse differed from all others of its species and color in two respects. First, it was no sort of a horse at all, neither hack nor hunter, and it picked up its feet in a queer way, and yet it had an arch to its neck and a small head and a wide nostril that were not entirely without distinction. And, second— and this distracted Ringwood from all curiosity as to breed and bloodline—this gray horse carried on its back a girl who was obviously and certainly the most beautiful girl he had ever seen in his life.

Ringwood looked at her, and as she came slowly through the dusk, she raised her eyes and looked at Ringwood. He at once forgot the little girl with the cows. In fact, he forgot everything else in the world.

The horse came nearer, and still the girl looked, and Ringwood looked, and it was not a mere exchange of glances, it was a wooing and a marriage, all complete and perfect in a mingling of the eyes.

Next moment, the horse had carried her past him, and, quickening its pace a little, it left him standing on the road. He could hardly run after it, or shout; in any case, he was too overcome to do anything but stand and stare.

He watched the horse and rider go on through the wintry twilight, and he saw her turn in at a broken gateway just a little way along the road. Just as she passed through, she turned her head and whistled, and Ringwood noticed that her dog had stopped by him and was sniffing about his legs. For a moment, he thought it was a smallish wolfhound, but then he saw it was just a tall, lean, hairy lurcher. He watched it run limping after her with its tail down, and it struck him that the poor creature had had an appalling thrashing not so long ago; he had noticed the marks where the hair was thin on its ribs.

However, he had little thought to spare for the dog. As soon as he got over his first excitement, he moved on in the direction of the gateway. The girl was already out of sight when he got there, but he recognized the neglected avenue that led up to the battered tower on the shoulder of the hill.

Ringwood thought that was enough for the day, so made his way back to the inn. Bates was still absent, but that was just as well. Ringwood wanted the evening to himself, in order to work out a plan of campaign.

That horse never cost two ten-pound notes of anybody's money, said he to himself. So she's not so rich. So much the better! Besides, she wasn't dressed up much; I don't know what she had on—a sort of cloak or something. Nothing out of Bond Street, anyway. And living in that old tower! I should have thought it was all tumbled down. Still, I suppose there's a room or two left at the bottom.

Poverty Hall! One of the old school, blue blood and no money, pining away in this godforsaken hole, miles away from everybody. Probably she doesn't see a man from one year's end to another. No wonder she gave me a look. God! If I was sure she was there by herself, I wouldn't need much of an introduction. Still, there might be a father or a brother or somebody. Never mind, I'll manage it.

When the landlady brought in the lamp, "Tell me," said he, "who's the young lady who rides the cobby-looking, old-fashioned-looking gray?"

"A young lady, sir?" said the landlady doubtfully. "On a gray?"

"Yes," said he. "She passed me in the lane up there. She turned in on the old avenue going up to the tower."

"Oh, Mary bless and keep you!" said the good woman. "That's the beautiful Murrough lady you must have seen."

"Murrough?" said he. "Is that the name? Well, well, well! That's a fine old name in the west here."

"It is so, indeed," said the landlady. "For they were kings and queens in Connaught before the Saxon came. And herself, sir, has the face of a queen, they tell me."

"They're right," said Ringwood. "Perhaps you'll bring me in the whiskey and water, Mrs. Doyle, and I shall be comfortable."

He had an impulse to ask if the beautiful Miss Murrough had anything in the shape of a father or a brother at the tower, but his principle was "Least said, soonest mended," especially in little affairs of this sort. So he sat by the fire, recapturing and savoring the look the girl had given him, and he decided he needed only the barest excuse to present himself at the tower.

Ringwood had never any shortage of excuses, so the next afternoon he spruced himself up and set out in the direction of the old avenue. He turned in at the gate and went along under the forlorn and dripping trees, which were so ivied and overgrown that the darkness was already thickening under them. He looked ahead for a sight of the tower, but the avenue took a turn at the end, and it was still hidden among the clustering trees.

Just as he got to the end, he saw someone standing there, and he looked again, and it was the girl herself, standing as if she were waiting for him.

"Good afternoon, Miss Murrough," said he, as soon as he got into earshot. "Hope I'm not intruding. The fact is I think I had the pleasure of meeting a relation of yours down in Cork, only last month." By this time, he had got close enough to see the look in her eyes again, and all this nonsense died away in his mouth, for this was something beyond any nonsense of that sort.

"I thought you would come," said she.

"My God!" said he. "I had to. Tell me—are you all by yourself here?"

"All by myself," said she, and she put out her hand as if to lead him along with her.

Ringwood, blessing his lucky stars, was about to take it when her lean dog bounded between them and nearly knocked him over.

"Down!" cried she, lifting her hand. "Get back!" The dog cowered and whimpered, and slunk behind her, creeping almost on its belly. "I don't trust him," she said.

"He's all right," said Ringwood. "He looks a knowing old fellow. I like a lurcher. . . .What? Are you trying to talk to me, old boy?" Ringwood always paid a compliment to a lady's dog, and in fact the creature really was whining and whimpering in the most extraordinary fashion.

"Be quiet!" said the girl, raising her hand again, and the dog was silent. "A cur," said she to Ringwood. "You did not come here to flatter a cur." With that, she gave him her eyes again, and he forgot the wretched dog, and she gave him her hand, and this time he took it, and they walked toward the tower.

Ringwood was in the seventh heaven. What luck! thought he. I might at this moment be fondling that little farm wench in some damp and smelly cowshed. And ten to one she'd be snivelling and crying and running home to tell her mammy. This is something different.

At that moment, the girl pushed open a heavy door, and, bidding the dog lie down, she led our friend through a wide, bare stone-flagged hall and into a small vaulted room, which certainly had no resemblance to a cowshed, except perhaps it smelled a little damp and moldy, as these old stone places so often do. All the same, there were logs burning on the open hearth, and a broad, low couch before the fireplace. For the rest, the room was furnished with the greatest simplicity, and very much in the antique style. A touch of the Kathleen ni Houlihan, thought Ringwood. Well, well! Sitting in the Celtic twilight, dreaming of love. She certainly doesn't make much bones about it.

The girl sat down on the couch and drew him down beside her. Neither of them said anything; there was no sound but the wind outside, and the dog scratching and whimpering timidly at the door of the chamber.

At last, the girl spoke. "You are of the Saxon," said she gravely.

"Don't hold it against me," said Ringwood. "My people came here in 1629. Of course, that's yesterday to the Gaelic League, but still I think we can say we have a stake in the country."

"Yes, through its heart," said she.

"Is it politics we're going to talk?" said he, putting an Irish turn to his tongue. "You and I, sitting here in the firelight?"

"Through the hearts, then," said the girl. "Through the hearts of the poor girls of Eire."

"You misjudge me entirely," said Ringwood. "I'm the man to live alone and sorrowful, waiting for the one love, though it seemed something beyond hoping for."

"Yes," said she. "But yesterday you were looking at one of the Connell girls as she drove her kine along the lane."

"Looking at her? I'll go so far as to say I did," said he. "But when I saw you, I altogether forgot her."

"That was my wish," said she, giving him both her hands. "Will you stay with me here?"

"Ah, that I will!" cried he in a rapture.

"Forever?" said she.

"Forever," cried Ringwood, for he felt it better to be guilty of a slight exaggeration than to be lacking in courtesy to a lady. But as he spoke, she fixed her eyes on him, looking so much as if she believed him that he positively believed himself. "Ah," he cried. "You bewitch me!" And he took her in his arms.

He pressed his lips to hers, and at once he was over the brink. Usually he prided himself on being a pretty cool hand, but this was an intoxication too strong for him; his mind seemed to dissolve in sweetness and fire, and at last the fire was gone, and his senses went with it. As they failed, he heard her saying "Forever! Forever!" and then everything was gone and he fell asleep.

He must have slept some time. It seemed he was wakened by the heavy opening and closing of a door. For a moment, he was all confused and hardly knew where he was.

The room was now quite dark, and the fire had sunk to a dim glow. He blinked, and shook his ears, trying to shake some sense into his head. Suddenly he heard Bates talking to him, muttering as if he, too, were half asleep—or half drunk, more likely. "You would come here," said Bates. "I tried hard enough to stop you."

"Hullo!" said Ringwood, thinking he must have dozed off by the fire in the inn parlor. "Bates? God, I must have slept heavy! I feel queer. Damn it—so it was all a dream! Strike a light, old boy. It must be late. I'll yell for supper."

"Don't, for heaven's sake," said Bates, in his altered voice. "Don't yell. She'll thrash us if you do."

"What's that?" said Ringwood. "Thrash us? What the hell are you talking about?"

At that moment, a log rolled on the hearth and a little flame flickered up, and he saw his long and hairy forelegs, and he knew.

GABRIEL-ERNEST

BY SAKI

And speaking of ol' Hector Hugh Munro . . . here he is now, with this charmingly calibrated slap in the face of polite society.

A man who never met a stiff upper lip he couldn't pinch, tickle, or otherwise set indignantly aquiver with his prose, The Artist Otherwise Known As Saki was one of my earliest heroes. Occupying a space neatly between Oscar Wilde and Edward Gorey, his black comic satires of Edwardian snootery are as sharp and funny today as they were when freshly minted, 100 years ago.

And so with "Gabriel-Ernest," a time-honored classic of cheeky lycanthropic lore. If you've read it, you're probably nodding and smiling already.

If you haven't, my friend, the time has come.

"There is a wild beast in your woods," said the artist Cunningham, as he was being driven to the station. It was the only remark he had made during the drive, but as Van Cheele had talked incessantly his companion's silence had not been noticeable.

"A stray fox or two and some resident weasels. Nothing more formidable," said Van Cheele. The artist said nothing.

"What did you mean about a wild beast?" said Van Cheele later, when they were on the platform.

"Nothing. My imagination. Here is the train," said Cunningham.

That afternoon Van Cheele went for one of his frequent rambles through his woodland property. He had a stuffed bittern in his study, and knew the names of quite a number of wild flowers, so his aunt had possibly some justification in describing him as a great naturalist. At any rate, he was a great walker. It was his custom to take mental notes of everything he saw during his walks, not so much for the purpose of assisting contemporary science as to provide topics for conversation afterwards. When the bluebells began to show themselves in flower he made a point of informing every one of the fact; the season of the year might have warned his hearers of the likelihood of such an occurrence, but at least they felt that he was being absolutely frank with them.

What Van Cheele saw on this particular afternoon was, however, something far removed from his ordinary range of experience. On a shelf of smooth stone overhanging a deep pool in the hollow of an oak coppice a boy of about sixteen lay asprawl, drying his wet brown limbs luxuriously in the sun. His wet hair, parted by a recent dive, lay close to his head, and his light-brown eyes, so light that there was an almost tigerish gleam in them, were turned towards Van Cheele with a certain lazy watchfulness. It was an unexpected apparition, and Van Cheele found himself engaged in the novel process of thinking before he spoke. Where on earth could this wild-looking boy hail from? The miller's wife had lost a child some two months ago, supposed to have been swept away by the mill-race, but that had been a mere baby, not a half-grown lad.

"What are you doing there?" he demanded.

"Obviously, sunning myself," replied the boy.

"Where do you live?"

"Here, in these woods."

"You can't live in the woods," said Van Cheele.

"They are very nice woods," said the boy, with a touch of patronage in his voice.

"But where do you sleep at night?"

"I don't sleep at night; that's my busiest time."

Van Cheele began to have an irritated feeling that he was grappling with a problem that was eluding him.

"What do you feed on?" he asked.

"Flesh," said the boy, and he pronounced the word with slow relish, as though he were tasting it.

"Flesh! What Flesh?"

"Since it interests you, rabbits, wild-fowl, hares, poultry, lambs in their season, children when I can get any; they're usually too well locked in at night, when I do most of my hunting. It's quite two months since I tasted child-flesh."

Ignoring the chaffing nature of the last remark Van Cheele tried to draw the boy on the subject of possible poaching operations.

"You're talking rather through your hat when you speak of feeding on hares." (Considering the nature of the boy's toilet the simile was hardly an apt one.) "Our hillside hares aren't easily caught."

"At night I hunt on four feet," was the somewhat cryptic response.

"I suppose you mean that you hunt with a dog?" hazarded Van Cheele.

The boy rolled slowly over on to his back, and laughed a weird low laugh, that was pleasantly like a chuckle and disagreeably like a snarl.

"I don't fancy any dog would be very anxious for my company, especially at night."

Van Cheele began to feel that there was something positively uncanny about the strange-eyed, strange-tongued youngster.

"I can't have you staying in these woods," he declared authoritatively.

"I fancy you'd rather have me here than in your house," said the boy.

The prospect of this wild, nude animal in Van Cheele's primly ordered house was certainly an alarming one.

"If you don't go. I shall have to make you," said Van Cheele.

The boy turned like a flash, plunged into the pool, and in a moment had flung his wet and glistening body half-way up the bank where Van Cheele was standing. In an otter the movement would not have been remarkable; in a boy Van Cheele found it sufficiently startling. His foot slipped as he made an involuntarily backward movement, and he found himself almost prostrate on the slippery weed-grown bank, with those tigerish yellow eyes not very far from his own. Almost instinctively he half raised his hand to his throat. The boy laughed again, a laugh in which the snarl had nearly driven out the chuckle, and then, with another of his astonishing lightning movements, plunged out of view into a yielding tangle of weed and fern.

"What an extraordinary wild animal!" said Van Cheele as he picked himself up. And then he recalled Cunningham's remark "There is a wild beast in your woods."

Walking slowly homeward, Van Cheele began to turn over in his mind various local occurrences which might be traceable to the existence of this astonishing young savage.

Something had been thinning the game in the woods lately, poultry had been missing from the farms, hares were growing unaccountably scarcer, and complaints had reached him of lambs being carried off bodily from the hills. Was it possible that this wild boy was really hunting the countryside in company with some clever poacher dogs? He had spoken of hunting "four-footed" by night, but then, again, he had hinted strangely at no dog caring to come near him, "especially at night." It was certainly puzzling. And then, as Van Cheele ran his mind over the various depredations that had been committed during the last month or two, he came suddenly to a dead stop, alike in his walk and his speculations. The child missing from the mill two months ago—the accepted theory was that it had tumbled into the mill-race and been swept away; but the mother had always declared she had heard a shriek on the hill side of the house, in the opposite direction from the water. It was unthinkable, of course, but he wished that the boy had not made that uncanny remark about child-flesh eaten two months ago. Such dreadful things should not be said even in fun.

Van Cheele, contrary to his usual wont, did not feel disposed to be communicative about his discovery in the wood. His position as a parish councillor and justice of the peace seemed somehow compromised by the fact that he was harbouring a personality of such doubtful repute on his property; there was even a possibility that a heavy bill of damages for raided lambs and poultry might be laid at his door. At dinner that night he was quite unusually silent.

"Where's your voice gone to?" said his aunt. "One would think you had seen a wolf."

Van Cheele, who was not familiar with the old saying, thought the remark rather foolish; if he HAD seen a wolf on his property his tongue would have been extraordinarily busy with the subject.

At breakfast next morning Van Cheele was conscious that his feeling of uneasiness regarding yesterday's episode had not wholly disappeared, and he resolved to go by train to the neighbouring cathedral town, hunt up Cunningham, and learn from him what he had really seen that had prompted the remark about a wild beast in the woods. With this resolution taken, his usual cheerfulness partially returned, and he hummed a bright little melody as he sauntered to the morning-room for his customary cigarette. As he entered the room the melody made way abruptly for a pious invocation. Gracefully asprawl on the ottoman, in an attitude of almost exaggerated repose, was the boy of the woods. He was drier than when Van Cheele had last seen him, but no other alteration was noticeable in his toilet.

"How dare you come here?" asked Van Cheele furiously.

"You told me I was not to stay in the woods," said the boy calmly.

"But not to come here. Supposing my aunt should see you!"

And with a view to minimising that catastrophe, Van Cheele hastily obscured as much of his unwelcome guest as possible under the folds of a Morning Post. At that moment his aunt entered the room.

"This is a poor boy who has lost his way—and lost his memory. He doesn't know who he is or where he comes from," explained Van Cheele desperately, glancing apprehensively at the waif's face to see whether he was going to add inconvenient candour to his other savage propensities.

Miss Van Cheele was enormously interested.

"Perhaps his underlinen is marked," she suggested.

"He seems to have lost most of that, too," said Van Cheele, making frantic little grabs at the Morning Post to keep it in its place.

A naked homeless child appealed to Miss Van Cheele as warmly as a stray kitten or derelict puppy would have done.

"We must do all we can for him," she decided, and in a very short time a messenger, dispatched to the rectory, where a page-boy was kept, had returned with a suit of pantry clothes, and the necessary accessories of shirt, shoes, collar, etc. Clothed, clean, and groomed, the boy lost none of his uncanniness in Van Cheele's eyes, but his aunt found him sweet.

"We must call him something til we know who he really is," she said. "Gabriel-Ernest, I think; those are nice suitable names."

Van Cheele agreed, but he privately doubted whether they were being grafted on to a nice suitable child. His misgivings were not diminished by the fact that his staid and elderly spaniel had bolted out of the house at the first incoming of the boy, and now obstinately remained shivering and yapping at the farther end of the orchard, while the canary, usually as vocally industrious as Van Cheele himself, had put itself on an allowance of frightened cheeps. More than ever he was resolved to consult Cunningham without loss of time.

As he drove off to the station his aunt was arranging that Gabriel-Ernest should help her to entertain the infant members of her Sunday-school class at tea that afternoon.

Cunningham was not at first disposed to be communicative.

"My mother died of some brain trouble," he explained, "so you will understand why I am averse to dwelling on anything of an impossibly fantastic nature that I may see or think that I have seen."

"But what DID you see?" persisted Van Cheele.

"What I thought I saw was something so extraordinary that no really sane man could dignify it with the credit of having actually happened. I was standing, the last evening I was with you, half-hidden in the hedgegrowth by the orchard gate, watching the dying glow of the sunset. Suddenly I became aware of a naked boy, a bather from some neighbouring pool, I took him to be, who was standing out on the bare hillside also watching the sunset. His pose was so suggestive of some wild faun of Pagan myth that I instantly wanted to engage him as a model, and in another moment I think I should have hailed him. But just then the sun dipped out of view, and all the orange and pink slid out of the landscape, leaving it cold and grey. And at the same moment an astounding thing happened--the boy vanished too!"

"What! Vanished away into nothing?" asked Van Cheele excitedly.

"No; that is the dreadful part of it," answered the artist; "on the open hillside where the boy had been standing a second ago, stood a large wolf, blackish in colour, with gleaming fangs and cruel, yellow eyes. You may think—"

But Van Cheele did not stop for anything as futile as thought. Already he was tearing at top speed towards the station. He dismissed the idea of a telegram. "Gabriel-Ernest is a werewolf" was a hopelessly inadequate effort at conveying the situation, and his aunt would think it was a code message to which he had omitted to give her the key. His one hope was that he might reach home before sundown. The cab which he chartered at the other end of the railway journey bore him with what seemed exasperating slowness along the country roads, which were pink and mauve with the flush of the sinking sun. His aunt was putting away some unfinished jams and cake when he arrived.

"Where is Gabriel-Ernest?" he almost screamed.

"He is taking the little Toop child home," said his aunt. "It was getting so late, I thought it wasn't safe to let it go back alone. What a lovely sunset, isn't it?"

But Van Cheele, although not oblivious of the glow in the western sky, did not stay to discuss its beauties. At a speed for which he was scarcely geared he raced along the narrow lane that led to the home of the Toops. On one side ran the swift current of the mill-stream, on the other rose the stretch of bare hillside. A dwindling rim of red sun showed still on the skyline, and the next turning must bring him in view of the ill-assorted couple he was pursuing. Then the colour went suddenly out of things, and a grey light settled itself with a quick shiver over the landscape. Van Cheele heard a shrill wail of fear, and stopped running.

Nothing was ever seen again of the Toop child or Gabriel-Ernest, but the latter's discarded garments were found lying in the road so it was assumed that the child had fallen into the water, and that the boy had stripped and jumped in, in a vain endeavour to save it. Van Cheele and some workmen who were near by at the time testified to having heard a child scream loudly just near the spot where the clothes were found. Mrs. Toop, who had eleven other children, was decently resigned to her bereavement, but Miss Van Cheele sincerely mourned her lost foundling. It was on her initiative that a memorial brass was put up in the parish church to "Gabriel-Ernest, an unknown boy, who bravely sacrificed his life for another."

Van Cheele gave way to his aunt in most things, but he flatly refused to subscribe to the Gabriel-Ernest memorial.

THE SHADOW OVER INNSMOUTH

BY H. P. LOVECRAFT

The vast and foreboding shadow of H. P. Lovecraft—hanging as it does over all of weird fiction ever since the 1920s, when his stories first appeared—is a precipitous and awe-inspiring one indeed. Few authors have been more deeply influential, with his strange and morally indifferent alternate metaphysics— the Cthulu mythos—seeping gradually but unstoppably into the popular dreamosphere.

Of all of his stories, "The Shadow over Innsmouth" has long been my favorite; and I suspect I'm giving nothing away by saying it's the ultimate atmospheric creepy-town-with-a-secret tale, replete with arduous ocean-reeking transformations far more icky and discomfiting than any nice fuzzy weremonsters you could possibly name.

That said, I recently snuggled a plush stuffed Cthulu that my awesome eldest daughter owns, and found myself helplessly wondering, what would those godless gods that Lovecraft called "the Old Ones" think?

During the winter of 1927-28 officials of the Federal government made a strange and secret investigation of certain conditions in the ancient Massachusetts seaport of Innsmouth. The public first learned of it in February, when a vast series of raids and arrests occurred, followed by the deliberate burning and dynamiting—under suitable precautions—of an enormous number of crumbling, worm-eaten, and supposedly empty houses along the abandoned waterfront. Uninquiring souls let this occurrence pass as one of the major clashes in a spasmodic war on liquor.

Keener news-followers, however, wondered at the prodigious number of arrests, the abnormally large force of men used in making them, and the secrecy surrounding the disposal of the prisoners. No trials, or even definite charges were reported; nor were any of the captives seen thereafter in the regular gaols of the nation. There were vague statements about disease and concentration camps, and later about dispersal in various naval and military prisons, but nothing positive ever developed. Innsmouth itself was left almost depopulated, and it is even now only beginning to show signs of a sluggishly revived existence.

Complaints from many liberal organizations were met with long confidential discussions, and representatives were taken on trips to certain camps and prisons. As a result, these societies became surprisingly passive and reticent. Newspaper men were harder to manage, but seemed largely to cooperate with the government in the end. Only one paper—a tabloid always discounted because of its wild policy—mentioned the deep diving submarine that discharged torpedoes downward in the marine abyss just beyond Devil Reef. That item, gathered by chance in a haunt of sailors, seemed indeed rather far-fetched; since the low, black reef lay a full mile and a half out from Innsmouth Harbor.

People around the country and in the nearby towns muttered a great deal among themselves, but said very little to the outer world. They had talked about dying and half-deserted Innsmouth for nearly a century, and nothing new could be wilder or more hideous than what they had whispered and hinted at years before. Many things had taught them secretiveness, and there was no need to exert pressure on them. Besides, they really knew little; for wide salt marshes, desolate and unpeopled, kept neighbors off from Innsmouth on the landward side.

But at last I am going to defy the ban on speech about this thing. Results, I am certain, are so thorough that no public harm save a shock of repulsion could ever accrue from a hinting of what was found by those horrified men at Innsmouth. Besides, what was found might possibly have more than one explanation. I do not know just how much of the whole tale has been told even to me, and I have many reasons for not wishing to probe deeper. For my contact with this affair has been closer than that of any other layman, and I have carried away impressions which are yet to drive me to drastic measures.

It was I who fled frantically out of Innsmouth in the early morning hours of July 16, 1927, and whose frightened appeals for government inquiry and action brought on the whole reported episode. I was willing enough to stay mute while the affair was fresh and uncertain; but now that it is an old story, with public interest and curiosity gone, I have an odd craving to whisper about those few frightful hours in that ill-rumored and evilly-shadowed seaport of death and blasphemous abnormality. The mere telling helps me to restore confidence in my own faculties; to reassure myself that I was not the first to succumb to a contagious nightmare hallucination. It helps me, too, in making up my mind regarding a certain terrible step which lies ahead of me.

I never heard of Innsmouth till the day before I saw it for the first and—so far—last time. I was celebrating my coming of age by a tour of New England— sightseeing, antiquarian, and genealogical—and had planned to go directly from ancient Newburyport to Arkham, whence my mother's family was derived. I had no car, but was traveling by train, trolley and motor-coach, always seeking the cheapest possible route. In Newburyport they told me that the steam train was the thing to take to Arkham; and it was only at the station ticket-office, when I demurred at the high fare, that I learned about Innsmouth. The stout, shrewd-faced agent, whose speech shewed him to be no local man, seemed sympathetic toward my efforts at economy, and made a suggestion that none of my other informants had offered.

"You could take that old bus, I suppose," he said with a certain hesitation, "but it ain't thought much of hereabouts. It goes through Innsmouth—you may have heard about that—and so the people don't like it. Run by an Innsmouth fellow— Joe Sargent—but never gets any custom from here, or Arkham either, I guess.

Wonder it keeps running at all. I s'pose it's cheap enough, but I never see mor'n two or three people in it—nobody but those Innsmouth folk. Leaves the square— front of Hammond's Drug Store—at 10 a.m. and 7 p.m. unless they've changed lately. Looks like a terrible rattletrap—I've never been on it."

That was the first I ever heard of shadowed Innsmouth. Any reference to a town not shown on common maps or listed in recent guidebooks would have interested me, and the agent's odd manner of allusion roused something like real curiosity. A town able to inspire such dislike in its neighbors, I thought, must be at least rather unusual, and worthy of a tourist's attention. If it came before Arkham I would stop off there and so I asked the agent to tell me something about it. He was very deliberate, and spoke with an air of feeling slightly superior to what he said.

"Innsmouth? Well, it's a queer kind of a town down at the mouth of the Manuxet. Used to be almost a city—quite a port before the War of 1812—but all gone to pieces in the last hundred years or so. No railroad now—B. and M. never went through, and the branch line from Rowley was given up years ago.

"More empty houses than there are people, I guess, and no business to speak of except fishing and lobstering. Everybody trades mostly either here or in Arkham or Ipswich. Once they had quite a few mills, but nothing's left now except one gold refinery running on the leanest kind of part time.

"That refinery, though, used to be a big thing, and old man Marsh, who owns it, must be richer'n Croesus. Queer old duck, though, and sticks mighty close in his home. He's supposed to have developed some skin disease or deformity late in life that makes him keep out of sight. Grandson of Captain Obed Marsh, who founded the business. His mother seems to've been some kind of foreigner—they say a South Sea islander—so everybody raised Cain when he married an Ipswich girl fifty years ago. They always do that about Innsmouth people, and folks here and hereabouts always try to cover up any Innsmouth blood they have in 'em. But Marsh's children and grandchildren look just like anyone else far's I can see. I've had 'em pointed out to me here— though, come to think of it, the elder children don't seem to be around lately. Never saw the old man.

"And why is everybody so down on Innsmouth? Well, young fellow, you mustn't take too much stock in what people here say. They're hard to get started, but once they do get started they never let up. They've been telling things about Innsmouth—whispering 'em, mostly—for the last hundred years, I guess, and I gather they're more scared than anything else. Some of the stories would make you laugh—about old Captain Marsh driving bargains with the devil and bringing imps out of hell to live in Innsmouth, or about some kind of devil-worship and awful sacrifices in some place near the wharves that people stumbled on around 1845 or thereabouts—but I come from Panton, Vermont, and that kind of story don't go down with me.

"You ought to hear, though, what some of the old-timers tell about the black reef off the coast—Devil Reef, they call it. It's well above water a good part of the time, and never much below it, but at that you could hardly call it an island. The story is that there's a whole legion of devils seen sometimes on that reef—sprawled about, or darting in and out of some kind of caves near the top. It's a rugged, uneven thing, a good bit over a mile out, and toward the end of shipping days sailors used to make big detours just to avoid it.

"That is, sailors that didn't hail from Innsmouth. One of the things they had against old Captain Marsh was that he was supposed to land on it sometimes at night when the tide was right. Maybe he did, for I dare say the rock formation was interesting, and it's just barely possible he was looking for pirate loot and maybe finding it; but there was talk of his dealing with demons there. Fact is, I guess on the whole it was really the Captain that gave the bad reputation to the reef.

"That was before the big epidemic of 1846, when over half the folks in Innsmouth was carried off. They never did quite figure out what the trouble was, but it was probably some foreign kind of disease brought from China or somewhere by the shipping. It surely was bad enough—there was riots over it, and all sorts of ghastly doings that I don't believe ever got outside of town— and it left the place in awful shape. Never came back—there can't be more'n 300 or 400 people living there now.

"But the real thing behind the way folks feel is simply race prejudice—and I don't say I'm blaming those that hold it. I hate those Innsmouth folks myself, and I wouldn't care to go to their town. I s'pose you know—though I can see you're a Westerner by your talk—what a lot our New England ships—used to have to do with queer ports in Africa, Asia, the South Seas, and everywhere else, and what queer kinds of people they sometimes brought back with 'em. You've probably heard about the Salem man that came home with a Chinese wife, and maybe you know there's still a bunch of Fiji Islanders somewhere around Cape Cod.

"Well, there must be something like that back of the Innsmouth people. The place always was badly cut off from the rest of the country by marshes and creeks and we can't be sure about the ins and outs of the matter; but it's pretty clear that old Captain Marsh must have brought home some odd specimens when he had all three of his ships in commission back in the twenties and thirties. There certainly is a strange kind of streak in the Innsmouth folks today—I don't know how to explain it but it sort of makes you crawl. You'll notice a little in Sargent if you take his bus. Some of 'em have queer narrow heads with flat noses and bulgy, stary eyes that never seem to shut, and their skin ain't quite right. Rough and scabby, and the sides of the necks are all shriveled or creased up. Get bald, too, very young. The older fellows look the worst—fact is, I don't believe I've ever seen a very old chap of that kind. Guess they must die of looking in the glass! Animals hate 'em—they used to have lots of horse trouble before the autos came in.

"Nobody around here or in Arkham or Ipswich will have anything to do with 'em, and they act kind of offish themselves when they come to town or when anyone tries to fish on their grounds. Queer how fish are always thick off Innsmouth Harbor when there ain't any anywhere else around—but just try to fish there yourself and see how the folks chase you off! Those people used to come here on the railroad—walking and taking the train at Rowley after the branch was dropped—but now they use that bus.

"Yes, there's a hotel in Innsmouth—called the Gilman House—but I don't believe it can amount to much. I wouldn't advise you to try it. Better stay over here and take the ten o'clock bus tomorrow morning; then you can get an evening bus there for Arkham at eight o'clock. There was a factory inspector who stopped at the Gilman a couple of years ago and he had a lot of unpleasant hints about the place. Seems they get a queer crowd there, for this fellow heard voices in other rooms—though most of 'em was empty—that gave him the shivers. It was foreign talk he thought, but he said the bad thing about it was the kind of voice that sometimes spoke. It sounded so unnatural—slopping like, he said—that he didn't dare undress and go to sleep. Just waited up and lit out the first thing in the morning. The talk went on most all night.

"This fellow—Casey, his name was—had a lot to say about how the Innsmouth folk watched him and seemed kind of on guard. He found the Marsh refinery a queer place—it's in an old mill on the lower falls of the Manuxet. What he said tallied up with what I'd heard. Books in bad shape, and no clear account of any kind of dealings. You know it's always been a kind of mystery where the Marshes get the gold they refine. They've never seemed to do much buying in that line, but years ago they shipped out an enormous lot of ingots.

"Used to be talk of a queer foreign kind of jewelry that the sailors and refinery men sometimes sold on the sly, or that was seen once or twice on some of the Marsh women-folks. People allowed maybe old Captain Obed traded for it in some heathen port, especially since he always ordered stacks of glass beads and trinkets such as seafaring men used to get for native trade. Others thought and still think he'd found an old pirate cache out on Devil Reef. But here's a funny thing. The old Captain's been dead these sixty years, and there's ain't been a good-sized ship out of the place since the Civil War; but just the same the Marshes still keep on buying a few of those native trade things—mostly glass and rubber gewgaws, they tell me. Maybe the Innsmouth folks like 'em to look at themselves—Gawd knows they've gotten to be about as bad as South Sea cannibals and Guinea savages.

"That plague of '46 must have taken off the best blood in the place. Anyway, they're a doubtful lot now, and the Marshes and other rich folks are as bad as any. As I told you, there probably ain't more'n 400 people in the whole town in spite of all the streets they say there are. I guess they're what they call 'white trash' down South—lawless and sly, and full of secret things. They get a lot of fish and lobsters and do exporting by truck. Queer how the fish swarm right there and nowhere else.

"Nobody can ever keep track of these people, and state school officials and census men have a devil of a time. You can bet that prying strangers ain't welcome around Innsmouth. I've heard personally of more'n one business or government man that's disappeared there, and there's loose talk of one who went crazy and is out at Danvers now. They must have fixed up some awful scare for that fellow.

"That's why I wouldn't go at night if I was you. I've never been there and have no wish to go, but I guess a daytime trip couldn't hurt you—even though the people hereabouts will advise you not to make it. If you're just sightseeing, and looking for old-time stuff, Innsmouth ought to be quite a place for you."

And so I spent part of that evening at the Newburyport Public Library looking up data about Innsmouth. When I had tried to question the natives in the shops, the lunchroom, the garages, and the fire station, I had found them even harder to get started than the ticket agent had predicted; and realized that I could not spare the time to overcome their first instinctive reticence. They had a kind of obscure suspiciousness, as if there were something amiss with anyone too much interested in Innsmouth. At the Y.M.C.A., where I was stopping, the clerk merely discouraged my going to such a dismal, decadent place; and the people at the library shewed much the same attitude. Clearly, in the eyes of the educated, Innsmouth was merely an exaggerated case of civic degeneration.

The Essex County histories on the library shelves had very little to say, except that the town was founded in 1643, noted for shipbuilding before the Revolution, a seat of great marine prosperity in the early 19th century, and later a minor factory center using the Manuxet as power. The epidemic and riots of 1846 were very sparsely treated, as if they formed a discredit to the county.

References to decline were few, though the significance of the later record was unmistakable. After the Civil War all industrial life was confined to the Marsh Refining Company, and the marketing of gold ingots formed the only remaining bit of major commerce aside from the eternal fishing. That fishing paid less and less as the price of the commodity fell and large-scale corporations offered competition, but there was never a dearth of fish around Innsmouth Harbor. Foreigners seldom settled there, and there was some discreetly veiled evidence that a number of Poles and Portuguese who had tried it had been scattered in a peculiarly drastic fashion.

Most interesting of all was a glancing reference to the strange jewelry vaguely associated with Innsmouth. It had evidently impressed the whole countryside more than a little, for mention was made of specimens in the museum of Miskatonic University at Arkham, and in the display room of the Newburyport Historical

Society. The fragmentary descriptions of these things were bald and prosaic, but they hinted to me an undercurrent of persistent strangeness. Something about them seemed so odd and provocative that I could not put them out of my mind, and despite the relative lateness of the hour I resolved to see the local sample—said to be a large, queerly-proportioned thing evidently meant for a tiara—if it could possibly be arranged.

The librarian gave me a note of introduction to the curator of the Society, a Miss Anna Tilton, who lived nearby, and after a brief explanation that ancient gentlewoman was kind enough to pilot me into the closed building, since the hour was not outrageously late. The collection was a notable one indeed, but in my present mood I had eyes for nothing but the bizarre object which glistened in a corner cupboard under the electric lights.

It took no excessive sensitiveness to beauty to make me literally gasp at the strange, unearthly splendor of the alien, opulent phantasy that rested there on a purple velvet cushion. Even now I can hardly describe what I saw, though it was clearly enough a sort of tiara, as the description had said. It was tall in front, and with a very large and curiously irregular periphery, as if designed for a head of almost freakishly elliptical outline. The material seemed to be predominantly gold, though a weird lighter lustrousness hinted at some strange alloy with an equally beautiful and scarcely identifiable metal. Its condition was almost perfect, and one could have spent hours in studying the striking and puzzlingly untraditional designs—some simply geometrical, and some plainly marine—chased or molded in high relief on its surface with a craftsmanship of incredible skill and grace.

The longer I looked, the more the thing fascinated me; and in this fascination there was a curiously disturbing element hardly to be classified or accounted for. At first I decided that it was the queer other-worldly quality of the art which made me uneasy. All other art objects I had ever seen either belonged to some known racial or national stream, or else were consciously modernistic defiances of every recognized stream. This tiara was neither. It clearly belonged to some settled technique of infinite maturity and perfection, yet that technique was utterly remote from any—Eastern or Western, ancient or modern—which I had ever heard of or seen exemplified. It was as if the workmanship were that of another planet.

However, I soon saw that my uneasiness had a second and perhaps equally potent source residing in the pictorial and mathematical suggestion of the strange designs. The patterns all hinted of remote secrets and unimaginable abysses in time and space, and the monotonously aquatic nature of the reliefs became almost sinister. Among these reliefs were fabulous monsters of abhorrent grotesqueness and malignity—half ichthyic and half batrachian in suggestion—which one could not dissociate from a certain haunting and uncomfortable sense of pseudomemory, as if they called up some image from deep cells and tissues whose retentive functions are wholly primal and awesomely ancestral. At times I fancied that every contour of these blasphemous fish-frogs was over-flowing with the ultimate quintessence of unknown and inhuman evil.

In odd contrast to the tiara's aspect was its brief and prosy history as related by Miss Tilton. It had been pawned for a ridiculous sum at a shop in State Street in 1873, by a drunken Innsmouth man shortly afterward killed in a brawl. The Society had acquired it directly from the pawnbroker, at once giving it a display worthy of its quality. It was labeled as of probable East-Indian or Indochinese provenance, though the attribution was frankly tentative.

Miss Tilton, comparing all possible hypotheses regarding its origin and its presence in New England, was inclined to believe that it formed part of some exotic pirate hoard discovered by old Captain Obed Marsh. This view was surely not weakened by the insistent offers of purchase at a high price which the Marshes began to make as soon as they knew of its presence, and which they repeated to this day despite the Society's unvarying determination not to sell.

As the good lady shewed me out of the building she made it clear that the pirate theory of the Marsh fortune was a popular one among the intelligent people of the region. Her own attitude toward shadowed Innsmouth—which she had never seen—was one of disgust at a community slipping far down the cultural scale, and she assured me that the rumours of devil-worship were partly justified by a peculiar secret cult which had gained force there and engulfed all the orthodox churches.

It was called, she said, "The Esoteric Order of Dagon," and was undoubtedly a debased, quasi-pagan thing imported from the East a century before, at a time when the Innsmouth fisheries seemed to be going barren. Its persistence among a simple people was quite natural in view of the sudden and permanent return of abundantly fine fishing, and it soon came to be the greatest influence in the town, replacing Freemasonry altogether and taking up headquarters in the old Masonic Hall on New Church Green.

All this, to the pious Miss Tilton, formed an excellent reason for shunning the ancient town of decay and desolation; but to me it was merely a fresh incentive. To my architectural and historical anticipations was now added an acute anthropological zeal, and I could scarcely sleep in my small room at the "Y" as the night wore away.

II

Shortly before ten the next morning I stood with one small valise in front of Hammond's Drug Store in old Market Square waiting for the Innsmouth bus. As the hour for its arrival drew near I noticed a general drift of the loungers to other places up the street, or to the Ideal Lunch across the square. Evidently the ticket-agent had not exaggerated the dislike which local people bore toward Innsmouth and its denizens. In a few moments a small motor-coach of extreme decrepitude and dirty grey color rattled down State Street, made a turn, and drew up at the curb beside me. I felt immediately that it was the right one; a guess which the half-illegible sign on the windshield—Arkham-Innsmouth-Newburyport—soon verified.

There were only three passengers—dark, unkempt men of sullen visage and somewhat youthful cast—and when the vehicle stopped they clumsily shambled out and began walking up State Street in a silent, almost furtive fashion. The driver also alighted, and I watched him as he went into the drug store to make some purchase. This, I reflected, must be the Joe Sargent mentioned by the ticket-agent; and even before I noticed any details, there spread over me a wave of spontaneous aversion which could be neither checked nor explained. It suddenly struck me as very natural that the local people should not wish to ride on a bus owned and driven by this man, or to visit any oftener than possible the habitat of such a man and his kinsfolk.

When the driver came out of the store I looked at him more carefully and tried to determine the source of my evil impression. He was a thin, stoop-shouldered man not much under six feet tall, dressed in shabby blue civilian clothes and wearing a frayed golf cap. His age was perhaps thirty-five, but the odd, deep creases in the sides of his neck made him seem older when one did not study his dull, expressionless face. He had a narrow head, bulging, watery-blue eyes that seemed never to wink, a flat nose, a receding forehead and chin, and singularly undeveloped ears. His long thick lip and coarse-pored, grayish cheeks seemed almost beardless except for some sparse yellow hairs that straggled and curled in irregular patches; and in places the surface seemed queerly irregular, as if peeling from some cutaneous disease. His hands were large and heavily veined, and had a very unusual grayish-blue tinge. The fingers were strikingly short in proportion to the rest of the structure, and seemed to have a tendency to curl closely into the huge palm. As he walked toward the bus I observed his peculiarly shambling gait and saw that his feet were inordinately immense. The more I studied them the more I wondered how he could buy any shoes to fit them.

A certain greasiness about the fellow increased my dislike. He was evidently given to working or lounging around the fish docks, and carried with him much of their characteristic smell. Just what foreign blood was in him I could not even guess. His oddities certainly did not look Asiatic, Polynesian, Levantine or negroid, yet I could see why the people found him alien. I myself would have thought of biological degeneration rather than alienage.

I was sorry when I saw there would be no other passengers on the bus. Somehow I did not like the idea of riding alone with this driver. But as leaving time obviously approached I conquered my qualms and followed the man aboard, extending him a dollar bill and murmuring the single word "Innsmouth." He looked curiously at me for a second as he returned forty cents change without speaking. I took a seat far behind him, but on the same side of the bus, since I wished to watch the shore during the journey.

At length the decrepit vehicle started with a jerk, and rattled noisily past the old brick buildings of State Street amidst a cloud of vapour from the exhaust. Glancing at the people on the sidewalks, I thought I detected in them a curious wish to avoid looking at the bus—or at least a wish to avoid seeming to look at it. Then we turned to the left into High Street, where the going was smoother; flying by stately old mansions of the early republic and still older colonial farmhouses, passing the Lower Green and Parker River, and finally emerging into a long, monotonous stretch of open shore country.

The day was warm and sunny, but the landscape of sand and sedge-grass, and stunted shrubbery became more and desolate as we proceeded. Out the window I could see the blue water and the sandy line of Plum Island, and we presently drew very near the beach as our narrow road veered off from the main highway to Rowley and Ipswich. There were no visible houses, and I could tell by the state of the road that traffic was very light hereabouts. The weather-worn telephone poles carried only two wires. Now and then we crossed crude wooden bridges over tidal creeks that wound far inland and promoted the general isolation of the region.

Once in a while I noticed dead stumps and crumbling foundation-walls above the drifting sand, and recalled the old tradition quoted in one of the histories I had read, that this was once a fertile and thickly settled countryside. The change, it was said, came simultaneously with the Innsmouth epidemic of 1846, and was thought by simple folk to have a dark connection with hidden forces of evil. Actually, it was caused by the unwise cutting of woodlands near the shore, which robbed the soil of the best protection and opened the way for waves of wind-blown sand.

At last we lost sight of Plum Island and saw the vast expanse of the open Atlantic on our left. Our narrow course began to climb steeply, and I felt a singular sense of disquiet in looking at the lonely crest ahead where the rutted road-way met the sky. It was as if the bus were about to keep on in its ascent, leaving the sane earth altogether and merging with the unknown arcana of upper air and cryptical sky. The smell of the sea took on ominous implications, and the silent driver's bent, rigid back and narrow head became more and more hateful. As I looked at him I saw that the back of his head was almost as hairless as his face, having only a few straggling yellow strands upon a gray scabrous surface.

Then we reached the crest and beheld the outspread valley beyond, where the Manuxet joins the sea just north of the long line of cliffs that culminate in Kingsport Head and veer off toward Cape Ann. On the far misty horizon I could just make out the dizzy profile of the Head, topped by the queer ancient house of which so many legends are told; but for the moment all my attention was captured by the nearer panorama just below me. I had, I realized, come face to face with rumor-shadowed Innsmouth.

It was a town of wide extent and dense construction, yet one with a portentous dearth of visible life. From the tangle of chimney-pots scarcely a wisp of smoke came, and the three tall steeples loomed stark and unpainted against the seaward horizon. One of them was crumbling down at the top, and in that and another there were only black gaping holes where clock-dials should have been. The vast huddle of sagging gambrel roofs and peaked gables conveyed with offensive clearness the idea of wormy decay, and as we approached along the now descending road I could see that many roofs had wholly caved in. There were some large square Georgian houses, too, with hipped roofs, cupolas, and railed "widow's walks." These were mostly well back from the water, and one or two seemed to be in moderately sound condition. Stretching inland from among them I saw the rusted, grass-grown line of the abandoned railway, with leaning telegraph-poles now devoid of wires, and the half-obscured lines of the old carriage roads to Rowley and Ipswich.

The decay was worst close to the waterfront, though in its very midst I could spy the white belfry of a fairly well preserved brick structure which looked like a small factory. The harbor, long clogged with sand, was enclosed by an ancient stone breakwater; on which I could begin to discern the minute forms of a few seated fishermen, and at whose end were what looked like the foundations of a bygone lighthouse. A sandy tongue had formed inside this barrier and upon it I saw a few decrepit cabins, moored dories, and scattered lobster-pots. The only deep water seemed to be where the river poured out past the belfried structure and turned southward to join the ocean at the breakwater's end.

Here and there the ruins of wharves jutted out from the shore to end in indeterminate rottenness, those farthest south seeming the most decayed. And far out at sea, despite a high tide, I glimpsed a long, black line scarcely rising above the water yet carrying a suggestion of odd latent malignancy. This, I knew, must be Devil Reef. As I looked, a subtle, curious sense of beckoning seemed superadded to the grim repulsion; and oddly enough, I found this overtone more disturbing than the primary impression.

We met no one on the road, but presently began to pass deserted farms in varying stages of ruin. Then I noticed a few inhabited houses with rags stuffed in the broken windows and shells and dead fish lying about the littered yards. Once or twice I saw listless-looking people working in barren gardens or digging clams on the fishy-smelling beach below, and groups of dirty, simian-visaged children playing around weed-grown doorsteps. Somehow these people seemed more disquieting than the dismal buildings, for almost every one had certain peculiarities of face and motions which I instinctively disliked without being able to define or comprehend them. For a second I thought this typical physique suggested some picture I had seen, perhaps in a book, under circumstances of particular horror or melancholy; but this pseudo-recollection passed very quickly.

As the bus reached a lower level I began to catch the steady note of a waterfall through the unnatural stillness, The leaning, unpainted houses grew thicker, lined both sides of the road, and displayed more urban tendencies than did those we were leaving behind. The panorama ahead had contracted to a street scene, and in spots I could see where a cobblestone pavement and stretches of brick sidewalk had formerly existed. All the houses were apparently deserted, and there were occasional gaps where tumbledown chimneys and cellar walls told of buildings that had collapsed. Pervading everything was the most nauseous fishy odor imaginable.

Soon cross streets and junctions began to appear; those on the left leading to shoreward realms of unpaved squalor and decay, while those on the right shewed vistas of departed grandeur. So far I had seen no people in the town, but there now came signs of a sparse habitation—curtained windows here and there, and an occasional battered motorcar at the curb. Pavement and sidewalks were increasingly well-defined, and though most of the houses were quite old—wood and brick structures of the early 19th century—they were obviously kept fit for habitation. As an amateur antiquarian I almost lost my olfactory disgust and my feeling of menace and repulsion amidst this rich, unaltered survival from the past.

But I was not to reach my destination without one very strong impression of poignantly disagreeable quality. The bus had come to a sort of open concourse or radial point with churches on two sides and the bedraggled remains of a circular green in the centre, and I was looking at a large pillared hall on the right-hand junction ahead. The structure's once white paint was now gray and peeling and the black and gold sign on the pediment was so faded that I could only with difficulty make out the words "Esoteric Order of Dagon". This, then was the former Masonic Hall now given over to a degraded cult. As I strained to decipher this inscription my notice was distracted by the raucous tones of a cracked bell across the street, and I quickly turned to look out the window on my side of the coach.

The sound came from a squat stone church of manifestly later date than most of the houses, built in a clumsy Gothic fashion and having a disproportionately high basement with shuttered windows. Though the hands of its clock were missing on the side I glimpsed, I knew that those hoarse strokes were tolling the hour of eleven. Then suddenly all thoughts of time were blotted out by an onrushing image of sharp intensity and unaccountable horror which had seized me before I knew what it really was. The door of the church basement was open, revealing a rectangle of blackness inside. And as I looked, a certain object crossed or seemed to cross that dark rectangle; burning into my brain a momentary conception of nightmare which was all the more maddening because analysis could not shew a single nightmarish quality in it.

It was a living object—the first except the driver that I had seen since entering the compact part of the town—and had I been in a steadier mood I would have found nothing whatever of terror in it. Clearly, as I realized a moment later, it was the pastor; clad in some peculiar vestments doubtless introduced since the Order of Dagon had modified the ritual of the local churches. The thing which had probably caught my first subconscious glance and supplied the touch of bizarre horror was the tall tiara he wore; an almost exact duplicate of the one Miss Tilton had shown me the previous evening. This, acting on my imagination, had supplied namelessly sinister qualities to the indeterminate face and robed, shambling form beneath it. There was not, I soon decided, any reason why I should have felt that shuddering touch of evil pseudo-memory. Was it not natural that a local mystery cult should adopt among its regimentals an unique type of head-dress made familiar to the community in some strange way—perhaps as treasure-trove?

A very thin sprinkling of repellent-looking youngish people now became visible on the sidewalks—lone individuals, and silent knots of two or three. The lower floors of the crumbling houses sometimes harbored small shops with dingy signs, and I noticed a parked truck or two as we rattled along. The sound of waterfalls became more and more distinct, and presently I saw a fairly deep river-gorge ahead, spanned by a wide, iron-railed highway bridge beyond which a large square opened out. As we clanked over the bridge I looked out on both sides and observed some factory buildings on the edge of the grassy bluff or part way down. The water far below was very abundant, and I could see two vigorous sets of falls upstream on my right and at least one downstream on my left. From this point the noise was quite deafening. Then we rolled into the large semicircular square across the river and drew up on the right-hand side in front of a tall, cupola crowned building with remnants of yellow paint and with a half-effaced sign proclaiming it to be the Gilman House.

I was glad to get out of that bus, and at once proceeded to check my valise in the shabby hotel lobby. There was only one person in sight—an elderly man without what I had come to call the "Innsmouth look"—and I decided not to ask him any of the questions which bothered me; remembering that odd things had been noticed in this hotel. Instead, I strolled out on the square, from which the bus had already gone, and studied the scene minutely and appraisingly.

One side of the cobblestoned open space was the straight line of the river; the other was a semicircle of slant-roofed brick buildings of about the 1800 period, from which several streets radiated away to the southeast, south, and southwest. Lamps were depressingly few and small—all low-powered incandescents—and I was glad that my plans called for departure before dark, even though I knew the moon would be bright. The buildings were all in fair condition, and included perhaps a dozen shops in current operation; of which one was a grocery of the First National chain, others a dismal restaurant, a drug store, and a wholesale fish-dealer's office, and still another, at the eastward extremity of the square near the river, an office of the town's only industry— the Marsh Refining Company. There were perhaps ten people visible, and four or five automobiles and motor trucks stood scattered about. I did not need to be told that this was the civic centre of Innsmouth. Eastward I could catch blue glimpses of the harbour, against which rose the decaying remains of three once beautiful Georgian steeples. And toward the shore on the opposite bank of the river I saw the white belfry surmounting what I took to be the Marsh refinery.

For some reason or other I chose to make my first inquiries at the chain grocery, whose personnel was not likely to be native to Innsmouth. I found a solitary boy of about seventeen in charge, and was pleased to note the brightness and affability which promised cheerful information. He seemed exceptionally eager to talk, and I soon gathered that he did not like the place, its fishy smell, or its furtive people. A word with any outsider was a relief to him. He hailed from Arkham, boarded with a family who came from Ipswich, and went back whenever he got a moment off. His family did not like him to work in Innsmouth, but the chain had transferred him there and he did not wish to give up his job.

There was, he said, no public library or chamber of commerce in Innsmouth, but I could probably find my way about. The street I had come down was Federal. West of that were the fine old residence streets—Broad, Washington, Lafayette, and Adams—and east of it were the shoreward slums. It was in these slums—along Main Street—that I would find the old Georgian churches, but they were all long abandoned. It would be well not to make oneself too conspicuous in such neighborhoods—especially north of the river since the people were sullen and hostile. Some strangers had even disappeared.

Certain spots were almost forbidden territory, as he had learned at considerable cost. One must not, for example, linger much around the Marsh refinery, or around any of the still used churches, or around the pillared Order of Dagon Hall at New Church Green. Those churches were very odd—all violently disavowed by their respective denominations elsewhere, and apparently using the queerest kind of ceremonials and clerical vestments. Their creeds were heterodox and mysterious, involving hints of certain marvelous transformations leading to bodily immortality—of a sort—on this earth. The youth's own pastor—Dr. Wallace of Asbury M. E. Church in Arkham—had gravely urged him not to join any church in Innsmouth.

As for the Innsmouth people—the youth hardly knew what to make of them. They were as furtive and seldom seen as animals that live in burrows, and one could hardly imagine how they passed the time apart from their desultory fishing. Perhaps—judging from the quantities of bootleg liquor they consumed—they lay for most of the daylight hours in an alcoholic stupor. They seemed sullenly banded together in some sort of fellowship and understanding—despising the world as if they had access to other and preferable spheres of entity. Their appearance—especially those staring, unwinking eyes which one never saw shut—was certainly shocking enough; and their voices were disgusting. It was awful to hear them chanting in their churches at night, and especially during their main festivals or revivals, which fell twice a year on April 30th and October 31st.

They were very fond of the water, and swam a great deal in both river and harbour. Swimming races out to Devil Reef were very common, and everyone in sight seemed well able to share in this arduous sport. When one came to think of it, it was generally only rather young people who were seen about in public, and of these the oldest were apt to be the most tainted-looking. When exceptions did occur, they were mostly persons with no trace of aberrancy, like the old clerk at the hotel. One wondered what became of the bulk of the older folk, and whether the "Innsmouth look" were not a strange and insidious disease-phenomenon which increased its hold as years advanced.

Only a very rare affliction, of course, could bring about such vast and radical anatomical changes in a single individual after maturity—changes invoking osseous factors as basic as the shape of the skull—but then, even this aspect was no more baffling and unheard-of than the visible features of the malady as a whole. It would be hard, the youth implied, to form any real conclusions regarding such a matter; since one never came to know the natives personally no matter how long one might live in Innsmouth.

The youth was certain that many specimens even worse than the worst visible ones were kept locked indoors in some places. People sometimes heard the queerest kind of sounds. The tottering waterfront hovels north of the river were reputedly connected by hidden tunnels, being thus a veritable warren of unseen abnormalities. What kind of foreign blood—if any—these beings had, it was impossible to tell. They sometimes kept certain especially repulsive characters out of sight when government and others from the outside world came to town.

It would be of no use, my informant said, to ask the natives anything about the place. The only one who would talk was a very aged but normal looking man who lived at the poorhouse on the north rim of the town and spent his time walking about or lounging around the fire station. This hoary character, Zadok Allen, was

96 years old and somewhat touched in the head, besides being the town drunkard. He was a strange, furtive creature who constantly looked over his shoulder as if afraid of something, and when sober could not be persuaded to talk at all with strangers. He was, however, unable to resist any offer of his favorite poison; and once drunk would furnish the most astonishing fragments of whispered reminiscence.

After all, though, little useful data could be gained from him; since his stories were all insane, incomplete hints of impossible marvels and horrors which could have no source save in his own disordered fancy. Nobody ever believed him, but the natives did not like him to drink and talk with strangers; and it was not always safe to be seen questioning him. It was probably from him that some of the wildest popular whispers and delusions were derived.

Several non-native residents had reported monstrous glimpses from time to time, but between old Zadok's tales and the malformed inhabitants it was no wonder such illusions were current. None of the non-natives ever stayed out late at night, there being a widespread impression that it was not wise to do so. Besides, the streets were loathsomely dark.

As for business—the abundance of fish was certainly almost uncanny, but the natives were taking less and less advantage of it. Moreover, prices were falling and competition was growing. Of course the town's real business was the refinery, whose commercial office was on the square only a few doors east of where we stood. Old Man Marsh was never seen, but sometimes went to the works in a closed, curtained car.

There were all sorts of rumors about how Marsh had come to look. He had once been a great dandy; and people said he still wore the frock-coated finery of the Edwardian age curiously adapted to certain deformities. His son had formerly conducted the office in the square, but latterly they had been keeping out of sight a good deal and leaving the brunt of affairs to the younger generation. The sons and their sisters had come to look very queer, especially the elder ones; and it was said that their health was failing.

One of the Marsh daughters was a repellent, reptilian-looking woman who wore an excess of weird jewelry clearly of the same exotic tradition as that to which the strange tiara belonged. My informant had noticed it many times, and had heard it spoken of as coming from some secret hoard, either of pirates or of demons. The clergymen—or priests, or whatever they were called nowadays— also wore this kind of ornament as a headdress; but one seldom caught glimpses of them. Other specimens the youth had not seen, though many were rumored to exist around Innsmouth.

The Marshes, together with the other three gently bred families of the town— the Waites, the Gilmans, and the Eliots—were all very retiring. They lived in immense houses along Washington Street, and several were reputed to harbor in concealment certain living kinsfolk whose personal aspect forbade public view, and whose deaths had been reported and recorded.

Warning me that many of the street signs were down, the youth drew for my benefit a rough but ample and painstaking sketch map of the town's salient features. After a moment's study I felt sure that it would be of great help, and pocketed it with profuse thanks. Disliking the dinginess of the single restaurant I had seen, I bought a fair supply of cheese crackers and ginger wafers to serve as a lunch later on. My program, I decided, would be to thread the principal streets, talk with any non-natives I might encounter, and catch the eight o'clock coach for Arkham. The town, I could see, formed a significant and exaggerated example of communal decay; but being no sociologist I would limit my serious observations to the field of architecture.

Thus I began my systematic though half-bewildered tour of Innsmouth's narrow, shadow-blighted ways. Crossing the bridge and turning toward the roar of the lower falls, I passed close to the Marsh refinery, which seemed to be oddly free from the noise of industry. The building stood on the steep river bluff near a bridge and an open confluence of streets which I took to be the earliest civic center, displaced after the Revolution by the present Town Square.

Re-crossing the gorge on the Main Street bridge, I struck a region of utter desertion which somehow made me shudder. Collapsing huddles of gambrel roofs formed a jagged and fantastic skyline, above which rose the ghoulish, decapitated steeple of an ancient church. Some houses along Main Street were tenanted, but most were tightly boarded up. Down unpaved side streets I saw the black, gaping windows of deserted hovels, many of which leaned at perilous and incredible angles through the sinking of part of the foundations. Those windows stared so spectrally that it took courage to turn eastward toward the waterfront. Certainly, the terror of a deserted house swells in geometrical rather than arithmetical progression as houses multiply to form a city of stark desolation. The sight of such endless avenues of fishy-eyed vacancy and death, and the thought of such linked infinities of black, brooding compartments given over to cob-webs and memories and the conqueror worm, start up vestigial fears and aversions that not even the stoutest philosophy can disperse.

Fish Street was as deserted as Main, though it differed in having many brick and stone warehouses still in excellent shape. Water Street was almost its duplicate, save that there were great seaward gaps where wharves had been. Not a living thing did I see except for the scattered fishermen on the distant break-water, and not a sound did I hear save the lapping of the harbor tides and the roar of the falls in the Manuxet. The town was getting more and more on my nerves, and I looked behind me furtively as I picked my way back over the tottering Water Street bridge. The Fish Street bridge, according to the sketch, was in ruins.

North of the river there were traces of squalid life—active fish-packing houses in Water Street, smoking chimneys and patched roofs here and there, occasional sounds from indeterminate sources, and infrequent shambling forms in the dismal streets and unpaved lanes—but I seemed to find this even more oppressive than the southerly desertion. For one thing, the people were more hideous and abnormal than those near the centre of the town; so that I was several times evilly reminded of something utterly fantastic which I could not quite place. Undoubtedly the alien strain in the Innsmouth folk was stronger here than farther inland— unless, indeed, the "Innsmouth look" were a disease rather than a blood stain, in which case this district might be held to harbor the more advanced cases.

One detail that annoyed me was the distribution of the few faint sounds I heard. They ought naturally to have come wholly from the visibly inhabited houses, yet in reality were often strongest inside the most rigidly boarded-up facades. There were creakings, scurryings, and hoarse doubtful noises; and I thought uncomfortably about the hidden tunnels suggested by the grocery boy. Suddenly I found myself wondering what the voices of those denizens would be like. I had heard no speech so far in this quarter, and was unaccountably anxious not to do so.

Pausing only long enough to look at two fine but ruinous old churches at Main and Church Streets, I hastened out of that vile waterfront slum. My next logical goal was New Church Green, but somehow or other I could not bear to repass the church in whose basement I had glimpsed the inexplicably frightening form of that strangely diademmed priest or pastor. Besides, the grocery youth had told me that churches, as well as the Order of Dagon Hall, were not advisable neighborhoods for strangers.

Accordingly I kept north along Main to Martin, then turning inland, crossing Federal Street safely north of the Green, and entering the decayed patrician neighborhood of northern Broad, Washington, Lafayette, and Adams Streets. Though these stately old avenues were ill-surfaced and unkempt, their elm-shaded dignity had not entirely departed. Mansion after mansion claimed my gaze, most of them decrepit and boarded up amidst neglected grounds, but one or two in each street shewing signs of occupancy. In Washington Street there was a row of four or five in excellent repair and with finely-tended lawns and gardens. The most sumptuous of these—with wide terraced parterres extending back the whole way to Lafayette Street—I took to be the home of Old Man Marsh, the afflicted refinery owner.

In all these streets no living thing was visible, and I wondered at the complete absence of cats and dogs from Innsmouth. Another thing which puzzled and disturbed me, even in some of the best-preserved mansions, was the tightly shuttered condition of many third-story and attic windows. Furtiveness and secretiveness seemed universal in this hushed city of alienage and death, and I could not escape the sensation of being watched from ambush on every hand by sly, staring eyes that never shut.

I shivered as the cracked stroke of three sounded from a belfry on my left. Too well did I recall the squat church from which those notes came. Following Washington street toward the river, I now faced a new zone of former industry and commerce; noting the ruins of a factory ahead, and seeing others, with the traces of an old railway station and covered railway bridge beyond, up the gorge on my right.

The uncertain bridge now before me was posted with a warning sign, but I took the risk and crossed again to the south bank where traces of life reappeared. Furtive, shambling creatures stared cryptically in my direction, and more normal faces eyed me coldly and curiously. Innsmouth was rapidly becoming intolerable, and I turned down Paine Street toward the Square in the hope of getting some vehicle to take me to Arkham before the still-distant starting-time of that sinister bus.

It was then that I saw the tumbledown fire station on my left, and noticed the red faced, bushy-bearded, watery-eyed old man in nondescript rags who sat on a bench in front of it talking with a pair of unkempt but not abnormal looking firemen. This, of course, must be Zadok Allen, the half-crazed, liquorish nonagenarian whose tales of old Innsmouth and its shadow were so hideous and incredible.

It must have been some imp of the perverse—or some sardonic pull from dark, hidden sources—which made me change my plans as I did. I had long before resolved to limit my observations to architecture alone, and I was even then hurrying toward the Square in an effort to get quick transportation out of this festering city of death and decay; but the sight of old Zadok Allen set up new currents in my mind and made me slacken my pace uncertainly.

I had been assured that the old man could do nothing but hint at wild, disjointed, and incredible legends, and I had been warned that the natives made it unsafe to be seen talking with him; yet the thought of this aged witness to the town's decay, with memories going back to the early days of ships and factories, was a lure that no amount of reason could make me resist. After all, the strangest and maddest of myths are often merely symbols or allegories based upon truth— and old Zadok must have seen everything which went on around Innsmouth for the last ninety years. Curiosity flared up beyond sense and caution, and in my youthful egotism I fancied I might be able to sift a nucleus of real history from the confused, extravagant outpouring I would probably extract with the aid of raw whiskey.

I knew that I could not accost him then and there, for the firemen would surely notice and object. Instead, I reflected, I would prepare by getting some bootleg liquor at a place where the grocery boy had told me it was plentiful. Then I would loaf near the fire station in apparent casualness, and fall in with old Zadok after he had started on one of his frequent rambles. The youth had said that he was very restless, seldom sitting around the station for more than an hour or two at a time.

A quart bottle of whiskey was easily, though not cheaply, obtained in the rear of a dingy variety-store just off the Square in Eliot Street. The dirty-looking fellow who waited on me had a touch of the staring "Innsmouth look", but was quite civil in his way; being perhaps used to the custom of such convivial strangers—truckmen, gold-buyers, and the like—as were occasionally in town.

Reentering the Square I saw that luck was with me; for—shuffling out of Paine street around the corner of the Gilman House—I glimpsed nothing less than the tall, lean, tattered form of old Zadok Allen himself. In accordance with my plan, I attracted his attention by brandishing my newly-purchased bottle: and soon realized that he had begun to shuffle wistfully after me as I turned into Waite Street on my way to the most deserted region I could think of.

I was steering my course by the map the grocery boy had prepared, and was aiming for the wholly abandoned stretch of southern waterfront which I had previously visited. The only people in sight there had been the fishermen on the distant breakwater; and by going a few squares south I could get beyond the range of these, finding a pair of seats on some abandoned wharf and being free to question old Zadok unobserved for an indefinite time. Before I reached Main Street I could hear a faint and wheezy "Hey, Mister!" behind me and I presently allowed the old man to catch up and take copious pulls from the quart bottle.

I began putting out feelers as we walked amidst the omnipresent desolation and crazily tilted ruins, but found that the aged tongue did not loosen as quickly as I had expected. At length I saw a grass-grown opening toward the sea between crumbling brick walls, with the weedy length of an earth-and-masonry wharf projecting beyond. Piles of moss-covered stones near the water promised tolerable seats, and the scene was sheltered from all possible view by a ruined warehouse on the north. Here, I thought was the ideal place for a long secret colloquy; so I guided my companion down the lane and picked out spots to sit in among the mossy stones. The air of death and desertion was ghoulish, and the smell of fish almost insufferable; but I was resolved to let nothing deter me.

About four hours remained for conversation if I were to catch the eight o'clock coach for Arkham, and I began to dole out more liquor to the ancient tippler; meanwhile eating my own frugal lunch. In my donations I was careful not to overshoot the mark, for I did not wish Zadok's vinous garrulousness to pass into a stupor. After an hour his furtive taciturnity shewed signs of disappearing, but much to my disappointment he still sidetracked my questions about Innsmouth and its shadow-haunted past. He would babble of current topics, revealing a wide acquaintance with newspapers and a great tendency to philosophize in a sententious village fashion.

Toward the end of the second hour I feared my quart of whiskey would not be enough to produce results, and was wondering whether I had better leave old Zadok and go back for more. Just then, however, chance made the opening which my questions had been unable to make; and the wheezing ancient's rambling took a turn that caused me to lean forward and listen alertly. My back was toward the fishy-smelling sea, but he was facing it and something or other had caused his wandering gaze to light on the low, distant line of Devil Reef, then showing plainly and almost fascinatingly above the waves. The sight seemed to displease him, for he began a series of weak curses which ended in a confidential whisper and a knowing leer. He bent toward me, took hold of my coat lapel, and hissed out some hints that could not be mistaken,

"Thar's whar it all begun—that cursed place of all wickedness whar the deep water starts. Gate o' hell—sheer drop daown to a bottom no saoundin'-line kin tech. Ol' Cap'n Obed done it—him that faound aout more'n was good fer him in the Saouth Sea islands.

"Everybody was in a bad way them days. Trade fallin' off, mills losin' business—even the new ones—an' the best of our menfolks kilt aprivateerin' in the War of 1812 or lost with the Elizy brig an' the Ranger scow—both on 'em Gilman venters. Obed Marsh he had three ships afloat—brigantine Columby, brig Hefty, an' barque Sumatry Queen. He was the only one as kep' on with the East-Injy an' Pacific trade, though Esdras Martin's barkentine Malay Bride made a venter as late as twenty-eight.

"Never was nobody like Cap'n Obed—old limb o' Satan! Heh, heh! I kin mind him a-tellin' abaout furren parts, an' callin' all the folks stupid for goin' to Christian meetin' an' bearin' their burdens meek an' lowly. Says they'd orter git better gods like some o' the folks in the Injies—gods as ud bring 'em good fishin' in return for their sacrifices, an' ud reely answer folks's prayers.

"Matt Eliot, his fust mate, talked a lot too, only he was again' folks's doin' any heathen things. Told abaout an island east of Othaheite whar they was a lot o' stone ruins older'n anybody knew anying abaout, kind o' like them on Ponape, in the Carolines, but with carven's of faces that looked like the big statues on Easter Island. Thar was a little volcanic island near thar, too, whar they was other ruins with diff'rent carvin'—ruins all wore away like they'd ben under the sea onct, an' with picters of awful monsters all over 'em.

"Wal, Sir, Matt he says the natives anound thar had all the fish they cud ketch, an' sported bracelets an' armlets an' head rigs made aout o' a queer kind o' gold an' covered with picters o' monsters jest like the ones carved over the ruins on the little island—sorter fish-like frogs or froglike fishes that was drawed in all kinds o' positions likes they was human bein's. Nobody cud get aout o' them whar they got all the stuff, an' all the other natives wondered haow they managed to find fish in plenty even when the very next island had lean pickin's. Matt he got to wonderon' too an' so did Cap'n Obed. Obed he notices, besides, that lots of the han'some young folks ud drop aout o' sight fer good from year to year, an' that they wan't many old folks around. Also, he thinks some of the folks looked durned queer even for Kanakys.

"It took Obed to git the truth aout o' them heathen. I dun't know haow he done it, but he begun by tradin' fer the gold-like things they wore. Ast 'em whar they come from, an' ef they cud git more, an' finally wormed the story aout o' the old chief — Walakea, they called him. Nobody but Obed ud ever a believed the old yeller devil, but the Cap'n cud read folks like they was books. Heh, heh! Nobody never believes me naow when I tell 'em, an' I dun't s'pose you will, young feller—though come to look at ye, ye hev kind o' got them sharp-readin' eyes like Obed had."

The old man's whisper grew fainter, and I found myself shuddering at the terrible and sincere portentousness of his intonation, even though I knew his tale could be nothing but drunken phantasy.

"Wal, Sir, Obed he 'lart that they's things on this arth as most folks never heerd about—an' wouldn't believe ef they did hear. It seems these Kanakys was sacrificin' heaps o' their young men an' maidens to some kind o' god-things that lived under the sea, an' gittin' all kinds o' favour in return. They met the things on the little islet with the queer ruins, an' it seems them awful picters o' frog-fish monsters was supposed to be picters o' these things. Mebbe they was the kind o' critters as got all the mermaid stories an' sech started.

"They had all kinds a' cities on the sea-bottom, an' this island was heaved up from thar. Seem they was some of the things alive in the stone buildin's when the island come up sudden to the surface, That's how the Kanakys got wind they was daown thar. Made sign-talk as soon as they got over bein' skeert, an' pieced up a bargain afore long.

"Them things liked human sacrifices. Had had 'em ages afore, but lost track o' the upper world after a time. What they done to the victims it ain't fer me to say, an' I guess Obed was'n't none too sharp abaout askin'. But it was all right with the heathens, because they'd ben havin' a hard time an' was desp'rate abaout everything. They give a sarten number o' young folks to the sea-things twice every year— May-Eve an' Hallawe'en—reg'lar as cud be. Also give some a' the carved knick-knacks they made. What the things agreed to give in return was plenty a' fish—they druv 'em in from all over the sea—an' a few gold like things naow an' then.

"Wal, as I says, the natives met the things on the little volcanic islet—goin' thar in canoes with the sacrifices et cet'ry, and bringin' back any of the gold-like jools as was comin' to 'em. At fust the things didn't never go onto the main island, but arter a time they come to want to. Seems they hankered arter mixin' with the folks, an' havin' j'int ceremonies on the big days—May-Eve an' Hallowe'en. Ye see, they was able to live both in ant aout o' water—what they call amphibians, I guess. The Kanakys told 'em as haow folks from the other islands might wanta wipe 'em out if they got wind o' their bein' thar, but they says they dun't keer much, because they cud wipe aout the hull brood o' humans ef they was willin' to bother—that is, any as didn't be, sarten signs sech as was used onct by the lost Old Ones, whoever they was. But not wantin' to bother, they'd lay low when anybody visited the island.

"When it come to matin' with them toad-lookin' fishes, the Kanakys kind o' balked, but finally they larnt something as put a new face on the matter. Seems that human folks has got a kind a' relation to sech water-beasts—that everything alive come aout o' the water onct an' only needs a little change to go back agin. Them things told the Kanakys that ef they mixed bloods there'd be children as ud look human at fust, but later turn more'n more like the things, till finally they'd take to the water an' jine the main lot o' things daown har. An' this is the important part, young feller—them as turned into fish things an' went into the water wouldn't never die. Them things never died excep' they was kilt violent.

"Wal, Sir, it seems by the time Obed knowed them islanders they was all full o' fish blood from them deep water things. When they got old an' begun to shew it, they was kep' hid until they felt like takin' to the water an' quittin' the place. Some was more teched than others, an' some never did change quite enough to take to the water; but mosily they turned out jest the way them things said. Them as was born more like the things changed arly, but them as was nearly human sometimes stayed on the island till they was past seventy, though they'd usually go daown under for trial trips afore that. Folks as had took to the water gen'rally come back a good deal to visit, so's a man ud often be a'talkin' to his own five-times-great-grandfather who'd left the dry land a couple o' hundred years or so afore.

"Everybody got aout o' the idee o' dyin'—excep' in canoe wars with the other islanders, or as sacrifices to the sea-gods daown below, or from snakebite or plague or sharp gallopin' ailments or somethin' afore they cud take to the water—but simply looked forrad to a kind o' change that wa'n't a bit horrible arter a while. They thought what they'd got was well wuth all they'd had to give up—an' I guess Obed kind o' come to think the same hisself when he'd chewed over old Walakea's story a bit. Walakea, though, was one of the few as hadn't got none of the fish blood—bein' of a royal line that intermarried with royal lines on other islands.

"Walakea he shewed Obed a lot o' rites an' incantations as had to do with the sea things, an' let him see some o' the folks in the village as had changed a lot from human shape. Somehaow or other, though, he never would let him see one of the reg'lar things from right aout o' the water. In the end he give him a funny kind o' thingumajig made aout o' lead or something, that he said ud bring up the fish things from any place in the water whar they might be a nest o' 'em. The idee was to drop it daown with the right kind o' prayers an' sech. Walakea allowed as the things was scattered all over the world, so's anybody that looked abaout cud find a nest an' bring 'em up ef they was wanted.

"Matt he didn't like this business at all, an' wanted Obed shud keep away from the island; but the Cap'n was sharp fer gain, an' faound he cud get them gold-like things so cheap it ud pay him to make a specialty of them. Things went on that way for years an' Obed got enough o' that gold-like stuff to make him start the refinery in Waite's old run-daown fullin' mill. He didn't dass sell the pieces like they was, for folks ud be all the time askin' questions. All the same his crews ud get a piece an' dispose of it naow and then, even though they was swore to keep quiet; an' he let his women-folks wear some o' the pieces as was more human-like than most.

"Well, come abaout thutty-eight—when I was seven year' old—Obed he faound the island people all wiped aout between v'yages. Seems the other islanders had got wind o' what was goin' on, and had took matters into their own hands. S'pose they must a had, after all, them old magic signs as the sea things says was the only things they was afeard of. No tellin' what any o' them Kanakys will chance to git a holt of when the sea-bottom throws up some island with ruins older'n the deluge. Pious cusses, these was—they didn't leave nothin' standin' on either the main island or the little volcanic islet excep' what parts of the ruins was too big to knock daown. In some places they was little stones strewed abaout—like charms—with somethin' on 'em like what ye call a swastika naowadays. Prob'ly them was the Old Ones' signs. Folks all wiped aout no trace o' no gold-like things an' none the nearby Kanakys ud breathe a word abaout the matter. Wouldn't even admit they'd ever ben any people on that island.

"That naturally hit Obed pretty hard, seein' as his normal trade was doin' very poor. It hit the whole of Innsmouth, too, because in seafarint days what profited the master of a ship gen'lly profited the crew proportionate. Most of the folks araound the taown took the hard times kind o' sheep-like an' resigned, but they was in bad shape because the fishin' was peterin' aout an' the mills wan't doin' none too well.

"Then's the time Obed he begun a-cursin' at the folks fer bein' dull sheep an' prayin' to a Christian heaven as didn't help 'em none. He told 'em he'd knowed o' folks as prayed to gods that give somethin' ye reely need, an' says ef a good bunch o' men ud stand by him, he cud mebbe get a holt o' sarten paowers as ud bring plenty o' fish an' quite a bit of gold. 0' course them as sarved on the Sumatry Queen, an' seed the island knowed what he meant, an' wa'n't none too anxious to get clost to sea-things like they'd heard tell on, but them as didn't know what 'twas all abaout got kind o' swayed by what Obed had to say, and begun to ast him what he cud do to sit 'em on the way to the faith as ud bring 'em results."

Here the old man faltered, mumbled, and lapsed into a moody and apprehensive silence; glancing nervously over his shoulder and then turning back to stare fascinatedly at the distant black reef. When I spoke to him he did not answer, so I knew I would have to let him finish the bottle. The insane yarn I was hearing interested me profoundly, for I fancied there was contained within it a sort of crude allegory based upon the strangeness of Innsmouth and elaborated by an imagination at once creative and full of scraps of exotic legend. Not for a moment did I believe that the tale had any really substantial foundation; but none the less the account held a hint of genuine terror if only because it brought in references to strange jewels clearly akin to the malign tiara I had seen at Newburyport. Perhaps the ornaments had, after all, come from some strange island; and possibly the wild stories were lies of the bygone Obed himself rather than of this antique toper.

I handed Zadok the bottle, and he drained it to the last drop. It was curious how he could stand so much whiskey, for not even a trace of thickness had come into his high, wheezy voice. He licked the nose of the bottle and slipped it into his pocket, then beginning to nod and whisper softly to himself. I bent close to catch any articulate words he might utter, and thought I saw a sardonic smile behind the stained bushy whiskers. Yes—he was really forming words, and I could grasp a fair proportion of them.

"Poor Matt—Matt he allus was agin it—tried to line up the folks on his side, an' had long talks with the preachers—no use—they run the Congregational parson aout o' taown, an' the Methodist feller quit—never did see Resolved Babcock, the Baptist parson, agin—Wrath 0' Jehovy—I was a mightly little critter, but I heerd what I heerd an, seen what I seen—Dagon an' Ashtoreth— Belial an' Beelzebub— Golden Caff an' the idols o' Canaan an' the Philistines—Babylonish abominations— *Mene, mene, tekel, upharsin*—."

He stopped again, and from the look in his watery blue eyes I feared he was close to a stupor after all. But when I gently shook his shoulder he turned on me with astonishing alertness and snapped out some more obscure phrases.

"Dun't believe me, hey? Hey, heh, heh—then jest tell me, young feller, why

Cap'n Obed an' twenty odd other folks used to row aout to Devil Reef in the dead o' night an' chant things so laoud ye cud hear 'em all over taown when the wind was right? Tell me that, hey? An' tell me why Obed was allus droppin' heavy things daown into the deep water t'other side o' the reef whar the bottom shoots daown like a cliff lower'n ye kin saound? Tell me what he done with that funny-shaped lead thingumajig as Walakea give him? Hey, boy? An' what did they all haowl on May-Eve, an', agin the next Hallowe'en? An' why'd the new church parsons— fellers as used to be sailors—wear them queer robes an' cover their-selves with them gold-like things Obed brung? Hey?"

The watery blue eyes were almost savage and maniacal now, and the dirty white beard bristled electrically. Old Zadok probably saw me shrink back, for he began to cackle evilly.

"Heh, heh, heh, heh! Beginni'n to see hey? Mebbe ye'd like to a ben me in them days, when I seed things at night aout to sea from the cupalo top o' my haouse. Oh, I kin tell ye' little pitchers hev big ears, an' I wa'n't missin' nothin' o' what was gossiped abaout Cap'n Obed an' the folks aout to the reef! Heh, heh, heh! Haow abaout the night I took my pa's ship's glass up to the cupalo an' seed the reef a-bristlin' thick with shapes that dove off quick soon's the moon riz?

"Obed an' the folks was in a dory, but them shapes dove off the far side into the deep water an' never come up. . .

"Haow'd ye like to be a little shaver alone up in a cupola a-watchin' shapes as wa'n't human shapes? . . .Heh? . . .Heh, heh, heh. . ."

The old man was getting hysterical, and I began to shiver with a nameless alarm. He laid a gnarled claw on my shoulder, and it seemed to me that its shaking was not altogether that of mirth.

"S'pose one night ye seed somethin' heavy heaved offen Obed's dory beyond the reef' and then learned next day a young feller was missin' from home. Hey! Did anybody ever see hide or hair o' Hiram Gilman agin. Did they? An' Nick Pierce, an' Luelly Waite, an' Adoniram Saouthwick, an' Henry Garrison Hey? Heh, heh, heh, heh. . . Shapes talkin' sign language with their hands . . . them as had reel hands. . .

"Wal, Sir, that was the time Obed begun to git on his feet agin. Folks see his three darters a-wearin' gold-like things as nobody'd never see on 'em afore, an' smoke stared comin' aout o' the refin'ry chimbly. Other folks was prosp'rin, too— fish begun to swarm into the harbour fit to kill an' heaven knows what sized cargoes we begun to ship aout to Newb'ryport, Arkham, an' Boston. T'was then Obed got the ol' branch railrud put through. Some Kingsport fishermen heerd abaout the ketch an' come up in sloops, but they was all lost. Nobody never see 'em agin. An' jest then our folk organised the Esoteric Order O' Dagon, an' bought Masonic Hall offen Calvary Commandery for it . . . heh, heh, heh! Matt Eliot was a Mason an' agin the sellin', but he dropped aout o' sight jest then.

"Remember, I ain't sayin' Obed was set on hevin' things jest like they was on that Kanaky isle. I dun't think he aimed at fust to do no mixin', nor raise no younguns to take to the water an' turn into fishes with eternal life. He wanted them gold things, an' was willin' to pay heavy, an' I guess the others was satisfied fer a while ...

"Come in' forty-six the taown done some lookin' an' thinkin' fer itself. Too many folks missin'—too much wild preachin' at meetin' of a Sunday—too much talk abaout that reef. I guess I done a bit by tellin' Selectman Mowry what I see from the cupalo. They was a party one night as follered Obed's craowd aout to the reef, an' I heerd shots betwixt the dories. Nex' day Obed and thutty-two others was in gaol, with everybody a-wonderin' jest what was afoot and jest what charge agin 'em cud be got to holt. God, ef anybody'd look'd ahead . . . a couple o' weeks later, when nothin' had ben throwed into the sea fer thet long . . .

Zadok was shewing signs of fright and exhaustion, and I let him keep silence for a while, though glancing apprehensively at my watch. The tide had turned and was coming in now, and the sound of the waves seemed to arouse him. I was glad of that tide, for at high water the fishy smell might not be so bad. Again I strained to catch his whispers.

"That awful night . . . I seed 'em. I was up in the cupalo . . . hordes of 'em ... swarms of 'em . . . all over the reef an' swimmin' up the harbour into the Manuxet . . . God, what happened in the streets of Innsmouth that night . . . they rattled our door, but pa wouldn't open . . . then he clumb aout the kitchen winder with his musket to find Selecman Mowry an' see what he cud do . . . Maounds o' the dead an' the dyin' . . . shots and screams . . . shaoutin' in Ol Squar an' Taown Squar an'

New Church Green—gaol throwed open . . . —proclamation . . . treason . . . called it the plague when folks come in an' faound haff our people missin' . . . nobody left but them as ud jine in with Obed an' them things or else keep quiet . . .never heard o' my pa no more. . . "

The old man was panting and perspiring profusely. His grip on my shoulder tightened.

"Everything cleaned up in the mornin'—but they was traces ... Obed he kinder takes charge an' says things is goin' to be changed . . . *others'll* worship with us at meetin'-time, an' sarten haouses hez got to *entertin "guests"* . . . they wanted to mix like they done with the Kanakys, an' he for one didn't feel baound to stop 'em. Far gone, was Obed . . . jest like a crazy man on the subjeck. He says they brung us fish an' treasure, an' shud hev what they hankered after . . .

"Nothin' was to be diff'runt on the aoutsid; only we was to keep shy o' strangers ef we knowed what was good fer us.

"We all hed to take the Oath o' Dagon, an' later on they was secon' an' third oaths that some o' us took. Them as ud help special, ud git special rewards—gold an' sech—No use balkin', fer they was millions of 'em daown thar. They'd ruther not start risin' an' wipin' aout human-kind, but ef they was gave away an' forced to, they cud do a lot toward jest that. We didn't hev them old charms to cut 'em off like folks in the Saouth Sea did, an' them Kanakys wudn't never give away their secrets.

"Yield up enough sacrifices an' savage knick-knacks an' harbourage in the taown when they wanted it, an' they'd let well enough alone. Wudn't bother no strangers as might bear tales aoutside—that is, withaout they got pryin'. All in the band of the faithful—Order O' Dagon—an' the children shud never die, but go back to the Mother Hydra an' Father Dagon what we all come from onct . . . *Ia! Ia! Cthulhu fhtagn! Ph'nglui mglw'nafh Cthulhu R'lyeh wgah-nagl fhtaga—*"

Old Zadok was fast lapsing into stark raving, and I held my breath. Poor old soul—to what pitiful depths of hallucination had his liquor, plus his hatred of the decay, alienage, and disease around him, brought that fertile, imaginative brain? He began to moan now, and tears were coursing down his channelled checks into the depths of his beard.

"God, what I seen senct I was fifteen year' old—*Mene, mene, tekel, upharsin!*—

the folks as was missin', and them as kilt theirselves—them as told things in Arkham or Ipswich or sech places was all called crazy, like you're callin' me right naow— but God, what I seen—They'd a kilt me long ago fer' what I know, only I'd took the fust an' secon' Oaths o' Dago offen Obed, so was pertected unlessen a jury of 'em proved I told things knowin' an' delib'rit . . . but I wudn't take the third Oath— I'd a died ruther'n take that—

"It got wuss araound Civil War time, *when children born senct 'forty-six begun to grow up*—some 'em, that is. I was afeared—never did no pryin' arter that awful night, an' never see one o'—them—clost to in all my life. That is, never no full-blooded one. I went to the war, an' ef I'd a had any guts or sense I'd a never come back, but settled away from here. But folks wrote me things wa'n't so bad. That, I s'pose, was because gov'munt draft men was in taown arter 'sixty-three. Arter the war it was jest as bad agin. People begun to fall off—mills an' shops shet daown— shippin' stopped an' the harbour choked up—railrud give up—but *they* . . . they never stopped swimmin' in an' aout o' the river from that cursed reef o' Satan—an' more an' more attic winders got a-boarded up, an' more an' more noises was heerd in haouses as wa'n't s'posed to hev nobody in 'em. . .

"Folks aoutside hev their stories abaout us—s'pose you've heerd a plenty on 'em, seein' what questions ye ast—stories abaout things they've seed naow an' then, an' abaout that queer joolry as still comes in from somewhars an' ain't quite all melted up—but nothin' never gits def'nite. Nobody'll believe nothin'. They call them gold-like things pirate loot, an' allaow the Innsmouth folks hez furren blood or is dis-tempered or somethin'. Beside, them that lives here shoo off as many strangers as they kin, an' encourage the rest not to git very cur'ous, specially raound night time. Beasts balk at the critters—hosses wuss'n mules—but when they got autos that was all right.

"In 'forty-six Cap'n Obed took a second wife *that nobody in the taown never see*—some says he didn't want to, but was made to by them as he'd called in—had three children by her—two as disappeared young, but one gal as looked like anybody else an' was eddicated in Europe. Obed finally got her married off by a trick to an Arkham feller as didn't suspect nothin'. But nobody aoutside'll hav nothin' to do with Innsmouth folks naow. Barnabas Marsh that runs the refin'ry now is Obed's grandson by his fust wife—son of Onesiphorus, *his eldest son, but his mother was another o' them as wa'n't never seen aoutdoors.*

"Right naow Barnabas is abaout changed. Can't shet his eyes no more, an' is all aout o' shape. They say he still wears clothes, but he'll take to the water soon. Mebbe he's tried it already—they do sometimes go daown for little spells afore they go daown for good. Ain't ben seed abaout in public fer nigh on ten year'. Dun't know haow his poor wife kin feel—she come from Ipiwich, an' they nigh lynched Barnabas when he courted her fifty odd year' ago. Obed he died in 'seventy-eight an' all the next gen'ration is gone naow—the fust wife's children dead, and the rest . . . God knows . . ."

The sound of the incoming tide was now very insistent, and little by little it seemed to change the old man's mood from maudlin tearfulness to watchful fear. He would pause now and then to renew those nervous glances over his shoulder or out toward the reef, and despite the wild absurdity of his tale, I could not help beginning to share his apprehensiveness. Zadok now grew shriller, seemed to be trying to whip up his courage with louder speech.

"Hey, yew, why dun't ye say somethin'? Haow'd ye like to be livin' in a taown like this, with everything a-rottin' an' dyin', an' boarded-up monsters crawlin' an' bleatin' an' barkin' an' hoppin' araoun' black cellars an' attics every way ye turn? Hey? Haow'd ye like to hear the haowlin' night arter night from the churches an' Order O' Dagon Hall, *an' know what's doin' part o' the haowlin'*? Haow'd ye like to hear what comes from that awful reef every May-Eve an' Hallowmass? Hey? Think the old man's crazy, eh? Wal, Sir, *let me tell ye that ain't the wust!*"

Zadok was really screaming now, and the mad frenzy of his voice disturbed me more than I care to own.

"Curse ye, dun't set thar a'starin' at me with them eyes—I tell Obed Marsh he's in hell, an, hez got to stay thar! Heh, heh . . . in hell, I says! Can't git me—I hain't done nothin' nor told nobody nothin'—

"Oh, you, young feller? Wal, even ef I hain't told nobody nothin' yet, I'm a'goin' to naow! Yew jest set still an' listen to me, boy—this is what I ain't never told nobody. . . I says I didn't get to do pryin' arter that night—*but I faound things about jest the same!*"

"Yew want to know what the reel horror is, hey? Wal, it's this—it ain't what them fish devils *hez done, but what they're a-goin' to do!* They're a-bringin' things up aout o' whar they come from into the taown—been doin' it fer years, an' slackenin' up lately. Them haouses north o' the river be-twixt Water an' Main Streets is full of 'em—them devils an' what they brung—an' when they git ready . . . I say, when they git. . . ever hear tell of a *shoggoth*?

"Hey, d'ye hear me? I tell ye I know what them things be—*I seen 'em one night when . . . eh-ahhh-ah! e'yahhh . . .* "

The hideous suddenness and inhuman frightfulness of the old man's shriek almost made me faint. His eyes, looking past me toward the malodorous sea, were positively starting from his head; while his face was a mask of fear worthy of Greek tragedy. His bony claw dug monstrously into my shoulder, and he made no motion as I turned my head to look at whatever he had glimpsed.

There was nothing that I could see. Only the incoming tide, with perhaps one set of ripples more local than the long-flung line of breakers. But now Zadok was shaking me, and I turned back to watch the melting of that fear-frozen face into a chaos of twitching eyelids and mumbling gums. Presently his voice came back— albeit as a trembling whisper.

"*Git aout o' here!* Get aout o' here! *They seen us*—git aout fer your life! Dun't wait fer nothin'—*they know naow*—Run fer it—*quick—aout o' this taown*—"

Another heavy wave dashed against the loosening masonry of the bygone wharf, and changed the mad ancient's whisper to another inhuman and blood-curdling scream. "*E-yaahhh! . . . Yheaaaaaa!. . .*"

Before I could recover my scattered wits he had relaxed his clutch on my shoulder and dashed wildly inland toward the street, reeling northward around the ruined warehouse wall.

I glanced back at the sea, but there was nothing there. And when I reached Water Street and looked along it toward the north there was no remaining trace of Zadok Allen.

IV

I can hardly describe the mood in which I was left by this harrowing episode—an episode at once mad and pitiful, grotesque and terrifying. The grocery boy had prepared me for it, yet the reality left me none the less bewildered and disturbed. Puerile though the story was, old Zadok's insane earnestness and horror had communicated to me a mounting unrest which joined with my earlier sense of loathing for the town and its blight of intangible shadow.

Later I might sift the tale and extract some nucleus of historic allegory; just now I wished to put it out of my head. The hour grown perilously late—my watch said 7:15, and the Arkham bus left Town Square at eight—so I tried to give my thoughts as neutral and practical a cast as possible, meanwhile walking rapidly through the deserted streets of gaping roofs and leaning houses toward the hotel where I had checked my valise and would find my bus.

Though the golden light of late afternoon gave the ancient roofs and decrepit chimneys an air of mystic loveliness and peace, I could not help glancing over my shoulder now and then. I would surely be very glad to get out of malodorous and fear-shadowed Innsmouth, and wished there were some other vehicle than the bus driven by that sinister-looking fellow Sargent. Yet I did not hurry too precipitately, for there were architectural details worth viewing at every silent corner; and I could easily, I calculated, cover the necessary distance in a half-hour.

Studying the grocery youth's map and seeking a route I had not traversed before, I chose Marsh Street instead of State for my approach to Town Square. Near the corner of Fall street I began to see scattered groups of furtive whisperers, and when I finally reached the Square I saw that almost all the loiterers were congregated around the door of the Gilman House. It seemed as if many bulging, watery, unwinking eyes looked oddly at me as I claimed my valise in the lobby, and I hoped that none of these unpleasant creatures would be my fellow-passengers on the coach.

The bus, rather early, rattled in with three passengers somewhat before eight, and an evil-looking fellow on the sidewalk muttered a few indistinguishable words to the driver. Sargent threw out a mail-bag and a roll of newspapers, and entered the hotel; while the passengers—the same men whom I had seen arriving in Newburyport that morning—shambled to the sidewalk and exchanged some faint guttural words with a loafer in a language I could have sworn was not English. I boarded the empty coach and took the seat I had taken before, but was hardly settled before Sargent re-appeared and began mumbling in a throaty voice of peculiar repulsiveness.

I was, it appeared, in very bad luck. There had been something wrong with the engine, despite the excellent time made from Newburyport, and the bus could not complete the journey to Arkham. No, it could not possibly be repaired that night, nor was there any other way of getting transportation out of Innsmouth either to Arkham or elsewhere. Sargent was sorry, but I would have to stop over at the Gilman. Probably the clerk would make the price easy for me, but there was nothing else to do. Almost dazed by this sudden obstacle, and violently dreading the fall of night in this decaying and half-unlighted town, I left the bus and reentered the hotel lobby; where the sullen queer-looking night clerk told me I could have Room 428 on next the top floor— large, but without running water— for a dollar.

Despite what I had heard of this hotel in Newburyport, I signed the register, paid my dollar, let the clerk take my valise, and followed that sour, solitary attendant up three creaking flights of stairs past dusty corridors which seemed wholly devoid of life. My room, a dismal rear one with two windows and bare, cheap furnishings, overlooked a dingy court-yard otherwise hemmed in by low, deserted brick blocks, and commanded a view of decrepit westward-stretching roofs with a marshy countryside beyond. At the end of the corridor was a bathroom—a discouraging relique with ancient marble bowl, tin tub, faint electric light, and musty wooded paneling around all the plumbing fixtures.

It being still daylight, I descended to the Square and looked around for a dinner of some sort; noticing as I did so the strange glances I received from the unwholesome loafers. Since the grocery was closed, I was forced to patronize the restaurant I had shunned before; a stooped, narrow-headed man with staring, unwinking eyes, and a flat-nosed wench with unbelievably thick, clumsy hands being in attendance. The service was all of the counter type, and it relieved me to find that much was evidently served from cans and packages. A bowl of vegetable soup with crackers was enough for me, and I soon headed back for my cheerless room at the Gilman; getting a evening paper and a fly-specked magazine from the evil-visaged clerk at the rickety stand beside his desk.

As twilight deepened I turned on the one feeble electric bulb over the cheap, iron-framed bed, and tried as best I could to continue the reading I had begun. I felt it advisable to keep my mind wholesomely occupied, for it would not do to brood over the abnormalities of this ancient, blight-shadowed town while I was still within its borders. The insane yarn I had heard from the aged drunkard did not promise very pleasant dreams, and I felt I must keep the image of his wild, watery eyes as far as possible from my imagination.

Also, I must not dwell on what that factory inspector had told the Newburyport ticket-agent about the Gilman House and the voices of its nocturnal tenants—not on that, nor on the face beneath the tiara in the black church doorway; the face for whose horror my conscious mind could not account. It would perhaps have been easier to keep my thoughts from disturbing topics had the room not been so gruesomely musty. As it was, the lethal mustiness blended hideously with the town's general fishy odor and persistently focused one's fancy on death and decay.

Another thing that disturbed me was the absence of a bolt on the door of my room. One had been there, as marks clearly shewed, but there were signs of recent removal. No doubt it had been out of order; like so many other things in this decrepit edifice. In my nervousness I looked around and discovered a bolt on the clothes press which seemed to be of the same size, judging from the marks, as the one formerly on the door. To gain a partial relief from the general tension I busied myself by transferring this hardware to the vacant place with the aid of a handy three-in-one device including a screwdriver which I kept on my key-ring. The bolt fitted perfectly, and I was somewhat relieved when I knew that I could shoot it firmly upon retiring. Not that I had any real apprehension of its need, but that any symbol of security was welcome in an environment of this kind. There were adequate bolts on the two lateral doors to connecting rooms, and these I proceeded to fasten.

I did not undress, but decided to read till I was sleepy and then lie down with only my coat, collar, and shoes off. Taking a pocket flash light from my valise, I placed it in my trousers, so that I could read my watch if I woke up later in the dark. Drowsiness, however, did not come; and when I stopped to analyze my thoughts I found to my disquiet that I was really unconsciously listening for something—listening for something which I dreaded but could not name. That inspector's story must have worked on my imagination more deeply than I had suspected. Again I tried to read, but found that I made no progress.

After a time I seemed to hear the stairs and corridors creak at intervals as if with footsteps, and wondered if the other rooms were beginning to fill up. There were no voices, however, and it struck me that there was something subtly furtive about the creaking. I did not like it, and debated whether I had better try to sleep at all. This town had some queer people, and there had undoubtedly been several disappearances. Was this one of those inns where travelers were slain for their money? Surely I had no look of excessive prosperity. Or were the towns folk really so resentful about curious visitors? Had my obvious sightseeing, with its frequent map-consultations, aroused unfavorable notice? It occurred to me that I must be in a highly nervous state to let a few random creakings set me off speculating in this fashion—but I regretted none the less that I was unarmed.

At length, feeling a fatigue which had nothing of drowsiness in it, I bolted the newly outfitted hall door, turned off the light, and threw myself down on the hard, uneven bed—coat, collar, shoes, and all. In the darkness every faint noise of the night seemed magnified, and a flood of doubly unpleasant thoughts swept over me. I was sorry I had put out the light, yet was too tired to rise and turn it on again. Then, after a long, dreary interval, and prefaced by a fresh creaking of stairs and corridor, there came that soft, damnably unmistakable sound which seemed like a malign fulfillment of all my apprehensions. Without the least shadow of a doubt, the lock of my door was being tried—cautiously, furtively, tentatively—with a key.

My sensations upon recognizing this sign of actual peril were perhaps less rather than more tumultuous because of my previous vague fears. I had been, albeit without definite reason, instinctively on my guard—and that was to my advantage in the new and real crisis, whatever it might turn out to be. Nevertheless the change in the menace from vague premonition to immediate reality was a profound shock, and fell upon me with the force of a genuine blow. It never once occurred to me that the fumbling might be a mere mistake. Malign purpose was all I could think of, and I kept deathly quiet, awaiting the would-be intruder's next move.

After a time the cautious rattling ceased, and I heard the room to the north entered with a pass key. Then the lock of the connecting door to my room was softly tried. The bolt held, of course, and I heard the floor creak as the prowler left the room. After a moment there came another soft rattling, and I knew that the room to the south of me was being entered. Again a furtive trying of a bolted connecting door, and again a receding creaking. This time the creaking went along the hall and down the stairs, so I knew that the prowler had realized the bolted condition of my doors and was giving up his attempt for a greater or lesser time, as the future would shew.

The readiness with which I fell into a plan of action proves that I must have been subconsciously fearing some menace and considering possible avenues of escape for hours. From the first I felt that the unseen fumbler meant a danger not to be met or dealt with, but only to be fled from as precipitately as possible. The one thing to do was to get out of that hotel alive as quickly as I could, and through some channel other than the front stairs and lobby.

Rising softly and throwing my flashlight on the switch, I sought to light the bulb over my bed in order to choose and pocket some belongings for a swift, valiseless flight. Nothing, however, happened; and I saw that the power had been cut off. Clearly, some cryptic, evil movement was afoot on a large scale—just what, I could not say. As I stood pondering with my hand on the now useless switch I heard a muffled creaking on the floor below, and thought I could barely distinguish voices in conversation. A moment later I felt less sure that the deeper sounds were voices, since the apparent hoarse barkings and loose-syllabled croakings bore so little resemblance to recognized human speech. Then I thought with renewed force of what the factory inspector had heard in the night in this moldering and pestilential building.

Having filled my pockets with the flashlight's aid, I put on my hat and tiptoed to the windows to consider chances of descent. Despite the state's safety regulations there was no fire escape on this side of the hotel, and I saw that my windows commanded only a sheer three story drop to the cobbled courtyard. On the right and left, however, some ancient brick business blocks abutted on the hotel; their slant roofs coming up to a reasonable jumping distance from my fourth-story level. To reach either of these lines of buildings I would have to be in a room two from my own—in one case on the north and in the other case on the south—and my mind instantly set to work what chances I had of making the transfer.

I could not, I decided, risk an emergence into the corridor; where my footsteps would surely be heard, and where the difficulties of entering the desired room would be insuperable. My progress, if it was to be made at all, would have to be through the less solidly-built connecting doors of the rooms; the locks and bolts of which I would have to force violently, using my shoulder as a battering-ram whenever they were set against me. This, I thought, would be possible owing to the rickety nature of the house and its fixtures; but I realized I could not do it noiselessly. I would have to count on sheer speed, and the chance of getting to a window before any hostile forces became coordinated enough to open the right door toward me with a pass-key. My own outer door I reinforced by pushing the bureau against it—little by little, in order to make a minimum of sound.

I perceived that my chances were very slender, and was fully prepared for any calamity. Even getting to another roof would not solve the problem for there would then remain the task of reaching the ground and escaping from the town. One thing in my favor was the deserted and ruinous state of the abutting building and the number of skylights gaping blackly open in each row.

Gathering from the grocery boy's map that the best route out of town was southward, I glanced first at the connecting door on the south side of the room. It was designed to open in my direction, hence I saw—after drawing the bolt and finding other fastening in place—it was not a favorable one for forcing. Accordingly abandoning it as a route, I cautiously moved the bedstead against it to hamper any attack which might be made on it later from the next room. The door on the north was hung to open away from me, and this—though a test proved it to be locked or bolted from the other side—I knew must be my route. If I could gain the roofs of the buildings in Paine Street and descend successfully to the ground level, I might perhaps dart through the courtyard and the adjacent or opposite building to Washington or Bates—or else emerge in Paine and edge around south-ward into Washington. In any case, I would aim to strike Washington somehow and get quickly out of the Town Square region. My preference would be to avoid Paine, since the fire station there might be open all night.

As I thought of these things I looked out over the squalid sea of decaying roofs below me, now brightened by the beams of a moon not much past full. On the right the black gash of the river-gorge clove the panorama, abandoned factories and railway station clinging barnacle-like to its sides. Beyond it the rusted railway and the Rowley road led off through a flat marshy terrain dotted with islets of higher and dryer scrub-grown land. On the left the creek-threaded country-side was nearer, the narrow road to Ipswich gleaming white in the moonlight. I could not see from my side of the hotel the southward route toward Arkham which I had determined to take.

I was irresolutely speculating on when I had better attack the northward door, and on how I could least audibly manage it, when I noticed that the vague noises underfoot had given place to a fresh and heavier creaking of the stairs. A wavering flicker of light shewed through my transom, and the boards of the corridor began to groan with a ponderous load. Muffled sounds of possible vocal origin approached, and at length a firm knock came at my outer door.

For a moment I simply held my breath and waited. Eternities seemed to elapse, and the nauseous fishy odor of my environment seemed to mount suddenly and spectacularly. Then the knocking was repeated—continuously, and with growing insistence. I knew that the time for action had come, and forthwith drew the bolt of the northward connecting door, bracing myself for the task of battering it open. The knocking waxed louder, and I hoped that its volume would cover the sound of my efforts. At last beginning my attempt, I lunged again and again at the thin paneling with my left shoulder, heedless of shock or pain. The door resisted even more than I expected, but I did not give in. And all the while the clamor at the outer door increased.

Finally the connecting door gave, but with such a crash that I knew those outside must have heard. Instantly the outside knocking became a violent battering, while keys sounded ominously in the hall doors of the rooms on both sides of me. Rushing through the newly opened connexion, I succeeded in bolting the northerly hall door before the lock could be turned; but even as I did so I heard the hall door of the third room—the one from whose window I had hoped to reach the roof below—being tried with a pass key.

For an instant I felt absolute despair, since my trapping in a chamber with no window egress seemed complete. A wave of almost abnormal horror swept over me, and invested with a terrible but unexplainable singularity the flashlight-glimpsed dust prints made by the intruder who had lately tried my door from this room. Then, with a dazed automatism which persisted despite hopelessness, I made for the next connecting door and performed the blind motion of pushing at it in an effort to get through and—granting that fastenings might be as providentially intact as in this second room—bolt the hall door beyond before the lock could be turned from outside.

Sheer fortunate chance gave me my reprieve—for the connecting door before me was not only unlocked but actually ajar. In a second I was though, and had my right knee and shoulder against a hall door which was visibly opening inward. My pressure took the opener off guard, for the thing shut as I pushed, so that I could slip the well-conditioned bolt as I had done with the other door. As I gained this respite I heard the battering at the two other doors abate, while a confused clatter came from the connecting door I had shielded with the bedstead. Evidently the bulk of my assailants had entered the southerly room and were massing in a lateral attack. But at the same moment a pass key sounded in the next door to the north, and I knew that a nearer peril was at hand.

The northward connecting door was wide open, but there was no time to think about checking the already turning lock in the hall. All I could do was to shut and bolt the open connecting door, as well as its mate on the opposite side—pushing a bedstead against the one and a bureau against the other, and moving a washstand in front of the hall door. I must, I saw, trust to such makeshift barriers to shield me till I could get out the window and on the roof of the Paine Street block. But even in this acute moment my chief horror was something apart from the immediate weakness of my defenses. I was shuddering because not one of my pursuers, despite some hideous panting, grunting, and subdued barkings at odd intervals, was uttering an unmuffled or intelligible vocal sound.

As I moved the furniture and rushed toward the windows I heard a frightful scurrying along the corridor toward the room north of me, and perceived that the southward battering had ceased. Plainly, most of my opponents were about to concentrate against the feeble connecting door which they knew must open directly on me. Outside, the moon played on the ridgepole of the block below, and I saw that the jump would be desperately hazardous because of the steep surface on which I must land.

Surveying the conditions, I chose the more southerly of the two windows as my avenue of escape; planning to land on the inner slope of the roof and make for the nearest sky-light. Once inside one of the decrepit brick structures I would have to reckon with pursuit; but I hoped to descend and dodge in and out of yawning doorways along the shadowed courtyard, eventually getting to Washington Street and slipping out of town toward the south.

The clatter at the northerly connecting door was now terrific, and I saw that the weak panelling was beginning to splinter. Obviously, the besiegers had brought some ponderous object into play as a battering-ram. The bedstead, however, still held firm; so that I had at least a faint chance of making good my escape. As I opened the window I noticed that it was flanked by heavy velour draperies suspended from a pole by brass rings, and also that there was a large projecting catch for the shutters on the exterior. Seeing a possible means of avoiding the dangerous jump, I yanked at the hangings and brought them down, pole and all; then quickly hooking two of the rings in the shutter catch and flinging the drapery outside. The heavy folds reached fully to the abutting roof, and I saw that the rings and catch would be likely to bear my weight. So, climbing out of the window and down the improvised rope ladder, I left behind me forever the morbid and horror-infested fabric of the Gilman House.

I landed safely on the loose slates of the steep roof, and succeeded in gaining the gaping black skylight without a slip. Glancing up at the window I had left, I observed it was still dark, though far across the crumbling chimneys to the north I could see lights ominously blazing in the Order of Dagon Hall, the Baptist church, and the Congregational church which I recalled so shiveringly. There had seemed to be no one in the courtyard below, and I hoped there would be a chance to get away before the spreading of a general alarm. Flashing my pocket lamp into the skylight, I saw that there were no steps down. The distance was slight, however, so I clambered over the brink and dropped; striking a dusty floor littered with crumbling boxes and barrels.

The place was ghoulish-looking, but I was past minding such impressions and made at once for the staircase revealed by my flashlight—after a hasty glance at my watch, which shewed the hour to be 2 a.m. The steps creaked, but seemed tolerably sound; and I raced down past a barnlike second storey to the ground floor. The desolation was complete, and only echoes answered my footfalls. At length I reached the lower hall at the end of which I saw a faint luminous rectangle marking the ruined Paine Street doorway. Heading the other way, I found the back door also open; and darted out and down five stone steps to the grass-grown cobblestones of the courtyard.

The moonbeams did not reach down here, but I could just see my way about without using the flashlight. Some of the windows on the Gilman House side were faintly glowing, and I thought I heard confused sounds within. Walking softly over to the Washington Street side I perceived several open doorways, and chose the nearest as my route out. The hallway inside was black, and when I reached the opposite end I saw that the street door was wedged immovably shut. Resolved to try another building, I groped my way back toward the courtyard, but stopped short when close to the doorway.

For out of an opened door in the Gilman House a large crowd of doubtful shapes was pouring—lanterns bobbing in the darkness, and horrible croaking voices exchanging low cries in what was certainly not English. The figures moved uncertainly, and I realized to my relief that they did not know where I had gone; but for all that they sent a shiver of horror through my frame. Their features were indistinguishable, but their crouching, shambling gait was abominably repellent. And worst of all, I perceived that one figure was strangely robed, and unmistakably surmounted by a tall tiara of a design altogether too familiar. As the figures spread throughout the courtyard, I felt my fears increase. Suppose I could find no egress from this building on the street side? The fishy odor was detestable, and I wondered I could stand it without fainting. Again groping toward the street, I opened a door off the hall and came upon an empty room with closely shuttered but sashless windows. Fumbling in the rays of my flashlight, I found I could open the shutters; and in another moment had climbed outside and was fully closing the aperture in its original manner.

I was now in Washington Street, and for the moment saw no living thing nor any light save that of the moon. From several directions in the distance, however, I could hear the sound of hoarse voices, of footsteps, and of a curious kind of pattering which did not sound quite like footsteps. Plainly I had no time to lose. The points of the compass were clear to me, and I was glad that all the street lights were turned off, as is often the custom on strongly moonlit nights in prosperous rural regions. Some of the sounds came from the south, yet I retained my design of escaping in that direction. There would, I knew, be plenty of deserted doorways to shelter me in case I met any person or group who looked like pursuers.

I walked rapidly, softly, and close to the ruined houses. While hatless and disheveled after my arduous climb, I did not look especially noticeable, and stood a good chance of passing unheeded if forced to encounter any casual wayfarer.

At Bates Street I drew into a yawning vestibule while two shambling figures crossed in front of me, but was soon on my way again and approaching the open space where Eliot Street obliquely crosses Washington at the intersection of South. Though I had never seen this space, it had looked dangerous to me on the grocery youth's map; since the moonlight would have free play there. There was no use trying to evade it, for any alternative course would involve detours of possibly disastrous visibility and delaying effect. The only thing to do was to cross it boldly and openly; imitating the typical shamble of the Innsmouth folk as best I could, and trusting that no one—or at least no pursuer of mine—would be there.

Just how fully the pursuit was organized—and indeed, just what its purpose might be—I could form no idea. There seemed to be unusual activity in the town, but I judged that the news of my escape from the Gilman had not yet spread. I would, of course, soon have to shift from Washington to some other southward street; for that party from the hotel would doubtless be after me. I must have left dust prints in that last old building, revealing how I had gained the street.

The open space was, as I had expected, strongly moonlit; and I saw the remains of a parklike, iron-railed green in its center. Fortunately no one was about though a curious sort of buzz or roar seemed to be increasing in the direction of Town Square. South Street was very wide, leading directly down a slight declivity to the waterfront and commanding a long view out at sea; and I hoped that no one would be glancing up it from afar as I crossed in the bright moonlight.

My progress was unimpeded, and no fresh sound arose to hint that I had been spied. Glancing about me, I involuntarily let my pace slacken for a second to take in the sight of the sea, gorgeous in the burning moonlight at the street's end. Far out beyond the breakwater was the dim, dark line of Devil Reef, and as I glimpsed it I could not help thinking of all the hideous legends I had heard in the last twenty-four hours—legends which portrayed this ragged rock as a veritable gateway to realms of unfathomed horror and inconceivable abnormality.

Then, without warning, I saw the intermittent flashes of light on the distant reef. They were definite and unmistakable, and awaked in my mind a blind horror beyond all rational proportion. My muscles tightened for panic flight, held in only by a certain unconscious caution and half-hypnotic fascination. And to make matters worse, there now flashed forth from the lofty cupola of the Gilman House, which loomed up to the northeast behind me, a series of analogous though differently spaced gleams which could be nothing less than an answering signal.

Controlling my muscles, and realizing afresh how plainly visible I was, I resumed my brisker and feignedly shambling pace; though keeping my eyes on that hellish and ominous reef as long as the opening of South Street gave me a seaward view. What the whole proceeding meant, I could not imagine; unless it involved some strange rite connected with Devil Reef, or unless some party had landed from a ship on that sinister rock. I now bent to the left around the ruinous green; still gazing toward the ocean as it blazed in the spectral summer moonlight, and watching the cryptical flashing of those nameless, unexplainable beacons.

It was then that the most horrible impression of all was borne in upon me—the impression which destroyed my last vestige of self-control and sent me running frantically southward past the yawning black doorways and fishily staring windows of that deserted nightmare street. For at a closer glance I saw that the moonlit waters between the reef and the shore were far from empty. They were alive with a teeming horde of shapes swimming inward toward the town; and even at my vast distance and in my single moment of perception I could tell that the bobbing heads and flailing arms were alien and aberrant in a way scarcely to be expressed or consciously formulated.

My frantic running ceased before I had covered a block, for at my left I began to hear something like the hue and cry of organized pursuit. There were footsteps and guttural sounds, and a rattling motor wheezed south along Federal Street. In a second all my plans were utterly changed—for if the southward highway were blocked ahead of me, I must clearly find another egress from Innsmouth. I paused and drew into a gaping doorway, reflecting how lucky I was to have left the moonlit open space before these pursuers came down the parallel street.

A second reflection was less comforting. Since the pursuit was down another street, it was plain that the party was not following me directly. It had not seen me, but was simply obeying a general plan of cutting off my escape. This, however, implied that all roads leading out of Innsmouth were similarly patrolled; for the people could not have known what route I intended to take. If this were so, I would have to make my retreat across country away from any road; but how could I do that in view of the marshy and creek-riddled nature of all the surrounding region? For a moment my brain reeled—both from sheer hopelessness and from a rapid increase in the omnipresent fishy odor.

Then I thought of the abandoned railway to Rowley, whose solid line of ballasted, weed-grown earth still stretched off to the northwest from the crumbling station on the edge at the river-gorge. There was just a chance that the townsfolk would not think of that; since its briar-choked desertion made it half-impassable, and the unlikeliest of all avenues for a fugitive to choose. I had seen it clearly from my hotel window and knew about how it lay. Most of its earlier length was uncomfortably visible from the Rowley road, and from high places in the town itself; but one could perhaps crawl inconspicuously through the undergrowth. At any rate, it would form my only chance of deliverance, and there was nothing to do but try it.

Drawing inside the hall of my deserted shelter, I once more consulted the grocery boy's map with the aid of the flashlight. The immediate problem was how to reach the ancient railway; and I now saw that the safest course was ahead to Babson Street; then west to Lafayette—there edging around but not crossing an open space homologous to the one I had traversed—and subsequently back northward and westward in a zigzagging line through Lafayette, Bates, Adam, and Bank streets—the latter skirting the river gorge—to the abandoned and dilapidated station I had seen from my window. My reason for going ahead to Babson was that I wished neither to recross the earlier open space nor to begin my westward course along a cross street as broad as South.

Starting once more, I crossed the street to the right-hand side in order to edge around into Babson as inconspicuously as possible. Noises still continued in Federal

Street, and as I glanced behind me I thought I saw a gleam of light near the building through which I had escaped. Anxious to leave Washington Street, I broke into a quiet dogtrot, trusting to luck not to encounter any observing eye. Next the corner of Babson Street I saw to my alarm that one of the houses was still inhabited, as attested by curtains at the window; but there were no lights within, and I passed it without disaster.

In Babson Street, which crossed Federal and might thus reveal me to the searchers, I clung as closely as possible to the sagging, uneven buildings; twice pausing in a doorway as the noises behind me momentarily increased. The open space ahead shone wide and desolate under the moon, but my route would not force me to cross it. During my second pause I began to detect a fresh distribution of vague sounds; and upon looking cautiously out from cover beheld a motor car darting across the open space, bound outward along Eliot Street, which there intersects both Babson and Lafayette.

As I watched—choked by a sudden rise in the fishy odor after a short abatement—I saw a band of uncouth, crouching shapes loping and shambling in the same direction; and knew that this must be the party guarding the Ipswich road, since that highway forms an extension of Eliot Street. Two of the figures I glimpsed were in voluminous robes, and one wore a peaked diadem which glistened whitely in the moonlight. The gait of this figure was so odd that it sent a chill through me—for it seemed to me the creature was almost hopping.

When the last of the band was out of sight I resumed my progress; darting around the corner into Lafayette Street, and crossing Eliot very hurriedly lest stragglers of the party be still advancing along that thoroughfare. I did hear some croaking and clattering sounds far off toward Town Square, but accomplished the passage without disaster. My greatest dread was in re-crossing broad and moonlit South Street—with its seaward view—and I had to nerve myself for the ordeal. Someone might easily be looking, and possible Eliot Street stragglers could not fail to glimpse me from either of two points. At the last moment I decided I had better slacken my trot and make the crossing as before in the shambling gait of an average Innsmouth native.

When the view of the water again opened out—this time on my right—I was half-determined not to look at it at all. I could not however, resist; but cast a sidelong glance as I carefully and imitatively shambled toward the protecting shadows ahead. There was no ship visible, as I had half-expected there would be. Instead, the first thing which caught my eye was a small rowboat pulling in toward the abandoned wharves and laden with some bulky, tarpaulin-covered object. Its rowers, though distantly and indistinctly seen, were of an especially repellent aspect. Several swimmers were still discernible; while on the far black reef I could see a faint, steady glow unlike the winking beacon visible before, and of a curious color which I could not precisely identify. Above the slant roofs ahead and to the right there loomed the tall cupola of the Gilman House, but it was completely dark. The fishy odor, dispelled for a moment by some merciful breeze, now closed in again with maddening intensity.

I had not quite crossed the street when I heard a muttering band advancing along Washington from the north. As they reached the broad open space where I had had my first disquieting glimpse of the moonlit water I could see them plainly only a block away—and was horrified by the bestial abnormality of their faces and the doglike sub-humanness of their crouching gait. One man moved in a positively simian way, with long arms frequently touching the ground; while another figure— robed and tiaraed—seemed to progress in an almost hopping fashion. I judged this party to be the one I had seen in the Gilman's courtyard—the one, therefore, most closely on my trail. As some of the figures turned to look in my direction I was transfixed with fright, yet managed to preserve the casual, shambling gait I had assumed. To this day I do not know whether they saw me or not. If they did, my stratagem must have deceived them, for they passed on across the moonlit space without varying their course—meanwhile croaking and jabbering in some hateful guttural patois I could not identify.

Once more in shadow, I resumed my former dog-trot past the leaning and decrepit houses that stared blankly into the night. Having crossed to the western sidewalk I rounded the nearest corner into Bates Street where I kept close to the buildings on the southern side. I passed two houses shewing signs of habitation, one of which had faint lights in upper rooms, yet met with no obstacle. As I turned into Adams Street I felt measurably safer, but received a shock when a man reeled out of a black doorway directly in front of me. He proved, however, too hopelessly drunk to be a menace; so that I reached the dismal ruins of the Bank Street warehouses in safety.

No one was stirring in that dead street beside the river-gorge, and the roar of the waterfalls quite drowned my foot steps. It was a long dog-trot to the ruined station, and the great brick warehouse walls around me seemed somehow more terrifying than the fronts of private houses. At last I saw the ancient arcaded station—or what was left of it—and made directly for the tracks that started from its farther end.

The rails were rusty but mainly intact, and not more than half the ties had rotted away. Walking or running on such a surface was very difficult; but I did my best, and on the whole made very fair time. For some distance the line kept on along the gorge's brink, but at length I reached the long covered bridge where it crossed the chasm at a dizzying height. The condition of this bridge would determine my next step. If humanly possible, I would use it; if not, I would have to risk more street wandering and take the nearest intact highway bridge.

The vast, barnlike length of the old bridge gleamed spectrally in the moonlight, and I saw that the ties were safe for at least a few feet within. Entering, I began to use my flashlight, and was almost knocked down by the cloud of bats that flapped past me. About half-way across there was a perilous gap in the ties which I feared for a moment would halt me; but in the end I risked a desperate jump which fortunately succeeded.

I was glad to see the moonlight again when I emerged from that macabre tunnel. The old tracks crossed River Street at grade, and at once veered off into a region increasingly rural and with less and less of Innsmouth's abhorrent fishy odour. Here the dense growth of weeds and briers hindered me and cruelly tore at my clothes, but I was none the less glad that they were there to give me concealment in case of peril. I knew that much of my route must be visible from the Rowley road.

The marshy region began very abruptly, with the single track on a low, grassy embankment where the weedy growth was somewhat thinner. Then came a sort of island of higher ground, where the line passed through a shallow open cut choked with bushes and brambles. I was very glad of this partial shelter, since at this point the Rowley road was uncomfortably near according to my window view. At the end of the cut it would cross the track and swerve off to a safer distance; but meanwhile I must be exceedingly careful. I was by this time thankfully certain that the railway itself was not patrolled.

Just before entering the cut I glanced behind me, but saw no pursuer. The ancient spires and roofs of decaying Innsmouth gleamed lovely and ethereal in the magic yellow moonlight, and I thought of how they must have looked in the old days before the shadow fell. Then, as my gaze circled inland from the town, something less tranquil arrested my notice and held me immobile for a second.

What I saw—or fancied I saw—was a disturbing suggestion of undulant motion far to the south; a suggestion which made me conclude that a very large horde must be pouring out of the city along the level Ipswich road. The distance was great and I could distinguish nothing in detail; but I did not at all like the look of that moving column. It undulated too much, and glistened too brightly in the rays of the now westering moon. There was a suggestion of sound, too, though the wind was blowing the other way—a suggestion of bestial scraping and bellowing even worse than the muttering of the parties I had lately overheard.

All sorts of unpleasant conjectures crossed my mind. I thought of those very extreme Innsmouth types said to be hidden in crumbling, centuried warrens near the waterfront; I thought, too, of those nameless swimmers I had seen. Counting the parties so far glimpsed, as well as those presumably covering other roads, the number of my pursuers must be strangely large for a town as depopulated as Innsmouth.

Whence could come the dense personnel of such a column as I now beheld? Did those ancient, unplumbed warrens teem with a twisted, uncatalogued, and unsuspected life? Or had some unseen ship indeed landed a legion of unknown outsiders on that hellish reef? Who were they? Why were they here? And if such a column of them was scouring the Ipswich road, would the patrols on the other roads be likewise augmented?

I had entered the brush-grown cut and was struggling along at a very slow pace when that damnable fishy odour again waxed dominant. Had the wind suddenly changed eastward, so that it blew in from the sea and over the town? It must have, I concluded, since I now began to hear shocking guttural murmurs from that hitherto silent direction. There was another sound, too—a kind of wholesale, colossal flopping or pattering which somehow called up images of the most detestable sort. It made me think illogically of that unpleasantly undulating column on the far-off Ipswich road.

And then both stench and sounds grew stronger, so that I paused shivering and grateful for the cut's protection. It was here, I recalled, that the Rowley road drew so close to the old railway before crossing westward and diverging. Something was coming along that road, and I must lie low till its passage and vanishment in the distance. Thank heaven these creatures employed no dogs for tracking—though perhaps that would have been impossible amidst the omnipresent regional odour. Crouched in the bushes of that sandy cleft I felt reasonably safe, even though I knew the searchers would have to cross the track in front of me not much more than a hundred yards away. I would be able to see them, but they could not, except by a malign miracle, see me.

All at once I began dreading to look at them as they passed. I saw the close moonlit space where they would surge by, and had curious thoughts about the irredeemable pollution of that space. They would perhaps be the worst of all Innsmouth types—something one would not care to remember.

The stench waxed overpowering, and the noises swelled to a bestial babel of croaking, baying and barking without the least suggestion of human speech. Were these indeed the voices of my pursuers? Did they have dogs after all? So far I had seen none of the lower animals in Innsmouth. That flopping or pattering was monstrous—I could not look upon the degenerate creatures responsible for it. I would keep my eyes shut till the sound receded toward the west. The horde was very close now—air foul with their hoarse snarlings, and the ground almost shaking with their alien-rhythmed footfalls. My breath nearly ceased to come, and I put every ounce of will-power into the task of holding my eyelids down.

I am not even yet willing to say whether what followed was a hideous actuality or only a nightmare hallucination. The later action of the government, after my frantic appeals, would tend to confirm it as a monstrous truth; but could not an hallucination have been repeated under the quasi-hypnotic spell of that ancient, haunted, and shadowed town? Such places have strange properties, and the legacy of insane legend might well have acted on more than one human imagination amidst those dead, stench-cursed streets and huddles of rotting roofs and crumbling steeples. Is it not possible that the germ of an actual contagious madness lurks in the depths of that shadow over Innsmouth? Who can be sure of reality after hearing things like the tale of old Zadok Allen? The government men never found poor Zadok, and have no conjectures to make as to what became of him. Where does madness leave off and reality begin? Is it possible that even my latest fear is sheer delusion?

But I must try to tell what I thought I saw that night under the mocking yellow moon—saw surging and hopping down the Rowley road in plain sight in front of me as I crouched among the wild brambles of that desolate railway cut. Of course my resolution to keep my eyes shut had failed. It was foredoomed to failure—for who could crouch blindly while a legion of croaking, baying entities of unknown source flopped noisomely past, scarcely more than a hundred yards away?

I thought I was prepared for the worst, and I really ought to have been prepared considering what I had seen before.

My other pursuers had been accursedly abnormal—so should I not have been ready to face a strengthening of the abnormal element; to look upon forms in which there was no mixture of the normal at all? I did not open my eyes until the raucous clamour came loudly from a point obviously straight ahead. Then I knew that a long section of them must be plainly in sight where the sides of the cut flattened out and the road crossed the track—and I could no longer keep myself from sampling whatever horror that leering yellow moon might have to shew.

It was the end, for whatever remains to me of life on the surface of this earth, of every vestige of mental peace and confidence in the integrity of nature and of the human mind. Nothing that I could have imagined—nothing, even, that I could have gathered had I credited old Zadok's crazy tale in the most literal way—would be in any way comparable to the demoniac, blasphemous reality that I saw—or believe I saw. I have tried to hint what it was in order to postpone the horror of writing it down baldly. Can it be possible that this planet has actually spawned such things; that human eyes have truly seen, as objective flesh, what man has hitherto known only in febrile phantasy and tenuous legend?

And yet I saw them in a limitless stream—flopping, hopping, croaking, bleating—surging inhumanly through the spectral moonlight in a grotesque, malignant saraband of fantastic nightmare. And some of them had tall tiaras of that nameless whitish-gold metal . . . and some were strangely robed . . . and one, who led the way, was clad in a ghoulishly humped black coat and striped trousers, and had a man's felt hat perched on the shapeless thing that answered for a head.

I think their predominant color was a grayish-green, though they had white bellies. They were mostly shiny and slippery, but the ridges of their backs were scaly. Their forms vaguely suggested the anthropoid, while their heads were the heads of fish, with prodigious bulging eyes that never closed. At the sides of their necks were palpitating gills, and their long paws were webbed. They hopped irregularly, sometimes on two legs and sometimes on four. I was somehow glad that they had no more than four limbs. Their croaking, baying voices, clearly used for articulate speech, held all the dark shades of expression which their staring faces lacked.

But for all of their monstrousness they were not unfamiliar to me. I knew too well what they must be—for was not the memory of the evil tiara at Newburyport still fresh? They were the blasphemous fish-frogs of the nameless design—living and horrible—and as I saw them I knew also of what that humped, tiaraed priest in the black church basement had fearsomely reminded me. Their number was past guessing. It seemed to me that there were limitless swarms of them and certainly my momentary glimpse could have shewn only the least fraction. In another instant everything was blotted out by a merciful fit of fainting; the first I had ever had.

It was a gentle daylight rain that awaked me from my stupor in the brush-grown railway cut, and when I staggered out to the roadway ahead I saw no trace of any prints in the fresh mud. The fishy odour, too, was gone, Innsmouth's ruined roofs and toppling steeples loomed up greyly toward the southeast, but not a living creature did I spy in all the desolate salt marshes around.   My watch was still going, and told me that the hour was past noon.

The reality of what I had been through was highly uncertain in my mind, but I felt that something hideous lay in the background. I must get away from evil-shadowed Innsmouth—and accordingly I began to test my cramped, wearied powers of locomotion. Despite weakness, hunger, horror, and bewilderment I found myself after a time able to walk; so started slowly along the muddy road to Rowley. Before evening I was in the village, getting a meal and providing myself with presentable clothes. I caught the night train to Arkham, and the next day talked long and earnestly with government officials there; a process I later repeated in Boston. With the main result of these colloquies the public is now familiar—and I wish, for normality's sake, there were nothing more to tell. Perhaps it is madness that is overtaking me—yet perhaps a greater horror—or a greater marvel—is reaching out.

As may well be imagined, I gave up most of the foreplanned features of the rest of my tour—the scenic, architectural, and antiquarian diversions on which I had counted so heavily. Nor did I dare look for that piece of strange jewelry said to be in the Miskatonic University Museum. I did, however, improve my stay in Arkham by collecting some genealogical notes I had long wished to possess; very rough and hasty data, it is true, but capable of good use later on when I might have time to collate and codify them. The curator of the historical society there—Mr. B. Lapham Peabody—was very courteous about assisting me, and expressed unusual interest when I told him I was a grandson of Eliza Orne of Arkham, who was born in 1867 and had married James Williamson of Ohio at the age of seventeen.

It seemed that a maternal uncle of mine had been there many years before on a quest much like my own; and that my grandmother's family was a topic of some local curiosity. There had, Mr. Peabody said, been considerable discussion about the marriage of her father, Benjamin Orne, just after the Civil War; since the ancestry of the bride was peculiarly puzzling. That bride was understood to have been an orphaned Marsh of New Hampshire—a cousin of the Essex County Marshes—but her education had been in France and she knew very little of her family. A guardian had deposited funds in a Boston bank to maintain her and her French governess; but that guardian's name was unfamiliar to Arkham people, and in time he dropped out of sight, so that the governess assumed the role by court appointment. The Frenchwoman—now long dead—was very taciturn, and there were those who said she would have told more than she did.

But the most baffling thing was the inability of anyone to place the recorded parents of the young woman—Enoch and Lydia (Meserve) Marsh—among the known families of New Hampshire. Possibly, many suggested, she was the natural daughter of some Marsh of prominence—she certainly had the true Marsh eyes. Most of the puzzling was done after her early death, which took place at the birth of my grandmother—her only child. Having formed some disagreeable impressions connected with the name of Marsh, I did not welcome the news that it belonged on my own ancestral tree; nor was I pleased by Mr. Peabody's suggestion that I had the true Marsh eyes myself. However, I was grateful for data which I knew would prove valuable; and took copious notes and lists of book references regarding the well-documented Orne family.

I went directly home to Toledo from Boston, and later spent a month at Maumee recuperating from my ordeal. In September I entered Oberlin for my final year, and from then till the next June was busy with studies and other wholesome activities—reminded of the bygone terror only by occasional official visits from government men in connection with the campaign which my pleas and evidence had started. Around the middle of July—just a year after the Innsmouth experience—I spent a week with my late mother's family in Cleveland; checking some of my new genealogical data with the various notes, traditions, and bits of heirloom material in existence there, and seeing what kind of a connected chart I could construct.

I did not exactly relish this task, for the atmosphere of the Williamson home had always depressed me. There was a strain of morbidity there, and my mother had never encouraged my visiting her parents as a child, although she always welcomed her father when he came to Toledo. My Arkham-born grandmother had seemed strange and almost terrifying to me, and I do not think I grieved when she disappeared. I was eight years old then, and it was said that she had wandered off in grief after the suicide of my Uncle Douglas, her eldest son. He had shot himself after a trip to New England—the same trip, no doubt, which had caused him to be recalled at the Arkham Historical Society.

This uncle had resembled her, and I had never liked him either. Something about the staring, unwinking expression of both of them had given me a vague, unaccountable uneasiness. My mother and Uncle Walter had not looked like that.

They were like their father, though poor little cousin Lawrence—Walter's son—had been an almost perfect duplicate of his grandmother before his condition took him to the permanent seclusion of a sanitarium at Canton. I had not seen him in four years, but my uncle once implied that his state, both mental and physical, was very bad. This worry had probably been a major cause of his mother's death two years before.

My grandfather and his widowed son Walter now comprised the Cleveland household, but the memory of older times hung thickly over it. I still disliked the place, and tried to get my researches done as quickly as possible. Williamson records and traditions were supplied in abundance by my grandfather; though for Orne material I had to depend on my uncle Walter, who put at my disposal the contents of all his files, including notes, letters, cuttings, heirlooms, photographs, and miniatures.

It was in going over the letters and pictures on the Orne side that I began to acquire a kind of terror of my own ancestry. As I have said, my grandmother and Uncle Douglas had always disturbed me. Now, years after their passing, I gazed at their pictured faces with a measurably heightened feeling of repulsion and alienation. I could not at first understand the change, but gradually a horrible sort of comparison began to obtrude itself on my unconscious mind despite the steady refusal of my consciousness to admit even the least suspicion of it. It was clear that the typical expression of these faces now suggested something it had not suggested before—something which would bring stark panic if too openly thought of.

But the worst shock came when my uncle shewed me the Orne jewellery in a downtown safe deposit vault. Some of the items were delicate and inspiring enough, but there was one box of strange old pieces descended from my mysterious great-grandmother which my uncle was almost reluctant to produce. They were, he said, of very grotesque and almost repulsive design, and had never to his knowledge been publicly worn; though my grandmother used to enjoy looking at them. Vague legends of bad luck clustered around them, and my great-grandmother's French governess had said they ought not to be worn in New England, though it would be quite safe to wear them in Europe.

As my uncle began slowly and grudgingly to unwrap the things he urged me not to be shocked by the strangeness and frequent hideousness of the designs.

Artists and archaeologists who had seen them pronounced their workmanship superlatively and exotically exquisite, though no one seemed able to define their exact material or assign them to any specific art tradition. There were two armlets, a tiara, and a kind of pectoral; the latter having in high relief certain figures of almost unbearable extravagance.

During this description I had kept a tight rein on my emotions, but my face must have betrayed my mounting fears. My uncle looked concerned, and paused in his unwrapping to study my countenance. I motioned to him to continue, which he did with renewed signs of reluctance. He seemed to expect some demonstration when the first piece—the tiara—became visible, but I doubt if he expected quite what actually happened. I did not expect it, either, for I thought I was thoroughly forewarned regarding what the jewelry would turn out to be. What I did was to faint silently away, just as I had done in that brier choked railway cut a year before.

From that day on my life has been a nightmare of brooding and apprehension, nor do I know how much is hideous truth and how much madness. My great-grandmother had been a Marsh of unknown source whose husband lived in Arkham—and did not old Zadok say that the daughter of Obed Marsh by a monstrous mother was married to an Arkham man through a trick? What was it the ancient toper had muttered about the likeness of my eyes to Captain Obed's? In Arkham, too, the curator had told me I had the true Marsh eyes. Was Obed Marsh my own great-great-grandfather? Who—or what—then, was my great-great-grandmother? But perhaps this was all madness. Those whitish-gold ornaments might easily have been bought from some Innsmouth sailor by the father of my great-grand-mother, whoever he was. And that look in the staring-eyed faces of my grandmother and self-slain uncle might be sheer fancy on my part—sheer fancy, bolstered up by the Innsmouth shadow which had so darkly colored my imagination. But why had my uncle killed himself after an ancestral quest in New England?

For more than two years l fought off these reflections with partial success. My father secured me a place in an insurance office, and I buried myself in routine as deeply as possible. In the winter of 1930-31, however, the dreams began. They were very sparse and insidious at first, but increased in frequency and vividness as the weeks went by. Great watery spaces opened out before me, and I seemed to wander through titanic sunken porticos and labyrinths of weedy cyclopean walls with grotesque fishes as my companions. Then the other shapes began to appear, filling me with nameless horror the moment I awoke. But during the dreams they did not horrify me at all—I was one with them; wearing their unhuman trappings, treading their aqueous ways, and praying monstrously at their evil sea-bottom temples.

There was much more than I could remember, but even what I did remember each morning would be enough to stamp me as a madman or a genius if ever I dared write it down. Some frightful influence, I felt, was seeking gradually to drag me out of the sane world of wholesome life into unnamable abysses of blackness and alienage; and the process told heavily on me. My health and appearance grew steadily worse, till finally I was forced to give up my position and adopt the static, secluded life of an invalid. Some odd nervous affliction had me in its grip, and I found myself at times almost unable to shut my eyes.

It was then that I began to study the mirror with mounting alarm. The slow ravages of disease are not pleasant to watch, but in my case there was something subtler and more puzzling in the background. My father seemed to notice it, too, for he began looking at me curiously and almost affrightedly. What was taking place in me? Could it be that I was coming to resemble my grandmother and uncle Douglas?

One night I had a frightful dream in which I met my grandmother under the sea. She lived in a phosphorescent palace of many terraces, with gardens of strange leprous corals and grotesque brachiate efflorescences, and welcomed me with a warmth that may have been sardonic. She had changed—as those who take to the water change—and told me she had never died. Instead, she had gone to a spot her dead son had learned about, and had leaped to a realm whose wonders— destined for him as well—he had spurned with a smoking pistol. This was to be my realm, too—I could not escape it. I would never die, but would live with those who had lived since before man ever walked the earth.

I met also that which had been her grandmother. For eighty thousand years Pth'thya-l'yi had lived in Y'ha-nthlei, and thither she had gone back after Obed Marsh was dead. Y'ha-nthlei was not destroyed when the upper-earth men shot death into the sea. It was hurt, but not destroyed. The Deep Ones could never be destroyed, even though the palaeogean magic of the forgotten Old Ones might sometimes check them. For the present they would rest; but some day, if they remembered, they would rise again for the tribute Great Cthulhu craved. It would be a city greater than Innsmouth next time. They had planned to spread, and had brought up that which would help them, but now they must wait once more. For bringing the upper-earth men's death I must do a penance, but that would not be heavy. This was the dream in which I saw a *shoggoth* for the first time, and the sight set me awake in a frenzy of screaming. That morning the mirror definitely told me I had acquired *the Innsmouth look*.

So far I have not shot myself as my uncle Douglas did. I bought an automatic and almost took the step, but certain dreams deterred me. The tense extremes of horror are lessening, and I feel queerly drawn toward the unknown sea-deeps instead of fearing them. I hear and do strange things in sleep, and awake with a kind of exaltation instead of terror. I do not believe I need to wait for the full change as most have waited. If I did, my father would probably shut me up in a sanitarium as my poor little cousin is shut up. Stupendous and unheard-of splendors await me below, and I shall seek them soon. *Iä-R'lyeh! Cthulhu fhtagn! Iä! Iä!* No, I shall not shoot myself—I cannot be made to shoot myself!

I shall plan my cousin's escape from that Canton madhouse, and together we shall go to marvel-shadowed Innsmouth. We shall swim out to that brooding reef in the sea and dive down through black abysses to Cyclopean and many-columned Y'ha-nthlei, and in that lair of the Deep Ones we shall dwell amidst wonder and glory for ever.

GRANDFATHER WOLF

BY STEVE RASNIC TEM

Family is family: the gene pool from which you rise or fall or learn to swim far, far away. Many are the stories that paddle there, duly noting their ancestry as they make their choices, coming to intimate grips with the personalities that life has imposed upon them.

Few—in this collection or any other—are more charmingly, alarmingly illustrative than this one.

Lifelong storytelling savant Steve Rasnic Tem's delightful "Grandfather Wolf" was the last freshly written story to howl and scratch outside my deadline window, once the book was already closed.

But once read, there was no way I could not admit it— nay, welcome it—inside.

After all, family is family.

Her grandfather sat in the big red chair in the living room, staring out the double windows at the back lawn where her father had put in tennis courts, a playground for her, and a workshop where he could make furniture whenever he wanted to. The chair was one of those old ones, with elaborate designs in gold thread, a high back, and wings. She thought it made her grandfather, especially with his long white hair, look like a king, or maybe a wizard.

Her grandfather had not spoken to anyone since arriving, except to the maid who had brought him a copper-colored drink in a tall crystal glass. He had smiled at the maid, but he hadn't smiled at anyone else since then. Abigail's mother told her she should go speak to him—after all, he was her grandfather, and she'd never met him before. Even though they all—her father and mother, her two younger brothers—now lived in his house, grandfather, himself, had been away for many years. No one ever explained why, and she had never asked. Perhaps another girl might have asked, but she was just that way. No one in her family ever asked anything.

"But you mustn't bother him," her mother warned, grasping Abigail's forearms tightly and speaking directly into her face, "and if he becomes angry with you, you must leave the room immediately."

How could Abigail know she was bothering him before it was too late? This was the sort of caution she'd received before when dealing with adults, and their dire warnings never helped her know how to behave. But there was obviously something more important about this particular warning, something in her mother's eyes and in her voice. Abigail just couldn't tell what it was. Instead of frightening her, her mother's warning led her to believe that her grandfather must be a very important adult indeed, which made her all the more eager to meet him.

As she'd been taught to do for parties, Abigail grabbed a plate full of cookies off the serving table and carried it to her grandfather with the intent of offering him one. She didn't know if this was *appropriate* for a family gathering or not, or if her grandfather even had a sweet tooth (What a *strange* expression—surely an entire mouth full of "sweet teeth" was what was required!), but at least it gave her an excuse, and something to hold between herself and this old man she'd never met before.

She stood in front of him, staring—he appeared to be asleep. His face was long, and serious, and outlined in whiskers the color of shiny steel pots. He had a wide mouth he kept cracked slightly open, providing just a glimpse of the mystery of his teeth. His lips were like velvet pillows, full and ripe and much more like a girl's than a man's, she thought, although she understood that was an opinion she best keep to herself.

His eyebrows were like fat spaniels, wiggling very slightly as they struggled to hold his wrinkled lids down.

"Grandfather, can I interest you in a cookie or two, perhaps?" She used her sweeter, politer voice, the one designed for important visitors and foreign dignitaries.

She wasn't sure if he'd heard her, but the top of one of his ears appeared to bulge slightly upward, like an ocean wave drawn by the moon. Then one big nostril twitched, followed by the other. His eyes crept out from behind their lids, shifted, and found her at the end of his long nose. "I never eat sweets, child," he said and looked away, closing his eyes again. So he didn't want a cookie. She understood that. But he could still talk to her. She stood there awhile, waiting. Finally he spoke again, his eyes still closed. "Was there something else?"

There was *everything* else, but she didn't know how to say that, so she asked, "How did you know I was still here? With your eyes closed?"

"Do not take this the wrong way, but I could *smell* you," he replied, eyes still shut.

"I took a bath this morning, before the party. Mother made me."

"That would not help. Nothing personal, you understand. Predator and prey, that sort of thing. It is, what you call, nature. And nature cannot be dissuaded."

She didn't understand what he was talking about, so she just said what she knew. "You're my grandpa, you know?"

He opened his eyes immediately, stared at her, studied her up and down, then loudly sniffed the air. "Yes. Of course I am. What was your name?"

"I have the same one I always had, Grandpa. It's Abigail."

"After your great-grandmother."

"I—think so." Abigail thought the air smelled kind of funny, like it did when their last dog had puppies, or how it smelled in the attic that time when she found a box some mice had eaten through and there had been three or four little mice still inside the box, sleeping in a mound of chewed paper.

"You sound like her as well, just a bit. You're a bit precocious for your age, aren't you? How old are you?"

"Thirteen. Daddy says I'm precocious, too. That's a compliment, isn't it? At

least when Daddy says it, it sounds like a compliment. I'm not so sure about you."
Her grandfather made a snuffling sound. She guessed that was supposed to be a
laugh. "Great-grandmother, she was your mother?"

Once again he sniffed the air loudly before he answered. "Yes, child. I take
after her in some ways. I think *you* take after her in some ways. But you're not
much like your father, or your mother, are you?"

"I don't know. My mother and I don't always get along, but I still love her."

"Child, I didn't mean it as an *insult*. Simple observation. Family members have
many differences. Sometimes you have more in common with an earlier generation
than a previous one."

"If you say so." She was beginning to feel bored, and unsure of exactly what he
was saying; she wanted to leave.

"Turn your head slightly to the left, please."

She did as she was told, although she didn't like it. She wondered if he was
checking to see if she'd done a good job washing her face.

"You do have Jackson's—your father's—eyes. But everything else—your nose,
the curve of jaw, that mouth—those are definitely all your great-grandmother
Abigail's. How interesting."

Abigail didn't understand what was so interesting about it. Weren't people in
the same family *supposed* to look like each other? She wasn't sure what she wanted
from her grandfather, if anything. Perhaps she just wanted to know more about her
family, why they were the way they were, and why her grandfather had always stayed
away. But she decided she wasn't going to learn anything from this strange old
man. She started to go—his eyes were closed again so obviously he wouldn't even
notice—when she saw the sketchpad and the pencil on the table by his chair.

"Do you draw, Grandpa?"

He opened his eyes again. "I sketch, yes. It relaxes me."

"Daddy is an artist—did you know? Except he says his canvas is wood."

"Is he? Then I assume these are his handiwork? They weren't here when I
kept up the place." Her grandfather gestured at the carvings around the doors and
windows, the fronts of the bookcases, even the rims and legs of the tables: deer and
bears and many dogs and people running, carrying torches, carrying guns, something leaping although you could never quite tell what it was.

Abigail nodded. "He made them when I was little."

"Very . . . impressive."

"*I* like to draw, too," she said. "Daddy says I inherited his talent. Maybe I inherited your talent as well." And so happy she was at discovering something in common between them, she boldly picked up the sketchpad and started flipping through it.

After she looked at a couple of the drawings it occurred to her that perhaps she'd been too forward. But her grandfather had made no attempt at stopping her, although that slightly dirty, slightly moist, hairy smell was even more intense in the room. "Wow, Grandpa! You're a much better draw-er than I am!"

"I've had practice, child," he said softly.

The drawings were a mix of pencil and charcoal. Many of them were of birds— robins, cranes, blue jays, doves—and so real Abigail thought she could see the flicker in their eyes, the rapid pulse in their throats. She put her longish nose close to the paper and could swear she smelled the smell of bird.

But there were other animals as well—a rabbit peeking out from behind a clump of grass, its nose swelling ever so slightly, a deer leaping between two trees—she was sure she saw its rib cage move. A slow-moving turtle, a fish dissolving into a wave, a dog with its ears suddenly alert.

And the last picture, the only human in the bunch, a little girl, a toddler, standing by the corner of a house, looking straight out from the paper, her eyes so, so wide. Abigail recognized her as a child who lived on the next street.

"Could you show me how to draw the way you do, Grandpa?"

"I suppose I could show you, oh, a few tricks. Pick up that pencil, please, and turn to a fresh page."

Even though she was eager, Abigail turned the page of the sketchpad carefully so as not to tear or smudge it. She gripped the pencil tightly. "Tell me what to do, Grandpa."

"First you have to hold the pencil properly, my dear, so that you may use your entire arm when you make your marks. Grasp it farther back, the way you might hold a paintbrush, and not so tightly."

But Abigail could not manage to position her fingers properly—they felt like sticks attached to her hand, and she dropped the pencil several times. Finally in frustration, she hopped up onto her grandfather's lap and snuggled her back up against him. It was a little kid thing to do, she knew, but he *was* her grandfather, and she really wanted to learn this. She held out her pencil. "Show me," she said.

Her grandfather said nothing for a moment, although she could hear his mouth making a creaking, wheezing sound as if he were having difficulty breathing. She started to turn and ask him if he was okay when his right hand came around and slowly enveloped hers, manipulating her fingers and molding her grip. His hand was long—it looked almost as long as her entire arm—and she could feel the strength of it, all kinds of hard muscles inside as if it were full of steel wires and rods. He guided her at first like she was a helpless puppet, making spheres and cones and long cylinders, but before she knew it she was connecting those shapes on her own, making long graceful curves that transformed cones and spheres and cubes and cylinders into hummingbird beaks and giraffe necks and gorilla torsos. "Help me make a rhinoceros," she said, and they did. "Help me make a hippo," she demanded, and soon a wet-backed hippo gazed out at her from a gleaming pool of pencil marks. "Now let's make a wolf," she cried, and her grandfather's long hand stopped, hovering patiently over the paper.

"Child, I will not draw a wolf," he murmured into her ear.

"Why not?" She held her breath.

"Because they are wretched and miserable and a plague upon the countryside, and cantankerous as they grow old, intolerant and most untrustworthy. I will not draw one."

"That's okay, Grandpa. How about a dog?"

"Dogs are fine animals, and loyal to a fault, I am told."

So together they drew dogs and cats and all the pets in the neighborhood. Abigail lost track of the time as they filled the sketchbook with every kind of animal she had ever seen or imagined, except wolves. Her grandfather nodded in and out of sleep with some bit of encouragement or instruction before another untroubled, gentle doze.

She was only vaguely aware of the dimming light and the first cooking smells drifting in from the kitchen when she heard the sound of tongue on lips behind her, and again caught that stench of animal life. "Do the smells make you hungry, Grandpa?"

But he did not answer. Instead she felt his electric shudder, and as she teetered from his lap, she grabbed hold of his arms on either side of her. She felt his skin ripple, then something prickly against her palms and the undersides of her fingers. She looked down at her hands as wirelike hair sprouted and grew around them.

"Away," he said, in the midst of a gargling noise. "Away, girl! Now!"

She sprang from his lap at the same moment he might have tumbled her, and turning around she saw him crouched in the windowsill, pushing out the double windows, leaping out into the yard, where he became a painful red blur skidding across her vision, disappearing behind her father's workshop.

Late that night she was vaguely aware of the commotion, the electricity of frantic activity as her family moved about the grand old house, but she was far too deep in sleep to investigate, and much too enthralled by her dreams of animals leaping out of pages, of penciled torsos heaving in fright or flight.

The next time Abigail saw her grandfather it was in that same living room, except the red chair was gone now, and an old-fashioned wooden wheelchair sat in its place. Her grandfather sat there, tied to the chair at his waist. Her mother had assured her it was for his safety, so that he wouldn't fall out when he fell asleep, and for no other reason.

The bright white bandages were thick on the stubs of his arms where his hands used to be, and even thicker around his ankles. Abigail thought they looked like those swami hats like people from India wear. One of the ones around his ankles had a little different shape. She'd overheard her daddy say that that was because Grandpa still had some of his foot left on that side.

Abigail carried the sketchpad over to her grandfather. She was very pleased with herself—she'd filled many more pages with drawings of animals. But she didn't want to smile in front of her grandfather, not just yet.

"I'm sorry, Grandpa."

He raised his head as if it weighed three times as much as it had before. "No worries, child. It had to be done. At least now I can stay awhile, get to know my grandchildren better, perhaps help you further your drawing studies."

"But Grandpa, you can't . . . hold my hand and help me."

"Oh, I think you're well beyond that stage. You can sit at my—you can sit in front of my chair and we'll chat. I'll look over your shoulder and provide suggestions from time to time. Now, will you show me what you've been drawing?"

"Sure!" She plopped down, folding her legs daintily beneath her.

"No drawings of wolves?"

"No wolves. But lots of dogs and cats, and squirrels. A big old hoot owl. A raccoon. A few snakes."

"Child, have you been walking in the woods?"

"A little, I guess. See my raccoon?"

The old wooden wheelchair creaked as he leaned over. She could feel his breath on her shoulders. She could smell the dank leaves in it, the rotting hearts of fallen trunks, the scattering corpses of small animals beneath running feet.

"It is very—detailed. Surprisingly so." He sniffed the air above her loudly. "Have you seen many raccoons, child?"

"A few. Look at my squirrel."

The squirrel was bent oddly, the head folded over so comically, Abigail had to stop herself from giggling. Its flattened head half-covered the large hole in its belly.

"Skillfully done, child. Very skillfully done. Child, have you been running in the woods?" He sniffed loudly again.

"Sometimes. Not too often, I don't think. See my rabbits? The way I have them all on their sides pointing in the same direction, lined up in a row? Aren't they cute?"

"Quite precious, my child. Your great-grandmother did something very similar, or so I was told."

She said no more then, turning the pages of the sketchbook slowly, showing her grandfather each new drawing, each carefully arranged final pose. Finally, without turning, she asked, "Grandpa, do you think your teeth could ever reach me now?"

"Oh, I hardly think so. I'm sure you could easily outrun me."

"I'm the best runner in my entire school. And I can jump farther than anyone I know."

"Oh, I'm sure you can."

"Did it hurt very much, Grandpa? When you lost your hands and feet?"

"The pain was—exquisite, child. As it should have been."

"I can't figure out how you did it. I've been thinking and thinking about my daddy's table saw, and I just can't figure out how you got all four."

Her grandfather made a sound behind her then. It sounded like a shudder, but she thought it was really a laugh. "I did the hands first, clasped together, with one quick sweeping movement of the arms. You have to use your entire arm, remember? It's easier that way. Then I leapt with all my might . . ."

"I'm a good leaper," Abigail said.

"I'm sure you are. I leapt straight up onto the table, directly down on the spinning blade. But I was slightly off balance, you see, and I fell off before the blade had eaten through the rest of the one foot."

Abigail was quiet for a time, then she asked, "May I draw a picture of all that? I can see things much more clearly if I can draw pictures of them."

"Yes, you may. But you must promise never to show them to anyone, especially not to other members of the family."

"I'm not a stupid little girl, Grandpa. I know better than *that*."

"I apologize."

"That's okay." Abigail stared out the window. "Grandpa, do you think if the time ever comes for me, I can do what needs to be done?"

"I cannot answer that for you, my child."

"I think I can. Daddy says I know how to do the right thing. I think I can do what needs to be done. I think I could even jump on a saw blade, if I needed to."

"Very well," her grandfather replied. "Very well."

And that's the last they ever spoke of it. They spent the rest of that day talking about art, and growing up, and changes, and the secrets that lay hidden beneath the muddy, leaf-trodden pathways of the forests beyond.

FIRE DOG

BY JOE E. LANSDALE

There's something about a man in a uniform, even if that uniform makes you less of a man every single time you wear it.

Dress codes are a form of social shape-shifting, in a workaday world where it seems the whole point of your job is to basically take over your life. Whether you're sporting business casual or a paper hat at a fast-food drive-thru, the same holds true. Clothes make the man.

And they can break him just as easily.

This leg-humping howler by the great Joe Lansdale is one of the funniest, saddest employment sagas I've ever had the pleasure to meet. If you're lucky, you'll get to hear him read it out loud some day, and laugh until you cry.

When Jim applied for the dispatcher job, the fire department turned him down, but the Fire Chief offered him something else. "Our fire dog, Rex, is retiring. You might want that job. Pays good and the retirement is great."

"Fire dog?" Jim said.

"That's right."

"Well, I don't know . . ."

"Suit yourself.

Jim considered. "I suppose I could give it a try—"

"Actually, we prefer greater dedication than that. We don't just want someone to give it a try. Being fire dog is an important job."

"Very well," Jim said. "I'll take it."

"Good."

The Chief opened a drawer, pulled out a spotted suit with tail and ears, pushed it across the desk.

"I have to wear this?"

"How the hell you gonna be the fire dog, you don't wear the suit?"

"Of course."

Jim examined the suit. It had a hole for his face, his bottom, and what his mother had called his pee-pee.

"Good grief," Jim said. "I can't go around with my . . . well, you know, my stuff hanging out."

"How many dogs you see wearing pants?"

"Well, Goofy comes to mind."

"Those are cartoons. I haven't got time to screw around here. You either want the job, or you don't."

"I want it."

"By the way. You sure Goofy's a dog?"

"Well, he looks like a dog. And he has that dog, Pluto."

"Pluto, by the way, doesn't wear pants."

"You got me there."

"Try on the suit, let's see if it needs tailoring."

The suit fit perfectly, though Jim did feel a bit exposed. Still, he had to admit there was something refreshing about the exposure. He wore the suit into the break room, following the Chief.

Rex, the current fire dog, was sprawled on the couch watching a cop show. His suit looked worn, even a bit smoke stained. He was tired around the eyes. His jowls drooped.

"This is our new fire dog," the Chief said.

Rex turned and looked at Jim, said, "I'm not out the door, already you got a guy in the suit?"

"Rex, no hard feelings. You got what, two, three days? We got to be ready. You know that."

Rex sat up on the couch, adjusted some pillows and leaned into them. "Yeah, I know. But, I've had this job nine years."

"And in dog years that's a lot."

"I don't know why I can't just keep being the fire dog. I think I've done a good job."

"You're our best fire dog yet. Jim here has a lot to live up to."

"I only get to work nine years?" Jim said.

"In dog years you'd be pretty old, and it's a decent retirement."

"Is he gonna take my name too?" Rex said.

"No," the Chief said, "of course not. We'll call him Spot."

"Oh, that's rich," said Rex. "You really worked on that one."

"It's no worse than Rex."

"Hey, Rex is a good name."

"I don't like Spot," Jim said. "Can't I come up with something else?"

"Dogs don't name themselves," the Chief said. "Your name is Spot."

"Spot," Rex said, "don't you think you ought to get started by coming over here and sniffing my butt?"

The first few days at work Spot found riding on the truck to be uncomfortable. He was always given a tool box to sit on so that he could be seen, as this was the fire department's way. They liked the idea of the fire dog in full view, his ears flapping in the wind. It was very promotional for the mascot to be seen.

Spot's exposed butt was cold on the tool box, and the wind not only blew his ears around, it moved another part of his anatomy about. That was annoying.

He did, however, enjoy the little motorized tail-wagging device he activated with a touch of a finger. He found that got him a lot of snacks from the fire men. He was especially fond of the liver snacks.

After three weeks on the job, Spot found his wife Sheila to be very friendly. After dinner one evening, when he went to the bedroom to remove his dog suit, he discovered Sheila lying on their bed wearing a negligee and a pair of dog ears attached to a hair band.

"Feel frisky, Spot?"

"Jim."

"Whatever. Feel frisky?"

"Well, yeah. Let me shed the suit, take a shower . . . "

"You don't need a shower . . . And baby, leave the suit on, will you?"

They went at it.

"You know how I want it," she said.

"Yeah. Doggie style."

"Good boy."

After sex, Sheila liked to scratch his belly and behind his ears. He used the tail-wagging device to show how much he appreciated it. This wasn't so bad, he thought. He got less when he was a man.

Though his sex life had improved, Spot found himself being put outside a lot, having to relieve himself in a corner of the yard while his wife looked in the other direction, her hand in a plastic bag, ready to use to pick up his deposits.

He only removed his dog suit now when Sheila wasn't around. She liked it on him at all times. At first he was insulted, but the sex was so good, and his life was so good, he relented. He even let her call him Spot all the time.

When she wasn't around, he washed and dried his suit carefully, ironed it. But he never wore anything else. When he rode the bus to work, everyone wanted to pet him. One woman even asked if he liked poodles because she had one.

At work he was well respected and enjoyed being taken to schools with the

Fire Chief. The Chief talked about fire prevention. Spot wagged his tail, sat up, barked, looked cute by turning his head from side to side.

He was even taken to his daughter's class once. He heard her say proudly to a kid sitting next to her, "That's my Daddy. He's the fire dog."

His chest swelled with pride. He made his tail wag enthusiastically.

The job really was the pip. You didn't have fires every day, so Spot laid around all day most days, on the couch sometimes, though some of the fireman would run him off and make him lie on the floor when they came in. But the floor had rugs on it and the television was always on, though he was not allowed to change the channels. Some kind of rule, a union thing. The fire dog can not and will not change channels.

He did hate having to take worm medicine, and the annual required trips to the vet were no picnic either. Especially the thermometer up the ass part.

But, hell, it was a living, and not a bad one. Another plus was after several months of trying, he was able to lick his balls.

At night, when everyone was in their bunks and there were no fires, Spot would read from *Call of the Wild, White Fang, Dog Digest*, or such, or lie on his back with all four feet in the air, trying to look cute.

He loved it when the firemen came in and caught him that way and ooohheeed and ahhhhhed and scratched his belly or patted his head.

This went on for just short of nine years. Then, one day, while he was lying on the couch, licking his ass — something he cultivated after three years on the job — the Fire Chief and a guy in a dog suit came in. "This is your replacement, Spot," the Chief said.

"What?"

"Well, it has been nine years."

"You didn't tell me. Has it been? You're sure? Aren't you supposed to warn me? Rex knew his time was up. Remember?"

"Not exactly. But if you say so. Spot, meet Hal."

"Hal? What kind of dog's name is that? Hal?"

But it was no use. By the end of the day he had his personal dog biscuits, pin ups from *Dog Digest*, and his worm-away medicine packed. There was also a spray can the firemen used to mist on his poop to keep him from eating it. The can of spray didn't really belong to him, but he took it anyway.

He picked up his old clothes, went into the changing room. He hadn't worn anything but the fire dog suit in years, and it felt odd to try his old clothes on. He could hardly remember ever wearing them. He found they were a bit moth-eaten, and he had gotten a little too plump for them. The shoes fit, but he couldn't tolerate them.

He kept the dog suit on. He caught the bus and went home.

"What? You lost your job?" his wife said.

"I didn't lose anything. They retired me."

"You're not the fire dog?"

"No. Hal is the fire dog."

"I can't believe it. I give you nine great years —"

"We've been married eleven."

"I only count the dog years. Those were the good ones, you know."

"Well, I don't have to quit being a dog. Hell, I am a dog."

"You're not the fire dog. You've lost your position, Spot. Oh, I can't even stand to think about it. Outside. Go on. Git. Outside."

Spot went.

After a while he scratched on the door, but his wife didn't let him in. He went around back and tried there. That didn't work either. He looked in the windows, but couldn't see her.

He laid down in the yard.

That night it rained, and he slept under the car, awakened just in time to keep his wife from backing over him on her way to work.

That afternoon he waited, but his wife did not return at the usual time. Five o'clock was when he came home from the fire house, and she was always waiting, and he had a feeling it was at least five o'clock, and finally the sun went down and he knew it was late.

Still, no wife.

Finally, he saw headlights and a car pulled into the drive. Sheila got out. He ran to meet her. To show he was interested, he humped her leg.

She kicked him loose. He noticed she was holding a leash. Out of the car came Hal.

"Look who I got. A real dog."

Spot was dumbfounded.

"I met him today at the fire house, and well, we hit it off."

"You went by the fire house?"

"Of course."

"What about me?" Spot asked.

"Well, Spot, you are a little old. Sometimes, things change. New blood is necessary."

"Me and Hal, we're going to share the house?"

"I didn't say that."

She took Hal inside. Just before they closed the door, Hal slipped a paw behind Sheila's back and shot Spot the finger.

When they were inside, Spot scratched on the door in a half-hearted way. No soap.

Next morning Sheila hustled him out of the shrubbery by calling his name. She didn't have Hal with her.

Great! She had missed him. He bounded out, his tongue dangling like a wet sock. "Come here, Spot."

He went. That's what dogs did. When the master called, you went to them. He was still her dog. Yes sirree, Bob. "Come on, boy." She hustled him to the car.

As he climbed inside on the back seat and she shut the door, he saw Hal come out of the house stretching. He looked pretty happy. He walked over to the car and slapped Sheila on the butt.

"See you later, baby."

"You bet, you, dog, you."

Hal walked down the street to the bus stop. Spot watched him by turning first to the back glass, then rushing over to the side view glass.

Sheila got in the car.

"Where are we going?" Spot asked.

"It's a surprise," she said.

"Can you roll down the window back here a bit?"

"Sure."

Spot stuck his head out as they drove along, his ears flapping, his tongue hanging.

They drove down a side street, turned and tooled up an alley.

Spot thought he recognized the place.

Why, yes, the vet. They had come from another direction and he hadn't spotted it right off, but that's where he was.

He unhooked the little tag that dangled from his collar. Checked the dates of his last shots.

No. Nothing was overdue.

They stopped and Sheila smiled. She opened the back door and took hold of the leash. "Come on, Spot."

Spot climbed out of the car, though carefully. He wasn't as spry as he once was.

Two men were at the back door. One of them was the doctor. The other an assistant.

"Here's Spot," she said.

"He looks pretty good," said the doctor.

"I know. But . . . well, he's old and has his problems. And I have too many dogs."

She left him there.

The vet checked him over and called the animal shelter. "There's nothing really wrong with him," he told the attendant that came for him. "He's just old, and well, the woman doesn't want to care for him. He'd be great with children."

"You know how it is, Doc," said the attendant. "Dogs all over the place."

Later, at the animal shelter he stood on the cold concrete and smelled the other dogs. He barked at the cats he could smell. Fact was, he found himself barking anytime anyone came into the corridor of pens.

Sometimes men and woman and children came and looked at him.

None of them chose him. The device in his tail didn't work right, so he couldn't wag as ferociously as he liked. His ears were pretty droopy, and his jowls hung way too low.

"He looks like his spots are fading," said one woman whose little girl had stuck her fingers through the grating so Spot could lick her hand.

"His breath stinks," she said.

As the days went by, Spot tried to look perky all the time. Hoping for adoption.

But one day, they came for him, wearing white coats and grim faces, brandishing a leash and a muzzle and a hypodermic needle.

PURE SILVER

BY A. C. CRISPIN AND KATHLEEN O'MALLEY

There is no horror like the slaughtering of innocents, no injustice more scarring or profound. And when you devote your whole life to defending the meek, how much more sacrifice can you be asked to make?

I don't wanna talk about A. C. Crispin and Kathleen O'Malley's wonderful story. I just want you to read it, and experience it as I did. It pushed all the right buttons for me, from animal love to outrage at our history's greatest crimes. Such are the burdens of humanity.

A beautiful gem, from a pair of wildly popular entertainers in the fantasy and science fiction field. This time, they made a fan out of me.

I first saw the werewolf at four A.M., Wednesday, on the A-8 Metrobus traveling from New York Avenue to my old one-room on Morris Road in Anacostia. It had been one of those days...there weren't any other kind with my job. I was exhausted, dozing as we lurched along, but suddenly I opened my eyes and he was there, across the aisle from me.

I knew what he was right off—but that's me. I see the animal in everyone. I'll meet someone and right away see a falcon deep inside, or a spider, maybe an otter or deer. But this was different. This guy didn't just have an animal's *spirit* inside him. . .no, no. Even though I'd never seen one before, I recognized that he was a real werewolf. I *knew* it, knew it as surely as I know I'm 5'6" and have reddish-blond hair.

His hair was pale silver, dipping low on his forehead in a pronounced widow's peak. Not just thick, it was *dense*—like a pelt. Shaggy, white brows met over his narrow, hooked nose. The eyes gleaming beneath them were steel gray, ringed with black like mine. The werewolf was old, seventy at a guess, more than twice my age, but his eyes were bright. . .ageless.

His grizzled stubble of beard started on top of his prominent cheekbones, continued down over well-chiseled features, then disappeared inside the neck of an enormous, mud-colored overcoat. I glanced at his hands; they were covered with rough, brindled hair. His fingernails were thick, raggedly sharp.

I dropped my eyes, wanting to ignore the werewolf, reminding myself that there were no such things, that I didn't believe in that stuff. I didn't go to horror flicks or read any scary books, and had no patience with crystals, pyramids, channeling or any of that crap. I didn't even believe in ghosts. . .and I saw those every day.

When I looked back at his face, our eyes met. Quickly, I looked up at the "DC is a Capital City" ad, but I was too late. By then, he was staring at me.

That's okay, I thought calmly, *he won't mess with me. He'll think I'm a cop.* I straightened my heavy navy-blue nylon bomber jacket with its fake fur collar. My navy pants, black vinyl shoes, blue shirt and imitation leather Harrison belt completed the uniform. I made sure he could see the silver badge over my left breast. I only wished my name wasn't under it. *Humane Officer Therese* (*not* Theresa, thank you) *Norris*.

Of course, my belt wasn't studded with cop toys, just a long, black flashlight and two old rope leashes. I might look like a cop, but I worked for the S.P.C.A., enforcing the animal control and cruelty laws of the District of Columbia. To the public, I was, at best, a dogcatcher—at worst, someone who gassed puppies for a living.

Not that we gassed them. Our animals were humanely euthanized with a painless injection of sodium pentobarbital, a powerful anesthetic pumped into the foreleg vein by a skilled technician. That it was merciful didn't make it easier.

Tonight's shift had been a *bitch*. The city's Animal Control Facility operates around the clock. I worked the night shift, driving a big, white van Tuesday through Saturday, five P.M. to one A.M. We called it the "nut" shift; the worst time to be on the streets, with the drug dealers, prostitutes, junkies, street people, headline-hungry politicians and—worse yet—tourists.

Tonight I'd had over forty calls, picked up thirty-two animals, and had had to euthanize twenty-seven before I could go home. The paperwork had taken me until three.

I'd barely walked in the door when I'd had to kill six three-day-old kittens with feline distemper. Then I did seven healthy mixed shepherds whose time had run out. We gave animals four days more than most places, so we were always cramped for space.

Around six-thirty I picked up three seriously injured strays (no collars, no tags) hit by cars in less than an hour. One of them had been neatly eviscerated. She looked at me gratefully as I talked soothingly to her, then pushed the plunger.

At nine, Linda, the night manager, said they couldn't hold the old stray hound any longer. I'd picked her up ten days ago. In spite of our posters, and ads in the *Post*, no one had claimed her. I loved her, but couldn't take her. My cat, Alfred, had died last year at seventeen, and I'd euthanized my fifteen-year-old Dobie, Dove, just six months ago, but my landlord had slapped a "no animals" clause on me before Dove got cold.

The hound licked our hands when Linda and I came to get her. She left this earth no doubt wondering where her people were.

At ten-fifteen I killed three raccoons we'd trapped, and one small brown bat who'd had his wings shattered by a terrified second-string Redskins linebacker wielding a broom. Each would have to be checked for rabies.

But the worst thing that'd happened tonight was that damned puppy. Even hours later, I found it hard to think about him. I'd chased his mother for half an hour, finally cornering her in an alley. She was nothing but drab fur, bones, and big nipples.

She led me to the nest where I found her pup safe and warm in a jumble of rags, paper and trash. He was fat and plush, about two weeks old, eyes just barely open—mixed beagle, mostly. I moved the trash off him. . .then I saw it.

It made me sick, and after ten years on the job, not much bothers me. He must've crawled through one of those plastic six-pack holders right after he was born. His head and right front leg were through one of the rings, and he was wearing it like a bizarre bandolier across his pudgy chest. Once in it, he couldn't get out, and he'd grown—but the plastic hadn't. The ring was sawing him neatly in half. Exposed muscles glistened red and swollen. . .intestines clearly visible. If I'd cut the damned thing, his entrails would've fallen out. All I could think of was Linda's favorite saying. . .there are worse things than death.

I put mom in the van, then sat in the alley, finding the tiny pup by the light of the street lamp, in spite of the danger. Clean needles pull junkies out of the woodwork, crazed cockroaches to sugar, and I'd been beaten and held up at gunpoint before for them. But I couldn't let his mom watch.

Both mom and I cried all the way back to the shelter. You'd have thought it was my first week on the job. At least she'd have a warm bed for a week and an endless supply of food. Then I'd probably have to do her. It killed me to think that those seven days would probably be the best in her short, bitter life.

I remembered all this and swallowed hard. I lived with ghosts every night. In my lap was that puppy with the ring; I could feel it squirm on my legs. At my feet the old hound wagged her tail. The mixed Shepherds and sick kittens watched me sadly. The raccoons stared. On my shoulder crouched the little bat. Every night I brought a crowd home—the ghosts of all the animals I killed. Every night for ten years.

Don't get me wrong, I didn't hate my job, but I didn't love it either. It was something I had to do because I loved animals. *Someone* had to kill the thousands of sick, injured and unwanted animals discarded annually, and who better than someone who loved them? I know. *You* love animals and *you* couldn't do it—well, that's why *I* had to.

While I was thinking this, the old werewolf touched me on the shoulder, nearly scaring me to death. He was hanging onto the overhead bar, staring at me. His expression was kindly, but I fingered my flashlight. I'd had to use it as a weapon before.

"You've had a hard night, haven't you, bubeleh?" he said in a sober, gravelly voice that was laced with a thick, Old World accent. It was the last thing I'd expected. A Jewish werewolf? In New York, maybe, but D.C.?

His unexpected sympathy hit me hard; tears welled up. I couldn't speak for fear I'd start bawling with ten years' backlogged heartache, so I just nodded. Here was this old man, homeless from the look of him, comforting *me*. I took a deep breath, glanced away, trying to pull myself together. That's when I noticed the number tattooed on the underside of his hairy arm as he held the bar. It was the old, faded, concentration camp number survivors of the Holocaust wear.

"You shouldn't work so hard, a nice girl like you," the old man rumbled, still smiling. "Goodnight, Therese." Therese. Not Theresa. Everybody said Theresa. Then he got off the bus.

I was still shaking my head as I stepped down onto Morris Road. I didn't believe in monsters. . .just like I didn't believe in ghosts. . .but when I thought of that old man, all I saw was a werewolf. A kindly Jewish werewolf. . .right. Sure.

I walked home, the ghosts of twenty-seven animals trailing behind me, wondering whether there'd been a full moon tonight.

"Hey, Tee, good to see you," the cop said the next night, as he opened my van door. Joseph WhiteCrane was a K-9 cop with Metro police. The shelter often supplied Metro with dogs, and Joe's dog, Chief, a big white shepherd, had been one of my finds. Joe was part Sioux, part Hispanic, and part Irish. About 5'8", he was handsome, with his hooked nose and pock-marked face, his dark skin, black hair and ice-black eyes that were magnetic, and alive. Inside, Joe was a red-tailed hawk.

A good night's sleep had erased any lingering willies I had from my odd delusion on the bus. I felt secure being back at work along with my normal run of real-life horrors.

"I just got the call," I said. "You impound a dog?" Drug dealers often protected themselves with bad dogs, so it wasn't unusual to be called to a crime scene to pick up animals. But this didn't look like a drug bust—for one thing, the coroner's van was sitting next to Joe's car. Inside the car, Chief lunged and whirled, frantically barking.

We were in the business district, the fourteen-hundred block of the street, so at this time of night, there weren't many bystanders. Besides the handful of street people and hookers gawking at the scene, there were a few businessmen who must've been in the social club that served lunch to the clericals during the day, and topless shows to the bosses at night.

"No dog for you tonight—at least, not yet," Joe said, then looked at me, frowning. "What's that smell?"

I'd been hoping he wouldn't notice. "Gasoline and burnt hair. The kids cooked a cat. I found her tied by her tail to a lamppost, smoldering. . .and screaming." I rubbed my hands on my pants, feeling bits of her still stuck to me. Her skin had sloughed off when I hit the vein.

He looked away, knowing better than to show any sympathy. "Well, like you say, there's worse things than death. Look, we need an expert opinion. An old guy's been killed, maybe by animals. We called the zoo, and nothing's loose. Would you look at the body and tell the coroner what you think of the wounds?"

I nodded. After the barbecued cat, nothing could bother me. At first, the coroner only wanted to show me the bites on the leg, but finally Joe convinced him to uncover the corpse. Damn right, there's worse things than death. The man's throat was torn out, but the coroner said he survived that, only to endure the rest without being able to scream. His chest was torn open. . .his heart ripped out.

"I've seen feral dogs do stuff like this to each other," I said, "but, eat *just* the heart? Weird." I stared at the bites. "Big jaws, wide muzzles, almost flat-faced."

"Pack of pit bulls?" Joe asked.

"Maybe. . .or bull mastiffs. How big are the paw prints?"

Joe and the coroner looked at each other. "No paw prints," the cop said finally.

"Come on. This guy had to bleed like a fountain."

"*Foot*prints," Joe said. "The victim's. Nothing else."

"Are you guys sharing this with the press?" I asked quietly.

Joe shrugged. "Don't know."

"C'mon, give a poor working girl a break," I urged. "Remember the rabies outbreak? The city'll go nuts if the media talks up a crazed pack of killer dogs."

Joe smiled. "I'll talk to the captain. We might be able to keep this on low profile until we know more about the victim."

As we left the coroner's wagon, I saw Joe's still-frantic dog. "What's wrong with Chief? I've never seen him like this."

The cop shrugged. "He's been crazy since we got here. Let's take him out. You got your pole?"

"Yeah." I retrieved the aluminum rabies pole with its plastic-covered cable loop that enabled me to snag animals and hold them at a distance.

Joe put Chief on a short lead and let him out. The dog was high-strung, hackles up, whining. Normally, the big shepherd was as steady as a brick.

"Think he can smell those dogs?" I asked.

Joe shrugged. "If we spot 'em we're going to catch them from a distance." He patted the pistol resting on his hip.

Chief pulled Joe for a few blocks, then turned up an alley. Suddenly, he rounded on a doorway, barking furiously. A huddled form was hiding in the shadows. I moved closer. Gray eyes, silver hair, muddy overcoat. . .the old man from the bus. . .Damn it, he *still* looked like a werewolf!

"Easy, Chief, easy!" Joe said to the frenzied dog. "Hey, grandfather, what're you doing here?"

"Resting, officer," he muttered tiredly. "Please, to hold your dog. Ach, Therese, tell him not to loose the dog!"

"You know this guy?" Joe asked me.

Something made me nod my head. "Grandfather," I said, using Joe's term, "It's not safe here. A man's been killed nearby. Did you see or hear anything?"

"Tsk, tsk." He shook his head. "Killed? *Such* a world!"

"Let us take you to the D Street shelter," Joe offered.

"In the same car with such a dog? Thank you, no."

I gazed at the old man—he seemed exhausted, weary to his soul, and my heart went out to him. Usually I only felt this kind of concern for animals, but. . .he was different. "Have you had anything to eat tonight, Grandfather? A hot meal?"

He smiled. "Say 'zeyde,' Therese. Yes. I've had a good, hot meal. . .Not kosher, but. . .how nice you should worry."

I wasn't sure I believed him. Impulsively, I shoved three dollars into his pocket. "Then this is for breakfast, Zeyde."

Joe and I walked back to my van. We had to drag Chief the whole way.

"So, is Zeyde his name?" I wondered to Joe.

He shook his head. "Means 'grandfather.' It's Yiddish."

Joe *would* know that. He was a mine of cultural knowledge. "What does 'bubeleh' mean?"

"Grandchild. It's an endearment." Joe paused. "Did you smell anything when you got near him?"

"Me? All I can smell is that poor cat. Why?"

Joe glanced back towards the alley. "I thought I caught a whiff of blood. Didn't see any, though. Might've been why Chief was spooked. Could've been his breath."

I looked at Joe, my eyes wide. "His *breath*?"

"Lots of street people are sick. . .ulcers, whatever."

Oh, I thought, embarrassed by my weird thoughts.

The next day was Friday, and by eleven forty-five P.M., Linda was helping me do my twentieth kill of the night. It was a full grown dobie, weighing thirty pounds. Should've weighed eighty. The people said they'd run out of dog food and couldn't afford more, so they just stopped feeding him. He couldn't even stand. Only his eyes looked alive.

Linda took him in her arms. "Hey, pretty dog," she crooned, petting him, her blond curls falling around her face. We ribbed Linda for looking like Jane Fonda. Lovely, quick and clever. . .inside she was a gray fox.

After filling the syringe, I turned to the dog. He had no muscles left, just hair, skin and bones. I'd found him tied in a closet, dumped like a pair of old shoes. He turned his liquid brown eyes on me and they were full of trust, ready to love again, in spite of everything he'd been through. Suddenly I saw Zeyde, ribs jutting, in the concentration camp.

"Tee, you okay?" Linda asked.

I swallowed. "Listen. . .uh, can we keep this one?"

She sighed tiredly. "He needs his own pen, vet care, it'd be *six months* before he'd be adoptable."

It was suddenly very important for me to save this dog. "I can't kill this one," I said, tightly. "He's so damned hungry."

Linda shook her head. "If we started saving every starvation case, we'd be packed to the rafters. . .." She must've seen something in my face then, something she recognized, because she stopped, giving in. "I don't know why I let you talk me into these things. We'll put a bed behind my desk—"

The phone rang, and she nodded at me to get it as she went to settle the dog in her office and fetch him some food.

"D.C. Animal Control, Officer Norris."

"It's Joe," a familiar deep voice said. "The guy that got killed by those dogs was on the Federal Witness Protection Program. Just got the word."

"Weird," I said. "Some kind of Mafia snitch?"

"Weirder," Joe said. "He was a former Nazi. Did some favors for the State Department at the end of the war. Homicide's calling it a random wild dog attack."

My fingers tightened on the phone, thinking how odd it was to run into a Nazi and a Holocaust survivor in the same night. "Think this has anything to do with Zeyde?" I asked, finally.

"Doubt it, but if you talk to him, call me."

I fought back an urge to ask Joe if there'd been a full moon that night. Joe would know.

"Be careful on the street tonight, Tee," Joe warned me.

"I'm always careful," I said defensively.

"The hell you are. I've seen you work. You take too many chances. I mean it, Tee."

"Yeah, yeah," I agreed impatiently. "Listen, I gotta go."

"Why can't you be nicer to that poor guy?" Linda asked, when I hung up the phone. "Every straight woman in this place would love to have him pay them half the attention he gives you."

"Get off my back," I said, good-naturedly.

With real pleasure I watched the dobie inhale a small meal from a soft bed of worn blankets. You had to start them slow, giving meals every two hours, to get their systems used to food again. Maybe it was time to look for an apartment that permitted pets, I thought as I walked out to the van.

I was startled out of my mental house-hunting when I found Zeyde waiting beside the vehicle, and had the sudden, uneasy feeling that my mentioning his name had conjured him up. Just like the movies, the old werewolf silently appeared out of the cold night air.

I gave myself a mental shake, irritated with my silly obsession with this helpless old man. The shelter was only a few blocks from the Hecht Company warehouse. All the street people knew they had the best dumpster in the city. He must've been down there foraging, and was now on his way back downtown.

"Therese, bubeleh," he greeted me warmly, like we were old friends, "still working hard?"

"Still, Zeyde," I agreed. "What can I do for you? Had anything to eat tonight?"

"Such a nice girl to worry about an old man. I was just walking by. . .I recognized your van." He must've watched me and Joe return to it the night of the murder. He smiled, and I felt funny. Why *was* I worried about him? I had enough to be concerned about taking care of the city's unwanted animals. "This is where you work, this place?" He indicated the shelter.

"Yeah, this is it."

"So, why does a nice girl like you do such a hard, dangerous job, chasing animals in the street at night?"

I shrugged. "Someone's got to do it."

"But you could get hurt by such big dogs, bitten terrible!"

"Not me, Zeyde," I reassured him. "I don't get bitten. Not in eight years. I'm good at this."

I found myself looking at the old mustard-colored cinderblock shelter. The huge walk-in refrigerator stuck out of its side garishly, all new stainless steel against the old block. That's where most of my night's work ended up, in the walk-in, waiting for the renderers. Big, plastic barrels filled with rigid animals curled in a mockery of sleep.

Suddenly, I was uncomfortably aware of the similarities between the shelter and a concentration camp. We warehoused animals until we had too many, then killed the sickest, weakest and oldest. Then we sent the bodies away to become soap and fertilizer. I didn't like thinking of myself as a *humane* Nazi.

"Ach, I've upset you, being the yenta, asking questions that are none of my business."

"Zeyde, I do this work because I *have* to, because I love animals. . . I *help* them. . . ." At least, I ended their suffering. He gave me a sad look and nodded. I thought of the dobie now sleeping behind Linda's desk who'd never again be hungry or dirty or cold. "I'm a complete vegan. I don't eat animals or eat *any* animal products."

He looked at me gently. "And people? You love them, too?"

I gritted my teeth. On a good day, I tolerated people. After a long shift, after picking up too many animals like that dobie, I despised them. The only reason this job existed was because of the cruelty and indifference of people. But, even before the job, I never had close relationships. I still hadn't recovered from Dove or Alfred's death, but my dad died ten years before, and I couldn't even remember the date.

Then I thought of Joe. I knew how he felt about me, but I didn't *want* to care. "So, how long have you been on the streets?" I asked the old man, wanting to change the subject.

"Since the war," he admitted, with an odd smile.

"*World War Two*?" Surviving that long, homeless?

"They took everything," he said softly. "Parents, wife, children, grand-children. . .our wealth, heritage. . .everything we were. Everything we would have been."

"Other people started over, remarried, rebuilt," I said.

He nodded. "Yes, but to see your loved ones destroyed, an entire family like ours. . .I did not have it in me."

"So, what've you been doing all these years?"

He smiled, showing long, yellow teeth. "Following the wind, bubeleh."

"Zeyde, what's your name?"

"Joshua Tobeck," he replied. "There are many Tobecks, but our branch of that honored line was. . .special. . .very old. First, we often said." He chuckled—a short, brittle sound.

"Listen, Zeyde, the other night, when that man was killed by dogs, weren't you close enough to hear anything?"

"Was *I* close enough?" he asked, slyly.

I watched him uneasily. "Did you know he was a Nazi?"

"Did I *know* he was a Nazi?" he repeated sarcastically.

I frowned. He was goading me. The hairs on the back of my neck stood on end. He wasn't a helpless old man anymore. . .and we both knew it. He was a werewolf. The feeling was on me stronger than ever, like instinct, like a sixth sense. "Did you kill that Nazi?" I asked softly, not wanting to know.

"Did I *kill* that Nazi?" He grinned wildly. "Did I *rip* his throat out? Did I *eat* his heart? Such a death is too *good* for a Nazi!" He spat angrily on the street. "Did *I* kill that Nazi?" His gray eyes gleamed with a feral light.

Fear made my skin crawl, but only for a moment. I got a grip on myself and felt embarrassed. It wasn't like me to let my imagination run away like that. I looked at Zeyde's thin form, his gnarled hands and stooped shoulders. He was so old, so worn.

Of course Zeyde knew about the corpse. News travels fast on the streets, and the street people who'd been there would've talked about it among themselves, sharing the grisly details. That's all it was. He was just raving, trying to scare me.

"So, how's your policeman, bubeleh?" Zeyde said, once more the sweet old man, as though nothing had happened. "Be nice to him, he has a good heart."

I watched the stooped figure shuffle away, telling myself that such conversations were typical with street people—confused memories laced with paranoia. But as I slid into the driver's seat, I switched on the radio to call Joe.

I never did tell Joe much. . .just that Zeyde wasn't a reliable witness. I didn't even consider discussing my uneasy imaginings. . .I'd have sounded even crazier than the old man. I could picture Joe's face. Werewolves, yeah, sure!

However, on impulse, I did let Joe take me to breakfast. We shared other meals over the next few weeks. We'd meet at the restaurant, go dutch, then separate from there. He had to be the world's most patient man, but I guess he could tell that was all I was up for. After the second week, I started really looking forward to seeing him and Chief, even though I suspected Joe was using my love for the dog to win me over. Linda couldn't believe I wasn't sleeping with him yet.

I kept running into Zeyde around the city. Sometimes he was lucid; others definitely not. He started telling me about his family, how the Nazis took them, how one minute they were together and the next, only he was alive. He hinted once that he'd helped other prisoners get away.

". . .when I had the strength to help them," he'd said. "The guards, they feared those bright silver nights."

"Bright silver? You mean moonli—" I'd started to ask.

"Searchlights!" he interrupted, smiling. Staring blankly, lost in memories, he muttered. "Six others, there were with me. . .three Jews, two gypsies, a political dissident. . .they hid me in the bad times, and I helped them get away. . .and revenge we exacted on sweet silver nights. . .."

"But, Zeyde," I'd said, when he trailed off, "why didn't *you* escape?"

He didn't answer.

Yet, I couldn't shake the crazy notion that he was a werewolf. Especially when he grinned, with all those long, yellow teeth. How could a man his age not have lost any teeth, especially in the camps?

We never found any large pack of dogs to explain that Nazi's death but, with the crush of work, it was easy to forget. I was averaging fifteen to twenty-five kills a night, average for fall. Then, one chilly Friday, almost a month to the day since I'd met him, Zeyde appeared at the shelter again, waiting by my van.

"Hi!" I greeted him, smiling. "Have you eaten?"

He nodded. "The people from *Bread for the City* had the trucks out early. The soup's not kosher, but. . ." He shrugged eloquently. "Do you have a minute to speak with me, Therese?"

"*Norris!*" Linda yelled out the front door. "Phone! It's *him!*" She batted her long lashes. I flipped her the bird.

"Sure, soon as I get this call. Come inside, it's warm." I went in to grab the phone. "Norris here."

"WhiteCrane," the baritone said. "Breakfast okay?"

I smiled, then realized Zeyde hadn't followed me inside. I poked Linda, who was leaning on me, trying to eavesdrop. "Bring Zeyde in," I hissed. "Sure," I told Joe. "Can we take Chief to the park later?"

"Yeah," he said, softly. "After the park. . .can Chief and I. . .take you home? Tell us at breakfast. Be careful tonight." He hung up quickly.

So, the world's most patient man had finally lost his patience. I was surprised to find how tempted I was. Then I noticed Linda still beckoning to the old man.

"Hey, come on, Zeyde," I called. "It's warm in here!"

Reluctantly, he stepped into the reception area, glancing at the array of brightly colored posters that admonished clients to neuter or spay—it's the only way. The cat kennel was on the left behind a glass wall, so clients could see the kitties. The dog kennel was out of sight, entered through a back hallway. Two small dogs were yapping, but the other sixty were still.

"Sit down, Zeyde, and tell me—"

The quiet shelter erupted in furious sound. The dog kennel exploded with hysterical barking. Linda and I stared wide-eyed at the cats. Every one of them stood facing Zeyde, backs arched, spitting and hissing.

Grabbing his elbow, I hustled him outside. Zeyde was shivering, looking sick and ancient. I sat him in the passenger seat of the van, then turned the heat up.

"I never had much of a way with animals," he muttered. There was a long, uncomfortable moment, until he finally said, "Therese, I've come to give you something. A gift."

I felt confused as he fumbled in the pockets of his huge coat. He pulled out something shiny, a small dagger, the blade maybe six inches long. It had a heavy handle, ornately carved.

"Pure silver," he said, touching it reverently. "It's been in my family since. . . since the family began, how far back no one knows. It's part of our legacy, this knife, like our name, and. . . To the strongest grandson, the knife is passed from grandfather, the zeyde. With the knife, the legacy, the blessing, is passed as well."

He took a shuddery breath and his young, gray eyes filled with tears. "Everything *they* took, but this. I hid it in the ground, and after the war, almost left it. Who needed the knife when there was no family, no legacy to pass? But, someday, I knew, I would want to pass it, so I took it. And now, I give it to you, bubeleh. I won't live much longer. If I die on the street, who gets the knife? You're all the family I have."

I didn't touch the knife, unsure if Zeyde was rational enough to give me the only thing of value he owned. "Uh. . .Zeyde, I'm honored. But. . .I'm not Jewish."

He chuckled. "Not even a little? Maybe once you went with a Jewish boy, we could say you were Jewish by injection?"

"Maybe once," I admitted, smiling.

"Take the knife, Therese," he begged, "with my love, my blessing. Then if I die tonight, I know the legacy is safe."

A month ago, I wouldn't have wanted that much connection to the old man. A month ago, I wouldn't have gone out with Joe. I held out my hand. He placed the handle in my palm.

"The inscription is Hebrew." He pointed to the ornately carved letters, reading from right to left. "It is *yod, he, vau, ??* English, it is YHVH—you would say 'Yahweh.'"

I wrapped my hand around the small, ancient knife, feeling the engraved name of God. I suddenly cared a great deal if Zeyde lived through the night. "Let me take you to the homeless shelter, okay?" I slid the knife into the pocket of my jacket.

His eyes glittered strangely. "No. The wind blows sweet tonight, like fresh hay sick with mold. You ever smelled that?"

I shook my head. I was a city girl, after all.

"I smelled it first in the camps. It's *their* smell, the Nazis, a smell to make you sick inside. I followed it all over the world, after the camps. In every city, I found the smell. . .I found them. But here. . .it leaks from the ground, from the big, fancy buildings. They come to make deals, and they carry the smell. Dictators come to make nice to the President. Last week, that one from South Africa—feh! The smell! And the monsters that make the bad drugs. . ." he smiled, shaking his head, lost in his memories. "To find a Nazi in this town is no easy thing. *So* much competition they have. Ach, tonight, the wind blows sweet and sick and I follow it."

Then, as if he'd said nothing bizarre at all, he smiled and said, "So, how's your fella, bubeleh? He's not Jewish, is he?"

After Zeyde had shuffled away, I started the van and went back to work. It wasn't a bad night for a Friday. By midnight, the van was only half full—no French-fried cats, no bad hit-by-cars. The air was cold and clean smelling. I was thinking about coming in, maybe even finishing on time. Then the radio crackled.

"Tee, we've got a police call," Linda's voice said. "In the alley between Vermont Avenue and Fourteenth Street, bordered by K and L. A possible feral dog attack.

Joe and Chief are on their way. He says to wait till he's on the scene before leaving the van. Says that's an order."

"Right!" I said, irritably, swinging the van around. "I'm not far away." Joe and I were going to have to talk about his mother-hen routine. A drug bust was one thing, but handling bad dogs was *my* business.

I pulled up to the alley, grabbed my pole and flashlight, then walked into the darkness. I peeked around a big dumpster that blocked most of my view. If I startled them, they'd all split and I'd never catch even one. If they came after me, I could always jump in the dumpster. I heard low growling, the kind a big, hairy-chested dog makes.

Then I saw him, and my breath stopped. I blinked, confused. It was Zeyde. Hunched over somebody, his back to me. The sounds had to be coming from him. The sprawled figure was moaning feebly, while the old man squatted on his haunches, hands to his mouth, growling.

"Zeyde!" I yelled, starting forward. "What the *hell* are you doing?" The old man would get busted if he was rolling this guy, and I didn't think Zeyde could handle being in the D.C. lock up.

He stopped, and turned, rising to his feet.

All that time I had spent with him, seeing the werewolf, I'd always talked myself out of it, not wanting to really *believe* it. I didn't see the moon, but it had to be full.

Zeyde was fully transformed. He filled up the huge coat, his thickly muscled arms thrusting out its sleeves, his coat and shirt wide open to accommodate his huge, furred chest. His clawed paws/hands were soaked with blood. He must've been six feet four, and weighed at least two hundred pounds. And his face! A wide-muzzled animal glared at me, with Zeyde's eyes shining out of dark fur. The teeth were huge, impossibly long and sharp.

As he faced me, the beast chewed the last bit of his victim's quivering heart and swallowed it.

You can't outrun him, I reminded myself, gripping my rabies pole and flashlight. I spoke quietly. "It's just me, Zeyde."

He grinned a bloody smile and I remembered Joe wondering about the smell of his breath. My knees got weak. He moved towards me, snarling. I couldn't help it. I backed up.

"Don't do it, Zeyde," I said softly. "Joe's coming. He'll kill you."

The werewolf growled a laugh and launched himself.

I swung the pole with everything I had, bending it double against him, but it had no effect. I backed away, clubbing him with the flashlight, but he ignored the blows and pulled me down. Instinctively, I threw up my left arm, protecting my throat, and he fastened his teeth into the heavy nylon sleeve, worrying it. The tough material ripped like ancient muslin. I grappled with him, trying to squeeze his windpipe one-handed, but his neck was steel, and my fingers tangled futilely in the coarse fur.

I brought my knee up, a solid blow to the groin, but he ignored it. He roared, deafening me, and his hot breath scorched my hand as I hammered my fist against his wet, black nose. He never flinched.

His claws tore my coat. "Zeyde!" I screamed. "Stop! It's Therese!" Then I shrieked as white-hot pain seared my arm.

I hadn't been bitten in eight years, and I'd *never* felt such pain. I screamed again, but he kept biting me, tearing me up. My blood filled his mouth, feeding him, giving him the hot meal he craved. Next it would be my throat, and then my beating heart.

As he clawed my coat open, I suddenly heard the clatter of his silver knife as it hit the ground. I scrabbled, searching for it blindly with my right hand.

My fingers enclosed the hilt, the name of God pressing against my palm, just as his hot, bloodied breath blew against my neck, and his teeth kissed the skin of my throat. The flare of sudden headlights brightened our bizarre coupling, as I drove the knife between his ribs right into his heart. His young, feral eyes widened, staring into mine. With a tired sigh, he sagged against me.

His expression was peaceful, just like the sick animals I killed. Hugging his body with my good arm, I wept.

They released me from the hospital only a few hours later. By the time I'd reached surgery, most of the wounds had healed. By tomorrow, I knew, there wouldn't even be a scar.

Joe came by to get me, but Chief wouldn't let me in the car. The moment he caught wind of me, he went crazy, lunging and barking. I can't tell you how bad that hurt.

One of Joe's buddies came and took Chief back to the station, so Joe could take me home. We drove in silence, but finally it overcame me, and I spoke. "What did the coroner say when he saw Zeyde?"

"Said it was amazing how much strength an old man can have under the right circumstances," he answered quietly.

"Like the full moon?" I asked, with a bitter laugh.

"He meant when they got crazy. All the coroner saw was an old, shriveled man."

"You knew about Zeyde," I said.

"I suspected," he said sully. "Native Americans have their own shape-changers. I was afraid you'd think I was nuts. I know, Therese." His jaw muscles tightened.

I couldn't stand his sympathy now; I'd fall apart. As we pulled up to my building, I reached for the door handle.

"You can't deal with this alone, Tee," Joe said, grabbing my hand. "Let me help you. Let me stay with you."

I choked on a sob. "Help me? How? Can you stop the changing of the moon?"

He hugged me tightly and let me cry. He smelled so good, like moonlight and nighttime, smells I'd never noticed before. Finally, I pulled away.

"The Navajo may know a rite," he insisted. "I'll find out. . ."

"Forget it, Joe," I said tiredly. "There's nothing to be done." I'd have to call Linda tomorrow and quit. I'd never be able to set foot in the shelter again. I'd lost everything. My career, the animals I loved, the man I might have had. . ..

"Joe, what happened to the knife?"

"There'll be a hearing. I'll bring it to you after that."

I saw myself as an old woman, transforming monthly into a healthy, strapping werewolf, killing and killing. The day after must be hell, as the aged body paid the price. Could I pass the knife to someone else, the way the Tobecks passed it to their strongest grandsons? "Give it to Linda," I said leadenly. "I'll get it from her. I can't see you again."

"Don't shut me out, Tee," he warned quietly.

"I *have* to. Or some night, I'll find you dead beside me."

"The full moon wanes tonight. Nothing will happen for twenty-seven days. We can. . ."

"Stop it!" I shouted. "The Tobecks carried this for centuries, generations! You're out of it, out of my life!" I stopped and took a deep breath. "I don't want your blood on my hands."

I climbed out of the car and walked away. Joe didn't call me back. As I reached my door, a silver stretch limo suddenly pulled out of a side street, then glided past, oddly out of place here in Anacostia, with its old buildings and trash-littered streets. The smell struck me like a blow, making my stomach clench. New-mown hay gone moldy. I almost puked.

After a moment I opened the door and climbed the stairs, but no animal ghost followed me tonight. I wondered dully if, in a month, there'd be two-legged ones. Inside, even Dove's and Alfred's ghosts were gone. I thought about the long years ahead of me, doing a job that had to be done, without the warmth of a friendly animal to relieve them. Without Joe's scent to perfume the night.

I pulled out my old, battered suitcase and, ignoring the tears splashing over it, methodically filled it, wondering where I'd be during the next full moon.

There are worse things than death.

GIFT WRAP

BY CHARLAINE HARRIS

This sweet, festive, frisky holiday treat comes courtesy of Charlaine Harris, the quadrillion-selling queen of shape-shifty paranormal romance, whose high-spirited crowd-pleasing literary love-fests have arm-wrestled no less than Stephen King to the ground.

*If popularity can be calculated—and I think that it can—*one happy purchase at a time, *then few contemporary writers can be accused of spreading more happiness throughout the modern readerly land.*

I am therefore delighted to participate in this gift that keeps on giving.

"Gift Wrap" provides fans old and new with the chance to hang out with Sookie Stackhouse—Harris's psychic, adorably trouble-shootin' seeker-after-love-so-true—in a twisty dalliance that just might be more trouble than it's worth.

It was Christmas Eve. I was all by myself.

Does that sound sad and pathetic enough to make you say, "Poor Sookie Stackhouse!"? You don't need to. I was feeling plenty sorry for myself, and the more I thought about my solitude at this time of the year, the more my eyes welled and my chin quivered.

Most people hang with their family and friends at the holiday season. I actually do have a brother, but we aren't speaking. I'd recently discovered I have a living great-grandfather, though I didn't believe he would even realize it was Christmas. (Not because he's senile—far from it—but because he's not a Christian.) Those two are it for me, as far as close family goes.

I actually do have friends, too, but they all seemed to have their own plans this year. Amelia Broadway, the witch who lives on the top floor of my house, had driven down to New Orleans to spend the holiday with her father. My friend and employer, Sam Merlotte, had gone home to Texas to see his mom, stepfather, and siblings. My childhood friends Tara and JB would be spending Christmas Eve with JB's family; plus, it was their first Christmas as a married couple. Who could horn in on that? I had other friends. . .friends close enough that if I'd made puppy-dog eyes when they were talking about their holiday plans, they would have included me on their guest list in a heartbeat. In a fit of perversity, I hadn't wanted to be pitied for being alone. I guess I wanted to manage that all by myself.

Sam had gotten a substitute bartender, but Merlotte's Bar closes at two o'clock in the afternoon on Christmas Eve and remains closed until two o'clock the day after Christmas, so I didn't even have work to break up a lovely uninterrupted stretch of misery.

My laundry was done. The house was clean. The week before, I'd put up my grandmother's Christmas decorations, which I'd inherited along with the house. Opening the boxes of ornaments made me miss my grandmother with a sharp ache. She'd been gone almost two years, and I still wished I could talk to her. Not only had Gran been a lot of fun, she'd been really shrewd and she'd given good advice—if she decided you really needed some. She'd raised me from the age of seven, and she'd been the most important figure in my life.

She'd been so pleased when I'd started dating the vampire Bill Compton. That was how desperate Gran had been for me to get a beau; even Vampire Bill was welcome. When you're telepathic like I am, it's hard to date a regular guy; I'm sure you can see why. Humans think all kinds of things they don't want their nearest and dearest to know about, much less a woman they're taking out to dinner and a movie. In sharp contrast, vampires' brains are lovely silent blanks to me, and werewolf brains are nearly as good as vampires', though I get a big waft of emotions and the odd snatch of thought from my occasionally furred acquaintances.

Naturally, after I'd thought about Gran welcoming Bill, I began wondering what Bill was doing. Then I rolled my eyes at my own idiocy. It was mid-afternoon, daytime. Bill was sleeping somewhere in his house, which lay in the woods to the south of my place, across the cemetery. I'd broken up with Bill, but I was sure he'd be over like a shot if I called him—once darkness fell, of course.

Damned if I would call him. Or anyone else.

But I caught myself staring longingly at the telephone every time I passed by. I needed to get out of the house or I'd be phoning someone, anyone.

I needed a mission. A project. A task. A diversion.

I remembered having awakened for about thirty seconds in the wee hours of the morning. Since I'd worked the late shift at Merlotte's, I'd only just sunk into a deep sleep. I'd stayed awake only long enough to wonder what had jarred me out of that sleep. I'd heard something out in the woods, I thought. The sound hadn't been repeated, and I'd dropped back into slumber like a stone into water.

Now I peered out the kitchen window at the woods. Not too surprisingly, there was nothing unusual about the view. "The woods are snowy, dark, and deep," I said, trying to recall the Frost poem we'd all had to memorize in high school. Or was it "lovely, dark, and deep"?

Of course, my woods weren't lovely *or* snowy—they never are in Louisiana at Christmas, even northern Louisiana. But it was cold (here, that meant the temperature was about thirty-eight degrees Fahrenheit). And the woods were definitely dark and deep—and damp. So I put on my lace-up work boots that I'd bought years before when my brother, Jason, and I had gone hunting together, and I shrugged into my heaviest "I don't care what happens to it" coat, really more of a puffy quilted jacket. It was pale pink. Since a heavy coat takes a long time to wear out down here, the coat was several years old, too; I'm twenty-seven, definitely past the pale pink stage. I bundled all my hair up under a knit cap, and I pulled on the gloves I'd found stuffed into one pocket. I hadn't worn this coat for a long, long time, and I was surprised to find a couple of dollars and some ticket stubs in the pockets, plus a receipt for a little Christmas gift I'd given Alcide Herveaux, a werewolf I'd dated briefly.

Pockets are like little time capsules. Since I'd bought Alcide the sudoku book, his father had died in a struggle for the job of packmaster, and after a series of violent events, Alcide himself ascended to the leadership. I wondered how pack affairs were going in Shreveport. I hadn't talked to any of the Weres in two months. In fact, I'd lost track of when the last full moon had been. Last night?

Now I'd thought about Bill *and* Alcide. Unless I took action, I'd begin brooding over my most recent lost boyfriend, Quinn. It was time to get on the move.

My family has lived in this humble house for over a hundred and fifty years. My much-adapted home lies in a clearing in the middle of some woods off Hummingbird Road, outside of the small town of Bon Temps, in Renard Parish. The trees are deeper and denser to the east at the rear of the house, since they haven't been logged in a good fifty years. They're thinner on the south side, where the cemetery lies. The land is gently rolling, and far back on the property there's a little stream, but I hadn't walked all the way back to the stream in ages. My life had been very busy, what with hustling drinks at the bar, telepathing (is that a verb?) for the vampires, unwillingly participating in vampire and Were power struggles, and other magical and mundane stuff like that.

It felt good to be out in the woods, though the air was raw and damp, and it felt good to be using my muscles.

I made my way through the brush for at least thirty minutes for any indication of what had caused the ruckus the night before. There are lots of animals indigenous to northern Louisiana, but most of them are quiet and shy: possums, raccoons, deer. Then there are the slightly less quiet but still shy mammals, like coyotes and foxes. We have a few more formidable creatures. In the bar, I hear hunters' stories all the time. A couple of the more enthusiastic sportsmen had glimpsed a black bear on a private hunting preserve about two miles from my house. And Terry

Bellefleur had sworn to me he'd seen a panther less than two years ago. Most of the avid hunters had spotted feral hogs, razorbacks.

Of course, I wasn't expecting to encounter anything like that. I had popped my cell phone into my pocket, just in case, though I wasn't sure I could get a signal out in the woods.

By the time I'd worked my way through the thick woods to the stream, I was warm inside the puffy coat. I was ready to crouch down for a minute or two to examine the soft ground by the water. The stream, never big to begin with, was level with its banks after the recent rainfall. Though I'm not Nature Girl, I could tell that deer had been here; raccoons, too; and maybe a dog. Or two. Or three. *That's not good*, I thought with a hint of unease. A pack of dogs always had the potential to become dangerous. I wasn't anywhere near savvy enough to tell how old the tracks were, but I would have expected them to look drier if they'd been made over a day ago.

There was a sound from the bushes to my left. I froze, scared to raise my face and turn in toward the right direction. I slipped my cell phone out of my pocket, looked at the bars. OUTSIDE OF AREA, read the legend on the little screen. *Crap*, I thought. That hardly began to cover it.

The sound was repeated. I decided it was a moan. Whether it had issued from man or beast, I didn't know. I bit my lip, hard, and then I made myself stand up, very slowly and carefully. Nothing happened. No more sounds. I got a grip on myself and edged cautiously to my left. I pushed aside a big stand of laurel.

There was a man lying on the ground, in the cold wet mud. He was naked as a jaybird, but patterned in dried blood.

I approached him cautiously, because even naked, bleeding, muddy men could be mighty dangerous; maybe *especially* dangerous.

"Ah," I said. As an opening statement, that left a lot to be desired. "Ah, do you need help?" Okay, that ranked right up there with "How do you feel?" as a stupid opening statement.

His eyes opened—tawny eyes, wild and round like an owl's "Get away," he said urgently. "They may be coming back."

"Then we'd better hurry," I said. I had no intention of leaving an injured man in the path of whatever had injured him in the first place. "How bad are you hurt?"

"No, *run*," he said. "It's not long until dark." Painfully, he stretched out a hand to grip my ankle. He definitely wanted me to pay attention.

It was really hard to listen to his words since there was a lot of bareness that kept my eyes busy. I resolutely focused my gaze above his chest. Which was covered, not too thickly, with brown hair. Across a broad expanse. Not that I was looking!

"Come on," I said, kneeling beside the stranger. A mélange of prints indented the mud, indicating a lot of activity right around him. "How long have you been here?"

"A few hours," he said, gasping as he tried to prop himself up on one elbow.

"In this cold?" Geez Louise. No wonder his skin was bluish. "We got to get you indoors," I said. "Now." I looked from the blood on his left shoulder to the rest of him, trying to spot other injuries.

That was a mistake. The rest of him—though visibly muddy, bloody, and cold—was really, really. . .

What was wrong with me? Here I was, looking at a complete (naked and handsome) stranger with lust, while he was scared and wounded. "Here," I said, trying to sound resolute and determined and neutered. "Put your good arm around my neck, and we'll get you to your knees. Then you can get up, and we can start moving."

There were bruises all over him, but not another injury that had broken the skin, I thought. He protested several more times, but the sky was getting darker as the night drew in, and I cut him off sharply. "Get a move on," I advised him. "We don't want to be out here any longer than we have to be. It's going to take the better part of an hour to get you to the house."

The man fell silent. He finally nodded. With a lot of work, we got him to his feet. I winced when I saw how scratched and filthy they were.

"Here we go," I said encouragingly. He took a step, did a little wincing of his own. "What's your name?" I said, trying to distract him from the pain of walking.

"Preston," he said. "Preston Pardloe."

"Where you from, Preston?" We were moving a little faster now, which was good. The woods were getting darker and darker.

"I'm from Baton Rouge," he said. He sounded a little surprised.

"And how'd you come to be in my woods?"

"Well. . ."

I realized what his problem was. "Are you a Were, Preston?" I asked. I felt his body relax against my own. I'd known it already from his brain pattern, but I didn't want to scare him by telling him about my little disability. Preston had a—how can I describe it?—a smoother, thicker pattern than other Weres I'd encountered, but each mind has its own texture.

"Yes," he said. "You know, then."

"Yeah," I said. "I know." I knew way more than I'd ever wanted to. Vampires had come out in the open with the advent of the Japanese-marketed synthetic blood that could sustain them, but other creatures of the night and shadows hadn't yet taken the same giant step.

"What pack?" I asked, as we stumbled over a fallen branch and recovered. He was leaning on me heavily. I feared we'd actually tumble to the ground. We needed to pick up the pace. He did seem to be moving more easily now that his muscles had warmed up a little.

"The Deer Killer pack, from south of Baton Rouge."

"What are you doing up here in my woods?" I asked again.

"This land is yours? I'm sorry we trespassed," he said. His breath caught as I helped him around a devil's walking stick. One of the thorns caught in my pink coat, and I pulled it out with difficulty.

"That's the least of my worries," I said. "Who attacked you?"

"The Sharp Claw pack from Monroe."

I didn't know any Monroe Weres.

"Why were you here?" I asked, thinking sooner or later he'd have to answer me if I kept asking.

"We were supposed to meet on neutral ground," he said, his face tense with pain. "A werepanther from out in the country somewhere offered the land to us as a midway point, a neutral zone. Our packs have been. . .feuding. He said this would be a good place to resolve our differences."

My brother had offered my land as a Were parley ground? The stranger and I struggled along in silence while I tried to think that through. My brother, Jason, was indeed a werepanther, though he'd become one by being bitten; his estranged wife was a born werepanther, a genetic panther. What was Jason thinking, sending such a dangerous gathering my way? Not of my welfare, that's for sure.

Granted, we weren't on good terms, but it was painful to think he'd actually want to do me harm. Any more than he'd already done me, that is.

A hiss of pain brought my attention back to my companion. Trying to help him more efficiently, I put my arm around his waist, and he draped his arm across my shoulder. We were able to make better time that way, to my relief. Five minutes later, I saw the light I'd left on above the back porch.

"Thank God," I said. We began moving faster, and we reached the house just as dark fell. For a second, my companion arched and tensed, but he didn't change. That was a relief.

Getting up the steps turned into an ordeal, but finally I got Preston into the house and seated at the kitchen table. I looked him over anxiously. This wasn't the first time I'd brought a bleeding and naked man into my kitchen, oddly enough. I'd found a vampire named Eric under similar circumstances. Was that not incredibly weird, even for my life? Of course, I didn't have time to mull that over, because this man needed some attention.

I tried to look at the shoulder wound in the improved light of the kitchen, but he was so grimy it was hard to examine in detail. "Do you think you could stand to take a shower?" I asked, hoping I didn't sound like I thought he smelled or anything. Actually, he did smell a little unusual, but his scent wasn't unpleasant.

"I think I can stay upright that long," he said briefly.

"Okay, stay put for a second," I said. I brought the old afghan from the back of the living room couch and arranged it around him carefully. Now it was easier to concentrate.

I hurried to the hall bathroom to turn on the shower controls, added long after the claw-footed bathtub had been installed. I leaned over to turn on the water, waited until it was hot, and got out two fresh towels. Amelia had left shampoo and crème rinse in the rack hanging from the showerhead, and there was plenty of soap. I put my hand under the water. Nice and hot.

"Okay!" I called. "I'm coming to get you!"

My unexpected visitor was looking startled when I got back to the kitchen. "For what?" he asked, and I wondered if he'd hit his head in the woods.

"For the shower. Hear the water running?" I said, trying to sound matter-of-fact. "I can't see the extent of your wounds until I get you clean."

We were up and moving again, and I thought he was walking better, as if the warmth of the house and the smoothness of the floor helped his muscles relax. He'd just left the afghan on the chair. No problem with nudity, like most Weres, I noticed. Okay, that was good, right? His thoughts were opaque to me, as Were thoughts sometimes were, but I caught flashes of anxiety.

Suddenly he leaned against me much more heavily, and I staggered into the wall. "Sorry," he said, gasping. "Just had a twinge in my leg."

"No problem," I said. "It's probably your muscles stretching." We made it into the small bathroom, which was very old-fashioned. My own bathroom off my bedroom was more modern, but this was less personal.

But Preston didn't seem to note the black-and-white-checkered tile. With unmistakable eagerness, he was eyeing the hot water spraying down into the tub.

"Ah, do you need me to leave you alone for a second before I help you into the shower?" I asked, indicating the toilet with a tip of my head.

He looked at me blankly. "Oh," he said, finally understanding. "No, that's all right." So we made it to the side of the tub, which was a high one. With a lot of awkward maneuvering, Preston swung a leg over the side, and I shoved, and he was able to raise the second leg enough to climb completely in. After making sure he could stand by himself, I began to pull the shower curtain closed.

"Lady," he said, and I stopped. He was under the stream of hot water, his hair plastered to his head, water beating on his chest and running down to drip off his. . . Okay, he'd gotten warmer everywhere.

"Yes?" I was trying not to sound like I was choking.

"What's your name?"

"Oh! Excuse me." I swallowed hard. "My name is Sookie. Sookie Stackhouse." I swallowed again. "There's the soap; there's the shampoo. I'm going to leave the bathroom door open, okay? You just call me when you're through, and I'll help you out of the tub."

"Thanks," he said. "I'll yell if I need you."

I pulled the shower curtain, not without regret. After checking that the clean towels were where Preston could easily reach them, I returned to the kitchen. I wondered if he would like coffee or hot chocolate or tea? Or maybe alcohol? I had some bourbon, and there were a couple of beers in the refrigerator. I'd ask him. Soup, he'd need some soup. I didn't have any homemade, but I had Campbell's Chicken Tortilla. I put the soup into a pan on the stove, got coffee ready to go, and boiled some water in case he opted for the chocolate or tea. I was practically vibrating with purpose.

When Preston emerged from the bathroom, his bottom half was wrapped in a large blue bath towel of Amelia's. Believe me, it had never looked so good. Preston had draped a towel around his neck to catch the drips from his hair, and it covered his shoulder wound. He winced a little as he walked, and I knew his feet must be sore. I'd gotten some men's socks by mistake on my last trip to Wal-Mart, so I got them from my drawer and handed them to Preston, who'd resumed his seat at the table. He looked at them very carefully, to my puzzlement.

"You need to put on some socks," I said, wondering if he paused because he thought he was wearing some other man's garments. "They're mine," I said reassuringly. "Your feet must be tender."

"Yes," said Preston, and rather slowly, he bent to put them on.

"You need help?" I was pouring the soup in a bowl.

"No, thank you," he said, his face hidden by his thick, dark hair as he bent to the task. "What smells so good?"

"I heated some soup for you," I said. "You want coffee or tea or. . ."

"Yes, please," he said.

I never drank tea myself, but Amelia had some. I looked through her selection, hoping none of these blends would turn him into a frog or anything. Amelia's magic had had unexpected results in the past. Surely anything marked LIPTON was okay? I dunked the tea bag into the scalding water and hoped for the best.

Preston ate the soup carefully. Maybe I'd gotten it too hot. He spooned it into his mouth like he'd never had soup before. Maybe his mama had always served homemade. I felt a little embarrassed. I was staring at him, because I sure didn't have anything better to look at. He looked up and met my eyes.

Whoa. Things were moving too fast here. "So, how'd you get hurt?" I asked. "Was there a skirmish? How come your pack left you?"

"There was a fight," he said. "Negotiations didn't work." He looked a little doubtful and distressed. "Somehow, in the dark, they left me."

"Do you think they're coming back to get you?"

He finished his soup, and I put his tea down by his hand. "Either my own pack or the Monroe one," he said grimly.

That didn't sound good. "Okay, you better let me see your wounds now," I said. The sooner I knew his fitness level, the sooner I could decide what to do. Preston removed the towel from around his neck, and I bent to look at the wound. It was almost healed.

"When were you hurt?" I asked.

"Toward dawn." His huge tawny eyes met mine. "I lay there for hours."

"But. . ." Suddenly I wondered if I'd been entirely intelligent, bringing a stranger into my home. I knew it wasn't wise to let Preston know I had doubts about his story. The wound had looked jagged and ugly when I'd found him in the woods. Yet now that he came into the house, it healed in a matter of minutes? What was up? Weres healed fast, but not instantly.

"What's wrong, Sookie?" he asked. It was pretty hard to think about anything else when his long wet hair was trailing across his chest and the blue towel was riding pretty low.

"Are you really a Were?" I blurted, and backed up a couple of steps. His brain waves dipped into the classic Were rhythm, the jagged, dark cadence I found familiar.

Preston Pardloe looked absolutely horrified. "What else would I be?" he said, extending an arm. Obligingly, fur rippled down from his shoulder and his fingers clawed. It was the most effortless change I'd ever seen, and there was very little of the noise I associated with the transformation, which I'd witnessed several times.

"You must be some kind of super werewolf," I said.

"My family is gifted," he said proudly.

He stood, and his towel slipped off.

"No kidding," I said in a strangled voice. I could feel my cheeks turning red.

There was a howl outside. There's no eerier sound, especially on a dark, cold night; and when that eerie sound comes from the line where your yard meets the woods, well, that'll make the hairs on your arm stand up. I glanced at Preston's wolfy arm to see if the howl had had the same effect on him, and saw that his arm had reverted to human shape.

"They've returned to find me," he said.

"Your pack?" I said, hoping that his kin had returned to retrieve him.

"No." His face was bleak. "The Sharp Claws."

"Call your people. Get them here."

"They left me for a reason." He looked humiliated. "I didn't want to talk about it. But you've been so kind."

I was not liking this more and more. "And that reason would be?"

"I was payment for an offense."

"Explain in twenty words or less."

He stared down at the floor, and I realized he was counting in his head. This guy was one of a kind. "Packleader's sister wanted me, I didn't want her, she said I'd insulted her, my torture was the price."

"Why would your packleader agree to any such thing?"

"Am I still supposed to number my words?"

I shook my head. He'd sounded dead serious. Maybe he just had a really deep sense of humor.

"I'm not my packleader's favorite person, and he was willing to believe I was guilty. He himself wants the sister of the Sharp Claw packmaster, and it would be a good match from the point of view of our packs. So, I was hung out to dry."

I could sure believe that the packmaster's sister had lusted after him. The rest of the story was not outrageous, if you've had many dealings with the Weres. Sure, they're all human and reasonable on the outside, but when they're in their Were mode, they're different.

"So, they're here to get you and keep on beating you up?"

He nodded somberly. I didn't have the heart to tell him to rewind the towel. I took a deep breath, looked away, and decided I'd better go get the shotgun.

Howls were echoing, one after another, through the night by the time I fetched the shotgun from the closet in the living room. The Sharp Claws had tracked Preston to my house, clearly. There was no way I could hide him and say that he'd gone. Or was there? If they didn't come in. . .

"You need to get in the vampire hole," I said. Preston turned from staring at the back door, his eyes widening as he took in the shotgun. "It's in the guest bedroom." The vampire hole dated from when Bill Compton had been my boyfriend, and we'd thought it was prudent to have a light-tight place at my house in case he got caught by day.

When the big Were didn't move, I grabbed his arm and hustled him down the hall, showed him the trick bottom of the bedroom closet. Preston started to protest—all Weres would rather fight than flee—but I shoved him in, lowered the "floor," and threw the shoes and junk back in there to make the closet look realistic.

There was a loud knock at the front door. I checked the shotgun to make sure it was loaded and ready to fire, and then I went into the living room. My heart was pounding about a hundred miles a minute.

Werewolves tend to take blue-collar jobs in their human lives, though some of them parlay those jobs into business empires. I looked through my peephole to see that the werewolf at my front door must be a semipro wrestler. He was huge. His hair hung in tight, gelled waves to his shoulders, and he had a trimmed beard and mustache, too. He was wearing a leather vest and leather pants and motorcycle boots. He actually had leather strips tied around his upper arms, and leather braces on his wrists. He looked like someone from a fetish magazine.

"What do you want?" I called through the door.

"Let me come in," he said, in a surprisingly high voice.

Little pig, little pig, let me come in!

"Why would I do that?" *Not by the hair of my chinny-chin-chin.*

"Because we can break in if we have to. We got no quarrel with you. We know this is your land, and your brother told us you know all about us. But we're tracking a guy, and we gotta know if he's in there."

"There was a guy here, he came up to my back door," I called. "But he made a phone call and someone came and picked him up."

"Not out here," the mountainous Were said.

"No, the back door." That was where Preston's scent would lead.

"Hmmmm." By pressing my ear to the door, I could hear the Were mutter, "Check it out," to a large dark form, which loped away. "I still gotta come in and check," my unwanted visitor said. "If he's in there, you might be in danger."

He should have said that first, to convince me he was trying to save me.

"Okay, but only you," I said. "And you know I'm a friend of the Shreveport pack, and if anything happens to me, you'll have to answer to them. Call Alcide Herveaux if you don't believe me."

"Oooo, I'm scared," said Man Mountain in an assumed falsetto. But as I swung open the front door and he got a look at the shotgun, I could see that he truly did look as if he was having second thoughts. Good.

I stood aside, keeping the Benelli pointed in his direction to show I meant business. He strode through the house, his nose working all the time. His sense of smell wouldn't be nearly as accurate in his human form, and if he started to change, I intended to tell him I'd shoot if he did.

Man Mountain went upstairs, and I could hear him opening closets and looking under beds. He even stepped into the attic. I heard the creak its old door makes when it swings open.

Then he clomped downstairs in his big old boots. He was dissatisfied with his search, I could tell, because he was practically snorting. I kept the shotgun level.

Suddenly he threw back his head and roared. I flinched, and it was all I could do to hold my ground. My arms were exhausted.

He was glaring at me from his great height. "You're pulling something on us, woman. If I find out what it is, I'll be back."

"You've checked, and he's not here. Time to go. It's Christmas Eve, for goodness' sake. Go home and wrap some presents."

With a final look around the living room, out he went. I couldn't believe it. The bluff had worked. I lowered the gun and set it carefully back in the closet. My arms were trembling from holding it at the ready. I shut and locked the door behind him.

Preston was padding down the hall in the socks and nothing else, his face anxious.

"Stop!" I said, before he could step into the living room. The curtains were open. I walked around shutting all the curtains in the house, just to be on the safe side. I took the time to send out my special sort of search, and there were no live brains in the area around the house. I'd never been sure how far this ability could reach, but at least I knew the Sharp Claws were gone.

When I turned around after drawing the last drape, Preston was behind me, and then he had his arms around me, and then he was kissing me. I swam to the surface to say, "I don't really. . ."

"Pretend you found me gift-wrapped under the tree," he whispered. "Pretend you have mistletoe."

It was pretty easy to pretend both those things. Several times. Over hours.

When I woke up Christmas morning, I was as relaxed as a girl can be. It took me a while to figure out that Preston was gone; and while I felt a pang, I also felt just a bit of relief. I didn't know the guy, after all, and even after we'd been up close and personal, I had to wonder how a day alone with him would have gone. He'd left me a note in the kitchen.

"Sookie, you're incredible. You saved my life and gave me the best Christmas Eve I've ever had. I don't want to get you in any more trouble. I'll never forget how great you were in every way." He'd signed it.

I felt let down, but oddly enough I also felt happy. It was Christmas Day. I went in and plugged in the lights on the tree and sat on the old couch with my grandmother's afghan wrapped around me, which still smelled faintly of my visitor. I had a big mug of coffee and some homemade banana nut bread to have for breakfast. I had presents to unwrap. And about noon, the phone began to ring. Sam called, and Amelia; and even Jason called just to say "Merry Christmas, Sis." He hung up before I could charge him with loaning my land out to two packs of Weres. Considering the satisfying outcome, I decided to forgive and forget—at least that one transgression. I put my turkey breast in the oven, and fixed a sweet potato casserole, and opened a can of cranberry sauce, and made some cornbread dressing and some broccoli and cheese.

About thirty minutes before the somewhat simplified feast was ready, the doorbell rang. I was wearing a new, pale blue pants and top outfit in velour, a gift from Amelia. I was feeling self-sufficient as hell.

I was astonished how happy I was to see my great-grandfather at the door. His name's Niall Brigant, and he's a fairy prince. Okay, long story, but that's what he is. I'd only met him a few weeks before, and I couldn't say we really knew each other well, but he was family. He's about six feet tall, he almost always wears a black suit with a white shirt and a black tie, and he has pale golden hair as fine as cornsilk; it's longer than my hair, and it seems to float around his head if there's the slightest breeze.

Oh, yeah, my great-grandfather is over a thousand years old. Or thereabouts. I guess it's hard to keep track after all those years.

Niall smiled at me. All the tiny wrinkles that fissured his fine skin moved when he smiled, and somehow that just added to his charm. He had a load of wrapped boxes, to add to my general level of amazement.

"Please come in, Great-grandfather," I said. "I'm so happy to see you! Can you have Christmas dinner with me?"

"Yes," he said. "That's why I've come. Though," he added, "I was not invited."

"Oh," I said, feeling ridiculously ill-mannered. "I just never thought you'd be interested in coming. I mean, after all, you're not. . ." I hesitated, not wanting to be tacky.

"Not Christian," he said gently. "No, dear one, but you love Christmas, and I thought I would share it with you."

"Yay," I said.

I'd actually wrapped a present for him, intending to give it to him when I next encountered him (for seeing Niall was not a regular event), so I was able to bask in complete happiness. He gave me an opal necklace, I gave him some new ties (that black one had to go) and a Shreveport Mudbugs pennant (local color).

When the food was ready, we ate dinner, and he thought it was all very good.

It was a great Christmas.

The creature Sookie Stackhouse knew as Preston was standing in the woods. He could see Sookie and her great-grandfather moving around in the living room.

"She really is lovely, and sweet as nectar," he said to his companion, the hulking Were who'd searched Sookie's house. "I only had to use a touch of magic to get the attraction started."

"How'd Niall get you to do it?" asked the Were. He really was a werewolf, unlike Preston, who was a fairy with a gift for transforming himself.

"Oh, he helped me out of a jam once," Preston said. "Let's just say it involved an elf and a warlock, and leave it at that. Niall said he wanted to make this human's Christmas very happy, that she had no family and was deserving." He watched rather wistfully as Sookie's figure crossed the window. "Niall set up the whole story tailored to her needs. She's not speaking to her brother, so he was the one who 'loaned out' her woods. She loves to help people, so I was 'hurt'; she loves to protect people, so I was 'hunted.' She hadn't had sex in a long time, so I seduced her." Preston sighed. "I'd love to do it all over again. It was wonderful, if you like humans. But Niall said no further contact, and his word is law."

"Why do you think he did all this for her?"

"I've no idea. How'd he rope you and Curt into this?"

"Oh, we work for one of his businesses as a courier. He knew we do a little community theater, that kind of thing." The Were looked unconvincingly modest. "So I got the part of Big Threatening Brute, and Curt was Other Brute."

"And a good job you did," Preston the fairy said bracingly. "Well, back to my own neck of the woods. See you later, Ralph."

"'Bye now," Ralph said, and Preston popped out of sight.

"How the hell do they do that?" Ralph said, and stomped off through the woods to his waiting motorcycle and his buddy Curt. He had a pocketful of cash and a story he was charged to keep secret.

Inside the old house, Niall Brigant, fairy prince and loving great-grandfather, pricked his ears at the faint sound of Preston's and Ralph's departures. He knew it was audible to only his ears. He smiled down at his great-granddaughter. He didn't understand Christmas, but he understood that it was a time humans received and gave gifts, and drew together as families. As he looked at Sookie's happy face, he knew he had given her a unique yuletide memory.

"Merry Christmas, Sookie," he said, and kissed her on the cheek.

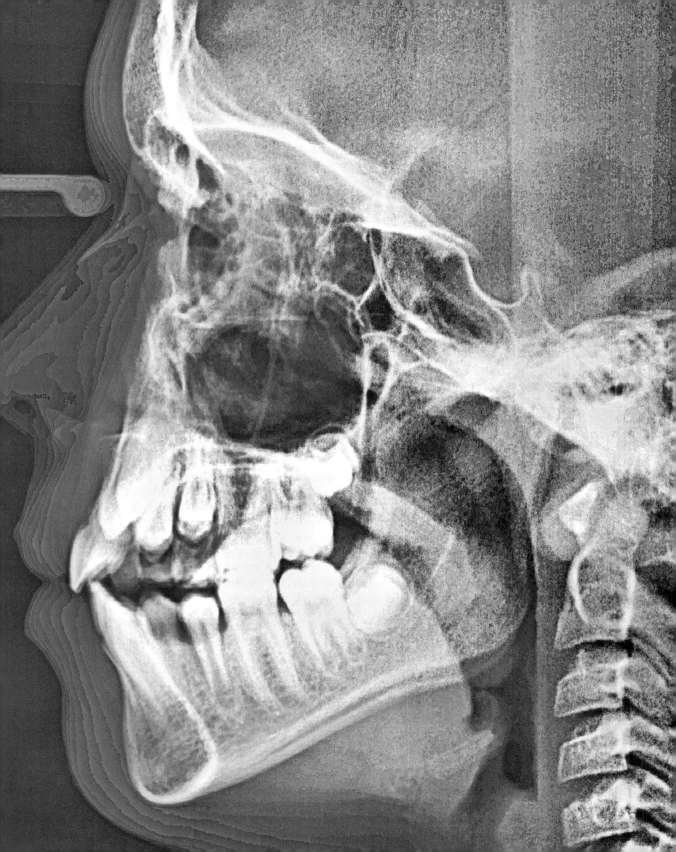

SIDE-EFFECTS MAY INCLUDE

BY STEVE DUFFY

I can attribute at least part of my love for this story to the fact that I had a broken tooth when I read it. So it wasn't a huge leap for me to empathize completely with its central dilemma. Cuz DAMN, does that hurt!

But put it all together with an exotic locale; an outsider's arrogant, bumbling perspective; a really weird drug; and the talented Steve Duffy; and (insert cheesy TV huckster's voice here) the side effects may include hilarity!

Flat out, this story is a hoot. Enjoy it painlessly, you lucky dog, you.

24-HOUR DENTIST said the sign, in Mandarin and English. Hayden tried to put out of his mind that awful old joke of his father's, when's your appointment, tooth-hurtee, and stepped inside. Though it was close on midnight, the streets were still bustling, tangy with exhaust fumes and the smell of the all-night noodle stalls. Inside the frosted-glass and brushed-metal reception area, it was air-conditioned and monastically quiet. The nurse who answered the buzzer installed him in a futuristic bucket chair, discreetly indicating the selection of reading matter spread on a nearby coffee-table. Running, for the hundredth time that day, his tongue along the edges of his teeth, Hayden noticed with little or no surprise that among the magazines was the very issue of Scientific American he'd been reading on the plane, back at the start of it all.

"MIRACLE" CHINESE DENTAL TREATMENT TO UNDERGO TRIALS IN WEST, announced the headline. Trapped in mid-flight hiatus, equidistant between London and Hong Kong, Hayden had been leafing through the magazine like the diligent sci-tech rep he tried to be, on the lookout for snappy, comprehensible articles free of algebra or chemical symbols. Medicine wasn't his area, so what drew him to this piece? Simply that long-distance plane travel often tended to set his teeth on edge, start up aches and twinges in his back fillings. Something to do with the cabin pressure, he wasn't quite sure. Did it matter that his crowns had been fitted at ground level, where the p.s.i. would be different? Perhaps the whole thing was psychosomatic, a displacement of some unconscious phobia to do with long-distance air travel. There wasn't really anyone he could ask: no-one he knew seemed to suffer the same problem. Unconsciously, Hayden stroked his jaw as he read on past the headline.

According to the text, scientists from the University of Hong Kong, using a groundbreaking mixture of ancient Chinese herbal lore and cutting-edge stem-cell procedures, had come up with a paradigm shift in the treatment of dental problems. Initial trials of the new medication, a simple rub-in gel, had exceeded all expectations, and already there was said to be a flourishing black market as small, pirate gene-tech labs churned out their own bootleg versions of the remedy. A side-bar explained the science part. The genes which controlled first and second dentitions in the human—milk teeth through wisdom teeth—had been identified several years previously, in the wave of slipstream discoveries subsequent to the Y2K breakthrough on the human genome. The Hong Kong scientists, experts in the field of transgenics, had concentrated their efforts on the so-called genetic switches which. . . here Hayden paused, distracted by a slowly increasing sense of no-longer subliminal apprehension.

He'd been grinding, ever so slightly, his teeth as he read. He knew this was something he did, not just in his sleep but when concentrating: both his girlfriend and his dentist had told him so. Now, if he clicked his top molars against his lower, he could feel. . . what was that? He tongued around furtively inside his mouth, inserting a finger once he was sure no-one was looking in his direction. There, just at the back. . . oh, great. Of course. Naturally. Six weeks on business in the Far East, and a wisdom tooth cracked clean down the middle.

It had been the Bombay mix back in the departure lounge, he recollected glumly; no doubt about it. He distinctly remembered chomping down on the bulletlike, roasted chickpea as his flight had been called, that suspicious splintering feeling he'd put to the back of his mind amidst all the check-in anxiety. . . that was the culprit, all right. Super. He didn't even like Bombay mix that much. Maybe he could sue Heathrow for the cost of the treatment.

Dismally he manipulated the injured tooth back and forth, feeling the broken surfaces grind together like shattered crockery. The tactful, near-subliminal voice of the flight attendant at his shoulder made him pull out his finger with an audible plop. "Have you got any painkillers?" Hayden asked, knowing in advance what the answer would be. Regretfully, the attendant explained the airline's strict policy with regard to passenger medications; Hayden nodded despondently, and stared out of the window at the cumulus clouds below. They looked like brilliant white molars in the cerulean gums of some unimaginably huge sky-troll.

The first actual sensations of pain had kicked in just prior to landing, after some four hours of incessant fiddling (tongue and fingertip) and an ill-advised glass of ice-cold mineral water. On the shuttle in from the airport, his cheek had begun to puff out; once in his hotel room he'd hooked open his mouth in front of the bathroom mirror, fearing the worst. And finding it, in spades. Hard up against the gum-line, there was a lump roughly the size and colour of a cherry tomato. It was hurting so badly, Hayden suspected it might actually be throbbing, visibly and palpably. Fully aware of what a stupid idea it would be, he inserted both index fingers, bracketed the swelling, and squeezed experimentally. The resultant right-hook of pain sent him staggering back from the mirror, cursing and whimpering through a mouthful of abscess and hurt.

In this way Hayden spent most of his first night in Hong Kong: alternately checking out the site of the damage in the mirror and pressed against the window in search of distraction. The waxing moon rose over the Island, soared across the tops of the skyscrapers and plunged into the fuzzy sink of light pollution above the western districts. Hayden followed its progress like a wounded timber-wolf, baying with each pulsing wave of toothache, the pain as relentless and regular as the jets that slid across the night sky, heading for Lantau and the International Airport.

He was up in plenty of time for his nine o'clock at Chen 2000 Industries. Unfortunately, between the sleeplessness and the jetlag, he looked like a homeless man who'd sneaked in off the street to panhandle cash in the atrium. With some difficulty—everyone at Chen 2000 spoke excellent English, but he was starting to sound more and more like the Elephant Man—he went through his sales pitch, careful not to let his molars clash as he spoke. Suffice it to say that the case for fast-surface gate conductors from England could have been better put. On the way out he tried to make a joke of it all, pointing ruefully to his swollen cheek, and was rewarded with polite nods and smiles from the junior executives assigned to see him off the premises. Their smooth, uncaring faces had showed marginally more interest in his Powerpoint slides and sales patter.

If the first night had been bad, then the second had been raw torture. As part of his duties, he'd been obliged to attend a banquet in the company of several important clients. Torn between not eating, which he understood would be disrespectful to the local culture, and eating, which he knew would probably end in tears, he'd chosen the latter, and had gingerly inserted a dressed tiger prawn into the opposite side of his mouth from the shattered tooth. Even before the chopsticks had cleared his lips the magnitude of his mistake became apparent. The hot hoi sin had sluiced around his tender mouth and gone straight to the root of the infection, where it had cut clean through the various analgesic treatments he'd been able to score from the pharmacy next door to the hotel. Like a dental probe wielded by some Nazi Doctor Death, the chilli sauce skewered straight into the flaming abscess. The pain that ran up the outraged nerve nearly split his head in two.

His involuntary moan of anguish had turned heads all around the table. Passing it off as a cough hadn't really helped, since even the slightest movement of his head was by now enough to make it feel as if his jaw was about to crack apart. Desperately, he'd searched the platters spread out before him for something—anything—he could reasonably appear to be eating (his plan was to nibble round the edges, and to smuggle the rest of it into his napkin), but whatever wasn't marinaded in chilli appeared to be crispy and/or chewy, and neither option was feasible for Hayden in his current predicament. He'd spent the evening with one hand clamped to his jaw, as if trying to suppress the mother of all belches. From time to time a more than usually vile blast of pain would cause him to make a squashy, razzing noise like an electrical buzzer under water, which he suspected was unacceptable in any social context the world over.

Somehow, he'd got back to the hotel. Things were starting to fray around the edges by this time, though no matter how much he drank, the numbing edge of the alcohol never quite kicked in. It was the pain that was blurring things; that, and the killer sleeplessness. He'd made yet another raid on the nearby pharmacy, triple-dosed on everything (ignoring the compendious lists of contraindications in the packaging), then retired for another night of horrors.

Sleep was out of the question: he was unable to set his head down on the pillow, not even on the nominally good side. The ache oscillated between thumping pressure and piercing intensity, and by daybreak he'd felt so wretched that even the transition from one variety of pain to another—throb to stab—seemed like a relief of sorts. A grey-faced zombie leered back at him from the mirror: was it possible, thought Hayden with the feverish, tearful wretchedness of a small child, for someone's entire head to go septic?

The next day he didn't even want to think about. Don't go there. And the night? Well, the night—

"Sir?" The nurse materialised at his side. "Dr Pang will see you now." Hayden nodded cautiously, and followed her through the translucent screens, carrying with him the copy of Scientific American from reception.

Dr Pang was a neat young man in immaculate whites who projected a powerful, slightly inhuman air of professionalism. Shaking his hand, Hayden found himself wishing he'd flossed more thoroughly, changed his shirt before leaving the hotel, and generally lived a better life. To his credit, the dentist spoke excellent English and seemed genuinely concerned for his patient; so he should at the price, Hayden reflected ungenerously.

He settled back in a high-tech treatment chair, tilted and swivelled to the precise pitch of accessibility; the gas-cylinder hydraulics of the chair, with their all-but-imperceptible hiss at each resettling, were probably the noisiest pieces of equipment in the surgery, which otherwise resembled nothing so much as the sterile assembly room at Intel—assuming, that is, Intel were keeping on top of all the latest thinking in interior design.

"So, Mr Hayden." Dr Pang perched on an adjustable stool at the side of the treatment chair, leaned slightly forward after the fashion of a father-confessor. "What seems to be the problem?"

Hayden settled back, taking absent-minded pleasure in the soft creak of the leather. He stared at the suspended ceiling, the gleaming baffled louvres of the light diffusers, and wondered where to begin. "I had this toothache," he began; and then thought: god, the toothache; yeah. What about that? Where does pain go, when it goes? We remember the fact of its having happened: rationally, its existence is accessible to us as a memory, and all the rest of it. But does the body itself remember on some cellular level, tissue, meat and pulp? Not in the same way; or else we'd surely go crazy. Imagine if each component part of us had 24-7 sentience in its own right, equal broadcasting time, like candidates in the Presidential debate. Suppose each bone, each nerve ending, had its own hotline to the sensorium; imagine the clamour, as the body became a Grand Central of sensation, a Babel of reaction. . .

". . .A toothache?" Dr Pang was waiting patiently. Hayden blinked, and tried to pick up his thread. "Er, sorry, yes: it started about a month ago, I suppose, just as I was arriving in Hong Kong."

"A month? My goodness." Dr Pang was the picture of respectful sympathy. "Four weeks is a very long time to be in pain. Was it perhaps not so bad at first?"

"No. . . I mean yes. It was very painful." If the Eskimos have all those words for snow, supposedly, then how come extreme discomfort boils down to a single syllable? True pain is irreducible, probably; indivisible, unchanging at the root.

There are modifiers, quantifiers, stabbing and throbbing, acute and severe and all the rest of them, but they really just serve to dress up the thing in itself: the monad constant and impregnable, the primordial principle of existence. Ouch. It hurts, therefore I am.

Dr Pang's alert, expressive face settled into a troubled moue. He shook his head slightly, as if in reproof. "Then you should have come to see me before now. Have you taken anything for the pain?"

Hayden felt in his pockets for the mangled remains of the various blister-packs he'd picked up at the pharmacy, and handed them to Dr Pang to be tutted over. "I was going through those a strip at a time at one point," he confessed, resettling himself in the dentist's chair, "popping them like M&Ms. The thing was, none of them were really working."

"Of course not." Dr Pang was shaking his head again, more in sorrow than in anger. "Over-the-counter medications such as these: you cannot expect them to deal with severe neuralgic pain. The problem must be dealt with at the root, Mr Hayden. Literally, in this case." He allowed himself an unpresumptuous smile.

"Yes. . ." Hayden was thinking. "Yes, I see that now, of course. Stupid of me, really." He rubbed a thumb experimentally along the point of his jaw. "I suppose it must have been around the third night when I just couldn't bear it any longer. . ."

Somewhere towards the witching hour, after the last of the cheap pills had worn off, he admitted to himself there was nothing for it but to seek help. He ought to have done it before, of course, but a quick status check had confirmed his worst fears: his bargain-basement traveller's insurance didn't cover emergency dental treatment. He'd have to pay for the treatment himself, and if the pricing policies of the first ten local dentists on the list he'd Googled on his laptop were at all representative, even a quick backstreet extraction sans anaesthetic would leave a hole in his current account roughly the size of Hong Kong harbour. This trip was running on the very edge of profitability as it was: one thumping dental bill would leave him dangerously out of pocket.

Over and above that—go on, admit it—he just didn't like dentists. They scared him: everything about them, their white coats, their whirring drills, the lights they shone in your eyes. Their cold unblinking stares, as they leaned over you and stuck sharp metal spikes into your soft, pink gums. The way they charged you an arm and a leg for the privilege of inflicting their medically sanctioned torture. Dentists? Monsters. Who else would volunteer for a job like that? It was a measure of the extremity of Hayden's predicament that he'd even considered going to one in the first place. Now, having come to the end of his tether, he was checking through the small-print of his freelance employment contract to see whether it might cover medical treatment. It didn't, of course: Hayden could almost hear the sniggers of the sadists in the legal department as they carefully precluded even the possibility of such a claim. Smug, toothy bastards. He stuffed the contract back in his briefcase, riffled through the rest of his papers—

—and came up with the Scientific American he'd bought for the flight. The magazine was folded open to the last article he'd been reading, back on the plane: "MIRACLE" CHINESE DENTAL TREATMENT TO UNDERGO TRIALS IN WEST. Squinting from the pain, he tried to focus on the headline: the final clause dissolved beneath his crosseyed scrutiny, leaving just four enormous words that filled the entire page, like newspaper declarations of war. "MIRACLE" CHINESE DENTAL TREATMENT. . . and as he stared, those super-cautious quotes, those weasel qualifiers, seemed to dwindle all the way into transparency and pop like tiny bubbles in champagne. A miracle; Christ, yes, that was what he wanted, a bucket of that, please.

The hotel porter, once buzzed up to the room and acquainted with the contents of Hayden's wallet, was gratifyingly eager to help. Hayden handed him the copy of Scientific American: scanning through the article intently, he nodded from time to time, then looked up. "You want—drugs!" he announced brightly.

"No—well, sort of, yes—look, I want medicine." Hayden pointed to the article, then to his swollen cheek. "Medicine. For toothache"

"Medicine. . .?" The porter (whose name was Jimmy Tsui) frowned. "You use up all your medicine already?" Only the night before, he'd pointed Hayden in the direction of the pharmacy round the corner.

"It's not strong enough," explained Hayden. "I need something much, much stronger—do you understand?"

"Sooo. . . you want drugs?"

"Not just any drugs," insisted Hayden "this drug. I want to know where in Hong Kong I can go to get some of this—look, here, this miracle Chinese dental treatment, see?" Why was everything so complicated?

Between Hayden's ravaged jaw and the magazine article, enlightenment gradually dawned on Jimmy Tsui. He jabbed a finger at the magazine and rattled off a musical burst of syllables. It might have been a brand name: it sounded pithy and to the point, *uuan-shan-dhol.* Hayden tried it out himself: "Wang-chang. . .wan-shang-dole? Is that this? The miracle thing?"

"Miracle, yes. . ." The porter nodded hard, his eyes saucer-wide in the wonderment of understanding. "You want—ask man about this?" He indicated the article, its illustration of a human head scanned by MRI into skull-like abstraction, all fangs and empty eyesockets. "Man who will sell you medicine. . . for this?" He pointed gingerly at Hayden's mouth.

"God, yes! Do you know anywhere I can get it? I can go up to five thousand Hong Kong, maybe seven. . ."

At long last, the porter seemed to have grasped it. "I know good doctor, yes, he got—all what you want! My shift—over, fifteen minutes! We take taxi into Mong Kok, you and me!" He tapped a finger against his nose, then laughed a trifle nervously as Hayden followed suit. Almost weeping at the prospect of relief, Hayden made to shake his hand, but the porter was already excusing himself, slipping backwards through the door in a deferential bow.

And so, soon after midnight, Hayden found himself crossing the harbour in the company of Jimmy Tsui. The taxi injected them directly into the rush and clamour of the Mong Kok strip, close by Sim City and the soaring Grand Tower. Even at this hour the bright sidewalks were chock-full of pedestrians jammed shoulder-to-shoulder, streets glittering and congested like the chutes of the fun machines in the slot parlours, all played out to a chorus of tinny chipmusic leaking from headphones and shop doorways. Above their heads neon advertisements flickered the length of Shantung Street, pulsing through the pollution layer, making rainbows on the oily tarmac underfoot. The night smelled of spent fireworks and overheated motherboards.

Jimmy tugged at his sleeve, once, twice. "Not far now! Follow me!" Hayden did his best to keep up with the porter as he dodged and shouldercharged across the road. Once he caught sight of himself in an unlit window: the surgical face-mask with which Jimmy had thoughtfully provided him—"Best you wear this—keep mouth hidden!"—made him look like the mad doctor in a Frankenstein movie. It was all in the eyes, he decided, before hastening on to follow Jimmy down a narrow entranceway between two buildings.

The walls on either side leaned in so close there was barely room for Hayden and Jimmy to walk line abreast. Optimistically, or else suicidally, a gang of kids came rollerblading at breakneck speed towards them: Hayden flattened himself against the graffitied concrete as they whizzed past, one hand raised to guard his face. Up ahead Jimmy had come to another right-turn; he waited for Hayden to catch up before gesturing theatrically and exclaiming, "This Night-town! You in Night-town now!"

Night-town took the form of another, wider alley running parallel to the strip. Each of the commercial premises stripside seemed to have its corresponding— probably unlicensed—counterpart round the back: some were simple stalls of wood-strut and canvas, while others were breezeblock lean-tos built straight on to the backs of the buildings. Jury-rigged lighting run illegally off the mains lit up the bustling alley: between that and whatever moonlight could reach the concrete canyon, Hayden could just about pick his way through the detritus underfoot. Dismembered cardboard boxes blocked his way; drifts of styrofoam packing beads, twisted snares of parcel strap, split plastic bags in the process of leaking their unguessable contents. Bedded down amongst the rubbish here and there were people lying slumped against the walls, needy or beyond need, it was impossible to tell. Whenever they passed one of these unfortunates, heads lolling anyhow, skins the colour and texture of mushrooms grown in tunnels, Jimmy would grab Hayden's arm and hurry him onwards. All the while, the ambulant dwellers of Night-town padded past on their backstreet errands, clustering briefly by each chop stall before disappearing off into the shadows.

Extractor fans heaved and whirred stale, second-hand odours at them: cigarette smoke, fast food, generator fumes. Hayden pulled his mask up over his nose and pressed on after Jimmy. Which of these booths was to be their destination? This one, perhaps: the concrete box with no door stacked floor to ceiling with cans of Kirin beer? Or the one opposite: racks of old iPods and Wiis, all scorched and heat-warped, the pinstriped proprietor perched toadlike on a tiny stool in the doorway, both hands permanently hidden inside the open briefcase that lay across his knees? Maybe this one: a whole wall full of Blu-Ray DVDs, no cases, the discs hung up on nails, their laser-etched data tracks scattering rainbow moirés of light across the faces of the teenagers who examined them.

None of these, of course. Instead, Jimmy stopped outside a plain doorway towards the end of the block, in between a dirty-looking noodle parlour and a tattooist's with a screaming demon shingle. "This way," he announced proudly: "the basement!" He ushered Hayden through the door, and followed after him down a flight of concrete stairs. At the first turn there lay sprawled another of the mushroom people: Hayden stepped gingerly over him, but Jimmy administered a sharp kick in the ribs that sent the man crashing against the wall. "Filthy monkey," he spat after the unfortunate indigent as he scrambled away up the steps. He turned to Hayden. "You follow me," he urged, and pushed past him down the stairway. By the light of red emergency bulbs, they continued their descent.

Down to an open fire-door, before which Jimmy stopped and looked round, nervously it seemed. Hayden smiled encouragingly, then realised he was still wearing the face mask. "You come please," said Jimmy, holding wide the door.

The corridor beyond was disturbingly dark, lit only by a crack of greenish light that shone through a door left ajar at the further end. It didn't look like normal room-lighting; Hayden was put in mind of the luminosity of certain sea creatures, or weird electrical discharges like St Elmo's fire. Jimmy jogged down the corridor and gave a sharp double-knock at the door, then vanished inside after signalling Hayden to wait.

Hayden heard voices through the open door, Jimmy's first of all, then that of another, much older-sounding man. After a few seconds Jimmy reappeared. He positioned himself very close to Hayden and spoke almost directly into his ear.

"Doctor has agree to see you. Make—examination! Ready in a little while."

"That's good," said Hayden uneasily. The subterranean consultant will see you now. They waited by the door, during which time Jimmy played a game of Tetris on his mobile phone. In the absence of chairs and magazines in this unorthodox waiting room, Hayden got bored; he made as if to take a look inside, but was blocked off rapidly by Jimmy. "Wait one minute!"

Frustrated, Hayden gestured with his hands at the bare corridor; Jimmy shrugged, I don't make the rules round here. But even as he spoke, a guttural word of command came from inside the room, and Jimmy clapped his hands in satisfaction. Taking Hayden by the shoulders, he propelled him through the doorway. "See you outside," he said, and vanished.

What had Hayden been expecting? Something stagey and traditional, a scene from the movies: a whiff of the mysterious East. An old-fashioned apothecary's with boxes of dried frogs, incense on braziers and twirling paper lanterns; or a smoky Triad opium den, the lair of Fu Manchu. What he actually found himself in was something else again.

It was a plain concrete bunker, dank and claustrophobic, lined floor to ceiling with industrial slotted shelving. There were no light-fittings, nor were there any candles or lanterns. The only illumination came from an enormous fish-tank, which was lit inside partly by electric light, and partly by the eerie bioluminescence of whatever was inside it—Hayden couldn't quite make it out, and wasn't really sure he wanted to know anyway. Silhouetted against the greenly glowing tank was a figure, standing very close to the glass but facing Hayden.

He'd sounded like an elderly man, but looking at him now he could have been any age. Between the green medical cap and a face-mask like Hayden's own, hardly any of his features were exposed, and over his eyes he wore tinted swimmer's goggles. The rest of his uniform consisted of a green smock and dark trousers, terminating an inch or so above his rope sandals; old man's ankles, noted Hayden, glad to have something to cling on to. The overall effect was deeply unsettling, and probably only a man in Hayden's sort of pain would have dreamed of going through with it. But he was desperate, and he wanted more than anything to get it over with, so he advanced a couple of steps into the room and bowed slightly.

The doctor said something brusque and croaky. Hayden thought of fetching Jimmy in to translate, then remembered that rolled up in his coat pocket was the invaluable copy of Scientific American. Bowing once more, he held out the magazine, indicating the article in question. The doctor made no attempt to look at it. Hayden gestured again for him to take it; this time the doctor extended a rubber-gloved hand and snatched the magazine away. He studied it for a minute, then rolled it up very tight as if wringing a chicken's neck. He stared at his patient blankly, waiting for him to acquire basic conversational Mandarin perhaps. Behind him, the air filtration unit in the tank bubbled softly.

Hayden had hoped the doctor would catch on sooner. What to do? Gingerly, he removed his face-mask, the better to articulate his wants. "Aaangh," he said, mouth wide open, finger pointing inside to the source of all his misery. "Naad toos. Agh ong." Surely the old codger could see what the matter was? "Bad tooth. That one." Please.

The doctor unrolled the magazine, looked from the article to the inside of Hayden's mouth and back again. He traced his finger along the text and read aloud, "Den-tee-shon. . . denteeshon?" He looked back up at Hayden. Hayden nodded his encouragement. "Denteeshon," the old man repeated pugnaciously. Again Hayden nodded. The doctor spread his hands wide in the universal mime for no idea, and threw the magazine at Hayden's feet.

Hayden scowled, then winced as his wrecked tooth yanked on its taproot of agony. How difficult was this going to be? "Look, I've got a toothache," he said, speaking slowly and emphasising words as if clarity alone would render them comprehensible to the doctor. To drive the point home, he pulled back his lips from his teeth to reveal the offending molar. "Hajg hju—" the doctor recoiled as if offended, and Hayden removed his fingers from his mouth—"Have you got any of this stuff?" He tapped the headline, ran his saliva-smeared finger beneath the familiar words, words that now only mocked him: MIRACLE CHINESE DENTAL TREATMENT. The old man shrugged, and Hayden felt like picking him up, all six stone of him, and shaking him till the medication fell out. Why couldn't everyone speak English, for God's sake?

On the verge of giving up and going back to the hotel, he tried one more time. "Jimmy, the man who brought me here? He said you'd be able to get me treatment for it. Like in the magazine?" Pointing at the Scientific American on the floor. "He called it wan-chang something. . . wang-shan-dole?"

Behind the face-mask came a sharp hiss of indrawn breath. The doctor had understood that part, all right. Emboldened, Hayden repeated it, pointing at his tooth: "Wang-shan-dole?" He smiled, hoping at last to get the consultation properly under way.

Quaveringly, the old man pointed at him, and fired off a breathy burst of Cantonese; something fast and high and wildly inflected. It ended in *uuan-shan-dhol* and a question mark, and a finger insistently jabbed in Hayden's direction.

Hayden seized eagerly on the one thing he thought he recognised. "Wan-shan-dole," he assented, pointing at himself.

Even under his mask there was something almost comically incredulous in the doctor's attitude—what, you?—as he let off another volley of Cantonese, again with that magic *uuan-shan-dhol* tucked away in it. Before Hayden could agree with him, the doctor was off and rooting through his shelves.

Without turning to Hayden he kept up a running commentary out of the corner of his mouth, shaking his head and throwing in the odd *uuan-shan'dhol* for good measure. At the time, Hayden was too impatient to register subtleties, but looking back later, he got the feeling the old man didn't really care to have him in the room much longer than was absolutely necessary, now he'd diagnosed the problem.

After all that fuss, it took the doctor less than a minute to come up with the goods: a pocket-sized cardboard box completely covered with small print in Pinyin and Standard Script. He held it out at arm's length; Hayden went to take it from him, and had to grab it as it fell. The old man had simply let it drop, before snatching his hand away as if afraid of catching Hayden's toothache.

Hayden turned the box round and round. "That's great," he said, hardly daring to believe he had the miracle cure in his hands at last. "Absolutely brilliant. How much do I owe you?" He took out his wallet and held it invitingly open.

The doctor, more animated and seemingly more nervous than before, scuttled forward and plucked out a few bills at random. Looking at what was left, Hayden realised he'd taken forty, fifty HK at most. The larger notes he'd withdrawn specially from the cash dispenser in the hotel lobby remained untouched. "Here," he urged, taking out one of the hundreds and waving it at him, "that's for your trouble," but the doctor wasn't having any. Backing away from Hayden, he jabbed a finger at the door and hit him with one last volley of croaky Yue dialect. Then he turned to the monster aquarium behind him. The consultation was at an end.

Slipping the cardboard box into his inside pocket, Hayden headed for the corridor. At the door he paused and tried to say goodbye: the old man turned impatiently around, lifted his face mask to reveal a flaccid maw lined with spiderish old-man's beard, and spat on the bare concrete floor at his feet. That seemed final enough: Hayden left him to his fishing.

Jimmy was practically jogging on the spot with nervous excitement. "Come on now! Time—to go!" Hayden had to hurry after him up the stairs and back outside. They barged down the alleyways to the main street, Hayden feeling oddly like a john might feel on being dismissed from some tart's parlour: surplus to requirements, something embarrassing to be got out of the way before the next punter showed up. At the taxi rank, Jimmy shook his hand for an unnaturally long time before relieving him of some of the high-denomination notes the doctor had spurned earlier. Once in the cab, Hayden couldn't wait: hands trembling ever so slightly, he reached into his pocket for the box with the medicine in it.

"So," said Dr Pang, his face rigid in barely-concealed disapproval, "you self-medicated with this black market treatment?"

"Yes," admitted Hayden. "Yes, I did. And it worked"

"Really?" One eyebrow expressively tilted.

"Really," confirmed Hayden. "What it said in the magazine? Miracle cure? They weren't exaggerating. Like turning a switch, and the pain just wasn't there any more. One dab of the gel, and. . . wow." Unconsciously, beneath the face-mask, he smiled at the memory.

"It's never quite as simple as 'wow'," Dr Pang informed him sternly. "There has been considerable trepidation as to possible side-effects of your 'miracle treatment', to say nothing of the ethical dimension of this new research in transgenics. Observations among the trial groups have pointed up several areas of grave concern—"

"Oh, I know," said Hayden, lying back in the chair and scratching his masked jaw ruminatively. "It's not as if there haven't been some side-effects. . ."

But who cared, if it wasn't hurting any more? Which it wasn't; he rubbed on gel from the tube, and the gel worked. It was cold going on, a snowball in the face, and within seconds you could feel it going to work, numbing, soothing; ah. Before he got back to the hotel he realised, with a sort of delirious disbelief, that he was pain-free. Experimentally he mouthed the words. His tooth didn't go ow. He said them aloud, until the taxi-driver turned round. Regally, Hayden waved away his curious stare.

No pain for Hayden that night, and for the whole of the marvellous day that followed. He slept in—he slept! and it didn't hurt—he slept in late, skipping his eight-thirty the following morning in favour of a lie-in, a long hot shower and an extra pot of coffee brought up to his room. And he drank the coffee, and his tooth didn't hurt any more. And he looked out of the window at the sun above the harbour, and no toothache. And he stuck his finger in his mouth, and the swelling had already gone down. It was fine.

The idea was that the gel would hold him till he got back to London, where his own dentist, a melancholy Welshman called Llewelyn, could deal with the tooth, cap it or drill it or yank it out. Whatever. That was one for the future, and Hayden was too busy relishing Hong Kong sans the agony. Padding across the room in bare feet, a lordly beast returning to its lair, he caught sight of himself in the mirror. His grin looked like something Jack Nicholson might sport at the winding-up of a particularly glorious orgy.

First thing on waking up, quite late in the afternoon; more gel. Mmmm. Rub it in, all nice and analgesic. And something to eat; Christ, he was hungry. Big hairy lumberjack portions, now, straightaway. He started to call room service, but halfway through he changed his mind, and bounded into the shower instead. Bathed and dressed, he loped down to the lobby in search of a taxi.

By the time Hayden was disembarking at Causeway Bay all the businesses on the Island were emptying out, each office block disgorging its load of commuter ants to jam up the streets below. Hayden took a deep breath and launched himself into the crowd, but his way seemed surprisingly easy; as if space were being cleared for him, somehow.

He dived into the first restaurant he saw, a gleaming 21st-century chow-parlour which seemed to be called the Futuristic Dragon. There he ordered up plate after plate of good things, all the protein he'd been denied over the last few days. Already all of that was starting to feel like a nightmare he'd once had, years and years ago: so complete was the current absence of pain, it seemed almost ludicrous to think that only yesterday he'd been desperate, maddened, panicking like a rat in a trap. . . hah. Absolutely ludicrous. He laughed out loud; some of the other diners glanced over before hastily averting their gazes. Supremely indifferent to everything except the contents of the platter laid before him, Hayden tore into the exquisite char sui pork.

Several meat courses and the best part of an hour later, Hayden untucked his napkin and pushed his chair back from the table. Sated for the time being, he felt like strolling some of his dinner off.

Though still busy by Western standards, the streets were appreciably less insane by the time he was stepping out in the direction of the Mid-levels. Pedestrians own the city, thought Hayden contentedly; car drivers slide through it untouched and unenlightened, subways are just burrows. Pedestrians lay claim to all the spaces; they flow through the arteries of the city and the city flows through them. As if to prove it, he took an unnecessary turn left at the next junction, following a sign that said Happy Valley. How long had it been since he'd walked anywhere just for fun?

For the next few blocks Hayden let chance determine his route. This he did by selecting, more or less at random, various passers-by, and following very close behind them, matching his stride exactly to their own, sometimes less than an arm's length away. As soon as they became aware of his presence, he would drop off, and select a new target. The fourth or fifth of his marks rumbled him almost immediately, though; they'd gone only a few paces when the man in front, a portly, respectable-looking type in a three-piece suit and, improbably, a white solar topee, suddenly became aware of Hayden's presence. He turned, saw Hayden falling back just a moment too late, and unloosed a string of indignant abuse in a hoarse high register. Along the street, people glanced in their direction, then turned, either incuriously or prudently, away. A couple of schoolgirls in pleated skirts and St Trinian's straw boaters had seen what Hayden was up to some blocks back;

smothering their laughter behind their hands, they were filming this latest alter-cation on their videophones. When they realised Hayden was looking at them, they screamed and ran away, *gwailo, gwailo*. With no immediate object in mind, Hayden followed them for a while.

By the time they'd vanished into some glitteringly meretricious megastore or other, he had no idea how far away from the hotel he was. His various diversions had led him uphill, which he supposed meant South and away from the harbour. Probably he was somewhere above Happy Valley by now, near Aberdeen Park perhaps, still a good few miles away from his hotel. Not that he was bothered: it was good just to walk, to stretch the muscles in his legs and fill his lungs with unprocessed air. He breathed in deep, relishing the stink of charcoal braziers and the savoury smell of street food, all the jostling aromas of a strange new city at dusk. He consulted the rising moon, and decided his hotel ought to lie in that direction. As he set off, three shadows subtracted themselves from the gloom of a nearby shop doorway and followed him.

Perhaps a mile later, Hayden found himself on the outskirts of some sort of public space, a closely planted grove of trees and bushes that fell away precipitately down the hillside. Beyond the topmost branches of the trees he could see the harbour down below, even pick out the landing lights of helicopters like fireflies round the cargo bays at Kai Tak. Hayden supposed he could waste time going round the park, or else he could just barrel right through it. Confidently—see what valorous animals we can be, when we're only free of pain?—Hayden set off along the path.

Underfoot was hard compacted sand, no slips, no trips. Even when the branches of the trees closed above his head, there was still enough moonlight for him to pick his way. (Had his night vision always been so acute? Damn, he was in good shape. Queue forms to the left, ladies.) The path wound down the hillside, til it was blocked all of a sudden by a wrought-iron gate set in a high hedge. Private property? Hayden thought not; and in any case the gate opened to his touch.

Inside was a small burial ground, very compact and quite grown-over. Small family shrines in serried ranks, with here and there a votive candle burning; white marble ghostly in the moonlight, and black tangles of bracken between the slabs.

Hayden stepped into the enclosure, closing the creaky gate behind him. Somewhere in the bushes, a nightbird sang out in alarm. There were flights of steps between the terraces; in no particular hurry, Hayden sat down and lit a cigarette. Behind him, the iron gate creaked. Hayden turned round. He had company among the dead.

Now for those of you who haven't been in a fight recently (as Hayden explained to an increasingly bemused Dr Pang), when it comes to mixing it the human male knows pretty much from the get-go how he'll behave. He'll either be emollient or abrasive, placatory or confrontational; he'll flee or fight. There's just something about the quality of the encounter that pre-determines these things—a hundred split-second decisions feeding into the adrenaline centres, instantaneous judgements based on the adversary's appearance, one's own state of preparedness, etc. And Hayden felt good tonight, dammit. He was enjoying his walk, and he did not appreciate being followed. And just in that moment, these simple factors out-weighed any more practical considerations: the fact that there were three of them, young and lean and vicious, and that the leader was waving a flick-knife in front of him as he advanced. No matter: there was no way Hayden was just handing over his wallet and his watch and his iPhone. Not tonight, no sir.

Instead he found himself up on his feet in a curious sort of crouching pose, leaning forward on the balls of his feet, his head canted to a slight angle. The one in the front—mean-looking bastard in a leather jacket, hair flopping down across his brow—snarled and said something in Mandarin. The other two laughed. Hayden ignored them entirely, and took a few steps back, feeling with one outstretched foot for obstructions, never taking his eyes off the thug in front.

Slowly, as the muggers advanced, he was retreating down a terrace of graves, letting them come after him. Bad tactics, if he was planning to run—nowhere to run. However, because the terrace was so narrow, they could only come at him one at a time, single file. That was better for fighting; it nullified their numerical advantage. And that was what it would come to, he had no doubt. Everything in him was drawn tight and singing; clenched, filled with energy and ready to spring.

Again the lead badass snarled something. Very clearly—very Englishly—Hayden said, "Come on, then, fuckface. Fucking have a go, then." Had he been paying less attention to the advancing roughneck, and more to the quality of his consonant sounds, he might have noticed some slight occlusion on the Cs and Fs, the sort of thing you associate with the wearers of new dentures, or the chewers of sticky toffee.

Thug Number One said something over his shoulder to the other two, advancing still in Indian file behind him. They nodded, and one of them leapt down between two graves to the next lowest terrace. The other one tried to clamber up to the next highest, but lost his footing and went over with a yell, twisting his ankle in the process. Hayden knew he had to act quickly, or else his one-on-one advantage would be lost.

Instinctively, he went for the high ground. From a standing start he leapt up to the higher terrace; no sooner had his feet found balance on top of the marble tombstone than he was kicking out like Jet Li, not connecting with Thug Number One but forcing him to stumble backwards in surprise. Behind him of course, was his mate, who'd tried but failed to scale the tombstones; he was kneeling down to rub his sprained ankle. The two of them went over together in a heap, and then Hayden was on them.

The impact of his landing drove all the breath out of Thug Number One, the one on top. An agonised squeal from the bottom of the pile suggested it wasn't doing much for his clumsy mate, Goon Number Two, either, but Hayden didn't care. First things first. Before he knew it he was close in and pinning the lead mugger down, forcing his arms away from his head to expose his face. In the brilliant moonlight Hayden could see the fear in the face of the kid—more than that, he felt it, tasted it rather—and it was the fear that set off some primordial time-bomb buried deep within him. Heedless of the snarl that disfigured his own features, he leaned in and bit, hard and deep and fierce.

Hayden remembered little else about the fight, to be honest; the who-did-what-to-who, the wirework and the stunts. But that feeling, when he first battened on to his opponent? The roaring, the struggling, the piteous screams and whimpers at the end; his strong and bulging jaws clamped down tight against the limited resistance of skin and flesh? The power of it. . . that he remembered well enough. And afterwards?

When the two least maimed of his muggers had scrambled away, snivelling and shrieking, he'd straightened up in amongst the gravestones, and tilted his head back to the fat enormous moon above the harbour. Never in his life had he known such transformative intensity; never before such focus and clarity. Beyond the graveyard, beneath the moon, there lay the radiant sweep of Hong Kong harbour. Everything he could see was his, it belonged to him and him alone—and he could see everything. No element of it escaped his hungry gaze; not the meanest, least significant scintilla. All his.

Involuntarily, he tilted back his head and howled, howled to the echo. The nightbirds rose from the branches and broke in a panicking spiral; away down the hill, even the tamest, most domesticated dogs twitched and grumbled in their sleep, hackles rising the length of their tensed spines, muzzles peeling back to reveal mottled gums and sharp teeth.

"But the teeth—! " Dr Pang was staring at him in amazement.

"Hang on," said Hayden mildly, and instantly the dentist closed his mouth. "I'm coming to that. Bear with me." He smiled, to convey reassurance. Dr Pang did not smile back.

Now, those things that take place in ancient graveyards after dark, under the appreciative sanction of the bleak and vengeful ancestor spirits, may end up looking very different beneath the bland pedestrian glow of electric light. When Hayden made it back to the hotel he was jacked up with energy still—he'd run the couple of miles from the hillside park to the Mid-levels in no time, and was up for another circuit of the harbour at least—but he was also exquisitely aware of the need for caution and discretion. Given the events of the last few hours, he realised that a low profile was essential at this stage of his adventures. In his jacket pocket, he'd found his old face-mask, proof against infection, ubiquitous amongst the passers-by during times of epidemic and contagion; before collecting his keycard at the desk he'd slipped it on, the better to conceal the focal point of his mysterious Shifting.

Up in his room Hayden made for the bathroom, where he used up a whole bottle of Listerine, rinsing and gargling. There was a sharp brassy taste in his mouth, charged, electric, like biting down on tinfoil. When he woke very early in the predawn of the next day after a short yet intense powernap filled with strenuously incomprehensible dreams, his morning coughs and snuffles drew the clotted tang of blood from the back of his throat. Again, he spat for a long time over the washbasin, looking at himself in the backlit mirror.

He looked good, though. Didn't he? A gloomy Gus no longer, freed from toothache pain and jet-lag; damn it, he was glowing, the way pregnant women are supposed to. Thoughtfully, Hayden squeezed a coiled blue blob of the miracle goo from its tube and applied it liberally to his gums. And another. No point in doing it by halves, was there? The gunk was menthol-cold going on—he could almost imagine his gumflesh shrinking back at its touch, which would at least account for the unusual prominence of his teeth in his grinning lean-mean-mother face. His teeth, oh yeah; warily, Hayden reviewed his exploits of the night before.

What had all that been about, then? The various cultural taboos governing use of the teeth while fighting were sufficiently well-established in Hayden's blokey superego to make him feel a little ambiguous about the whole affair. The only habitual biter he could remember having come across was back in school, a pale malnourished lad with more-or-less permanent pinkeye and impetigo. Nigel Tavers was his name; he used to smell of piss and stand by the radiators, and when cornered he would first of all whine, then try to kick you in the goolies, then use teeth and nails til he drew blood. Not the most admirable role model. So how, Hayden asked himself, did you square that inbred distaste for a dirty-fighter with those goings-on in the graveyard last night?

And found, without too much need for soul-searching and self-examination, the answer, or at least an answer. It was a knife, Hayden told himself; the bad bastard in the cemetery was waving a knife at him, with every intention of using it. This being the case, he, Hayden, a nice guy who carried no weapon, was obliged to use the implements to hand; or in this case, to mouth. Nature's equaliser, in the face of the strong threat. No biggie.

This was true up to a point; at which Hayden stopped short, and threw himself back on the bed for a luxuriously bone-cracking stretch among the sheets. Had he been only slightly more open to self-examination, he might have gone on to consider both the nature of the attack—the damage done, the extent of the retribution—and the way it made him feel at the time. The buzz, the mega bloody buzz: he could still feel its aftermath, like the tail-end of a marathon coke binge. As it was, all he could think about was breakfast.

Naturally, only the full English would do. Hayden called room service to see if it could be fetched up now, immediately, right away; no question of waiting. When it appeared some minutes later—brought up by Jimmy Tsui, of all people—Hayden was waiting at the door like a zoo animal that hadn't been fed in a fortnight.

"How you feeling?" inquired Jimmy, wheeling the trolley through into the bedroom before Hayden could wrest it from his grip and fall on the contents there and then. "Hope your medicine is—working out?"

"It's fine," Hayden assured him through a mouthful of undercooked sausage. "Look—" pulling back his cheek to reveal the problem grinder. "Worked overnight. Amazing."

Jimmy stared at Hayden's exposed dentistry; and as he stared, his own mouth fell indecorously open. Backing up rapidly, he waved away the proffered tip, and was out of the door before Hayden could press the folded bills into his hand. His parting shot came back along the corridor: "All part of the service! Enjoy!"

Shrugging it off, Hayden returned to his breakfast. God, it was great to be able to eat like a man again, and not some toothless old dear! He bit down hard on a crispy slice of bacon, and felt with lupine pleasure the action of his teeth reducing it to pulp. Not the slightest twinge from his damaged molar; all that was in the past now. Good riddance. He had a busy day ahead of him.

Meetings, mostly, rescheduled and rejigged, clean through to half six in the evening, at which point Hayden passed on a corporate dinner with clients. He had to run an errand, he explained; which was true, so far as it went. A quick taxi ride over to Mong Kok, chop-chop, and after half an hour's wandering the strip, the right back alley and the right set of stairs. As it had been the night before last, the door at the end of the corridor was ajar.

Hayden knocked, and waited till the old man poked his head out like a hermit crab ready to defend its shell against all-comers. Before the door was slammed in his face, Hayden put his weight to it, forcing it open and sending the old man staggering back into the room. Following him inside, Hayden closed the door behind them and pulled out the package from his jacket. "More," he said, holding it up so the old man could see. "I need more."

The old man's response—a near-breathless tirade of what sounded to Hayden like every curse and swear-word in the Chinese language—was pretty clearly in the negative. When Hayden asked him again, politely still, it was like standing in the way of a hosepipe of abuse. He tried cajoling him; he tried flashing his wallet, he made increasingly heated demands, but all to no avail. In the end, not knowing what else to do, Hayden ripped off his face mask. "Look!" he said, thickly, as if through a mouthful of something hard and uncomfortable. Immediately, the old man shut up.

Towards dusk he'd started to feel it, deep in the roots of his teeth. At first it had been bearable, actually not at all unpleasant: that rigid crackling sensation like popping your knuckles, only this was taking place inside his mouth, inside his jaw. Then the pressure, the constant pushing upwards, flesh and bone stretching, resettling. Probably nothing could stop it, that was the feeling he had. That was okay, though; that was fine, so long as he had some more of that blue stuff. More gel, now. Surely the old man must understand?

"You did this," said Hayden, stretching his lips wide open and showing the old man what lay concealed behind the second mask, the mask of his own skin. "You did this," advancing on him now, and the old man retreating, retreating, till he was backed up against the fish-tank, yammering frantically; and then the tank tipped over and everything went flying, and the underground chamber was plunged into dark. . .

"So, anyway, I took all of the stuff he had left," explained Hayden. "That's lasted me until now, but. . ." He spread his hands and looked at Dr Pang.

The dentist frowned. "Mr Hayden. I have to tell you, this account of yours raises the gravest questions. The science of transgenic pharmaceuticals is still very much in its infancy; goodness knows what unauthorised, possibly toxic substances you may have received from this, this street vendor. I must urge you to stop self-medicating forthwith, and I shall now examine you to assess the extent of the problem. Please remove your mask."

Above the antiseptic face-mask, Hayden's eyes creased in disappointment. "Doctor," he said wheedlingly, "isn't there some way we can, you know, come to an agreement on this? You know the right people, I'm sure. Can't you get hold of some of this?" He waved his scrap of paper from the Scientific American. "I need it. I'd be prepared to pay."

"It would be more than my licence is worth," Dr Pang assured him frowningly. "Now it would be best for me to examine you, to see the extent of the problem."

"It's almost full moon," said Hayden, shifting slightly upright on the chair. "It'll get worse before it gets better."

Dr Pang stared at him. "What did you call that. . .that thing the hotel porter said to you? You repeated it to the street vendor. What was it again?"

"Wanchang dhole," said Hayden, with none of his former awkwardness. The foreign words seemed to slip more easily between his swollen lips than his birth-language. "I looked it up on the internet, afterwards."

"Then. . . you know what that means?" Dr Pang had pushed his chair slightly back from the side of the recliner. The castors rolled silently across the gleaming tiles, till he came to a halt against the wall. No sound in all that antiseptic space except the hum of the air conditioning, a white clock ticking towards one a.m., and the fast, slightly ragged breathing of the dentist.

Hayden swung his legs over the side of the chair and sat up, directly facing Dr Pang. "Yes," he said, with difficulty. "Yes, I know what it means. But do you?" Lips parted in what might have passed for a grin, he stripped off his mask.

Dr Pang gave an involuntary cry, and tried to get to his feet. The chair skidded sideways on its castors, and he lost his balance for a crucial second; then Hayden was upon him.

UNLESS you CHANGE

BY FRANCESCA LIA BLOCK

No writer, for me, has captured the second-by-second fragrance and flavor and soul of modern Los Angeles like Francesca Lia Block. From her earliest YA novel, Weetzy Bat, *through her increasingly complex more recent work, she has always ensnared me with her sensual acuity. She writes through her senses, in ways that make most of us look like we're only guessing.*

The profoundly personal story that follows is an achingly rich little masterpiece of woe and will.

I hope it makes you feel as deeply, and gratefully, as it did me.

She was so bombarded by the sounds of the TV, the video games, the computer, the Ipod, the different salsa-opera-classic rock-carnival ring tones of all the cell phones, the mortgage payments, the utility bills, the grocery shopping, the driving the kids to school and soccer and ballet, the constant pre-occupation with youth and beauty—going to the gym every day, getting haircuts and colors, facials, cosmetic injections and laser hair removal—the fears about hydrogenated oils, carcinogens in plastic, mercury in fish and hormones in milk that might make her daughters develop too early, that she did not notice that she was going blind.

One night at dinner, she shouted, "Jasper! Maribelle! Stop messing with the lights! Sadie!" and her kids kept fighting over who had gotten more dessert the night before until she shouted again, "Someone turn on the lights!" and then her kids got quiet, giggled nervously and waited. She stood up and stumbled toward the wall.

"Mom?" they said. "Mommy? Are you okay?"

She was rushed to the hospital. On the way she remembered something a psychic friend had said to her the month before.

"I tried to see into February and all I could see was black."

The woman liked to believe in magic, but only good magic. She liked to believe in fairies and fairy tales, goddesses and spirit guides and beautiful shape-shifters. But she did not like to think about evil. It made sense to believe in evil if you believed in the good magic, but she had refused. The psychic said that a dark, demonic energy was coming, invading their world, attacking them at their most vulnerable spots. A djinn, the psychic said. Energy of a smokeless fire. Seen by horses, dogs and wolves. The woman had chosen to ignore this but it unsettled her. Now she wished she had paid more attention.

They admitted her into surgery immediately. She lay shaking on the gurney in a hospital gown and cap while her husband held her hand and her best friend sat with the kids in the waiting room. The woman thought, I probably look like shit, and then realized how sick it was to be concerned with that, but it was how she had come to think, no matter what else was happening.

A voice—the anesthesiologist—said, "You will still be a little awake but you won't feel much." The anesthesiologist had a bright green, jangling energy that made her feel unsafe.

"I don't want to be awake at all," she said. "I don't want to feel anything."

"Oh, don't worry," said the jovial anesthesiologist. "You'll have lots of drugs."

She began to tremble like a small dog and couldn't stop. The world was black and she wondered if she would ever see her children's faces again. Already, part of her was leaving them. She said to her husband, "Make sure you take good care of my babies."

"You aren't going anywhere," he said.

She wanted to tell him she had already gone somewhere. She imagined that her best friend would get her good shoes and bags and jackets. Her husband would have her photography and poetry books. Her daughters, Maribelle and Sadie, would have her antique jewelry. Jasper would have her camera. He liked to take random pictures of his feet, his sister's blue jeanned bottoms, his friends jumping on the trampoline, and every dog he saw. Her children always begged her for a dog but her husband said no; it would mess up the house and yard, he told them.

Besides the pictures she took for work there were baby albums full of pictures of the kids—just hundreds of up-close shots of their faces. There were very few pictures of anything or anyone else, and almost none of her; she was always the photographer, although it was her husband's profession as well, and Jasper had started showing an interest lately.

She thought of vision—the tyranny of it and the great joy. How she had scrutinized her face her whole life, trying to find ways to make it look better. Her older daughter's face looked like perfection to her with the deep-set blue-gray eyes, pale brows and lashes, the smattering of freckles over the already strong nose, the small, melancholy purse to the lips. But even her beautiful daughter at nine scrutinized her own face for what she believed were imperfections. Was it just a female disease? Would it hit her younger daughter in a few years, her girl whose red hair now tangled into elflocks that she would rather wear than suffer the tug of the brush? Her son seemed oblivious to the effect of his small, light features, his feline cheekbones and green eyes shaped like half moons when he smiled. Her eyes had given her a prize-winning career—spreads in elegant magazines of fresh plum pies and dahlias, jade beads and silk kimonos, peonies and antique perfume bottles. Her eyes had given her green-trimmed windows peeking out at gardens with weather-peeled wrought iron furniture and earthen pots of lemon trees, morning glories tangled in their branches, doorways leading through to sun-filled kitchens where soup cooked on stoves in heavy orange pots, bedrooms with lace curtains letting in the green light of trees through cut-work; her eyes had given her dawns, sunsets, coastlines, highways, fields, rainstorms, lightning, fire, and all the eyes she had ever loved looking back into hers. And all the animals. When she shot the animals, she imagined what it was like to be them, to have fur and claws and sharp teeth and a tail, to hear the magnified sounds of the world, to see the world through smell. Her eyes had given her the animals as they lived; the fierce, quiet rituals of their lives, lives she admired and even envied. Sometimes, when things seemed too much, she wanted that world more than her own. But without her vision she had no world; therefore it felt as if she had no self.

A woman's voice—the nurse—said, "Do you still have your period?" The nurse's energy was pastel-colored but jarring, like panda bears printed on a hospital scrub.

"No," she said, meaning she didn't have her period right then.

"Then you don't need to pee for me," the nurse said.

"No, wait, I still get my period. I just don't have it now." This seemed suddenly very important although really it didn't matter at all. She wasn't going to have any more children and she was blind.

"She doesn't need a pregnancy test," her husband said flatly.

They hadn't had sex in a year. This made her feel even more as if she didn't really exist.

When she and her husband had first met they had gone to photograph the wolves together. They had waited very quietly on their bellies in the snow breathing icy clouds and finally her husband had fastened his mittened hand to her shoulder and they had seen the animals appear from behind the dark trees. The big gray wolf stood poised, sniffing the air, then raised his throat to the sky and howled with snow-pure love and melancholy. The female wolf had nuzzled his neck. Her pale eyes were rimmed with black as if she had eyeliner on.

The woman and her husband had clicked their cameras again and again, trying to capture what they saw. There was no way a photograph could really capture it. But it had gone deep into her soul. At the time she believed it had gone into both of their souls and that they were bonded forever, especially when the three cubs appeared, loping drunkenly up the slope, coming into view, puffs of fur with bright eyes. And then when, years later, first one child, then two, then three, were born. But after Sadie's fourth birthday it seemed as if the woman had dreamed the wolves and that if they brought an omen it was not of what she could have but of what was lost to her.

That night after they had seen the wolves, they had made love by firelight in a cabin in the woods and she had growled with pleasure into his ear. His back had arched above her, lupine, his unshaven face had scratched her cheeks. By crackling firelight his eyes looked feral and he bared his teeth as he came inside her. At this moment she loved him with all of her intact, seeing soul.

Her husband was a fashion photographer now. His portfolio was filled with shots of young, lithe models dressed in animal skins, their eyes heavily lined with black paint. He almost never photographed his wife at all. And never the wolves.

The gurney was wheeled along. Then it stopped. The room was dark and she wondered how they could operate on her in such bad light.

"I wouldn't have bothered to wear makeup if I knew the light was this bad," she joked.

The anesthesiologist laughed.

She begged him for more drugs. She didn't want to feel them cutting into her eyes.

A man's voice—the doctor—spoke softly to her. He said they would do everything they could. He asked if she needed anything.

She said, "Now I'm supposed to bond with you." She tried to smile. She had read that the outcome of surgery could be affected by the bond one formed with one's surgeon. She couldn't tell if the doctor was smiling back or not.

"I have three children," she said. "I use my eyes for my work. I'm a photographer. I'm terrified."

The doctor had a cool, detached, metallic feel to him. "We'll do everything we can, Mrs. March," he said.

She was not Mrs. March. "Call me Jennifer. While you are operating, call me Jennifer."

"Okay, Jennifer."

But she was not really Jennifer either.

The world goes away and then you are gone. Unless you change.

When she woke she was on her side with her head tilted down. It was dark. There were tubes attached to her. She couldn't move. She tried to speak but no sound came. Her mouth was dry and bitter-tasting.

She heard a woman's voice—her mother-in-law—say, "I knew someone who had this happen, went through three surgeries, and she never recovered. But she should have seen it coming. There are always warning signs." The color around this voice was red.

She heard a man—her husband—say, "Thank you so much for everything." His voice was much deeper than usual, the voice he used with clients and to flirt with women. His energy was a storm cloud, dark but crackling with dangerous electricity. He was speaking to the woman's best friend.

She answered him, "Oh, I'm here for you. If there's anything I can do, let me know." Her voice sounded much higher than usual, the voice she used when she was comforting her children or talking to dogs and cats, almost artificially sweet, almost sexy. There was a brightness about her the woman had never noticed so clearly before.

The woman had the disconcerting sensation that parts of herself had lodged inside of her husband and her best friend as they flirted with each other. She wanted to retrieve herself from their bodies but, at the same time, she did not want to go back into her own body.

She realized she had not said a proper goodbye to her family. She had not said, I love you. But, strangely, they did not seem like her family any more. A husband and three beautiful children. Someone else's three beautiful children. She had never felt this before. She had never even been apart from her children at all, except for the few nights when she went to the hospital to birth Jasper and then Sadie. When they were born she had realized that she would no longer worry so much about her own health and safety. It was only their health and safety that mattered. But she had not been honest with herself. Without her vision she did not want to exist any more, at least not like this, in this body, in this life. She could not work, she could not drive, she could not care-take as she had, she could not see her loved ones. Her soul had fragmented, going into the souls of her husband and of her friend, those who could care for her children. She had always thought that there was nothing that could make her give up, abandon them. But now she was not sure it was going to be possible for her to stay. She felt incapable of caring for them herself.

You are shattering into fragments like the devil's mirror shards in the story you once read to your children. You are the devil's mirror and the fragments lodge in your own eyes as well. Death is a snow queen and you want her to kiss you. Because of the broken mirror shards, she looks like what you desire. In the distance you hear the brutal coyote eviscerating the young thing in the road but you are not sure if that is the sound of the devil or the sound of human music. Are your ears cursed by trolls as well? Your eyes smoke. Sylvia, beset by demons, put her head in an oven and Anne asphyxiated. They were no less beautiful or gifted because of it, perhaps more so. Frida disemboweled by that pole through her pelvis. Diane Arbus took barbiturates and slit her wrists in a bathtub. Paint poet saints of grief. You did not want to be that, fighting for joy in your green and white house, your circle of flowers and children, spread open to your husband's missed kisses. Birch trees whiten the fairy sky, the young faes have left the pond for fear of your smokeless fire. But you can't see any of it. You are shaking like a Chihuahua with eyeballs that roll out of its head. Pills slide beneath your bitter tongue. You stink of your medicated terror-stricken sweat. Where your legs press together infections grow, pus in your place of sacred loving. The black things in your eyes are demons that want to obliterate you, spot you out. This body can diminish to nothing but this soul is infected, too and won't survive it either. When you broke off into the bodies of the others you became shards of your ability to care for your beloveds. Lodged in the sternum and temples and groins and hearts of others so if you left they—in their health and sightednes—could feed and tend to the children. What is left of you is only this shaking half corpse without sight. You want to be touched all over with the salt silk of tongue and wild angel fur. Your skin starves like a stomach sack without nourishment. You go black, you go black; the tears of love that gave you sustenance are dried up. You grow fur and fangs, a tail of pain and permanent shadows. The cup dipped full of myth was spilled out onto the sand. You don't even bother to lick the dregs. Aging before your time. This thing happens to old, fragile people without young children and big careers. Does it? You've taken enough pictures and birthed enough babies to earn your death. But don't let anyone know you said that. Perhaps the only thing that could save you is you.

Time went by; she couldn't tell how much. She was falling deeper down a dark well toward nothing. She couldn't move. If you cannot see or move there is no point in being alive, she thought. People put their hands on her head and administered stinging drops into her eyes. Who were they? She did not hear her husband's voice anymore, or her friend's.

She had always wanted to be an animal. You could be instead of having to do, instead of having to become. You had instincts toward feeding yourself, mating, caring for your young. But you did not eat compulsively, or starve yourself to look better, or wait for months and months for your husband to touch you, or see your children look at you with shame and contempt and disappointment. You had fear of starvation, of being attacked. But you did not have doubts about your worth, about what you were. You did not worry about getting old and ugly, about being betrayed. If you became sickly and weak your pack might leave you behind but you did not think of that until it happened. Perhaps it did not always happen. Sometimes your pack would rescue you. Perhaps they waited for you.

As a child she had a dog named Sia that resembled a wolf. She loved this dog with a desperate love that brought tears to her eyes. Sia slept at the foot of her bed, warming the top of her feet, and walked with her through the hills every day. When the woman, the girl then, was sad, she pressed her head into Sia's fur and wept and Sia stayed perfectly still until the ruff around her neck was drenched and her owner was done crying and then Sia licked the tears off the girl's face. When the girl was sick Sia lay with her head on the girl's chest, her eyes flicking anxiously from side to side, keeping watch. Once, when she was old and arthritic, Sia fell down a flight of stairs and cut herself. The girl carried Sia all the way to the veterinarian's office because no one was home to drive them. Sia was a large, heavy dog and the girl's arms shook with her weight. The dog's blood dripped down the girl's bare legs in streaks so it looked as if it was the girl who bled. It felt as if she was the one who had been hurt. When Sia had to be put to sleep the girl bathed her and kissed her and held her head on her lap and stroked her while the vet gave her the injection. The girl wanted the vet to inject her, instead. She wanted to give her soul to Sia and leave her own body behind. But the vet only told her to leave the room with her parents while he wrapped Sia up in plastic and took her away.

One day, or night, whichever it was, the woman heard her children's voices. She felt their little hands in hers. This brought her back into her body for a moment. She could tell who was who by the different sizes, textures and temperatures of their hands. Her son's hand was wiry and he held on tight. Maribelle's hand was soft, round and gentle. Sadie's hand was so tiny and a little sticky.

"How are you, my loves?" the woman asked in a muffled voice. It was the first thing she had said.

"More importantly, how are you?" said Jasper soberly. His energy was green-gold light, like sun through leaves.

The woman smiled into the pillow that into which her head hung down.

"How is school?" she asked them. Maribelle told her an idea for a story she was writing about a little girl with no friends who wanted love and passion in her life. "Love and passion," were the actual words Maribelle used and they made a lump form in the woman's throat. She suggested that Maribelle write about how the girl finds a friend at a place where they do something the girl loves, something like dancing, or singing.

"She could play the piano," Maribelle said. She was violet.

The woman told her that was a good idea. She tickled Sadie's hand so she could hear her youngest daughter giggle. It made your stomach clench with joy to hear it. Maribelle said they were studying Greek mythology. When she and her brother and sister played the game at home, she was Aphrodite or Artemis, Jasper was Hermes because he was fast or Zeus because he was king and Sadie had to be whomever they needed to finish the game.

"I like to play wolf best," Sadie said. Sadie like a sunflower.

Sometimes the children pretended to be wild animals, running around the house howling at the top of their lungs and baring their teeth fiercely at their mother when she refused to give them chocolate.

"Wolves don't eat chocolate," the woman usually said. "Do you want a raw elk steak?" This time she said, "Make sure daddy gives you some chocolate."

She told her children she loved them.

After awhile, they left the room and she felt herself slipping out of her body again.

Djinn from a smokeless fire I banish thee in the name of Tara, Quan Yin, Shekinah, Mary, Mab, Aphrodite, Astarte, Inanna, Hera, Juno, Artemis, Diana, Persephone, Demeter, Hecate. Goddesses, release the elflocks painlessly from my baby's hair. Teach my daughter to love herself, value her beauty. My son has built a totem of tigers, bears and wolves to guard the house. Make sure they watch over him when he sleeps. Tell my friend to smudge the rooms and shut tight the closet door. In the name of Titania and her court release me, lift the shade from my eyes, the screams buried in my chest. Or set me free. Safe be my beloveds. The world is oily, black, slick and cold. Here at the periphery I cannot see my attacker's face. He will draw into himself and hide, waiting to throw his length upon me. The horse dog with the yellow flower in its mane runs bounding beside us on the highway. He is telling me who you are. Go in peace back to your domain. I seek a bed without traps. If I can still tell my story you can't take my soul. It is small but stronger than you imagined. You wanted me to give up and leave. To escape you, my soul fragments into the souls of others until I am left as nothing. Fear, I thought I knew you before. I knew nothing of your true countenance. Now I burn but not of my own volition. Are the trappings forever? I ask this: if I cannot be as I was, let me altogether different, as I should have always been.

She heard voices but she could not tell what they were saying. Still tied down, she was, still on her side with her head lowered off the table and her tongue lolling out of her mouth. Her neck ached. Someone touched her and spoke to her in words she did not understand. Large, cold hands wearing gloves removed something from her eyes with a ripping sound. She saw dim shadows and light— blurry shapes. Large, oily black bubbles blocked her sight, expanding and dispersing into smaller black bubbles. She still didn't understand the words that were being spoken. Someone put something around her neck and pulled her up. Her back jerked. She was placed on the ground. Four small feet held her upright. Four thin legs wobbled. Her body shook. She was lead out doors.

The air felt cool and she could smell a world that had never been before. Maybe the world could exist as scent. Her sense of smell had sharpened to the intensity of sight. She smelled green and blue and brown and mineral and vegetable and blood and musk. Sounds crackled in her ears, not the unknown sounds of the black tunnel but sounds of wind and trees, leaves, distant footsteps, bark crackling, petals falling, stars awakening. And then the howls. And the scents! The scents!

The muzzles were wet, soft, prodding her gently. Four of them. One larger and three smaller ones. The hair was bristling, coarse and lush. The throats pulsed. The powerful jaws trembled with howls. She felt the soft, damp lick of tongue on her eye, the great tenderness of that. They were not going to leave her.

Her mate and their three cubs. Nothing had ever been so beautiful.

Her body was heavy and warm; her sides heaved with relief. Love rose up in her with the force of a howl.

FORGIVEN

BY ERIC SHAPIRO

Once again, writer-filmmaker Eric Shapiro does me in with this little miracle of narrative economy. It's a neat emotional riff on David Case's authentic werewolf classic "The Cage," only at one-thirtieth the running time, and with a whisper beneath its voice that harkens back to young Bradbury.

Very short story means very short introduction.

Enjoy, and be haunted in turn.

Long ago, it was me who made the winning kicks. Me who made the cute girls laugh. Me who spent four Sundays in a row ladling bean soup for homeless men. Me, also, who stepped over the finish line in two annual Marches of Dimes.

That, and a whole many other things.

But none of them cancel out what has gone on since.

Come the dawn, I feel okay. That's when, pun intended, it "dawns" on me: I'm here for a good purpose. And Grandma is capable of helping me.

She's without fear when opening the basement door. Her march down the stairs isn't marked by slowness. As is her way, she makes no eye contact. Just comes over to me, key outstretched, scoops up the chains.

My mind, at this time, is bent in its center. Even though I slept all night, I've been wide awake, also. Instinctively, before looking at Grandma, I look at the flesh about my torso. Check for scrapes or sunray blotches, any possible remnants of an attempted escape. Grandma concentrates on the lock and key.

I find no injuries.

With Grandma, you don't just listen to what she says. There's always something she's getting at in the meantime.

Over breakfast, she picks the corners of her toast, says to me, "I saw a wolf once."

"Oh, yeah?" I ask. Head's still uneven, but my interest is real.

"Oh, yes, yes," she says. That accent she has. "I was in the car with your mother. She was driving. There was snow all around. And she said, 'Look,' and pointed off.

"Such a beautiful face on that creature. The way it looked at us."

Then her fingers work toward the center of the bread. She chews so softly that her teeth don't touch. Do I detect a smile?

As warm breath squeezes my esophagus, I dare suspect I just received a compliment.

I then almost ask what I've been meaning to ask.

But I've only been here for several nights— and these eggs on my plate are looking plump. She makes them just the way I like.

Come the afternoon, I feel less okay. The day seems heavier, like the sky's bloating in on the house. I find myself near the home's front window. All that land. A sheet of snow. An ache at the rears of my calves. Two calves / one ache.

The sounds I must make down there at night.

Does she put in earplugs before she sleeps?

(The boy screamed for me to stop. Told me he wouldn't tell on me. Said that he liked being alive, and that he liked being himself. But my adrenaline gushed too hard. I needed the smell of his blood stabbed up my brain.)

I'm relieved when I see the mailman's pickup. Out here, there aren't enough houses to validate a postal vehicle. The smile he gives me through the window is far better than what I got back home. The district attorney. Threats of silver-bullet murder.

"Hey, Pete," he says, as he hands me the mail.

I don't know this guy enough to like him, but maybe if I knew more I'd like him less. "Hey," I say.

This because I don't know his name, either.

He says good-bye. Mostly ads and coupons. Grandma doesn't keep up very many relations. Reason number one for Mom's sending me.

The TV lies at me. Everybody acting official. Everyone talking like they're in on something. How many amid these talking heads and pharmaceutical pastures have ever known the crush of the totally real?

At least the DA isn't on today, reassuring us all about "concerted manhunts."

Rip-roaring laughter from the kitchen. Grandma's on the yellow phone, has it between her ear and shoulder. She's on with my mom. Something about an old man they once knew.

Rip. Roar.

But do they mention what I did to Nicole?

What I did to that boy?

What I almost did to my mother, when it started getting dark on the long drive up?

The zonked perversion of my even being here?

Click. Nope, not today. Maybe never. Or maybe right after a word from our sponsors . . .

The afternoon's when I get fed the herbs. They come straight from a spoon in Grandma's hand. She doesn't seem to recall my age. And even if she does, she's too caught up thinking about my case. Mutters things like, "A virus, probably. Just clean the blood."

But when my eyeballs are crackling outward—when my palms are fast shedding their native pinkness—it doesn't feel like any virus I've known. More like a curse, you want my opinion.

We're in close proximity. Her breath curves through mints before reaching my face. I adore the fact that she keeps so clean. But she looks only at the herb bowl, and at her spoon. The wood table supporting both items.

Another spoonful. I swallow, a good boy. I try to believe.

"I hope it works," I say. "It has to, I guess."

"It will," she says, but is that confidence or an impression thereof? She then says, "You still have a lot to do in this life."

A charge goes through me. Something like willpower. The best sensation I'll feel all day. I start to ask her the question, finally. "Grandma . . . ?" I say.

And now she looks at me. Chestnut brown, her eyes.

"Yes, dear?" she asks, though her eyes are gone again before the *s*. She clears her throat, then—a little less forcefully than I'd prefer.

Mucus, running-dripping in there.

Why won't she look? Agitation bends me. I get up before the final spoonful.

On my way out the doorway, I clear my throat hard, hoping that she'll get the hint and mimic me.

(Nicole's nipples were like flesh razors on my palms. I wanted to think I turned her on, but it was also cold outside. The freeze coming off her breast lobes was heaven. Her sweater was tight, kept my hands pressed inside.

"Pete?" she said.

"Yeah?"

"Pete?" Again.

Seemed the word began in between her legs.

I looked at her. Her visible breath. "Is someone outside the car?" she asked.

Not someone, it turned out. Some-thing. And my bite marks still often leak beneath their dressings.)

Night skies no longer greet my sight. Once the sun goes rosy, we know it's time. Two flights of stairs, joined by an L-curve, on the way down to the basement.

Though I'm awake all night, dreams still come in floods. Usually Nicole is in them, asking-asking-asking why I did that to her spine.

(She begged to know why I was doing this to her. Assured me, in screams, that she wasn't my enemy. No one would ever know if I just-stopped-right-now. But as more hair grew from me, she stopped making sounds. Her stares overtook her; her eyes tried to escape.)

"That wasn't me, Nicky," I try to say in my dreams. But my vocal cord cavity's hollow. And my breath's funneling in the wrong direction.

And try saying that again come the morning, when you're exhausted from sleeping, and your fingernail sockets ache and crust.

The sun's a pink yolk. My grandmother, catching its rays, is our home's true beauty. She nears me in the living room. I stand at attention. She's got the key. A sparkle dives off its tip.

I move ahead of her, toward the cellar's deep door. Before I walk through it, I turn and face her.

Now, at last, the question—it rolls out in too many sounds. Spittle tucks into my lips' humid corners—

"How-are-you-able-to-do-this-with-me,-Grandma?"

Now she's not walking. Her eyes find her shoes.

"You have to answer." I'm not asking.

"Do what?" Her eyes, for me. But she presents them in flashes.

"I killed Nicole."

"No." Shake of her head / click of her neck.

"And the boy," I step back toward her, "from Robin's Path. I opened his mouth till his skull caved in."

Tears, now. My own skull might just cave.

"My mother. *Your daughter.*"

"She's fine!"

"I could've ended her l—!"

A finger, upward. Wrinkled yet dense. At least her eyes will be mine until we're through. "It wasn't you," my grandma insists. "Sweet boy," she says, as I rain more tears, "those things were not of you."

Behind her, the pinkness runs away from the foyer. I feel rage that could stiffen a Nazi's boot.

"More talk later," she says to me.

My chest is spreading. A zillion tiny bites about my scalp. But my throat's not yet done with its tender swell.

"How can you love me?" I say to her (growl).

She steps toward me. I back toward the door. She's ready to shove me if the moment insists. Come the doorway, though, I plan not to move.

"How c—?"

"You did those things?" she asks, her face in mine.

"Yes, I did."

"You think *I* haven't done some things?"

Dimes of my wetness hit the hardwood.

And I retreat still backward, let the darkness shade me.

"You," she says, with a swift step forward, "are *Peter*.

"You are more than those things."

As we submit to the darkness, her words bring light:

"People are more than the worst things they've ever done."

THE COLD THAT FLAYS THE SKIN

BY TESSA GRATTON

Tessa Gratton writes tough, smart, imaginative, beautiful, and emotionally wise stories for young adults. She picked that audience, she says, because, "I've never loved books as much as I did as a teenager. I've never needed books as much as I did then, either."

Her work is the best possible payment forward, as evidenced by "The Cold That Flays the Skin": a gorgeously played contemporary fantasia of love and resilience that made me cry, and I ain't ashamed to say it. Like a five-minute version of Eternal Sunshine of the Spotless Mind, *stripped down to its wide-open heart combined with one enormously great idea.*

I see the Christmas lights go up, and I know my time is running short.

When I was a child, it was easier. I'd be found, and coddled by kind folk or child services for a few days, then sent to a foster family. Sometimes they were awful, and I knew I only needed to bear it until Christmas. Sometimes they were wonderful, and I cried when the first plastic reindeer appeared in a neighbor's yard.

I've never met anyone like me, but I often wonder how many of the missing children whose faces line the exit at Walmart have a similar affliction.

The year I was six (I think—I don't have my original birth certificate, only the paperwork Mr. Fax gave me), I saw my own face on the TV and begged my new mom to take me to the mall parking lot to help with the search. I watched my old mom drink hot cocoa, her eyes red-rimmed, and try to speak coherently with reporters. My old dad huddled with the preacher, and they waited. And waited. I was right there, but they couldn't see.

I had a different face.

Mrs. Hannah, who took me in when I was nine, believed in angels, and I told her that I would never leave her. No matter what happened, she'd know because I would recite to her the thing she prayed with me every night: *Little angel, formed of Joy and Mirth, go love without the help of anything on earth.*

And after it happened, I ran home through the ice and crept in the back door. I brought her tea with a shot of Irish Cream, and put it down next to the rocker where she sat reading her Blake. "Mrs. Hannah," I whispered.

Her wide eyes found me and she didn't shrink away at all. I told her the poem, and she touched my new cheeks with her papery old hands. "A miracle," she said.

I lived with her for almost three years, but she died in the autumn, and I was sent to a creaking house with five other foster kids. The Partriges were kind, but harried, and after them I lived with Maris Lakes. I tried the same trick with her, that following winter, but she kicked me out into the snow and called the police.

At fifteen, I stopped trying. I lived in libraries and bus stations, occasionally in police stations, worked wherever I could, and didn't let myself get attached to anything.

I attended five different universities, transferring between the fall and spring semesters so I never had an advisor or professor who'd notice that Will Everson didn't match the kid from last year's design seminar. At the end, I cycled back around to my first alma matter to get around the school's residency requirement. That was the year I met Emma.

"Hey, do you know if this is the right form for graduation?"

I turned around to the short girl behind me in line at the Registrar's office. "Uh," I said.

She had a dimple in her left cheek, and purple hair. When she realized I was only going to stare at her, she scoffed and asked the boy behind her instead. Silver barrettes glinted in the otherwise dull hallway. They reminded me of Christmas lights, and I didn't let myself ask her out, because I only had a few weeks before it wouldn't matter if she wanted to kiss me like I wanted to kiss her.

I've always been a sucker for moments. Like when you leap into a murky lake and startle the bluegills. Like when the sun bursts out from behind the rainclouds and this relief pours through you that you don't have to sleep wet again. Like watching the baby bluejays hop around after they've been pushed from their nest. Like finishing the hardest essay exam ever. Like seeing a girl with purple hair and falling in love. Like the crackle of fire and the heat of cocoa sliding down your throat. Like when your favorite basketball team wins in overtime. Like selling your first website.

Those kinds of moments.

Like standing in a snowy field, when the coldest wind of the year snaps over your cheeks so sharply it feels like your skin will peel away.

I got to have a lot of first moments with Emma. For five years, I had them. I met her for the second time in a coffee shop, where I engineered a mix-up between my double-tall mocha and her double-tall cinnamon latte. (Emma's hair was long and apple-red.) We dated that year, but I chickened out around Labor Day and said I had a rare blood disease. She saw it for the lie it was, and dumped me.

The third time we met, she picked me up at a bar. Her hair was pink and she had a stud pierced through her tongue. I was eager and slept with her right away. She never answered my calls after that, though. She didn't like to think of herself as being so easy, though I'd never, ever have considered her so. It wasn't like I could tell her we'd known each other for a couple of years.

The fourth time, I was hired to design her boyfriend's webpage. It sucked.

The fact that she had a boyfriend, not the site I designed. We hung out anyway, and she laughed at all my jokes. She said, "You remind me of someone," every other week. Her hair was still red, but streaked with black. I only saw the dimple in her cheek when her boyfriend wasn't around.

I kissed her at a Christmas party, knowing I had nothing to lose. Her eyelashes tingled against my cheeks and for a moment, I was afraid I was going to cry. I smiled and pointed up at some mistletoe. We laughed it off, but she turned away after that and didn't talk to me for the rest of the night.

Then, ten months ago, I was walking my dog around the park, staring at the trees as if I could will the fuchsia blossoms on the redbuds to remain forever, to never let the cold come back. I turned the corner onto St. Peter's and there she was, sitting at the bus stop. Her hair was about fifteen shades of blond.

I sat down next to her, pretending to take a break. We chatted, and she said, "You remind me of someone I used to know."

"Someone from your dreams?" I smiled.

Her eyes narrowed, a little. Curiously. "He had a Scottie dog, too." She held out her hand and Summer licked her fingers like they were best friends. Which they had been.

"You're absolutely beautiful," I said.

It's easy to be what I am in the age of the internet. Designing websites doesn't require any face time, and as long as I renew my driver's license every January, nobody in any sort of authority notices. Certainly not the landlord's at my massive complex, not the people at the gas station, or the vet's office. Not anybody who reads my blog or chats with me at one in the morning. I use screennames and nicknames, so most people never notice my bank statements read William Everson. They know me as Ever, or Liam, or Bill. Never Will.

But that afternoon, at the bus stop, Emma asked my name and I told her.

"Will." She repeated it three times. I noticed she'd removed the tongue ring. Emma held out her hand to me, and I took it. "I'm Emma."

That whole year was a moment. Thousands of them.

The hardest thing I've ever done was to tell Emma I didn't love her.

It was three days ago. I put my hands on her face, and said, "I never want to see you again."

"I don't believe you," she said. She kissed me, and I closed my eyes and pretended it would last forever.

I pushed her away, and shrugged. "Believe what you want."

Now, I'm standing alone.

The moon is a hard, sharp diamond in the sky and the skeletal trees clack together in the biting breeze.

My feet break through layers of ice and snow, and as I walk into the grove, I shed clothes. It used to be I left them on, only to trash them later when they're too sticky and crusted. But back then, I feared the cold. Now I just hate it.

Tears freeze on my lashes and I try not to think about her. I touch my face with my fingers, running them over the curve of my cheeks and the square of my jaw. I feel the scar next to my ear—it will be gone in an hour. I feel the mole just inside my hairline. I feel the wrinkles at the corners of my eyes. My skin is tight and chapping.

I drop my shirt and unbutton my pants. I kick it all away and stand on the frozen ground, toes burning and going numb. The wind explodes against my back and I moan. It's a reedy sound, quiet and pleading. I just want this over fast. In the morning I'm moving to Chicago, so I'll never see Emma again.

The moonlight dims and I raise my face. Clouds blow across the sky and I see the first drops of ice seconds before they hit my forehead. Then my nose. My lips. My shoulders. Each flake, every crystal, slices open my skin.

I burn all over, jaw clenched, eyes closed.

Winter flays me.

It ends with numbness. First I bend and stretch my muscles, joints cracking, blood flowing again. I pull up my jeans and throw my shirt on, then my socks and boots. When I am covered up, I touch my new face. The skin is smooth, baby-fresh. And warm.

I feel a sharper chin, with a cleft. That's good. I like it when I have a cleft. I sigh and run my fingers up into my hair. When the sun rises, I'll glance in the mirror.

I turn around to leave the park.

"Will," Emma whispers. She's standing there in her blue parka. Her hands are pressed to her face so hard. Her hair is white in the moonlight.

IL DONNAIOLO

BY BRAD C. HODSON

Sexual obsession is an all-too-human response to an all-too-animal impulse. It's also a running thread throughout much of this book.

But when you're in love, and in Rome, beneath the moon . . . well, you can see how one might get carried away.

As is the case in this breakthrough story by a gifted young writer named Brad C. Hodson. Just another instance of a guy I never heard of, slipping in sideways and delivering the elegant goods, with language so lovely you'd think he'd been writing for a hundred years.

This one gets a little dark and sweaty, the way sex with a stranger should.

She found Giovanni in the Piazza Navona, sipping coffee with his bitch and waiting out the rain. Amanda stood under the eaves of a closed *gelateria* and stared through Bernini's Four Rivers. His face was fragile from here, nestled between the Danube's marble triceps and its back. Or was it the Nile? The Baroque had never been her strong suit.

He laughed, crystal eyes catching the moonlight and sparkling like stars. Even if he had been close enough for her to hear, the trickle of rain and the roar of the fountain would have drowned the noise out. But the air vibrated around her, the laugh tickling its way along her skin. It wasn't possible, she knew, but that had been his gift: bringing the impossible to life.

Her phone rang. It was David or Jen, wondering where she was. They would be at one of the jazz clubs lining the Campo di Fiori by now with a hundred other students, drinking and dancing until sunrise. She silenced it. What would she tell them? I'm out in the rain and dark, stalking Giovanni?

They had warned her about him. Hell, everyone had warned her about him. *He* had warned her about him. But staying away from him, she always said, would be like not eating if she were starving and someone placed roasted boar in front of her.

"Anticipation," he had told her once while kissing her neck, "makes the meal burst with flavor."

In her blood, she knew it was true. That's what this was, she reminded herself. Not stalking, but anticipation.

She wiped a damp hand across her face and tried to focus.

When she looked back toward the café, he was gone.

She stepped into the rain and scanned the piazza. Panic crawled into her stomach. Where was he?

There. By the fountain of Neptune, standing between the God and a dolphin bursting from the water, his body little more than shadow. The girl faced him, back arched, hands braced against the fountain behind her. He brushed the back of his hand down her face.

Amanda bit her cheek. The pain was sharp, and the blood bitter, but all she could think about was how that soft hand felt. How it had been her just a month ago, her dress wet and filthy from leaning against the wall of the Trevi, a thousand tourists chattering and snapping pictures around them as he bent in and the world disappeared.

The rain eased.

His shadow pressed against the girl's.

Amanda's head trembled. Her arms shook.

The rain stopped.

He took the girl's hand and walked south on the Corso, toward the Tiber and then, Amanda knew, on to his apartment.

Her steps clicked on the cobblestone, the noise echoing around her. She stopped by the café and let them walk farther down the alley. She wasn't afraid of losing them. She knew the way.

Two young waiters stood by empty tables and smoked. The harsh smell of their cigarettes mixed with the heady aroma of gnocchi and tiramisu seeping from inside. One of them nudged the other and pointed at her.

"*Bella*," he said.

The other one nodded. "*Scusi?*"

His face was young, thin, the features placed in an awkward pattern that suggested he might one day be handsome, but not now. Not while Giovanni's laughing face still burned in her eyes. Bernini would have recognized Giovanni's hard lines and piercing eyes. This boy would be more familiar to Picasso.

"Yes?"

"*Americana?*"

Across the piazza, Giovanni and his bitch were swallowed by shadows.

"*Si.*"

The smell grew stronger, more inviting. Would it be so bad to step inside, eat and drink and enjoy the night, and forget Giovanni?

"The blond hair that is short tells me you are. Is not the fashion here." He smiled. "You are a student?"

"I was." She had been studying for her master's. The test had been two weeks ago back in Boston. She had canceled her flight when Giovanni stopped returning her calls.

"Want to have a seat? We are done with work soon and maybe the three of us will share *una botiglia del rosso?*"

A bottle of red did sound good right now.

She pictured the cold, black iron frame of Giovanni's bed. The dark satin sheets.

"*Non voglio,*" she said and headed for the Corso.

His cologne lingered in the alley like it had been embedded in the walls. Far ahead two shapes pressed against each other as they walked. Amanda kept a hard pace, the ancient stones beneath her sending aches up her calves.

She had met Giovanni on the Spanish Steps. The sun was sinking, the purple sky shot through with veins of orange, as she leaned against the pink brick of the Keats-Shelley house and read Cicero's *On Friendship*. He sat beside her, his smell a sharp musk as if he had just been with a woman.

"Poor Chickpea," he said and pointed to the book.

"Why do you say that?"

"He was too much of an idealist, do you not think?"

"I don't know if that's possible."

"Being too much of an idealist?" He looked down where a group of older women laughed at the foot of the stairs, their photo being snapped by one of the Moroccans milling about. "Oh, yes."

He patted her knee and motioned his chin toward the women. She looked down and watched as two small children, no older than five, slipped wallets and cell phones from the women's purses.

"They are idealists," he said, leaning in to whisper. "They want to think no one will take advantage of them here. But this is the Eternal City. It has survived this long because it takes advantage of anyone it pleases."

His voice was two pieces of silk rubbed together.

She closed her book. "And me?"

"What about you?"

"Will I be taken advantage of?"

"Oh, most certainly."

They came to the Ponte Garibaldi and stopped under a dull yellow lamp. Their shadows were long and thin on the bridge's white stones. Giovanni leaned in and pressed his lips against the girl's.

Amanda closed her eyes and pushed her head against the wall hard enough to see stars explode.

The slut took his hand and pulled him away. Why weren't they crossing the bridge? Ponte Garibaldi was his usual route home. He had taken Amanda that way countless times, over the dark Tiber and down into the narrow medieval streets of Trastevere. A few times they hadn't even made it to his apartment, stopping in an alley to grope each other like drunken teenagers.

She followed, sticking to the dark on the opposite side of the street. They must be going to the girl's place. This was likely *her* routine. The whore no doubt brought men back this way night after night. Some stupid American slut who spread her legs for any man who spoke English with an accent. All anyone had to do was watch the sway of her hips, see how she shoved her breasts against him when she spoke, to see what a tramp she was. Amanda couldn't believe that Giovanni had fallen for it.

That's wrong. She knew he hadn't fallen for it. He was an animal. He had urges. To deny them would have been like denying sleep, or . . .

Not eating if he were starving and someone put roasted boar in front of him.

The soft notes of a violin floated through the streets. She couldn't tell where they came from, but it wasn't a strange sound. There was always music in this city, always some street performer out with his hat. It was one of the things she loved about Rome.

The first night they had spent together a violin had played. Teeth clenched, sweat soaking the sheets, the cool breeze rushing down from the Aventine and into his window, wrapping their hot flesh and carrying the sounds of Rome, music and laughter and car horns, as he melted into her, over and over, the night as eternal as the city. They had held each other sometime before dawn. One finger trailed up and down her spine as soft as breath.

She had opened up to him, told him things her closest friends didn't know. She told him about her early years in foster homes, about her adoption, how she wished she knew who her birth parents were. She told him why she really left home, how she didn't understand her adopted mother and was afraid of becoming her.

"Tell me a secret," she'd said, the tears still drying on her face.

He pulled her close to him, kissed her forehead, and ran a hand through her hair. "I cannot have children," he said, his voice hollow and aching. It broke her heart.

There was a comfort in his arms, a vulnerability awakened in her by his kiss, and they had shared far more than their bodies in those few hours.

Giovanni turned down an alley, tugging the girl behind him. The bitch seemed confused, her head darting around. Maybe they weren't going to her apartment after all.

The dark was thick, and the streets twisting, but Amanda was sure they were in the Ancient City. She passed more and more shops displaying tacky T-shirts and gaudy ceramic gladiators in the windows. What were they doing here? There weren't many apartments near the Colosseum.

She followed them out onto the street. They darted across traffic and up the steep staircase of the Campidoglio. Amanda waited.

Giovanni and his slut disappeared over the hill and into the piazza.

Amanda held her breath and darted across traffic. She crested the hill and stopped when she saw the crowd. Blue light bathed the piazza, washing over the assembly and spilling into the cracks of the marble equestrians guarding the stairs. The hard beat of dance music blasted from speakers lining the square. A stage with white backdrop had been erected across from her, a waif in a thin, silver dress with spiked hair sauntering onto it. The crowd applauded.

Amanda almost wept. It would be impossible to find Giovanni in this crowd. Her eyes flooded and threatened to burst. She refused to cry. Not here, not in front of three hundred strangers. She sucked in a deep breath.

His smell tickled her nostrils. Taunted her. His cologne. His musk. It took her and pulled her past the crowd, behind the museum, and into the brush and broken Roman columns of the Capitoline. It had to be a figment of her imagination. It was impossible to follow someone by scent, especially in such a crowd.

Yet there he was, the girl at his side, stepping down the hill.

He brought the impossible to life.

From the top of the hill, the moon burned bright and swollen above Imperial Rome. Trajan's Market stood across the way, its red brick gray in the moonlight like a tombstone for a forgotten world.

She hurried down the hill.

They stood against a wall overlooking the Forum. She inched to the corner of the Mamertine Prison and watched them. Giovanni pulled the girl into an embrace, the moonlight glowing from his skin.

Amanda pressed her hand against the cold stone of the ancient building. Inside, she knew, was a deep dark pit where Rome threw her enemies and let them rot. It was too easy to imagine herself in there, weeping in the black and waiting to die.

She fumbled in her purse.

"Never worry about becoming her," he had said once. "Not your adopted mother, not any of them. You will never become what is not already inside you."

The knife was cool in her hand. She squeezed it until her knuckles burned.

The girl leaned back over the wall, moonlight flooding over her breasts and onto Giovanni's face. His hand ran up her thigh, bunching her dress high on the curve of her hip.

Acid burned the back of Amanda's throat.

Anticipation.

Six quick steps and Amanda was with them. The girl's fear was sharp, the smell of beef soaked in vinegar.

The knife slipped between the bitch's ribs. Her face was a frightened *O*. She stumbled back, fell against the stone.

Blood spread out beneath her like wings unfolding.

Amanda dropped the knife. "No . . . what did I—"

"The hunt," Giovanni said, "must always end in death."

He grabbed Amanda by the back of the head, his fingers knotting in her hair, and shoved her face down toward the wound.

Wheezing breath came in a weak rhythm from the girl. She was slumped against the wall, the handle of Amanda's knife standing tall from her ribs, her dress stained and bloody bubbles popping on her lips.

"Look," Giovanni said.

Amanda's breath caught in her throat. Tears burst and ran hot down her cheeks. The girl's eyes were vacant, glassy, but still managed to burn a hole in Amanda.

Giovanni forced her closer. "See what you've done."

"No," Amanda's voice was cracked and small. "God, I'm so sorry, I didn't—"

His scent was overwhelming, the musk pouring off of him in streams. "You did, *cara mia*. You meant it. You hunted her and you killed her."

Below, the ruins of the Forum were painted with thick shadow, the edges tipped with moonlight. Amanda stared away to the House of Vestal Virgins and tried to stop the world from spinning.

His smell crashed over her, the scent of the girl's meat riding it, and her bones trembled. He pulled her closer, his hair falling into her face, and forced her to her knees. The tremor in her bones grew, the joints popping and bulging, and a ripple passed through her flesh like a thousand spider's legs scrambling across her.

Giovanni crouched over the girl.

Amanda closed her eyes.

The sound of meat slapping. Fabric ripping. Chewing. Tearing. Slurping. Low growls. Teeth gnashing. Jaws snapping.

She fought to find her voice. "I didn't want her to . . . to . . ."

"I told you, you cannot be what is not already in you."

The sharp scent of blood hit her, the rancid odor of an open stomach following behind. Giovanni was beside her, his eyes burning her, his jaw dripping red. He leaned in close, sniffed her throat. She fell against him, crying, shaking, muttering apologies. He kissed her. His taste was unmistakable even through the blood.

His tongue darted around her mouth, painting the girl's insides onto her face. Anticipation.

The girl lay sprawled on the cobblestone, knees akimbo, mouth open, bowels exposed, jagged ribs pointing to the sky. The sight made Amanda's mouth water.

A howl erupted from her throat.

They fell to all fours and dragged the girl into the safety of the Forum to crack her bones and roll in her blood. The two wolves nipped at one another and licked her mess from each other's fur.

Others watched from ruined temples. As she and Giovanni ate, they crept close, but his growls pushed them away. She was grateful. It was intimate, just the two of them. She was whole. This was passion. Purpose. It was how she felt in Giovanni's bed, pressed against him, the world outside kept at arm's length. She was glad to share it only with him.

He brought the impossible to life.

When she was a woman again she tried to stand but her body screamed at her. She ground her teeth and took deep breaths. The air was cold against her bare skin. She hugged her knees to her chest, the salty tang of meat still on her tongue, and marveled at the blood caked on her.

Around her the cold marble columns and temple walls were rinsed in black. She fought to her feet and sucked in a sharp breath. She hurt, ached all over, but nothing seemed to be broken. She wondered about internal bleeding.

The wind sighed through the ruins. They were out there, she knew. Watching. Waiting for scraps.

She turned to find Giovanni, naked, standing on the steps of the ancient Senate House. The giant green doors were thrown open and a light from inside danced against his skin.

Wolves shuffled through pebbles in the ruins around her.

"They are curious about you," he said. He turned and walked inside.

She glanced back into the dark. The breeze carried an unfamiliar scent, strong and heady like Giovanni's. The other wolves crept closer, hovering in the shadows.

She stepped through the doors and into the heart of the Republic. Torches circled the room, their light flickering across the red and green marble floor. White stone seats were tiered around the walls. She stood there, one foot inside, and tried to catch her breath.

"Did you ever think," Giovanni said as he slumped on one of the seats, "when you came to study the Republic, that you would ever be in here?" He spread his arms and gestured around the room.

Amanda walked inside. Iron grating along the upper walls allowed moonlight to trickle in. A bronze relief of Romulus and Remus suckling at a wolf's tit caught the light from above the door.

"We were kings once," he said, his voice soft and fragile.

She glanced back at the others waiting outside the door. "Why does it hurt?"

Giovanni stood and held out his hand. She stepped closer. This close, she could see the blood staining his skin. She fought the urge to taste it, to lick him clean.

"You hurt," he said, "because you let the dream go." He pulled her into an embrace and rocked her back and forth.

The air in the room changed. Soft steps padded around her.

"You don't remember your parents," he said, pulling her to her knees, "because they never existed the way you think they should have."

The other wolves grew closer.

"You are a wolf who dreamed she was a woman."

Soft fur brushed the backs of her legs.

"You let the dream go and tasted that girl with me."

She licked her lips. The blood there was sweet, the taste overpowering. The memory of the girl's flesh, salty with sweat, and fear, sent a tremor through her.

Giovanni kissed her. "There are so few of us. We have been waiting for someone like you."

"Like me?"

"Yes." He held her hand against his cheek and closed his eyes.

Hot breath washed over the back of her neck. A wet snout nudged her ribs.

"A bitch in heat," he said.

Her heart fluttered. Tears streamed down her face.

"I love you," she said.

He kissed her hand.

The memory of him pressed against her that first night flooded over her. "I cannot have children," he had said.

He stood.

"Giovanni?"

"For the pack," he said.

He stepped away.

A heavy paw thumped against her back. She fell to her stomach. Yellow eyes bored into her. Hot breath carried the odor of rot into her face.

Giovanni was still, silent.

"I'm sorry," he whispered.

His hard, perfect lines formed a beautiful silhouette against the light behind him. If not for his breath, she would have mistaken him for marble.

The weight of the others pressed down on her, the smells of their lust tangling together.

The sound of the bronze doors closing echoed in the room. A single tear caught the light as it rolled down Giovanni's face.

The sight broke her heart.

WEREWOLF 101

BY MERCEDES M. YARDLEY

Relationships are tricky, and it doesn't pay to be too picky, if you ever wanna wind up having any fun at all.

This is the important message relayed by the hilarious "Werewolf 101," by Mercedes M. Yardley, a young writer who is knocking me out with her wonky snapshot tales of cheerfully violent, wayward women.

She first came to my attention in Shock Totem #1, *a 2009 small-press digest of odd fiction with unusually strong writing throughout. Yardley's "Murder for Beginners" had me rolling from start to finish, and I was praying she would mess me up again if I asked her real nice.*

So I asked her, and she did.

THANKS, CRAZY LADY!

Please enjoy.

"So guess what?" Harley asked me. She toasted me with her beer bottle. "I snagged a live one this time."

"No kidding," I said.

"Yep. Tall, dark, handsome. Tortured, I think. Something to do with his family. Whatever." She took a pull of her beer. "I sorta stopped listening after a while. Interested in other things."

"You trollop."

"Ain't that the truth." She leaned back, shook her blond hair out. "Life's too short, y'know? In another ten years I'll be all saggy, and then what will I land?"

I shrugged. "Bored middle-aged office workers?"

She snorted and pretended to throw the bottle at me. "Shut up, Lil." Harley drained her drink, slammed it down. "So how about you? What are you up to?"

I thought about what I should tell her, finally decided to try the truth. "Shane turned into an animal last night and tried to kill me. It got pretty nasty. I finally stabbed him in the neck with a kitchen knife and he ran off." I checked my nails. Broken. "I'm pissed. Took off with my best Wüsthof knife sticking out of him. You have any idea how much those things cost?"

I glanced at her. She was studying my face.

"They cost, like, a lot," I explained.

She kept watching me.

"They're pretty nice," I said. "Only have to sharpen them once a year."

"So you stabbed him in the neck?"

I nodded.

"Is he still alive?"

"He was when he left."

She was quiet for a moment. Then, "Well, bummer. He was pretty."

"I know."

Two more drinks and she was off to collect her tortured love. "Tonight is my 'I'm here if you need me' speech," she told me. "I'll be all warm and heartfelt. Then I'll drag him off to bed to wile away his sorrows."

"I'll stay here in case Shane comes back," I said. "I really ought to apologize for the whole knife thing."

"You do that. 'Night."

I was watching a Spanish soap opera with the sound off when I heard a knock at the door. I checked the peephole. Shane stood there in a red plaid shirt.

"Can I come in?" he called through the door.

"Don't know. Are you gonna eat me?"

He held a bag of Chinese takeout to the peephole. "Nah, I brought something a little less tough."

I unlocked the bolt and chain. He sauntered past me, set the food on the table.

"Hey, love," he said.

"Hi. Sorry that I got all stabby back there. Is that Almond Chicken?"

"And egg foo yong. No, you did the right thing. I was going to rip your throat out with my teeth." He dropped into a kitchen chair, grabbed a pair of chopsticks. "So I guess we'd better talk about this whole 'turning into a werewolf' thing. It's only responsible."

"If you want to. Hit me with Werewolf 101." I opened a carton of chow mein and dug in. "Did you bring my knife back?"

"No. Sorry. I'll get you a new one."

"Okay."

"You're not a very good stabber."

"I'll work on it."

He sighed, leaned back. "Listen, so this is something new for me. It's only happened for the last couple of months or so. I don't know why, really."

I talked around my mouth of noodles. "Think it's genetic?"

He raised one shoulder and dropped it. "I'm not sure. Toss over that beef, will you? Thanks. Anyway, it comes on without much of a warning. Like this one time? I was in the subway, right? That totally bit."

"What did you do?"

He shook his head sadly. "Actually, I think that *I* totally bit. Like, I ate a couple of nuns. I'm not a hundred percent clear about it, though. It all gets kinda hazy when I wolf out."

I speared a piece of broccoli from his carton and snickered. "'Wolf out?'"

"What, you don't like it?"

"It sounds a little *Teen Wolf* to me."

"Huh. I'll have to think of something better. "

I pushed the food out of his hands and sat on his lap. "I don't care that you're a wolf. I still totally dig you."

His eyes lit up. "Yeah?"

"Yeah."

I was showing him just how much I dug when the doorbell rang. It was Harley.

"Lousy prude," she sniffed, throwing her purse on the table. "He was going to be content sobbing into my arms all night. I bailed."

"Hey, Harley."

"Hey, Shane. Heard that Lil here almost iced you last night."

He blinked slowly. "Yeah, well, I deserved it."

She grabbed his chopsticks and started eating. "Most men do. Did you bring her knife back? She's been whining about it all day."

Shane's eyes narrowed.

I looked from Harley to Shane and back again. "Uh, Harley, I'd give that food back to him if I were you."

Harley stuffed a piece of beef in her mouth. "There's enough. Like, he can't share because he's a *guy*?"

I took a step backward. "I'd really, really put that down."

Harley jabbed at me with her chopsticks. "Listen, it was a lousy night, okay? Give it up. And as for you," she began, but Shane leapt across the table and knocked her to the ground. His eyes were glowing.

"Shane!" I looked around for some sort of a weapon. Too bad my Wüsthof couldn't come to the rescue again.

Harley hit him with her fist. "What has gotten into you?"

He snarled, baring his newly pointed teeth. Harley paled.

"Bad! Bad Shane!" I smacked him across the back with my broom. He turned to face me, tufts of hair sprouting from his ears. His face contorted, growing longer and leaner until he had a snout. It was even more fascinating to watch the second time. I hoped I lived to see it a third.

Harley's eyes were teary by now, but I could tell that she was also really angry.

And an angry Harley is a wild, unpredictable Harley. Soon I'd have two animals on my hands.

Shane lunged at me, clawing at me with fingers that were quickly turning into paws. I beat at them with my broom.

"Harley! Get away!" I knew she wouldn't listen to me.

With a scream as wild as anything that the Shane-wolf could have made, Harley rushed forward and kicked him with her pointy Manolos. I winced.

Shane turned from me and lunged at her. Harley shrieked and ducked under the table.

"You stupid dog!" she screamed, holding her shoe threateningly in her hand. "If you so much as come near me, I'll take out your eye!"

Shane barked and stepped forward. Harley yelled back and raised her shoe even higher.

I was done with this.

"Harley, can it! Shane, to the room. Go!" I smacked at his rump and legs with the broom handle. He turned to growl at me, but I wasn't having it. "No. Down. To the room. Or no sex for you." He cocked his head, snorted at me, and then trotted off.

"Yeah, Shane! Go to your room." Harley staggered to her feet, and sent the shoe flying at Shane's head. He growled and leapt into the air.

I blocked his way with the broom. "I said no! Room. Now." I glared at him. "I mean it, Shane." He huffed and slunk into the bedroom. I reached over and shut the door. Then I turned to Harley. "Get out."

Her eyes widened. "What?"

I held the broom like a baseball bat. "Out, Harley. You're not helping."

She blinked a few times, frowned. I snapped the broom against her bare calf. "Ouch!"

"I'm not kidding."

She reached out and I smacked her hands.

"I was only getting my shoe!"

"Leave it."

She backed toward the doorway. "You're enjoying this."

I felt my lips twitch. "A little."

She tried to hide her smile. "Well then. Don't let Shane chew that shoe, will you? It cost me almost seven hundred bucks."

"Got it. Call you tomorrow."

"All right." She shut the door behind her. I stood there with my broom for a minute.

"Hey, Shane," I called. "Are you human yet?"

There was a thud, a growl, and desperate scrabbling on the door.

"No hurry," I said. "I'll wait."

I sat down, propped my boots on the table, and rested the broom across my lap. In the other room, Shane howled.

"Don't feel bad, baby," I yelled. "All relationships have their quirks. We'll work it out."

He howled again. Right. This one could take a while.

But screw it. We had all night.

MANDIBLE

BY ALICE HENDERSON

Sometimes the most hideous, inexplicable changes take place for a very good reason. We may not understand it at the time—we may not ever understand it completely—but that doesn't mean that, sometimes, bad news isn't good news in disguise.

Or at least the best bad news we could possibly hope for, in a world madly changing beyond our control.

Alice Henderson's brain-twisting "Mandible" is an excellent case in point.

Henderson broke into the biz doing top-ranked fan-faved Buffy the Vampire Slayer *tie-ins, after stints in academia and the Lucasfilm fields. But her first "solo" novel,* Voracious—*written largely in tents during weeks of immersive solo research in Glacier National Park—was itself a romantic and sometimes shockingly violent twist on shapeshiftobilia, with unusually fine taste in victims.*

This little berserkoid narrative is something else entirely—no hot kick-ass heroines here—but her propulsively twisty narrative rigor and big-picture sf fascination are clearly on tap. And have never been stranger. Which is good news for all.

The stench hit me first. I stopped in the darkness of my kitchen, only the faint ticking of the wall clock filling the quiet. The smell hung heavily, reeking like something left festering too long in a drain. I'd just taken off my tuxedo jacket, and I draped it over a barstool next to the center island. I turned toward the sink, peering down, and caught a flash of movement in the reflection of the kitchen window. *Intruder.* Pivoting wildly, I searched the gloom. I saw now that the back door stood open a crack, leading out to the yard. Something clicked in the darkness, over near the pantry door.

I moved silently along the counter, eager fingers searching out the light switch near the microwave. Something stirred closely in the darkness, then more clicking and the smell growing even stronger now of rancid meat and curdled milk. The clicking sounded right next to my ear then, and in a panic, I flipped on the light, whirling around to face it.

My mind registered it in pieces. A spindly, chitonous arm rose up, shielding the thing's eyes from the light. Its mouth, full of too many moving parts, whirred and glistened, mandibles clicked and snapped.

The thing was huge. Taller than me, walking upright, but impossibly insectoid. It advanced, sleek black mandibles, flexing and clacking. I backed around the center island of the kitchen, keeping the tiled surface between myself and the thing. Black, shiny eyes stared down at me, the overhead light reflecting back in dozens of facets. A strange quivering stalk of a tongue lolled inside its mouth. The thing moved around the side of the island. On its thin, ungainly legs it staggered forward, its underside like a multisegmented shield.

I reached for the kitchen drawer, pulling out the sharpest knife I could find with my groping hands. I couldn't look away from the thing. It held up its two upper, hooked limbs toward me.

The mandibles clacked again, and it rounded the corner, eyes narrowing on me. The tongue came out again, and with a loud gush of air that stank of the sewer, it chittered, loud and suddenly, causing me to start. My hip hit the drawer painfully.

The creature saw the knife in my hand, started shaking its head furiously in some kind of frenzy. Antennae, covered in numerous bristling hairs, uncurled from its head and quivered in anticipation of the fight.

I continued to circle the island, feeling the reassuring bulk of the counter between us. The thing moved one top appendage downward, tugging at something sticking out of its carapace. It hissed in frustration, trying again to remove it. I could see now something purple stuck out there, probably from some previous altercation. It looked at me then, held one hand out toward me, then tried to pull out the purple thing again. I continued to back away.

It buzzed loudly, and the black-brown shell of its back split open down the middle. Four translucent wings sprang out, black veins pulsing through them. In an instant it was in the air, flying right over the island straight at me, a stinger or ovipositor or whatever the hell now visible as its body arced toward mine.

The creature hit me heavily, and I flew back into the kitchen table behind me, knocking over two chairs and stumbling into the cabinetry. I lifted the knife, slashing out with it blindly, as I regained my balance. I felt it connect with the soft underbelly of the thing. It let out a piercing, shrill cry, and the putrid stink of rotten meat blossomed into my nose as viscous white fluid spilled out of the wound.

Those glistening eyes locked on me, eyes pleadingly pathetic, and then it gave a final quiver, falling backward onto the tile floor and rocking to a halt on its rounded back.

I got up, still gripping the knife, watching for any twitch or sign of life. I peered at the thing, leaning over it, catching my breath. I took off my bow tie and undid the top two buttons of my dress shirt.

I wasn't sure what to do then. Call the cops? Animal control? What the hell was it? Some roach grown to mutated proportions in the sewer tunnels?

As I stared closer at its carapace, I saw again the edge of something purple peeking out from between two plates of the exoskeleton. Paper. It was a folded piece of paper. I leaned over carefully, nudging the thing with my dress shoe before I got too close. It didn't react. It was dead.

Carefully I pulled the sheet out from between the plates. I set the knife down and unfolded the note. It had been ripped from a tablet of pale purple paper. A cartoon sun smiled out from the bottom right corner. A handful of words had been written across the note in a scrawling hand.

It read: "Don't let them take you. It's not a flu shot."

I stared down at it, rereading the note.

The sudden pounding on my front door made me jump. I shoved the note in my pocket and turned toward the door. Incessant pounding continued.

"It's the National Guard, sir. Please open up. We have an emergency," said a man's voice from the other side of the door. My house was still dark inside, except for the kitchen at the far back. I crept to a window in the living room and peered out through a tiny gap in the curtains.

Outside the night was split with spotlights, and the usually quiet street was host to a caravan of army vehicles. People in white Hazmat suits led my neighbors out of their houses, directing them toward several white medical vans.

The pounding continued. "Open up, please, sir. We have a medical emergency. A pathogen has been released, and everyone needs to be inoculated before it hits this area."

Inoculated. I could feel the crumpled note in my pocket.

I watched as they ushered my next-door neighbors into one of the medical vans. I was just deciding how to proceed when my door suddenly splintered inward. Two men in Hazmat suits stormed inside, grabbing me. "Please do not be alarmed, sir," the taller one urged me. "Allow us to help you. I know this must be confusing and frightening, but we are dealing with a dangerous emergency."

"What is it?" I asked.

They pulled me toward my front door. I couldn't see his face through the face shield, nor that of his silent companion.

"It's nothing to be alarmed about, as long as you comply."

They pushed me out of my front door, tugging me along the sidewalk to the street. Several Humvees and other personnel trucks were being loaded up with my neighbors. "But you still haven't told me what it is," I said.

"A dangerous strain of the flu has been released into the atmosphere about thirty miles from here. A vaccine was already in the works, and we simply need to inoculate the population as quickly and expediently as possible," the taller man told me. They shoved me inside a waiting Humvee, along with fifteen of my neighbors. Someone pounded on the side of the vehicle and the engine roared up, taking off with us. My cross-the-street neighbor, Phyllis O'Brien, sat near the back. She smiled at me, though it was a nervous smile that belied her fear. Then her smile faded. Fear hung between us.

"I need some time to think about this," I protested, turning toward the only communicative med tech, the same one who had pulled me out of my house. "There hasn't been anything on the news."

People murmured in agreement around me. One drunken man cried out that he wasn't going to take this shit for another minute. The Hazmat suits moved to restrain him immediately. We rode on for a minute in silence, and I wondered if the tech was going to answer at all. At last he said wearily, "We have requested the media merely suggest people receive the inoculation," he explained. "To avoid panic, they were instructed not to speak of the danger level of the virus or of how it was released." He gestured at my tuxedo. "Looks like you've been out, not at home watching the news."

That was true enough. I'd been at a black-tie dinner party all night. Godzilla could have devastated New York and none of us at the party would have known. As usual, we'd drunk too much champagne and danced until we shut the place down. "How was it released?" I pressed.

"Terrorist action," he responded curtly.

"Domestic or . . . ?"

"We don't know yet." We rode on in silence, all of us staring at each other nervously. At last we pulled up and they opened the back of the Humvee. We piled out and the Hazmat suits directed us toward an open medical van, where four people from another neighborhood already stood in line, waiting for the vaccine. I hesitated. The med tech pushed me forward. "Please sir. We have so many people to inoculate. I understand you have questions, but we really must hurry."

Some of my neighbors, including Phyllis, had been directed to a different med van. They injected her with the vaccine, and she turned away, meeting my eyes again. But they didn't point her back to the Humvee. Instead, they ushered her toward a large brick building that stood nearby. Was she already infected? They pointed two more of my neighbors toward it, as well.

"What's that?" I asked the med tech, pointing at the building.

The woman in front of me held out her arm, and the med tech inside the van injected her with the vaccine. "The inoculation has an allergic reaction in a tiny percentage of the population. People wait in the building for an hour to be sure they aren't affected like that." The woman looked nervous, and my talkative friend directed her toward the building. I was next in line, watching them as they prepared my syringe. I couldn't get my feet to move forward. "Please sir," said the tech inside the van. "We have many more people to inoculate before the night is over."

The crumpled note in my pocket pressed against my leg. My gut turned sour.

I backed away from the van. "Sorry, I'll pass."

Immediately the med-tech who had dragged me out of my house signaled to three other people in Hazmat suits. One grabbed my arm, and I twisted away, turning to run. But three more stood behind me, seizing my arms. I bucked my legs, kicking at them. And then I felt the sting of the needle go into my neck.

I turned around, white rage spilling into me.

The tall med tech stood behind me, the spent vaccination syringe in his hand. "I'm sorry to do that, sir. It really is for your protection. Please go to the building with the others."

The three men dragged me in that direction. More of my neighbors joined us, old Mr. Smith who always walked his Rottweiler at three a.m., and the young couple who bought the fixer upper on the corner.

They led us into the brick building, down a series of corridors, past innumerable steel doors. "What is this place?" I asked one of the faceless men in the Hazmat suits. He didn't answer.

Our journey ended in a large room, big as a gymnasium, full of cots and makeshift buffet tables with granola bars, fruit, bottles of water and juice. The roar of conversation was deafening. Worried people paced and talked, some cried in corners.

Not a single cot was still available. Between the fight in my kitchen and having too much to drink at my dinner party, exhaustion was claiming me. Finally I slumped down on the floor against a wall. I watched people in horror, feeling hopeless and wishing I had my cell phone with me.

My head lolled and I fell into a fitful sleep. I jerked awake to the loud sound of buzzing. A nightmare about that thing in my kitchen still gripped me, my body clammy and sweating. I screamed, wrenching away from the wall. The buzzing remained, though, following me out from the dream into the waking world.

Then I saw why.

On the far side of the large room stood another one of those things, buzzing and flopping against one of the doors. Like the one in my kitchen, it walked on its hind legs, exposing that white underbelly carapace. A few people stood around it, staring in horror. It flung itself against the door over and over again, the shiny black back open, wings buzzing and thrumming in the stale air.

The familiar clack of mandibles ripped my attention away from that far corner to much closer. On a cot about a dozen feet away, another of the things lay on its back, legs twitching, bristling antennae feeling along the iron rail headboard of the bed. An even closer clacking and sudden eruption of putrid meat stench made me snap my head to the right. Only ten feet away, scrabbling desperately against the door I had entered through, struggled another one, its antennae quivering in its efforts to force the door open.

I felt something cold and thick drip onto my face, and I started, looking up. Nestled there on the bare metal rafters of the ceiling hung dozens more of the creatures, bustling together in a single quivering mass of wings and legs.

I brought my hand up to wipe away the viscous fluid and cried out in surprise. My hand was no longer a hand. Two of my fingers had knit together in a single, fleshy casing, while thick, black spurs jutted out of my arms and wrist. I leapt to my feet, but struggled to balance. I lifted up my black tuxedo pants, revealing legs horribly deformed, one still fleshy and pink, the other dwindled away into a thin, black stalk that ended in three sharp barbs jutting out of my dress shoe.

Terror sweeping over me, I ran forward, joining the scuttling creature by the closest door. Our eyes met, his glistening and wet, full of fear. I tried to tell him we could smash the door in unison, but my mouth felt round and thick, my tongue unable to form the words. A keening trill, followed by a clicking sound, came out of my mouth. Tentatively, afraid of what I'd find there, I reached what was left of my right hand up to my mouth. My lower lip still felt human, but growing out from under my greatly diminished nose jutted a sharp, chitonous mandible. I tried to scream, to curse, but only shrill whistles came out.

I looked again at the other creature, and he gave me a slight nod. Then we ran at the door together, hearing metal snap and groan. It gave way, spilling us into the hallway beyond.

A man in a Hazmat suit stood there, armed with a submachine gun. He turned on us. "I don't want to shoot," he shouted.

We ran straight at him. He fired his P90, the bullets tearing through my comrade. One white-hot bullet grazed my leg, and I hopped to the side in pain, clicking like a locust flying from one blade of grass to the other.

I bowled into the man, sending him and his gun sprawling. My newfound companion skittered off in a different direction, following a hallway. I continued the way I'd come in. I raced toward the exit, running down the passageway as fast as I could. Constantly slipping on the tile, my one bad leg was nearly impossible to control. I kicked off my ruined shoe, but that did little to help.

Instead of reaching the exit, I came to a fresh brick wall. I retraced my steps, sneaking around the corridors, and was sure this was where the entrance to the building had been. I could see the old doorframe, smell the fresh mortar. It was a massive amount of work, one that couldn't have been accomplished during my nap. How long had I been out?

I skittered back along the hallways, searching for another exit. At the next intersection of corridors, a pair of swinging doors led to a glassed-in room. A line of people in Hazmat suits stood before a huge machine. In the machine's center stood a large metal square bristling with dials, buttons, and electrical cables. And in the open center of this square gleamed a spiraling, bright window of energy. A green indicator light of some kind glowed brightly above the machine.

Above the contraption hung a digital calendar and clock. I stared, my mouth falling open. I'd been unconscious for six days.

The Hazmat tech at the head of the line paused in front of the wall of light, picked up a metal case from a table there and stepped into the dazzling brightness. The green light turned to red.

He vanished completely.

When the indicator light returned to green, the next tech did the same thing, then another and another. I recognized those same metal cases as holding the vaccine that I'd been injected with. I dove through the swinging doors, the Hazmat techs spinning as I entered.

"Get him!" someone yelled.

"He can't be allowed to pass through!"

A hand grabbed my arm, and I flung it off. My strength was ten times what it had been before I was taken. A dozen arms seized me, trying to pull me down to the ground. I thrashed, throwing them off me as if they weighed no more than stuffed animals.

Several of them slammed into me, throwing me off balance. I skittered across the floor, sliding to a halt in front of the table holding the silver cases. Gripping a table leg in my ruined hands, I pivoted wildly, smashing the techs around me. Then I jumped into the light.

The dazzling brightness blinded me for a moment, and I felt my feet step down onto metal. My eyes adjusted, taking in my surroundings. I was inside a medical van. Several techs turned their shielded faces up to me. I shoved them aside and barged out of the van's back doors. The vehicle was stopped on a suburban street. Several techs gasped as I tumbled into view, though their faces remained hidden behind their masks.

"Don't let him leave this area!" one of them shouted.

I shoved him aside and ran, bursting through the line of techs and moving as fast as I could into the streets. I didn't recognize the neighborhood.

I ran into someone's side yard, leaping over their ten-foot privacy fence as if it were a tiny dog gate. I ran on, hearing their voices grow distant. But I kept running, leaping over fence after fence, not stopping until twelve blocks lay between me and my pursuers.

Then I stopped to catch my breath. I'd just entered the yard of a darkened house. In the distance a dog barked. Thirst burned my throat, and the thought of water beckoned me like a siren. I crept up to the patio door and stared in. No cars parked in the garage, and no lights within. I smashed through the glass and hobbled into the house.

At the sink I drank and drank until my stomach felt heavy and painful.

I turned off the faucet, finally catching my breath. A newspaper lay open on the counter top. It was old, dated a week before all this madness had started. The house owners must have been on vacation. Headlines read of the war in the Middle East, of poverty here at home.

Next to the paper lay a TV remote, and I fumbled to turn it on, to see news of any of this.

CNN winked into view, the news scrolling across the bottom. It talked of the president's visit to Japan, which I thought had happened last week. None of it mentioned an outbreak. Were they suppressing this whole thing? The next news scroll dealt with a scandal unfolding in Texas, a congressman caught cheating on his wife. I was sure that was old news, too. I looked down at the date next to the scrolling news. It was the same as the newspaper. I flipped the channel. A weather display reported the same date, with coverage of a tornado that had devastated part of Oklahoma. I was sure that had been a week before.

I seized the phone, not sure who I was going to call, and my eyes fell on a portable weather station standing on the kitchen counter. It gave the temperature and humidity, and was one of those units that displayed atomic time, synced every day to be absolutely accurate. It, too, thought it was a week ago.

I flipped around on the channels until I found a local station. The identification in the corner told me I was in the town that neighbored on my own. I looked down at my watch, now hanging loosely around the spindly thing that had become my arm. At this time right now, I was having dinner with my friends Steve and Linda at the local brewpub. Tomorrow I'd be reorganizing my garage. And in a week I'd be at my black-tie dinner party, before all this began. I could stop all this. I could warn myself.

Desperately I threw upon drawers, pulling out paper clips and flashlights and refrigerator magnets and dumping them on the floor. Inside the third drawer I found a pad of paper and ripped off a sheet. I grabbed a pen, struggling to hold it in my deformed fingers. I started to scratch out a note to myself, finding writing nearly impossible. Then I saw the emblem at the bottom right of the paper. A cartoon sun smiled back of me.

My mouth gone dry and my heart transformed into a leaden weight, I reached my hand into my pocket and pulled out the note that thing had tucked in its carapace.

I smoothed it out, placing it next to my piece of identical paper. It had even been torn off in the same way, leaving a frayed edge along the left top. With what was left of my right hand, I gripped the pen. Trembling, I scrawled on my new sheet, "Don't let them take you. It's not a flu shot." I closed my eyes, hoping desperately I was wrong, then held up the two notes to compare.

They were identical.

A sudden stabbing pain in my stomach seized me, and my body doubled over. My waist erupted outward, stomach and back ripping through my pants, shredding them. I cried out, feeling a second mandible tear free from my upper lip and meet the other beneath my deformed nose. Tearing through my dress shirt, my back arched and flexed, growing round and hard. Tentatively, I felt back there, what was left of my fingers finding a single, thin quivering wing.

The pain finally subsided and panicked, I ran into the hallway, searching desperately for a mirror. When I found one, inside a closet upstairs, I stared into watery black eyes that were all too familiar. I'd killed the owner of those eyes in my kitchen.

I stood there breathing, not sure what to do. With no clothing now, I had nowhere to put the matching notes, so I tucked them as best I could between two layers of chitonous armor.

I couldn't go back and warn myself, at least not in the same way.

I had to know what was happening, how I could stop it.

Leaving the sanctuary of the house, I rushed back to where the medical vans lined the street, where I'd come bursting out of that strange square of light.

Three med techs stood around the back of one van, talking over a laptop. I crept closer, staying in the shadows, trying to overhear them. I could smell them now, a sickly sweet smell of decay. My forehead quivered, no, something *above* my forehead quivered. I wasn't smelling them with my nose, but with hundreds of tiny little hairs along two long stalks that had sprouted out of my head.

And I could hear them now, too, their voices on the wind.

They talked of infecting a few more thousand people tonight. I boggled as I heard genuine joy and happiness in their voices.

An uncontrollable anger swept over me. I rushed forward, my arms upraised, careening into them. Bringing down those serrated spurs along my arms, I connected violently with their bodies. I tore through the white material of their suits, ripping flesh and bone beneath.

I slashed at their helmets, at last exposing their faces. That sickly sweet smell of death bloomed outward even more powerfully. I couldn't even tell if they were men or women. Couldn't tell ethnicity or age. Lidless eyes stared out from a mass of lesions and sores. Bloody, bald pates shed blistered skin inside the helmets. None of them had any hair at all. White cheekbones jutted out from glistening muscle. The shouts of other med-techs demanded my attention, and I saw about twenty of them running over to me. I grabbed the laptop and ran, feeling my back open up involuntarily. My single wing hummed, trying to take flight. I leapt over fences again, moving through suburbia like some chitonous insect borne of nightmares. I bounded up to a roof, then to another roof, able to leap so far that I found myself trilling uncontrollably with excitement at each freefalling sail through the air.

I landed finally on the edge of town, escaping into the woods there, weaving between trees and leaping over logs.

Finally, sure I wasn't followed, I sat down with my rounded back against a tree and opened the computer.

My mind took in the information there. Maps. Radiation zones. Nuclear fallout. I found my city, my neighborhood, my house. The zone was red, which the legend declared meant, "Unable to survive."

I zoomed out on the map, seeing red covering most of the country. I zoomed farther out, and saw it covered Europe, Asia, Africa, Australia, South America. The whole goddamn world was going up in flames.

I moused down to the lower right-hand corner, wanting to double-check the day. But the time there didn't make sense. The laptop thought it was some five years in the future.

I returned to the maps, studying them. The incident date on the red map read little more than a week from now.

Exhaustion took me as I sat there, puzzling over the map.

When I awoke, it was still dark. I didn't know if I'd been asleep for minutes or days, like before. The laptop, still sitting on the ground next to me, had gone to sleep. I could barely focus on it, my eyes seeing the image of a dozen or more laptops. Tentatively, I brought a black, clawed hand up to my face and felt there. My eyes had grown huge. I could see a dozen versions of my hand as I waved it in front of my face.

I closed my eyes, concentrated. When I opened them again, I struggled to convince my mind to see the multitude of images as a single picture. I narrowed my eyes, the dozen laptops becoming a single one. I reached for it and woke it up, finding it surviving on the dregs of the battery. I examined the maps again as a window popped up, warning me of imminent battery failure. I scrolled along the bottom of the map, reading below the legend. Next to the incident date, it read: "Time of Incident: 2:45 a.m." I looked at my digital watch, still hanging on my stalk of an arm next to one of the serrated spurs. The date and time was today. In fact, it was twenty minutes ago.

A high-pitched whistle brought my eyes up to the sky. My gaze staggered to pull the picture into a single one. At first I thought my brain was unable to process the multifaceted image. But I was wrong. The sky was alive with hundreds of missiles, all streaking down to earth, their bright green trails glowing in the night sky.

The human race would not survive.

Only roaches could survive a holocaust like this.

FAR AND WEE

BY KATHE KOJA

Kathe Koja has long been one of my favorite authors, with a writerly voice unlike any other. Over the years, she has split her work between jaw-dropping high-end sf/horror/modern phantasmagoria for discerning grown-ups and powerfully wise novels for the smart young adult set.

With "Far and Wee" she buries her signature style in the unsophisticated voice of a priceless young fellow who, as it turns out, has more than a little explaining to do.

The results are surprising and, to my mind, hilarious. YOWCH!

Oh, you sexy, sexy beasts . . .

My job, senhor, was to pull the drapes. Smooth and slow when the shows began, and quickly when they ended; sometimes very quick, the men got too excited, they wanted to climb onstage. The players laughed about it, after: *Did you see him? The walrus belly, yes, did you see? And the old one, Old Cheeseface, why I thought he would die!* They laughed as they scooped up the flowers and the calling-cards, the shiny tokens stamped with a C. Sometimes I picked up the tokens, too, but not to keep; that would be stealing, and I am no thief.

I told him that, Master Konstantin, the first night I came, out of the snow. The last few miles, before the City, felt to me like a dream, what is it called, the very bad dream? A nightmare. I had wrapped my boots with strips of rag, my fingers were so cold they had stopped bleeding. *When did you last eat, sonny boy?* Master Konstantin asked me. *We could cast you as Rawhead and Bloody Bones. . . .All these beggars. It is bad in the City, now.*

Oh no, I said. I remember I could hardly stand upright, the room—orange coals in the grate, the smell of hair oil and hot tea, the electric candles, Annelise yawning and tugging her curls —it was all like heaven to me, being inside, being warm. *I came here to work. The soldiers told me, go to the theatre. And I am strong, messire, I can work hard, I am no thief—*

That will be a nice change for us here. Annelise, call Ambrose, have him take sonny boy here belowstairs. . . .Keep your hands off the players, Sonny Boy. That was the way I came to the Capitalia.

At first I did only the work no one else wanted: emptied slops, filled the grates, carried hod and water, cleaned the vomit in the jakes. The players treated me like part of the wall, sweeping on and off the stage all shiny in their costumes, their masks like the faces of birds and beasts, of demons. Some of those faces frightened me, the horns and the painted fangs, but I never showed it; I am not a child, I am a man. And some of the costumes the players wore. . ..The Capitalia makes a special kind of show, you see, it is all about love, you see, between men and women. That kind of love. You understand these kinds of shows, senhor, I know; you live in the City.

And at the Capitalia, the players are the most beautiful of all, the most skillful in their acting, they can make anything seem real, as if it is really happening right there in front of you. This is why the men come night after night, past the soldiers, through the snow, this is why they stamp their feet and whistle and throw jewelry, and silver cigarette cases, and their calling-cards, and the tokens Master Konstantin sells. Because they watch Alma, and Suzette, and Geraldina, they watch the things that they do and think *Oh, that could be me up there, holding that beautiful lady, that could be me* doing all the things that they do. . .. So the men get hot, watching. And no one made them hotter than Annelise.

It is not only that she is beautiful, senhor, although she is very beautiful, there is no one more beautiful at the Capitalia, in the whole City. It is the way she holds herself, the way she walks, the way she looks over her shoulder that makes you think you are the only man in the world, the only man for her....The men throw so many tokens, I have seen her wince up her eyes: "Like a hailstorm," she said, it was the first time she really spoke to me, stepping off the stage, fanning herself with the feathers of her bird-mask; some of her curls were stuck to her forehead, little half-circles of gold. "Look—they hit me," turning her bare pink shoulder to show me the red marks there. "Idiots."

I did not answer her, I did not know what to say. That Annelise would speak to me! All I could do was smile, and help her gather up the tokens, dozens of tokens, we made sure to get them all. The players cash the tokens with Master Konstantin, to pay for their food and their lodging in the theatre, buy scents and silks, corn plasters for their blisters, all those things that ladies need. At first they slapped me off the tokens, but then they saw that I did not steal, so they trusted me, the ladies. Annelise trusted me.

Master Konstantin trusted me, too, more and more as the weeks went on. He put me on the door, to help Ambrose with the men; some nights he let me watch him count the money. He gave me a frock coat like his own to wear, with silver thread on the arms, and pomade to put on my hair; he showed me how to use powder to wash my teeth "—to ease the carrion whiff. We will civilize you yet, Sonny Boy," he said, and I smiled; Ambrose frowned. Later, on the door, Ambrose said to me, "Don't mind him, that old vulture. You are civil enough already, for this place, Sonny. . ..What was your name in your village?" but I only shrugged. I did not want to lie to Ambrose, but I did not want to talk about the village, ever, about the fields and the mud, the shit on my bare feet — I was nearly grown before I had boots to wear, the ragged boots I wore into the City, tied to my ankles with rags. I was Dusan, there, and here I am Sonny. Would Annelise let Dusan run her errands, or lace up her little shoes for her, sweet little shoes, like a child's? Would she smile at him, the way she does at me? I never want to be Dusan again.

"I am done with that," I told Ambrose, "the farm and the beasts. I am in the City now."

"Plenty beasts in the City, young man."

At first I thought he was just a drummer, one of those who go from place to place selling sundries, candies and horse tobacco, poultices for the tooth-ache and such. Except he carried a rusty flute, and he was so dirty, he looked as if he had never been in a city before, never slept inside. His cart was dirty too, its paint worn away, one side missing a wheel, and he pulled it himself, crookedly, like a beast. He looked like a beast, the players laughed about it: "See those woolly arms," Geraldina said. "Like a ram's. All he needs are the curly horns."

"Do you speak?" Alma asked, tugging at his coat-sleeve, ragged like the rest of him. "Or can you only bray, mm?" and she laughed, and Geraldina laughed, and Suzette, and he laughed with them; Annelise did not laugh, only sat watching and smoking, letting the smoke drift out from between her pink lips.

They all bought things from the old man, Ambrose too; even Master Konstantin bought tobacco from "Pyotr," he said his name was, rumbling it out past his beard, the red mouth deep inside like a smelly cave and "Don't you ever wash your teeth?" I asked him. My voice was louder than I wanted. "For the, the carrion whiff?"

"What's biting Sonny?" Geraldina asked, head to one side, smirking, Suzette giggled and I stomped away, angry; Master Konstantin asked me as well: "What ails you?" after the night's shows were over, counting out the money in his office. On his desk was the bottle of gin, he always drank while he counted. That night he offered me some. It tasted sour.

"You don't like old Drummer Pyotr and his flute, do you? That song he plays,

'Far and Wee,' it's an old song, isn't it? Ancient airs and graces. . .. He's staying only for the night, tomorrow he'll be on his way. So what ails you?"

I shrugged. I did not know how to answer. No I did not like him, the way he dragged his ugly cart behind him, the devilish way he smelled. The way he looked at the ladies, at Annelise; the way she looked at him but "He can stay or go," I said. "Either way, I don't care."

"That's the first time you've lied to me, Sonny Boy." He was smiling, counting through the coins, something was funny to him; was it me? "It's our Christian duty, is it not, to offer shelter to the vagabond and the orphan? Go on, have another drink," and I did; in the end I drank quite a lot, enough to make me dizzy, to send me into the jakes, I thought I was going to vomit so I closed my eyes as the walls spun around me, listening to the sound of water dripping, the sound of heels click-clacking on the floor, clip-clopping like hooves—

—and I opened my eyes, senhor, I swear I opened my eyes and I swear I saw what I saw: that man, that Drummer Pyotr with his hairy legs ending not in shoes or boots or even feet but hooves, I swear that man had hooves like a goat's. And I looked up, straight up into his face, his laughing face beneath the shadow of the horns, and "Shall I play you a song?" he said, and his laugh was the sound the goats make when they breed. I jumped up to grab him, but I fell, face-down and filthy, and by the time I scrambled up again he was gone.

First thing dawn, my head hurting, I went to Ambrose in his little room by the door, Ambrose who sat on his cot and listened, scratching his chest and "You were drunk, young man, that's all. Drink does that to a person, helps them see what is not. Like Geraldina and her belladonna—"

"No. I mean, yes, I drank gin with Master Konstantin, but I know what I saw." Ambrose did not say more, but I knew he did not credit me. Who would? Master Konstantin? He would laugh, *Oh the drunken farmboy saw a goat, no surprises there.* No use to tell Geraldina or the others, to tell Annelise—

—who I saw that very evening, before the show, in the courtyard beside the goat-man, as he filled his little bucket at the pump. They spoke, or at least she spoke to him, what did she say? with her hand on his arm and her head to one side, like a cunning bird, a bird flirting for crumbs so when she had gone I went out to where he sat, cross-legged before his cart; he wore boots, stout workingman's boots, but that did not fool me.

"I saw you," I said. "I know what you are. You should go away, quickly, before I tell Master Konstantin." He did not answer me. "You don't belong here, in the City."

"Nor do you." His voice was serious but his eyes were laughing, laughing at me. "You are not from the City either. You are a creature of the fields, just like the beasts."

"I, I am civilized! I work here!"

"I work everywhere," and he laughed as I walked away, back into the theatre, what could I do? when no one would believe me? and all the players liked him, Suzette and Geraldina, silly Alma sitting on his lap, giggling as he pretended to feed her like a baby, chocolate smeared on her face but everyone thought it was funny, even Master Konstantin laughed. Even Annelise laughed, then smiled at me when "That drummer," I said to her, quiet in her ear. "That man is not good."

"What man is?" but she was smiling still, teasing me. She wore her spangled costume, the ribbons trailing black down her back, her pink skin flushed with sweat; I could smell her, a sweet, clean, secret smell. "He is a traveler," she said softly, as if to herself. "He has been everywhere, St. Petersburg, everywhere, every city in the world."

"Did he tell you that? Out by the pump?"

Her smile changed. "How do you know I spoke to him? Do you watch me, Sonny? Are you like those men in the theatre, do you like to watch?" and she left me there in the hallway, her smell still in the air, like something I could almost touch.

And I went out to the courtyard, to watch some more: for what? his empty cart? which was all I saw, there in the moonlight, the three-wheeled cart like a broken promise, Ambrose found me there asleep in the morning when "Get up," he said to me, not unkindly. "Move that cart into the shed, Pyotr will stay with us awhile."

"Stay? Why?"

"Ask Konstantin," but when I went to him Master Konstantin arched his eyebrows: "We can always use a musician, mm? And the girls like him."

"He stinks like the mating barn."

"That must be why," and Master Konstantin smiled, but grew curt when I kept talking, tried how I could to say what I knew but "How is it your affair?" if the old man, old goat, old Pyotr made music for the ladies, tootling his stupid flute, the music made the girls wilder, which made the men throw more tokens, which meant more coins to count at the end of the evening so "What ails you, Sonny Boy?" Master Konstantin said, drinking gin; this time he did not offer me any. "Shall I pull you off the door, send you back to the slops? Or all the way back to your greasy little village? Don't ask me about Pyotr again."

What could I do, senhor? as the days turned into weeks, as the spring came on, the time of power for things like him. I kept watch as best I could, trying to find proof of what I knew: as he played his music, the creeping, tootling, dirty noise of his flute; as he ate like the beast he was, that red mouth dripping spit, once I threw down a handful of straw before him to see if he would gobble it up, but he only laughed at me.

And I watched as one by one the players crossed the courtyard in secret, Alma and Suzette and Geraldina, it was no secret what they did there, all of them. All of them. Even Annelise. Watching her walk back to her room, wobbling like a foal, I cried, senhor, I know it is not manly but I cried. Because I had so much wanted— I had thought that perhaps one day, if I was civilized enough, I might go to her, Annelise, and we, she and I—

—but *him*, Pyotr, rutting there in the cobbles and the mud—and he was *old*, grizzled and dirty and old and so I went to Geraldina instead, Geraldina who laughed but was not surprised, who did not say no to me; Geraldina never said no. Afterwards she asked, "But how will you pay me, Sonny? It can't be free, even for you."

"I'll give you something," I said, something for us all, because something must be done, and quickly. Because now Pyotr was wearing a player's hat, with golden braid, he was sleeping inside, under the stairs, boots on always but I did not need to see again, I knew what he was. And he would end by making beasts of us all, Annelise, everyone. Even me.

But senhor, truly, I gave him one last chance. As God is my witness, I went to him where he sat beneath the stairs, wrapped in a stable blanket, still wearing the braided hat and "Go away," I said to him, through my teeth. "Go away from here now, tonight."

"From *her*, don't you mean?" but he did not laugh, only crinkled up his eyes at me and "Your name, your true name, is not Sonny, is it? What did they call you, back on your farm?"

"Yours is not Pyotr. Is it?"

"Wise child," and he did laugh then, showing me his ground-down teeth, nubs in the jaw and "Tonight," I said. "I won't warn you again," and I left him there, to collect what I needed, to finish my evening tasks. Geraldina tried to stop me in the hallway but I put up my hand at her, to say *Wait*, wait until after the show—

—which that night was very wild, I had to close the curtains early, Ambrose and even Master Konstantin had to help me, yanking them shut on the backs of the gasping, grasping men, tokens spilling out of their pockets, the players fleeing: Alma got her ankle wrenched, Suzette was stripped almost bare—

—as the flute shrieked on, old Pyotr on the side of the stage staring over all our heads as if he saw something amusing out in the darkness, playing on and on as the men were herded out, cursing and pushing, as Master Konstantin came back wiping his brow, stood shouting at Pyotr which was what I needed, all I needed, to go and fetch the gin and the wine and "When it begins to cost instead of pay," Master Konstantin said, "that is where I draw the line. You see Alma hobbling? She's finished for the week. And Geraldina will have a black eye, the stupid cow.— Ah, that's good," as he took the drink from me, his bottle of gin, and the little tin bucket, Pyotr's own bucket half-filled with wine that I took from the cask in the cellar, took and mixed and mingled and "None for you," Master Konstantin scowled at me, "you can't hold your liquor, go on," back to the doors to sit with Ambrose and to wait, wait until it was later, very late and they were all asleep, even him. Especially him, snoring like a bull under the stairs.

And then I did what I know how to do, what Dusan knows, from the mud and the shit and the farm: to make a he-goat a wether, a neuter, all you need is a knife. A sharp knife, and some wine mixed with belladonna, and the job is done. If you do it swiftly and well, there is not even very much blood. . .. I know you say you took his boots from him, and that his feet were not hooves, his head had no horns, but I swear to you, senhor, and the Lieutenant too, I saw what I saw and I did what was right. And civilized, too, senhor, I was civilized. I buried what I took from him, and I made sure to place his flute inside his coat.

BRAIDS

BY MELANIE TEM

There's some seriously magical realism at play in this stunning, surreal equine coming-of-age tale by Melanie Tem. Like Angela Carter, she cuts to the core of provincial folk wisdom and subversively shows us how its heart beats today. The results are alternately creepy, marvelous, and empowering, depending on how you wear your hat.

"Braids" was the first original story I received for this book (her husband's "Grandfather Wolf" was the last). And the moment I finished it, I knew this book would be the editorial ride of a lifetime.

Thank you, Melanie, for blowing through the gates.

When Siguanaba dropped me off in the alley, I could hear the little kids in the yard getting ready to do the piñata, so the party'd been going on for a while. I went in the gate and looked around for my mom. She waved from where she was putting hot dogs on the grill. My Grandma Jerrie called out, "Where you been, girl?" so everybody'd know she knew I was late.

Marcus was sitting on the edge of the porch, strumming his tiny guitar, with his feet dangling and his stupid straw hat with the cross made of pins on the front of it pulled down practically over his face. When I went past him he was saying, "Women'll steal your fuckin' soul, man, if you don't steal theirs first." My boy cousins were laughing. Some of my girl cousins, too, which I totally didn't get.

I've known Marcus since I was, like, five. He's friends with my cousins. We used to ride bikes and play catch. But lately I didn't like how he was watching me.

My mom called me over. "Did you have fun?" She doesn't like horses but she knows how much I do. She's never met Siguanaba. I made up a different name and said she's my teacher and my mom assumed I meant from school.

Talking about the horses was safe. I told my mom about the new chestnut filly with the white blaze. She didn't remember what a filly or a blaze was, so I told her again. She'd forget this time, too. When I was little I used to wish she'd pay more attention. Now I'm glad she doesn't. "My teacher says I get to name the filly," I said.

I'd been thinking maybe I'd name the filly Rosie after my mom, but she didn't even ask what names I had in mind, so I decided not to bother. She smoothed my hair even though it was tied back. I hate it when she does that.

All my little girl cousins except the baby have long hair straight down to their butts even when it's really hot. Once you get a boyfriend you braid your hair. My mom's got braids, and all my aunties. I'm the oldest girl cousin. Don't have a boyfriend. Don't want one.

Old ladies cut their hair short. My Grandma Jerrie always says she's not old, and her hair's blacker than mine and longer and thicker and wilder than anybody's. One time when I was little I think she had braids, but they didn't last long.

I'd have had my hair short like an old grandma if I could. It was a pain long, always in my face, got all tangled, and it was heavy, weighed me down, gave me a headache. Sometimes I put a ponytail down my back through the hole in my extra-large baseball cap—a horsetail, Marcus called it, and one time he twisted it till it hurt. When I stomped on his foot he let go and he called me a name and then my cousin punched him. I didn't need somebody to punch him for me. I was going to wait till later, when he didn't expect it. Too bad I didn't get the chance.

"I rode the mare today," I told my mom. There was no way I could explain how cool this was, about those silver flecks in her black coat or how big and strong she is, or how fast we went through the woods, or how I held onto Siguanaba and we were flying. Really. Flying. So I just said yeah, it was fun.

Marcus got up and started toward us, and my mom said, "Gina, go inside and get some napkins." I wasn't sure it had anything to do with Marcus, but her voice sounded funny and her eyes were hard. She's a watcher like me, but that's not all I am, not all I'm going to be in my life. There was a whole big stack of napkins right there on the picnic table, but I did what she said. I had to go past Marcus and he tried to pull my cap off but he missed. He's really short, not even up to my shoulder.

I stayed in the house for a while. When I went back outside with the napkins, Marcus said, "Why don't you take off that cap, girlie," and he reached for it again and I grabbed his wrist. "What the hell—Goddamn, she's strong as a man!" He didn't mean it as a compliment. He whooped and swung the guitar at me with the arm I wasn't digging my nails into. The women in my family are kind of obsessed with their nails, so I'd always kept mine short, until Siguanaba showed me what all they can be used for.

"Leave her alone," my mom told Marcus. Since I had him under control, there was no reason for her to say that, and anyway she didn't sound very tough.

"Girl's almost grown, Rose." That was my Grandma Jerrie. By this time she was dancing like she does, waving her beer can up over her head like one of those fancy fans. Her hair was practically hiding her face and I wondered how she could breathe. A couple of my uncles and boy cousins whistled. She tossed her hair and wiggled her butt and pretended like she almost fell down and my cousin pretended like he had to catch her. My mom and I didn't look at each other. My Grandma Jerrie is fun, but she can also be embarrassing.

Nobody could break the piñata, even the kids that were really too old for the blindfold and all that stuff. "Let Gina try," my mom called out, like she was proud of how strong I am. Siguanaba is. She likes the wind in her hair when she rides the mare really fast. I do, too, sitting behind her and holding on tight. I don't wear a cap when we're riding fast, or when she's teaching me about other stuff like men and love and magic and how to muck out a stall, which I used to think was gross but I don't mind anymore.

Instead of the wimpy cardboard stick with pink and green crepe paper stuck on it that came with the piñata, I got my baseball bat and took a couple of hard swings and the piñata split open and the candy spilled out. Marcus played a loud, obnoxious chord and yelled, "Girl's got an arm on her! Look at them muscles, man!" and I said thank you back at him in that same nasty-pretending-to-be-nice voice.

My little cousins jumped in like the candy was a swimming pool and filled up their bags and their mouths. I made sure the birthday girl got the most, then grabbed a couple of pieces for myself and sat on the picnic table with my feet on the bench and picked at the wrappers with my nails. One was strawberry and I saved it for Siguanaba.

My Grandma Jerrie swatted at me. "Get your butt off the table, girl, what's the matter with you?" She popped the top on another beer and told me to "act like a lady for once in your life."

"I'm not a lady." I didn't exactly know what I meant by that, but it sounded good.

"Yeah, I can see that."

"Don't want to be a lady."

"You know something, Regina?" She said my whole name like it was a cuss word. She was standing really close and I could smell her perfume and the beer on her breath and the sun on her hair, but she was talking loud. "It's about time somebody braided that hair for you."

I said, "I'd like to see somebody try," and she said back, "You better watch yourself, girl," and everybody but my mom went, "Oooooh," and I didn't get what just happened. I looked over at my mom but she had her back to me and her head bent over her plate.

The party finally got over. The birthday girl needed a nap. Everybody went home except the aunties and cousins that were staying at our house that night. Our landlord says we can't have company overnight but we're family and my mom doesn't like a quiet house. It's better since I got my own room, and my mom says no matter how many people are at our house, I don't have to share it.

Grandma Jerrie announced that she had plans for the evening. Somebody called, "Who's the lucky guy?" and she said she didn't know yet and giggled and flounced off down the street singing a Beyoncé song really loud. I didn't want to know what the neighbors would say.

I had trouble falling asleep because I was thinking about riding the mare and holding on to Siguanaba and singing the words she taught me in some other language. In the middle of the night Marcus woke me up singing under my window. I recognized his guitar first, and then his voice like when Siguanaba's donkey brays. At first I pretended I was asleep. Then I got up and whispered out at him to shut up. From my window, in the streetlight, he looked like he was all hat, with just these two little legs and the tiny guitar poking out. He made his voice sound like he was crying and begging, but he wasn't. He put my name into his songs. Like that would impress me. After a while he went away, but not because I told him to, just because he was done. He sang over his shoulder that he'd be back.

For a while then I tried to dream about riding. Siguanaba says you can tell yourself what to dream, but I'm not very good at it yet. Siguanaba says she can even make other people dream stuff, and she'll teach me how.

I dreamed I was a horse, or at least I had the head of a horse, I couldn't tell about my body. It wasn't a bad dream. It was from Siguanaba. I was sad when I had to leave it to go to the bathroom. What I saw in the mirror was what I always saw—round face with a couple of zits, flat nose, big shoulders, messy hair pulled back with a hair tie because a baseball cap won't stay on in bed. The dream was better.

Then I couldn't get the dream back, so finally I gave up and got a bag of chips and started outside to eat them. But through the window I saw my mom on the porch and I thought I'd just go back to my room before she knew I was up. Instead I went out to sit on the steps and said hi without looking at her. She didn't seem surprised that I was out there in the middle of the night, and I wasn't surprised that she was.

She said did I have trouble sleeping, too? I said something woke me up, it was kind of noisy outside. She said, "Yeah, I heard," and we both sort of laughed like we had a secret together and I guessed she meant she heard Marcus and I was ashamed like I called him here or something. The street was quiet. It was cool and dark out there. "I got something to show you," my mom said, and I didn't want to know what it was, and I wanted to know more than anything, and I wished Siguanaba was there with me.

It was a photo. My mom held it out to me but I didn't get up so she came over and put it on my knee. I finished the chips and wiped my hands on my shirt. I was thirsty. Should have brought a Coke out, too.

The picture was of my mom when she was a few years older than me and a few years younger than Siguanaba, maybe nineteen or twenty. She was pretty. I mean, she's still pretty, but she didn't look so worried back then. A thick braid went all the way down her back. There was some dude, too, he was a lot shorter than her and he had on a big hat. "Is that my dad?" That was a weird thing to ask.

"No, Gina, I don't know who your dad was. I told you."

"Who is that, then?"

"The first man I ever loved. The only."

"You didn't love my dad?" When she didn't answer I said, "Looks like Marcus."

"Marcus's cousin." The way my family talks, everybody's everybody's cousin, so that didn't help much.

I tried to look close at the picture without her knowing I was. She drank her coffee and smoked her cigarette, and I made myself stay there even with the smoke stinging my eyes and probably giving me lung cancer, not to mention her.

"He serenaded me under my bedroom window one night."

"What's 'serenaded'?"

"He had this great big hat and this little tiny guitar, and he didn't sing very good, but he was singing to *me*, you know? And the songs were about me, they had my name in them. And then I let him come up and he braided my hair, and then he went away, and I been waiting for him ever since. Can't love any other man. He took my soul." It wouldn't have been so weird if she'd said her heart.

Her shoulder was warm against mine. I tried to move away without her noticing. Somebody was clomping around inside the house. My Grandma Jerrie yelled at whoever it was to quiet down, people were trying to sleep, goddammit.

That woke up some of my little cousins and they sounded like ducks at the lake. I asked my mom, "He took it or you gave it to him?"

She asked me back, "Do you understand what I'm telling you, Gina?"

To make her happy I started to say yes, but what I said was, "Not really."

"Watch out, daughter. He'll ruin you for love. He'll love you and leave you and he'll make it so you can't love any other man in your whole life."

I was thinking, what about Siguanaba? Can I love Siguanaba? But I didn't know what that meant in my own head and for sure I was not going to say it out loud to my mom. I never used to have secrets from my mom. What I said was, "Don't worry. Not a chance. Marcus is a fool."

I gave her back the picture and she looked at it for a long time and then she went inside to make my cousin and my Grandma Jerrie stop yelling at each other. I had to get out of there. "Mom!" I called through the screen door. "I'm going to the stable," and it was fine with me that she didn't hear me.

I'd never walked to Siguanaba's before and I'd never been there at night. Maybe it was dangerous. Maybe I'd get lost. Maybe she'd have company or she wouldn't be home or she'd get mad if I woke her up. I'd probably get in trouble from my mom. But there I was, walking to Siguanaba's at night, and after a while I could feel her in my head showing me part of the way and letting me figure out the rest.

It wasn't all that far, I didn't think. It was a little chilly and I didn't bring a jacket. I also didn't bring my cap and the hair tie came loose and my hair was all over the place.

All the way to the end of our street where it turns into a dirt road, I didn't see a single other person. The school looked different at night, like it'd turned inside out. Some of the houses had lights on but I couldn't tell if somebody was up or they just left a light on at night. Dogs barked at me but as soon as I was past their territory they quit like they did their job and chased me away.

There's only one way you can turn onto the road, good thing because I was not totally sure which way the stable was from there and Siguanaba wasn't telling me. I told myself I better pay attention. Nothing was familiar, or maybe it was, familiar but different—fields and trees, a white fence, the river I could smell and hear off to my right. It was really quiet out there, but full. My hair was in my face and I held it back with one hand and then the other hand and my arms ached. I was getting tired. I wished I was on a horse with Siguanaba. I wished I was a horse flying with Siguanaba.

The road split. I stood there looking for clues, and then I was pretty sure it was the left-hand road I wanted, the stable was just around the bend if the road actually bent, which I couldn't see. When I squatted to dump the dirt out of my sandals, I could smell weeds Siguanaba used and what I guessed was hay, and I could hear little animals rustling, which was cool. Siguanaba hadn't exactly told me but I had a suspicion she could talk to animals and someday she'd teach me.

The road did bend, and there was Siguanaba's place down along the river with the big old willow tree in front. And Marcus was following me.

I'd been hearing the plinking like some weird night bird. Then all of a sudden I realized it was his ridiculous little guitar, and I heard him singing but I couldn't make out the words, and then I heard him singing my name. *Gina, look at him* came into my head. When I turned around, he was quite a ways back and mostly it was his hat I saw, like a spaceship flying low to the ground but wiggling like he was doing a little dance.

I broke into a run. *Don't run away.* I slowed back down because I was not going to run from anybody and, besides, I've known Marcus practically my whole life. Now I could hear, "Beautiful lady," and "Don't try to run from me" and "I would never hurt you," which let me know he would. And, "Let me braid your hair."

He was right behind me. How'd he catch up so fast? I said over my shoulder, "Go away and leave me alone." He laughed and kept on singing. That really made me mad. "Go away or I'll beat your ass!"

He hooted and hollered and stopped playing the guitar long enough to grab my hair. I swung my elbow and knocked off his hat and then I was running. Running away from him, running to get to the mare because what I wanted most right then was to be on her back in the night with her black mane and her tail and my hair flying out behind us, running to Siguanaba, then running just to be running, just because I could and the way my leg muscles hurt felt good, and I was really out of breath when I got to the top of the hill but I didn't stop, I raced through the corral and the stable yard and pushed open the stable door and then I bent over with my hands on my knees to catch my breath and my hair fell almost to the floor in front of me. The mare whinnied. *Pay attention*, Siguanaba said in my head.

From right by my hip came one note on the guitar again and again and again high and hard, and Marcus sang in my ear, "Beautiful lady, strong lady, I love you, I've been waiting for you, now's the time." He took a chunk of my hair in both hands and started to twist and braid it. When I straightened up and pulled away from him I could feel that some of my hair stayed in his hands.

I jerked open the stall door, got a bridle on the mare, didn't bother with any other tack, and pulled myself up onto her back. I never rode bareback before. She was warm and breathing between my thighs. I leaned low over her neck and whispered, "Let's fly, girl!" and touched her with my heels, and she shot out of the stall and we knocked Marcus down and his big hat went flying again. He was cussing and I was laughing as the mare and I took off up the road.

We galloped full-out down a hill and up the next one before I realized Marcus was on the horse behind me with his legs spread and me with no choice but to press back into him if I wanted to stay on. How'd that happen? You'd think I'd have noticed when he jumped on. Already he had one side of my hair braided tight with a rubber band or something on the end so the braid banged against my back.

I pulled hard on the right rein and the mare swerved, and I slid sideways and grabbed onto her mane, and I thought we'd lost Marcus but then he was in front of me, his hat keeping me from seeing where we were going. One good thing was he lost his stupid guitar. He was still singing and the wind threw his voice back in my face. "You're almost mine, girl! You're gonna be mine tonight! Before this ride is over you'll be mine!"

"In your dreams!" I yelled. In my head Siguanaba laughed. I love how she laughs.

 He grabbed the reins. The horse stumbled but like Siguanaba says she's sure-footed, *you've got to be sure-footed in this world or any world*. Her hooves clattered on the gravel. The wind was really wild now. Maybe it would blow Marcus's hat off his head. Something close to a song was loud and strong in my throat and out into the night, "I am not! I am not yours! I am mine!" Siguanaba harmonized.

I had to wrap my arms around his waist to keep from falling off but that was okay when I dug my nails into his belly. He yelled something disgusting and I squeezed hard and stabbed him deeper and he swore. The unbraided side of my hair blew around both of us. The mare's muscles made waves and then she was jumping high and long over a little arroyo, and when we landed both Marcus and I fell off, but his hat was still on his head. The mare went to get a drink from the river.

The side of my face felt funny where my hair was loose. It didn't exactly hurt, but it felt weird, and when I touched it there was something like grass stuck to it and it was all out of shape, my eye and ear on that side in different places than usual and that part of my mouth kind of swollen like it wasn't big enough for my teeth all of a sudden.

Marcus was limping, but he was on top of me before I could get away and he had his hands in my hair and I screamed at him without words. He backhanded me. I tried to knee him in the crotch but he was so short that my knee caught him in the belly and knocked the wind out of him. He doubled over and said a lot of curse words and called me ugly names in what sounded like different languages.

Then he stopped and stared at me. "Holy shit," he whispered, and pulled his hat lower over his face.

My head felt lopsided, heavier on that one side. Now I was hearing and seeing and smelling different than usual. My ear was more on the top of my head and my eye was pointed sideways instead of forward. Lots of smells were coming in my nose. My hair and that grassy stuff covered my neck.

Marcus was backing away from me. I bet he didn't mean to be singing right then, but his voice went way up and way down when he cried out, "Spirit of woman! Half horse and half beautiful woman! You stay away from me!"

Then I was madder than I'd ever been in my whole life, mad for my mom and for my Grandma Jerrie and for my girl cousins and for my boy cousins, too, and for myself. I grabbed his hat and tossed it away. I didn't think I threw it all that hard but it disappeared. He grabbed his little head with his little hands and made a little noise. I chased him, all the way to the river where he tore off all his clothes and jumped in howling.

I haven't seen him since that night, but I heard they found him in the river the next morning, still buck naked and afraid to get out, and he's still not right in the head. I don't know if anybody ever found his guitar and his hat or not. My Grandma Jerrie says he lost his soul. My mom watches me.

I caught the mare and she let me get back on and we went at a nice easy lope back to the stable. Siguanaba was waiting. When I slid off we touched fists and she whispered, "You go, girlfriend!" Together we wiped the mare down and gave her water and a little oats. Both of us pretended we didn't hear Marcus screaming and moaning down there in the river, and she didn't say anything about half of my face looking like a horse, and I didn't ask if it did. Then we went and sat under the willow tree and she unbraided my hair and brushed it out, and my face felt normal again where she laid her hand on it, and I wanted her to kiss me, and she did.

NOT FROM AROUND HERE

BY DAVID J. SCHOW

When David J. Schow gets inducted into the Horror Hall of Fame, I think it should be like a Viking funeral, except that Davey isn't dead; and so, instead of burning his body, we all just spontaneously burst into flames.

That's just my little way of saying that for those of us who regularly perform in the club scene of literary horror, Schow is like an evil Stevie Ray Vaughn, whose blistering verbal solos (or "air sculptures," as Frank Zappa used to call them) make us feel as if we're drawing with crayons. The jazz pianist Art Tatum also comes to mind: a guy with a lightning bolt in either hand, who played complex rhythms and melodies with uncanny velocity and pinpoint precision, and who schooled every keyboard player in town wherever he played.

This is a slice of vintage '80s Schow, its venom and shred undiminished by time. Prepare to get your ass whipped by a master and like it.

This morning I saw an alley cat busily disemboweling a rail lizard. I watched much longer than I had to in order to get the point.

Townies call little hamlets like Point Pitt "bedroom communities." Look west from San Francisco, and you'll see the Pacific Ocean. Twenty minutes by car to any other compass point will bring you to the population-signless borders of a bedroom community. El Granada. Dos Piedras. Half Moon Bay. Summit. Pumpkin Valley (no kidding).

Point Pitt rated a dot on the roadmaps only because of a NASA tracking dish, fenced off on a stone jetty, anchored rock-solid against gales, its microwave ear turned toward the universe. Gatewood was four and three-quarter miles to the north. To drive from Point Pitt to Gatewood you passed a sprawling, loamy-smelling acreage of flat fields and greenhouses, where itinerant Mexicans picked mushrooms for about a buck an hour. I saw them working every morning. They were visible through my right passenger window as I took the coast road up to San Francisco, and to my left every evening when I drove home. On the opposite side of the road, the ocean marked time. The pickers never gazed out toward the sea; they lacked the leisure. My first week of commuting eroded my notice of them. The panorama of incoming surf proved more useful for drive-time meditation. I no longer lacked the leisure.

You had to lean out a bit, but you could also see the Pacific from the balcony rail of our new upstairs bedroom, framed between two gargantuan California pines at least eighty years old. Suzanne fell for the house as soon as we toured it under the wing of the realtor. Our three-year-old, Jilly, squealed "Cave!" and jumped up and down in place, in hyperactive circles of little kid astonishment. Hard to believe, that this cavernous place was ours, that we weren't visiting a higher social class and would soon have to go home. This *was* home, and we were in love. . .goofy as that may sound.

I did not fall in love with the idea that all the decent movies, restaurants, and other urban diversions were still up in San Francisco. Gatewood boasted a single grease-griddle coffee shop that opened two hours before my morning alarm razzed and went dark promptly at five—up here, dinner was obviously a meal eaten at home, with family. Nearby was a mom-and-pop grocery that locked up at 9:00

p.m. Several miles away, in Dos Piedras, was an all-nighter where you could get chips and beer and bread and milk.

It sure wasn't the city. As a town, it wasn't vast enough to merit a stoplight. Point Pitt was no more than a rustic clot of well-built older homes tucked into a mountainside, with an ocean view. Voilá—bedroom community. Any encapsulation made it sound like a travel-folder wet dream, or an ideal environment in which to raise a child. I suspect my shrink knew this. He fomented this conspiracy, with my doctor, to get me away from my beloved city for the sake of my not-so-beloved ulcers.

I became a commuter. The drive was usually soothing, contemplative. I calmed my gut by chugging a lot of milk from the all-night market. We popped for cable TV—sixty channels. We adjusted fast.

It was required that I buy a barn-shaped rural mailbox. Suzanne jazzed it up with our name in stick-on weatherproof lettering: TASKE. The first Sunday after we moved in, I bolted it to the gang post by the feeder road, next to the boxes of our nearest neighbors. The hillside lots were widely separated by distance and altitude, fences and weald. There was much privacy to be had here. The good life, I guessed.

When a long shadow fell across the gang post from behind, I looked up at Creighton Dunwoody for the first time. His box read MR. & MRS. C. DUNWOODY. He had the sun behind him; I was on my knees, wrestling with a screwdriver. It just wouldn't have played for me to say, *You have me at a disadvantage, sir*, so I gave him something else sparkling, like, "Uh. . .hello?"

He squinted at my shiny white mailbox, next to his rusty steel one. It had a large, ancient dent in the top. "You're Taske?" He pronounced it like *passkey*; it was a mistake I'd endured since the first grade.

I gently corrected him. "Carl Taske, right." I stood and shifted, foot-to-foot, the essence of nervous schmuckdom, and finally stuck out my hand. Carl Taske, alien being, here.

I almost thought he was going to ignore it when he leaned forward and clasped it emotionlessly. "Dunwoody. You're in Meyer Olson's old house. Good house." He was taller than me, a gaunt farmer type. His skin was stretched over his bones in that brownly weathered way that makes thirty look like fifty, and fifty like a hundred and ten. Like a good neighbor coasting through meaningless chat, I was about to inquire as to the fate of Meyer Olson when Dunwoody cut in, point-blank. "You got any kids?"

"My daughter Jill's the only one so far." And Jilly had been well-planned. I couldn't help thinking of farm families with fourteen kids, like litters.

He chewed on that a bit. His attention seemed to stray. This was country speed, not city rush, but I felt like jumping in and filling the dead space. It wouldn't do to appear pushy. I might have to do this a lot with the hayseed set from now on.

"Any pets?" he said.

"Not today." A partial lie. Suzanne had found an orphaned Alsatian at the animal shelter and was making the drive to collect it the next day.

"Any guns in your house?"

"Don't believe in guns." I shook my head and kept my eyes on his. The languid, directional focus of his questions made my guard pop up automatically. This was starting to sound like more than the standard greenhorn feel-up.

"That's good. That you don't." We traded idiotic, uncomfortable smiles.

In my new master bedroom there were his and hers closets. A zippered case in the back of mine held a twelve-gauge Remington pumpgun loaded with five three-inch Nitro Mag shells. My father had taught me that this was the only way to avoid killing yourself accidentally with an "unloaded" gun, and Suzanne was giving me hell about it now that Jilly was walking around by herself. It was none of Dunwoody's business, anyway.

"How old's your girl?"

"Three, this past May."

"She's not a baby anymore, then."

"Well, technically no." I smiled again and it hurt my face. The sun was waning and the sky had gone mauve. Everything seemed to glow in the brief starkness of twilight gray.

Dunwoody nodded as though I'd given the correct answers on a geography test. "That's good. That you have your little girl." He was about to add something else when his gaze tilted past my shoulder.

I turned around and saw nothing. Then I caught a wink of reflected gold light. Looking more intently, I could see what looked to be a pretty large cat, cradled in the crotch of a towering eucalyptus tree uphill in the distance. Its eyes tossed back the sunset as it watched us.

Dunwoody was off, walking quickly up the slope without further comment. Maybe he had to feed the cat. "I guess I'll see. . .you later," I said to his back. I doubt if he heard me. His house stood in shadow off a sharp switchback in the road. A wandering, deeply-etched dirt path wound up to the front porch.

Not exactly rudeness. Not the city brand, at least.

The moon emerged to hang full and orange on the horizon, like an ebbing sun. High in its arc it shrank to a hard silver coin, its white brilliance filtering down through the treetops and shimmering on the sea-ripple. Suzanne hopped from bed and strode naked to the balcony, moving out through the French doors. Moonbeams made foliage patterns on her skin; the cool nighttime breeze buffeted her hair, in a gentle contest.

Her thin summer nightgown was tangled up in my feet, beneath the sheets. We'd dispensed with it about midnight. The one advantage to becoming a homeowner I'd never anticipated was the nude perfection of Suzanne on the balcony. She was a blue silhouette, weight on one foot and shoulders tilted in an unconsciously classical pose. After bearing Jilly and dropping the surplus weight of pregnancy, her ass and pelvis had resolved into a lascivious fullness that I could not keep my hands away from for long.

We fancied ourselves progressive parents, and Jilly had been installed in our living room from the first. We kept our single bedroom to ourselves. On hair triggers for the vaguest noise of infant distress, Mommy and Daddy were then besieged with the usual wee-hour fire drills and some spectacular demonstrations of eliminatory functions. Marital spats over the baby came and went like paper cuts; that was normal, too. Pain that might spoil a whole day, but was not permanent. Jilly's crib was swapped for a loveseat that opened into a single bed. And now she did not require constant surveillance, and was happily ensconced in her first private, real-life room.

Recently, Suzanne had shed all self-consciousness about sex, becoming adventurous again. There was no birth control to fret over. That was a hitch we still didn't discuss too often, because of the quiet pain involved—the permanent kind.

"Carl, come here and look." She spoke in a rapid hush, having spied something odd. "Hurry up!"

I padded out to embrace her from behind, nuzzling into the bouquet of her hair, then looking past her shoulder.

A big man was meandering slowly up the road. The nearest streetlamp was more than a block away, and we saw him as he passed through its pool of light, down by the junction with the coast highway. He was large and fleshy and fat and as naked as we were.

I pulled Suzanne back two paces, into the darkness of the bedroom. The balcony was amply private. Neither of us wanted to be caught peeking.

He seemed to grow as he got closer, until he was enormous. He was bald, with sloping mountain shoulders and vast pizza-dough pilings of flesh pulled into pendant bags by gravity. His knotted boxer's brow hid his eyes in shadow, as his pale belly hung to obscure his sex, except for a faint smudge of pubic hair. The load had bowed his knees inward, and his *lumpen* thighs jiggled as he ponderously hauled up one leg to drop in front of the other. We heard his bare feet slapping the pavement. His tits swam to and fro.

"There's something wrong with him," I whispered. Before Suzanne could give me a shot in the ribs for being a smartass, I added, "No—something else. *Look* at him. Closely."

We hurried across to the bedroom's south window so we could follow his progress past the mailboxes in front of the house. He was staring up into the sky as he walked, and his chin was wet. He was drooling. His arms hung dead dumb at his sides as he gazed upward, turning his head slowly one way, then another, as though trying to record distant stars through faulty receiving equipment.

"He's like a great big *baby*." Suzanne was aghast.

"That's what I was thinking." I recalled Jilly, when she was only a month out of the womb. The slack, stunned expression of the man below reminded me of the way a baby stares at a crib trinket—one that glitters, or revolves, or otherwise captures the eye of a being who is seeing this world for the first time.

"Maybe he's retarded."

A shudder wormed its way up my backbone but I successfully hid it. "Maybe he's a local boy they let run loose at night, y'know, like putting out the cat."

"Yeeugh, don't say that." She backed against me and my hands enfolded her, crossing to cup her breasts. Her body was alive with goosebumps; her nipples condensed to solid little nubs. She relaxed her head into the hollow of my shoulder and locked her arms behind me. Thus entangled, we watched the naked pilgrim drift up the street and beyond the light. My hands did their bit and she purred, closing her eyes. Her gorgeous rump settled in. "Hm. I seem to be riding the rail again," she said, and chuckled.

She loved having her breasts kneaded, and we didn't lapse into the dialogue I'd expected. The one about how her bosom *could* be a *little bit* larger, didn't I think so? (What I thought was that every woman I'd ever known had memorized this routine, like a mantra. Suzanne played it back every six weeks or so.) Nor did she lapse into the post-sex melancholy she sometimes suffered when she thought of the other thing, the painful one.

Eighteen months after Jilly was born, Suzanne's doctor discovered ovarian cysts. Three, medium-sized, successfully removed. The consensus was that Jilly would be our only child, and Suzanne believed only children were maladjusted. While there was regret that our power of choice had been excised, Suzanne still held out hope for a happy accident someday. I was more pragmatic, or maybe more selfish. I wasn't sure I wanted more than one child, and in a sense this metabolic happenstance had neatly relieved me of the responsibility of the vasectomy I'd been contemplating. I was hung up on getting my virility surgically removed in an operation that was, to me, a one-way gamble with no guarantees. Frightening. I prefer guarantees—hard-line, black-and-white, duly notarized. A hot tip from a realtor on a sheer steal of a house had more to do with reality than the caprices of a body that turns traitor and hampers your emotional life.

And when Suzanne's tumors were a bad memory, a plague of superstitions followed. For several months she was convinced that I considered her leprous, sexually unclean. From her late mother she had assimilated the irrational fear that says once doctors slice into your body with a scalpel, it's only a matter of borrowed time before the Big *D* comes pounding at the drawbridge.

The whole topic was a tightly twined nest of vipers neither of us cared to trespass upon anymore. God, how she could bounce back.

Passion cranked up its heat, and she shimmied around so we were face-to-face. The way we fit together in embrace was comfortingly safe. Her hand filled and fondled, and I got a loving squeeze below. "This gets enough of a workout," she slyly opined. Then she patted my waistline. "But we need to exert this. When we get the dog, you can go out running with it, like me."

It was depressingly true. Bucking a desk chair had caused a thickening I did not appreciate. "Too much competition," I muttered. I was afraid to challenge the ulcerations eating my stomach wall too soon. She was in much better physical shape than me. Those excuses served, for now. Her legs were short, well-proportioned, and athletic. Her calves were solid and sleek. Another turn-on.

"Mmm." Her hands slid up, around, and all over. "In that case, come back to bed. I've got a new taste sensation I know you're just dying to try."

The following morning, I met the huge bald man.

He was wearing a circus-tent-sized denim coverall, gum-soled work boots, and an old cotton shirt, blazing white and yellowed at the armpits. He was busily rummaging in Dunwoody's mailbox.

I played it straight, clearing my throat too loudly and standing by.

He started, looking up and yanking his hand out of the box. His head narrowed at the hat-brim line and bulged up and out in the back, as though his skull had been bound in infancy, ritually deformed. His tiny black eyes settled on me and a wide grin split his face. Too wide.

"G'morn," he said with a voice like a foghorn. My skin contracted. I got the feeling he was sniffing me from afar. His lips continued meaningless movements while he stared.

"*Ormly!*"

Creighton Dunwoody was hustling down the path from his house. The hillside was steep enough to put his cellar floor above the level of our roof. He wore an undershirt and had a towel draped around his neck; he had obviously interrupted his morning shave to come out and yell. Drooping suspenders danced around his legs as he mountaineered down the path.

Ormly cringed at the sound of his name, but did not move. Birds twittered away the morning, and he grinned hugely at their music.

For one frozen moment we faced off, a triangle with Ormly at the mailboxes. I thought of the three-way showdown at the climax of *The Good, the Bad and the Ugly*.

Dunwoody stopped to scope us out, made his decision with a grunt, and resumed his brisk oldster's stride toward me. He realized the burden of explanation was his, and he motioned me to approach the mailboxes. Maybe disgust. But he bulled it through.

"Mister Taske. This here's Ormly. My boy." He nodded from him to me and back again. "Ormly, Mister Taske is from the city. You should shake his hand."

Dunwoody's presence did not make it any easier to move into Ormly's range. Without the workboots he would still be a foot taller than I was. I watched as his brain obediently motivated his hand toward me. It was like burying my own hand in a catcher's mitt. He was still grinning.

The social amenities executed, Dunwoody said, "You get on back up the house now. Mail ain't till later."

Ormly minded. I've seen more raw intelligence in the eyes of goldfish. As he clumped home, I saw a puckered fist of scar tissue nested behind his left ear. It was a baseball-sized hemisphere, deeply fissured and bone white. A big bite of brains was missing there. Maybe his pituitary gland had been damaged as part of the deal.

Dunwoody batted shut the lid to his mailbox; it made a hollow *chunk* sound. "S'okay," he said. "Ormly's not right in the head."

I was suddenly embarrassed for the older man.

"Sometimes he gets out. He's peaceful, though. He has peace. Ain't nothing to be afraid of."

I took a chance and mentioned what I'd seen last night. His eyes darted up to lock onto mine for the first time.

"And what were *you* doin' up that time of night anyhow, Mister Taske?" That almost colonial mistrust of newcomers was back.

"I woke up. Thought I heard something crashing around in the woods." The lie slipped smoothly out. So far, I'd aimed more lies at Dunwoody than truth. It was stupid for me to stand there in my C&R three-piece, calfhide attaché case in hand, judging his standards of honesty.

"This ain't the city. Animals come down from the hills to forage. Make sure your garbage-can lids are locked down or you'll have a mess to clean up."

I caught a comic picture of opening the kitchen door late at night and saying howdy-do to a grizzly bear. Not funny. Nearly forty yards up the hill, I watched Ormly duck the front door lintel and vanish inside. Dunwoody's house cried out for new paint. It was as decrepit as his mailbox.

Dunwoody marked my expression. "Ormly's all I got left. My little girl, Sarah, died a long time ago. The crib death. Primmy—that's my wife; her name was Primrose—is dead, too. She just didn't take to these parts. . . .." His voice trailed off.

I felt like the shallow, yuppie city slicker I was. I wanted to say something healing, something that would diminish the gap between me and this old rustic. He was tough as a scrub bristle. His T-shirt was frayed but clean. There was shaving lather drying on his face, and he had lost a wife, a daughter, and from what I'd seen, ninety percent of a son. I *wanted* to say something. But then I saw his bare arms, and the blood drained from my face in a flood.

He didn't notice, or didn't care.

I checked my watch, in an artificial, diversionary move Dunwoody saw right through. It was a Cartier tank watch. I felt myself sinking deeper.

"Mind if I ask you a question?"

"Uh—no." I shot my cuff to hide the watch, which had turned ostentatious and loud.

"Why do you folks want to live here?" There it was: bald hostility, countrified, but still as potent as snake venom. I tried to puzzle out some politic response to this when he continued. "I mean, why live here when it makes you so late for everything?" His eyes went to my shirtsleeve, which concealed my overpriced watch.

He shrugged and turned toward his house with no leave-takings, as before. All I could register in my brain were his arms. From the wrists to where they met his undershirt, Dunwoody's arms were seeded with more tiny puncture marks than you would have found on two hundred junkies up in the Mission district. Thousands and thousands of scarred holes.

My trusty BMW waited, a sanctuary until the scent of leather upholstery brought on new heartstabs of class guilt. It was simple to insulate oneself with the trappings of upward mobility, with *things*. My grand exit was marred by sloppy shifting. The closer I drew to the city the better I felt, and my deathgrip on the wheel's racing sleeve gradually relaxed.

Maybe our other neighbors would make themselves apparent in time. Oh bliss oh joy.

Brix became the dog's name by consensus. I stayed as far away from that decision as politely possible. Dad the diplomat.

Jilly had thrilled to its reddish-brown coat, which put her in mind of "bricks," you see. Suzanne went at tedious length about how Alsatians reacted best to monosyllabic names containing a lot of hard consonants. In a word, that was Brix—and he was already huge enough for Jilly to ride bareback. He could gallop rings around Suzanne while she jogged. He never got winded or tired. He looked great next to the fireplace. A Christmas card snapshot of our idyllic family unit would have made you barf from the cuteness: shapely, amber-haired Mom; angelic blond Jillian Heather; Brix the Faithful Canine. . .and sourpuss Dad with his corporate razor cut and incipient ulcers. We were totally nuclear.

I didn't bother with Dunwoody or Ormly again until the night Brix got killed.

It was predestined that the dog's sleeping mat would go at the foot of Jilly's hide-a-bed. While Suzanne and I struggled patiently to indoctrinate the animal to his new name and surroundings, he'd snap to and seek Jilly the instant she called him. They were inseparable, and that was fine. The dog got a piece of Jilly's life; Suzanne and I were fair-traded a small chunk of the personal time we'd sacrificed in order to be called Mommy and Daddy. This payoff would accrue interest, year by year, until the day our daughter walked out the door to play grownup for the rest of her life. It was a bittersweet revelation: starting right now, more and more of her would be lost to us. On the other hand, the way she flung her arms around Brix's ruff and hugged him tight made me want to cry, too.

Since we'd assumed residence in Point Pitt, our lives really *had* begun to arrange more agreeably. Our city tensions bled off. We were settling, healing. Sometimes I must be forced to drink the water I lead myself to.

Brix quickly cultivated one peculiar regimen. At Jilly's bedtime he'd plunk his muzzle down on the mat and play prone sentry until her breathing became deep and metered. Then he'd lope quietly out to hang with the other humans. When our lights went down, he'd pull an about-face and trot back to his post in Jilly's room. Once or twice I heard him pacing out the size of the house in the middle of the night, and when the forest made its grizzly-bear commotions, Brix would return one or two barks of warning. He never did this while in Jilly's room, which was considerate of him. Barks sufficed. In his canine way, he kept back the dangers of the night.

So when he went thundering down the stairs barking loudly enough to buzz the woodwork, I woke up knowing something was not normal. Suzanne moaned and rolled over, sinking her face into the pillows. I extricated myself from the sleepy grasp of her free arm in order to punch in as Daddy the night watchman. The digital clock merrily announced 3:44 A.M. And counting.

Point Pitt was not a place where residents bolted their doors at night, although that was one habit I was in no danger of losing, ever. Because the worst of summer still lingered, we had taken to leaving a few windows open. It wasn't completely foolish to assume some thief might be cruising for a likely smash-and-grab spot. By the time the sheriffs (the district's only real law enforcement) could be summoned, even an inept burglar would have ample time to tip off all the goodies in the house and come back for seconds. While this sort of social shortcoming was traditionally reserved for the big bad city, there was no telling who might start a trend, or when.

Besides, if there were no bad guys, I might be treated to the surreal sight of a live bear consuming my rubbish.

Downstairs a window noisily ceased existence. Breaking glass is one of the ugliest sounds there is. I picked up speed highballing down the stairs.

I thought of the claw hammer Suzanne had been using while hanging plants in her little conservatory and hung the corner wildly, skidding to a stop and embedding a flat wedge of glass into the ball of my right foot. I howled, keeled over, and obliterated a dieffenbachia mounted in a wire tripod. The entire middle section of leaded-glass panes was blown out into the night. Pots swung crookedly in their macramé slings where Brix had leapt through.

Somewhere in the backyard he was having it rabidly out with the interloper, scrabbling and snapping.

Grimacing, I stumped into the kitchen and hit the backyard light switches. Nothing. The floodlamps were still lined up on the counter in their store cartons, with a Post-it note stuck to the center one, reminding me of another undone chore. Outside the fight churned and boiled and I couldn't see a damned thing.

My next thought was of the shotgun. I limped back to the stairs, leaving single footprints in blood on the hardwood floor. Brix had stopped barking.

"Carl?"

"I'm okay," I called toward the landing. To my left was the shattered conservatory window, and the toothless black gullet of the night beyond it. "*Brix!* Hey, Brix! C'mon, guy! Party's over!"

Only one sound came in response. To this day I can't describe it accurately. It was like the peal of tearing cellophane, amplified a thousand times, or the grating rasp a glass cutter makes. It made my teeth twinge and brought every follicle on my body to full alert.

"Carl!" Suzanne was robed and halfway down the stairs.

"Get me a bandage and some peroxide, would you? I've hacked my goddamn foot wide open. Don't go outside. Get my tennis shoes."

I sat down on the second stair with a thump. When Suzanne extracted the trapezoidal chunk of glass, I nearly puked. There was a gash two inches wide, leaking blood and throbbing with each slam of my heartbeat. I thought I could feel cold air seeking tiny, exposed bones down there.

"Jesus, Carl." She made a face, as though I'd done this just to stir up a boring night. "Brixy whiffs a bobcat, or some fucking dog game, and you have to ruin our new floor by bleeding all over it. . .."

"Something turned him on enough to take out the conservatory window. Jesus Christ in a Handi-Van. Ouch! Even if it *is* a bobcat, those things are too bad to mess with."

She swept her hair back, leaving a smear of blood on her forehead. She handed over the peroxide and left my foot half taped. "You finish. Let me deal with Jilly before she freaks out."

"Mommy?" Jilly's voice was tiny and sleep-clogged. She'd missed the circus. I sure hadn't heard her roll out of the sack, but Suzanne apparently had. Mommy vibes, she'd tell me later.

After gingerly pulling on my shoes, I stumped to the kitchen door and disordered some drawers looking for a flashlight. Upstairs, Suzanne was murmuring a soothing story about how Daddy had himself an accident and fell on his ass.

I didn't have to look far to find Brix. He was gutted and strewn all over the backyard. The first part I found was his left rear leg, lying in the dirt like a gruesome drumstick with a blood-slicked jag of bone jutting from it. My damaged foot stubbed it; pain shot up my ass and blasted through the top of my head. His carcass was folded backward over the east fence, belly torn lengthwise, organs ripped out. The dripping cavern in the top of his head showed me where his brain had been until ten minutes ago.

The metallic, shrieking noise sailed down from the hills.

And the lights were on up at Dunwoody's place.

When the sheriffs told me Brix's evisceration was nothing abnormal, I almost lost it and started punching. Calling the cops had been automatic city behavior; a conditioned reaction that no longer had any real purpose. Atavistic. There hadn't been enough of Brix left to fill a Hefty bag. What wasn't in the bag was missing, presumed eaten. Predators, they shrugged.

In one way I was thankful we'd only had the dog a few days. Jilly was still too young to be really stunned by the loss of him, though she spent the day retreated into that horrible quiet that seizes children on the level of pure instinct. I immediately promised her another pet. Maybe that was impulsive and wrong, but I wasn't tracking on all channels myself. It did light her face briefly up.

I felt worse for Suzanne. She had been spared most of the visceral evidence of the slaughter, but those morsels she could not avoid seeing had hollowed her eyes and slackened her jaw. She had taken to Brix immediately, and had always militated against anything that caused pain to animals. There was no way to bleach out the solid and sickeningly large bloodstain on the fence, and I finally kicked out the offending planks. Looking at the hole was just as depressing.

The sheriffs were cloyed, too fat and secure in their jobs. All I had done was bring myself to their attention, which is one place no sane person wants to be. Annoyed at my cowardly waste of their time, they marked up my floor with their boots and felt up my wife with their eyes.

Things were done differently here. That was what impelled me to Dunwoody's place, at a brisk limp.

I had not expected Ormly to answer the door; I couldn't fathom what tasks were outside his capabilities and simply assumed he was too stupid to wipe his own ass. He filled up the doorway, immense and ugly, his face blank as a pine plank (with a knot on the flip side, I knew). He was dressed exactly as before. Perhaps he had not changed. It took a couple of long beats, but he did recognize me.

"Fur paw," he said.

The back of my neck bristled. When Ormly's brain changed stations, he haunted the forest, starkers, in the dead of night; what other pastimes might his damaged imagination offer him? When he spoke, I half expected him to produce one of Brix's unaccounted for shanks from his back pocket and gnaw on it. Then I realized what he had said: *For pa*.

"Yeah." I tried to clear the idiocy out of my throat. "Is he home?"

"Home. Yuh." He lurched dutifully out of the foyer, Frankenstein's Monster in search of a battery charge.

I waited on the stoop, thinking it unwise to go where I wasn't specifically beckoned or invited. Another urban prejudice. Wait for the protocol, go through the official motions. Put it through channels. That routine was what had won me the white-lipped holes blooming in my stomach.

Dunwoody weaved out of the stale-smelling dimness holding half a glass of peppermint schnapps. He was wearing a long-sleeved workshirt with the cuffs buttoned.

"I'm sorry to bother you, Mr. Dunwoody, but my dog was killed last night." No reaction. He showed the same disinterest the cops had, and that brought my simmering anger a notch closer to boiling. "More to the point, he was pelted and hung on my back fence with his head scooped out and his guts spread all over the yard. The fence bordering *your* property, Mr. Dunwoody."

"I heard him barking." He looked down and away. "Saw you kick the slats out." His words billowed toward me in minty clouds; he was tying on a nice, out-of-focus afternoon drunk. "You said you didn't have no pets."

It was an accusation: *If you hadn't lied, this would not have happened.*

I felt obligated to be pissed off, but my soul wasn't really in it. My need to know was stronger. "Sorry—but look, you mentioned wildcats coming out of the hills. Or bears. Maybe I'm no authority on wildlife feeding habits, but what happened was. . ." I flashed on Brix's corpse again and my voice hitched. "That was far beyond killing for food."

"I didn't see it." His voice wasn't a full slur. Not yet, but soon. "Woke me up. But I didn't see it. I'm glad I didn't. That part I don't fancy, sir." He scratched an eyebrow. "I think y'all should leave. Go."

"You mean leave Point Pitt?"

"Move somewhere else. Don't live here." He took a long drag on his glass and grimaced, as though choking down cough medicine. "See what happens? This ain't for boys like you, with your fag hairdos and your little Japanese cars and your satellite TV. . .aahhh, Christ. . ."

Ormly loomed behind him, recording all the pain with oddly sad eyes, so much like a dog himself.

A cloudy tear slipped down Dunwoody's face, but his own eyes were clear and decisive as they looked from me to the north. "Go home," he said. "Just go home, please." Then he shut the door in my face.

Dinner was flavorless, by rote. Suzanne had tried to nap and only gotten haggard. Jilly told me she missed Brix.

After bestowing my customary bedtime smackeroo, Jilly asked again about getting another pet *right now*. Her mom had run the same idea past me downstairs. Between them I'd finally be goaded into some reparation.

Suzanne reached for me as soon as I hit my side of the bed. She had already divested herself of clothing, and her movements were brazen and urgent. She wanted to outrun the last twenty-four hours in a steambath of good therapeutic fucking. Her nerves were rawed, and close to the surface; she climaxed with very little effort and kept me inside her for a long, comforting while. Then she kissed me very tenderly, ate two sleeping pills, and chased oblivion in another direction.

My foot felt as if I had stomped on a sharpened pencil. I hobbled to the bathroom, pretending I was Chester in *Gunsmoke*. The dressing was yellowed from drainage and shadowed with dry brown blood. It gave off a carrion odor. I took my time washing and swabbing and winding on new gauze. I was still pleasantly numb everywhere else.

There was a low thrumming, like that of a large truck idling on the street outside. I felt it before I actually heard it. I checked the window across from the bathroom door, but there was nothing, not even Ormly making his uniformless predawn rounds. With my Bay City paranoid's devotion to ritual, I hobbled downstairs and jiggled all the locked doors. The boarded-up plant nook was secure. I sneaked a couple of slugs of milk straight from the carton. Ulcer maintenance.

Jilly's room was on the far side of the bathroom. When I peeked stealthily in, the vibrational noise got noticeably louder.

Triplechecking everything constantly was as much a habit of new parenthood as security insecurity. Jilly was wound up in her Sesame Street sheets. I decided to shut the window, which was curtained but half-open.

The sheet-shape was grotesque enough to suggest that Jilly's entire platoon of stuffed animals was bunking with her tonight. I'd tucked in Wile E. Coyote myself. No more Brix. My throat started to close up with self-pity. I crept closer to plant a sleeptime kiss on Jilly's temple—another parental privilege, so Suzanne told me. Jilly's hair was just beginning to shade closer to the coloring of my own.

The low, fluttering noise was coming from beneath her sheets. And something smelled bad in the room. Perhaps she had soiled herself in sleep.

Hunched into Jilly's back was a mass of oily black fur as big as she was. At first my brain rang with a replay of Brix's horrifying inside-out death. The thing spooning with my daughter had one fat paw draped over her sleeping shoulder, and was alive. And purring.

I had the sheet peeled halfway down to reveal more of it when it twisted around and bit me on the wrist.

I took one panicked backward step, jerking away. Jilly's plush brontosaurus was feet-up on the floor; I stumbled over it, savaging my injured foot and crashing, sprawl-assed, down on Brix's rug, which smelled doggish and was dusted with his red hair. I had to get up, fast, tear the thing from her back, get the shotgun, to—

I tried to chock my good leg under me and could not. Both had gone thick and unresponsively numb. Then, shockingly, warmth spread at my crotch as my belly was seized by a sudden and powerful orgasm. My arms became as stupid as my legs. Then even my neck muscles lost it, and my forehead thunked into Brix's rug. And I came again.

And again.

Within seconds it was like receiving a thorough professional battering. I was having one orgasm for every three beats of my heart. My useless legs twitched. Saliva ran from the corner of my mouth to pool in my ear; even my vocal cords were iced into nonfunction. And while I lay curled up on the floor, coming and shuddering and coming, the creature that had been in bed with my daughter climbed down to watch.

Its eyes were bronze coins, reflecting candlefire. I thought of the thing I had seen monitoring me from the tree on my first day as a Point Pitt resident.

It was bigger than a bobcat, stockier, low-slung. The fur or hair was backswept, spiky-stiff and glistening, as though heavily lubricated. Thick legs sprouted out from the body rather than down, making its carriage ground-gripping and reptilian. I heard hard leather pads scuff the floor as it neared, saw hooked claws, hooded in pink ligatures, close in on my face.

It was still purring. The head was a cat's, all golden eyes and pointed felt ears, but the snout was elongated into a canine coffin shape. The chatoya pupils were X-shaped, deep-glowing crosscuts in the iris of each eye, and they widened like opening wounds to drink me in. It yawned. Less than a foot from my face I saw two bent needle fangs, backed by triangular, sharkish teeth in double rows. Its breath was worse than the stink of the congealed bandage I had stripped from my foot.

One galvanic sexual climax after another wrenched my insides apart. I was dry-coming; about to ejaculate blood. The creature dipped its head to lick some spittle from my cheek. Its tongue was sandpapery.

I had to kill it, bludgeon its monster skull to mush, blast it again and again until its carcass could hold no more shot. I orgasmed again. I could barely breathe.

It ceased tasting me and the hideous eyes sparked alive, hot yellow now. It padded back to the bed and leaped silently up. Jilly remained limp. I didn't even know if she was already dead or not.

It looked, to make sure I could see. Then it settled in, gripping Jilly's shoulders from above with its claws and licking her hair. It opened its mouth. Cartilage cracked softly as its jawbones separated, and the elastic black lips stretched taut to engulf the top of her head.

It sensed how much I hated it. Hate glittered back at me from those molten gash-eyes—my own hate, absorbed, made primal and total, and sent back to me.

Of hate, it knew.

My traitorous body continued its knifing spasms, and tears of pain blurred the view that I was incapable of commanding my eyelids to block out. The lips wormed forward, side-to-side, the slanted teeth seating, then pulling backward. The mouth elongated to full bore and the eyes fixed in a forward stare, glazed as though intoxicated by this meal.

With a mindless alien malice, it looked like it was smiling.

Blackness sucked me down before I could hear the abrasive, porcelain sound of those teeth grinding together, meeting at last through the pale flesh of my little girl's throat.

Moonlight delineated the window in blue-white.

I tried to sit up and rub my face. I was sweat-soaked, and lacquered in scales of dry semen. My balls were crushed grapes. Half my mind tried to wheedle me back into unconsciousness, begging to flee from what it had recorded. The less craven half had kicked me until I awoke, feeling like a frayed net loaded with broken bones, unable to stand or walk. I sprawled on my belly to Jilly's bed. Lowering groans slipped from my throat.

I've seen snakes eat their prey. I didn't have to see what was left in Jilly's bed to know what had happened. But to get my legs back, and finish the work begun this night, I forced myself to look.

I took it all in without even a gasp. Only the drapes whispered furtively together, unable to remain still or quiet.

So much blood, blackening the Sesame Street sheets. Her tiny outthrust hand was speckled with it, and cold to the touch. Her pillow was a saturated dark sponge.

I slumped and vomited into my own lap. Nothing much came up as my guts were rent, the sore muscles pulling themselves to tatters. My hand went out and skidded into something like warm gelatin next to the bedpost.

It was the skin of our visitor, piled there like an enormous scalp, greasy black spines rooted in an opaque membrane. It reminded me of Brix's empty pelt. Here was the broad, flat sheath of the back; here, the sleeve of each leg. The reversed tissue was coated with a kind of thick, veined afterbirth that smelled like shit, and the pain almost put me under again. I swallowed a surge of bile and held.

It was slippery, as heavy as a waterlogged throw rug when I dragged it out of the room.

I knew there was a handful of speed and painkillers waiting for me in the bathroom. I filled the basin from the cold tap and immersed my head. I stared into the clean white gorge of the toilet and decided not to heave.

Suzanne was still safe in the depths of drugged sleep, where there are no true nightmares. On wobbly wino's feet I locked the balcony doors. The bedroom door had a two-way skeleton-key lock that could be engaged from the outside.

My Levi's jacket and shoes were downstairs on the sofa. And the shotgun was where it had been patiently waiting since the day we moved in.

Dunwoody's house was just up the hill.

My shoulder stung as the Remington's recoil pad kicked it, and the works on Dunwoody's back door, mostly shit, blew away to floating wood chaff and fused shrapnel. The door skewed open on its upper hinge, and the inside knob rebounded from the kitchen wall with a clacking cueball noise. It spun madly in place until its energy was used up. The echo of the blast returned softly from the hills.

Two rooms down a narrow hallway, Dunwoody sat watching a black-and-white television that displayed only test-pattern bars. The screen bounced rectangles of light off his wire-rim glasses and made his old-fashioned undershirt glow blue in the darkness. He turned to look at the intruder stepping through the hanging wreckage of his back door, his gaze settling with resigned indifference on the twelve-gauge in my hand. He sighed.

My right wrist was throbbing as though fractured; mean red coronas of inflammation had blossomed around the twin punctures there, and I didn't know how many more shots it could stand before breaking. The smell of dry puke swam richly through my head, chased by the fetor of my prize. My eyes were pinpricks; the black capsules were doing their dirty work in the solvents of my stomach. It was the dope as much as the backwash of nausea that made me giddy—dark, toxic waves slopping up on a polluted beach, then receding.

Stiff-legged, lead-footed, I moved into the house. I knew where I was going and what to do when I arrived. My life had a purpose.

I jacked back the slide to reload, retrieved the reeking mess of shed skin with my free hand, and clumped forward. I was going to nestle the barrel right on the bridge of Dunwoody's thin hickory nose. He just sat there, watching my approach. There were no hidey-holes, and Ormly was probably out cruising at this time of night.

"You look foolish with that pumpgun, city boy."

"Foolish enough to spread your reedy old ass all over the wallpaper." My voice was dry and coarse, a rusted thing.

"You want all kind of answers." He spoke like the keeper of knowledge and wisdom, shifting in his easy chair with a snort of contempt. "Big-city know-it-all finds out he *don't* know it all. Don't know shit." He gulped schnapps from a finger-printy glass.

I couldn't buy his casual disdain for the gun. Perhaps he thought I wouldn't use it. To dash that little misconception from his mind, I stepped into the room and brought the shotgun to bear.

It tore violently out of my grasp like a runaway rocket, skinning my index finger on the trigger guard. Momentum yanked me the rest of the way into the room, and I got my crippled foot down to keep from falling. It wasn't worth it.

Ormly had been stationed in ambush behind the doorway and had acted with a speed startling for his bulk and presumed intellect. He stood there with the shotgun locked in his bulldozer grip, upside down, while Dunwoody watched drops of blood from my hand speckle the floor like small change.

"Get Mister Taske a cloth for his hand, Ormly." Each order was slow, metered, portioned out at rural speed. "Take care of his pumpgun; I'm sure he paid a lot of money for it. And bring me my bottle. You might as well have a seat, Mister Taske. And we'll talk."

The tar-colored pelt had slithered from my grasp and piled up in an oily heap on the floor. It slid around itself, never settling, as if it refused to give up the life it once contained. Dunwoody looked at it.

"It's stronger now, quicker. At its best, since it dropped a hide. Don't gawp at me like *I'm* nuts. You saw it the first day you was here, and you didn't pay it no mind."

"I thought it was. . .some kind of cat," I stammered lamely. "Mountain lion, or. . ."

"Yeah, well, you know so goddamn much about mountain cats, now don't you?" he said with derision. "You said you didn't have no pets, no guns. See what happens? It ain't no cat."

Jesus. Anybody with two dendrites of intelligence could see that it *weren't no cat*. Arguing that now would only keep the old man off the track. I decided to shut up, and he seemed satisfied that I was going to let him talk without any know-it-all city-boy interruptions. Ormly lumbered back with the schnapps, which Dunwoody offered to me perfunctorily. *Let's retch!* my stomach announced, and I waved the bottle away.

Ormly backed into his corner like the world's largest Saint Bernard sentry, keeping his eyes on me.

"Ormly was whip-smart," Dunwoody began. "He was my Primmy's favorite. Then she had Sarah. Little Sarah. You'da seen that baby girl, Mister Taske, she woulda busted your heart left and right, she was so perfect. Like your little girl."

"Jilly's dead." It was shockingly easy to say it so soon. "It—that thing, it—"

"I know. And I know you think me and Ormly is up to something, squirreled away up here, that we're somehow responsible. We ain't. I'd never hurt a little girl, and Ormly's never harmed no person nor animal. It's just. . .there's a certain order of things, here."

I had begun watching the ugly shed skin, still yielding, relaxing. It might reinflate and attack.

"Primmy and I kept a henhouse. We loved fryers and fresh eggs. One day I went out and all our chickens had been killed." The drama replayed behind his eyes. "You know how chickens run around after you cut off their heads, too dumb to know they're dead? Christ almighty. Twenty chickens, and half of them still strutting around when I got there. Without heads. It came down that night to eat the heads. And left the chickens. We'd been living in Point Pitt about two months."

My brain dipped sickeningly toward blackout. It was an almost pleasing sensation. Ebb tide of the mind; time to go to sleep. I sat down hard in the chair next to Dunwoody's and swallowed some schnapps without even tasting it.

"I had two hounds, Homer and Jethro, and an old Savage and Fox double-barrel, not as fancy as that pumpgun you got, but mean enough to stop a runaway truck dead. I laid up in the chicken coop the next night. 'Long about two in the morning, it stuck its head in and I let it have both barrels in the face. It was as close as you are to me. It yowled and ran off into the woods, and I set Homer and Jethro on it. Next morning, I found them. That thing took two loads of double-ought buckshot in the face and still gutted both my dogs. Ormly loved them old mutts."

I remembered the sound it made, the ground-glass screech. I didn't have to ask whether Dunwoody's dogs had been found with their heads intact.

Dunwoody cleared his throat phlegmatically and hefted himself out of the chair, to pry open a stuck bureau drawer behind the TV set. "Next night, it came back again. Walked into my home bold as you please and took my baby Sarah. It was slow getting out the window. Sluggish, with its belly full. I shot it again like a fool. Didn't do no good. Let me show you something."

He handed across a brown-edged, fuzzy piece of sketchbook paper. "Careful with it. It's real old."

It was a pencil rendering of the Dunwoody house, done in a stark and very sophisticated woodcut style. The trim and moldings stood out in relief. The building was done in calm earth tones, complimented by trees in full bloom. The forest shaded up the hillside in diminishing perspective. The strokes and chiaroscuro were assured. The drawing deserved a good matte and frame. I tilted it toward the light of the television and made out a faded signature in the lower right, done with a modest but not egocentric flourish.

O. Dunwoody.

He handed me a photograph, also slightly foxed, in black-and-white with waffled snapshot borders. A furry diagonal crease bisected a robustly pregnant woman packed into a paisley maternity dress. She had the bun hairdo and slight bulb nose that had always evoked the 1940s for me—World War II wives, the Andrews Sisters, all of that. Hugging her ferociously was a slim, dark-haired boy of nine or so, smiling wide and unselfconsciously. He had his father's eyes, and they blazed with what Dunwoody would call the smarts.

I tried to equate the boy in the photo with Ormly's overgrown, cartoonish body, or to the imbecilic expression on his face as he stood placidly in his corner. No match.

"Night after it took baby Sarah, it came back. We were laying to bushwhack it outside. It flanked us. Ormly came in for a drink of water, and there it was, all black and bristly and eating away on his mamma. He couldn't do nothing but stand there and scream; all the starch had run right out of him. He looked kinda like you do right now. I ran back in. That was the first time it bit me."

I extended my wrist for him to see, and his eyes lowered with guilt.

"Then you know that part already," he said.

Ormly stood parked like a wax dummy while his father went to him and looked over the wasteland of his son, hoping perhaps to read a glimmer of the past in the dull eyes. There was no light there, only the reflected snow of the TV set, now turned to nothingness.

"Ormly was crazy with fear and wanted to run. He loved his mamma and his little sister and the dogs, but he knew the sense in running. I was full up with ideas of what a man should do. A man didn't go beggin' to the police. The police don't understand nothing; they don't care and don't want to. A man should settle with his own grief, I thought, and Ormly wanted to be a man, so he hung with me."

Brave kid, I thought. *Braver than me.*

"Ormly came up with the idea of setting it on fire. He'd seen some monster movie where they'd doused the monster with kerosene and touched it off with a flare gun. We set up for it. We knew it was coming back, because it knew we didn't like it and would try to kill it. It *knew* how we felt. We were the ones that had intruded on its territory, and when you do that, you either make peace or you make a stand. Or you run. And that's what we shoulda done, because we were prideful and we didn't know what we were up against. We shoulda run like hell."

Dunwoody was stoking his own coals now, like a stump revival preacher getting ready to rip Satan a new asshole.

"Sure enough, the son of a bitch came down after us that night. You couldn't have convinced me there was another human soul in Point Pitt. All the houses were dark. They all *knew*, that is, everyone but me. When I spotted it crossing the backyard, in the moonlight, it was different than before. It'd dropped its hide, just like a bullsnake." He indicated the rancid leftover on the floor with a weak wave of his hand, not wanting to see it.

He did not look at Ormly, either, even as he spoke of him.

"The boy was perfect, by god. He stepped out from his hiding place, exposed himself to danger just so he could dump his pail of gasoline right smack into that thing's open mouth. I set my propane torch to it and it tagged me on the back of the hand—just a scratch; no venom. Or maybe the gas all over my hand neutralized it. We watched it shag ass into the hills, shrieking and dropping embers, setting little fires in the bushes as it ran. We hooted and jumped and clapped each other on the back like we were big heroes or something, and the next morning we tried to find it. All we turned up was a shed skin, like that one. And when the sun went down again, it came back. For Ormly. I swear to you, Mister Taske, it knew who had thought of burning it. But it didn't kill Ormly." The memory shined in Dunwoody's welling eyes. He had witnessed what had happened. "Didn't kill him. It took a big, red mouthful out of the back of his head, and. . .and. . ."

He extended his scarred arms toward me, Christ-like, seeking some absolution I could not give. Bite marks peppered them everywhere, holes scabbing atop older ones.

"You get so you can't go without," he said dully. "You won't want to. You'll see."

I was aware of speaking in an almost sub-aural whisper. "Why didn't you leave?"

He shook his head sadly, ignoring me. "One day it just showed up. That's all anybody knows. Whether it came down out of the hills or crawled out of the ocean don't really matter. What matters is it came here and decided to stay. Maybe somebody fed it."

The speed maxed out in my bloodstream, hitting its spike point. The murky room resolved to sharp-edged clarity around me in a single headlong second. I'd broken through, and rage sprang me from my chair, to brace Dunwoody so he could no longer retreat into obfuscations or babble.

"Why the hell didn't you leave?" I screamed in his face.

He flinched, then considered his ruined arms again, and avoided the easy answer. "We don't like the city."

I remembered Suzanne, browsing the house. All her remarks about getting back to nature, slowing down, escaping the killer smog, hightailing it from the city as though it was some monster that had corrupted us internally and conspired to consume us. The big, bad neon nightmare. What penetrated now was the truth— that the state of nature is the last thing any thinking being would want. The true state of nature is not romantic. It is savage, primal, unforgivingly hostile. Mercy is a quality of civilization. Out here, stuck halfway between the wilds and the cities, a man had to settle his own grief. And if he could not. . .

My father, the guy who'd taught me to keep all guns loaded, had another adage I'd never had to take seriously yet: *If you can't kill it with a gun, son—run.*

"You've squared off with it," Dunwoody said. "That choice was yours. Believe me when I say it knows you don't like it." The provincial superiority was seeping back into his tone. "Have you figured it out yet, or has all that toe-food crap turned your brain to marl?"

Near the nub of his right elbow, the old man had sustained a fresh bite. It was all I could see. The thing had bitten Dunwoody recently—and Dunwoody had let it.

He sighed at my thickness. "It's coming back. Might even come back tonight. You're new here, after all."

I bolted then, with a strangled little cry. It was a high sound, childish, womanish. A coward's bleat, I thought.

Ormly had left my shotgun on the kitchen table, and I snatched it up as I ran, hurdling the demolished door, heedless of the stabbing pains in my hand, or the blood I could feel welling from the ruptured wound on my foot. My shoe had turned crimson. I ran so fast I did not see Dunwoody nodding to himself, like a man who has made the desired impression, and I missed his final words to his huge, dim-witted son.

"Ormly, you go on with Mister Taske, now. You know what you have to do."

Three feet more.

Three feet more, and the world would be set right. Three feet more to reach the hole in the fence, where Brix had died. Then came three more feet to reach the back door, to the stairs, to our bedroom. Three seconds more and I could shake Suzanne awake, pack her into the BMW, and bust posted limits red-lining it out of this nightmare. If the city wanted us back, no problem. We could scoot by on our plastic for months. My life was not a spaghetti western; I did not bash through my degree and get ulcers so I could do symbol-laden combat with monsters.

And Jilly. . .

The south window had been shoved neatly up. The drapes fluttered and there was no hint of broken glass, of the horrorshow trespass my brain had pictured for me. The creature was snuggled between Suzanne's legs on the bed. Eating. It looked very different without its skin.

Thick braids of exposed sinew coiled up each of its legs, filament cable that bunched and flexed. The knobs of its spine were strapped down by double wrapping of inflated, powerful muscle tissue as smoothly grooved and perfect as plastic. It no longer required an envelope of skin. An absurd little triangular flap covered its anus like a pointed tail.

Suzanne's eyes were slitted, locked. She was beyond feeling what was being done to her. Another orgasm hissed past her teeth, gutturally. Nothing more.

The skeleton key dropped from my trembling fingers and bounced on the hardwood floor. The thing on the bed had cranked its blood-slathered muzzle around to dismiss me. I was no big deal.

With a sidelong yank of its head, it worried loose some morsel anchored by stubborn tendons to the chest cavity. It was about halfway to its favorite part. The scraps it had sampled and discarded littered the bed wetly. If it had chanced across any tumors during it methodical progress toward the brain, I was sure it had crunched them up like popcorn. Piggishly, it lapped and slurped.

Suzanne looked at me as she came again, convulsing as much as her sundered body would let her. A thin stringer of frothy lung blood leapt into her chest.

I kept my eyes in contact with hers as I snapped the trigger of the Remington, thinking how much I loved her.

The Nitro Mag load tore our bed to smithereens. Suzanne's dead arm jerked up, flopped back. Bloodstained goosedown took to the air, drifting. I worked the slide one-handed and fired again. The French doors disintegrated. Rickrack jumped from the bedstands to shatter on the floor.

The creature eased out its caked snout and saw what had just befallen that part of the feast it had been saving for last. Its impossibly wide, hinged maw dropped open to screech at me, as though I owed it something and had reneged. I shot it in the face, as Dunwoody had years ago. It snapped at the incoming shot like a bloodhound at gnats, then obstinately sank its nose back into its grisly dinner.

Suzanne was no longer on the bed. The corpse was not identifiable as anything but dead, butchered meat.

I slammed the bedroom door hard; don't ask why. There was an instant when I might have jammed the barrel between my teeth and swallowed that last shot myself. Instead, a pungent odor hauled me, staggering, to the stair landing.

Downstairs, the floor was wet and sloppy, glistening. Ormly waited for me, a ten-gallon jerry can of gasoline in each massive hand, smiling.

The buffeting heat was so intense that we had to back across the street to avoid getting our eyebrows flash-fried.

I watched the south window of our bedroom grow dreamy behind a sheet of orange flame. There was absolutely no exterior access. The thing had crawled up the front of the house like a fly, and clinging, had opened the window with one paw.

Neither of us saw it jump out, trailing sparks. The expression on Ormly's face frightened me. It was the closest thing to a glimmer of abstract thought I'd yet seen mar his slablike, mannequin countenance. He stared, unblinking, into the skyrocketing licks of fire.

"Hotter," he said. "Stronger. Better this time."

By dawn we were down to smoldering debris. I did not want to scrutinize the wreckage too closely, for fear of recognizing blackened bones.

Ormly stood in the backyard, his face dead with a kind of infinite sadness. I followed his gaze to the ground, and saw a deeply-dug, charred clawprint. The foot that had embossed itself there had been so hot that the grass had been cooked into an unmistakable pattern.

Ormly's mitt-sized hands pushed me toward my BMW, parked past the mailboxes. When I dug in my heels, he plucked me up and carried me. It was too easy to know why.

When night fell, the ground-glass shriek would waft down from the forest, and Point Pitt's new god would return.

Back in the arms of the city, I waited around for fate to come crashing down on my head with charges of murder and arson. Civilized accusations. No one came knocking.

Like I said earlier, this morning I sat and watched a cat disembowel a rail lizard. I watched much longer than I had to in order to get the point. Then my eyelids pushed down to allow swatches of stop-and-go sleep.

The nightmares of my past replaced those of the here and now.

A week after I'd turned thirteen, the school sadist at my junior high decreed that the day had come to pound every last speck of shit out of my rasty white body. Ross Delaney was the eldest son of a local garbageman—to be fair, he took a lot of socially maladjusting crap just for that. He was coasting through his third encore performance at the seventh-grade level. A seventh-grader who had a down mustache, drove his own jalopy to school, smoked, and hung out with peers destined for big things: aggravated assault, rape, grand theft auto. . .

Ross had made me loan him a pen once in study hall and he'd dismantled it after scrawling on the back of my shirt and laughing like I was the world's biggest a-hole. My buddy Blake and I had discovered a bunch of disposable hypodermic needles while scrounging for intriguing goodies in the trash dumpster of a health clinic, reasoning that it was against some law for them to throw out anything really *dangerous*, right? Those hypos made primo mini-squirt guns, and that's all Blake and I thought of using them for. They were tech, they were cool. They were enormously appealing to Ross, who threatened to put out my eye with a Lucky if I didn't give him one. Right before lunch, Ross was scooped up by Mr. Shanks, *El Principal* of the humorless specs and full-length gray plastic raincoat. Needles in school were serious business, and I soon found myself being paged for an interview. I denied everything. Ross's eyes, yellow-brown, settled on me like a pronouncement of execution by hanging.

He laid for me in the parking lot. There was no way around him. He loomed above me. I wanted to say something pacifying, babble that might exonerate us both as rebels cornered by an unfair system. Ross' brain lacked the logic links such a ploy needed to work. Trying to appease him had always been a pussy's game with an automatic loser. Guess who.

The next thing I knew, I was catching Ross' hand with my face.

My neckbones popped as my head snapped around, and my hand made the mistake of contracting into a fist. My left eye filled up with knuckles and stopped seeing. He snagged a handful of my hair and used his knee to loosen all the molars on the side of my head nearest the pavement. I bit tarmac and tasted blood. I curled up. He started kicking me with his Mexican pimp boots, shouting incoherently, his face totally glazed.

My deck was discarded, so I called for my mom. I honestly thought it was my moment to die, and so reverted to instant babyhood, bawling and dribbling and yowling for my mother. Ross' cohorts ate it up. What a queer, what a pussy, he wants he momma. Ross kicked again and I felt a lung try to jump out my throat. He yelled for me to shut up. Something cracked sharply inside me.

Then something *burst* inside me.

It wasn't my liver exploding. It was something slag-hot, bursting brightly outward, filling me, popping on full bore like sprinkler systems during a fire, or an airbag in a car crash. The only sensation I can compare it to is the time my cardiologist broke an ampule of amyl nitrate under my nose, to test my pump. Only my internal ampule was full of something more like PCP. I was flooded to the brim—wham! My fingertips tingled. Both hands locked into fists. I scared the crap out of myself; I think I yelped. Instead of stopping the tip of Ross' next incoming bonebreaker, I rolled out, stood up, and faced him.

Then I kicked the shit out of him, impossibly enough.

Hesitation scampered behind his eyes when he saw me get up. But there was no mystery in it for him. The medulla section of his primate mind saw an opportunity to stomp some serious ass and would not be denied. If I could stand, the massacre would just be more interesting. Ross roared and came in like a freight train. His fist was black and sooty and callused.

I snatched that meteor out of the air and diverted his momentum, planting my elbow in his mouth, then whip-cracking him into a one-eighty snap that left his gonads open to my foot. They decompressed with a squish and he hit the pavement on hands and knees. . .and then *I* was kicking *him*, blood flushing my face. Every bullshit, picayune adolescent injustice ever suffered now rushed home, and I went at Ross like a berserk wolverine spiked on crank. Ribs staved inward. Snot and blood lathered his chin.

And I felt *good*.

Mr. Shanks, the principal, yanked me off of Ross Delaney, school tyrant. He was too horrified by the damage he saw to wonder how I'd done it. I got my fine white ass suspended.

That school had been my introduction to life in the city. Since then, the city had treated me right. My apartment never got robbed; my car never got boosted. Degree. Master's. Wife. Promotion, Child. Success. Suzanne and Jilly had been excited by our move to Point Pitt; I had been the reluctant one.

Now my city had repudiated me. I'd come crawling back after giving it the finger, and the only thing it would show me was an ugly orange tabby tearing the intestines out of a lizard that wasn't dead all the way yet.

In its reptile eyes, the suffering as it was eaten.

I wanted to file a complaint. To protest that none of this was my fault. I didn't want to leave; they made me do it. That would be like trying to make nice to Ross Delaney. Too late for that.

I had spent the night in a parking lot and there was dry snot on my face, from crying. Returning to the city had not erased Suzanne or Jilly or poor old goddamn Brix. So much for the snapshot.

The BMW's motor caught on the third try. I noticed blood staining the walnut of the gearshift as I backed out of the alleyway.

I wanted my mommy. But she wasn't around this time, either. Not here.

The blackened garbage dump that, yesterday, had been my new home had cooled. If anyone had come out to investigate, they were gone now. Birds twittered in the forest, above all this folly.

Dunwoody finally spotted me and came out; I have to credit him for having that much iron left. He motioned me into his squalid little home and we sat drinking until the sun went down. I watched Ormly shamble about. Such a waste, there.

The shrieking I expected began to peal down from the woods after dusk. My hands quivered on the arms of Dunwoody's dusty easy chair. They had not stopped shaking since last night.

"You forgot your pumpgun," said Dunwoody. "Had Ormly fetch it. Only two loads innit though." He drained his schnapps glass and burped, half-in, half-out, a state he clearly wanted to maintain.

The clear liquor trickled into me like kerosene. I thought of it as fuel. I noticed the barrels of the shotgun were warm; that seemed odd, somehow.

Clutching the Remington, I left limping, favoring my gashed foot. Breathing was a chore. My eyes pulsed in time to the pounding of my metabolism as I picked my way to the center of my burned-out grave of a home. One end of the barbequed sofa jutted from the debris like the stern of a sinking ship. Here was the banister—fissured, carbonized, its stored heat energy bled free. Over here, smashed shards of terra cotta from Suzanne's conservatory. Skeletal junk, all exuding the reek of an overflowing ashtray. Soft clouds of soot puffed up with each step I took.

On the border of the feeder road, the streetlamp sputtered blue, then white, throwing tombstone shadows down from the row of mailboxes. The residents of Point Pitt had drawn their curtains. The houses on the hillside were dark against whatever might come in the night. Not secure. Just lacking light and any form of human sympathy.

Dunwoody was the exception. I saw his drawn face appear in a crack of drape, then zip away, then return. I'd lost my Cartier watch, so I used Dunwoody's periodic surveillance to mark time. I couldn't recall losing the watch, not that it mattered. Night vapors tingled the hair on my arms. My last bath had been yesterday afternoon, eons ago, and by now I was as aromatic as stale beef bouillon.

"Come on, come *on!*" I lashed out at a fire-ravaged plank and it crumbled into brittle charcoal cinders. My voice echoed back from the treeline twice.

Lava-colored eyes emerged to assess me from behind the still-standing brick chimney. Chatoyant pupils tossed back the street light in dual crosscut shapes.

A conventional defensive move would draw it out, confident of its own invincibility. I chambered a round as loudly as I could. "This is for you! Come on—it's what you want, right?"

Motion, hesitant, like Ross Delaney, unsure. There was a smear of bright bronze as the eyes darted to a new vantage.

"Come on, bag of shit!" Fuck reaction time. The gun went boom and a mean bite leapt out of the chimney. Pointed chunks of brick flew into the creature's face. It did not blink. The Remington's report settled debris all around.

I dropped the gun into the ashes.

Its outer tissue was pinkish, as though battened with blood from an earlier feed. The alien eyes blazed. When it saw me lose the shotgun, it decided, and in three huge bounds the distance between us was reduced to nothing. I saw it in mid-air, rippling, its thorny claws extruded from their cowls and coming for my face.

I braced myself, the memory of grabbing Ross Delaney's deadly fist still hot. I spoke softly to the woods, to the forest in the distance, to the sea behind me.

"Help me. Mother."

It smashed me down like a truck pasting an old lady in a crosswalk. The opaque talons sank to their moorings in my shoulder. I grabbed, to keep the jaws from my throat, and its fangs pierced the palm of my hand, one-two.

"Mother! Help me!"

I got my other hand up and seized its snout, which was feverishly hot. Stale blood-breath misted into my eyes and the black lips yawned wide for me. Those lips had caressed my daughter's face as they engulfed her. They had made an intimate, ghastly smorgasbord of Suzanne.

I clenched my fist. It tried to jerk its paw back to slash me into confetti, but the claws were trapped in my muscle tissue and would not slide free. The X-shaped eyes dimmed in surprise. It backpedaled, preparing to dig in with its hind legs and free my intestines.

I sat up with its movement, taking a firmer grip and twisting until its lower jaw came away in my hand. Think of halving a head of lettuce; that was the sound it made. Think of pulling a drumstick from a whole tom turkey. It jammed, then wrenched loose, dripping, trailing ruptured tatters of sinew.

It shrieked. Without a mouth, in pain.

Purple blood, thick and gelid, spurted into my face. Under the vapor lamp it looked like chocolate syrup; it stank of vomit or hydrochloric acid. The eyes went from golden to dead ochre, the color of dry leaves.

"You're done here," I rasped in its face. Still holding the snout, I punched my fist down the ruined wet maw of glottis. My fingers locked around something slick and throbbing and I tore it out. The body on top of me shuddered hideously and lost tension. The legs scrabbled, then went slack, pitching more feebly.

I stared fixedly into the eyes as their incandescence waned.

The residents of Point Pitt had come out at last, to watch. My new neighbors. They dotted the street, milling uncertainly, none daring closer than the mailboxes. They watched as their old god screeched and died. As with department-store mannequins, it had been so simple for them to be led, to be arranged.

What difference? That was ended now.

When I extracted the claws from my shoulder, my own blood jetted briefly out. I was still that human. Eyes cold, the limp and stinking carcass slid as I rose. Another shedding. A steel rail of an erection was trying to fight its way out of my pants.

They all stood, nothing more declarative. Silently they waited. The last to arrive were Dunwoody and Ormly, coming down the trail from their home. No one else moved to attack, or assist, or anything. It was not their place to.

Thank you. . .

Reflexively, the dead claws had folded in upon themselves. When I picked up the corpse, it crackled, still seeming to weigh too much for its mass. I remembered the awful sound its discarded skin had made. Purple goo dripped from the jawless mouth. The flat paws dangled harmlessly as I lifted the fatal wound to my lips and drank in long, soul-kiss draughts, quaffing with a passion almost primitive in its purity.

Thank you. Mother.

My communion raced through me to work its changes. My arm ceased bleeding and clotted up. I stopped shaking at last; all of me at once. My vision began to blur. Soon I would be able to see things imperceptible to normal, circular pupils.

I motioned to Ormly and he dutifully clumped forward. He had to be the first one. There was plenty for everybody, but Ormly had to be first.

Things evolve. Always have. Even in the country, things change when it's time. There was growth potential here.

Dunwoody nodded his old man's brand of approval. If I needed any indication that I was going to be benevolent, that was it.

THE SKIN TRADE

BY GEORGE R. R. MARTIN

And now we come to the centerpiece of the book. The full-tilt action fulcrum around which the rest of the stories spin, like pups encircling Daddy when he brings home the kill.

George R. R. Martin's "The Skin Trade" is the proverbial 800-pound werewolf in the room that everybody wants to talk about. Which is why it's a legend unto itself.

Like the Schow that precedes it, it's vintage blood-soaked '80s pulp that transcends itself at every turn, through sheer narrative propulsion and the skillfulness by which it's steered.

In ordinary hands, the genre tropes—police procedural, spooky mansion on the hill—could easily reduce this to run-of-the-mill fun. But in Martin's masterful grasp, we hit a Chandler-esque quintessence.

Which is to say: THIS is how this kind of story ought to be told. Beginners, take note.

So come for the werewolves. Stay for the things that even werewolves *are scared of.*

And feel free to let Hollywood know you're waiting.

Willie smelled the blood a block away from her apartment.

He hesitated and sniffed at the cool night air again. It was autumn, with the wind off the river and the smell of rain in the air, but the scent, *that* scent, was copper and spice and fire, unmistakable. He knew the smell of human blood.

A jogger bounced past, his orange sweats bright under the light of the full moon. Willie moved deeper into the shadows. What kind of fool ran at this hour of the night? *Asshole*, Willie thought, and the sentiment emerged in a low growl. The man looked around, startled. Willie crept back further into the foliage. After a long moment, the jogger continued up the bicycle path, moving a little faster now.

Taking a chance, Willie moved to the edge of the park, where he could stare down her street from the bushes. Two police cruisers were parked outside her building, lights flashing. What the hell had she gone and done?

When he heard the distant sirens and saw another set of lights approaching, flashing red and blue, Willie felt close to panic. The blood scent was heavy in the air, and set his skull to pounding. It was too much. He turned and ran deep into the park, for once not caring who might see him, anxious only to get away. He ran south, swift and silent, until he was panting for breath, his tongue lolling out of his mouth. He wasn't in shape for this kind of shit. He yearned for the safety of his own apartment, for his La-Z-Boy and a good shot of Primateen Mist.

Down near the riverfront, he finally came to a stop, wheezing and trembling, half-drunk with blood and fear. He crouched near a bridge abutment, staring at the headlights of passing cars and listening to the sound of traffic to soothe his ragged nerves.

Finally, when he was feeling a little stronger, he ran down a squirrel. The blood was hot and rich in his mouth, and the flesh made him feel ever so much stronger, but afterwards he got a hairball from all the goddamned fur.

"Willie," Randi Wade said suspiciously, "if this is just some crazy scheme to get into my pants, it's not going to work."

The small man studied his reflection in the antique oval mirror over her couch, tried out several faces until he found a wounded look he seemed to like, then turned back to let her see it. "You'd think that? You'd think that of *me?* I come to you, I need your help, and what do I get, cheap sexual innuendo. You ought to know me better than that, Wade, I mean, Jesus, how long we been friends?"

"Nearly as long as you've been trying to get into my pants," Randi said. "Face it, Flambeaux, you're a horny little bastard."

Willie deftly changed the subject. "It's very amateur hour, you know, doing business out of your apartment." He sat in one of her red velvet wingback chairs. "I mean, it's a nice place, don't get me wrong, I love this Victorian stuff, can't wait to see the bedroom, but isn't a private eye supposed to have a sleazy little office in the bad part of town? You know, frosted glass on the door, a bottle in the drawer, lots of dust on the filing cabinets. . ."

Randi smiled. "You know what they charge for those sleazy little offices in the bad part of town? I've got a phone machine, I'm listed in the Yellow Pages. . ."

"AAA-Wade Investigations," Willie said sourly. "How do you expect people to find you? Wade, it should be under W, if God had meant everybody to be listed under A, he wouldn't have invented all those other letters." He coughed. "I'm coming down with something," he complained, as if it were her fault. "Are you going to help me, or what?"

"Not until you tell me what this is all about," Randi said, but she'd already decided to do it. She liked Willie, and she owed him. He'd given her work when she needed it, with his friendship thrown into the bargain. Even his constant, futile attempts to jump her bones were somehow endearing, although she'd never admit it to Willie. "You want to hear about my rates?"

"Rates?" Willie sounded pained. "What about friendship? What about old times' sake? What about all the times I bought you lunch?"

"You never bought me lunch," Randi said accusingly.

"Is it my fault you kept turning me down?"

"Taking a bucket of Popeye's extra spicy to an adult motel for a snack and a quickie does not constitute a lunch invitation in my book," Randi said.

Willie had a long, morose face, with broad rubbery features capable of an astonishing variety of expressions. Right now he looked as though someone had just run over his puppy. "It would not have been a quickie," he said with vast wounded dignity. He coughed, and pushed himself back in the chair, looking oddly childlike against the red velvet cushions. "Randi," he said, his voice suddenly gone scared and weary, "this is for real."

She'd first met Willie Flambeaux when his collection agency had come after her for the unpaid bills left by her ex. She'd been out of work, broke, and desperate, and Willie had taken pity on her and given her work at the agency. As much as she'd hated hassling people for money, the job had been a godsend, and she'd stayed long enough to wipe out her debt. Willie's lopsided smile, endless propositions, and mordant intelligence had somehow kept her sane. They'd kept in touch, off and on, even after Randi had left the hounds of hell, as Willie liked to call the collection agency.

All that time, Randi had never heard him sound scared, not even when discoursing on the prospect of imminent death from one of his many grisly and undiagnosed maladies. She sat down on the couch. "Then I'm listening," she said. "What's the problem?"

"You see this morning's *Courier*?" he asked. "The woman that was murdered over on Parkway?"

"I glanced at it," Randi said.

"She was a friend of mine."

"Oh, Jesus." Suddenly Randi felt guilty for giving him a hard time. "Willie, I'm so sorry."

"She was just a kid," Willie said. "Twenty-three. You would have liked her. Lots of spunk. Bright too. She's been in a wheelchair since high school. The night of her senior prom, her date drank too much and got pissed when she wouldn't go all the way. On the way home he floored it and ran head-on into a semi. Really showed her. The boy was killed instantly. Joanie lived through it, but her spine was severed, she was paralyzed from the waist down. She never let it stop her. She went on to college and graduated with honors, had a good job."

"You knew her through all this?"

Willie shook his head. "Nah. Met her about a year ago. She'd been a little overenthusiastic with her credit cards, you know the tune. So I showed up on her doorstep one day, introduced her to Mr. Scissors, one thing led to another and we got to be friends. Like you and me, kind of." He looked up into her eyes. "The body was mutilated. Who'd do something like that? Bad enough to kill her, but. . ." Willie was beginning to wheeze. His asthma. He stopped, took a deep breath. "And what the fuck does it mean? *Mutilated*, Jesus, what a nasty word, but mutilated *how?* I mean, are we talking Jack the Ripper here?"

"I don't know. Does it matter?"

"It matters to me." He wet his lips. "I phoned the cops today, tried to get more details. It was a draw. I wouldn't tell them my name and they wouldn't give me any information. I tried the funeral home too. A closed casket wake, they say the body is going to be cremated. Sounds to me like something getting covered up."

"Like what?" she said.

Willie sighed. "You're going to think this is real weird, but what if. . ." He ran his fingers through his hair. He looked very agitated. "What if Joanie was. . .well, savaged. . .ripped up, maybe even. . .well, partially eaten. . .you know, like by. . .some kind of animal."

Willie was going on, but Randi was no longer listening.

A coldness settled over her. It was old and gray, full of fear, and suddenly she was twelve years old again, standing in the kitchen door listening to her mother make that sound, that terrible high thin wailing sound. The men were still trying to talk to her, to make her understand. . .*some kind of animal*, one of them said. Her mother didn't seem to hear or understand, but Randi did. She'd repeated the words aloud, and all the eyes had gone to her, and one of the cops had said, *Jesus, the kid*, and they'd all stared until her mother had finally gotten up and put her to bed. She began to weep uncontrollably as she tucked in the sheets. . .her mother, not Randi. Randi hadn't cried. Not then, not at the funeral, not ever in all the years since.

"Hey. Hey! Are you okay?" Willie was asking.

"I'm fine," she said sharply.

"Jesus, don't scare me like that, I got problems of my own, you know? You looked like. . .hell, I don't know what you looked like, but I wouldn't want to meet it in a dark alley."

Randi gave him a hard look. "The paper said Joan Sorenson was murdered. An animal attack isn't murder."

"Don't get legal on me, Wade. I don't know, I don't even know that an animal was involved, maybe I'm just nuts, paranoid, you name it. The paper left out the grisly details. The fucking paper left out a lot." Willie was breathing rapidly, twisting around in his chair, his fingers drumming on the arm.

"Willie, I'll do whatever I can, but the police are going to go all out on something like this, I don't know how much I'll be able to add."

"The police," he said in a morose tone. "I don't trust the police." He shook his head. "Randi, if the cops go through her things, my name will come up, you know, on her rolodex and stuff."

"So you're afraid you might be a suspect, is that it?"

"Hell, I don't know, maybe so."

"You have an alibi?"

Willie looked very unhappy. "No. Not really. I mean, not anything you could use in court. I was supposed to. . .to see her that night. Shit, I mean, she might have written my name on her fucking *calendar* for all I know. I just don't want them nosing around, you know?"

"Why not?"

He made a face. "Even us turnip-squeezers have our dirty little secrets. Hell, they might find all those nude photos of you." She didn't laugh. Willie shook his head. "I mean, god, you'd think the cops would have better things to do than go around solving murders—I haven't gotten a parking ticket in over a year. Makes you wonder what the hell this town is coming to." He had begun to wheeze again. "Now I'm getting too worked up again, damn it. It's you, Wade. I'll bet you're wearing crotchless panties under those jeans, right?" Glaring at her accusingly, Willie pulled a bottle of Primateen Mist from his coat pocket, stuck the plastic snout in his mouth, and gave himself a blast, sucking it down greedily.

"You must be feeling better," Randi said.

"When you said you'd do anything you could to help, did that include taking off all of your clothes?" Willie said hopefully.

"No," Randi said firmly. "But I'll take the case."

River Street was not exactly a prestige address, but Willie liked it just fine. The rich folks up on the bluffs had "river views" from the gables and widow's walks of their old Victorian houses, but Willie had the river itself flowing by just beneath his windows. He had the sound of it, night and day, the slap of water against the pilings, the foghorns when the mists grew thick, the shouts of pleasure-boaters on sunny afternoons. He had moonlight on the black water, and his very own rotting pier to sit on, any midnight when he had a taste for solitude. He had eleven rooms that used to be offices, a men's room (with urinal) *and* a ladies' room (with Tampax dispenser), hardwood floors, lovely old skylights, and if he ever got that loan, he was definitely going to put in a kitchen. He also had an abandoned brewery down on the ground floor, should he ever decide to make his own beer. The drafty red brick building had been built a hundred years ago, which was about how long the flats had been considered the bad part of town. These days what wasn't boarded up was industrial, so Willie didn't have many neighbors, and that was the best part of all.

Parking was no problem either. Willie had a monstrous lime-green Cadillac, all chrome and fins, that he left by the foot of the pier, two feet from his door. It took him five minutes to undo all his locks. Willie believed in locks, especially on River Street. The brewery was dark and quiet. He locked and bolted the doors behind him and trudged upstairs to his living quarters.

He was more scared than he'd let on to Randi. He'd been upset enough last night, when he'd caught the scent of blood and figured that Joanie had done something really dumb, but when he'd gotten the morning paper and read that she'd been the victim, that she'd been tortured and killed and mutilated. . .*mutilated*, dear god, what the hell did that *mean*, had one of the others. . .no, he couldn't even think about that, it made him sick.

His living room had been the president's office back when the brewery was a going concern. It fronted on the river, and Willie thought it was nicely furnished, all things considered. None of it matched, but that was all right. He'd picked it up piece by piece over the years, the new stuff usually straight repossession deals, the antiques taken in lieu of cash on hopeless and long-overdue debts. Willie nearly always managed to get *something*, even on the accounts that everyone else had written off as a dead loss. If it was something he liked, he paid off the client out of his own pocket, ten or twenty cents on the dollar, and kept the furniture. He got some great bargains that way.

He had just started to boil some water on his hotplate when the phone began to ring.

Willie turned and stared at it, frowning. He was almost afraid to answer. It could be the police. . .but it could be Randi or some other friend, something totally innocent. Grimacing, he went over and picked it up. "Hello."

"Good evening, William." Willie felt as though someone was running a cold finger up his spine. Jonathan Harmon's voice was rich and mellow; it gave him the creeps. "We've been trying to reach you."

I'll bet you have, Willie thought, but what he said was, "Yeah, well, I been out."

"You've heard about the crippled girl, of course."

"*Joan*," Willie said sharply. "Her name was Joan. Yeah, I heard. All I know is what I read in the paper."

"I own the paper," Jonathan reminded him. "William, some of us are getting together at Blackstone to talk. Zoe and Amy are here right now, and I'm expecting Michael any moment. Steven drove down to pick up Lawrence. He can swing by for you as well, if you're free."

"No," Willie blurted. "I may be cheap, but I'm never free." His laugh was edged with panic.

"William, your life may be at stake."

"Yeah, I'll bet, you sonofabitch. Is that a threat? Let me tell you, I wrote down everything I know, *everything*, and gave copies to a couple of friends of mine." He hadn't, but come to think of it, it sounded like a good idea. "If I wind up like Joanie, they'll make sure those letters get to the police, you hear me?"

He almost expected Jonathan to say, calmly, 'I *own* the police,' but there was only silence and static on the line, then a sigh. "I realize you're upset about Joan—"

"Shut the fuck up about Joanie," Willie interrupted. "You got no right to say jackshit about her, I know how you felt about her. You listen up good, Harmon, if it turns out that you or that twisted kid of yours had anything to do with what happened, I'm going to come up to Blackstone one night and kill you myself, see if I don't. She was a good kid, she. . .she. . ." Suddenly, for the first time since it had happened, his mind was full of her—her face, her laugh, the smell of her when she was hot and bothered, the graceful way her muscles moved when she ran beside him, the noises she made when their bodies joined together. They all came back to him, and Willie felt tears on his face. There was a tightness in his chest as if iron bands were closing around his lungs. Jonathan was saying something, but Willie slammed down the receiver without bothering to listen, then pulled the jack. His water was boiling merrily away on the hotplate. He fumbled in his pocket and gave himself a good belt of his inhaler, then stuck his head in the steam until he could breathe again. The tears dried up, but not the pain.

Afterwards he thought about the things he'd said, the threats he made, and he got so shaky that he went back downstairs to double-check all his locks.

Courier Square was far gone in decay. The big department stores had moved to suburban malls, the grandiose movie palaces had been chopped up into multi-screens and given over to porno, once-fashionable storefronts now housed palm readers and adult bookstores. If Randi had really wanted a seedy little office in the bad part of town, she could find one on Courier Square. What little vitality the Square had left came from the newspaper.

The Courier Building was a legacy of another time, when downtown was still the heart of the city and the newspaper its soul. Old Douglas Harmon, who'd liked to tell anyone who'd listen that he was cut from the same cloth as Hearst and Pulitzer, had always viewed journalism as something akin to a religious vocation, and the "gothic deco" edifice he built to house his newspaper looked like the result of some unfortunate mating between the Chrysler Building and some especially grotesque cathedral. Five decades of smog had blackened its granite facade and acid rain had eaten away at the wolfshead gargoyles that snarled down from its walls, but you could still set your watch by the monstrous old presses in the basement and a Harmon still looked down on the city from the publisher's office high atop the Iron Spire. It gave a certain sense of continuity to the square, and the city.

The black marble floors in the lobby were slick and wet when Randi came in out of the rain, wearing a Burberry raincoat a couple sizes too big for her, a souvenir of her final fight with her ex-husband. She'd paid for it, so she was damn well going to wear it. A security guard sat behind the big horseshoe-shaped reception desk, beneath a wall of clocks that once had given the time all over the world. Most were broken now, hands frozen into a chronological cacophony. The lobby was a gloomy place on a dark afternoon like this, full of drafts as cold as the guard's face. Randi took off her hat, shook out her hair, and gave him a nice smile. "I'm here to see Barry Schumacher."

"Editorial. Third floor." The guard barely gave her a glance before he went back to the bondage magazine spread across his lap. Randi grimaced and walked past, heels clicking against the marble.

The elevator was an open grillwork of black iron; it rattled and shook and took forever to deliver her to the city room on the third floor. She found Schumacher alone at his desk, smoking and staring out his window at the rain-slick streets. "Look at that," he said when Randi came up behind him. A streetwalker in a leather miniskirt was standing under the darkened marquee of the Castle. The rain had soaked her thin white blouse and plastered it to her breasts. "She might as well be topless," Barry said. "Right in front of the Castle too. First theater in the state to show *Gone with the Wind*, you know that? All the big movies used to open there." He grimaced, swung his chair around, ground out his cigarette. "Hell of a thing," he said.

"I cried when Bambi's mother died," Randi said.

"In the Castle?"

She nodded. "My father took me, but he didn't cry. I only saw him cry once, but that was later, much later, and it wasn't a movie that did it."

"Frank was a good man," Schumacher said dutifully. He was pushing retirement age, overweight and balding, but he still dressed impeccably, and Randi remembered a young dandy of a reporter who'd been quite a rake in his day. He'd been a regular in her father's Wednesday night poker game for years. He used to pretend that she was his girlfriend, that he was waiting for her to grow up so they could get married. It always made her giggle. But that had been a different Barry Schumacher; this one looked as if he hadn't laughed since Kennedy was president. "So what can I do for you?" he asked.

"You can tell me everything that got left out of the story on that Parkway murder," she said. She sat down across from him.

Barry hardly reacted. She hadn't seen him much since her father died; each time she did, he seemed grayer and more exhausted, like a man who'd been bled dry of passion, laughter, anger, everything. "What makes you think anything was left out?"

"My father was a cop, remember? I know how this city works. Sometimes the cops ask you to leave something out."

"They ask," Barry agreed. "Them asking and us doing, that's two different things. Once in a while we'll omit a key piece of evidence, to help them weed out fake confessions. You know the routine." He paused to light another cigarette.

"How about this time?"

Barry shrugged. "Hell of a thing. Ugly. But we printed it, didn't we?"

"Your story said the victim was mutilated. What does that mean, exactly?"

"We got a dictionary over by the copyeditor's desk, you want to look it up."

"I don't want to look it up," Randi said, a little too sharply. Barry was being an asshole; she hadn't expected that. "I know what the word means."

"So you are saying we should have printed all the juicy details?" Barry leaned back, took a long drag on his cigarette. "You know what Jack the Ripper did to his last victim? Among other things, he cut off her breasts. Sliced them up neat as you please, like he was carving white meat off a turkey, and piled the slices on top of each other, beside the bed. He was very tidy, put the nipples on top and everything." He exhaled smoke. "Is that the sort of detail you want? You know how many kids read the *Courier* every day?"

"I don't care what you print in the *Courier*," Randi said. "I just want to know the truth. Am I supposed to infer that Joan Sorenson's breasts were cut off?"

"I didn't say that," Schumacher said.

"No. You didn't say much of anything. Was she killed by some kind of animal?"

That did draw a reaction. Schumacher looked up, his eyes met hers, and for a moment she saw a hint of the friend he had been in those tired eyes behind their wire-rim glasses. "An animal?" he said softly. "Is that what you think? This isn't about Joan Sorenson at all, is it? This is about your father." Barry got up and came around his desk. He put his hands on her shoulders and looked into her eyes.

"Randi, honey, let go of it. I loved Frank too, but he's dead, he's been dead for. . . hell, it's almost twenty years now. The coroner said he got killed by some kind of rabid dog, and that's all there is to it."

"There was no trace of rabies, you know that as well as I do. My father emptied his gun. What kind of rabid dog takes six shots from a police .38 and keeps on coming, huh?"

"Maybe he missed," Barry said.

"He didn't miss!" Randi said sharply. She turned away from him. "We couldn't even have an open casket, too much of the body had been. . ." Even now, it was hard to say without gagging, but she was a big girl now and she forced it out. ". . .eaten," she finished softly. "No animal was ever found."

"Frank must have put some bullets in it, and after it killed him the damned thing crawled off somewhere and died," Barry said. His voice was not unkind. He turned her around to face him again. "Maybe that's how it was and maybe not. It was a hell of a thing, but it happened eighteen years ago, honey, and it's got nothing to do with Joan Sorenson."

"Then tell me what happened to her," Randi said.

"Look, I'm not supposed to. . ." He hesitated, and the tip of his tongue flicked nervously across his lips. "It was a knife," he said softly. "She was killed with a knife, it's all in the police report, just some psycho with a sharp knife." He sat down on the edge of his desk, and his voice took on its familiar cynicism again. "Some weirdo seen too many of those damn sick holiday movies, you know the sort, *Halloween*, *Friday the 13th*, they got one for every holiday."

"All right." She could tell from his tone that she wouldn't be getting any more out of him. "Thanks."

He nodded, not looking at her. "I don't know where these rumors come from. All we need, folks thinking there's some kind of wild animal running around, killing people." He patted her shoulder. "Don't be such a stranger, you hear? Come by for dinner some night. Adele is always asking about you."

"Give her my best." She paused at the door. "Barry. . ." He looked up, forced a smile. "When they found the body, there wasn't anything missing?"

He hesitated briefly. "No," he said.

Barry had always been the big loser at her father's poker games. He wasn't a bad player, she recalled her father saying, but his eyes gave him away when he tried to bluff. . .like they gave him away right now.

Barry Schumacher was lying.

The doorbell was broken, so he had to knock. No one answered, but Willie didn't buy that for a minute. "I know you're there, Mrs. Juddiker," he shouted through the window. "I could hear the TV a block off. You turned it off when you saw me coming up the walk. Gimme a break, okay?" He knocked again. "Open up, I'm not going away."

Inside, a child started to say something, and was quickly shushed. Willie sighed. He hated this. Why did they always put him through this? He took out a credit card, opened the door, and stepped into a darkened living room, half-expecting a scream. Instead he got shocked silence.

They were gaping at him, the woman and two kids. The shades had been pulled down and the curtains drawn. The woman wore a white terrycloth robe, and she looked even younger than she'd sounded on the phone. "You can't just walk in here," she said.

"I just did," Willie said. When he shut the door, the room was awfully dark. It made him nervous. "Mind if I put on a light?" She didn't say anything, so he did. The furniture was all ratty Salvation Army stuff, except for the gigantic big-screen projection TV in the far corner of the room. The oldest child, a little girl who looked about four, stood in front of it protectively. Willie smiled at her. She didn't smile back.

He turned back to her mother. She looked maybe twenty, maybe younger, dark, maybe ten pounds overweight but still pretty. She had a spray of brown freckles across the bridge of her nose. "Get yourself a chain for the door and use it," Willie told her. "And don't try the no-one's-home game on us hounds of hell, okay?" He sat down in a black vinyl recliner held together by electrical tape. "I'd love a drink. Coke, juice, milk, anything, it's been one of those days." No one moved, no one spoke. "Aw, come on," Willie said, "cut it out. I'm not going to make you sell the kids for medical experiments, I just want to talk about the money you owe, okay?"

"You're going to take the television," the mother said.

Willie glanced at the monstrosity and shuddered. "It's a year old and it weighs a million pounds. How'm I going to move something like that, with my bad back? I've got asthma too." He took the inhaler out of his pocket, showed it to her. "You want to kill me, making me take the damned TV would do the trick."

That seemed to help a little. "Bobby, get him a can of soda," the mother said. The boy ran off. She held the front of her robe closed as she sat down on the couch, and Willie could see that she wasn't wearing anything underneath. He wondered if she had freckles on her breasts too, sometimes they did. "I told you on the phone, we don't have no money. My husband run off. He was out of work anyway, ever since the pack shut down."

"I know," Willie said. The pack was short for meat-packing plant, which is what everyone liked to call the south side slaughterhouse that had been the city's largest employer until it shut it doors two years back. Willie took a notepad out of his pocket, flipped a few pages. "Okay, you bought the thing on time, made two payments, then moved, left no forwarding address. You still owe two-thousand-eight-hundred-sixteen dollars. And thirty-one cents. We'll forget the interest and late charges." Bobby returned and handed him a can of Diet Chocolate Ginger Beer. Willie repressed a shudder and cracked the pop top.

"Go play in the back yard," she said to the children. "Us grown-ups have to talk." She didn't sound very grown-up after they had left, however; Willie was half-afraid she was going to cry. He hated it when they cried. "It was Ed bought the set," she said, her voice trembling. "It wasn't his fault. The card came in the mail."

Willie knew that tune. A credit card comes in the mail, so the next day you run right out and buy the biggest item you can find. "Look, I can see you got plenty of troubles. You tell me where to find Ed, and I'll get the money out of him."

She laughed bitterly. "You don't know Ed. He used to lug around those big sides of beef at the pack, you ought to see the arms on him. You go bother him and he'll just rip your face off and shove it up your asshole, mister."

"What a lovely turn of phrase," Willie said. "I can't wait to make his acquaintance."

"You won't tell him it was me that told you where to find him?" she asked nervously.

"Scout's honor," Willie said. He raised his right hand in a gesture that he thought was vaguely Boy-Scoutish, although the can of Diet Chocolate Ginger Beer spoiled the effect a little.

"Were you a Scout?" she asked.

"No," he admitted. "But there was one troop that used to beat me up regularly when I was young."

That actually got a smile out of her. "It's your funeral. He's living with some slut now, I don't know where. But weekends he tends bar down at Squeaky's."

"I know the place."

"It's not real work," she added thoughtfully. "He don't report it or nothing. That way he still gets the unemployment. You think he ever sends anything over for the kids? No way!"

"How much you figure he owes you?" Willie said.

"Plenty," she said.

Willie got up. "Look, none of my business, but it is my business, if you know what I mean. You want, after I've talked to Ed about this television, I'll see what I can collect for you. Strictly professional, I mean, I'll take a little cut off the top, give the rest to you. It may not be much, but a little bit is better than nothing, right?"

She stared at him, astonished. "You'd do that?"

"Shit, yeah. Why not?" He took out his wallet, found a twenty. "Here," he said. "An advance payment. Ed will pay me back." She looked at him incredulously, but did not refuse the bill. Willie fumbled in the pocket of his coat. "I want you to meet someone," he said. He always carried a few cheap pairs of scissors in the pocket of his coat. He found one and put it in her hand. "Here, this is Mr. Scissors. From now on, he's your best friend."

She looked at him like he'd gone insane.

"Introduce Mr. Scissors to the next credit card that comes in the mail," Willie told her, "and then you won't have to deal with assholes like me."

He was opening the door when she caught up to him. "Hey, what did you say your name was?"

"Willie," he told her.

"I'm Betsy." She leaned forward to kiss him on the cheek, and the white robe opened just enough to give him a quick peek at her small breasts. Her chest was lightly freckled, her nipples wide and brown. She closed the robe tight again as she stepped back. "You're no asshole, Willie," she said as she closed the door.

He went down the walk feeling almost human, better than he'd felt since Joanie's death. His Caddy was waiting at the curb, the ragtop up to keep out the off-again on-again rain that had been following him around the city all morning. Willie got in and started her, then glanced into the rearview mirror just as the man in the back seat sat up.

The eyes in the mirror were pale blue. Sometimes, after the spring runoff was over and the river had settled back between its banks, you could find stagnant pools along the shore, backwaters cut off from the flow, foul-smelling places, still and cold, and you wondered how deep they were and whether there was anything living down there in that darkness. Those were the kind of eyes he had, deepset in a dark, hollow-cheeked face and framed by brown hair that fell long and straight to his shoulders.

Willie swiveled around to face him. "What the hell were you doing back there, catching forty winks? Hate to point this out, Steven, but this vehicle is actually one of the few things in the city that the Harmons do not own. Guess you got confused, huh? Or did you just mistake it for a bench in the park? Tell you what, no hard feelings, I'll drive you to the park, even buy you a newspaper to keep you warm while you finish your little nap."

"Jonathan wants to see you," Steven said, in that flat, chill tone of his. His voice, like his face, was still and dead.

"Yeah, good for him, but maybe I don't want to see Jonathan, you ever think of that?" He was dogmeat, Willie thought; he had to suppress the urge to bolt and run.

"Jonathan wants to see you," Steven repeated, as if Willie hadn't understood. He reached forward. A hand closed on Willie's shoulder. Steven had a woman's fingers, long and delicate, his skin pale and fine. But his palm was crisscrossed by burn scars that lay across the flesh like brands, and his fingertips were bloody and scabbed, the flesh red and raw. The fingers dug into Willie's shoulder with ferocious, inhuman strength. "Drive," he said, and Willie drove.

"I'm sorry," the police receptionist said. "The chief has a full calendar today. I can give you an appointment on Thursday."

"I don't want to see him on Thursday. I want to see him now." Randi hated the cophouse. It was always full of cops. As far as she was concerned, cops came in three flavors: those who saw an attractive woman they could hit on, those who saw a private investigator and resented her, and the old ones who saw Frank Wade's little girl and felt sorry for her. Types one and two annoyed her; the third kind really pissed her off.

The receptionist pressed her lips together, disapproving. "As I've explained, that simply isn't possible."

"Just tell him I'm here," Randi said. "He'll see me."

"He's with someone at the moment, and I'm quite sure that he doesn't want to be interrupted."

Randi had about had it. The day was pretty well shot, and she'd found out next to nothing. "Why don't I just see for myself?" she said sweetly. She walked briskly around the desk, and pushed through the waist-high wooden gate.

"You can't go in there!" the receptionist squeaked in outrage, but by then Randi was opening the door. Police Chief Joseph Urquhart sat behind an old wooden desk cluttered with files, talking to the coroner. Both of them looked up when the door opened. Urquhart was a tall, powerful man in his early sixties. His hair had thinned considerably, but what remained of it was still red, though his eyebrows had gone completely gray. "What the hell—" he started.

"Sorry to barge in, but Miss Congeniality wouldn't give me the time of day," Randi said as the receptionist came rushing up behind her.

"Young lady, this is the police department, and I'm going to throw you out on your ass," Urquhart said gruffly as he stood up and came around the desk, "unless you come over here right now and give your Uncle Joe a big hug."

Smiling, Randi crossed the bearskin rug, wrapped her arms around him, and laid her head against his chest as the chief tried to crush her. The door closed behind them, too loudly. Randi broke the embrace. "I miss you," she said.

"Sure you do," he said, in a faintly chiding tone. "That's why we see so much of you."

Joe Urquhart had been her father's partner for years, back when they were both in uniform. They'd been tight, and the Urquharts had been like an aunt and uncle to her. His older daughter had babysat for her, and Randi had returned the favor for the younger girl. After her father's death, Joe had looked out for them, helped her mother through the funeral and all the legalities, made sure the pension fund got Randi through college. Still, it hadn't been the same, and the families drifted apart, even more so after her mother had finally passed away. These days Randi saw him only once or twice a year, and felt guilty about it. "I'm sorry," she said. "You know I mean to keep in touch, but—"

"There's never enough time, is there?" he said.

The coroner cleared her throat. Sylvia Cooney was a local institution, a big brusque woman of indeterminate age, built like a cement mixer, her iron-gray hair tied in a tight bun at the back of her smooth, square face. She'd been coroner as long as Randi could remember. "Maybe I should excuse myself," she said.

Randi stopped her. "I need to ask you about Joan Sorenson. When will autopsy results be available?"

Cooney's eyes went quickly to the chief, then back to Randi. "Nothing I can tell you," she said. She left the office and closed the door with a soft click behind her.

"That hasn't been released to the public yet," Joe Urquhart said. He walked back behind his desk, gestured. "Sit down."

Randi settled into a seat, let her gaze wander around the office. One wall was covered by commendations, certificates, and framed photographs. She saw her father there with Joe, both of them looking so achingly young, two grinning kids in uniform standing in front of their black-and-white. A moose head was mounted above the photographs, peering down at her with its glassy eyes. More trophies hung from the other walls. "Do you still hunt?" she asked him.

"Not in years," Urquhart said. "No time. Your Dad used to kid me about it all the time. Always said that if I ever killed anyone on duty, I'd want the head stuffed and mounted. Then one day it happened, and the joke wasn't so funny anymore." He frowned. "What's your interest in Joan Sorenson?"

"Professional," Randi said.

"Little out of your line, isn't it?"

Randi shrugged. "I don't pick my cases."

"You're too good to waste your life snooping around motels," Urquhart said. It was a sore point between them. "It's not too late to join the force."

"No," Randi said. She didn't try to explain; she knew from past experience that there was no way to make him understand. "I went out to the precinct house this morning to look at the report on Sorenson. It's missing from the file; no one knows where it is. I got the names of the cops who were at the scene, but none of them had time to talk to me. Now I'm told the autopsy results aren't being made public either. You mind telling me what's going on?"

Joe glanced out the windows behind him. The panes were wet with rain. "This is a sensitive case," he said. "I don't want the media blowing this thing all out of proportion."

"I'm not the media," Randi said.

Urquhart swiveled back around. "You're not a cop either. That's your choice. Randi, I don't want you involved in this, do you hear?"

"I'm involved whether you like it or not," she said. She didn't give him time to argue. "How did Joan Sorenson die? Was it an animal attack?"

"No," he said. "It was not. And that's the last question I'm going to answer." He sighed. "Randi," he said, "I know how hard you got hit by Frank's death. It was pretty rough on me too, remember? He phoned me for back-up. I didn't get there in time. You think I'll ever forget that?" He shook his head. "Put it behind you. Stop imagining things."

"I'm not imagining anything," Randi snapped. "Most of the time I don't even think about it. This is different."

"Have it your way," Joe said. There was a small stack of files on the corner of the desk near Randi. Urquhart leaned forward and picked them up, tapped them against his blotter to straighten them. "I wish I could help you." He slid open a drawer, put the file folders away. Randi caught a glimpse of the name on the top folder: *Helander*. "I'm sorry," Joe was saying. He started to rise. "Now, if you'll excuse—"

"Are you just rereading the Helander file for old times' sake, or is there some connection to Sorenson?" Randi asked.

Urquhart sat back down. "Shit," he said.

"Or maybe I just imagined that was the name on the file."

Joe looked pained. "We have reason to think the Helander boy might be back in the city."

"Hardly a boy anymore," Randi said. "Roy Helander is three years older than me. You're looking at him for Sorenson?"

"We have to, with his history. The state released him two months ago, it turns out. The shrinks said he was cured." Urquhart made a face. "Maybe, maybe not. Anyway, he's just a name. We're looking at a hundred names."

"Where is he?"

"I wouldn't tell you if I knew. He's a bad piece of business, like the rest of his family. I don't like you getting mixed up with his sort, Randi. Your father wouldn't either."

Randi stood up. "My father's dead," she said, "and I'm a big girl now."

Willie parked the car where 13th Street dead-ended, at the foot of the bluffs. Blackstone sat high above the river, surrounded by a ten-foot high wrought iron fence with a view of forbidding spikes along its top. You could drive to the gatehouse easily enough, but you had to go all the way down Central, past downtown, then around on Grandview and Harmon Drive, up and down the hills and all along the bluffs where aging steamboat-gothic mansions stood like so many dowagers staring out over the flats and river beyond, remembering better days. It was a long, tiresome drive.

Back before the automobile, it had been even longer and more tiresome. Faced with having to travel to Courier Square on a daily basis, Douglas Harmon made things easy for himself. He built a private cable car: a two-car funicular railway that crept up the gray stone face of the bluffs from the foot of 13th below to Blackstone above.

Internal combustion, limousines, chauffeurs, and paved roads had all conspired to wean the Harmons away from Douglas's folly, making the cable car something of a back door in more recent years, but that suited Willie well enough. Jonathan Harmon always made him feel like he ought to come in by the servant's entrance anyway.

Willie climbed out of the Caddy and stuck his hands in the sagging pockets of his raincoat. He looked up. The incline was precipitous, the rock wet and dark. Steven took his elbow roughly and propelled him forward. The cable car was wooden, badly in need of a whitewash, with bench space for six. Steven pulled the bell cord; the car jerked as they began to ascend. The second car came down to meet them, and they crossed halfway up the bluff. The car shook and Willie spotted rust on the rails. Even here at the gate of Blackstone, things were falling apart.

Near the top of the bluff, they passed through a gap in the wrought iron fence, and the New House came into view, gabled and turreted and covered with Victorian gingerbread. The Harmons had lived there for almost a century, but it was still the New House, and always would be. Behind the house the estate was densely forested, the narrow driveway winding through thick stands of old growth. Where the other founding families had long ago sold off or parceled out their lands to developers, the Harmons had held tight, and Blackstone remained intact, a piece of the forest primeval in the middle of the city.

Against the western sky, Willie glimpsed the broken silhouette of the tower, part of the Old House whose soot-dark stone walls gave Blackstone its name. The house was set well back among the trees, its lawns and courts overgrown, but even when you couldn't see it you knew it was there somehow. The tower was a jagged black presence outlined against the red-stained gray of the western horizon, crooked and forbidding. It had been Douglas Harmon, the journalist and builder of funicular railways, who had erected the New House and closed the Old, immense and gloomy even by Victorian standards, but neither Douglas, his son Thomas, nor his grandson Jonathan had ever found the will to tear it down. Local legend said the Old House was haunted. Willie could just about believe it. Blackstone, like its owner, gave him the creeps.

The cable car shuddered to a stop, and they climbed out onto a wooden deck, its paint weathered and peeling. A pair of wide French doors led into the New House. Jonathan Harmon was waiting for them, leaning on a walking stick, his gaunt figure outlined by the light that spilled through the door. "Hello, William," he said. Harmon was barely past sixty, Willie knew, but long snow-white hair and a body wracked by arthritis made him look much older. "I'm so glad that you could join us," he said.

"Yeah, well, I was in the neighborhood, just thought I'd drop by," Willie said. "Only thing is, I just remembered, I left the windows open in the brewery. I better run home and close them, or my dust bunnies are going to get soaked."

"No," said Jonathan Harmon. "I don't think so."

Willie felt the bands constricting across his chest. He wheezed, found his inhaler, and took two long hits. He figured he'd need it. "Okay, you talked me into it, I'll stay," he told Harmon, "but I damn well better get a drink out of it. My mouth still tastes like Diet Chocolate Ginger Beer."

"Steven, be a good boy and get our friend William a snifter of Remy Martin, if you'd be so kind. I'll join him. The chill is on my bones." Steven, silent as ever, went inside to do as he was told. Willie made to follow, but Jonathan touched his arm lightly. "A moment," he said. He gestured. "Look."

Willie turned and looked. He wasn't quite so frightened anymore. If Jonathan wanted him dead, Steven would have tried already, and maybe succeeded. Steven was a dreadful mistake by his father's standards, but there was a freakish strength in those scarred hands. No, this was some other kind of deal.

They looked east over the city and the river. Dusk had begun to settle, and the streetlights were coming on down below, strings of luminescent pearls that spread out in all directions as far as the eye could see and leapt across the river on three great bridges. The clouds were gone to the east, and the horizon was a deep cobalt blue. The moon had begun to rise.

"There were no lights out there when the foundations of the Old House were dug," Jonathan Harmon said. "This was all wilderness. A wild river coursing through the forest primeval, and if you stood on high at dusk, it must have seemed as though the blackness went on forever. The water was pure, the air was clean, and the woods were thick with game. . .deer, beaver, bear. . .but no people, or at least no white men. John Harmon and his son James both wrote of seeing Indian campfires from the tower from time to time, but the tribes avoided this place, especially after John had begun to build the Old House."

"Maybe the Indians weren't so dumb after all," Willie said.

Jonathan glanced at Willie, and his mouth twitched. "We built this city out of nothing," he said. "Blood and iron built this city, blood and iron nurtured it and fed its people. The old families knew the power of the blood and iron, they knew how to make this city great. The Rochmonts hammered and shaped the metal in smithies and foundries and steel mills, the Anders family moved it on their flatboats and steamers and railroads, and your own people found it and pried it from the earth. You come from iron stock, William Flambeaux, but we Harmons were always blood. We had the stockyards and the slaughterhouse, but long before that, before this city or this nation existed, the Old House was a center of the skin trade. Trappers and hunters would come here every season with furs and skins and beaver pelts to sell the Harmons, and from here the skins would move downriver. On rafts, at first, and then flatboats. Steam came later, much later."

"Is there going to be a pop quiz on this?" Willie asked.

"We've fallen a long way," he said, looking pointedly at Willie. "We need to remember how we started. Black iron and red, red blood. You need to remember. Your grandfather had the Flambeaux blood, the old pure strain." Willie knew when he was being insulted. "And my mother was a Pankowski," he said, "which makes me half-frog, half-polack, and all mongrel. Not that I give a shit. I mean, it's terrific that my great-grandfather owned half the state, but the mines gave out around the turn of the century, the Depression took the rest, my father was a drunk, and I'm in collections, if that's okay with you." He was feeling pissed off and rash by then. "Did you have any particular reason for sending Steven to kidnap me, or was it just a yen to discuss the French and Indian War?"

Jonathan said, "Come. We'll be more comfortable inside, the wind is cold." The words were polite enough, but his tone had lost all faint trace of warmth. He led Willie inside, walking slowly, leaning heavily on the cane. "You must forgive me," he said. "It's the damp. It aggravates the arthritis, inflames my old war wounds." He looked back at Willie. "You were unconscionably rude to hang up on me. Granted, we have our differences, but simple respect for my position—"

"I been having a lot of trouble with my phone lately," Willie said. "Ever since they deregulated, service has turned to shit." Jonathan led him into a small sitting room. There was a fire burning in the hearth; the heat felt good after a long day tromping through the cold and the rain. The furnishings were antique, or maybe just old; Willie wasn't too clear on the difference.

Steven had preceded them. Two brandy snifters, half-full of amber liquid, sat on a low table. Steven squatted by the fire, his tall, lean body folded up like a jackknife. He looked up as they entered and stared at Willie a moment too long, as if he'd suddenly forgotten who he was or what he was doing there. Then his flat blue eyes went back to the fire, and he took no more notice of them or their conversation.

Willie looked around for the most comfortable chair and sat in it. The style reminded him of Randi Wade, but that just made him feel guilty. He picked up his cognac. Willie was couth enough to know that he was supposed to sip but cold and tired and pissed-off enough so that he didn't care. He emptied it in one long swallow, put it down on the floor, and relaxed back into the chair as the heat spread through his chest.

Jonathan, obviously in some pain, lowered himself carefully onto the edge of the couch, his hands closed round the head of his walking stick. Willie found himself staring, Jonathan noticed. "A wolf's head," he said. He moved his hands aside to give Willie a clear view. The firelight reflected off the rich yellow metal. The beast was snarling, snapping.

Its eyes were red. "Garnets?" Willie guessed.

Jonathan smiled the way you might smile at a particularly doltish child. "Rubies," he said, "set in 18 karat gold." His hands, large and heavily veined, twisted by arthritis, closed round the stick again, hiding the wolf from sight.

"Stupid," Willie said. "There's guys in this city would kill you as soon as look at you for a stick like that."

Jonathan's smile was humorless. "I will not die on account of gold, William." He glanced at the window. The moon was well above the horizon. "A good hunter's moon," he said. He looked back at Willie. "Last night you all but accused me of complicity in the death of the crippled girl." His voice was dangerously soft. "Why would you say such a thing?"

"I can't imagine," Willie said. He felt light-headed. The brandy had rushed right to his mouth. "Maybe the fact that you can't remember her name had something to do with it. Or maybe it was because you always hated Joanie, right from the moment you heard about her. My pathetic little mongrel bitch, I believe that was what you called her. Isn't it funny the way that little turns of phrase stick in the mind? I don't know, maybe it was just me, but somehow I got this impression that you didn't exactly wish me well. I haven't even mentioned Steven yet."

"Please don't," Jonathan said icily. "You've said quite enough. Look at me, William. Tell me what you see."

"You," said Willie. He wasn't in the mood for asshole games, but Jonathan Harmon did things at his own pace.

"An old man," Jonathan corrected. "Perhaps not so old in years alone, but old nonetheless. The arthritis grows worse every year, and there are days when the pain is so bad I can scarcely move. My family is all gone but for Steven, and Steven, let us be frank, is not all that I might have hoped for in a son." He spoke in firm, crisp tones, but Steven did not even look up from the flames. "I'm tired, William. It's true, I did not approve of your crippled girl, or even particularly of you. We live in a time of corruption and degeneracy, when the old truths of blood and iron have been forgotten. Nonetheless, however much I may have loathed your Joan Sorenson and what she represented, I had no taste of her blood. All I want is to live out my last years in peace."

Willie stood up. "Do me a favor and spare me the old sick man act. Yeah, I know all about your arthritis and your war wounds. I also know who you are and what you're capable of. Okay, you didn't kill Joanie. So who did? Him?" He jerked a thumb toward Steven.

"Steven was here with me."

"Maybe he was and maybe he wasn't," Willie said.

"Don't flatter yourself, Flambeaux, you're not important enough for me to lie to you. Even if your suspicion was correct, my son is not capable of such an act. Must I remind you that Steven is crippled as well, in his own way?"

Willie gave Steven a quick glance. "I remember once when I was just a kid, my father had to come see you, and he brought me along. I used to love to ride your little cable car. Him and you went inside to talk, but it was a nice day, so you let me play outside. I found Steven in the woods, playing with some poor sick mutt that had gotten past your fence. He was holding it down with his foot, and pulling off its legs, one by one, just ripping them out with his bare hands like a normal kid might pull petals off a flower. When I walked up behind him, he had two off and was working on the third. There was blood all over his face. He couldn't have been more than eight."

Jonathan Harmon sighed. "My son is. . .disturbed. We both know that, so there is no sense in my denying it. He is also dysfunctional, as you know full well. And whatever residual strength remains is controlled by his medication. He has not had a truly violent episode for years. Have you, Steven?"

Steven Harmon looked back at them. The silence went on too long as he stared, unblinking, at Willie. "No," he finally said.

Jonathan nodded with satisfaction, as if something had been settled. "So you see, William, you do us a great injustice. What you took for a threat was only an offer of protection. I was going to suggest that you move to one of our guest rooms for a time. I've made the same suggestion to Zoe and Amy."

Willie laughed. "I'll bet. Do I have to fuck Steven too, or is that just for the girls?"

Jonathan flushed, but kept his temper. His futile efforts to marry off Steven to one of the Anders sisters was a sore spot. "I regret to say they declined my offer. I hope you will not be so unwise. Blackstone has certain. . .protections. . .but I cannot vouch for your safety beyond these walls."

"Safety?" Willie said. "From what?"

"I do not know, but I can tell you this—in the dark of night, there are things that hunt the hunters."

"Things that hunt the hunters," Willie repeated. "That's good, has a nice beat, but can you dance to it?" He'd had enough. He started for the door. "Thanks but no thanks. I'll take my chances behind my own walls." Steven made no move to stop him.

Jonathan Harmon leaned more heavily on his cane. "I can tell you how she was really killed," he said quietly.

Willie stopped and stared into the old man's eyes. Then he sat back down.

It was on the south side in a neighborhood that made the flats look classy, on an elbow of land between the river and that old canal that ran past the pack. Algae and raw sewage choked the canal and gave off a smell that drifted for blocks. The houses were single-story clapboard affairs, hardly more than shacks. Randi hadn't been down here since the pack had closed its doors. Every third house had a sign on the lawn, flapping forlornly in the wind, advertising a property for sale or for rent, and at least half of those were dark. Weeds grew waist-high around the weathered rural mailboxes, and they saw at least two burned-out lots.

Years had passed, and Randi didn't remember the number, but it was the last house on the left, she knew, next to a Sinclair station on the corner. The cabbie cruised until they found it. The gas station was boarded up, even the pumps were gone, but the house stood there much as she recalled. It had a For Rent sign on the lawn, but she saw a light moving around inside. A flashlight, maybe? It was gone before she could be sure.

The cabbie offered to wait. "No," she said. "I don't know how long I'll be." After he was gone, she stood on the barren lawn for a long time, staring at the front door, before she finally went up the walk.

She'd decided not to knock, but the door opened as she was reaching for the knob. "Can I help you, miss?"

He loomed over her, a big man, thick-bodied but muscular. His face was unfamiliar, but he was no Helander. They'd been a short, wiry family, all with the same limp, dirty blonde hair. This one had hair black as wrought iron, and shaggier than the department usually liked. Five o'clock shadow gave his jaw a distinct blue-black cast. His hands were large, with short blunt fingers. Everything about him said cop.

"I was looking for the people who used to live here."

"The family moved away when the pack closed," he told her. "Why don't you come inside?" He opened the door wider. Randi saw bare floors, dust, and his partner, a beer-bellied black man standing by the door to the kitchen.

"I don't think so," she said.

"I insist," he replied. He showed her a gold badge pinned to the inside of his cheap gray suit.

"Does that mean I'm under arrest?"

He looked taken aback. "No. Of course not. We'd just like to ask you a few questions." He tried to sound friendlier. "I'm Rogoff."

"Homicide," she said.

His eyes narrowed. "How—?"

"You're in charge of the Sorenson investigation," she said. She'd been given his name at the cophouse that morning. "You must not have much of a case if you've got nothing better to do than hang around here waiting for Roy Helander to show."

"We were just leaving. Thought maybe he'd get nostalgic, hole up at the old house, but there's no sign of it." He looked at her hard and frowned. "Mind telling me your name?"

"Why?" she asked. "Is this a bust or a come-on?"

He smiled. "I haven't decided yet."

"I'm Randi Wade." She showed him her license.

"Private detective," he said, his tone carefully neutral. He handed the license back to her. "You working?"

She nodded.

"Interesting. I don't suppose you'd care to tell me the name of your client."

"No."

"I could haul you into court, make you tell the judge. You can get that license lifted, you know. Obstructing an ongoing police investigation, withholding evidence."

"Professional privilege," she said.

Rogoff shook his head. "PIs don't have privilege. Not in this state."

"This one does," Randi said. "Attorney-client relationship. I've got a law degree too." She smiled at him sweetly. "Leave my client out of it. I know a few interesting things about Roy Helander I might be willing to share."

Rogoff digested that. "I'm listening."

Randi shook her head. "Not here. You know the automat on Courier Square?" He nodded. "Eight o'clock," she told him. "Come alone. Bring a copy of the coroner's report on Sorenson."

"Most girls want candy or flowers," he said.

"The coroner's report," she repeated firmly. "They still keep the old case records downtown?"

"Yeah," he said. "Basement of the courthouse."

"Good. You can stop by and do a little remedial reading on the way. It was eighteen years ago. Some kids had been turning up missing. One of them was Roy's little sister. There were others—Stanski, Jones, I forget all the names. A cop named Frank Wade was in charge of the investigation. A gold badge, like you. He died."

"You saying there's a connection?"

"You're the cop. You decide." She left him standing in the doorway and walked briskly down the block.

Steven didn't bother to see him down to the foot of the bluffs. Willie rode the little funicular railway alone, morose and lost in thought. His joints ached like nobody's business and his nose was running. Every time he got upset his body fell to pieces, and Jonathan Harmon had certainly upset him. That was probably better than killing him, which he'd half expected when he found Steven in his car, but still. . .

He was driving home along 13th Street when he saw the bar's neon sign on his right. Without thinking, he pulled over and parked. Maybe Harmon was right and maybe Harmon had his ass screwed on backwards, but in any case Willie still had to make a living. He locked up the Caddy and went inside.

It was a slow Tuesday night, and Squeaky's was empty. It was a workingman's tavern. Two pool tables, a shuffleboard machine in back, booths along one wall. Willie took a bar stool. The bartender was an old guy, hard and dry as a stick of wood. He looked mean. Willie considered ordering a banana daiquiri, just to see what the guy would say, but one look at that sour, twisted old face cured the impulse, and he asked for a boilermaker instead. "Ed working tonight?" he asked when the bartender brought the drinks.

"Only works weekends," the man said, "but he comes in most nights, plays a little pool."

"I'll wait," Willie said. The shot made his eyes water. He chased it down with a gulp of beer. He saw a pay phone back by the men's room. When the bartender gave him his change, he walked back, put in a quarter, and dialed Randi. She wasn't home; he got her damned machine. Willie hated phone machines. They'd made life a hell of a lot more difficult for collection agents, that was for sure. He waited for the tone, left Randi an obscene message, and hung up.

The men's room had a condom dispenser mounted over the urinals. Willie read the instructions as he took a leak. The condoms were intended for prevention of disease only, of course, even though the one dispensed by the left-hand slot was a French tickler. Maybe he ought to install one of these at home, he thought. He zipped up, flushed, washed his hands.

When he walked back out into the taproom, two new customers stood over the pool table, chalking up cues. Willie looked at the bartender, who nodded. "One of you Ed Juddiker?" Willie asked.

Ed wasn't the biggest—his buddy was as large and pale as Moby Dick—but he was big enough, with a real stupid-mean look on his face. "Yeah?"

"We need to talk about some money you owe." Willie offered him one of his cards.

Ed looked at the hand, but made no effort to take the card. He laughed. "Get lost," he said. He turned back to the pool table. Moby Dick racked up the balls and Ed broke.

That was all right, if that was the way he wanted to play it. Willie sat back on the bar stool and ordered another beer. He'd get his money one way or the other. Sooner or later Ed would have to leave, and then it would be his turn.

Willie still wasn't answering his phone. Randi hung up the pay phone and frowned. He didn't have an answering machine either, not Willie Flambeaux, that would be too sensible. She knew she shouldn't worry. The hounds of hell don't punch time-clocks, as he'd told her more than once. He was probably out running down some deadbeat. She'd try again when she got home. If he still didn't answer, they she'd start to worry.

The automat was almost empty. Her heels made hollow clicks on the old linoleum as she walked back to her booth and sat down. Her coffee had gone cold. She looked idly out the window. The digital clock on the State National Bank said 8:13. Randi decided to give him ten more minutes.

The red vinyl of the booth was old and cracking, but she felt strangely comfortable here, sipping her cold coffee and staring off at the Iron Spire across the square. The automat had been her favorite restaurant when she was a little girl.

Every year on her birthday she would demand a movie at the Castle and dinner at the automat, and every year her father would laugh and oblige. She loved to put the nickels in the coin slots and make the windows pop open, and fill her father's cup out of the old brass coffee machine with all its knobs and levers.

Sometimes you could see disembodied hands through the glass, sticking a sandwich or a piece of pie into one of the slots, like something from an old horror movie. You never saw any people working at the automat, just hands; the hands of people who hadn't paid their bills, her father once told her, teasing. That gave her the shivers, but somehow made her annual visits even more delicious, in a creepy kind of way. The truth, when she learned it, was much less interesting. Of course, that was true of most everything in life.

These days, the automat was always empty, which made Randi wonder how the floor could possibly stay so filthy, and you had to put quarters into the coin slots beside the little windows instead of nickels. But the banana cream pie was still the best she'd ever had, and the coffee that came out of those worn brass spigots was better than anything she'd ever brewed at home.

She was thinking of getting a fresh cup when the door opened and Rogoff finally came in out of the rain. He wore a heavy wool coat. His hair was wet. Randi looked out at the clock as he approached the booth. It said 8:17. "You're late," she said.

"I'm a slow reader," he said. He excused himself and went to get some food. Randi watched him as he fed dollar bills into the change machine. He wasn't bad-looking if you liked the type, she decided, but the type was definitely cop.

Rogoff returned with a cup of coffee, the hot beef sandwich with mashed potatoes, gravy, and overcooked carrots, and a big slice of apple pie.

"The banana cream is better," Randi told him as he slid in opposite her.

"I like apple," he said, shaking out a paper napkin.

"Did you bring the coroner's report?"

"In my pocket." He started cutting up the sandwich. He was very methodical, slicing the whole thing into small bite-sized portions before he took his first taste. "I'm sorry about your father."

"So was I. It was a long time ago. Can I see the report?"

"Maybe. Tell me something I don't already know about Roy Helander."

Randi sat back. "We were kids together. He was older, but he'd been left back a couple of times, till he wound up in my class. He was a bad kid from the wrong side of the tracks and I was a cop's daughter, so we didn't have much in common. . . until his little sister disappeared."

"He was with her," Rogoff said.

"Yes, he was. No one disputed that, least of all Roy. He was fifteen, she was eight. They were walking the tracks. They were off together, and Roy came back alone. He had blood on his dungarees and all over his hands. His sister's blood."

Rogoff nodded. "All that's in the file. They found blood on the tracks too."

"Three kids had already vanished. Jessie Helander made four. The way most people looked at it, Roy had always been a little strange. He was solitary, inarticulate, used to hook school and run off to some secret hideout he had in the woods. He liked to play with the younger kids instead of boys his own age. A degenerate from a bad family, a child molester who had actually raped and killed his own sister, that was what they said. They gave him all kinds of tests, decided he was deeply disturbed, and sent him away to some kiddie snakepit. He was still a juvenile, after all. Case closed, and the city breathed easier."

"If you don't have any more than that, the coroner's report stays in my pocket," Rogoff said.

"Roy said he didn't do it. He cried and screamed a lot, and his story wasn't coherent, but he stuck to it. He said he was walking along ten feet or so behind his sister, balancing on the rails and listening for a train, when a monster came out of a drainage culvert and attacked her."

"A monster," Rogoff said.

"Some kind of big shaggy dog, that was what Roy said. "He was describing a wolf. Everybody knew it."

"There hasn't been a wolf in this part of the country for over a century."

"He described how Jessie screamed as the thing began to rip her apart. He said he grabbed her leg, tried to pull her out of its jaws, which would explain why he had her blood all over him. The wolf turned and looked at him and howled. It had red eyes, burning red eyes, Roy said, and he was real scared, so he let go. By then Jessie was almost certainly dead. It gave him one last snarl and ran off, carrying the body in its jaws." Randi paused, took a sip of coffee. "That was his story. He told it over and over, to his mother, the police, the psychologists, the judge, everyone. No one ever believed him."

"Not even you?"

"Not even me. We all whispered about Roy in school, about what he'd done to his sister and those other kids. We couldn't quite imagine it, but we knew it had to be horrible. The only thing was, my father never quite bought it."

"Why not?"

She shrugged. "Instincts, maybe. He was always talking about how a cop had to go with his instincts. It was his case, he'd spent more time with Roy than anyone else, and something about the way the boy told the story had affected him. But it was nothing that could be proved. The evidence was overwhelming. So Roy was locked up." She watched his eyes as she told him. "A month later, Eileen Stanski vanished. She was six."

Rogoff paused with a forkful of the mashed potatoes, and studied her thoughtfully. "Inconvenient," he said.

"Dad wanted Roy released, but no one supported him. The official line was that the Stanski girl was unconnected to the others. Roy had done four, and some other child molester had done the fifth."

"It's possible."

"It's bullshit," Randi said. "Dad knew it and he said it. That didn't make him any friends in the department, but he didn't care. He could be a very stubborn man. You read the file on his death?"

Rogoff nodded. He looked uncomfortable.

"My father was savaged by an animal. A dog, the coroner said. If you want to believe that, go ahead." This was the hard part. She'd picked at it like an old scab for years, and then she'd tried to forget it, but nothing ever made it easier. "He got a phone call in the middle of the night, some kind of lead about the missing kids. Before he left he phoned Joe Urquhart to ask for back-up."

"Chief Urquhart?"

Randi nodded. "He wasn't chief then. Joe had been his partner when he was still in uniform. He said Dad told him he had a hot tip, but not the details, not even the name of the caller."

"Maybe he didn't know the name."

"He knew. My father wasn't the kind of cop who goes off alone in the middle of the night on an anonymous tip. He drove down to the stockyards by himself. It was waiting for him there. Whatever it was took six rounds and kept coming. It tore out his throat and after he was dead it ate him. What was left by the time Urquhart got there. . .Joe testified that when he first found the body he wasn't even sure it was human."

She told the story in a cool, steady voice, but her stomach was churning. When she finished Rogoff was staring at her. He set down his fork and pushed his plate away. "Suddenly I'm not very hungry anymore."

Randi's smile was humorless. "I love our local press. There was a case a few years ago when a woman was kidnapped by a gang, held for two weeks. She was beaten, tortured, sodomized, raped hundreds of times. When the story broke, the paper said she'd been quote *assaulted* unquote. It said my father's body had been mutilated. It said the same thing about Joan Sorenson. I've been told her body was intact." She leaned forward, looked hard into his dark brown eyes. "That's a lie."

"Yes," he admitted. He took a sheet of paper from his breast pocket, unfolded it, passed it across to her. "But it's not the way you think."

Randi snatched the coroner's report from his hand, and scanned quickly down the page. The words blurred, refused to register. It wasn't adding up the way it was supposed to.

Cause of death: exsanguination.

Somewhere far away, Rogoff was talking. "It's a security building, her apartment's on the fourteenth floor. No balconies, no fire escapes, and the doorman didn't see a thing. The door was locked. It was a cheap spring lock, easy to jimmy, but there was no sign of forced entry."

The instrument of death was a blade at least twelve inches long, extremely sharp, slender and flexible, perhaps a surgical instrument.

"Her clothing was all over the apartment, just ripped to hell, in tatters. In her condition, you wouldn't think she'd put up much of a struggle, but it looks like she did. None of the neighbors heard anything, of course. The killer chained her to her bed, naked, and went to work. He worked fast, knew what he was doing, but it still must have taken her a long time to die. The bed was soaked with her blood, through the sheets and mattress, right down to the box spring."

Randi looked back up at him, and the coroner's report slid from her fingers onto the formica table. Rogoff reached over and took her hand.

"Joan Sorenson wasn't devoured by any animal, Miss Wade. She was flayed alive, and left to bleed to death. And the part of her that's missing is her skin."

It was a quarter past midnight when Willie got home. He parked the Caddy by the pier. Ed Juddiker's wallet was on the seat beside him. Willie opened it, took out the money, counted. Seventy-nine bucks. Not much, but it was a start. He'd give half to Betsy this first time, credit the rest to Ed's account. Willie pocketed the money and locked the empty wallet in the glovebox. Ed might need the driver's license. He'd bring it by Squeaky's over the weekend, when Ed was on, and talk to him about a payment schedule.

Willie locked up the car and trudged wearily across the rain-slick cobbles to his front door. The sky above the river was dark and starless. The moon was up by now, he knew, hidden somewhere behind those black cotton clouds. He fumbled for his keys, buried down under his inhaler, his pillbox, a half-dozen pairs of scissors, a handkerchief, and the miscellaneous other junk that made his coat pocket sag. After a long minute, he tried his pants pocket, found them, and started in on his locks. He slid the first key into his double deadbolt.

The door opened slowly, silently.

The pale yellow light from a streetlamp filtered through the brewery's high, dusty windows, patterning the floor with faint squares and twisted lines. The hulks of rusting machines crouched in the dimness like great dark beasts. Willie stood in the doorway, keys in hand, his heart pounding like a triphammer. He put the keys in his pocket, found his Primateen, took a hit. The hiss of the inhaler seemed obscenely loud in the stillness.

He thought of Joanie, of what happened to her.

He could run, he thought. The Cadillac was only a few feet behind him, just a few steps, whatever was waiting in there couldn't possibly be fast enough to get him before he reached the car. Yeah, hit the road, drive all night, he had enough gas to make Chicago, it wouldn't follow him there. Willie took the first step back, then stopped, and giggled nervously. He had a sudden picture of himself sitting behind the wheel of his big lime-green chromeboat, grinding the ignition, grinding and grinding and flooding the engine as something dark and terrible emerged from inside the brewery and crossed the cobblestones behind him. That was silly, it was only in bad horror movies that the ignition didn't turn over, wasn't it? Wasn't it?

Maybe he had just forgotten to lock up when he'd left for work that morning. He'd had a lot on his mind, a full day's work ahead of him and a night of bad dreams behind, maybe he'd just closed the fucking door behind him and forgotten about his locks.

He never forgot about his locks.

But maybe he had, just this once.

Willie thought about changing. Then he remembered Joanie, and put the thought aside. He stood on one leg, pulled off his shoe. Then the other. Water soaked through his socks. He edged forward, took a deep breath, moved into the darkened brewery as silently as he could, pulling the door shut behind him. Nothing moved. Willie reached down into his pocket, pulled out Mr. Scissors. It wasn't much, but it was better than bare hands. Hugging the thick shadows along the wall, he crossed the room and began to creep upstairs on stockinged feet.

The streetlight shone through the window at the end of the hall. Willie paused on the steps when his head came up to the level of the second-story landing. He could look up and down the hallway. All the office doors were shut. No light leaking underneath or through the frosted-glass transoms. Whatever waited for him waited in darkness.

He could feel his chest constricting again. In another moment he'd need his inhaler. Suddenly he just wanted to get it over with. He climbed the final steps and crossed the hall in two long strides, threw open the door to his living room, and slammed on the lights.

Randi Wade was sitting in his beanbag chair. She looked up blinking as he hit the lights. "You startled me," she said.

"I startled *you!*" Willie crossed the room and collapsed into his La-Z-Boy. The scissors fell from his sweaty palm and bounced on the hardwood floor. "Jesus H. Christ on a crutch, you almost made me lose control of my personal hygiene. What the hell are you doing here? Did I forget to lock the door?"

Randi smiled. "You locked the door and you locked the door and then you locked the door some more. You're world class when it comes to locking doors, Flambeaux. It took me twenty minutes to get in."

Willie massaged his throbbing temples. "Yeah, well, with all the women who want this body, I got to have some protection, don't I?" He noticed his wet socks, pulled one off, grimaced. "Look at this," he said. "My shoes are out in the street getting rained on, and my feet are soaking. If I get pneumonia, you get the doctor bills, Wade. You could have waited."

"It was raining," she pointed out. "You wouldn't have wanted me to wait in the rain, Willie. It would have pissed me off, and I'm in a foul mood already."

Something in her voice made Willie stop rubbing his toes to look up at her. The rain had plastered loose strands of light brown hair across her forehead, and her eyes were grim. "You look like a mess," he admitted.

"I tried to make myself presentable, but the mirror in your ladies' room is missing."

"It broke. There's one in the men's room."

"I'm not that kind of girl," Randi said. Her voice was hard and flat. "Willie, your friend Joan wasn't killed by an animal. She was flayed. The killer took her skin."

"I know," Willie said, without thinking.

Her eyes narrowed. They were gray-green, large and pretty, but right now they looked as cold as marbles. "You *know?*" she echoed. Her voice had gone very soft, almost to a whisper, and Willie knew he was in trouble. "You give me some bullshit story and send me running all around town, and you *know? Do you know what happened to my father too, is that it? It was just your clever little way of getting my attention?"

Willie gaped at her. His second sock was in his hand. He let it drop to the floor. "Hey, Randi, gimme a break, okay? It wasn't like that at all. I just found out a few hours ago, honest. How could I know? I wasn't there, it wasn't in the paper." He was feeling confused and guilty. "What the hell am I supposed to know about your father? I don't know jackshit about your father. All the time you worked for me, you mentioned your family maybe twice."

Her eyes searched his face for signs of deception. Willie tried to give his warmest, most trustworthy smile. Randi grimaced. "Stop it," she said wearily. "You look like a used car salesman. All right, you didn't know about my father. I'm sorry. I'm a little wrought up right now, and I thought. . ." She paused thoughtfully. "Who told you about Sorenson?"

Willie hesitated. "I can't tell you," he said. "I wish I could, I really do. I can't. You wouldn't believe me anyway." Randi looked very unhappy. Willie kept talking. "Did you find out whether I'm a suspect? The police haven't called."

"They've probably been calling all day. By now they may have an APB out on you. If you won't get a machine, you ought to try coming home occasionally." She frowned. "I talked to Rogoff from Homicide." Willie's heart stopped, but she saw the look on his face and held up a hand. "No, your name wasn't mentioned. By either of us. They'll be calling everyone who knew her, probably, but it's just routine questioning. I don't think they'll be singling you out."

"Good," Willie said. "Well, look, I owe you one, but there's no reason for you to go on with this. I know it's not paying the rent, so—"

"So what?" Randi was looking at him suspiciously. "Are you trying to get rid of me now? After you got me involved in the first place?" She frowned. "Are you holding out on me?"

"I think you've got that reversed," Willie said lightly. Maybe he could joke his way out of it. "You're the one who gets bent out of shape whenever I offer to help you shop for lingerie."

"Cut the shit," Randi said sharply. She was not amused in the least, he could see that. "We're talking about the torture and murder of a girl who was supposed to be a friend of yours. Or has that slipped your mind somehow?"

"No," he said, abashed. Willie was very uncomfortable. He got up and crossed the room, plugged in the hotplate. "Hey, listen, you want a cup of tea? I got Earl Grey, Red Zinger, Morning Thunder—"

"The police think they have a suspect," Randi said.

Willie turned to look at her. "Who?"

"Roy Helander," Randi said.

"Oh, boy," Willie said. He'd been a PFC in Hamburg when the Helander thing went down, but he'd had a subscription to the *Courier* to keep up on the old hometown, and the headlines had made him ill. "Are you sure?"

"No," she said. "They're just rounding up the usual suspects. Roy was a great scapegoat last time, why not use him again? First they have to find him, though. No one's really sure that he's still in the state, let alone the city."

Willie turned away, busied himself with hotplate and kettle. All of a sudden he found it difficult to look Randi in the eye. "You don't think Helander was the one who grabbed those kids."

"Including his own sister? Hell no. Jessie was the last person he'd ever have hurt, she actually *liked* him. Not to mention that he was safely locked away when number five disappeared. I knew Roy Helander. He had bad teeth and he didn't bathe often enough, but that doesn't make him a child molester. He hung out with younger kids because the older ones made fun of him. I don't think he had any friends. He had some kind of secret place in the woods where he'd go to hide when things got too rough, he—"

She stopped suddenly, and Willie turned toward her, a teabag dangling from his fingers. "You thinking what I'm thinking?"

The kettle began to scream.

Randi tossed and turned for over an hour after she got home, but there was no way she could sleep. Every time she closed her eyes she would see her father's face, or imagine poor Joan Sorenson, tied to that bed as the killer came closer, knife in hand. She kept coming back to Roy Helander, to Roy Helander and his secret refuge. In her mind, Roy was still the gawky adolescent she remembered, his blonde hair lank and unwashed, his eyes frightened and confused as they made him tell the story over and over again. She wondered what had become of that secret place of his during all the years he'd been locked up and drugged in the state mental home, and she wondered if maybe sometimes he hadn't dreamt of it as he lay there in his cell. She thought maybe he had. If Roy Helander had indeed come home, Randi figured she knew just where he was.

Knowing about it and finding it were two different things, however. She and Willie had kicked it around without narrowing it down any. Randi tried to remember but it had been so long ago, a whispered conversation in the schoolyard. A secret place in the woods, he'd said, a place where no one ever came that was his and his alone, hidden and full of magic. That could be anything, a cave by the river, a treehouse, even something as simple as a cardboard lean-to. But where were these woods? Outside the city were suburbs and industrial parks and farms, the nearest state forest was forty miles north along the river road. If this secret place was in one of the city parks, you'd think someone would have stumbled on it years ago. Without more to go on, Randi didn't have a prayer of finding it. But her mind worried it like a pit bull with a small child.

Finally her digital alarm clock read 2:13, and Randi gave up on sleep altogether. She got out of bed, turned on the light, and went back to the kitchen. The refrigerator was pretty dismal, but she found a couple of bottles of Pabst. Maybe a beer would help put her to sleep. She opened a bottle and carried it back to bed.

Her bedroom furnishings were a hodge-podge. The carpet was a remnant, the blonde chest-of-drawers was boring and functional, and the four-poster queen-sized bed was a replica, but she did own a few genuine antiques—the massive oak wardrobe, the full-length clawfoot dressing mirror in its ornate wooden frame, and the cedar chest at the foot of the bed. Her mother always used to call it a hope chest. Did little girls still keep hope chests? She didn't think so, at least not around here. Maybe there were still places where hope didn't seem so terribly unrealistic, but this city wasn't one of them.

Randi sat on the floor, put the beer on the carpet, and opened the chest.

Hope chests were where you kept your future, all the little things that were part of the dreams they taught you to dream when you were a child. She hadn't been a child since she was twelve, since the night her mother woke her with that terrible inhuman sound. Her chest was full of memories now.

She took them out, one by one. Yearbooks from high school and college, bundles of love letters from old boyfriends and even that asshole she'd married, her school ring and her wedding ring, her diplomas, the letters she'd won in track and girls' softball, a framed picture of her and her date at the senior prom.

Way, way down at the bottom, buried under all the other layers of her life, was a police .38. Her father's gun, the gun he emptied the night he died. Randi took it out and carefully put it aside. Beneath it was the book, an old three-ring binder with a blue cloth cover. She opened it across her lap.

The yellowed *Courier* story on her father's death was Scotch-taped to the first sheet of paper, and Randi stared at that familiar photograph for a long time before she flipped the page. There were other clippings: stories about the missing children that she'd torn furtively from *Courier* back issues in the public library, magazine articles about animal attacks, serial killers, and monsters, all sandwiched between the lined pages she'd filled with her meticulous twelve-year-old's script. The handwriting grew broader and sloppier as she turned the pages; she'd kept up the book for years, until she'd gone away to college and tried to forget. She'd thought she'd done a pretty good job of that, but now, turning the pages, she knew that was a lie. You never forget. She only had to glance at the headlines, and it all came back to her in a sickening rush.

Eileen Stanski, Jessie Helander, Diane Jones, Gregory Corio, Erwin Weiss. None of them had ever been found, not so much as a bone or a piece of clothing. The police said her father's death was accidental, unrelated to the case he was working on. They'd all accepted that, the chief, the mayor, the newspaper, even her mother, who only wanted to get it all behind them and go on with their lives. Barry Schumacher and Joe Urquhart were the last to buy in, but in the end even they came around, and Randi was the only one left. Mere mention of the subject upset her mother so much that she finally stopped talking about it, but she didn't forget. She just asked her questions quietly, kept up her binder, and hid it every night at the bottom of the hope chest.

For all the good it had done.

The last twenty-odd pages in the back of the binder were still blank, the blue lines on the paper faint with age. The pages were stiff as she turned them. When she reached the final page, she hesitated. Maybe it wouldn't be there, she thought. Maybe she had just imagined it. It made no sense anyway. He would have known about her father, yes, but their mail was censored, wasn't it? They'd never let him send such a thing.

Randi turned the last page. It was there, just as she'd known it would be.

She'd been a junior in college when it arrived. She'd put it all behind her. Her father had been dead for seven years, and she hadn't even looked at her binder for three. She was busy with her classes and her sorority and her boyfriends, and sometimes she had bad dreams but mostly it was okay, she'd grown up, she'd gotten real. If she thought about it at all, she thought that maybe the adults had been right all along, it had just been some kind of an animal.

. . .some kind of animal. . .

Then one day the letter had come. She'd opened it on the way to class, read it with her friends chattering beside her, laughed and made a joke and stuck it away, all very grown-up. But that night, when her roommate had gone to sleep, she took it out and turned on her Tensor to read it again, and felt sick. She was going to throw it away, she remembered. It was just trash, a twisted product of a sick mind.

Instead she'd put it in the binder.

The Scotch tape had turned yellow and brittle, but the envelope was still white, with the name of the institution printed nearly in the left-hand corner. Someone had probably smuggled it out for him. The letter itself was scrawled on a sheet of cheap typing paper in block letters. It wasn't signed, but she'd known who it was from.

Randi slid the letter out of the envelope, hesitated for a moment, and opened it.

IT WAS A WEREWOLF

She looked at it and looked at it and looked at it, and suddenly she didn't feel very grown-up any more. When the phone rang she nearly jumped a foot.

Her heart was pounding in her chest. She folded up the letter and stared at the phone, feeling strangely guilty, as if she'd been caught doing something shameful. It was 2:53 in the morning. Who the hell would be calling now? If it was Roy Helander, she thought she might just scream. She let the phone ring.

On the fourth ring, her machine cut in. "This is AAA-Wade Investigations, Randi Wade speaking. I can't talk right now, but you can leave a message at the tone, and I'll get back to you."

The tone sounded. "Uh, hello," said a deep male voice that was definitely not Roy Helander.

Randi put down the binder, snatched up the receiver. "Rogoff? Is that you?"

"Yeah," he said. "Sorry if I woke you. Listen, this isn't by the book and I can't figure out a good excuse for why I'm calling you, except that I thought you ought to know."

Cold fingers crept down Randi's spine. "Know what?"

"We've got another one," he said.

Willie woke in a cold sweat.

What was that?

A noise, he thought, Somewhere down the hall.

Or maybe just a dream? Willie sat up in bed and tried to get a grip on himself. The night was full of noises. It could have been a towboat on the river, a car passing by underneath his windows, anything. He still felt sheepish about the way he'd let his fear take over when he found his door open. He was just lucky he hadn't stabbed Randi with those scissors. He couldn't let his imagination eat him alive. He slid back down under the covers, rolled over on his stomach, closed his eyes.

Down the hall, a door opened and closed.

His eyes opened wide. He lay very still, listening. He'd locked all the locks, he told himself, he'd walked Randi to the door and locked all his locks, the springlock, the chain, the double deadbolt, he'd even lowered the police bar. No one could get in once the bar was in place, it could only be lifted from inside, the door was solid steel. And the back door might as well be welded shut, it was so corroded and unmovable. If they broke a window he would have heard the noise, there was no way, no way. He was just dreaming.

The knob on his bedroom door turned slowly, clicked. There was a small metallic rattle as someone pushed at the door. The lock held. The second push was slightly harder, the noise louder.

By then Willie was out of bed. It was a cold night, his jockey shorts and undershirt small protection against the chill, but Willie had other things on his mind. He could see the key still sticking out of the keyhole. An antique key for a hundred-year-old lock. The office keyholes were big enough to peek through. Willie kept the keys inside them, just to plug up the drafts, but he never turned them. . .except tonight. Tonight for some reason he'd turned that key before he went to bed and somehow felt a little more secure when he heard the tumblers click. And now that was all that stood between him and whatever was out there.

He backed up against the window, glanced out at the cobbled alley behind the brewery. The shadows lay thick and black beneath him. He seemed to recall a big green-metal dumpster down below, directly under the window, but it was too dark to make it out.

Something hammered at the door. The room shook.

Willie couldn't breathe. His inhaler was on the dresser across the room, over by the door. He was caught in a giant's fist and it was squeezing all the breath right out of him. He sucked at the air.

The thing outside hit the door again. The wood began to splinter. Solid wood, a hundred years old, but it split like one of your cheap-ass hollow-core modern doors.

Willie was starting to get dizzy. It was going to be real pissed off, he thought giddily, when it finally got in here and found that his asthma had already killed him. Willie peeled off his undershirt, dropped it to the floor, hooked a thumb in the elastic of his shorts.

The door shook and shattered, falling half away from its hinges. The next blow snapped it in two. His head swam from lack of oxygen. Willie forgot all about his shorts and gave himself over to the change.

Bones and flesh and muscles shrieked in the agony of transformation, but the oxygen rushed into his lungs, sweet and cold, and he could breathe again. Relief shuddered through him and he threw back his head and gave it voice. It was a sound to chill the blood, but the dark shape picking its way through the splinters of his door did not hesitate, and neither did Willie. He gathered his feet up under him, and leapt. Glass shattered all around him as he threw himself through the window, and the shards spun outward into the darkness. Willie missed the dumpster, landed on all fours, lost his footing, and slid three feet across the cobbles.

When he looked up, he could see the shape above him, filling his window. Its hands moved, and he caught the terrible glint of silver, and that was all it took. Willie was on his feet again, running down the street faster than he had ever run before.

The cab let her off two houses down. Police barricades had gone up all around the house, a dignified old Victorian manor badly in need of fresh paint. Curious neighbors, heavy coats thrown on over pajamas and bathrobes, lined Grandview, whispering to each other and glancing back at the house. The flashers on the police cars lent a morbid avidity to their faces.

Randi walked past them briskly. A patrolman she didn't know stopped her at the police barrier. "I'm Randi Wade," she told him. "Rogoff asked me to come down."

"Oh," he said. He jerked a thumb back at the house. "He's inside, talking to the sister."

Randi found them in the living room, Rogoff saw her, nodded, waved her off, and went back to his questioning. The other cops looked at her curiously, but no one said anything. The sister was a young-looking forty, slender and dark, with pale skin and a wild mane of black hair that went half down her back. She sat on the edge of a section couch in a white silk teddy that left little to the imagination, seemingly just as indifferent to the cold air coming through the open door as she was to the lingering glances of the policemen.

One of the cops was taking some fingerprints off a shiny black grand piano in the corner of the room. Randi wandered over as he finished. The top of the piano was covered with framed photographs. One was a summer scene, taken somewhere along the river, two pretty girls in matching bikinis standing on either side of an intense young man. The girls were dappled with moisture, laughing for the photographer, long black hair hanging wetly down across wide smiles. The man, or boy, or whatever he was, was in a swimsuit, but you could tell he was bone thin. He was gaunt and sallow, and his blue eyes stared at the lens with a vacancy that was oddly disturbing. The girls could have been as young as eighteen or as old as twenty. One of them was the woman Rogoff was questioning, but Randi could not have told you which one. Twins. She glanced at the other photos, half-afraid she'd find a picture of Willie. Most of the faces she didn't recognize, and she was still looking them over when Rogoff came up behind her.

"Coroner's upstairs with the body," he said. "You can come up if you've got the stomach."

Randi turned away from the piano and nodded. "You learn anything from the sister?"

"She had a nightmare," he said. He started up the narrow staircase, Randi close behind him. "She says that as far back as she can remember, whenever she had bad dreams, she'd just cross the hall and crawl in bed with Zoe." They reached the landing. Rogoff put his hand on a glass doorknob, then paused. "What she found when she crossed the hall this time is going to keep her in nightmares for years to come."

He opened the door. Randi followed him inside.

The only light was a small bedside lamp, but the police photographer was moving around the room, snapping pictures of the red twisted thing on the bed. The light of his flash made the shadows leap and writhe, and Randi's stomach writhed with them. The smell of blood was overwhelming. She remembered summers long ago, hot July days when the wind blew from the south and the stink of the slaughterhouse settled over the city. But this was a thousand times worse.

The photographer was moving, flashing, moving, flashing. The world went from gray to red, then back to gray again. The coroner was bent over the corpse, her motions turned jerky and unreal by the strobing of the big flash gun. The white light blazed off the ceiling, and Randi looked up and saw the mirrors there. The dead woman's mouth gaped open, round and wide in a silent scream. He'd cut off her lips with her skin, and the inside of her mouth was no redder than the outside. Her face was gone, nothing left but the glistening wet ropes of muscle and here and there the pale glint of bone, but he'd left her her eyes. Large dark eyes, pretty eyes, sensuous, like her sister's downstairs. They were wide open, staring up in terror at the mirror on the ceiling. She'd been able to see every detail of what was being done to her. What had she found in the eyes of her reflection? Pain, terror, despair? A twin all her life, perhaps she'd found some strange comfort in her mirror image, even as her face and her flesh and her humanity had been cut away from her.

The flash went off again, and Randi caught the glint of metal at wrist and ankle. She closed her eyes for a second, steadied her breathing, and moved to the foot of the bed, where Rogoff was talking to the coroner.

"Same kind of chains?" he asked.

"You got it. And look at this." Coroner Cooney took an unlit cigar out of her mouth and pointed.

The chain looped tightly around the victim's ankle. When the flash went off again, Randi saw the other circles, dark, black lines, scored across the raw flesh and exposed nerves. It made her hurt just to look.

"She struggled," Rogoff suggested. "The chain chafed against her flesh."

"Chafing leaves you raw and bloody," Cooney replied. "What was done to her, you'd never notice chafing. That's a burn, Rogoff, a third-degree burn. Both wrists, both ankles, wherever the metal touched her. Sorenson had the same burn marks. Like the killer heated the chains until they were white hot. Only the metal is cold now. Go on, touch it."

"No thanks," Rogoff said. "I'll take your word for it."

"Wait a minute," Randi said.

The coroner seemed to notice her for the first time. "What's she doing here?" she asked.

"It's a long story," Rogoff replied. "Randi, this is official police business, you'd better keep—"

Randi ignored him. "Joan Sorenson had the same kind of burn marks?" she asked Cooney. "At wrist and ankle, where the chains touched her skin?"

"That's right," Cooney said. "So what?"

"What are you trying to say?" Rogoff asked her.

She looked at him. "Joan Sorenson was a cripple. She had no use of her legs, no sensation at all below the waist. So why bother to chain her ankles?"

Rogoff stared at her for a long moment, then shook his head. He looked over to Cooney. The coroner shrugged. "Yeah. So. An interesting point, but what does it mean?"

She had no answer for them. She looked away, back at the bed, at the skinned, twisted, mutilated thing that had once been a pretty woman.

The photographer moved to a different angle, pressed his shutter. The flash went off again. The chain glittered in the light. Softly, Randi brushed a fingertip across the metal. She felt no heat. Only the cold, pale touch of silver.

The night was full of sounds and smells.

Willie had run wildly, blindly, a gray shadow streaking down black rain-slick streets, pushing himself harder and faster than he had ever pushed before, paying no attention to where he went, anywhere, nowhere, everywhere, just so it was far away from his apartment and the thing that waited there with death shining bright in its hand. He darted along grimy alleys, under loading docks, bounded over low chain-link fences. There was a cinder-block wall somewhere that almost stopped him, three leaps and he failed to clear it, but on the fourth try he got his front paws over the top, and his back legs kicked and scrabbled and pushed him over. He fell onto damp grass, rolled in the dirt, and then he was up and running again. The streets were almost empty of traffic, but as he streaked across one wide boulevard, a pick-up truck appeared out of nowhere, speeding, and caught him in its lights. The sudden glare startled him; he froze for a long instant in the center of the street, and saw shock and terror on the driver's face. A horn blared as the pick-up began to brake, went into a skid, and fishtailed across the divider.

By then Willie was gone.

He was moving through a residential section now, down quiet streets lined by neat two-story houses. Parked cars filled the narrow driveways, realtor's signs flapped in the wind, but the only lights were the streetlamps. . .and sometimes, when the clouds parted for a second, the pale circle of the moon. He caught the scent of dogs from some of the back yards, and from time to time he heard a wild, frenzied barking, and knew that they had smelled him too. Sometimes the barking woke owners and neighbors, and then lights would come on in the silent houses, and doors could open in the back yards, but by then Willie would be blocks away, still running.

Finally, when his legs were aching and his heart was thundering and his tongue lolled redly from his mouth, Willie crossed the railroad tracks, climbed a steep embankment, and came hard up against a ten-foot chain-link fence with barbed wire strung along the top. Beyond the fence was a wide, empty yard and a low brick building, windowless and vast, dark beneath the light of the moon. The smell of old blood was faint but unmistakable, and abruptly Willie knew where he was.

The old slaughterhouse. The pack, they'd called it, bankrupt and abandoned now for almost two years. He'd run a long way. At last he let himself stop and catch his breath. He was panting, and as he dropped to the ground by the fence, he began to shiver, cold despite his ragged coat of fur.

He was still wearing jockey shorts, Willie noticed after he'd rested a moment. He would have laughed, if he'd had the throat for it. He thought of the man in the pick-up and wondered what he'd thought when Willie appeared in his headlights, a gaunt gray spectre in a pair of white briefs, with glowing eyes as red as the pits of hell.

Willie twisted himself around and caught the elastic in his jaws. He tore at them, growling low in his throat, and after a brief struggle managed to rip them away. He slung them aside and lowered himself to the damp ground, his legs resting on his paws, his mouth half-open, his eyes wary, watchful. He let himself rest. He could hear distant traffic, a dog barking wildly a half-mile away, could smell rust and mold, the stench of diesel fumes, the cold scent of metal. Under it all was the slaughterhouse smell, faded but not gone, lingering, whispering to him of blood and death. It woke things inside him that were better left sleeping, and Willie could feel the hunger churning in his gut.

He could not ignore it, not wholly, but tonight he had other concerns, fears that were more important than his hunger. Dawn was only a few hours away, and he had nowhere to go. He could not go home, not until he knew it was safe again, until he had taken steps to protect himself. Without keys and clothes and money, the agency was closed to him too. He had to go somewhere, trust someone.

He thought of Blackstone, thought of Jonathan Harmon sitting by his fire, of Steven's dead blue eyes and scarred hands, of the old tower jutting up like a rotten black stake. Jonathan might be able to protect him, Jonathan with his strong walls and his spiked fence and all his talk of blood and iron.

But when he saw Jonathan in his mind's eye, the long white hair, the gold wolf's head cane, the veined arthritic hands twisting and grasping, then the growl rose unbidden in Willie's throat, and he knew Blackstone was not the answer.

Joanie was dead, and he did not know the others well enough, hardly knew all their names, didn't want to know them better.

So, in the end, like it or not, there was only Randi.

Willie got to his feet, weary now, unsteady. The wind shifted, sweeping across the yards and the runs, whispering to him of blood until his nostrils quivered. Willie threw back his head and howled, a long shuddering lonely sound that rose and fell and went out through the cold night until the dogs began to bark for blocks around. Then, once again, he began to run.

Rogoff gave her a lift home. Dawn was just starting to break when he pulled his old black Ford up to the front of her six-flat. As she opened the door, he shifted into neutral and looked over at her. "I'm not going to insist right now," he said, "but it might be that I need to know the name of your client. Sleep on it. Maybe you'll decide to humor me."

"Maybe I can't," Randi said. "Attorney-client privilege, remember?"

Rogoff gave her a tired smile. "When you sent me to the courthouse, I had to look at your file too. You never went to law school."

"No?" She smiled back. "Well, I meant to. Doesn't that count for something?" She shrugged. "I'll sleep on it, we can talk tomorrow." She got out, closed the door, moved away from the car. Rogoff shifted into drive, but Randi turned back before he could pull away. "Hey, Rogoff, you have a first name?"

"Mike," he said.

"See you tomorrow, Mike."

He nodded and pulled away just as the streetlamps began to go out. Randi walked up the stoop, fumbling for her key.

"Randi!"

She stopped, looked around. "Who's there?"

"Willie." The voice was louder this time. "Down here by the garbage cans."

Randi leaned over the stoop and saw him. He was crouched down low, surrounded by trash-bins, shivering in the morning chill. "You're naked," she said.

"Somebody tried to kill me last night. I made it out. My clothes didn't. I've been here an hour, not that I'm complaining mind you, but I think I have pneumonia and my balls are frozen solid. I'll never be able to have children now. Where the fuck have you been?"

"There was another murder. Same m.o."

Willie shook so violently that the garbage cans rattled together. "Jesus," he said, his voice gone weak. "Who?"

"Her name was Zoe Anders."

Willie flinched. "Fuck fuck fuck," he said. He looked back up at Randi. She could see the fear in his eyes, but he asked anyway. "What about Amy?"

"Her sister?" Randi said. He nodded. "In shock, but fine. She had a nightmare." She paused a moment. "So you knew Zoe too. Like Sorenson?"

"No. Not like Joanie." He looked at her wearily. "Can we go in?"

She nodded and opened the door. Willie looked so grateful she thought he was about to lick her hand.

The underwear was her ex-husband's, and it was too big. The pink bathrobe was Randi's, and it was too small. But the coffee was just right, and it was warm in here, and Willie felt bone-tired and nervous but glad to be alive, especially when Randi put the plate down in front of him. She'd scrambled the eggs up with cheddar cheese and onion and done up a rasher of bacon on the side, and it smelled like nirvana. He fell to eagerly.

"I think I've figured out something," she said. She sat down across from him.

"Good," he said. "The eggs, I mean. That is, whatever you figured out, that's good too, but Jesus, I *needed* these eggs. You wouldn't believe how hungry you get—" He stopped suddenly, stared down at the scrambled eggs, and reflected on what an idiot he was, but Randi hadn't noticed. Willie reached for a slice of bacon, bit off the end. "Crisp," he said. "Good."

"I'm going to tell you," Randi said, as if he hadn't spoken at all. "I've got to tell somebody, and you've known me long enough so I don't think you'll have me committed. You may laugh." She scowled at him. "If you laugh, you're back out in the street, minus the boxer shorts and the bathrobe."

"I won't laugh," Willie said. He didn't think he'd have much difficulty not laughing. He felt rather apprehensive. He stopped eating.

Randi took a deep breath and looked him in the eye. She had very lovely eyes, Willie thought. "I think my father was killed by a werewolf," she said seriously, without blinking.

"Oh, Jesus," Willie said. He didn't laugh. A very large invisible anaconda wrapped itself around his chest and began to squeeze. "I," he said, "I, I, I." Nothing was coming in or out. He pushed back from the table, knocking over the chair, and ran for the bathroom. He locked himself in and turned on the shower full blast, twisting the hot tap all the way around. The bathroom began to fill up with steam. It wasn't nearly as good as a blast from his inhaler, but it did beat suffocating. By the time the steam was really going good, Willie was on his knees, gasping like a man trying to suck an elephant through a straw. Finally he began to breathe again.

He stayed on his knees for a long time, until the spray from the shower had soaked through his robe and his underwear and his face was flushed and red. Then he crawled across the tiled floor, turned off the shower, and got unsteadily to his feet. The mirror above the sink was all fogged up. Willie wiped it off with a towel and peered in at himself. He looked like shit. Wet shit. Hot wet shit. He felt worse. He tried to dry himself off, but the steam and the shower spray had gone everywhere and the towels were as damp as he was. He heard Randi moving around outside, opening and closing drawers. He wanted to go out and face her, but not like this. A man has to have some pride. For a moment he just wanted to be home in bed with his Primateen on the end table, until he remembered that his bedroom had been occupied the last time he'd been there.

"Are you ever coming out?" Randi asked.

"Yeah," Willie said, but it was so weak that he doubted she heard him. He straightened and adjusted the frilly pink robe. Underneath the undershirt looked as though he'd been competing in a wet T-shirt contest. He sighed, unlocked the door, and exited. The cold air gave him goosepimples.

Randi was seated at the table again. Willie went back to his place. "Sorry," he said. "Asthma attack."

"I noticed," Randi replied. "Stress related, aren't they?"

"Sometimes."

"Finish your eggs," she urged. "They're getting cold."

"Yeah," Willie said, figuring he might as well, since it would give him something to do while he figured out what to tell her. He picked up his fork.

It was like the time he'd grabbed a dirty pot that had been sitting on top of his hotplate since the night before and realized too late that he'd never turned the hotplate off. Willie shrieked and the fork clattered to the table and bounced, once, twice, three times. It landed in front of Randi. He sucked on his fingers. They were already starting to turn red. Randi looked at him very calmly and picked up the fork. She held it, stroked it with her thumb, touched its prongs thoughtfully to her lip. "I brought out the good silver while you were in the bathroom," she said. "Solid sterling. It's been in the family for generations."

His fingers hurt like hell. "Oh, Jesus. You got any butter? Oleo, lard, I don't care, anything will. . ." He stopped when her hand went under the table and came out again holding a gun. From where Willie sat, it looked like a very big gun.

"Pay attention, Willie. Your fingers are the least of your worries. I realize you're in pain, so I'll give you a minute or two to collect your thoughts and try to tell me why I shouldn't blow off your fucking head right here and now." She cocked the hammer with her thumb.

Willie just stared at her. He looked pathetic, like a half-drowned puppy. For one terrible moment Randi thought he was going to have another asthma attack. She felt curiously calm, not angry or afraid or even nervous, but she didn't think she had it in her to shoot a man in the back as he ran for the bathroom, even if he was a werewolf.

Thankfully, Willie spared her that decision. "You don't want to shoot me," he said, with remarkable aplomb under the circumstances. "It's bad manners to shoot your friends. You'll make a hole in the bathrobe."

"I never liked that bathrobe anyway. I hate pink."

"If you're really so hot to kill me, you'd stand a better chance with the fork," Willie said.

"So you admit that you're a werewolf?"

"A lycanthrope," Willie corrected. He sucked at his burnt fingers again and looked at her sideways. "So sue me. It's a medical condition. I got allergies, I got asthma, I got a bad back, and I got lycanthropy, is it my fault? I didn't kill your father. I never killed anyone. I ate half a pit bull once, but can you blame me?" His voice turned querulous. "If you want to shoot me, go ahead and try. Since when do you carry a gun anyway? I thought all that shit about private eyes stuffing heat was strictly television?"

"The phrase is *packing* heat, and it is. I only bring mine out for special occasions. My father was carrying it when he died."

"Didn't do him much good, did it?" Willie said softly.

Randi considered that for a moment. "What would happen if I pulled the trigger?" The gun was getting heavy, but her hand was steady.

"I'd try to change. I don't think I'd make it, but I'd have to try. A couple bullets in the head at this range, while I'm still human, yeah, that'd probably do the job. But you don't want to miss and you *really* don't want to wound me. Once I'm changed, it's a while different ballgame."

"My father emptied his gun on the night he was killed," Randi said thoughtfully.

Willie studied his hand and winced. "Oh fuck," he said. "I'm getting a blister."

Randi put the gun on the table and went to the kitchen to get him a stick of butter. He accepted it from her gratefully. She glanced toward the window as he treated his burns. "The sun's up," she said, "I thought werewolves only changed at night, during the full moon?"

"Lycanthropes," Willie said. He flexed his fingers, sighed. "That full moon shit was all invented by some screenwriter for Universal, go look at your literature, we change at will, day, night, full moon, new moon, makes no difference. Sometimes I *feel* more like changing during the full moon, some kind of hormonal thing, but more like getting horny than going on the rag, if you know what I mean." He grabbed his coffee. It was cold by now, but that didn't stop Willie from emptying the cup. "I shouldn't be telling you all this, fuck, Randi, I like you, you're a friend, I care about you, you should only forget this whole morning, believe me, it's healthier."

"Why?" she said bluntly. She wasn't about to forget anything. "What's going to happen to me if I don't? Are you going to rip my throat out? Should I forget Joanie Sorenson and Zoe Anders too? How about Roy Helander and all those missing kids? *Am I supposed to forget what happened to my father?*" She stopped for a moment, lowered her voice. "You came to me for help, Willie, and pardon, but you sure as hell look as though you still need it."

Willie looked at her across the table with a morose hangdog expression on his long face. "I don't know whether I want to kiss you or slap you," he finally admitted. "Shit, you're right, you know too much already." He stood up. "I got to get into my own clothes, this wet underwear is giving me pneumonia. Call a cab, we'll go check out my place, talk. You got a coat?"

"Take the Burberry," Randi said. "It's in the closet."

The coat was even bigger on him than it had been on Randi, but it beat the pink bathrobe. He looked almost human as he emerged from the closet, fussing with the belt. Randi was rummaging in the silver drawer. She found a large carving knife, the one her grandfather used to use on Thanksgiving, and slid it through the belt of her jeans. Willie looked at it nervously. "Good idea," he finally said, "but take the gun too."

The cab driver was the quiet type. The drive crosstown passed in awkward silence. Randi paid him while Willie climbed out to check the doors. It was a blustery overcast day, and the river looked gray and choppy as it slapped against the pier.

Willie kicked his front door in a fit of pique, and vanished down the alley. Randi waited by the pier and watched the cab drive off. A few minutes later Willie was back, looking disgusted. "This is ridiculous," he said. "The back door hasn't been opened in years, you'd need a hammer and chisel just to knock through the rust. The loading docks are bolted down and chained with the mother of all padlocks on the chains. And the front door. . .there's a spare set of keys in my car, but even if we got those, the police bar can only be lifted from inside. So how the hell did it get in, I ask you?"

Randi looked at the brewery's weathered brick walls appraisingly. They looked pretty solid to her, and the second floor windows were a good twenty feet off street level. She walked around the side to take a look down the alley. "There's a window broken," she said.

"That was me getting out," Willie said, "not my nocturnal caller getting in."

Randi had already figured out that much from the broken glass all over the cobblestones. "Right now I'm more concerned about how *we're* going to get in." She pointed. "If we move that dumpster a few feet to the left and climb on top, and you climb on my shoulders, I think you might be able to hoist yourself in."

Willie considered that. "What if it's still in there?"

"What?" Randi said.

"Whatever was after me last night. If I hadn't jumped through that window, it'd be me without a skin this morning, and believe me, I'm cold enough as it is." He looked at the window, at the dumpster, and back at the window. "Fuck," he said, "We can't stand here all day. But I've got a better idea. Help me roll the dumpster away from the wall a little."

Randi didn't understand, but she did as Willie suggested. They left the dumpster in the center of the alley, directly opposite the broken window. Willie nodded and began unbolting the coat she'd lent him. "Turn around," he told her. "I don't want you freaking out. I've got to get naked and your carnal appetites might get the best of you."

Randi turned around. The temptation to glance over her shoulder was irresistible. She heard the coat fall to the ground. Then she heard something else. . . soft padding steps, like a dog. She turned. He'd circled all the way down to the end of the alley. Her ex-husband's old underwear lay puddle across the cobblestones atop the Burberry coat. Willie came streaking back toward the brewery, building speed. He was, Randi noticed, not a very prepossessing wolf. His fur was a dirty gray-brown color, kind of mangy, his rear looked too large and his legs too thin, and there was something ungainly about the way he ran. He put on a final burst of speed, leapt on top of the dumpster, bounded off the metal lid, and flew through the shattered window, breaking more glass as he went. Randi heard a rough *thump* from inside the bedroom.

She went around to the front. A few moments later, the locks began to unlock, one by one, and Willie opened the heavy steel door. He was wearing his own bathrobe, a red tartan flannel, and his hand was full of keys. "Come on," he said. "No sign of night visitors. I put on some water for tea."

"The fucker must have crawled out of the toilet," Willie said. "I don't see any other way he could have gotten in."

Randi stood in front of what remained of his bedroom door. She studied the shattered wood, ran her finger lightly across one long, jagged splinter, then knelt to look at the floor. "Whatever it was, it was strong. Look at these gouges in the wood, look at how sharp and clean they are. You don't do that with a fist. Claws, maybe. More likely some kind of knife. And take a look at this." She gestured toward the brass doorknob, which lay on the floor amidst a bunch of kindling.

Willie bent to pick it up.

"Don't touch," she said, grabbing his arm. "Just look."

He got down on one knee. At first he didn't notice anything. But when he leaned close, he saw how the brass was scored and scraped.

"Something sharp," Randi said, "and hard." She stood up. "When you first heard the sounds, what direction were they coming from?"

Willie thought for a moment. "It was hard to tell," he said. "Toward the back, I think."

Randi walked back. All along the hall, the doors were closed. She studied the banister at the top of the stairs, then moved on, and began opening and closing doors. "Come here," she said, at the fourth door.

Willie trotted down the hall. Randi had the door ajar. The knob on the hall side was fine; the knob on the inside displayed the same kind of scoring they'd seen on his bedroom door. Willie was aghast. "But this is the *men's room*," he said. "You mean it *did* come out of the toilet? I'll never shit again."

"It came out of this room," Randi said. "I don't know about the toilet." She went in and looked around. There wasn't much to look at. Two toilet stalls, two urinals, two sinks with a long mirror above them and antique brass soap dispensers beside the water taps, a paper towel dispenser, Willie's towels and toiletries. No window. Not even a small frosted-glass window. No window at all.

Down the hall the tea kettle began to whistle. Randi looked thoughtful as they walked back to the living room. "Joan Sorenson died behind a locked door, and the killer got to Zoe Anders without waking her sister right across the hall."

"The fucking thing can come and go as it pleases," Willie said. The idea gave him the creeps. He glanced around nervously as he got out the teabags, but there was nobody there but him and Randi.

"Except it can't," Randi said. "With Sorenson and Anders, there was no damage, no sign of a break-in, nothing but a corpse. But with you, the killer was stopped by something as simple as a locked door."

"Not stopped," Willie said, "just slowed down a little." He repressed a shudder and brought the tea over to the coffee table.

"Did he get the right Anders sister?" she asked.

Willie stood there stupidly for a moment holding the coffee poised over the cups. "What do you mean?"

"You've got identical twins sharing the same house. I presume it's a house the killer's never visited before. Somehow he gains entry, and he chains, murders, and skin's only one of them, without even waking the other." Randi smiled up at him sweetly. "You can tell them apart by sight, he probably didn't know which room was which, so the question is, did he get the werewolf?"

It was nice to know that she wasn't infallible. "Yes," he said, "and no. They were twins, Randi. Both lycanthropes." She looked honestly surprised. "How did you know?" he asked her.

"Oh, the chains," she said negligently. Her mind was away, gnawing at the puzzle. "Silver chains. She was burned wherever they'd touched her flesh. And Joan Sorenson was a werewolf too, of course. She was crippled, yes. . .but only as a human, not after her transformation. That's why her legs were chained, to hold her if she changed." She looked at Willie with a baffled expression on her face. "It doesn't make sense, to kill one and leave the other untouched. Are you sure that Amy Anders is a werewolf, too?"

"A lycanthrope," he said. "Yes. Definitely. They were even harder to tell apart as wolves. At least when they were human they dressed differently. Amy liked white lace, frills, that kind of stuff, and Zoe was into leather." There was a cut-glass ashtray in the center of the coffee table filled with Willie's private party mix: aspirin. Allerest, and Tums. He took a handful of pills and swallowed them dry.

"Look, before we go on with this, I want one card on the table," Randi said.

For once he was ahead of her. "If I knew who killed your father, I'd tell you, but I don't, I was in the service, overseas. I vaguely remember something in the *Courier*, but to tell the truth I'd forgotten all about it until you threw it at me last night. What can I tell you?" He shrugged.

"Don't bullshit me, Willie. My father was killed by a werewolf. You're a werewolf. You must know something."

"Hey, try substituting *Jew* or *diabetic* or *bald man* for werewolf in that statement, and see how much sense it makes. I'm not saying you're wrong about your father because you're not, it fits, it all fits, everything from the condition of the body to the empty gun, but even if you buy that much, then you got to ask *which* werewolf."

"How many of you *are* there?" Randi asked incredulously.

"Damned if I know," Willie said. "What do you think, we get together for a lodge meeting every time the moon is full? The purebloods, hell, not many, the pack's been getting pretty thin these last few generations. But there's lots of mongrels like me, halfbreeds, quarterbreeds, what have you, the old families had their share of bastards. Some can work the change, some can't. I've heard of a few who change one day and never do manage to change back. And that's just from the old bloodlines, never mind the ones like Joanie."

"You mean Joanie was different?"

Willie gave her a reluctant nod. "You've seen the movies. You get bitten by a werewolf, you turn into a werewolf, that is assuming there's enough of you left to turn into anything except a cadaver." She nodded, and he went on. "Well, that part's true, or partly true, it doesn't happen as often as it once did. Guy gets bit nowadays, he runs to the doctor, gets the wound cleaned and treated with antiseptic, gets his rabies shots and his tetanus shots and penicillin and fuck-all knows what else, and he's fine. The wonders of modern medicine."

Willie hesitated briefly, looking in her eyes, those lovely eyes, wondering if she'd understand, and finally he plunged ahead. "Joanie was such a good kid, it broke my heart to see her in that chair. One night she told me that the hardest thing of all was realizing that she'd never know what it felt like to make love. She'd been a virgin when they hit that truck. We'd had a few drinks, she was crying, and. . .and, I couldn't take it. I told her what I was and what I could do for her, she didn't believe a word of it, so I had to show her. I bit her leg, she couldn't feel a damned thing down there anyway, I bit her and I held the bite for a long time, worried it around good. Afterwards I nursed her myself. No doctors, no antiseptic, no rabies vaccine. We're talking major infection here, there was a day or two when her fever was running so high I thought maybe I'd killed her, her leg had turned nearly black, you could see the stuff going up her veins. I got to admit it was pretty gross, I'm in no hurry to try it again, but it worked. The fever broke and Joanie changed."

"You weren't just friends," Randi said with certainty. "You were lovers."

"Yeah," he said. "As wolves. I guess I look sexier in wolf. I couldn't even begin to keep up with her, though. Joanie was a pretty active wolf. We're talking almost every night here."

"As a human, she was still crippled," Randi said.

Willie nodded, held up his hand. "See." The burns were still there, and a blood blister had formed on his index finger. "Once or twice the change has saved my life, when my asthma got so bad I thought I was going to suffocate. That kind of thing doesn't cross over, but it's sure as hell waiting for you when you cross back. Sometimes you even get nasty surprises. Catch a bullet as a wolf and it's nothing, a sting and a slap, heals up right away, but you can pay for it when you change into human form, especially if you change too soon and the damn thing gets infected. And silver will burn the shit out of you no matter what form you're in. LBJ was my favorite president, just *loved* them cupro-nickle-sandwich quarters."

Randi stood up. "This is all a little overwhelming. Do you *like* being a werewolf?"

"A lycanthrope." Willie shrugged. "I don't know, do you like being a woman? It's what I am."

Randi crossed the room and stared out his window at the river. "I'm very confused," she said. "I look at you and you're my friend Willie. I've known you for years. Only you're a werewolf too. I've been telling myself that werewolves don't exist since I was twelve, and now I find out the city is full of them. Only someone or something is killing them, flaying them. Should I care? Why should I care?" She ran a hand through her tangled hair. "We both know that Roy Helander didn't kill those kids. My father knew it too. He kept pressing, and one night he was lured to the stockyards and some kind of animal tore out his throat. Every time I think of that I think maybe I ought to find this werewolf killer and sign up to help him. Then I look at you again." She turned and looked at him. "And damn it, you're *still* my friend."

She looked as though she was going to cry. Willie had never seen her cry, and he didn't want to. He hated it when they cried. "Remember when I first offered you a job, and you wouldn't take it, because you thought all collection agents were pricks?"

She nodded.

"Lycanthropes are skinchangers. We turn into wolves. Yeah, we're carnivores, you got it, you don't meet many vegetarians in the park, but there's mean and there's meat. You won't find nearly as many rats around here as you will in other cities this size. What I'm saying is the skin may change, but what you do is still up to the person inside. So stop thinking about werewolves and werewolf-killers and start thinking about murderers, 'cause that's what we're talking about."

Randi crossed the room and sat back down. "I hate to admit it, but you're making sense."

"I'm good in bed too," Willie said with a grin.

The ghost of a smile crossed her face. "Fuck you."

"Exactly my suggestion. What kind of underwear are you wearing?"

"Never mind my underwear," she said. "Do you have any ideas about these murderers? Past *or* present?"

Sometimes Randi had a one track mind, Willie thought; unfortunately, it never seemed to be the track that led under the sheets. "Jonathan told me about an old legend," he said.

"Jonathan?" she said.

"Jonathan Harmon, yeah, that one, old blood and iron, the *Courier*, Blackstone, the pack, the founding family, all of it."

"Wait a minute. He's a were—a lycanthrope?"

Willie nodded. "Yeah, leader of the pack, he—"

Randi leapt ahead of him. "And it's hereditary?"

He saw where she was going. "Yes, but—"

"Steven Harmon is mentally disturbed," Randi interrupted. "His family keeps it out of the papers, but they can't stop the whispering. Violent episodes, strange doctors coming and going at Blackstone, shock treatments. Steven's some kind of pain freak, isn't he?"

Willie sighed. "Yeah. Ever see his hands? The palms and fingers are covered with silver burns. Once I saw him close his hand around a silver cartwheel and hold it there until smoke started to come out between his fingers. It burned a big round hole right in the center of his palm." He shuddered. "Yeah, Steven's a freak all right, and he's strong enough to rip your arm out of your socket and beat you to death with it, but he didn't kill your father, he couldn't have."

"Says you," she said.

"He didn't kill Joanie or Zoe either. They weren't just murdered, Randi. They were skinned. That's where the legend comes in. The word is *skinchangers*, remember?

What if the power was *in* the skin? So you catch a werewolf, flay it, slip into the bloody skin. . .and change."

Randi was staring at him with a sick look on her face. "Does it really work that way?"

"Someone thinks so."

"Who?"

"Someone who's been thinking about werewolves for a long time. Someone who's gone way past obsession into full-fledged psychopathy. Someone who thinks he saw a werewolf once, who thinks werewolves done him wrong, who hates them, wants to hurt them, wants revenge. . .but maybe also, down deep, someone who wants to know what's it like."

"Roy Helander," she said.

"Maybe if we could find this damned secret hideout in the woods, we'd know for sure."

Randi stood up. "I wracked my brains for hours. We could poke around a few of the city parks some, but I'm not sanguine on our prospects. No. I want to know more about these legends, and I want to look at Steven with my own eyes. Get your car, Willie. We're going to pay a visit to Blackstone."

He'd been afraid she was going to say something like that. He reached out and grabbed another handful of his party mix. "Oh, Jesus," he said, crunching down on a mouthful of pills. "This isn't the Addams Family, you know. Jonathan is for real."

"So am I," said Randi, and Willie knew the cause was lost.

It was raining again by the time they reached Courier Square. Willie waited in the car while Randi went inside the gunsmith's. Twenty minutes later, when she came back out, she found him snoring behind the wheel. At least he'd had the sense to lock the doors of his mammoth old Cadillac. She tapped on the glass, and he sat right up and stared at her for a moment without recognition. Then he woke up, leaned over, and unlocked the door on the passenger side. Randi slid beside him.

"How'd it go?"

"They don't get much call for silver bullets, but they know someone upstate who does custom work for collectors," Randi said in a disgusted tone of voice.

"You don't sound too happy about it."

"I'm not. You wouldn't believe what they're going to charge me for a box of silver bullets, never mind that it's going to take two weeks. It was going to take a month, but I raised the ante." She looked glumly out the rain-streaked window. A torrent of gray water rushed down the gutter, carrying its flotilla of cigarette butts and scraps of yesterday's newspaper.

"Two weeks?" Willie turned the ignition and put the barge in gear. "Hell, we'll both probably be dead in two weeks. Just as well, the whole idea of silver bullets makes me nervous."

They crossed the square, past the Castle marquee and the Courier Building, and headed up Central, the windshield wipers clicking back and forth rhythmically. Willie swung a left on 13th and headed toward the bluff while Randi took out her father's revolver, opened the cylinder, and checked to see that it was fully loaded. Willie watched her out of the corner of his eye as he drove. "Waste of time," he said. "Guns don't kill werewolves, werewolves kill werewolves."

"Lycanthropes," Randi reminded him.

He grinned and for a moment looked almost like the man she'd shared an office with, a long time ago.

Both of them grew visibly more intense as they drove down 13th, the Caddy's big wheels splashing through the puddles. They were still a block away when she saw the little car crawling down the bluff, white against the dark stone. A moment later, she saw the lights, flashing red-and-blue.

Willie saw them too. He slammed on the brakes, lost traction, and had to steer wildly to avoid slamming into a parked car as he fishtailed. His forehead was beading with sweat when he finally brought the car to a stop, and Randi didn't think it was from the near-collision. "Oh, Jesus," he said, "Oh, Jesus, not Harmon too, I don't *believe* it." He began to wheeze, and fumbled in his pocket for an inhaler.

"Wait here, I'll check it out," Randi told him. She got out, turned up the collar of her coat, and walked the rest of the way, to where 13th dead-ended flush against the bluff. The coroner's wagon was parked amidst three police cruisers. Randi arrived at the same time as the cable car. Rogoff was the first one out. Behind him she saw Cooney, the police photographer, and two uniforms carrying a body bag. It must have gotten pretty crowded on the way down.

"You." Rogoff seemed surprised to see her. Strands of black hair were plastered to his forehead by the rain.

"Me," Randi agreed. The plastic of the body bag was slick and wet, and the uniforms were having trouble with it. One of them lost his footing as he stepped down, and Randi thought she saw something shift inside the bag. "It doesn't fit the pattern," she said to Rogoff. "The other killings have all been at night."

Rogoff took her by the arm and drew her away, gently but firmly. "You don't want to look at this one, Randi." There was something in his tone that made her look at him hard. "Why not? It can't be any worse than Zoe Anders, can it? Who's in the bag, Rogoff? The father or the son?"

"Neither one," he said. He glanced back behind them, then toward the top of the bluff, and Randi found herself following his gaze. Nothing was visible of Blackstone but the high wrought iron fence that surrounded the estate. "This time his luck ran out on him. The dogs got to him first. Cooney says the scent of blood off of. . .of what he was wearing. . .well, it must have driven them wild. They tore him to pieces, Randi." He put his hand on her shoulder, as if to comfort her.

"No," Randi said. She felt numb, dazed.

"Yes," he insisted. "It's over. And believe me, it's not something you want to see."

She backed away from him. They were loading the body in the rear of the coroner's wagon while Sylvia Cooney supervised the operation, smoking her cigar in the rain. Rogoff tried to touch her again, but she whirled away from him, and ran to the wagon. "Hey!" Cooney said.

The body was on the tailgate, half-in and half-out of the wagon. Randi reached for the zipper on the body bag. One of the cops grabbed her arm. She shoved him aside and unzipped the bag. His face was half gone. His right cheek and ear and part of his jaw had been torn away, devoured right down the bone. What features he had left were obscured by blood.

Someone tried to pull her away from the tailgate. She spun and kicked him in the balls, then turned back to the body and grabbed it under the arms and pulled. The inside of the body bag was slick with blood. The corpse slid loose of the plastic sheath like a banana squirting out of its skin and fell into the street. Rain washed down over it, and the runoff in the gutter turned pink, then red. A hand, or part of a hand, fell out of the bag almost like an afterthought. Most of the arm was gone, and Randi could see bones peeking through, and places where huge hunks of flesh had been torn out of his thigh, shoulder, and torso. He was naked, but between his legs was nothing but a raw red wound where his genitalia had been.

Something was fastened around his neck, and knotted beneath his chin. Randi leaned forward to touch it, and drew back when she saw his face. The rain had washed it clean. He had one eye left, a green eye, open and staring. The rain pooled in the socket and ran down his cheek. Roy had grown gaunt to the point of emaciation, with a week's growth of beard, but his long hair was still the same color, the color he'd shared with all his brothers and sisters, that muddy Helander blonde.

Something was knotted under his chin, a long twisted cloak of some kind, it had gotten all tangled when he fell. Randi was trying to straighten it when they caught her by both arms and dragged her away bodily. "No," she said wildly. "What was he wearing? What was he wearing, damn you! I have to see!" No one answered. Rogoff had her right arm prisoned in a grip that felt like steel. She fought him wildly, kicking and shouting, but he held her until the hysteria had passed, and then held her some more as she leaned against his chest, sobbing.

She didn't quite know when Willie had come up, but suddenly there he was. He took her away from Rogoff and led her back to his Cadillac, and they sat inside, silent, as first the coroner's wagon and then the police cruisers drove by one by one. She was covered with blood. Willie gave her some aspirin from a bottle he kept in his glove compartment. She tried to swallow it, but her throat was raw, and she wound up gagging it back up. "It's all right," he told her, over and over. "It wasn't your father, Randi. Listen to me, please, it *wasn't your father!*"

"It was Roy Helander," Randi said to him at last. "And he was wearing Joanie's skin."

Willie drove her home; she was in no shape to confront Jonathan Harmon or anybody. She'd calmed down, but the hysteria was still there, just under the surface, he could see it in the eyes, hear it in her voice. If that wasn't enough, she kept telling him the same thing, over and over. "It was Roy Helander," she'd say, like he didn't know, "and he was wearing Joanie's skin."

Willie found her keys and helped her upstairs to her apartment. Inside, he made her take a couple of sleeping pills from the all-purpose pharmaceutical in his glove box, then turned down the bed and undressed her. He figured if anything would snap her back to herself, it would be his fingers on the buttons of her blouse, but she just smiled at him, vacant and dreamy, and told him that it was Roy Helander and he was wearing Joanie's skin. The big silver knife jammed through her belt loops gave him pause. He finally unzipped her fly, undid her buckle, and yanked off the jeans, knife and all. She didn't wear panties. He'd always suspected as much.

When Randi was finally in bed asleep, Willie went back to her bathroom and threw up.

Afterward he made himself a gin-and-tonic to wash the taste of vomit out of his mouth, and went and sat alone in her living room in one of her red velvet chairs. He'd had even less sleep than Randi these past few nights, and he felt as though he might drift off at any moment, but he knew somehow that it was important not to. It was Roy Helander and he was wearing Joanie's skin. So it was over, he was safe.

He remembered the way his door shook last night, a solid wood door, and it split like so much cheap paneling. Behind it was something dark and powerful, something that left scars on brass doorknobs and showed up in places it had no right to be. Willie didn't know what had been on the other side of his door, but somehow he didn't think that the gaunt, wasted, half-eaten travesty of a man he'd seen on 13th Street quite fit the bill. He'd believe that his nocturnal visitor had been Roy Helander, with or without Joanie's skin, about the same time he'd believe that the man had been eaten by dogs. *Dogs!* How long did Jonathan expect to get away with that shit? Still, he couldn't blame him, not with Zoe and Joanie dead, and Helander trying to sneak into Blackstone dressed in a human skin.

. . .there are things that hunt the hunters.

Willie picked up the phone and dialed Blackstone.

"Hello." The voice was flat, affectless, the voice of someone who cared about nothing and no one, not even himself.

"Hello, Steven," Willie said quietly. He was about to ask for Jonathan when a strange sort of madness took hold of him, and he heard himself say, "Did you watch? Did you see what Jonathan did to him, Steven? Did it get you off?"

The silence on the other end of the line went on for ages. Sometimes Steven Harmon simply forgot how to talk. But not this time. "Jonathan didn't do him. I did. It was easy. I could smell him coming through the woods. He never even saw me. I came around behind him and pinned him down and bit off his ear. He wasn't very strong at all. After a while he changed into a man, and then he was all slippery, but it didn't matter, I—"

Someone took the phone away. "Hello, who is this?" Jonathan's voice said from the receiver.

Willie hung up. He could always call back later. Let Jonathan sweat awhile, wondering who it had been on the other end of the line. "After a while he changed into a man," Willie repeated aloud. Steven did it himself. Steven didn't do it himself. Could he? "Oh Jesus," Willie said.

Somewhere far away, a phone was ringing.

Randi rolled over in her bed. "Joanie's skin," she muttered groggily in low, half-intelligible syllables. She was naked, with the blankets tangled around her. The room was pitch dark. The phone rang again. She sat up, a sheet curled around her neck. The room was cold, and her head pounded. She ripped loose the sheet, threw it aside. Why was she naked? What the hell was going on? The phone rang again and her machine cut in. "This is AAA-Wade Investigations, Randi Wade speaking. I can't talk right now, but you can leave a message at the tone, and I'll get back to you."

Randi reached out and speared the phone just in time for the *beep* to sound in her ear. She winced. "It's me," she said. "I'm here. What time is it? Who's this?"

"Randi, are you all right? It's Uncle Joe." Joe Urquhart's gruff voice was a welcome relief. "Rogoff told me what happened, and I was very concerned about you. I've been trying to reach you for hours."

"Hours?" She looked at the clock. It was past midnight. "I've been asleep. I think." The last she remembered, it had been daylight and she and Willie had been driving down 13th on their way to Blackstone to. . .*It was Roy Helander and he was wearing Joanie's skin.*

"Randi, what's wrong? You sure you're okay? You sound wretched. Damn it, *say* something."

"I'm here," she said. She pushed hair back out of her eyes. Someone had opened her window, and the air was frigid on her bare skin. "I'm fine," she said. "I just. . .I was asleep. It shook me up, that's all. I'll be fine."

"If you say so." Urquhart sounded dubious.

Willie must have brought her home and put her to bed, she thought. So where was he? She couldn't imagine that he'd just dump her and then take off, that wasn't like Willie.

"Pay attention," Urquhart said gruffly. "Have you heard a word I've said?"

She hadn't. "I'm sorry. I'm just. . .disoriented, that's all. It's been a strange day."

"I need to see you," Urquhart said. His voice had taken on a sudden urgency. "Right away. I've been going over the reports on Roy Helander and his victims. There's something out of place, something disturbing. And the more I look at these case files and Cooney's autopsy report, the more I keep thinking about Frank, about what happened that night." He hesitated. "I don't know how to say this. All these years. . .I only wanted the best for you, but I wasn't. . .wasn't completely honest with you."

"Tell me," she said. Suddenly she was a lot more awake.

"Not over the phone. I need to see you face to face, to show it to you. I'll swing by and get you. Can you be ready in fifteen minutes?"

"Ten," Randi said.

She hung up, hopped out of bed and opened the bedroom door. "Willie?" she called out. There was no answer. "Willie!" she repeated more loudly. Nothing. She turned on the lights, passed barefoot down the hall, expecting to find him snoring away on her sofa. But the living room was empty.

Her hands were sandpaper dry, and when she looked down she saw that they were covered with old blood. Her stomach heaved. She found the clothes she'd been wearing on a heap on the bedroom floor. They were brown and crusty with dried blood as well. Randi started the shower, and stood under the water for a good five minutes, running it so hot that it burned the way that silver fork must have burned in Willie's hand. The blood washed off, the water turning faintly pink as it whirled away and down. She toweled off thoroughly, and found a warm flannel shirt and a fresh pair of jeans. She didn't bother with her hair; the rain would wet it down again soon enough. But she made a point of finding her father's gun and sliding the long silver carving knife through the belt loop of her jeans.

As she bent to pick up the knife, Randi saw the square of white paper on the floor by her end table. She must have knocked it off when she'd reached for the phone.

She picked it up, opened it. It was covered with Willie's familiar scrawl, a page of hurried, dense scribbling. *I got to go, you're in no condition*, it began. *Don't go anywhere or talk to anyone. Roy Helander wasn't sneaking in to kill Harmon. I finally figured it out. The damned Harmon family secret that's no secret at all. I should have twigged, even—*

That's as far as she'd gotten when the doorbell rang.

Willie hugged the ground two-thirds of the way up the bluff, the rain coming down around him and his heart pounding in his chest as he clung to the tracks. Somehow the grade didn't seem nearly as steep when you were riding the cable car as it did now. He glanced behind him, and saw 13th Street far below. It made him dizzy. He wouldn't even have gotten this far if it hadn't been for the tracks. Where the slope grew almost vertical, he'd been able to scrabble up from tie to tie, using them like rungs on a ladder. His hands were full of splinters, but it beat trying to crawl up the wet rock, clinging to ferns for dear life.

Of course, he could have changed, and bounded up the tracks in no time at all. But somehow he didn't think that would have been such a good idea. *I could smell him coming*, Steven had said. The human scent was fainter, in a city full of people. He had to hope that Steven and Jonathan were inside the New House, locked up for the night. But if they were out prowling around, at least this way Willie thought he had a ghost of a chance.

He'd rested long enough. He craned his head back, looking up at the high black iron fence that ran along the top of the bluff, trying to measure how much further he had to go. Then he took a good long shot off his inhaler, gritted his teeth, and scrambled for the next tie up.

The windshield wipers swept back and forth almost silently as the long dark car nosed through the night. The windows were tinted a gray so dark it was almost black. Urquhart was in civvies, a red-and-black lumberjack shirt, dark woolen slacks, and bulky down jacket. His police cap was his only concession to uniform. He stared straight out into the darkness as he drove. "You look terrible," she told him.

"I feel worse." They swept under an overpass and around a long ramp onto the river road. "I feel old, Randi. Like this city. This whole damn city is old and rotten."

"Where are we going?" she asked him. At this hour of night, there was no other traffic on the road. The river was a black emptiness off to their left. Streetlamps swam in haloes of rain to the right as they sailed past block after cold, empty block stretching away toward the bluffs.

"To the pack," Urquhart said. "To where it happened."

The car's heater was pouring out a steady blast of warm air, but suddenly Randi felt deathly cold. Her hand went inside her coat, and closed around the hilt of the knife. The silver felt comfortable and comforting. "All right," she said. She slid the knife out of her belt and put it on the seat between them.

Urquhart glanced over. She watched him carefully. "What's that?" he said.

"Silver," Randi said. "Pick it up."

He looked at her. "What?"

"You heard me," she said. "Pick it up."

He looked at the road, at her face, back out at the road. He made no move to touch the knife.

"I'm not kidding," Randi said. She slid away from him, to the far side of the seat, and braced her back against the door. When Urquhart looked over again, she had the gun out, aimed right between his eyes. "Pick it up," she said very clearly.

The color left his face. He started to say something, but Randi shook her head curtly. Urquhart licked his lips, took his hand off the wheel, and picked up the knife. "There," he said, holding it up awkwardly while he drove with one hand. "I picked it up. Now what am I supposed to do with it?"

Randi slumped back against the seat. "Put it down," she said with relief.

Joe looked at her.

He rested for a long time in the shrubs on top of the bluff, listening to the rain fall around him and dreading what other sounds he might hear. He kept imagining soft footfalls stealing up behind him, and once he thought he heard a low growl somewhere off to his right. He could feel his hackles rise, and until that moment he hadn't even known he *had* hackles, but it was nothing, just his nerves working on him, Willie had always had bad nerves. The night was cold and black and empty.

When he finally had his breath back, Willie began to edge past the New House, keeping to the bushes as much as he could, well away from the windows. There were a few lights on, but no other sign of life. Maybe they'd all gone to bed. He hoped so.

He moved slowly and carefully, trying to be as quiet as possible. He watched where his feet came down, and every few steps he'd stop, look around, listen. He could change in an instant if he heard anyone. . .or *anything*. . .coming toward him. He didn't know how much good that would do, but maybe, just maybe, it would give him a chance.

His raincoat dragged at him, a water-logged second skin as heavy as lead. His shoes had soaked through, and the leather squished when he moved. Willie pushed away from the house, further back into the trees, until a bend in the road hid the lights from view. Only then, after a careful glance in both directions to make sure nothing was coming, did he dare risk a dash across the road.

Once across he plunged deeper into the woods, moving faster now, a little more heedless. He wondered where Roy Helander had been when Steven had caught him. Somewhere around here, Willie thought, somewhere in this dark primal forest, surrounded by old growth, with centuries of leaves and moss and dead things rotting in the earth beneath his feet.

As he moved away from the bluff and the city, the forest grew denser, until finally the trees pressed so close together that he lost sight of the sky, and the raindrops stopped pounding against his head. It was almost dry here. Overhead, the rain drummed relentlessly against a canopy of leaves. Willie's skin felt clammy, and for a moment he was lost, as if he'd wandered into some terrible cavern far below the earth. A dismal cold place where no light ever shone.

Then he stumbled between two huge, twisted old oaks. He felt air and rain against his face again, and raised his head, and there it was ahead of him, broken windows gaping down like so many blind eyes from walls carved from rock that shone like midnight and drank all light and hope. The tower loomed up to his right, some monstrous erection against the stormclouds, leaning crazily.

Willie stopped breathing, groped for his inhaler, found it, dropped it, picked it up. The mouthpiece was slimy with humus. He cleaned it on his sleeve, shoved it in his mouth, took a hit, two, three, and finally his throat opened again.

He glanced around, heard only the rain, saw nothing. He stepped forward toward the tower. Toward Roy Helander's secret refuge.

The big double gate in the high chain-link fence had been padlocked for two years, but it was open tonight, and Urquhart drove straight through. Randi wondered if the gate had been opened for her father as well. She thought maybe it had.

Joe pulled up near one of the loading docks, in the shadow of the old brick slaughterhouse. The building gave them some shelter from the rain, but Randi still trembled with the cold as she climbed out. "Here?" she asked. "This is where you found him?"

Urquhart was staring off into the stockyard. It was a large area, subdivided into a dozen pens along the railroad landing. There was a maze of chest-high fencing they called the "runs" between the slaughterhouse and the pens, to force the cows into a single line and herd them along inside, where a man in a blood-spattered apron waited with a hammer in his hand. "Here," Joe said, without looking back at her.

There was a long silence. Somewhere far off, Randi thought she heard a faint, wild howl, but maybe that was just the wind and the rain. "Do you believe in ghosts?" she asked Joe.

"Ghosts?" The chief sounded distracted.

She shivered. "It's like. . .I can feel him, Joe. Like he's still here, after all this time, still watching over me."

Joe Urquhart turned toward her. His face was wet with rain, or maybe tears. "I watched over you," he said. "He asked me to watch over you, and I did, I did my best."

Randi heard a sound somewhere off in the night. She turned her head, frowning, listening. Tires crunched across gravel and she saw headlights outside the fence. Another car coming.

"You and your father, you're a lot alike," Joe said wearily. "Stubborn. Won't listen to nobody. I took good care of you, didn't I take good care of you? I got my own kids, you know, but you never wanted nothing, did you? So why the hell didn't you listen to me?"

By then Randi knew. She wasn't surprised. Somehow she felt as though she'd known for a long time. "There was only one phone call that night," she said. "You were the one who phoned for back-up, not Dad."

Urquhart nodded. He was caught for a moment in the headlights of the on-coming car, and Randi saw the way his jaw trembled as he worked to get out the words. "Look in the glove box," he said.

Randi opened the car door, sat on the edge of the seat, and did as he said. The glove compartment was unlocked. Inside was a bottle of aspirin, a tire pressure gauge, some maps, and a box of cartridges. Randi opened the box and poured some bullets out into her palm. They glimmered pale and cold in the car's faint dome light. She left the box on the seat, climbed out, kicked the door shut. "My silver bullets," she said. "I hadn't expected them quite so soon."

"Those are the ones Frank ordered made up, eighteen years ago," Joe said. "After he was buried, I went by the gunsmith and picked them up. Like I said, you and him, you were a lot alike."

The second car pulled to a stop, pinning her in its high beams. Randi threw a hand across her eyes against the glare. She heard a car door opening and closing.

Urquhart's voice was anguished. "I told you to stay away from this thing, damn it. I *told* you! Don't you understand? They *own* this city!"

"He's right. You should have listened," Rogoff said, as he stepped into the light.

Willie groped his way down the long dark hall with one hand on the wall, placing each foot carefully in front of the other. The stone was so thick that even the sound of the rain did not reach him. There was only the echo of his careful steps, and the rush of blood inside his ears. The silence within the Old House was profound and unnerving, and there was something about the walls that bothered him as well. It was cold, but the stones under his fingers were slick and curiously warm to the touch, and Willie was glad for the darkness.

Finally he reached the base of the tower, where shafts of light fell across crabbed, narrow stone steps that spiraled up and up and up. Willie began to climb. He counted the steps at first, but somewhere around two hundred he lost the count, and the rest was a grim ordeal that he endured in silence. More than once he thought of changing. He resisted the impulse.

His legs ached from the effort when he reached the top. He sat down on the steps for a moment, his back to a slick stone wall. He was breathing hard, but when he groped for his inhaler, it was gone. He'd probably lost it in the woods. He could feel his lungs constricting in panic, but there was no help for it.

Willie got up.

The room smelled of blood and urine and something else, a scent he did not place, but somehow it made him tremble. There was no roof. Willie realized that the rain had stopped while he'd been inside. He looked up as the clouds parted, and a pale white moon stared down.

And all around other moons shimmered into life, reflected in the tall empty mirrors that lined the chamber. They reflected the sky above and each other, moon after moon after moon, until the room swam in silvered moonlight and reflections of reflections of reflections.

Willie turned around in a slow circle and a dozen other Willies turned with him. The moon-struck mirrors were streaked with dried blood, and above them a ring of cruel iron hooks curved up from the stone walls. A human skin hung from one of them, twisting slowly in some wind he could not feel, and as the moonlight hit it seemed to writhe and change, from woman to wolf to woman, both and neither.

That was when Willie heard the footsteps on the stairs.

"The silver bullets were a bad idea," Rogoff said. "We have a local ordinance here. The police get immediate notice any time someone places an order for custom ammunition. Your father made the same mistake. The pack takes a dim view of silver bullets."

Randi felt strangely relieved. For a moment she'd been afraid that Willie had betrayed her, that he'd been one of them after all, and that thought had been like poison in her soul. Her fingers were still curled tight around a dozen of the bullets. She glanced down at them, so close and yet so far.

"Even if they're still good, you'll never get them loaded in time," Rogoff said.

"You don't need the bullets," Urquhart told her. "He only wants to talk. They promised me, honey, no one needs to get hurt."

Randi opened her hand. The bullets fell to the ground. She turned to Joe Urquhart. "You were my father's best friend. He said you had more guts than any man he ever knew."

"They don't give you any choice," Urquhart said. "I had kids of my own. They said if Roy Helander took the blame no more kids would vanish, they promised they'd take care of it, but if we kept pressing, one of my kids would be the next to go. That's how it works in this town. Everything would have been all right, but Frank just wouldn't let it alone."

"We only kill in self-defense," Rogoff said. "There's a sweetness to human flesh, yes, a power that's undeniable, but it's not worth the risk."

"What about the children?" Randi said. "Did you kill them in self-defense too?"

"That was a long time ago," Rogoff said.

Joe stood with his head downcast. He was beaten, Randi saw, and she realized that he'd been beaten for a long time. All those trophies on his walls, but somehow she knew that he had given up hunting forever on the night her father died. "It was his son," Joe muttered quietly, it a voice full of shame. "Steven's never been right in the head, everyone knows that, he was the one who killed the kids, *ate* them. It was horrible, Harmon told me so himself, but he still wasn't going to let us have Steven. He said he'd. . .he'd control Steven's. . .appetite. . .if we closed the case. He was good as his word too, he put Steven on medication, and it stopped, the murders stopped."

She ought to hate Joe Urquhart, she realized, but instead she pitied him. After all this time, he still didn't understand. "Joe, he lied. It was never Steven."

"It was Steven," Joe insisted, "it had to be, he's insane. The rest of them. . .you can do business with them, Randi, listen to me now, you can talk to them."

"Like you did," she said. "Like Barry Schumacher."

Urquhart nodded. "That's right. They're just like us, they got some crazies, but not all of them are bad. You can't blame them for taking care of their own, we do the same thing, don't we? Look at Mike here, he's a good cop."

"A good cop who's going to change into a wolf in a minute or two and tear out my throat," Randi said.

"Randi, honey, listen to me," Urquhart said. "It doesn't have to be like that. You can walk out of here, just say the word. I'll get you onto the force, you can work with us, help us to. . .to keep the peace. Your father's dead, you won't bring him back, and the Helander boy, he deserved what he got, he was *killing* them, skinning them alive, it was self-defense. Steven is sick, he's always been sick—"

Rogoff was watching her from beneath his tangle of black hair. "He still doesn't get it," she said. She turned back to Joe. "Steven is sicker than you think. Something is missing. Too inbred, maybe. Think about it. Anders and Rochmonts, Flambeauxes and Harmons, the four great founding families, all werewolves, marrying each other generation after generation to keep the lines pure, for how many centuries? They kept the lines pure all right. They bred themselves Steven. He didn't kill those children. Roy Helander saw a *wolf* carry off his sister, and Steven can't change into a wolf. He got the bloodlust, he got inhuman strength, he burns at the touch of silver, but that's all. The last of the purebloods *can't work the change!*"

"She's right," Rogoff said quietly.

"Why do you think you never found any remains?" Randi put in. "Steven didn't kill those kids. His father carried them off, up to Blackstone."

"The old man had some crazy idea that if Steven ate enough human flesh, it might fix him, make him whole," Rogoff said.

"It didn't work," Randi said. She took Willie's note out of her pocket, let the pages flutter to the ground. It was all there. She'd finished reading it before she'd gone down to meet Joe. Frank Wade's little girl was nobody's fool.

"It didn't work," Rogoff echoed, "but by then Jonathan had got the taste. Once you get started, it's hard to stop." He looked at Randi for a long time, as if he were weighing something. Then he began. . .

. . .to change. Sweet cold air filled his lungs, and his muscles and bones ran with fire as the transformation took hold. He'd shrugged out of pants and coat, and he heard the rest of his clothing ripping apart as his body writhed, his flesh ran like hot wax, and he reformed, born anew.

Now he could see and hear and smell. The tower room shimmered with moonlight, every detail clear and sharp as noon, and the night was alive with sound, the wind and the rain and the rustle of bats in the forest around them, and traffic sounds and sirens from the city beyond. He was alive and full of power, and something was coming up the steps. It climbed slowly, untiring, and its smells filled the room. The scent of blood hung all around it, and beneath he sensed an aftershave that masked an unwashed body, sweat and dried semen on its skin, a heavy tang of wood smoke in its hair, and under it all the scent of sickness, sweetly rotten as a grave.

Willie backed all the way across the room, staring at the latched door, the growl rising in his throat. He bared long yellowed teeth, and slaver ran between them.

Steven stopped in the doorway and looked at him. He was naked. The wolf's hot red eyes met his cold blue ones, and it was hard to tell which were more inhuman. For a moment Willie thought that Steven didn't quite comprehend. Until he smiled, and reached for the skin that twisted above him, on an iron hook.

Willie leapt.

He took Steven high in the back and bore him down, with his hand still clutched around Zoe's skin. For a second Willie had a clear shot at his throat, but he hesitated and the moment passed. Steven caught Willie's foreleg in a pale scarred fist, and snapped it in half like a normal man night break a stick. The pain was excruciating. Then Steven was lifting him, flinging him away. He smashed up hard against one of the mirrors, and felt it shatter at the impact. Jagged shards of glass flew like knives, and one of them lanced through his side.

Willie rolled away, the glass spear broke under him, and he whimpered. Across the room, Steven was getting to his feet. He put out a hand to steady himself.

Willie scrambled up. His broken leg was knitting already, though it hurt when he put his weight on it. Glass fragments clawed inside him with every step. He could barely move. Some fucking werewolf he turned out to be.

Steven was adjusting his ghastly cloak, pulling flaps of skin down over his own face. The skin trade, Willie thought giddily, yeah, that was it, and in a moment Steven would use that damn flayed skin to do what he could never manage on his own, he would *change*, and then Willie would be meat.

Willie came at him, jaws gaping, but too slow. Steven's foot pistoned down, caught him hard enough to take his breath away, pinned him to the floor. Willie tried to squirm free, but Steven was too strong. He was bearing down, crushing him. All of a sudden Willie remembered that dog, so many years ago.

Willie bent himself almost double and took a bite out of the back of Steven's calf.

The blood filled his mouth, exploding inside him. Steven reeled back. Willie jumped up, darted forward, bit Steven again. This time he sank his teeth in good and held, worrying at the flesh. The pounding in his head was thunderous. He was full of power, he could feel it swelling within him. Suddenly he knew that he could tear Steven apart, he could taste the fine sweet flesh close to the bone, could hear the music of his screams, could imagine the way it would feel when he held him in his jaws and shook him like a rag doll and felt the life go out of him in a sudden giddy rush. It swept over him, and Willie bit and bit and bit again, ripping away chunks of meat, drunk on blood.

And then, dimly, he heard Steven screaming, screaming in a high shrill thin voice, a little boy's voice. "No, daddy," he was whining, over and over again. "No, please, don't bite me, daddy, don't bite me any more."

Willie let him go and backed away.

Steven sat on the floor, sobbing. He was bleeding like a sonofabitch. Pieces were missing from thigh, calf, shoulder, and foot. His legs were drenched in blood. Three fingers were gone off his right hand. His cheeks were slimy with gore.

Suddenly Willie was scared.

For a moment he didn't understand. Steven was beaten, he could see that, he could rip out his throat or let him live, it didn't matter, it was over. But something was wrong, something was terribly, sickeningly wrong. It felt as though the temperature had dropped a hundred degrees, and every hair on his body was prickling and standing on end. What the hell was going on? He growled low in his throat and backed away, toward the door, keeping a careful eye on Steven.

Steven giggled. "You'll get it now," he said. "You called it. You got blood on the mirrors. You called it back again."

The room seemed to spin. Moonlight ran from mirror to mirror to mirror, dizzyingly. Or maybe it wasn't moonlight.

Willie looked into the mirrors.

The reflections were gone. Willie, Steven, the moon, all gone. There was blood on the mirrors and they were full of fog, a silvery pale fog that shimmered as it moved.

Something was moving through the fog, sliding from mirror to mirror to mirror, around and around. Something hungry that wanted to get out.

He saw it, lost it, saw it again. It was in front of him, behind him, off to the side. It was a hound, gaunt and terrible; it was a snake, scaled and foul; it was a man, with eyes like pits and knives for its fingers. It wouldn't hold still, every time he looked its shape seemed to change, and each shape was worse than the last, more twisted and obscene. Everything about it was lean and cruel. Its fingers were sharp, so sharp, and he looked at them and felt their caress sliding beneath his skin, tingling along the nerves, pain and blood and fire trailing behind them. It was black, blacker than black, a black that drank all light forever, and it was all shining silver too. It was a nightmare that lived in a funhouse mirror, the thing that hunts the hunters.

He could feel the evil throbbing through the glass.

"Skinner," Steven called.

The surface of the mirrors seemed to ripple and bulge, like a wave cresting on some quicksilver sea. The fog was thinning, Willie realized with sudden terror; he could see it clearer now, and he knew it could see him. And suddenly Willie Flambeaux knew what was happening, knew that when the fog cleared the mirrors wouldn't be mirrors anymore, they'd be doors, *doors*, and the skinner would come. . .

. . .sliding forward, through the ruins of his clothing, slitted eyes glowing like embers from a muzzle black as coal. He was half again as large as Willie had been, his fur thick and black and shaggy, and when he opened his mouth, his teeth gleamed like ivory daggers.

Randi edged backward, along the side of the car. The knife was in her hand, moonlight running off the silver blade, but somehow it didn't seem like very much. The large black wolf advanced on her, his tongue lolling between his teeth, and she put her back up against the car door and braced herself for his leap.

Joe Urquhart stepped between them.

"No," he said. "Not her too, you owe me, talk to her, give her a chance, I'll make her see how it is."

The wolf growled a warning.

Urquhart stood his ground, and all of a sudden he had his revolver out, and he was holding it in two shaky hands, drawing a bead. "Stop. I mean it. She didn't have time to load the goddamned silver bullets, but I've had eighteen fucking years. I'm the fucking police chief in this fucking city, and you're under arrest."

Randi put her hand on the door handle, eased it open. For a moment the wolf stood frozen, baleful red eyes fixed on Joe, and she thought it was actually going to work. She remembered her father's old Wednesday night poker games; he'd always said Joe, unlike Barry Schumacher, ran one hell of a bluff.

Then the wolf threw back his head and howled, and all the blood went out of her. She knew that sound. She'd heard it in her dreams a thousand times. It was in her blood, that sound, an echo from far off and long ago, when the world had been a forest and humans had run naked in fear before the hunting pack. It echoed off the side of the old slaughterhouse and trembled out over the city, and they must have heard it all over the flats, heard it and glanced outside nervously and checked their locks before they turned up the volumes on their TVs.

Randi opened the door wider and slid one leg inside the car as the wolf leapt.

She heard Urquhart fire and fire again, and then the wolf slammed into his chest and smashed him back against the car door. Randi was half into the car, but the door swung shut hard, crunching down on her left foot with awful force. She heard a bone break under the impact, and shrieked at the sudden flare of pain. Outside Urquhart fired again, and then he was screaming. There were ripping sounds and more screams and something wet spattered against her ankle.

Her foot was trapped, and the struggle outside slammed her open door against it again and again and again. Each impact was a small explosion as the shattered bones grated together and ripped against raw nerves. Joe was screaming and droplets of blood covered the tinted windows like rain. Her head swam, and for a moment Randi thought she'd faint from the pain, but she threw all her weight against the door and moved it just enough and drew her foot inside and when the next impact came it slapped the door shut *hard* and Randi pressed the lock.

She leaned against the wheel and almost threw up. Joe had stopped screaming, but she could hear the wolf tearing at him, ripping off chunks of flesh. *Once you get started it's hard to stop*, she thought hysterically. She got out the .38, cracked the cylinder with shaking hands, flicked out the shells. Then she was fumbling around on the front seat. She found the box, tipped it over, snatched up a handful of silver.

It was silent outside. Randi stopped, looked up.

He was on the hood of the car.

Willie *changed*.

He was running on instinct now, he didn't know why he did it, he just did. The pain was there waiting for him along with his humanity, as he'd known it would be. It shrieked through him like a gale wind, and sent him whimpering to the floor. He could feel the glass shard under his ribs, dangerously close to a lung, and his left arm bent sickeningly downward at a place it was never meant to bend, and when he tried to move it, he screamed and bit his tongue and felt his mouth fill with blood.

The fog was a pale thin haze now, and the mirror closest to him bulged outward, throbbing like something alive.

Steven sat against the wall, his blue eyes bright and avid, sucking his own blood from the stumps of his fingers. "Changing won't help," he said in that weird flat tone of his. "Skinner don't care. It knows what you are. Once it's called, it's got to have a skin." Willie's vision was blurry with tears, but he saw it again then, in the mirror behind Steven, pushing at the fading fog, pushing, pushing, trying to get through.

He staggered to his feet. Pain roared through his head. He cradled his broken arm against his body, took a step toward the stairs, and felt broken glass grind against his bare feet. He looked down. Pieces of the shattered mirror were everywhere.

Willie's head snapped up. He looked around wildly, dizzy, counting. Six, seven, eight, nine. . .the tenth was broken. Nine then. He threw himself forward, slammed all his body weight into the nearest mirror. It shattered under the impact, disintegrated into a thousand pieces. Willie crunched the biggest shards underfoot, stamped on them until his heels ran wet with blood. He was moving without thought. He caromed around the room, using his own body as a weapon, hearing the sweet tinkling music of breaking glass. The world turned into a red fog of pain, and a thousand little knives sliced at him everywhere, and he wondered, if the skinner came through and got him, whether he'd even be able to tell the difference.

Then he was staggering away from another mirror, and white hot needles were stabbing through his feet with every step, turning into fire as they lanced up his calves. He stumbled and fell, hard. Flying glass had cut his face to ribbons, and the blood ran down into his eyes.

Willie blinked, and wiped the blood away with his good hand. His old raincoat was underneath him, bloodsoaked and covered with ground glass and shards of mirror. Steven stood over him, staring down. Behind him was a mirror. Or was it a door?

"You missed one," Steven said flatly.

Something hard was digging into his gut, Willie realized. His hand fumbled around beneath him, slid into the pocket of his raincoat, closed on cold metal.

"Skinner's coming for you now," Steven said.

Willie couldn't see. The blood had filled his eyes again. But he could still feel. He got his fingers through the loops and rolled and brought his hand up fast and hard, with all the strength he had left, and put Mr. Scissors right through the meat of Steven's groin.

The last thing he heard was a scream, and the sound of breaking glass.

Calm, Randi thought, *calm*, but the dread that filled her was more than simple fear. Blood matted his jaws, and his eyes stared at her through the windshield, glowing that hideous baleful red. She looked away quickly, tried to chamber a bullet. Her hands shook, and it slid out of her grip, onto the floor of the car. She ignored it, tried again.

The wolf howled, turned, fled. For a moment she lost sight of him. Randi craned her head around, peering nervously out through the darkness. She glanced into the rearview mirror, but it was fogged up, useless. She shivered, as much from the cold as from fear. *Where was he?* she thought wildly.

Then she saw him, running toward the car.

Randi looked down, chambered a bullet, and had a round in her fingers when he came flying over the hood and smashed against the glass. Cracks spiderwebbed out from the center of the windshield. The wolf snarled at her. Slaver and blood smeared the glass. Then he hit the glass again. Again. Again. Randi jumped with every impact. The windshield cracked and cracked again, then a big section in the center went milky and opaque.

She had the second bullet in the cylinder. She slid in a third. Her hands were shaking as much from cold as from fear. It was freezing inside the car. She looked out into the darkness through a haze of cracks and blood smears, loaded a fourth bullet, and was closing the cylinder when he hit the windshield again and it all caved in on her.

One moment she had the gun and the next it was gone. The weight was on her chest and the safety glass, broken into a million milky pieces but still clinging together, fell across her face like a shroud. Then it ripped away, and the blood-soaked jaws and hot red eyes were right there in front of her.

The wolf opened his mouth and she was feeling the furnace heat of his breath, smelling awful carnivore stench. "You fucker!" she screamed, and almost laughed, because it wasn't much as last words go.

Something sharp and silvery bright came sliding down through the back of his throat.

It went so quickly Randi didn't understand what was happening, no more than he did. Suddenly the bloodlust went out of the dark red eyes, and they were full of pain and shock and finally fear, and she saw more silver knives sliding through his throat before his mouth filled with blood. And then the great black-furred body shuddered, and struggled, as something pulled it back off her, front paws beating a tattoo against the seat. There was a smell like burning hair in the air. When the wolf began to scream, it sounded almost human.

Randi choked back her own pain, slammed her shoulder against the door, and knocked what was left of Joe Urquhart aside. Halfway out the door, she glanced back.

The hand was twisted and cruel, and its fingers were long bright silver razors, pale and cold and sharp as sin. Like five long jointed knives the fingers had sunk through the back of the wolf's neck, and grabbed hold, and pulled, and the blood was coming out between his teeth in great gouts now and his legs were kicking feebly. It yanked at him then, and she heard a sickening wet *crunching* as the thing began to *pull* the wolf through the rearview mirror with inexorable, unimaginable force, to whatever was on the other side. The great black-furred body seemed to waver and shift for a second, and the wolf's face took on an almost human case.

When his eyes met hers, the red light had gone out of them; there was nothing there but pain and pleading.

His first name was Mike, she remembered.

Randi looked down. Her gun was on the floor.

She picked it up, checked the cylinder, closed it, jammed the barrel up against his head, and fired four times.

When she got out of the car and put her weight on her ankle, the pain washed over her in great waves. Randi collapsed to her hands and knees. She was throwing up when she heard the sirens.

". . .some kind of animal," she said.

The detective gave her a long, sour look, and closed his notebook. "That's all you can tell me?" he said. "That Chief Urquhart was killed by some kind of animal?"

Randi wanted to say something sharp, but she was all fucked up on painkillers. They'd had to put two pins in her ankle and it still hurt like hell, and the doctors said she's have to stay another week. "What do you want me to tell you?" she said weakly. "That's what I saw, some kind of animal. A wolf."

The detective shook his head. "Fine. So the chief was killed by some kind of animal, probably a wolf. So where's Rogoff? His car was there, his blood was all over the side of the chief's car, so tell me. . .*where the fuck is Rogoff?*"

Randi closed her eyes, and pretended it was the pain. "I don't know," she said.

"I'll be back," the detective said when he left.

She lay with her eyes closed for a moment, thinking maybe she could drift back to sleep, until she heard the door open and close. "He won't be," a soft voice told her. "We'll see to it."

Randi opened her eyes. At the foot of the bed was an old man with long white hair leaning on a gold wolf's head cane. He wore a black suit, a mourning suit, and his hair fell to his shoulders. "My name is Jonathan Harmon," he said.

"I've seen your picture. I know who you are. And what you are." Her voice was hoarse. "A lycanthrope."

"Please," he said. "A werewolf."

"Willie. . .what happened to Willie?"

"Steven is dead," Jonathan Harmon said.

"Good," Randi spat. "Steven and Roy, they were doing it together, Willie said. For the skins. Steven hated the others, because they could work the change and he couldn't. But once your son had his skin, he didn't need Helander anymore, did he?"

"I can't say I will mourn greatly. To be frank, Steven was never the sort of heir I might have wished for." He went to the window, opened the curtains, and looked out. "This was once a great city, you know, a city of blood and iron. Now it's all turned to rust."

"Fuck your city," Randi said. "What about Willie?"

"It was a pity about Zoe, but once the skinner has been summoned, it keeps hunting until it takes a skin, from mirror to mirror to mirror. It knows our scent, but it doesn't like to wander far from its gates. I don't know how your mongrel friend managed to escape it twice, but he did. . .to Zoe's misfortune, and Michael's." He turned and looked at her. "You will not be so lucky. Don't congratulate yourself too vigorously, child. The pack takes care of its own, The doctor who writes your next prescription, the pharmacist who fills it, the boy who delivers it. . .any of them could be one of us. We don't forget our enemies, Miss Wade. Your family would do well to remember that."

"You were the one," she said with a certainty. "In the stockyards, the night my father. . ."

Jonathan nodded curtly. "He was a crack shot, I'll grant him that. He put six bullets in me. My war wounds, I call them. They still show up on X rays, but my doctors have learned not to be curious."

"I'll kill you," Randi said.

"I think not." He leaned over the bed. "Perhaps I'll come for you myself some night. You ought to see me, Miss Wade. My fur is white now, pale as snow, but the stature, the majesty, the power, those have not left me. Michael was a halfbreed, and your Willie, he was hardly more than a dog. The pureblood is rather more. We are the dire wolves, the nightmares who haunt your racial memories, the dark shapes circling endlessly beyond the light of your fires."

He smiled down at her, then turned and walked away. At the door he paused. "Sleep well," he said.

Randi did not sleep at all, not even when night fell and the nurse came in and turned out the lights, despite all her pleading. She lay there in the dark staring up at the ceiling, feeling more alone than she'd ever been. He was dead, she thought. Willie was dead and she'd better start getting used to the idea. Very softly, alone in the darkness of the private room, she began to cry.

She cried for a long time, for Willie and Joan Sorenson and Joe Urquhart and finally, after all this time, for Frank Wade. She ran out of tears and kept crying, her body wracking with dry sobs. She was still shaking when the door opened softly, and a thin knife of light from the hall cut across the room.

"Who's there?" she said hoarsely. "Answer, or I'll scream."

The door closed quietly. "Ssssh. Quiet, or they'll hear." It was a woman's voice, young, a little scared. "The nurse said I couldn't come in, that it was after visiting hours, but he told me to get to you right away." She moved close to the bed.

Randi turned on her reading light. Her visitor looked nervously toward the door. She was dark, pretty, no more than twenty, with a spray of freckles across her nose. "I'm Betsy Juddiker," she whispered. "Willie said I was to give you a message, but it's all crazy stuff. . ."

Randi's heart skipped a beat. "Willie. . .tell me! I don't care how crazy it sounds, just tell me."

"He said that he couldn't phone you hisself because the pack might be listening in, that he got hurt bad but he's okay, that he's up north, and he's found this vet who's taking care of him good. I know, it sounds funny, but that's what he said, a vet."

"Go on."

Betsy nodded. "He sounded hurt on the phone, and he said he couldn't. . . couldn't *change* right now, except for a few minutes to call, because he was hurt and the pain was always waiting for him, but to say that the vet had gotten most of the glass out and set his leg and he was going to be fine. And then he said that on the night he'd gone, he'd come by *my* house and left something for you, and I was to find you and bring it here." She opened her purse and rummaged around. "It was in the bushes by the mailbox, my little boy found it." She gave it over.

It was a piece of some broken mirror, Randi saw, a shard as long and slender as her finger. She held it in her hand for a moment, confused and uncertain. The glass was cold to the touch, and it seemed to grow colder as she held it.

"Careful, it's real sharp," Betsy said. "There was one more thing, I don't understand it at all, but Willie said it was important. He said to tell you that there were no mirrors where he was, not a one, but last he'd seen, there were plenty up in Blackstone."

Randi nodded, not quite grasping it, not yet. She ran a finger thoughtfully along the shiny sliver of glass.

"Oh, look," Betsy said. "I told you. Now you've gone and cut yourself."

THE ANIMAL ASPECT OF HER MOVEMENT

BY ADAM GOLASKI

This is only the second Adam Golaski story I've ever read, which makes him two for two. (The first one, "The Dead Gather on the Bridge to Seattle," was in my last anthology.) So at least for me, this boy is on one really weird roll.

I can't help it. In a field known for unusual thinkers whose prose lets you know how they see the world, Golaski's literary camera angles never fail to startle me with the oddness of their compositions. And then you get to the things he has his characters think and do and say . . .

In that sense, he reminds me of the Canadian filmmaker Guy Maddin, whose compositions often Vaseline-smear off the edges of the frame. And whose tales feel very much like deranged yet lucid dreams.

Case in point: this loopy dreamscape meditation on animal attraction and the unseemly emotions that it stirs.

BRIAN

Sun caught the chrome bumper of the little red car that cut in front of me, my eyes drawn, then dazzled, and for miles that little red car seemed to settle in, locked into my line of sight. I only kind of noticed, my mind stuck on the failed sales call I'd made an hour earlier. I guess I really started to pay attention to the little red car when it signaled for an exit, seconds before I signaled, and I thought, that little red car has been ahead of me for a while.

Better than worry over my customer's dismissal ("I've never heard anything about your company"), I played a game with the little red car. I sped up to pass; the little red car blocked my advance in the passing lane. I slowed, to let another car in between us; the little red car slowed till we were nearly bumper to bumper. I changed lanes without signaling; so did the little red car. Odd, but not outrageous. Nonetheless, and backwards, surely, I felt followed.

A sign for a scenic turnout (three miles) presented a course of action. From the leftmost lane and at full speed I'd exit without warning, let the little red car get far ahead, get gone so I didn't have to think about it anymore. Determined not to give myself away, I moved only my eyes, from odometer to the little red car to the dirt and pine along the right side of the road. A quick scan of my mirrors—

—and the little red car crossed the highway traffic and exited. So. Simple enough. All I needed to do was not exit. But I did exit, unable not to, unable to change my plan.

And there was the little red car, parked, stopped for a while so its driver could enjoy the scene, valley, river, mountain. Whatever. The sky. I parked alongside the little red car, afraid, adrenaline-jittery, eyes forward, a bird, some raptor, its path, down. I was in that little red car, years ago. The nose of my car touched the wood guardrail set a few yards from the lip of the cliff that fell to the valley bottom. I remembered, I knew the little red car. A few folks had spread a picnic across a shaded wooden table. They paid us no mind. I'd been a passenger in the little red car many times. I became aroused.

The driver-side door of the little red car opened. A girl, seventeen years old, emerged from the little red car. She stood at the guardrail like anyone would who stopped at a scenic view on the way to. . . on the way to wherever. I didn't get out of my car. I was too afraid. But I didn't turn the engine over and escape, either. The girl stepped over the guardrail—her skirt, very tight, very short, rose and stretched. Near the cliff-edge, she kicked at the dirt. Dust rose up around her feet. In heels, her action was horse-like, only, she was far too delicate to be a horse, she was more like a fawn. Finally, my hands, fists pushed hard against my thighs, the girl turned her back on the valley and I saw who I knew she must be, Marianne Ferris, and—impossible. Marianne Ferris was in my high school graduating class and so should be thirty-four, or thirty-three, or thereabouts. My age. Instead: seventeen year-old Marianne Ferris returned to her car, shut the door, turned on the ignition, drove through the wood guardrail, and over the edge of the cliff.

I followed. With deliberation, I backed up and drove my car through the gap she'd made in the guardrail, across a few yards of crumbling dirt, over, down. I caught a glimpse of the picnickers, a delightfully absurd sight, as my stomach laughed its way up my throat to my brain. My car hit the dirt, nose-first. The river loud, a short distance from my shattered windshield.

The little red car lay on its back, to the left of my car. Marianne drove the little red car to school every day. I rode with her many times.

I was unharmed, awake, alert. The engine and other under-the-hood-inner-workings of my car were shoved into the passenger seat beside me, stinking hot oil. My legs were free, the driver's side foot-well untroubled by the impact. I unbuckled my seatbelt and clumsily tumbled out of my car. Marianne's dusty high heeled shoes; she stood over me. Marianne smiled and tilted her head—just a hair, as she'd often done, a gesture she may once have cultivated but by the time I met her was her own, a gesture I loved. I got up on my knees and she sprinted, her skirt (I recognized that skirt) rose and stretched as it had before, rose high and tightened around her buttocks as she ran, accentuated the animal aspect of her movement. She ran through the grass that grew tall along the river's edge, followed a secret path.

I raised my right leg, angled forward, my instinct to run after her—I resisted, planted my feet, dug into the soft of the muddy river's edge. A while—Marianne gone, the tires of her dead car still—sirens and people shouting down at me. I couldn't understand the words.

I was later coming home than expected.

And I expected Janie to be worried, to have called and left escalating messages on my phone (lost in and with the car), but when I parked the rental in our driveway, the house was dark. The car clattered as it cooled. Janie must be asleep, I was relieved she was asleep, I hated when she worried, her worry made me feel guilty, and I wasn't sure how to explain why I was late or why I didn't call because I didn't know what had happened that morning. Marianne, Marianne Ferris, I'd thought of her often, grown erect and sleepy with nostalgia on long drives, remembering her as she was, as somehow she was still.

Janie was in the backyard, I caught her movement at the corner of my eye.

Janie was my wife. Her name was Jane and no one, not even her mother, called her Janie. Except me. It's a babyish thing to call a woman, I suppose, but I did once and it stuck, for us, she gave me permission to call her Janie, and from that permission came a pleasure hard to quantify or explain.

Janie stood in the yard, at the far end where the grass met a small stretch of trees. My mouth opened to call to her, but something about the way she moved—slightly, with her hands up in front of her face—caused me to shut my mouth.

As quietly as I tried to approach, Janie spotted me before I was halfway across the yard. Beyond her, something large and hidden among the trees, quickly moved away. Janie's body relaxed; her head dropped, her stance made it look as if she were sleepwalking, but she called my name, so I knew she wasn't. She wore jeans and a sweatshirt. I asked, "What are you doing out here?" She didn't reply right away, but walked to close the gap between us. She put her arms around me and pressed her face into my chest (except for her breasts, she was very small). Her hair was wet and it glistened. She'd just showered, the perfume of her shampoo. "Are you okay?" I asked. She nodded. I put my arm over her shoulder and we walked toward the house.

"Whose car is that?" she asked.

"It's a rental."

"Where's our car?"

"Our car is totaled."

She stopped and looked up at me, eyes wide.

"Janie, I'm fine. Look at me. I'm fine."

We resumed our walk to the house. The grass shushed as we moved over it. A branch snapped—Janie tensed, relaxed. She asked, "How did our car get totaled?"

"It fell off a cliff."

Janie laughed, then stopped mid-stride. "You're serious."

"I am." I told her the official story, which while more reasonable than the true story, didn't add up, didn't explain why next to my car was an abandoned little red car, or why I was unharmed after driving my car off a cliff, but the police didn't seem to want to know, didn't ask a lot of question and, when I think back, they supplied more answers than I did. Ultimately, the official story became: "I stopped at a scenic turnout to enjoy the view. Something in the car malfunctioned. The car accelerated on its own and drove through a gap in the guardrail." Janie interrupted and stumbled out an, "Oh my God." I squeezed her shoulders and urged her to keep on toward the house. We walked up a slope to the driveway. She touched the rental car as we passed. I continued: "The police think that the car was angled just so, and so while the front of the car was crushed, the driver's side was largely undamaged and me, I mean, I was undamaged."

In the kitchen, Janie squeezed me around my middle, squeezed tight enough to expel breath from my lungs and that felt good. She released me, a little, arms still around me, and we went upstairs to our bedroom where I took off her clothes (she'd worn no underwear) and we made love, quick, not great sex but good, and I thought of Marianne Ferris as I'd seen her today, exactly as I remembered her. Janie and I lay side by side, eyes open in our dark bedroom, eyes to the humming white ceiling, and I asked, "What were you doing in the yard?"

To which she replied:

"There was a deer in the yard."

She said, "I was undressed, about to put on pajamas, when I spotted a deer in the yard."

"A deer."

"Hmm," she said. "I almost went out naked."

I didn't understand why she almost went out naked, I almost asked but instead at that moment it occurred to me what I should have told my customer when he said he wasn't going to let my company manage his money. I should have said, "All you don't know is how good we are." To that, I smiled, woozy with exhaustion.

Janie said, "I went out into the yard. The deer didn't run away. It stood, with its head turned so it could look at me over its shoulder. I got really close. The deer moved away from me. I got close again. It led me, slowly, across the yard. And then you came home."

"Huh," was all I managed before I vanished into sleep. I felt sleep rise up around me and with it, memory.

Marianne Ferris was great looking and wore short skirts and I steered clear of her for the longest time. I thought, she's way more sophisticated than I am, and I'll never know her in any way at all. Next year she and I were in a class together and I found myself in brief, exhilarating, class-related contact. Senior year she often approached me during the free minutes before class to say hello and maybe to ask a question. History class, for instance:

"Hey, Brian."

"Hi."

"I can't remember the name of Otto von Bismarck's dog."

She leaned over my desk and her hair fell against my face as I flipped through our history text. I pointed to a caption: "Tyras," I read. "But, didn't he have lots of dogs?"

My thick-headed belief that Marianne Ferris could not possibly be romantically interested in me died one afternoon when she and I ran into each other in the city. Dressed in her street clothes, I didn't recognize her at first. The jeans she wore were not tight like her skirts, and instead of a blouse she wore a man's plaid shirt. Her hair was down, just straight. She said my name and I stopped. "Marianne Ferris," I said. With only a few months left of high school, we were still declared class couple, and girls said things to me like, "I can't even remember what it was like when you weren't together," and asked, "What are you buying her for your one-month anniversary?" I bought Marianne nothing. We laughed at our breathy classmates. Guys asked other questions, which, had I not actually cared about Marianne, I would have gladly answered. But I did care about her. And in that way we were mysterious. We were glad when school was over, both of us going to local colleges, me with a summer job at a movie theater. She worked at an ice cream stand. She was seventeen.

That day that we ran into each other in the city she bought the skirt that she would wear fifteen-plus years later, on the day she drove her little red car off a cliff and I followed. I was with her when she bought it; she stepped out of the dressing room, plaid shirt bunched up in her hand to better show the skirt and revealing a slim line of her belly—she turned—a slim line of her back. Of course I liked it, and said so, I was still amazed she'd said my name and further amazed she'd asked me to wait for her while she tried on some skirts. "That'll make Mrs. Kirk flinch," she said. "It is short," I said. Marianne twirled for me.

While with Marianne, my confidence emerged, but was unwieldy, and thus the screw up, at a summer party, the last house party Marianne's cohorts at the ice cream stand threw (they had the best parties, they knew everyone). I went to the party late, the last show over after midnight, sweeping popcorn well after the ice cream stand was shuttered. I walked over in my theater uniform, bow tie unhooked (a clip-on). The girl who answered the door was Susan, she answered with a drink in hand and said, "I made this just for you," though it was half gone, obviously her own, and she touched my nose with her pinkie before she gave me the glass, rum and diet Coke-a-Cola. Susan led me to Marianne, who was sweetly drunk and happy to see me, in the middle of extra-soft couch with two co-workers, girls like Susan. Marianne tried to get up, failed, she took my hand and I pulled her up and we kissed and danced, and her co-workers teased us and all was good for a while, until Marianne and I were separated, somehow, and I wound up in the backyard on a hammock, very drunk, and Susan climbed into the hammock with me, and Susan and I kissed, my eyes half closed, my hands on Susan's breasts and down the back of her pants as far as my reach allowed. I blacked out some of the time, distant party noise, glass beer bottles, a television. Marianne found us like that. I was too drunk to apologize or to show remorse or even to take my hand out of Susan's pants. A week later Marianne and I met for coffee, not a cup drunk. A couple weeks after that we went to college, both broken-hearted (I think she was; I was, and I felt stupid, too. I felt stupid and bad for a long time).

The night of the party, after Marianne found me with Susan, after Susan crept away, I hung in the hammock, struggled with my drunk, and heard an animal knocking trash cans.

When I woke up, next to my wife, the morning after the accident, I felt guilty. I put a tie around my collar, looked at Janie as she slept a little extra, and I went down to the kitchen for a bowl of cereal. I felt guilty. Not for the car, but because Marianne Ferris was on my mind all the time, I couldn't remember when she wasn't my mind, maybe, maybe for a while when I first met Janie, when Janie and I were first married, but ever since, Marianne Ferris. I didn't want breakfast. I said to myself, I did nothing wrong. That wasn't quite true, but I knew what I meant. I hadn't hurt Janie.

Before I left, Janie joined me in the kitchen, bathrobe, hair up, sloppy. She asked, "You totaled the car? Are you sure you're okay? Shouldn't you take the day off? Are you okay to drive today? Our car malfunctioned?" I said, "Everything's fine."

JANIE

From the bedroom window I saw a girl as she walked along the far end of the backyard. She moved along the tree line, in and out of shadow. I knew some of the high school girls in the neighborhood, sometimes they came to me for advice, I wasn't too old, and I was always around. The girls would walk into my yard when they saw me out on the back steps drinking vodka/pomegranate/soda. There was Kathy, Carrie, and Maureen, and there was Jenny and Darla. They all lived in nearby houses. Once or twice a girl showed up late in the day, shadowing our house, looking in windows to see if I was around. I turned off the lights to better see the yard. Brian was very late coming home from work. The bedroom clock: 9:37. I was undressed, still damp from a bath. I stood at the window, put my forehead to the cool glass and watched. The girl moved slow, her steps herky-jerky, as if her feet were asleep/not her own. She wore a blouse and a short skirt. Heels would explain that walk.

I was downstairs and at the kitchen door before I noticed I was naked. I put on the jeans and sweatshirt that I'd draped over the back of a chair to dry after an afternoon sun shower and went out into the yard. Barefoot, I enjoyed the shock of cold grass. I said, "Kathy," though I was sure it wasn't Kathy, and I said, "Jenny," though sure the girl was not her, either; the names were a comfort to me, real girls I knew and cared for, silly girls.

I stood halfway between the house and the tree line, in a pool of shadow where the yard dipped, and so no girl at all, and felt lost. The air smelled of gasoline and of something else. Popcorn. A cool breeze caused the trees to shiver, their leaves turning, dark green/black, dark green/black. A deer moved along the tree line. Had I mistaken a deer for a girl?

The deer took a step away from me, stopped, looked to where I stood, and I very nearly pointed to myself, as if to ask, *me?* I approached the animal. My first feelings were this deer is a beautiful creature, how special this moment is, etc., but all those sentimental, automatic feelings were gradually replaced by lust. Not desire: bloodlust. I wanted to kill the deer, but I did not know how.

Brian touched my shoulder, I started, the deer disappeared among trees. My bloodlust transferred briefly onto Brian, then dissipated, almost wholly, but not completely, and so I was glad Brian wanted sex, quick and simple.

The next day, Brian at the office, doing the horrible job that sustained us ("I sell asset management plans"), I slept on the couch till noon, ate lunch, felt gross and forced myself to take a walk around the block. I considered walking into the woods behind our house, a little nothing patch of trees that kept the main road from sight, but the overgrown ferns and vines and probably poison ivy put me off. I stood at the end of a deer path and looked but did nothing. The sun filtered through green, lots of green and was pretty, and the green nearly put me to sleep where I stood. Around three I sat on the back steps with a glass of vodka/pomegranate/soda staring out at the yard, which I needed to mow and would later or the next day if I could muster the energy. Darla, sans her gal pal Jenny, stood at the edge of my backyard, with her hand up to shade her eyes and she waved when she saw me.

"Hey Jane," she said, as if she'd bumped into me. She lit a cigarette, a recently developed habit, some stupid boy's fault, so I gathered from Jenny, who would surely be carrying her own cigarettes soon enough. Darla didn't ask if it was okay to smoke, nor did she offer me a cigarette; she was low on etiquette. I vaguely wanted one, but mostly didn't.

"Darla," I said. "Where's Jenny?"

"David, *I think*." Darla touched her lip and asked, "What're you drinking?"

I held my glass up to my eyes: "This has a stupid name I won't say. It's vodka, pomegranate, and soda." I tipped the glass to my lips.

She wanted some; I would give her none. She'd never ask but she added:

"I like vodka." She paused for my reaction. I sipped. She sat down beside me. "So," she said.

She pulled and puffed at her cigarette, then bent over and rubbed out her cigarette on the last of the steps where I sat. She didn't know what to do with the butt or with the black smudge she'd left on my step. She rubbed at the smudge with her foot and slipped the butt into a little coin pocket on the front of her jeans. There was hope.

"Don't worry about it, Darla."

She folded her arms.

"What's on your mind?"

Her lips moved, a little. I looked out across the backyard and decided I wouldn't have the energy to mow the lawn. I squeezed my eyes a little and the trees bent together. Or: did an animal move behind the trees?

"Darla, did you see something?"

"Where?"

I pointed with my glass.

Darla leaned forward, squinted, put her hand up to her forehead as she'd done from the street: was it really so sunny? Darla's lipstick was too orange. I asked, "What's on your mind?"

"David."

She touched her pack of cigarettes but I guess she decided not to smoke. I was a little sorry because I would've had a puff, but I didn't want to ask for a cigarette because that seemed too much like encouraging her, and I felt some vague urge, as an adult, I guess, to promote not smoking, or something to that effect. Perhaps, I thought for an instant, I didn't care at all, and I should pour Darla some vodka, and the two of us should get really drunk together, and watch television until her parents sent the police out looking for her, if her parents cared, and if they didn't then I don't know what.

She said, "David and Jenny are going out. They've been going out for two weeks. Last night the three of us went out to see a movie. Before the movie started Jenny went out to the lobby to talk to Sarah, who had some news she wanted to tell Jenny, and while she was gone I put my hand on David's leg."

"You did?"

"Yeah. I put my hand on his leg and, you know, I felt it get hard."

I finished my drink and said, "On his leg?"

"You know."

"Sure."

"So?"

"Um?"

"What should I do?"

I took Darla's cigarettes and put one in my mouth. Lighting my bummed cigarette did not occur to her, so I put it to my mouth and tapped the filter with the tip of my tongue, waited a second, took the cigarette from my mouth and said, "Maybe, don't touch David's penis?" I tucked the cigarette behind my ear.

"I know that."

"Why did you?"

"I like David."

"Trust me. You don't like David more than you like Jenny. She's your friend. Come on. I need to get a refill." In the kitchen, Darla watched me make another vodka/pomegranate/soda. Not offering her a drink, of any kind, was my revenge for her not offering a light. I lit my cigarette off a stove burner, smoked for the first time in. . . I couldn't remember, I wondered if I'd smoked with Darla before, felt woozy, then calm, then guilty: in Brian's kitchen, I thought. From the back step I saw movement in the woods. "Darla, do you see something?" I pointed.

"Yeah, a deer," she said. "How sweet," she added.

"Yeah."

Then Darla said, "I know Jenny's my friend, but I don't think you realize."

"Maybe not, Darla." I saw the next few months of Darla's life play out: summer would come, she'd be at a party with Jenny, and David, no doubt Jenny's ex by then, would be there, and late at night, in the backyard of whomever was throwing the party, Darla would make out with David. And Jenny would be pissed off and

Jenny and Darla wouldn't return to school as friends, and David, stupid, stupid David, well what could it possibly matter?

Darla stayed longer than she usually did. Eventually, we shared things: Darla, my drink, me, her cigarettes and her lighter. When Brian came home Darla said, "Hi," and then wandered off, coin pocket full of cigarette butts, hers and mine. She wandered across our backyard, to a spot where the trees were parted, a little doorway in the woods.

"What's wrong with her?" Brian asked.

"A boy," I said. And I said, "Let's order Chinese, shall we? I was too tired to go to the grocery store today and besides I don't feel like cooking."

Oh, Brian, the way you sighed. If only you knew how I exhausted I was all of the time. Pour me another! But I didn't ask for another. I nibbled at the steamed vegetables. Later, I thought, I'd eat all the fried rice. I would sit on the back steps with a tablespoon and shovel rice into my mouth. Soon after dinner, Brian went to bed. I sat in the living room, television on but the sound down—occasionally a glimmer of laughter. The book on my knee was spent, damp, pages dropped out onto the floor. When the television screen went dark between programs, I saw reflected the living room. And beside the television, the window, blinds up, it also reflected the living room, and me, but in that reflection was the dark grassy backyard. A deer put its face to the window and I screamed.

The deer's oval-shaped face emerged, like something floating up from the bottom of a murky pool. A white, ragged stripe from the deer's nose to its forehead. No horns, a female, the same, I knew, as I'd seen the night before. And possibly that afternoon.

Brian did not come down the stairs. My scream had not been enough to rouse him after an exhausting, dreadful day calling potential investors, most smart enough to know that the firm Brian worked for was worthless.

The deer's face disappeared from the window. I carried my drink, less pomegranate, less soda, and went out into the backyard. The grass, black. Faint light only exaggerated the darkness of the woods where I was sure I saw movement, the deer or the girl. I rushed across the lawn, my drink sloshed onto my hand, cold; it dried and that felt good. I stumbled, that dip in the yard, and very nearly dropped my glass. A sip. I walked on, into the woods, I crashed into branches, and my drink slipped from my hand and the glass shattered. Brian, you idiot, I thought, you wrecked our car. I stepped into a stream. The water was cold and polluted, and soon my bare feet were sticky. Again, I'd rushed from the house without shoes. At least I was dressed, I thought, and I laughed, a kind of a snort. I walked without caution and soon my feet stopped hurting, didn't hurt when I stepped on sharp rocks or sticks, when my foot went sideways into a hole, some animal's burrow. The trees were luminescent with a mossy light. I waked through a shallow pond, felt slime coated stones and living things, they swam up the cuffs of my pants, attached themselves to my legs. My heart beat hard and steady. Ahead of me the trees fell away—

—a backyard.

Jenny's.

Jenny and Darla and I had walked in Jenny's backyard once before, on a calm afternoon. A cool afternoon. Even night, now, was warm. My body was hot and prickled.

The yard was a dark plane, the house ahead was white. A single window on the ground floor was lit, the blinds up, a hot square. Jenny's bedroom. From the dark yard my view was perfect, Jenny on her bed, sitting up on her knees, and a boy— surely, David—in Jenny's bedroom. Her parents out or asleep. From where I stood, beneath her window, they moved without sound, but I put two fingers to the window and felt the glass vibrate and so I knew, they talked, there was sound. The yard was endlessly silent, no clicking crickets and frogs, only black grass growing up around my bare feet.

David wasn't naked—why was that?—her shirt, off, her bra, unclasped (it un-hooked in the front), her belt undone and he pulled at her jeans, tugged while she sat up and wriggled her little hips, helped him to undress her. She reached for the buttons of his shirt. He dipped forward and kissed her clavicle, her breasts. Jenny's head back, she sighed; her excitement breathy and sick, my terror for her huge:

I slapped the glass and shouted,

I shouted, "Jenny! Don't!"

Jenny and David turned to the window, frightened, blind. With the light so brilliant in Jenny's room, they surely couldn't see me, or saw only a shape, an animal tapping its head on the glass. I slapped the glass again, with both hands, "Jenny! Don't ruin everything!"

She didn't cover herself, as I would've. Nor did David panic. He dashed for the light switch and I ran, a flash burning across the yard. I burned through the little forest, through the muck and wet, stopped for a breath only when I at last stood in my kitchen. And though the kitchen was cool I could not get cool, I sweated and my abdomen turned, I felt my intestines working feverishly to expel some rotten thing I'd consumed. At the kitchen table, I put my hands palm-down, tried to push the table into the linoleum. I could imagine pouring a vodka, but I could not get up from where I sat until—

—I heard a noise from the bedroom upstairs; a noise like an animal crashing through a forest.

As complex as the sound was, it did not last. But it had been real and real enough to move me from my seat, bare feet sticking to the floor, wet pant-cuffs stiffly shifting with each step I took, up, upstairs to the bedroom. I opened the door.

My husband, Brian, lay asleep, naked and uncovered, his penis semi-erect and wet—it glistened as it had the night before. Beside him, on my side of the bed, was a deer. (All our bedclothes on the floor in a heap at the foot of the bed). I squinted in the dim-lit room. A doe, that's what they're called, lay on her side, peacefully, I supposed, sleeping. Eyes shut, belly (flank) rising up and down as she breathed, a doe, and from between her hind legs a slick trail to Brian that would dry white and stain.

I clapped my hands together once. The doe started, her head rose quick from my pillow, her legs, too. Brian stirred, but did not wake. She was awake, though. The doe scrambled upright, stood ridiculously on my bed, caused the mattress to sink deep where I usually slept so lightly. Brian woke when she trotted off the bed onto the hardwood floor. The noise her hooves made—

Brian shouted, then he shouted my name, "Janie!" and yelled, "Look out!" as if I might not have noticed the deer, as if he was surprised we were all there.

I ran at her. She dodged my attack with ease, her reflexes fast and natural. My wet pants tripped me up, they were loose on me and heavy, so I stepped out of them, free now half-naked.

I ran out of the bedroom, after the doe. She stumbled in the hallway, her big body crashed into the wall (the plaster cracked), and I caught up enough to give her a big push: I put my hands on her rump and shoved and she stumbled forward, toward the stairs, and at the top step she lost her balance, crashed down the stairs and collapsed, a disaster in our living room, broken legs, more than that, probably. She writhed, turned her head up—I glared down from the top step. She mewled, pitifully, and I felt sorry for her, a dumb animal.

And yet, she had tricked me, lured me into the woods she knew so well, saw me lost and double-backed. So, perhaps not so dumb, not so dumb as Brian, wrecker-of-cars, foolish enough to keep a dreadful job and to fall asleep with his girl-animal, when he must have known I wouldn't be lost forever.

Brian stood in the doorway of our bedroom. He wore only his slippers. His thick, dark hair was matted, pushed flat. He held out his arms and said, "That was terrible, how horrifying, are you okay? I just can't believe, I just don't know how she got in. Oh, Janie."

"Don't call me that!" I shouted.

And then I said, "Brian."

And I said, "You will drag her carcass out. You will put her carcass in the car you've rented. You will leave, and you will never come back."

Brian wanted to explain but instead told me about a girl he dated when he was in high school. I said nothing. He told me he needed clothes. I said, "You're perfect the way you are." His pitiful, pale, naked butt exposed, he followed his girlfriend down the stairs.

STRANGE SKIN

BY BENTLEY LITTLE

Rumor has it that this previously unpublished tale by the astonishing Bentley Little has been sitting on his desk for many years, unwanted and unloved. That he wrote it during his college days, where he may or may not have subsidized his education with titillating tales for the gentlemen's rags. And that for decades, it has been rejected by every single editor *that laid eyes upon its terribly,terribly twisted pages.*

I don't know if a word of this is true, or whether it's just another red herring stacked up around the legend of Bentley Little: the most reclusive, mysterious giant in the field of modern horror.

I will say that this story is a punch right in the teeth, another in the gut, and then one in the you-know-where. Or do *you?*

I am fiercely proud to publish this malformed classic for the very first time.

It had been a dry summer. He and Felicia had broken up back in May, at the end of the semester, and he hadn't found anyone since. It was not for lack of trying. He'd gone with his friends to clubs, he'd hung out at the beach, he'd even tried hitting on some of the customers in the store, although his boss, when she caught him, had rebuked him for it.

He supposed that was why he decided to try the hooker.

He had never understood before why men would visit prostitutes. Particularly these days, with AIDS and everything. But as he knew now, the sex drive was very strong. Sex was addicting and almost impossible to give up, especially once you'd gotten used to experiencing it regularly.

Masturbation only went so far, and after having real sex, it was like going back to riding a tricycle after you'd been an Indy racer.

He'd started out by surfing the Internet, content at first merely to see naked females again.

But looking at beautiful women and not being able to touch them had been incredibly frustrating.

Rather than sate his desires, it had increased them. He'd graduated to porno newspapers, the ones they sold in front of the post office, and after looking at the photos of gorgeous, willing women adorning the ads, he'd finally broken down and called what was euphemistically referred to as an "escort service." They did not talk specifics over the phone. He was given an "appointment," a time and place where they would meet, and he grabbed a pen and wrote down the instructions on his hand.

The location was a coffee shop not that far from his apartment. He had assumed for some reason that he would be given directions to a secret bordello somewhere in the sleazy part of Hollywood or downtown L.A., and the fact that this woman suggested a nearby restaurant—without even knowing where he lived—surprised him. Obviously, she was a local.

He hoped to God it wasn't one of the store's customers. He'd never be able to live that down.

The appointment wasn't until tomorrow, and he worried about it all day and all night. He considered canceling several times and once even made an effort to call, but he hung up when she answered. He was not sure if he *wanted* to go through with this or was afraid *not* to go through with it, but he was committed, and at the appointed time he went down to the coffee shop to wait.

He'd scanned the restaurant when he first walked in, and he kept an eye on everyone who walked through the door, but no one looking even remotely like a prostitute entered or left the building. It was twenty minutes past the meeting time and he was about to bail when a nondescript young woman from one of the rear booths stopped by his table on her way out the door. "Excuse me," she said. "Are you Reed?" He nodded, looking up. She was nothing like he'd expected. In his mind, he'd seen a cinematic sexpot, all blond hair and high heels, short skirt and tight blouse, but this woman looked more like a secretary or librarian. She was wearing a conservative business ensemble that covered up almost everything. Her eyes were hidden behind glasses, her hair pulled back in a brown ponytail.

Somehow, that made it seem more exciting.

She appeared nervous, almost as though this was her first time, and that, too, seemed exciting.

"I'm Jen," she said.

They talked for a few moments, he hesitant and unsure of how to proceed, she acting as though this was a regular date.

Finally, she suggested that they leave, and he paid the bill and met her outside. She quoted a price and told him to follow her; they'd drive in separate cars.

She led him to a motel on Beach Boulevard. She already had a room key, and he parked his car next to hers and followed her into a dingy little suite. There was a pot on the small stove, women's clothes in the open closet, and he wondered if this was where she lived.

The thought depressed him.

They talked terms again, and he paid her eighty dollars up front. She made it clear she would not perform oral or anal, but "you can do anything else you want," she told him. She walked into the bathroom, closing the door. "Make yourself comfortable," she said. "I'll be out in a minute." He pulled down the bedspread and sheet, took off his clothes, and crawled under the covers.

She emerged from the bathroom a moment later, wearing only a white silk chemise. There was still something of the innocent about her, an incongruity between her appearance and her profession, and he was already hard by the time she reached the bed.

She pulled down the covers, smiled at his erect organ, and slowly slipped off her chemise.

He stared at her crotch.

She had no pubic hair.

No vagina.

No penis.

Nothing.

Reaching out, he rubbed his hands wonderingly between her legs, feeling only smooth skin, a soft, pliant warmth that was unlike anything he'd ever touched before.

She seemed self-conscious about her body, and he stopped caressing her as she crawled into bed. Was she a freak? He supposed she was, but it was not a repellant aberration. Her physical abnormality did not repulse him. On the contrary, he found it quite exciting, sensuous in a weird way, and he was even more aroused than he had been before.

She tried to pull the covers over the two of them, but he pushed them back, over and off the side of the mattress. "I want to see," he said.

She nodded, reached for him. Her hands were soft, but not as soft as the smooth skin between her legs, and even as she manipulated his penis with her fingers, he was rolling her onto her back, climbing on top.

His erection slid against her, pressing against that strange skin. He longed desperately for penetration and it was maddeningly frustrating not to be able to enter her, but it was also highly erotic, and he had never felt anything like it. The sensation grew, the warm softness affecting him in a way that nothing else ever had. He realized almost instantly that he was not going to be able to hold out, and, hole or no hole, he began thrusting.

He moved up onto his knees as he climaxed, crouching between her spread legs, pressing his spurting organ where her vagina should be.

His semen was absorbed into her skin.

He watched the thick milky liquid melt into her pale unblemished flesh, individual drops seeming to evaporate, larger squirts being visibly sucked into invisible pores.

A moment later, her crotch and belly were clean and dry. There was no indication that his semen had ever landed on her body.

She smiled up at him.

How did she pee? he wondered. Did she have a menstrual cycle? Maybe everything oozed *out* of the skin the same way his sperm had oozed in.

The skin.

It was the skin that intrigued him so, that smooth patch between her legs where her sex should have been. He had never felt, never seen, never heard of anything even remotely like it.

No one else on earth had that skin.

Was that possible? He supposed it was. In this media-saturated society where uniformity was not only admired but considered a worthy goal, uniqueness had become something exotic, something excitedly reported upon by tabloid news programs, sleazy magazines, and unattributable Internet sources. If this had been a recognized medical condition—even a rare one—chances were that he would have heard about it before, would have at least come across hints and whispers on the porno sites if nowhere else.

She might be the only one like this.

That intrigued him even more, and he felt himself stiffening again as he stared down at that hairless unblemished skin. She looked up, saw his arousal, and started to sit up, but once again he lay down on top of her, and though she struggled a little, tried to squirm away, she didn't tell him to get off, didn't say no.

Could you rape a hooker? He didn't know, didn't think so, but at this point he didn't really care. He could feel the warm giving smoothness against the underside of his penis, and he moved faster, rubbing harder, aching for release. He had never been able to come more than once with Felicia, had not thought he was able to do so, but the sense of draining tiredness he usually experienced after orgasm was nowhere in evidence, and he was as excited as he had been the first time.

He looked into her face as he moved. Her eyes were closed, her mouth open and gasping, but the expression on her face was not one of ecstasy, not even feigned ecstasy. It was more like . . . hunger.

Before he could think about that, before he could analyze it, he was coming, and he pulled up, away from her, not wanting to climax while their bodies were pressed together, not wanting the sticky sperm to adhere to his hairy stomach.

Wanting to watch it be absorbed into her skin.

He spurted between her legs again, holding himself, pointing, and once more the thick milky liquid sank into the clear skin, the small outer drops disappearing first, the main mass of puddled semen sucked more slowly into the invisible pores of her featureless groin.

Breathing deeply, feeling a satisfying emptiness in his testicles that was just this side of pain, he flopped down on the bed next to her, rolling onto his back.

Jen got up immediately, without speaking, swinging her legs off the bed, pulling on her chemise and hurrying into the bathroom.

She emerged a few moments later, dressed once again like a librarian, sorting through her purse. He heard the jingle of keys.

"Hey," he said. "Where're you going?" She spoke rapidly, embarrassedly, not looking at him. "I have to get back: Just close the door when you leave. It'll lock automatically." "Wait." "I can't. I have to get back." "Get back?" "To work." "I thought this was your work." "Just make sure the door's locked." She hurried out of the motel room, closing the door behind her, and Reed scrambled to find his clothes on the floor. He quickly pulled on his pants, slipped into his shirt, grabbed his underwear, socks, and shoes, and ran out of the room. He saw her across the parking lot, getting into her car, and, still holding his socks and underwear, he forced his bare feet into his Nikes and dashed across the asphalt to his Honda. He fumbled for his keys, found them, started the car.

She backed up and pulled out of the parking lot, moving onto Beach, heading south.

He followed her.

She drove first to a strip mall on the edge of Buena Park, parking in front of a convenience store and walking next door to a small unmarked office sandwiched between the store and a nail parlor. He parked on the street, slumping low in his car seat, and watched as she knocked on the shaded glass door. It opened.

His eyes remained focused on the shifting material covering her thighs and buttocks, and once again he felt a stirring between his legs.

Were there others? he wondered. And, if so, what were they? Women with a genetic mutation? An alternate race of creatures? Aliens who had infiltrated human society? One seemed just as plausible to him as the other.

She did not go in the office but stood in the open doorway, and he watched her hand an envelope to a dark-haired woman in a red business suit. Was this one of her peers? Was this one of *them?* He didn't have time to think about it. She waved good-bye, turned back toward her car, and he ducked down even further so as not to be seen.

This time he followed her across Orange County to an area of Irvine comprised of recently constructed high-rises. She parked in a gated lot adjacent to the Automated Interface office complex, and he watched from the street as she walked into the only single-story building on the property.

The letters above the ultrawide doors spelled out RON STEWART MEMORIAL TECH LIBRARY. She *was* a librarian.

He sat there for a minute, thinking, then drove away, heading back home.

He knew where she worked.

That was good enough for now.

Finances were tight and his checking account was overdrawn, but three days later he called the "escort service" once again, asking specifically for Jen. He was told that she was unavailable and he almost hung up then but when the woman on the other end of the line asked if there was someone else she could set him up with, he said, "Do you have anyone else *like* Jen?" He stressed the word *like*, hoping the woman would catch his meaning, and his heart rate sped up as she said, "There's Leece." "Fine," he said.

He met Leece in Anaheim, in a motel bar, and he recognized her immediately. This one looked like a hooker, provocative clothes, heavy makeup, and all, and at first her appearance turned him off, but as his gaze moved down to the tight skirt covering her crotch, he felt himself responding.

Maybe she had the skin, too.

Again, they retired to a motel. He paid the woman in advance, asked her to disrobe, and was disappointed to learn when she slipped off her panties that she had a vagina. It was bald, shaved, but it was there nevertheless, traditional women's sex organs, and he felt as though he'd been somehow cheated as he looked at the overly large lips of her vulva. He saw no resemblance to Jen at all, and the realization came to him that the woman on the phone had lied.

He'd paid, though, and he was determined to go through with it, and he lay there as the woman worked on him with her tongue. It took a long time, and he could sense that she was getting annoyed, so he closed his eyes, thought of Jen's featureless crotch, and felt his penis stiffen as he imagined thrusting against that smooth skin. Crying out, he grabbed the hooker's head and spurted into her mouth.

He was the first one to leave this time, quickly putting on his clothes and hurrying away without saying a word.

He drove to Irvine.

Waited by her car in the Automated Interface parking lot.

She saw him as she walked out after work, the expression on her face hardening as she approached. There was a sinking feeling in the pit of his stomach, but he forced himself to smile at her as she took the keys from her purse. "Jen," he said. "Hi." She ignored him, walked by him, unlocked the driver's door.

"Jen?" he said, reaching for her arm.

She pulled away. "Get out of here," she said. "Or I'll call security." "I asked for you," he told her. "When I called the service." "No," she said. "Only once to a customer." "'Once to a customer?' What the hell does that mean?" "It means I don't have regulars. It means I don't do the same john twice. It means that you can call and ask for me all you want, but you're not going to get me." "I'll pay extra!" She took a deep breath, looked at him. "No. Thanks for the offer. I'm very flattered and everything, but no." She opened her car door, got in.

He followed her home.

He cut her after he killed her, slicing off the skin between her legs. He was afraid he'd damage it with his clumsiness, but he couldn't exactly hire a surgeon to come out to a murder scene and perform an emergency genital excision, so he had no choice but to perform the procedure himself.

She hadn't lived in the motel room after all, but in a quiet suburban neighborhood in Orange. She'd screamed as he leaped the low hedge bordering her lawn and forced his way into the house immediately after she'd unlocked the door, and he'd covered her mouth at first only because he wanted her to stop screaming. But he realized even as he mentally mapped out the logistics of his planned rape that he didn't really need her at all. It was not the hooker he wanted but her crotch, the skin between her legs. So instead of forcing her to the floor, he'd increased the pressure of his hand on her mouth, took the back of her head in his other hand, and twisted her neck.

Then he'd cut her.

Her entryway was covered with puddled blood, and that was a turnoff, but even unattached to a body, her crotch was almost unbearably sexy. He couldn't help himself, and he made sure the door was locked, then quickly pulled down his pants.

Closing his eyes, he held the chunk of flesh with both hands, rubbing it over his penis. It felt just as he remembered—warm and soft and unlike anything else in the world—and he climaxed almost immediately, unable to hold back and prolong his pleasure.

He opened his eyes, watched his semen being absorbed into the skin.

Part of him was horrified by what he had done, and he stared at Jen's mutilated body in abhorrence and shocked disgust, unable to believe that he had actually killed her, but then he looked down at the bloody severed crotch in his hands and he knew that he had done the right thing.

It was the only thing he *could* have done.

He cleaned up before he left.

And did it once more in the kitchen.

Reed kept it in the refrigerator.

He used it several times a day—morning, noon and night—and he realized sometime after the third day that he no longer thought about finding a woman anymore. It was not love he'd been after, not companionship, but sex, pure and simple, and Jen's excised crotch met all of his needs. It was all he wanted, all he desired, and it provided him with a pleasure that neither Felicia nor his own hands had ever been able to match.

A week later, he discovered that the meat behind the skin was beginning to rot.

He'd just finished using it, had just warmed up the cold crotch with his hot lust, had just watched the endlessly fascinating spectacle of his seed being drawn into the smooth featureless skin, when he detected in the air a soft whiff of decay, a subtle hint of degeneration and incipient putrefaction. He knew instantly what it was, of course, but he didn't want to believe it, and he pushed the thought out of his mind and replaced Jen's groin on the middle refrigerator shelf next to the milk.

But when he took it out again later that night, he turned it over, examining the ragged backing flesh into which he usually sunk his hands as he pressed the skin against his penis. The red edges of clumsily cut fat and muscle were beginning to turn a sort of grayish brown, and he touched that area with a tentative finger. The flesh felt slightly hardened to him, as though it were drying out.

Panic threatened to overwhelm him. He was not a doctor, not a scientist, hell, not even a meat cutter. He didn't know what to do. He didn't know how long body parts stayed fresh or how to keep them from rotting. He felt physically ill at the thought of losing the skin, and he thought of freezing it, wrapping it, sealing it and putting it in the freezer, taking it out only when he could no longer hold back and *had* to have sex, but he knew that would not work. For one thing, freezing would only prolong the degeneration, not stop it. And for another, he was using Jen's crotch three or four times a day. Even if he cut that in half—something that was doubtful in itself—he would still be taking it out of the freezer at least once or twice in every twelve-hour period.

He had to think of something else.

It came to him as he came.

He finished up, placed the flesh on the kitchen counter, and got out his sharpest knife.

He peeled the skin from the meat, carefully sliding it off in a single creased sheet.

There was no blood left by this time, and the fat and muscle separated easily from the skin, much more easily than he would have expected. He worked slowly, not wanting to nick or cut the skin at all, wanting only to remove the rotting material behind it. He had not made up his mind what to do with the skin afterward, was half-thinking of drying it out like parchment or beef jerky so it would not rot, but he figured he had time to sort that out later. This would buy him some extra days, maybe even some extra weeks, and he could do some research, find out what needed to be done.

He had just climaxed a few moments before, but there was no trace of his semen on the front of the skin or on the back of it. There was nothing on the chunks of meat either, and once again he marveled at how the skin just seemed to absorb his sperm and make his fluids a part of it.

There was also something sensuous about cutting the crotch, dissecting the remaining parts of Jen's groin, and though his penis was still throbbing with pain from the power of his last orgasm, it was also stiffening again, and he ran his hands over the smooth skin, touching his fingertips lightly against the soft substance.

Picking up the skin, he wrapped it around his engorged organ. He didn't plan or think about it, just did it, and the skin adhered to his erection like a smooth soft sheath created expressly for that purpose. Already he was spurting, hot painful jets squirting out of his penis, and the warm wetness that lingered for a few seconds before being replaced by a slight sucking dryness was even more erotic than his previously vigorous thrusting had been. He wondered why he had not cut off the skin and wrapped it around his cock before.

He stood there for a moment, unmoving, until the last tentative tremors of orgasm had passed through him, then attempted to pull the skin from his penis.

He could not get it off.

He tugged on the edge he'd been holding, bracing himself, expecting it to hurt, prepared for the adhesion of the skin to rip away as though held by superglue, but the feeling instead was one of soft caressing. He yanked with all his might, but the skin would not come off and the sensation that was translated to his penis was a velvety feather touch that seemed to revive his sore and tired organ.

Again, he felt himself hardening.

He did not want another orgasm. He wanted only to be free of this unnatural stimulation, and he drew on the *skin*, grasping his penis as hard as he could and pulling it up, down, to the left, to the right.

He came.

He was practically crying, overcome with a sense of panic. He didn't know what to do, and for the first time Reed regretted what he'd done to Jen, regretted ever *meeting* Jen. Despite the great sex, he wished he'd never encountered that smooth, hairless crotch.

He glanced around the kitchen, looking for something he could use to get the integument off him. He found vegetable oil and doused his covered genitals with it to try to slide his penis out, used a knife to try to slice the skin off, but neither plan worked, and he spent the next hour running around the house, trying everything and anything to extricate himself, before finally ending up in his bedroom and falling back on the bed, sobbing in pain and frustration.

The orgasms had not abated, and the overwhelming sense of panic that had overtaken him was stronger. He closed his eyes against the pain, against the horrid reality of what was happening to him, and he fell asleep, still climaxing, though by now nothing was coming out and his penis burned as though his urethra were filled with broken glass.

In the morning, his penis was gone.

He could tell the difference immediately, and he reached a hand between his legs and felt only smooth skin where his cock and balls had been. He jumped up, hurried over to the full-length mirror on the back of the bedroom door, and examined his pubic area.

The skin had merged with his own.

There was no way to tell where his real epidermis left off and Jen's crotch began.

A dull sinking feeling settled in the pit of his stomach, and he touched himself, rubbed himself, poked himself, and it was a full five minutes before his brain allowed him to recognize what he knew to be true.

He no longer had any sexual feeling in his body.

He no longer had any sexual desire.

He looked like a Ken doll or a G.I. Joe. There was not even a slight bulge between his legs, and he continued to stare at and examine himself in the mirror.

Had Jen done the same thing he had? Had she killed someone for the skin? He didn't know, but it didn't seem that implausible, and for the first time since he had met her, since all of this had started, he was afraid. The sheer irrationality of it, the bizarre incomprehensibility, had never really registered before. He'd accepted it too easily, bought into it unquestioningly, and now he realized just how big a mistake that had been. He had no idea what had happened to him, no idea why. This was not a simplistic O. Henry horror-story payback, not a personalized example of karma going around and coming around. It was more impersonal, more . . . inevitable, and he understood that he would never know where the skin had come from or what it really did.

He had used it.

And now it was using him.

He urinated through his mouth, he discovered. It was like vomiting, only backward, and the disgusting thing was that his taste buds continued to work perfectly. They were not impaired in any way and there was no possibility of shutting them off.

He could no longer eat. He tried to. He shoved crackers in his mouth, crackers and chips, chewing them, but his body would not allow him to swallow. He could not even get the food down far enough to throw it up. Meat, pasta, soup, bread, all of it sat in his mouth and dribbled back over his lips. He was unable to ingest either solids or liquids. He had to obtain his nourishment from . . . a woman's juices.

The knowledge was instinctive, not a rational thought but an understanding that seemed to be long-held, and as the first day passed, and the second, and the third, and he remained in his house, growing weaker and hungrier, he realized that he was going to have to go out and find a woman.

And eat her.

That old slang phrase was far more apt than he wanted it to be.

He went to a bar, a singles bar he'd frequented in earlier, more innocent times, and he met a woman, and he bought her a drink, and he took her to a motel. It was not the same motel in which he'd gone with Jen, but the similarities were impossible not to miss, and he thought numbly, *This is how it starts.*

They sat on the bed, talked for a while, kissed, touched, began rolling around, and he knew it was time to make his move.

He stood, unbuttoned his shirt. "I won't do oral or anal," he told her, the words emerging from his mouth of their own accord. He realized it was the same thing Jen had said.

"What?" she said, confused.

He pulled down his pants and the woman stared at the smooth, unblemished skin between his legs. He recognized on her face the same excited fascination he himself had experienced the first time he'd seen Jen, and he took off his clothes, pulled her up off the bed, undressed her. They lay down again, kissing and her hand strayed between his thighs, stroking him. There was still no feeling, no sexual feeling, but his stomach was growling with hunger.

He scissored his legs sideways, and she slid between them so her hairy crotch was pressed against his. She began moving, and he felt every ridge and indentation of her vulva, the tingling skin between his legs registering the soft protrusions of her vaginal lips, the moistening slit of her opening.

She was moving faster now, using his smooth groin to rub herself to climax, and he could feel her secretions, her juices, seeping into him, being absorbed into his flesh. He felt stronger already, the nourishment reviving him, and as she began bucking, pressing herself hard onto him, the skin between his legs sopped up every last drop of moisture that her orgasm produced.

Finally, she rolled away from him, sated.

Glancing over at the woman—a woman whose name he had not even asked—he realized why Jen had not been willing to be with him more than once. There was something distasteful to him now about her presence, the sense that what remained were leftovers, those gross and pitifully insubstantial remainders of a meal that had been successfully consumed.

He also felt empty, emotionally drained, used.

She started asking him about who he was, *what* he was, all of the questions he'd asked Jen, and this time he was the one to quickly put on his clothes and hurriedly exit the motel room.

"Can I see you again?" she called after him.

He looked back at her. There was something in her eyes that he didn't like, something that seemed somehow . . . familiar.

"Please?" she said.

He stopped in the doorway. She was pulling on her panties, trying to seem as sexy as possible, but she looked to him like a cold, half-eaten string bean sitting on an empty plate in a puddle of mingled gravy and corn juice. Gagging, he turned away, shaking his head.

He strode across the parking lot, got into his car, feeling disgusted and abused and humiliated. He started the vehicle, pulled onto Lincoln Avenue, heading toward home.

A few seconds later, the woman followed.

BREAK-UP

BY RICHARD CHRISTIAN MATHESON

You can't invoke the art of the short-short shocker without invoking Richard Christian Matheson, an author whose name is actually longer than some of his tales. *Which is why his friends get to call him R.C.*

He says this is a story about the single life.

And it happens just like that.

They were in bed, curled together like children.

That was when he whispered it and her expression quietly tore open. She asked how long he'd felt this way. He gestured without detail and guessed two or three weeks. She stared at him, wanting to know how soon he intended to break things off.

"Now," he answered, a silhouette.

She gathered the comforter around herself like a funeral shroud and started to cry when he told her the relationship was good but that for reasons he couldn't name, he wanted out.

"I'll change," she offered, sitting higher, ready to negotiate. She grasped a glass of water from her bedside table with pale fingers and told him she could be more what he wanted. She'd find a way. She watched for his reaction, optimism trapping her.

He rose and began to dress, telling her it was too late. He needed something different. But even as he said it, in some odd sense he didn't relate to the words. Still, he made no effort to correct the message, though it frightened him.

She tried to understand and told him if he needed time off, to take as much as he required. A weekend. A year. She would wait.

He began buttoning his shirt, tying his tie. She watched as he laced his wing-tips and asked if he would call.

". . .no." He wouldn't say more.

"You can't do this to us!" Her eyes were wide, angry. He was an executioner, sentencing them.

He pulled on his suit coat, sat on the bedside, spoke softly.

"Try to understand. It's not us. It's me. People grow. They want different things. Nothing's forever." He didn't know where the ideas were coming from and felt himself in some grotesque trance.

Sun struck the brass headboard, as if controlled by a catwalk technician and lit her bloodless lips. They parted to free a sound of drowning; assassination. "It's someone else, isn't it?"

"No. I'm just feeling different from when we met." He tried to remember when or how they'd met and couldn't. He felt sick.

"We've known each other six months and you've already fallen out of love? What about all the promises? Our plans? *Damn* you!" She tried to slap him but thoughtlessly drew her fingers into claws and swiped his skin. Three uneven scratches etched warpaint stripes under one eye and he wiped his cheek, smearing a cuff red. He tried to say something as she watched the blood glide down his face.

"I'm sorry, Jill. . .maybe you're right, maybe I don't love you anymore. . . I don't know. If I could explain it. . ." he sounded lost; unable to translate himself. ". . . I just have to move on."

She looked poisoned. "Get out. *Now.*"

He grabbed his wallet and keys, looked at her one last time and closed the door behind himself. She caught her reflection in the mirror and threw the bedside clock at her deserted image.

Outside her apartment, he walked toward his car and stopped to lean against the wall in the underground garage. He was suddenly nauseous and a spasm broke glass in his stomach. He began to vomit and as he arched over the greasy cement, the sensation felt somehow familiar, the pains like dim memories. He became more sick and tried to think about the conversation he'd just had with. . .but he couldn't recall her name.

Or who she was. Or what they'd been doing.

He stared down at his right hand, which supported him against the wall as he coughed. But he no longer recognized it; where it had been slight of structure, covered with fine, blond fuzz, it now had black hair on its back and knuckles. The wrists were growing thicker, fingers more powerful, tendons sleek beneath the now tanned skin. He tried to concentrate on where he was and saw an I.D. bracelet on his wrist. It grew gradually more tight and he unclasped it. On one side was an engraving:

"I Love You, *Madly*. Jill."

He stared at it, thinking, concentrating, unable to place the name. He flipped it and on the other side was another name: *David*. He felt a flicker of recollection but it vanished in seconds and he was quickly distracted by the feeling of growing taller, more sinewed. He felt an aggressive stream of ideas and sensations filling his mind; things deep inside dying, other things replacing them, taking over, taking control. He sensed he'd been through this hundreds of times, somehow even knew it, as the change spread like a perverse warmth, becoming more potent, settling within his cells; becoming them.

He stopped vomiting. Stood straight.

He was inches taller, pounds heavier. His face had broadened, the nose more flat. A heavy stubble had come in and he felt his face, probing at the red wounds on his cheek as they filled in and closed. He ran strong hands through hair that was now long and curly as a woman came up behind him.

"Excuse me? I'm looking for my boyfriend?"

He turned and Jill stared at him, hoping he could help. But he didn't remember anything about her and in a deep voice said he'd seen no one. Then he walked away, not knowing to take his car. As he exited the garage and moved down the street, he felt a wallet against his thigh, withdrew it. He looked at the face on the driver's license and felt nothing as he bellowed the wallet wide, took the cash and tossed it aside.

Then, feeling the morning sun on his new life, he walked on, good for another six months.

THE BETTER HALF:
A LOVE STORY

BY SCOTT BRADLEY AND PETER GIGLIO

In preparing for this book, I spent some quality time sleuthing in the library shelves of my good friend Scott Bradley. As the instigating coeditor of The Book of Lists: Horror, *he's a walking encyclopedia of haunted fiction and film, with whom I often confab.*

So I'm looking at the William Goldman section, and I say, "Damn! Can you imagine what a Goldman shape-shifting story would be like?"

Little knowing the seed I had just casually planted.

So Scott got together with lifelong pal Peter Giglio, and together they whipped up this sneaky little bastard, which only admirers of Goldman's trickiest, most unfilmable books (Control, Brothers, The Color of Light) would ever have thought to conceive.

This is, for both gentlemen, their first published story. DRINKS ARE ON SCOTT AND PETE!

A moment before the listless buzz of the alarm clock, a perpendicular slash of sunlight found Evan's eyes and pulled him from sleep.

I forgot to draw the curtains shut, he thought. And in that instant he was glad Hope wasn't with him yet. She wouldn't be angry, that wasn't her style. Just disappointed. "The blinds always let the morning in too soon," he could almost hear her say.

Evan smiled. While he never wanted to disappoint her, any more than she wanted to disappoint him, Hope always had a lazy cat languor in the morning. A stretching pout that he found delicious.

He reached out for her, but only found the alarm clock's snooze button.

There was so much to do today. And tomorrow. And the day after that. So much to prepare before The Change.

That was what both of them called it— capital *T*, capital *C*—though Evan couldn't remember which one of them had suggested that name. Not that it mattered. It was synchronicity or chemistry or what the poets call Love.

Love was what Evan and Hope shared. But love—True Love—meant struggles as well as snuggles, and for them the big struggle was The Change.

You don't understand The Change, Evan thought.

He slipped out of bed, a tremor of nausea passing through him. Two minutes of dry heaves before he steadied enough to sit at the computer. He opened the web browser and began to type.

Date: July 21, 2010
Time: 7:43 am CDT
FROM: EvanSterling@CompuNet.com
TO: HopeSterling@CompuNet.com
SUBJECT: The Change

Good morning, sweetie! Just woke up. Missing you something fierce. I can feel it beginning, and I'm so grateful I have this link to you. When I feel sick, you always tell me I'll be better. And you're always right! LOL! :) But—seriously—tell me it will be okay again? XO—E

Evan and Hope loved good wine. But neither of them was an expert on the subject. For advice they sought the expertise of Richard, a man who had been a wine steward for the better part of thirty years. Conveniently, the Wine Connection—Richard's place of business—was only a short walk from Evan and Hope's elegant downtown condo.

"Where's your better half?" asked Richard.

"Hope," Evan responded weakly, "will be . . . returning soon. Thank God."

Evan didn't like the way Richard was looking at him today. It was as if the man were scrutinizing the bouquet of a particular vintage and realizing, to his disdain, that the wine had become vinegar.

"Is anything wrong, Evan?"

"Come again?"

"You don't .. . . well, don't take this the wrong way, but . . . you don't look so good."

Evan tilted his head and tried to smile. He did everything in his power to look amused rather than hurt. And if he succeeded it wasn't because of a special inner strength, but rather because he knew that Richard was right. He'd seen himself in the mirror and considered not leaving home. But he had to leave. There were things to do. Everything had to be right before The Change.

Evan managed to say, "I have an appointment for later today."

Richard nodded.

"With a doctor," Evan added, just to be clear. But it wasn't true.

"Well, how can I help you today?"

"I want something special for Hope. She's a wonderful girl, and . . . I just need something that she'll adore."

Richard nodded. His brow furrowed in concentration, then he snapped his fingers. "Bordeaux. I have a nice 2000 Château Margaux. Pencil lead and beeswax nose, tight, but nice midpalate, with flavors of fig and anise. Long finish."

"Sounds good to me. You know how much we hate short finishes."

"You don't know what the hell I'm talking about," Richard said with a grin, "do you?"

"I know you have good taste. And you know our taste."

Fetching the bottle, Richard explained that the 2000 First Growth tended to be damned expensive, but due to the depressed market he could give Evan the Château Margaux for $400—"a steal," Richard assured him.

"I'll take it," Evan said.

Evan studied his work one last time, as the last light of the day faintly illuminated his generous offering for Hope. Evan understood generosity, his notwithstanding, was usually as much for the benefit of the giver as for the receiver.

Hope is worth the adoration, he thought.

On the coffee table was the bottle of wine. Leaning against the bottle, an envelope addressed to her in calligraphy.

It was a long-standing tradition in the relationship for Evan and Hope to compose notes for each other, especially around The Change. "It keeps the relationship fresh," she would say at times. "I know you love me, but I like to have a document of it," she said at others, like a joke but meaning it. He prayed she would like the handwritten note half as much as she loved the e-mails he sent her. He suspected that she might love it even more.

He smiled, safe in knowing that he had done well.

And then a terrible pain pierced his abdomen, causing him to double over.

Gingerly, he made his way into the bathroom, where he wound up staring blankly into his own feverish reflection for too long. How long? He didn't know. He considered taking his temperature, but sleep, he knew, was the only cure. Why cause himself stress in the meantime? What he was experiencing was, after all, only The Change.

Evan squeezed some toothpaste—a brand that promised to be ultra whitening—onto his brush. Using what was left of his energy, he began to scour his teeth and gums. He wanted to tend to the pain that was spreading through his midsection, but he blocked it out. It was more important that his mouth be extra fresh for Hope.

Inexplicably, a tear trickled from his eye and rolled down his cheek.

Strange, he thought, *I'm not sad.*

But he wasn't sure what he was.

A rush of anxiety seemed to take over, causing him to throw his toothbrush into the sink.

Calm down, he reminded himself.

It's only The Change.

The alarm clock's listless drone repeated for several minutes before Hope became aware of it. Her eyes opened hesitantly and her body—bathed in thin slats of early morning light—sprawled and stretched with feline grace.

"You're so beautiful when you wake," she could almost hear Evan say. Thoughts of his strong, reassuring voice were all she needed by way of encouragement. She could face the new day, no matter what.

Her eyes were still adjusting when she saw the line. It seemed to connect her body to the depression that had been made by Evan's. It made her think of an umbilical cord, but the thought—so counterintuitive to the couple's feelings about children—was fleeting. The line was thin and dark. And she became aware of— though not surprised by—the feeling of something wet and sticky between her thighs. Hope reached out, touched the line, and discovered that it was a thick liquid.

Blood.

"Tsk, tsk," she whispered.

But she didn't chide Evan for long. Even if an expensive set of silk sheets would have to be sacrificed to the trash gods, she was only a little annoyed. How could she be mad? After all, weren't most men naturally averse in matters of feminine hygiene? It was built into their DNA, wasn't it?

She tenderly kissed the pillow where Evan's head had rested.

I love you, she thought dreamily, the faint curl of a smile beginning to form on one side of her trembling mouth.

The Change was getting easier all the time.

Date: July 24, 2010
Time: 8:07 am CDT
FROM: HopeSterling@CompuNet.com
TO: EvanSterling@CompuNet.com
RE: The Change

I have to tell you how much I love you! The wine is amazing—no doubt a recommendation from Richard, right? I'll have to stop by the store and thank him. But most of all — Thank you! Thank you! Thank you! The note you left me was so lovely. It reminded me of the letters that you used to write when we were still young. And you're right; we are so lucky to have this connection. And I am so lucky to have you. As long as we have each other, sweetheart, we'll always be okay. I promise. Love, Hope

PLASTIC FANTASTIC

BY DIETER MEYER AND MAXWELL HART

Some people are never satisfied. Can never be too rich, too thin, or too phony. And if it truly is what's on the outside that counts, who needs the real you, anyhoo?

From Los Angeles, the cosmetic surgery capital of the universe, comes "Plastic Fantastic": a squishy narrative nugget with a distinctive chemical odor, brought to you by noted fictional authors Dieter Meyer and Maxwell Hart.

Jesse awoke, and knew she was alone on the boat. Scratches on her locked cabin door. Still drunk, she stumbled over trash in the galley. All food and water gone. A party—they went wild when they couldn't get to her, and then jumped overboard to swim in the moonlight.

Out on the deck, in the sick, silver starshine, indigo sky and black sea, she saw Tom off the port bow. He was walking on the water.

He was walking toward her.

"It's perfection, Jess," he said. "A miracle."

Words failed her, but the flare gun spoke loud and clear. Green phosphorus melted his perfect plastic mouth, but his eyes bubbled over with pity.

"An undiscovered country," he said through oozing magnesium sparks. "Let it perfect you."

The four of them had come two hundred miles south from Maui to document the solid waste sink in the center of the Pacific: the fatally clogged colon of the modern world. It mottled and choked the surface, formed a dense lilypad island nation of inorganic waste. She'd seen it from the air, and gasped at its nefarious spread. Twice the size of Texas, and growing faster than Facebook.

Up close in yesterday's daylight, it had struck her as merely banal and sad, the infinite waste of water jugs, baby bottles, shoe soles, diapers, condoms, syringes and cigarette lighters, mired in a glutinous soup of plastic chewed past recognition but utterly undecayed. Immortal.

"Everything here was useful once," he'd told her then. "Essential, yet disposable. It's come together here to be useful again." Winking. "Like us."

"Oh, Tom," she'd thrown back. "We were never useful."

That was then, but this was the new forever, glimmering slick beneath the ancient moon. Forever changed, not dying, never dead, its kingdom extended into the sky. Swarms of shopping-bag jellyfish played on the lunar updrafts, scattered from a swooping, translucent manta ray. Schools of eyeless vinyl fish darted across the jigsaw surface of the sea on spider-legs and curling tentacles, nibbling naugahyde kelp with Velcro teeth.

The others hid beneath the heaving sea for now, evidently waiting her out.

Never strong to begin with, thirst and hunger and terror made her weaker by the hour. She was dehydrated long before the sun came up. The engines were clogged with wads of trash bags and tampon applicators, the props snarled in pantyhose cobwebs.

They didn't try to storm the boat again. When she was starving, she would join them.

When she looked into a mirror, she would beg them to take her.

They'd gone out broken, the four of them: rootless rich kids with nothing to do but wander, indulge, and obsess for no good reason on whatever impulse compelled them next.

In that sense, Nina and Lono fit together like a broken glass puzzle. She never thought there were such girls, who really did long for the bare-knuckled smack, adding much-needed drama to their otherwise vacant life experience. And Lono, like a mad, bad sculptor, crazed and mournful because his fists couldn't fix her, make her turn out the way he thought they should.

And her own Tom Chaykin, homely-handsome and callow and nearly half as smart as he thought he was, who claimed he loved Jesse for her mind. Which was why, after all, he'd brought her here. To put her beautiful mind in a more lovable body, one less sickly and frail and altogether unworthy than the one she'd suffered from the moment of birth—

It came back with her hangover. She'd gotten ill, and gone to bed, and then they went out without her, whooping it up as they dove into the new plasma pool.

When the laughter and screams were swallowed up by the slurping petroleum waves, she was too drunk to find her way out of bed. But then they came back.

They came back perfect.

Just as they suddenly came back now: rising up from the depths, even shinier and less authentic than before.

Tom's melted face had hardened into a messianic Ken-doll smirk that both mimicked and amplified the original. Wind-up hermit crabs scuttled out of his empty eye sockets, flooding her with a flesh-crawling terror. But the sculpted features, impeccable, commanded her eyes.

"It can be whatever we want it to be," he said. Polyvinyl washboard abs and tire-tread pecs rippled with a queasy rainbow sheen in the morning light. "Meat wrinkles and rots and dies," he went on, godlike arms spread wide in all-encompassing embrace. "But not us. Not ever again."

Nina and Lono lurked at his feet, their beckoning mermaid tails churning out foamy scum-angels.

"You want this," said Lono. "Stop being such a prig, you ugly, stuck-up little bitch."

"Come on in," Nina cooed. "It feels sooooo goooood…"

"And baby?" Tom concluded. "I want this for you. "'Cause this is what you want to be. You know you do."

They couldn't smell or see it coming. Maybe senses no longer mattered, the old neural pathways gummed up, shut down, or otherwise rendered passé. Maybe their upgrade came with an even greater sense of entitlement, you-can't-touch-me pushed to its ultimate, laminated extreme.

Or maybe they were still just stupid, self-absorbed human flotsam. In which case, nothing had really changed, but only retrofitted to fleshless, empty perfection.

Jesse shuddered, reloaded the flare gun, and fired into the water around the stern of the boat. The gasoline fumes inhaled the flare and leapt out across the water, climbed her replicant friends and drove her back into the cabin.

They urged, taunted, and cajoled her to come out until they were only sputtering candles of slag on the scabby glacier of melted trash around the smoldering fiberglass boat. A tower of noxious black smoke split the sky with a toxic arrow that must be visible from space. Surely, someone would come.

And within the hour, they did.

She heard the roar of rotor blades and crawled out onto the deck, into the shadow of a dragonfly thirty feet long.

Out on the horizon, vast plastic crabs clattered across the wet desert toward the burning boat.

She started to both laugh and scream, her fine spoiled useless meat-mind unraveling. The dragonfly barked at her in eight languages before she understood. "—Prepare to be boarded and surrender to customs authorities—"

Even the undiscovered country had an immigration policy.

And all the money in the world couldn't help her now.

Still she howled and fought back with the last of her flares and her feeble, fierce humanity, for whatever that was worth.

Slowly, the boat sank, left her clawing at the surface till the boiling plastic closed over her head, drowning her old self, filling her lungs with something she needed more than air.

As the promised reconstruction began.

And she had to admit, by the time it was done, she looked pretty fucking fantastic.

WARM IN YOUR COAT

BY VIOLET GLAZE

The first I ever heard of Violet Glaze, she was informing me (and I paraphrase only slightly), "If anyone else wrote you a bulimic lesbian werewolf story, I am going to be *so pissed."*

Needless to say, there could be only one.

And I doubt that there will ever be another quite like this.

Violet Glaze makes me laugh and swear out loud, goggle my eyes, and think of running for cover. It's as if she has an army of unbridled geniuses packed inside one single, screaming skull. I haven't seen this much superstar hot and unhinged since Angelina Jolie in Girl, Interrupted. *Only no one's interrupting this time.*

Ladies and gentlemen, you have been warned.

Suzy Parker's panties glistened with dabs of crème fraîche and rose water. The sebum from her pores stained fool's gold black, and the carbon dioxide she exhaled brought dried marigolds back from the dead.

They squeezed one of her christened tampons into the lipstick batch at Revlon. White-coated lab techs took it out of her with diamond-crusted forceps, paid her thirty thou in 1950 dollars for the privilege. (Plus half a point of stock. It split in 1963. Made her rich.) Charles Revson applauded and popped the champagne magnum himself, *pow*, as blades swirled the scarlet potion in the stainless-steel tank. Ten thousand women buying dime-store lipstick a lunar month later blotted their pout and tasted the goddess. Cochineal, tallow, uterine lining. Cherries in the Snow.

"Scarlet, what a funny word," the girl who was not Suzy Parker whispered to herself as she ran a dreamy hand along the lipstick rack. Black plastic bullets rattled in their slots, *ta-rack-a-rack-a-rack*. "The color of what's let from a scar."

"Hey, lightfingers," the drugstore clerk yelled. "Go get your touchy-feelies somewhere else."

And so she did, ducking into Boston wind with secret ammo in her pockets. Shoplifted: Orange You Glad and Mauvelous and Eldorado Red, *click clack* in her dry little palms like worry beads, tucked in the pocket of a Windbreaker thin enough to gird a kite's bamboo bones. The way the wind skinned the heat off her body in sharp lashes made her heart soar, made her think of the joy of not eating and not sleeping and the hard thudding pace of thin shoes on knee-rattling concrete, every step across the Harvard Bridge taking her out of her body and into a soft distracting thrum of pain.

The girl who was not Suzy Parker thought of *body* not in inches and pounds but new units, invented just for her sad and sick case. A *revolt* is the measure of energy required to fuss, displeased, at one's reflection. Her hair was chopped and snipped like mange at 5.5 revolts, a force of hate so strong it made her thrilled to not recognize the ugly gamine in the mirror. Scissor cuts on her arms (6.1 revolts). A too-thin T-shirt (3.4 revolts) wrapped around her bony chest. An empty stomach (4.0) and hiccupy pulse (4.9) and third-eye-awake daze deep in her glucose-starved brain.

In Central Square the Namu My h Renge Ky Buddhist Society hung a sign in the storefront. *It's the void in the vase that makes it valuable.* She saw her reflection in the storefront glass and winced.

"Find me a merciful mirror," she incanted into the ragged prayer flags and crossed the street to Harvard Square.

The Brattle Theater opens at noon, next show at two. She waited until the popcorn clerk's back was turned and slipped inside. Dark swallowed her. Dolby rattled. Out of body, for one weightless, guiltless moment once again. She turned her face to the screen, like a plant seeking light.

Jack Warner presents. Crashing waves. *Mildred Pierce.*

She was too hungry to follow the plot, but the plot didn't matter. The plot was the story of light on dark, of swooping shadows and slivers of venetian blind crossing a woman's face. Mildred Pierce, wreathed in fur like a beast, stepping in and out of ink like a seal in black water, surfacing and diving. That fur was a monster. It shimmied and undulated and wrapped around Mildred Pierce like a bodyguard. It tucked her weapon into its pockets and kept her secrets. *Veda's convinced me that alligators have the right idea*, Mildred Pierce scoffed. *They eat their young.*

A hard hand on her shoulder pulled the girl who was not Suzy Parker back into her detestable body. She flinched. Joe from the hospital stood beside her. An aide stood behind. "Come on, Gwen." He pulled her to standing. "Let's go."

Back at the center her punishment sat on an orange cafeteria tray. "It's not a punishment," said the aide. Cardboard milk box, skinned orange, three slices of hemorrhaging pizza. Cubes of cheese, gray succotash, salt crackers slathered with waxy peanut butter and clots of strawberry jam. "You missed dinner. Food is life."

The girl who was not Suzy Parker set her jaw.

The aide sighed. "You're not as bad as some girls here, Gwen. I know there's hope for you." She leaned in conspiratorially. "You're not Tricia."

Tricia was eighty ghostly pounds, a matchstick marionette wrapped in dead cat sinew. She just got a nasogastric bag, a plastic bladder pumping beige pulp up her nose and into the thimble of her anorexic stomach. The girls were jealous. They all wanted one. Tricia was Empress Upchuck now, shuffling through the linoleum halls of the center, clinging to her electrolyte IV pole like a pope's scepter. Her legs in Ugg boots looked like chopsticks in flower pots.

"I don't like Tricia," said Gwen. Starvation made her senses sharp. The paper carton smelled like udders. The peanut butter smelled like hair conk, that same salty peanut smell. *Don't put it in your mouth*, her stomach twisted.

"And you don't want to be like her. That I know. But if you don't eat . . ." The aide nudged the tray meaningfully toward her. "Or if there's something else you'd like?"

Silence.

"Sneaking out isn't acceptable, Gwen. Day leave is a privilege. You earn it when you prove you're trying to get well."

Something stirred inside her, a witchy finger crooking something closer. She thought of pious Pope Tricia, turning up her feeding tube-stuffed nose at the sausage on her breakfast plate. "Meat is murder," she'd whine, and her lower lip would quiver. Remembering that feigned, masturbatory empathy made vomiting up breakfast a real cakewalk. She could do it all by herself, now. Earned her PhBulimia. No need for finger tickles and ipecac and gouging her uvula with the bristle end of a toothbrush. Just think of something awful and up it came. *What smells in here? Oh, Jesus, Gwen, not behind the radiator.*

"Meatballs," said the girl who was not Suzy Parker.

"Eat a cracker first and drink some milk." The aide slid from her chair. "I'll tell the chef."

She came back five minutes later, a sextet of marinara-draped meatballs wreathed in lank spaghetti on a Styrofoam plate. "Eat one," she said. "And keep it down."

The meatball steamed when she cut into it, breathed out a spurt of moist perfume. Savor, grease, tomato tang. She ignored the starch on her plate and devoured all the balls but one, slowly but with hypnotic purpose. They tasted magnificent but sat like lead shot inside her. The beatific haze in her brain went away as her underused stomach lurched to work. Back down to earth, heavy and thick and cramping in her gut. Loss of heaven made her cry.

"Easy now," the aide said, handing her a tissue. "You did good."

They sat and watched TV as she digested, forty postmeal minutes certified purge-free by a smiley sticker on her progress sheet. There was talk of privileges retained as she shuffled down the hall. "Can't sneak out. Can't come back late," the aide refrained. "Can't skip mealtime. You know the rules. But you're doing well. This was your first major infraction. Let it just be a slip." She hovered at the door of her cage, the peach-walled dorm with one low bunk. Bleach and the Roquefort stink of vomit still colored the air. "When your mother comes tomorrow we'll talk again with your caseworker. The three of us. About whether your behavior merits the supervised outing next week."

Mother. Another funny word. So crossword-close to *monster.*

Gwen's face darkened. "Can't wait a week."

The aide gave her a *shoulda-done-better* smile. "Privilege is as privilege does. 'Night, Gwen."

"Stop calling me Gwen," she growled, low as earthquakes rumble. Lost in the closing *clik* of the door.

The girl who was not Suzy Parker jumped on the bed and scooped the stash from underneath. They would take them away if they found them. The staff here bans the golden calf, the ribsy supermodels and lanky colt-women torn from glossy magazines that stink like perfume samples. No *Vogue*, no *Elle*. No problem. The girl who was not Suzy Parker didn't care about those gut-fuck *haute cunture* bitches, their too-smooth limbs taffy-stretched to spider legs by too much Photoshop. Pixels never touched Suzy Parker. The hourglass of her waist was real, a true treacherous swerve of Texarkana highway. Her cheekbones cut light because of grace and fate, not surgery, and her sanguine hair never touched henna. *Are you a redhead all over?*

Not-Suzy-P was sure of it. The meatballs combusting inside her flushed her face, pumped her veins with caloric heat. She tapped the pack of cigarettes she never smoked, kicking out not coffin nails but tiny printouts rolled into white cylinders. She unrolled them reverently. Suzy Parker ads from the 1950s. Thanks, Flickr, thanks, Google. *Revlon's new fabulous Futurama case with lipstick refill*, the effusive copy gushed in ladylike cursive at the top of the paper. That same something stirred inside her, an electrified quaver above and below where the thick meatballs seethed in her gut. She could evict dinner with one unsavory thought—men's farts, smashed roaches, *mother*—but something made her want to keep meat down.

She lay on her bed atop her pictures, swaddled in the glow of Suzy Parker. She touched her own arm. Fine hair, herringboning down her arm like baby stalks of wheat. Darker than before. Maybe lanugo. The starving girls got lanugo, the defatted body's last ditch effort to keep heat in. Tricia had it, skin head to toe dusted with needle-thin hair like a cactus. *Don't touch.* Not-Suzy frowned at her own arm. The bobcat fur flecks there were probably not lanugo. She wasn't thin enough anymore for that.

Nok-nok. The night aide's knuckles on the outside of the closed door. "Lights out, Gwen." She could hear her muffled voice behind the safety glass. "You're on random checks tonight. I'll be back in fifteen."

"All right," she said, cheerful as could be as she rolled her narrow hips coolly over the pile of contraband. The aide didn't notice and went away.

Lights out.

Not Suzy lay in the dark, still dressed, hands twitching on her belly, an itchiness that spread to her twisting ankles and quivering thighs. The thought seized her, surged inside her, powered itself to caged-animal-frantic pitch by the hot meatballs splintering into diesel gasoline in her gut and the ghost of Mildred Pierce. *I can't wait a week. I must go out again. I must go out tonight.* Suzy Parker underneath her burned like an electric blanket.

I must have a fur coat.

Sneaking out was easy with meat and glamour in her veins. *I am Jean Harlow*, her thoughts thrummed as she crouched low and slipped through the cracked door. *I am Barbara LaMarr and Theda Bara and Louise Brooks.* She skipped on four legs, a half-crawl that felt as easy as a squirrel undulating in sinusoid leaps. *I 'm no squirrel*, she laughed to herself. *I'm the hunter, not the lunch.* The front door was alarmed. She went out the back, thudding down the service entrance stairs and landing on light bones as soft as a cat. Too easy. Her eroded bulimic teeth still had enough enamel to gnaw the ID bracelet off her wrist. She spit it onto the floor as she hit the back corridors, orderlies mopping and smoking and flirting and ignoring a thin white girl slipping out of the hospital. Out the loading dock, bored fat nurses slapped cigarette packs on their palm and paid no attention as she slid into the night like a shadow.

She ran and ran. January wind meant nothing. The icy snap in the air only fueled her stride, made her senses predator sharp. Her ruined teeth sang out when she sucked in the air and still she grinned, thrilling to the sidewalk scrolling underneath her. She ran down the Fenway, through the park, and the night around her whispered *go, go, go*. Tennis shoes thudding on soft dark grass, meat-plumped muscles full of power, wind whipping the short dense fur of her hair. No one behind. Clean getaway. The scent of the river blossomed up ahead—*dead fish, oil slick, sewage, wild fresh air*. She ran for the bridge. The throbbing red triangle of the Citgo sign lit her way, like a blood-gorged constellation.

She knew where to find her quarry. Furriers are alarmed, wary, their luxury goods protected like dumb chickens in a razor wire pen. Back in Baltimore her uncle had a dry cleaner on Eutaw Street. The pungent scent sprung from some childhood memory: glycol ethers, hydrocarbon, the uncapped marker smell of perchloroethylene. She smelled it again. She turned.

Butterfly Cleaners, the sign spelled in turquoise script. Trust Us with Your Finest Mink.

Not Suzy grabbed a chunk of broken pavement and smashed the window. No alarm besides the tortured chime of shattering glass.

The furs hung in clear plastic like sides of beef, a snaking monorail of corpses. Otter and fox, rabbit and beaver, plush pelts sealed like supermarket meat. She ground her jaw, some secret reflex slavering for the kill as she tore frantic hands through easy pickings. Faun, sienna, warm black like coffee. Then white fur flashed in the moonlight and she gasped. She tore off the plastic like a lover's shirt. The fur's guard hairs were sharp and wild and scratched her face as she buried her nose in its rich nap. She breathed in as if drowning. It smelled like ice and deep woods. It smelled like spotlights and face powder. It smelled like crème fraîche and rose water, and the secret within.

Hello, the coat said. *Put me on. Become me.*

The fur was heavy on her shrunken shoulders but nothing could slow her down now. As she ran through the Fenway on bare feet, her nipples scratching against the coat's silk lining with every step, Beauty flowered up inside her. Beauty wasn't self-control. It was wild and bad and unbehaved. It was leaving your clothes on the floor of a dry cleaner's and tucking three stolen lipsticks and your naked body into a purloined fur coat. It was Alla Nazimova surfacing between an ingenue's legs in the Black Sea–shaped pool in the Garden Of Allah. It was Clara Bow fucking the entire USC football team. It was Frances Farmer kicking the police in a Benzedrine frenzy and writing down her occupation as "cocksucker."

The meatballs welled in Not-Suzy's throat at the thought. *Cocksucker, ugh.* She stopped, gagging for breath. She felt that push again, that easy tip of the gut that spilled the bag of her stomach into her grateful esophagus. It was all she could do to stop voiding all over the sumptuous coat. *Keep it in, keep it in.* She bent down and put a hand to her stomach, genuflecting on cold ground and calming herself, ignoring the hot sweat sprouting on her upper lip and the warm gush of saliva washing her mouth. *It's your kill*, she thought, and though the words surprised her they calmed her as well. *You'll need it. Keep it in.* She calmed her stomach with thoughts of moonlight on the face of Garbo and Dietrich and Lupe Velez. *María Guadalupe Villalobos Vélez. Town of wolves, valley of wolves. She died throwing up sleeping pills and drowned in the toilet bowl.*

I will not throw up.

I will not drown.

"My name is Scarlet," she whispered to herself, and willed herself to run on. Where do I run? An ancestral memory skidded her feet to a stop, turned her path like a compass swinging wildly back to true north. *Return to the ones who are like you. They may nip and bite from fear but alone you are carrion. In sisterhood you will survive.*

Return to the pack.

When she sneaked into her room, Tricia was sleeping. Fatless bones swaddled in sweatshirts, feeding tube snaking into her nose from a maggot-fat bag of tan glop suspended from an IV pole. The nurses pulverize heavy cream and protein powder and peanut butter, drip it into her stomach at night, and hope she keeps it down, hope she won't wake up and rip it out of her face. She saw where Tricia's chickenbone wrists were bound to the hospital bed.

Tricia had a window in her room. The window was open. *A room with a window,* she thought, bitterness melting to pity. *Big enough to escape through. That's how much they trust Tricia'll never leave. That's how much they believe she'll never get well.*

"Wake up," she barked. Tricia's eyes snapped open.

She stood before her, magnificent fur coat split so Tricia could see the naked body within. Thin and pale but breasts proud. Flesh getting stronger.

"Come away with me," said the girl whose name was Scarlet.

Tricia gulped. The words scratched out of her tube-scarred throat.

"Fur is murder."

Scarlet opened her eyes wide. Yellow, hard like the moon.

"*I* am murder."

She tore the tube out of her face and Tricia said *shluuuuuck* and *ghhhluup* and gave a deep, choking gasp. Burgundy-streaked mucus smeared all over her sweatshirt. Nutritional paste spilled like an artery all over the floor. Scarlet looked into Tricia's pale blue eyes and saw the puppyish fear. Something pitying dredged up inside her. Half-digested meat churned inside her like lava in one great maternal spasm . . .

It heaved up out of love. The great ripping exodus of dinner in her stomach surged up in a yawning red cascade, a tenderhearted waterfall of puke splattering at Tricia's feet. *This is how wolves do it,* Scarlet thought, woozy and pure in a postvomit haze. *The females stuff their gullet with fresh kill and bring it back in their belly, back to the den for the new-weaned pups. The sight and the smell of those weaker than them, the members of the pack that need their help . . .* Stomach acid and tomato sauce seared the tender lining of her nose. She popped a lipstick from her pocket and smeared Grand Guignol Red on her burning wet mouth. *The cries of pups in need makes them chuck it up. They heave it up so quickly the hot killed meat still steams in the arctic air . . .*

She smacked her greased lips together, looked at Tricia.

"Eat," said Scarlet. She snapped Tricia's restraints.

Commotion in the hallway outside. Escape alarm, intercom paging. *All staff alert. Security breach. Paging Dr. Strong and Dr. Meds and Dr. Straitjacket.*

"Now," said Scarlet.

Tricia slid on spidery legs to the floor, kneeling before the chunky puddle. Something gelled in her brain, some spark of jungle survival surfacing out of a mountain of ash. For a moment she looked as if she would scoop up a delicate fingerful, take a sacramental taste off her fingertip. Then her eyes flashed amber and she dove in face-first, lapping up great mouthfuls of still-hot vomit, her trembling arms barely able to support her infant-big head as she devoured Scarlet's offering off the linoleum floor.

She stared up at Scarlet, jaws stained red. Eyes big and pleading.

I am alpha to her, thought Scarlet.

"Take off the clothes they give you," she barked.

The tumble of sensible shoes squeaking down the hall. *Nurses coming.* Tricia slid her cadaver arms out of her fleece sweatshirt and lowered her sweatpants past the obscene crag of her hipbones. She hooked her thumbs under her grotesquely flat training bra and Scarlet helped her. Her shriveled breasts were empty. Like a nursing wolf starving in winter.

Tricia shuddered violently, a skeleton clutching herself. "I'm cold."

"Be warm in my coat," said Scarlet, parting the fur. "Until you grow your own."

In a flash she was inside, Scarlet's warm flesh on skin-and-bones. Their mouths cleaved together, nipping, snapping, yipping. Scarlet slid her palms over the knobbly landscape of Tricia's body, the gouge of her hips and the Braille of her spine and the *ta-rack-a-rack-a-rack* of her ribs. Cold as a corpse. She tweaked her empty nipples.

"Fuck that feeding tube," said Scarlet, and fixed her mouth over hers. This time her alpha offering didn't spill but flowed in one warm kiss, and Tricia's throat pumped tight and swallowed every drop.

Scarlet held Tricia tight, clutching her into the warm cocoon of her coat, pressing the leather skull of her head into the warm diamond of heat between her breasts. She stroked her brittle hair and thought of Virginia Rappe's bad doctors, Lana Turner kissing Stompanato's fist, Frances Farmer's lobotomy, Marilyn face down with a stomach full of cum and a barbiturate enema in her ass. "It won't happen to you," she whispered into her packmate's mouth. "I won't let it." Lanugo bristled, grew thick and real enough to scare the cold. Enamel grew back on ruined eyeteeth. In a moment the two women melted and snarled and it didn't hurt a bit.

The nurse with the straitjacket slammed the door open and it was too late. They'd already gone, two silver bitches fleeing into the moonlit night.

ALL I REALLY NEED TO KNOW I LEARNED IN PIGGY CLASS

BY NICOLE CUSHING

Nicole Cushing is one of my faves in the new wave of Bizarro authors. There's a focused intelligence and clarity at play throughout even the deepest patches of delirium—a genuine method to the unadulterated madness—that makes it so much more than merely weird. (Although frankly, excellent weirdness is its own reward.)

And so it is with the following tale of social conditioning at its most nakedly transparent, which opens with a kick and just keeps on kicking. Making points I've never seen made more clearly or strangely about how society actually works.

Hello, teacher tell me what's my lesson. Look right through me. Look right through me.

—Tears for Fears, "Mad World"

I. PIGGY CLASS

We'd made the papier-mâché Piggy masks in art class. All the way back in middle school. It had been career day, and we'd just taken a vocational aptitude test. My cousin Cheyenne's results had told her that she'd make a good Hen. David (my older brother) who'd taken a similar test five years before me, had been told he'd make a good Bull. The butcher who prepared his body for market sent a kind note informing us that he'd proven a fine specimen, and had not so much as flinched before entering the abattoir.

The treasure of our family, though—the one who made us all proud—was my *eldest* brother, Donnie (at fifteen years my senior, he always treated me more like a niece than a sister). His aptitude test said he'd make a good farmhand. And so off he went one day, to a farm up around Cherry Hill. He consoled us by pointing out that they mostly grew feed corn and soybeans up there, with a few goats thrown in as a hobby. So the chances of him being put in the awkward position of farming a sibling were remote.

My aptitude test said I'd make a good Piggy. As soon as I'd received the results, the Enforcer escorted me out of the principal's office to join the other Piggies in Ms. Tinsman's art class. That's when we made our masks.

It didn't make any sense to me at the time that Ms. Cafferty (our principal) confiscated them before we could try them on. "Not yet, my little Piglets! Wallow in summertime before you don your masks," she'd said.

That didn't make any sense at all. Not until the first day at Lagrange High School, when I opened my assigned locker and discovered the Piggy mask I'd made three months before dangling from a coat hook, awaiting me. A mimeographed sheet read: *Wear This Now! Be This Now! If You Are Not Piggy Enough, You Will Be Expelled!*

I'd never known anyone in school who'd been Expelled, but one heard stories over the years. Rumor had it that the school system liked to dissect the expelled to find out just what had gone wrong. Rumor had it they started the procedure with you alive. I can't imagine why, unless one's response to the dissection was part of the data collected. The school system did so love testing.

To be Expelled meant you had failed to fulfill your niche in life—a fate most people in town considered worse than death due to the dishonor it inflicted on the entire family. If I were ever to join the ranks of the Expelled, I would bring great shame to my mom and dad.

So I put on the Piggy mask, and went to visit my new homeroom teacher (and, it turned out, my new everything-else teacher) Ms. Landres. She'd been in the employ of the school system for decades, and had all the mechanical add-ons to prove it. Gears in her eyes. All the better to see us with. Gears in her heart. All the better to hate us with.

When I tell people about it *now*, I'm told I shouldn't be surprised I got Expelled. Maybe it all started on September 1, the day of our first class inspection (right after lunch and a fire drill). The first day I saw Ms. Landres' Scaramouche mask. The day I pissed her off by calling it a Bird mask.

"I'm not a filthy animal like you, Swine. Now repeat after me: Scar-a-mouche," she'd snarled, glaring down at me with those gear-eyes of hers.

"Sc-scare-a-Moose," I'd stammered, my voice muffled under the papier-mâché Piggy mask.

"Close enough, you worthless Piggy!" she'd said just before she hocked an oily loogie onto my new school dress. The rest of the Piggy class broke out in a chorus of condescending snorts and squeals.

After that, I did everything Ms. Landres said and limited my communication with the other kids to a stray whisper every other day or so. "Stop looking at me," I'd croak.

I'd learned my lesson, I thought. I wasn't about to call her Scaramouche mask a Bird mask anymore. I would just do my best to be a good Piggy and blend in. On inspection days, in particular, that was the best strategy.

It was November 1, when it happened. The first of the month, just a couple of weeks shy of fall break. Ms. Landres hissed directions for us to line up for inspection, boy-girl-boy-girl, same as always this day of the month, at high noon. Each of us stood in queue, struggling to project the aura of the quintessential papier-mâché Piggy.

Ms. Landres' gear-wheel-eyes churned with deliberate machination on such days. They made slow, safe-tumbler sounds. Click-click-click-click-click. Each "click" an indication of her sensation, her perception, her *judgment* of us. Each click rendered the true status of our souls harder and harder to hide.

"Scara-you-scara-me-scara-mouche!" the braver, less browbeaten Piggies whispered to each other at the bus stop that morning. Although well on their way to Pigginess, I took solace in thinking that they must have had enough human kid still in them to find a way to defuse their dread with a lame joke. After all, Piggies don't whistle past the graveyard.

If we passed inspection, Ms. Landres would shriek that we were (in her singular, but sufficient opinion) "Piggy!"

"Piggy!" Ms. Landres hollered with approval at she stared into the soul of Natalie Simmons. Then Natalie smiled and snorted and skipped off to her seat.

"Piggy!" Ms. Landres yipped as she took a quick glance at Aiden Addison—a Piggy so brimming with Pigginess that inspection itself seemed an unnecessary formality. He squealed long and longingly, crawling back to his seat.

Then she got to me. That mean old hag placed one gnarled arthritic finger under my chin and brought my reluctant eyes to hers. I looked up, past the Scaramouche mask, into her eye-gears. Gears that started to go faster. Gears that seemed able to ground up my soul.

"Not Piggy enough!" she'd wailed, reaching her claws into the holes of my mask (and nearly scratching my eyeballs with her ragged, untrimmed nails in the process). Her gears clicked away faster still, like a roller coaster approaching the plunge. *Click-click-click-click-click-click-click.* "No! No! Not Piggy enough! Click-click No! No! Not Piggy enough!" she roared. She yanked for all she was worth, unmasking me.

For a few moments I just stood there, adjusting to the odd, unwelcome kiss of air against my cheeks. Just stood there, not understanding the implications of the monthly judgment.

"Expelled! Expelled!" Ms. Landres screeched, her eyes clicking with manic judgment. She pushed a red button on her desk

My face flushed. My face ached. My face must have expressed, at that moment, all the aggregate horrors encountered during my days in Piggy class. I don't know how long I stood there, stunned still, until I heard the first slap of the Enforcer's boot against the linoleum floor. That reminded me of all the agonies (both of the flesh and of the soul) awaiting me.

I ran.

Ran out of the high school, pulse pumping, arms pumping, my face ablaze with the wince-worthy pain induced by air rushing onto it. Air hitting raw nerve. The extra weight I'd put on since September jiggled around my midsection.

I ran past the ball field, past the tree line, and splashed into the shallow creek nearby. I'd heard somewhere on TV that if you did that it would make it hard for someone to track you; that your scent would disappear. And disappear is exactly what I wanted to do.

I ran along the soft creek bottom, splashing for a bit, nervous that what the Enforcer's hounds couldn't smell the Enforcers themselves could plainly hear. I decided after a bit of running that I'd best make it to land. There was a cemetery nearby, and then some woods past that. Where I'd go after that, I did not know.

I made a leap out of the creek onto the waiting bank and slipped. My new girth pulled me backward, and I fell into the water. The splash of water onto my face stung like a hundred bee stings. I yelped. My fall kicked up a vomit of sediment from the sandy creek bottom, and minnows scattered in its wake. As the water stilled, I caught a rippling reflection of myself.

My face was scarred and deformed, with nerves and muscles visible (and throbbing) under my eyes and cheeks. But even with that mess, I could see a few suggestions of Pigginess. My nose had become more upturned than it ever had been before, and it had grown in length about half an inch. I could see where it began to bear a resemblance to a snout. Likewise, my ears possessed a suggestion of pointedness. I'd gotten a double chin.

But it struck me that there was something about my transformation that had gone awry. That Ms. Landres had been right, if not in her pedagogy than in her perception, that I *was* "not Piggy enough!" It was as though the mask had suggested the change to my facial features, but my face—by some vestigial sense of fixed identity—had compromised. Had talked back to the mask. Had said, "This far, no further."

Looking down at my reflection, I felt the whole world wobble. The aptitude test had said I'd make a good Piggy, but there I sat, looking into a reflection that at best looked like some sort of Piggy-abortion. I began sobbing. I'd failed. I'd been Expelled. This meant disgrace for my family. Mom had already told me that if I washed out and didn't fulfill my potential, I shouldn't bother coming back home. She said that if I did come home, she'd have no choice but to turn me in.

What could I do? If I could have found a way to drown myself right there, in the foot or so of creek, I would have.

Instead I crawled up the creek bank and ran. Past the cemetery, past the woods, darting behind one house and another to catch my breath and evade detection. It was this way, sleeping in cornfields and stealing melons, that I survived as I found my way out of town. To the city.

II. FREAK-CATCHER'S MODELING SCHOOL

When you're young, Expelled, and of ambiguous species, you end up surviving in some of the worst possible ways. You are, after all, a fugitive. Even worse, you're naive, and willing to glom onto any facsimile of family. You're willing to set aside gut feelings about people you'd ordinarily see as shady because you are, after all, a freak.

You buy into society's hype about the Expelled. You learn to stop trusting yourself. You trust clichés instead ("beggars can't be choosers," "any port in a storm").

So it was that I ended up with Freak-Catcher.

He fancied himself an underground artist. He taunted the authorities by taking grainy photographs of the Expelled and posting them on telephone poles in the arts district. Freak-Catcher and his wife (Freak-Watcher, they called her) "discovered" me scrounging through the trash outside a trendy artist's restaurant. They offered me a free meal and a place to stay the night if I'd participate in a photo session.

By then fall had turned to winter. The temperature had plunged to ten degrees, and the thin, calf-length sweater I'd recycled from the trash wasn't cutting it.

Meals recycled from the trash weren't cutting it either. Still, the idea of trusting Freak-Catcher to photograph me and still somehow keep my location a secret from the authorities gave me pause.

After all, Freak-Catcher wasn't a freak. That is, no matter how much of an affinity he had for the Expelled, he wasn't one. His liked to tell us (over and over) that his aptitude test told him that he was to be an artist, but I doubted that the aptitude test told anyone to be an artist. Aptitude tests just weren't like that.

Besides, he didn't exactly dress the way I expected an artist to dress. He wore a black leather jacket over top of a grease-stained NASCAR T-shirt. He bragged on having been a sailor once, and he wore his salt-and-pepper hair in a mop top. He said he could be my new dad, and that Freak-Watcher could be my new mom. Together, they'd take pictures of me.

I stood there paralyzed for a moment.

"Trust him—he won't turn you in," a voice said from behind me. "He never snitched on me or Huck." The voice sounded young and deep—exuding confidence. Confidence was a commodity in short supply in my life, so I turned to meet it.

The boy was maybe a year or two older than me. He had a long face with big teeth, prominent nostrils, and bulging eyes. Bulging eyes that just kept *looking* down at me from a height of about six foot four. Eyes that wouldn't let go. At that moment, I felt relieved that poverty had taken off the weight I'd gained during my brief time in high school. From the moment he opened his mouth, I liked this Horse-abortion-boy (even if his face itself didn't exactly conform to universal standards of handsomeness). I liked that he noticed me.

"He rescues us," the tall Horse-boy said.

A much-shorter dude with a bushy, blood-red Mohawk and sagging jowls emerged from behind the Horse-boy and made a coughing, crowing sound that I thought might have been a laugh. "He recycles us," the Rooster-boy said.

Huck the Rooster-boy, Champ the Horse-boy, and I only spent three months with Mama Freak-Watcher and Daddy Freak-Catcher before they kicked us out. I know it sounds mean, but I don't think they meant it that way. I think they just got bored with us. I think that the entire city got bored with us. We were over-exposed. We weren't even newsworthy anymore (Freak-Catcher had showed us the clippings back when we'd been the talk of the town). Even an *underground* artist had to introduce enough novelty to keep the audience interested.

A month or two after he evicted me, I noticed that Freak-Catcher had moved on to using transvestite hookers in his photography. Champ had to explain to me what a transvestite hooker was. We didn't have those in the country. Once again, Freak-Catcher's art was the stuff of headlines. One day, when I glanced up a telephone pole and saw Freak-Catcher's grainy rendering of a transvestite's meaty, man-foot in a high-heeled shoe, I had to stop and wonder—had the transvestite's aptitude test *told* her she'd be a transvestite?

Anyway, three months wasn't a lot, but it was enough time for me to learn the ropes of life in the city. Champ and Huck seemed to know what to do when we got kicked out. They'd heard of an acting troupe that sometimes hired creatures like us to portray burn victims, ghouls, and other monstrosities. The pay wasn't much, of course, but between the three of us we could afford a shabby one-bedroom apartment within walking distance to the theater. We had just enough left over to buy the cheapest store-brand bread and eggs at the market.

III. INDUSTRIAL ARTS (TODAY)

We've lived this way for about three years now. During that time, I've played every variety of disfigured monster the theater has to offer. I've had every combination of wild, half-bestial sex with Champ, Huck, and any other Expelled creature I've run into.

I think the only reason I've never gotten pregnant is that I like to party pretty hard. Okay—*extremely* hard. I've tried every flavor of liquor (in copious amounts, each and every night) and have sampled enough pills to start a pharmacy. Whenever I pop one into my mouth, I tell myself that I'm taking the cure for my freakishness and I pretend—for a half-second—that the pills undo the work of that high school mask. Sometimes, if I take the right combination, I get high enough that they seem (for a few minutes) to do just that.

I try to not show my face during broad daylight, and that's why theater—the ultimate second-shift job—works for me.

Yeah, I know it's not the greatest life in the world. But I'm pretty sure that it's better than live dissection.

I mean, I *do* want more than this hand-to-mouth existence. I think I want Champ's baby, someday. But that will mean changes. I'll need to stop drinking and pill-popping. We'll need more than bread and eggs to feed a child. Champ knows all of this. He wants to ditch Huck and get a place for the two of us, but it's awfully expensive and dangerous for two Expelled folks like ourselves. But I'm convinced that, for once, we need to drop all pretense of our life as artists and redouble our efforts to find the niche we never did in high school. Maybe we could even find more than just a niche. Maybe we could find redemption.

Champ agrees with this wholeheartedly. Today he brought home a brochure for a local industrial arts college. "No more struggling, Babe," he said. Promises abounded amidst the brochure's glossy pages. New careers. New vistas.

One could be a piston, a spark plug, crank shaft, or rod. One could even aspire to be a entire wheel onto oneself (some day). Perhaps a gear, or whole collection of gears. Our education will require multiple surgeries, the transformation of some aspects of our bodies into a liquid state, and the pouring of those parts into molds.

There will be sacrifice (but then again, no worthwhile calling is without it). I just have to keep in mind the end result: a future in which Champ and I would have parts to play in the real world. A future for *just* Champ and me (no more Huck), with our shiny gears intermeshed with those of our offspring. Usefulness and prosperity for all three of us.

Only time will tell. The industrial arts school seems quite promising. The possibilities are limited only by our scores on the entrance aptitude test.

HOWL OF THE SHEEP

BY CODY GOODFELLOW

WOO-HOO! Welcome to Hormone Hell! C'mon! Take a ride on the Puberty Flume, where every teenage body launches into monstrous rebellion, careening on a stream of inchoate consciousness replete with zits, inexplicable urges, dank sexual secretions, and ungainly tufts of fur.

It's an awesome ride, as everyone who's ever been on it knows all too well. For many, middle school IS werewolf time, with biological transformations every bit as excruciating as the gnarliest FX sequence in An American Werewolf in London.

Count on noted literary troublemaker Cody Goodfellow to take this ball and run it across the finish line, then set it on fire, kick it into the stands, and dance as the stadium burns.

This is a cunning "what-if" intramural inversion of "Boobs," the lycanthropic gurl-power classic by Suzy McKee Charnas that inspired Ginger Snaps, *the greatest teenage werewolf film ever made.*

She couldn't wait to change. Hours before moonrise, she stripped and took to the streets.

Looking for a fight.

On her own, but she wasn't alone. High school kids pissed everywhere and prowled the alleys in Berserker war paint, pounding beers and painkillers to numb the coming change, or just pounding each other and anyone passing by in full-throated anticipation of it.

Vanessa itched with burning sweat that burned like her pelt coming in early, but she made herself walk down the street toward the park. Running would only attract them, and whatever they did to her before she changed would be permanent.

She was stupid to be out alone, but the impending change had been working her mind for days, and she couldn't wait at home any longer. The raging intensity of new sensations, the slippery, sickening nature of linear thought, made it impossible to control herself, but at least it focused her previously scattered impulses.

She no longer knew what she was, but at least she knew what she wanted.

This was the last full moon of the summer, and Vanessa meant to make the most of it. The rest of the girls on her football team would want to go play grab-ass games like hunting rabbits in the canyons or scrapping with stuck-up cheerleader bitches, but next week, they would start at Schwarzenegger High, and try out for the JV Berserkers squad. Everyone knew that high school was different. The sports were co-ed. They would be fresh meat.

Her friend Trista's brother Heath made first-string varsity his sophomore year. Varsity played Full Moon Ball. He got his foreleg ripped off in the first game against Valhalla and missed three games until it grew back stunted, and all his dreams of playing pro ball were dashed.

High school was serious. To survive and thrive as Berserkers, they would have to come in with blood on their paws.

To that end, Vanessa had simmered upon a course of action, but her febrile teenage mind could not cut through the bullshit and make itself clear. Now that she knew what they had to do, she only hoped she could find her friends and transmit the urgency and excellence of her plan, before it was too late for words.

She was in the office—for fighting, again—when Richard Pilcher's mom came in to see the principal, only that afternoon. They closed the door, but Vanessa scooted her chair up to the door and pressed her ear to the claw-scarred Formica. Mrs. Pilcher started sobbing, and the principal shouted at her to harden the fuck up.

"Your son's condition is not as rare as all that, Mrs. Pilcher, but . . . it's just rare for someone with his condition to survive this long—"

"His father was an alpha pack leader—"

"And what does *he* have to say about his son's progress?"

More sobbing. "I don't know. . . . I was r-r-r—*casually impregnated* . . . in the *daytime*." Wow. Ms. Pilcher almost used that dirty, illegal whine-word, *rape*. She should have been proud. Less than half of adult Americans could change at will, and maybe one in ten could do it in sunlight.

"That's just too bad, Ms. Pilcher, but facts are facts. Richard shows no ability, or willingness, to change. His grades may be top-notch, but he flunked the physical aptitude tests. He flatlined on the instinct tests. And he's a fucking vegetarian, to boot. He's not one of us. And if I send him on to high school as he is, I'll be ringing the dinner bell—"

The secretary tasered Vanessa away from the door, but she had already heard enough to set her head spinning.

Richard "Rabbit" Pilcher was the smartest kid in school, but he was a freak. Long before the first twinges of puberty sharpened their senses, everybody knew there was something wrong with the scrawny, nearsighted kid whose torrential dandruff fluttered after him like skywriting.

Vanessa was briefly his friend in kindergarten, and had to pound him almost daily until fourth grade before anybody forgot about it. The abuse only got worse after the other kids got their first changes in seventh grade, so he kept to himself. He spent all his free time reading the few unburned books in the library and twanging away on a queer little mandolin thing, when he wasn't running from a beating.

She saw Richard on her way home. He sat high up on the jungle gym in the playground, halfheartedly ducking clods of mud and rocks some kids from Norris Elementary threw at him as he read another of his infuriating books. No pictures, just words like dead bugs in a row that came alive in your brain when you looked at them. Ugh.

Perched up there with his head down, too scared to run away from a pack of hairless cubs, Pilcher didn't look so smart.

"Whatcha reading, Rabbit?" Vanessa shouted.

Without looking down, Pilcher waved and held up *The Foxfire Book*. Cool enough title, but the cover was a plain brown snore: *Hog dressing, log cabin building, mountain crafts*, zzzzz.

"Looks like a pretty shitty book," she sagely observed.

"No, actually, it's quite—Oh, I get it." He sat resigned as Vanessa threw the punch line. He brushed the clods of month-old wolf shit off the book, then wiped his glasses on his scarf. The scars on his neck and hands were flushed and angry as Richard Pilcher himself never was. Bite marks and claw-stripes from all the kids who tried to make him one of them.

The Norris kids howled and high-fived Vanessa. "You got any special plans for tonight, Rabbit?"

Shaking as if it was winter, Pilcher said, "I was thinking I might try to get out and do a little hunting . . ."

That cracked Vanessa up, but later it made her mad, because she couldn't think of anything smart to say. But as the sun went down and the electrified darkness of the Bright Night began to fall over the howling town, she knew what she had to do.

But first, she had homework.

U.S. history was Vanessa's favorite subject, after PE. Her textbook was thinner than most coloring books.

History made simple: once, the world was complicated by the weak and the weird; and overwhelmed, it ground on toward its own destruction, until one full moon twenty-five years ago, when the revolution came.

They called it a plague, but it would be the cure for all that ailed America. Nobody left alive was positive what caused it, but the shady data from that first fateful full-moon election night pointed to red meat, domestic beer, and cable news as contributing factors. The brave patriots who first rose up on all fours and tore out the throats of the weaklings in their midst were proud core consumers of all three, and little else. The armed forces were routed from within, but resurrected with new purity after savaging the feeble civilian hands that had starved and misused them for centuries.

When America emerged from its first cycle of the Werewolf "Plague," 77 percent of the population had fled to Canada or been eaten, but the remaining whatever percent restored a new order and integrated a golden age of freedom in the true spirit of the Founding Fathers. And not those fruits in the powdered wigs, either, but the *real* founding fathers, who first swore the sacred blood oath of the pack in the forest primeval.

Still quarantined and shunned by the rest of the world, America had returned to embrace its purest core values—and one or two nights a month, it lived them.

Vanessa recklessly blasted through the word searches in her homework and copied her Bible verses, then scarfed down the steak tartar cuts Mom left for her, and stripped down to her shorts.

Mom and Dad were off to the Santee Drive-In again, and hadn't invited her along. The stress of raising a girl in a world of wolves had left them tearing each other's ears off, and ever since she could fend for herself, they went out wilding on mule deer at the Barona reservation or rutting with strange mates at the drive-in at least twice a season.

When the sirens began to bay all over town, most of the howls that answered it were from thickened, bestial throats. Vanessa was already in the park, sniffing trees for the spoor of her friends, when the fat, mustard bulk of the harvest moon first peered down on them over the shoulder of Cowles Mountain.

She dropped to all fours and buried her face in the parched brown grass. Wrenching agony wrung the last gasps of humanity out of her mind, flooded it with pain so pure it obliterated any trace of self. Vanessa ripped the grass and dug into the dirt with her knurled, shrinking hands, and rolled on her warped spine to kick all four twisting, trembling limbs at the sky.

In health class, they told you how to handle the changes and showed a stupid video, *What's Happening to Me?* (2nd Ed). It was a painful but natural part of growing up, just like whelping pups or honor killings. They talked about their estrus cycles and their wet red dreams and practiced their breathing, but nothing prepared her for this. And each time, as her human body grew up, it hurt worse. As if she wasn't changing, but birthing the wolf, and dying.

When it was over, she could barely remember her name and who she was. The sudden unfolding rush of the world, the scintillant brightness of the moonlit night, the blazing mosaic of heat and the sweet scents of predator and prey made her forget the pain, but pushed her even further from the pimply, nervous, two-legged thing she'd been before.

She bounded around the park, chasing a few other young wolves and marking everything in sight, when she scented her teammates. They came bounding up in a bunch, panting as if they'd just returned from a fire in the boy's locker room.

She hunched down on her forelegs and snarled, daring them to run after her, but their anxiety pricked her nerve. They were spoiling for a hunt, and rats and raccoons were for kids.

Damn. What had she been thinking? What was it that seemed so important, just a while ago?

The black-faced wolf who always ran at her wing, her best friend, Trista, reminded her. In her mouth, dangling from slavering jaws, she carried a dead rabbit.

In PE, they teach you everything you need to know: the breathing exercises to ride out the initial trauma of becoming a wolf, the mnemonic tricks to hold onto some crust of one's human self, the dos and don'ts of prey selection and courtship. The thing they didn't actually teach you, but smugly winked about and said to let Nature take its course, was how to actually *kill* something.

It should come naturally, and in a natural world, no doubt it would. If you were the lone predator and lord of all you surveyed, et cetera, you'd run across all kinds of small game in the scrub canyons around town. But there were about two hundred thousand werewolves in San Diego County, and they had exercised their 38th Amendment rights to the hilt until nothing but rodents ran wild in the hills. The only game bigger than a rat that Vanessa had ever run down was the hobbled baby deer at her coming-out party, last year.

But she hungered to be something more than another bitch at the back of the pack, or an old gray, skeevy mutt alone with a litter like . . . like Richard Pilcher's mother.

Rabbit.

Her mind was a scarlet fever swamp, but while she chased her tail through it, her divine animal body raced ahead of her mates over fences and down the game trails of extinct coyotes to the bluffs of lower San Carlos. The trails stank of sugary lupine piss, but they didn't see another wolf. It felt heavenly to dig her claws into soft sand instead of clicking on pad-punishing concrete.

Most of the tract homes out here had burned down or been abandoned as their owners either got eaten or moved to better digs. A few houses were occupied and had electric fences and huge halogen lights on motion detectors. Dog breeders and other malcontents lived on the bluffs, but they were out wilding with the rest tonight. If there was anyone still human by the light of the full moon, they had to be more mole than human by now.

The Pilcher household didn't leave a light on, but Vanessa knew he'd be home. Ms. Pilcher was a fundamentalist, and did her wilding at the First Lunar Revival Temple in Allied Gardens. They rolled in thorns and broken glass to keep themselves from enjoying the glories of becoming a beast.

Stupid. So stupid . . .

She'd heard all the tall tales about what it was like to eat human flesh. The laws were foggy about charging people for crimes committed in animal form, and no humans had been seen on full moon nights in San Diego since Vanessa was a cub.

They said that if you ate human flesh, you might never change back. She knew they said that just to scare you, but she wished it were true.

If she could, Vanessa would never change back.

The bloodthirsty whirligig in Vanessa's streamlined skull skidded to a stop at the chorus of howls from before and behind her. The trail petered out on a cactus-studded ridge overlooking a ghost town of empty cul-de-sacs and naked foundations. Nothing stirred or shed heat anywhere in the terraced gulch below, but she could smell the goatish spoor of their prey in tantalizing traces of his sweat, piss, and even blood in the sand, where he'd run home like a hunted thing from school every day. They all could smell it, and in their quickened state it drove them crazy.

It was a wonder every wolf in the zip code hadn't scented Richard Pilcher and circled his door; but Vanessa suspected that most werewolves were like any other animal. Once they started chasing the nearest vermin or licking their own balls, they forgot whatever cares troubled their two-legged selves. Vanessa was simply gifted, or perhaps not so lucky. She barked and bit her mates to silence and led them down through the brush and burned-out cars choking the ravine, down onto the cracked blacktop game trail of Golfcrest Avenue.

Slinking from pothole to pileup like quicksilver shadows, they fanned out and surrounded the crappy stucco two-story tract home on the corner. She didn't know why anyone would stay out in the middle of nowhere, in such a shithole. Unless they had something to hide . . .

Trista bolted for the front picture window, but Vanessa bit her ear hard enough to draw blood. They circled each other for a tense moment before Vanessa stared her down and reasserted herself as the alpha.

Behind the curtains blocking all the upstairs windows, she saw the glow of candles. Downstairs was dark, and probably booby-trapped. He'd be up there reading, thinking himself safe.

Vanessa padded cautiously into the yard, hugging the rusty chain-link fence and sniffing for traps. Strange urine trails clouded her palate. Not wolves, and not human, either. An ugly smell, it chafed her nose and bristled her hackles, but she wouldn't let the doubt turn into the crippling animal fear that would turn her away. She skulked past the garbage cans and the locked-down garage to the backyard.

A drained swimming pool had been filled with soil and turned into a nice little vegetable garden. Bear traps lay all around it, and the perimeter fence was electrified. Crispy bird carcasses lay everywhere to bear witness to the effectiveness of the voltage. The ground-floor windows were boarded up, and the back door had a ten-key box on it. A big dead oak tree stood up close to the house, and a thick jute rope dangled from its highest branches. It stank of how he got in and out of the house.

Digging her claws into the iron-hard bark got her nowhere, but when she backed up and charged it, she was able to get halfway up the trunk before a wire noose dropped around her slim snout. She snapped at it, but it drew snug around her throat, then fed her enough electricity to power a roller coaster.

Vanessa yelped and went ragdoll. She fell from the tree, but missed the ground. Swinging by the noose like a fish, Vanessa danced for the chuckling amusement of someone hanging out the window. She couldn't see his face through her tears, and he wore a white sheep mask anyway. He dangled her from a Taser on a fishing pole.

Vanessa bit the wire. The jolt shot through her teeth and turned her whiskers to ash, but she fell to the ground and sounded the alarm.

So much for hide-and-seek.

Vanessa shook herself and crept up close to the back door. A flapping dog door in the bottom panel let something dart out into the yard. It moved too fast for Vanessa's shock-treated eyes to track, but it yowled and hissed like an angry dead thing and was over the fence before it could get shocked.

Vanessa stuck her head through the dog door, expecting to catch a shotgun blast to the face, but she saw only a jungle of uninhabited clutter. Squeezing through the low, narrow hole in the door, Vanessa stalked the Pilcher house.

Her snout wrinkled in repulsion at the ammoniac reek that saturated every fiber of the carpet, every stick of furniture, the overstuffed bookshelves. She only recognized the stench from the scratch-and-sniff cards in health class. Cats. Incredible. They were wiped out before she was born, supposedly.

These people were freaks.

Outside the house, she heard her mates baying and scratching around the property. Her simmering fear went away at the sound. She was not alone. The pack would back her play.

Almost immediately, a chorus of yipping and the clang of steel jaws snapping on clumsy paws and snouts sent her cringing in the corner.

She pissed on the crumbling plaster until the smell made her feel in command of at least of tiny piece of the world.

Before something else could catch her, she darted up the hall, and climbed the stairs.

Weird. His weak, deviant smell was alpha here. It was a cloying, musky goat smell, devoid of even the faintest trace of tangy predator edge that every boy in school exuded even at the bottom of his cycle. She quivered with rage, but it only masked something deeper, that even her worldly-wise animal self could not explain.

That he was anything but helpless here, that his retiring, sheepish public clothing had been only bait, she knew, but she didn't care. She knew what she had to do next, and why health and PE teachers couldn't tell her. She was ready to kill.

Rabbit stepped into the hall and jumped back as if electrified. The vapid sheep mask only magnified his surprise. His legs tangled up and spun him around like a top. What a spaz. On two legs, she would've busted a gut laughing.

She unleashed a proper roar that pinned him to the spot, then pounced on him. Her jaws wide to accept his neck, she hung above him in the air for an instant.

Her snarling snout smashed into a mirror and crashed through glass instead of hot, soft flesh.

He stood in the open doorway to her right and watched her fall through the angled mirror and the hole in the floor and into a darkness even her wide, nocturnal eyes could not penetrate.

She landed hard on cold concrete. Her left foreleg folded under her funny and snapped cleanly through her auburn-black fur. Shrieking and licking the sweet marrow, Vanessa could try to climb the walls or she could heal, but not both at once.

Growling and gagging on tears as the bone set itself, she turned and looked up at the hole in the ceiling just in time to see Richard peek down at her and drop something on her head.

A net snarled her flailing limbs and bit into her furry hide with teeth that stung her to paralysis. The barbed hooks woven into the net were pure silver.

Suddenly, the room was filled with light. Headlights painted the walls of the garage. The door opened with a grating skirmish of bent metal, and an army of remote control cars squealed out of the garage and down the driveway.

Vanessa barked to summon her mates, but those who weren't caught in traps were too bewitched by the lights and wailing sirens of the speeding RC cars to heed her call.

They raced barking into the street after the cars. Trista shagged one before it jumped the curb. It exploded in her mouth and blew her snout off. She quivered and rolled up whining, but the others were too far gone to notice her. They raced off out of sight to end in muffled bangs and whimpers in the dark.

Richard came down the hall and entered the garage. He wasn't wearing a sheep mask anymore. He had a long, tapered snout; big, batlike ears; and twinkling, opalescent yellow eyes. She recognized it from magazine pictures and museum dioramas. It was the face of a coyote.

And it wasn't a mask.

"I hoped you'd come," he said, and kneeling beside her, took out a huge, serrated combat knife.

She growled warningly, but the sound came out like a purr. Her foreleg was shaky, but the bone felt strong under her. Any movement caused the silver hooks to dig deeper into her pelt.

Set deep under a sloping brow covered in fine copper-blond fur, his yellow eyes twinkled at her. She ached to have his heart in her mouth, but that head-spinning something else swelled up inside her, almost smothering her pain, and transmuting her hate.

"Lie still, Vanessa. Yes, I know it's you." Laying the flat of the shark-toothed blade against the downy fur of her throat, he skinned back his lips from his needle teeth as he let her think he was about to kill her. "I could always kind of tell," he said, "when you were picking on me with the others, that you were different from the rest. You knew I was different, too."

Petrified, she trembled under his gentle, tawny hand. He slid the razor-thin knife up the net, slitting it like pantyhose to set her free. Delicately as a mother, he pulled the hooks from her hide and scratched behind her ears. The pits behind her ears throbbed and oozed arousal scent. The goatish stink of him no longer made her hackles rise; now, it had taken on a whole new meaning.

He worked her nerves like the strings of his instrument, settling the tension and stealing away her pain, so that she felt only the quivering, queasy wash of strange sensations pouring out of her loins. She burned for words, but her wolf tongue betrayed her, straying out from her jaws to lap at his paw.

"I'm not like the rest of you," he said, "But I'm not weaker. I'm a child of Coyote, the Trickster God, who was the lord of this land. We can control how often we change," he added, pinching her with the opposable thumb on his paw. "I've been hiding among you to find someone who was special, to run with me and hunt wolves as wolves hunted men, forever and ever. Does that sound crazy?"

His gently relentless paws stroked the sweaty softness of her belly. She lifted her throat to him and turned to present her inflamed hindquarters. Whimpering as he mounted her, she felt no defeat in surrender.

He was her first, and nothing about it felt like the health videos said it would. His thing was all wrong, and far larger than a canine's ought to be, and it didn't shoot out of a sheath or lock inside her, like she expected. But neither was it the kind of gross doggy-style mounting that she'd always dreaded. He drove her mad with his dexterous forepaws as he thrust with a maddening delicacy into her trembling hindquarters.

At long last, Richard uttered a tortured howl and spent so deep inside her she felt his seed racing through her heart. She howled deliriously, whined with a joy too powerful for human words. She had come here to kill this strange boy who haunted her dreams, and discovered so much more. He was not weaker, but just different, and so much smarter than the rest. Instinct had drawn her to him, and now she had found a mate like no other, her destiny could only be something awesome.

Still stroking her, he smiled wide, his pink tongue lolling out like a broken party favor. His grin got even wider, and he reached up to pull his ears back until his grin split his face apart. Ripping off the furry mask and peeling away the gooey gum that held it in place, Richard Pilcher spat out his coyote dentures and grinned at her with his blunt, crooked rabbit teeth.

His muscle-melting massage turned into a bee sting between her shoulder blades, and frigid fog poured into her bloodstream.

She tried to get up, but couldn't even make a sound. Skinning off the furry-paw gloves, Richard turned to face the shadowy figures watching from the corner of the garage. "So, how was that?"

They had no scent at all. They wore black dappled fatigues that rendered them completely invisible to her until they moved. They shed no heat, and their faces, behind big goofy black sheep masks, might have been figments of her drugged, despairing mind. Apparently, they'd watched—and *ewww*, videotaped— the whole thing.

"Points for originality and daring," one of them said, "but hardly a challenge. These suburban bitches are dumb enough to fall for anything."

"She's as smart as they come, out here," Richard answered, and Vanessa felt sickened at a tremor of love for him, even now. "I can't stay here, after this."

"Fine then, kid," said the other black sheep. "But wrap it up. We've got to be out of the county before the wolves wake up."

Richard turned back to her and sat beside her. "I'm sorry about all of this, Vanessa. I wish I could take you with me. But you're just not all that special. Mostly, I'm sorry this isn't going to hurt."

Out came the knife, slicing into the tender flesh under her ears and plowing a red furrow down her shaggy flanks to her tail, as neatly as any diagram in *The Foxfire Book*.

But Richard was wrong. It hurt like hell.

His sheepish smile wet warm and wicked, and it might be another trick, but she could see the wolf inside him. He might be immune, or he might just have it so locked down that it never came out to play. But it raced behind his eyes, just the same. He only looked like a sheep on the outside.

"Ask yourself," he said in a jocular tone, his knife chattering off the shivering bones of her ribs, "why you have to be dumb, to be strong."

The day after every full moon was a National Day of Rest. Only the 7-Eleven, the churches, the butcher shops, and the emergency rooms were open in town. Most folks slept in until noon, when the NFL preseason games from the night before replayed. The Chargers looked to have a decent offensive package for once, but the Raiders sacked the quarterback in his own end zone, cracked his ribs and ate his heart for a safety. He was expected to miss the rest of the season.

Vanessa woke up in her bed, and stayed there.

The next day, she tried to weasel out of school, but Mom made her go. She wore a hooded sweatshirt to cover her bald head and the scabby, itchy pink mess of her half-healed back.

Trista's parents let her stay home. Lucky bitch got her face blown off, but at least she didn't know what really happened in Richard's house. That, at least, somehow took care of itself.

Everyone was talking about Richard, but there was no announcement in homeroom. His desk sat empty. Someone with a radio said the sheriff was investigating and would make an announcement, but it was pretty obvious what was coming. The bloody rags in the house matched Richard Pilcher's scent. His murderers were not identified, but from the lingering stares she got as she slinked down the hall, Vanessa thought she had somehow got the credit. Richard's devious black sheep friends must've turned on him.

Unless it was another trick, she thought uneasily, and he was still out there. She should tell someone what he really was, and the danger he posed, and warn the world that he wasn't alone.

She could do this and still take credit for killing him, maybe. She was still chewing this over when the intercom razzed health class and ordered her to the nurse's office.

That was a new one. Fights and trouble, she knew, but the nurse's office? She wasn't sick, and the nurse's office wasn't allowed to give out anything stronger than aspirin, anyway.

Two sheriff's deputies and a bunch of angry, red-eyed parents huddled in the back of the room. She really didn't believe any of it could be about her, until she saw her father sulking among them.

So they were spotted at Pilcher's house. So what? Full-moon nights were like Carnival in Rio. Crimes of passion didn't count for shit. They would probably just hit her for a stool sample, and when none of Richard's teeth or toenails came out in the wash, she could come clean. Anyway, she'd be entering Berserker country as a celebrity.

The sheriff came over with the nurse and requested some privacy. They took her behind a screen and he ordered her to strip. Vanessa howled, "Daddy!" but he didn't come. "Just do what they say, honey."

She stripped and the nurse slipped on rubber gloves and gave her a pelvic exam. The pervy sheriff stood close enough to spit his tobacco juice into her, squinting at her junk as if it was modern art until her last atom of dignity floated away on the wind.

"Looks like a natural girl to me," the sheriff finally said. *Gee, thanks, Sheriff. So glad it's finally official.* "Now missy, I suppose you better tell us what you remember about last night."

Vanessa snarled, "Fuck you sideways." The nurse backhanded her off the gurney, then yanked her up by the hood. When they saw her freshly scalped head, the sheriff said, "Ah shit. Now it adds up."

He ordered Vanessa to get cleaned up and go back to class. The nurse slapped the Red Man out of his jowl. He reluctantly took off his hat and apologized, then explained.

Trista, Bristol, and Britney had each come back to their respective homes yesterday morning, torn up and tired and pleading total amnesia on the entire night. But after they all ended up at the hospital, they grudgingly gave her up. Any loyalty was out the window, anyway, after what she'd allegedly done to them.

They all told the same story. Vanessa—or someone who looked and smelled just like Vanessa—had come and sprung them out of traps or saved them from bleeding out from their toy car injuries . . . and then forced herself on them.

None of them said it was a male wolf, and the hair and blood samples from each girl matched Vanessa, though it was anyone's guess whose semen it was. That kind of God-mocking witchcraft was just one more thing the weaklings had taken with them, when Vanessa's parents' generation ate them.

Vanessa hugged herself for fear she would transform and kill everyone in the room, right there and then. He'd used her, then used her skin to casually impregnate her friends. And this . . .examination. She'd have to change schools. Her clique was ruined. Trista and the others would drop PE for extra family planning classes. Abortion, even of a deviant's litter, was out of the question.

"It was him!" she screamed. "Rabbit! I mean, Richard Pilcher!"

"That's impossible, miss," the sheriff said. "He was, er, roughed up in his bed. By the volume of blood at the scene, we're pretty sure he was in no shape—"

"You can't be sure of shit, with that boy!" She got up off the gurney and came at the sheriff with her cracked nails out. Her dad and the nurse grabbed her and held her back. "He's smarter than you and he doesn't need to change, but he's out there, and he's not alone, and he's going to come back—"

The sheriff asked the nurse to give Vanessa something strong to help her relax, and then backed out of the school with his hat on backward. Vanessa's dad slipped out in the commotion without saying good-bye.

The nurse gave her a pill and stroked Vanessa's flayed back with chubby, rough palms covered in tufts of wiry black hair.

"You'll be back to normal in no time, sweetie," she said. Her nostrils flared and took in Vanessa's scent. Her orange eyes bugged with alarm, but then she smiled, as she realized the strange blood she smelled on Vanessa was not on her claws, but in her belly. "On second thought, I suppose congratulations are in order."

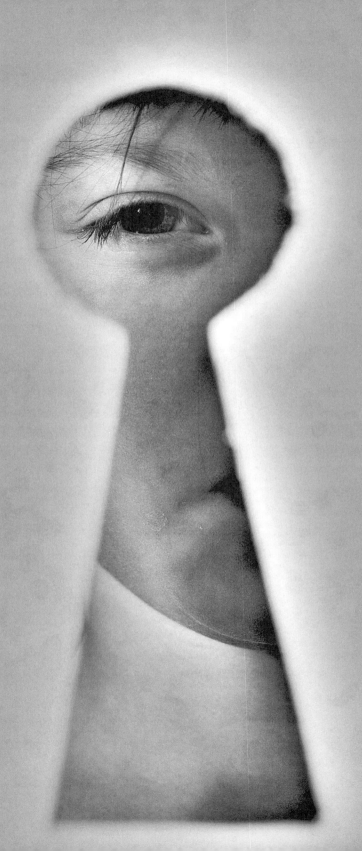

PIECES OF ETHAN

BY ADAM-TROY CASTRO

Here's a family snapshot you won't soon forget, from the prodigious Adam-Troy Castro. This one distills the essence of secrets and surprises I promised you, way back in the introduction to this book. And so, about it I will only say this:
Love is long suffering. But hate doesn't age well.
Now enjoy this modern classic, seeing print here for the very first time.

Ethan's condition swallowed him whole on the day of his sixth birthday. You could say that he was dead from that moment on, though he lingered for many years afterward, dragging all of us into the same black hole with him. Maybe we were entitled to hate him for what he became, and what that did to us: but how was he entitled to feel about us, the ones who would go on after he was gone?

It happened at the place on Sunny Creek where the river turned wide enough and calm enough and deep enough to become our natural playground on those days when the afternoons were more generous with hours than chores. This was of course still many years before that creek was dried to a fraction of its former glory by the dams greedy developers constructed upstream to turn our little valley from a refuge on the edge of wilderness to yet another overcrowded place for city folks to breed their litters of vacant-eyed suburban tots. We could splash around in our underwear or even outside of it without fear of offending neighborhood prudes or attracting neighborhood pederasts. Until that day Ethan changed we considered the site one of the great landmarks of our childhood, and I suppose we still did after Ethan, though what it meant to us had irrevocably changed by then.

I returned to the spot just once within the last couple of years, just to see if it had continued to get worse after Ethan died and our family moved away forever. I found rust on the rocks, stagnant water that stank of sewage, and abandoned crack pipes in the dirt. Highway traffic was audible over the trickle that remained of the waterfall. The ruination of our childhood playground made the lives we had lived before Ethan's transformation look even more like what it was: an idyll we had known but lost.

But back then, it was still a family refuge beloved by all of us. And so Mom had felt no misgivings over asking me to take him there and keep him occupied until it was time to get him dressed for his party. He'd been driving her crazy for hours with his constant talk of the presents to come, and she needed him taken out of the house as an acceptable alternative to strangling him. It was a choice between watching him or helping her clean the living room, so I agreed. She packed some sandwiches and sodas, and let me take Ethan and our middle sister Jean out to where the water was cold and white.

We enjoyed a few hours of innocent fun going over the falls and dunking one another under the water, before taking a break on the flat rocks that overlooked the pool so we could feel the droplets tingle as they turned to vapor on our skin. During those hours, the last unspoiled hours of our lives, I'd dared Ethan to jump from the highest cliff, something he hadn't ever worked up the nerve to do before and might actually be able to steel himself to attempt some visit soon. I'd splashed Jean in the face and endured her promises to go running to Mom. I'd endured the inevitable payback in the form of the fistful of mud she'd mined from the pond bottom. We teased and played and pretended that time wasn't passing at all as the sun rose high in the sky and started to sink again, changing only the pattern of the light that shone like diamonds on the rippled surface.

Many years later, I think about the first part of the day and reflect that if the bad thing hadn't come along to ruin it we would now remember it as one of the perfect, transcendent moments of our lives; one of those days that we all keep as permanent snapshots in our heads, when we define what was best about our childhood.

But then the bad thing did happen, and form a snapshot of a different kind.

I remember having nothing in mind but scaring Ethan silly with a cannonball landing, right next to where he paddled around in circles, wondering where I had gone. Grinning, I shouted Geronimo and leaped off the rocks twenty feet above him, striking the water with the kind of concussive force that made the impact feel less like a splash and more like an explosion. The bubbles rose all around me, like a fleet of spaceships taking flight. I hit the soft ooze at the bottom and pushed off, grinning, happy, in what I now recognize as the last uncomplicated moment of my youth.

I broke surface just behind Ethan, with a fine view of the back of his head. Jean was screaming. I didn't know right away that this meant anything was wrong, as shrieking girls are just part of the fun of horseplay in water. But when I tracked the sound to Jean, who was paddling around in the water twenty strokes beyond Ethan, nothing in her face testified to play; she was pale and wide eyed, her lips peeled back as far as they would go in a grimace of horrified denial.

My first thought was that I'd just scared her more than I'd intended to scare Ethan. My second, more serious, was that some kind of animal had bitten her underwater and that I'd catch hell from Mom for not being sufficiently watchful.

Then she screamed, *"It's Ethan!"*

The back of Ethan's head looked the same as it had always looked. It looked like the back of any little kid's head, jug ears and all. I figured it couldn't be too bad, since he was still treading water just fine, but Jean was still screaming, so I grabbed his shoulder and pulled him toward me.

The only warning I had that I would not be seeing a human face where his should have been was a sudden shift of the bone where my palm touched his shoulder. It felt like the bulge of a rat scurrying around underneath a throw rug. It flattened and became something other than a shoulder just before Ethan completed his turn and blinked at me through the one eye that remained recognizable, an eye that had somehow migrated, socket and all, farther down his cheek, and now blinked at me from the vicinity of his lips. That eye begged me for explanation. Then the skin on both sides of that eye rose up and swallowed it whole beneath a curtain of bubbling flesh.

I was away at college when word arrived that Ethan had taken a turn for the worse and that I needed to hurry home right away.

That was a hell of a way to put it. The phrase "taking a turn for the worse" implies that the state before it could be somehow counted as better. With Ethan, all developments were bad; some were worse than others, but every day brought a fresh nadir, a brand-new visit to countries more terrible.

This was cram week, so it took me the better part of a morning's negotiating with various academic offices before I could get a hardship leave that would allow me to postpone finals without flunking out or taking incompletes. I made sandwiches before I left, borrowed a junker from a friend in the dorm, and made it home in just over twenty hours, feeling like a failure as a brother whenever I had to stop to stretch my legs or fill up the gas tank or even take a shit. On the way back I got regular updates by cell phone. Ethan was awake and coherent now; he was asking for me. Then he was insane and ripping holes in the walls. Then he was flat on his back and gasping for air, unable to take in enough to feel anything but slow strangulation. Then he was expected to be dead within the hour. Then he was dead. Then he was alive again (or rather still, the half hour he'd spent mistaken as corpse now explained away as an understandable mistake, given that he'd been something nobody could bear to think of as alive).

Twenty hours, and then I pulled off the highway and into the cookie-cutter template the old neighborhood had become, rows and rows and rows of ugly houses without enough space between them to pass sunlight except as isolated stripes. As always after a long absence, I hated the families in all those houses, for what they'd done to the special place where I'd grown up. My folks might have still had a couple of dozen acres left over from the days when land was cheap, and they'd kept the original homestead inside it as pristine as possible behind stone walls crawling with ivy, but even as I pulled past the automatic gate, what I found past it no longer felt like a homey refuge on the edge of a forest; rather, the last threatened keep protecting itself from invaders who had ruined a once enchanted country.

It was a much smaller estate than it had been, once upon a time. Mother had been selling off our acreage, both to pay taxes and to support us when all her energies went to Ethan and no other form of income was possible.

I left the pavement of the hated outside, pulled onto the gravel of the family's circular drive, and after another minute or so came to a stop behind a small fleet of parked cars clustered at the base of the wraparound porch. Jean, who'd been up all night providing intermittent companionship via cell phone, slammed the screen door and came running to meet me, her waist-length scarlet hair bouncing behind her like a banner. She was hugging me tight even before I was all the way out of the car.

Her voice broke as our cheeks touched and her tears mingled with mine. "Oh, Lawrence. It's been so *long*."

I knew she wasn't talking about the months since my last visit home; rather, of these last days since Ethan started to fail. We'd lost our father to emphysema a couple of years back, and had learned back then what Jean and the rest of the family had been relearning now; that deathbed vigils have a way of trapping time in amber, turning each passing tick of the clock into another slice of eternity.

I didn't have to ask how bad it had been. Life with our afflicted brother had always been bad, but my sister's beautiful green eyes looked like the last night, alone, had aged her twenty years. "I should have taken a plane."

Had I been anybody else, Jean might have said, *damn straight you should have taken a plane*. But Jean had been with me the one and only time I'd been a passenger on a commercial aircraft, and knew that flying with me was a nightmare. I didn't take well to enclosed places. "It wouldn't have made a difference. Most of the time he wouldn't have known you were here. You're here for the end; that's what matters."

The screen door slammed again, and Mom appeared. She was tall, slender, an older version of Jean, who had aged in the way most beautiful women hope to age, becoming more golden where others just become more lined. Unlike Jean, who had come at a run, Mom came at a measured walk: calm, regal, as measured in every movement as only a woman who had discovered her own iron strength could be. She wore her own long hair, as scarlet as Jean's without a touch of dye, in a tight wrap behind her head, more for convenience than any aged dignity. Her tight-lipped, tired smile was as warm to me as any embrace. "It's good to see you, Lawrence. You made good time. I was afraid that you'd have to stop in a motel for a few hours. Do you need to sleep before you see him?"

"No, I think I had about twenty cups of coffee on the road. I'm about to jump out of my skin—you're looking good, Mom."

"Nice of you to say. But I know I look like hell."

This was both true and untrue. Physically, Mom had never come close to looking like what women mean when they say they *look like hell*. More than once, doing her grocery run in town, she'd had been mistaken for Jean's older sister instead of her mother; more than once, she'd received come-ons from young men who would have been mortified to find out just how old she was; more than once, she had admitted to being lonely enough to want to take them up on their offers, if only for a night of anonymous release. It hadn't been loyalty to the memory of my father, or fear of our disapproval, that stopped her. It was the tormented presence in the upstairs room, the sense that allowing herself to take pleasure in anything outside the family while he still lived, amounted to failing him.

As for the other part, the price taking care of a doomed boy enacts on the mother who loves him—well, in that sense, you could say that my mother looked like the hell she'd been through. She wore every moment of the last ten years on her face, and anybody with an ounce of sensitivity could see it. But again, on her, it didn't mean what women usually mean when they say they look like hell. Hell hadn't aged her. Hell had just brought out what she was. Hell became her.

She put her hands on my shoulders. "Whatever you say, I won't have you driving yourself to exhaustion. You can bring your bag inside later. You'll pay your respects to your brother, and then you'll come downstairs for a hot breakfast, and then you'll go up to your room and catch some of that sleep you've been missing. I won't take any argument on this. Is that clear?"

I nodded, and then hugged her. "It's good to be home."

I could see how close she came to contradicting me, to saying that she knew damned sure it wasn't—as it hadn't been; being home wouldn't be good as long as Ethan remained what he was—but she allowed the lie to stand, as she hugged me back and told me, as she told me out loud only in times of great celebration or sorrow, that she loved me.

There was no point in expending tears now, not with the sight of Ethan still ahead of me, and so I gave her one last squeeze and let her and Jean lead me into the house, where I nodded hello at the gathered forms of my cousins and uncles and aunts, all gathered out of grim sense of family duty for these last hours of the long vigil my mother had endured, almost without rest, for so many years. Then I went to the stairs, putting my hand on the polished banister that Ethan had once used to slide down with giggles, and holding on to it as I ascended toward the attic floor with the locked and soundproofed door that had never been able to cage the sound of splintering bones.

On the day Ethan changed, Jean had run home to get Mom and Dad while I stayed with him, watching him shift from one terrible shape to another, enduring the sounds his insides made as they fractured and reformed into new configurations. I shooed flies away from the lungs that had burst from his chest, glistening with blood and foaming with fugitive breath. I lied to him about everything going to be okay when his spine contracted like a salted slug and bent him over backward, with the back of his head melting into the bare skin of his buttocks. I vomited with revulsion, for the first of what turned out to be many times in our relationship, when all his connective tissue dissolved and he became a mound of disembodied organs, pulsing on the rocks where a boy had been, with nothing but a boiling puddle of blood between them to identify them as parts of the same tormented body and not as separate butchered pieces of meat..

I had thought that nothing in my life could ever be as horrible as that half hour, and had gone away for a little while when Jean returned with our parents and a plastic tub to carry our brother in. I surrendered myself to shock and catatonia as the three of them helped me collect Ethan's pieces, as we squared him away in an upstairs bathtub, and as we called the family physician, Dr. Zuvicek.

My ability to form new memories went away for a while. I know intellectually what happened. I suppose you can even say I remember it, in the way one remembers a favorite movie. But in another way it never really happened to me. It never recorded. I can't really call forth anything else until much later that day, until Dr. Zuvicek trudged down from upstairs to enter a living room still festooned with multicolored balloons and HAPPY BIRTHDAY banners.

Zuvicek's status as our family doctor bore a double meaning, as he was related to us via some arcane spider's web of genealogy that had always escaped me and frankly always would. I knew little else about him except that he specialized in treating members of our family, and in fact traveled throughout our region to pay house calls on those who had settled in the six closest states. He was broad-shouldered and thick-armed and wore a sculpted red beard with silvery flares at the pointed tips. Today he had pieces of bloody Ethan tissue on his sideburns and glistening patches of worse things on his conservative black suit. He looked colorless, which for him was like being another person, because Zuvicek had always been one of the ruddiest men I'd ever known.

As he entered the living room, he put his big black bag on the coffee table and faced my sister and myself with a look of almost infinite pity.

Jean, who was still young enough to seek hope even in hopeless situations, said, "Is he going to be okay?"

He rubbed at his dark eyes with one gloved hand. He always wore black gloves, even indoors: something to do with a skin condition that made his fingers sensitive. "No."

"Is he gonna die?"

"Yes," Zuvicek said, with a sharpness that surprised me. "But that's true of you and me as well. It might happen tonight and it might happen fifty years from now. Your brother, I think he'll still be with us for another few years yet."

I heard in his voice the admission that this would not be good news for us. "But what's wrong with him, exactly?"

We heard footsteps on the stairs, and Zuvicek said, "Your father will wish to speak to you on this, I think."

Unlike my mother, who would remain youthful even after years of fighting for her damaged son, my father looked like he had aged four decades in as many hours. Ethan's plight had ripped a hole in his life, one that had already leeched the color from his skin and the spark from his eyes. In the short time he had left, before daily existence in the same house as my damaged brother put him in his grave, he'd age still more, developing a stoop, a lingering wheeze, and a patina of exhaustion that turned every breath he took into a fresh burden he only shouldered out of habit. But on that day, as he came down the stairs, there was still some of the man he'd been left on his bones, and as he lowered himself into the overstuffed armchair that had always been his alone, it seemed less the attitude of a man without strength to stand than that of a father who now had to address his two undamaged children from across a common table.

Father massaged his temples with forefinger and thumb. "I am sorry. In any other family, you would have been able to live your entire lives without seeing this."

"Seeing what?"

"This . . . curse," he said, spitting the word as if he would have liked to wrap both his hands against the disease, and strangle the life from it, if he could. Then he heard himself, seemed to realize that anger at the fates would only frighten us, and softened. "This disorder. It is known to our family, from the old country, but it is very, very rare. Most of us have lived an entire lifetime without ever hearing of a case, except in old stories. A distant cousin you have likely never met had a child with the condition, about twenty years ago. Your grandmother, may she rest in peace, once told me it had happened to a grand-uncle of hers, when she was a girl even younger than Ethan is now; and a hundred years before that it happened to some other poor child, whose name and exact relationship to us have been lost to history. Records only go back so far, but it has always been the hidden devil inside us, the one that slept for generations."

I had been learning genetics in my science classes. "You're talking about a recessive trait."

My father looked blank for a moment, as if I'd just tossed a few words of quantum physics into the conversation.

Zuvicek answered for him. "You are a smart boy. Yes. That is exactly what your father is talking about."

"And . . . it only happens to our family? To no one else?"

"As far as I know," Zuvicek said. "There are rumored to be other families who suffer something like it. But they may be obscure offshoots of our own. There are, as I say, few records. In the old country, these things were always kept private."

Jean shivered and hugged herself, which was not just a fearful gesture, because she had donned her clothes while still wet and had caught a chill running back from the creek. "Why would anybody even want to be part of our family, then? Why would anybody in our family ever have children, if this could happen to us?"

I saw pain and anger flare in my father's eyes, reactions he tried to hide by looking away. Years later, I still wonder if that was the moment when death first planted its terrible seed in him. Maybe. It still feels like the moment when it was first planted in me.

But Zuvicek was patient. "I understand that you are upset. I don't expect you to take much comfort in this right away, but every family in the world has a history of increased susceptibility to one ailment or another. To compensate, they also all harbor areas of high congenital resistance. In our own family's case, the childhood cancer rate is much lower than the norm, and the same can be said of our personal incidence of epilepsy, diabetes, and degenerative muscle disease. Nor is that all we have to be thankful for. There are many things we have to worry about less, that are much more important in the scheme of things, than this one ailment that almost never happens."

Jean was not mollified. "Are we going to get it?"

My father was even more stricken by this question than he had been by her last one, but Zuvicek was firm. "Absolutely not. You are already older than you would be if you were ever going to get it—as are you, Lawrence. This ailment only attacks very young children, most of them infants or toddlers; tragically, Ethan was himself almost old enough to be considered out of danger. It is next to certain that your own children, should either of you have children, will also never have to worry about such a thing. All you have to worry about now is your poor brother . . . and how much your poor mother and father will now depend on you, to help take care of him. It—"

Ethan screamed. The inhuman sounds from upstairs, which would never stop in the long years that followed, had been audible since long before Zuvicek came down. But most of them had been cracking and grinding noises, as well as sudden exhalations, that had not sounded like anything in particular and had been almost impossible to identify as product of any particular little boy's voice.

This shriek was Ethan's voice, returned to him: a cry of almost unimaginable pain that would not have been inappropriate coming from a boy set on fire, or one swarmed by hornets, or one simply locked in a cramped black place along with the sound of vicious things scrabbling in the dark. There was no sanity in it, or hope. But it was, for a second, recognizable as Ethan's voice. I suddenly remembered that it was my little brother we were talking about, and half-stood, determined to race up the stairs to his side. But then the sound of his pain changed to something far worse, something with barbed wire and broken glass in it, and all my instinctive protectiveness fled, replaced by paralysis and shame as a stream of warm piss ran down my leg.

My father saw it. So did Jean, and so did Zuvicek. Not one of them blamed me. They had all heard the same thing I'd heard, and may have come close to the same involuntary release.

In the end, Zuvicek could only finish the sentence he had started before Ethan's scream.

"—will not be easy for any of you, I'm afraid."

Now I was an adult, home from the university my mother had insisted I leave home to attend, as inured to horror as only one who had lived his life steeped in horror could ever come to be.

I stood at the locked door of Ethan's room, gripping the deadbolt, closing my eyes when one of the wet sounds from within reminded me of rending flesh.

As always, standing at this threshold felt like facing a long drop into formless darkness. Even if I'd taken the next step on more days than I could count, even I knew from long experience that I'd survive an encounter with my brother, there was no way of quantifying how much it was going to hurt. The only certainty was that it would.

As always, I waited for the first cry that sounded recognizably human before I peered through the spy hole.

Even allowing for the distortion of the panoramic lens, Ethan's room no longer looked like the toy-strewn sanctuary decorated with spacemen and superheroes that it had been on the day of his sixth birthday. The colorful boy-size bed frame and desk and toy chest had not long survived his illness unbroken; they had been removed, and replaced with padded walls and a steel trunk equipped with padlock and air holes, for those times when only absolute confinement would be enough. The padding covered walls that had been rebuilt to cover what had once been windows open to morning light, with a fine view of the trees at the edge of our backyard forest. Now the only light was a circular fluorescent ring within a reinforced cage. One of its segments flickered and one of the others gave off a dim glow brightest at the center, like the sun trying to break through a blanket of clouds. Stains of various colors, some recognizable as the things that come out of a human body, and some not, streaked from the ceiling and puddled on the knit seams between the padded places on the floor.

It was, I knew, impossible to keep the room looking or smelling like anything but an open sewer. By its very nature, Ethan's disorder meant that he leaked. Sometimes, when he transformed into whatever he became next, he reabsorbed whatever he'd spilled last. Sometimes he didn't. It was the only consistent way to tell the difference between what was part of Ethan and what was just his waste fluids.

It took me a second or two to find the twitching, half-melted form, like a man wrenched into a Möbius strip, that bubbled at the room's farthest corner. Even as I watched, it tried to grow spikes, but they deflated with a hiss. The shape softened, becoming as close to the shape of a human boy as Ethan ever got anymore: a lot like a plastic army man that somebody had melted on a hot stove and then allowed to cool.

I threw the bolt and entered, wincing as always at the sheer stench of the place. My mother and father had installed a state-of-the-art air-filtration system early on, using what would have been Ethan's college fund, but the atmosphere in here was always like a deep whiff of a sweaty sneaker that had been allowed to marinate in rotten bananas and then soaked in a puree made from the contents of a rancid diaper.

It was as impossible to get used to the stench as it was to get used to the things Ethan changed into, because fresher and more offensive perfumes were always being added to the soup. You can get used to living inside an open sewer, if you have to. Your sense of smell adapts, if only by turning off. But if shit is only the least offensive of all the possible things you have to wade through, and everything new that comes dribbling down the pipes attacks some remaining vulnerability in your gag reflex, then adaptation doesn't work. There's nothing to get used to.

I had lost one of my college girlfriends because our evening walk had taken us past a golden retriever who'd been split open by a passing car. It was still alive, and whining, even as its parts leaked from its flattened belly. The septic release of its split bowels made the site of its imminent death like the inside of a toilet. My girlfriend vomited out the General Tso's Chicken I'd just paid for and later called me cold and inhuman because the sight of the poor pooch had left me unaffected. I hadn't been able to explain to her that I'd long since grown used to obscene sights and smells like that, because my little brother spent most of his life as obscene sights and smells like that.

Now, fighting back the nausea I hadn't been able to feel then, that Ethan could still wrench from me, I padded across the sodden canvas to the place where the throbbing shape lay, trying to grow a face. Dark patches that could have been embryonic eyes, a nose, and mouth, as captured in a drawing by an ungifted first grade cartoonist, appeared just below the thing's semiliquid chest, and seemed about to congeal into something capable of speech . . . but then they faded, leaving only an oozing green patch, like a gasoline spill on a driveway.

Ethan quivered, that little failed attempt at coherence exhausting him utterly.

My vision blurred. "Hey, kid. I drove a long way to get here. Can you spare a little hello for me?"

He gurgled like an infant, and exploded.

There's a certain sight popular in Hollywood comedies: the hapless character who gets drenched by something slimy and malodorous—shit or fertilizer or paint or, in gooier fantasies, alien bodily fluids that have never been included in the usual list of substances produced by the human body. The victim's eyes always blink multiple times in the middle of a face otherwise obscured by muck, eloquently communicating an offended dignity that encourages the ticket holders in the audience to howl in disgust and delight.

Ever since Ethan turned six, my family no longer considers that kind of scene funny. We've all been through it too many times.

This time I was lucky; not only did none get inside me, but what got on me decided that it didn't want to stick. The layers of little brother flowed off my skin like quicksilver, forming another queasy puddle at my feet before pieces of him became the snout of a rat, the leg of a dog, the cock of a stallion. Two beautiful cat's eyes, with irises of green and gold, blinked on his surface, communicating a calm amazement that could have meant anything I wanted it to mean; then they disappeared and—in what I could only think of as a little miracle—the vomitous ooze congealed, forming an oversize, bodiless portrait of a little boy's face.

"Hello," he said.

It was the first coherent word my little brother had spoken to me in three years.

He looked like he would stay this way for a while, so I touched him on his oversize cheek. My hand looked like an infant's against that larger-than-life canvas.

A lump formed in my throat. "Hi, kid. How's it going?"

He gulped, a gesture more about seeming to swallow than actually swallowing, as his big face fronted no throat and no gullet. "That's a fucking . . . stupid question, Lawrence. You know . . . how I'm doing."

"I know. I'm sorry."

"Fuck your sorry." He coughed, struggled for voice, moaned with a supreme effort of will as his mouth tried to go away. Several seconds later he managed to bring it back, but by then his eyes had dropped several sizes and assumed normal human dimensions, which made them comical on that oversize face already beginning to run like wax at the edges. "Fuck you. Fuck Mom. Fuck Dad. Fuck Jean. Fuck all of those fucking vultures downstairs. Fuck your pity in your fucking ass. I hope your fucking kids get what I fucking have. I hope you have to fucking watch them live with this. I hope you have to fucking hope for them to die. I fucking wish it had been you all along. I fucking wish I could look down at you the way you're looking down at me. I fucking wish I could piss on you. I fucking wish you'd get cancer. Fuck you. Fuck you. Fuck you. Fuck you. Fuck you."

He tried to say more, but his moment of coherency was done. His body was too busy becoming a succession of specific things, all of them terrible. A bloody Jesus, writhing on the cross. A burned man, crawling across an expanse of broken glass, his trail marked by the pieces of himself he left behind. A little girl having her eyes gouged out by hooks. A dog trying to crawl on the bleeding stumps of amputated legs. A pregnant woman giving birth to a spiked asterisk of a thing, all bristling needles and barbs, that crawled from her bloody womb only to sink its claws into her flesh and drag itself up her body, so it could force itself down her throat and enjoy being born a second time. A little boy paddling around a favorite swimming hole on his birthday, and beaming with an innocent delight that was about to be ruined, forever, by the terrible fatal flaw that cruel nature had built into him.

None of them surprised me.

They were all things that I'd seen him become before.

I left Ethan's cell after another half an hour, feeling as unclean as I always felt whenever I visited my little brother. It never mattered whether I'd managed to avoid getting any of him on me. I was contaminated by the sight of him, sometimes the very idea of him.

I took a shower with the water hot just a sliver short of scalding. I let it burn. There was no stain of Ethan on me—that quicksilver retreat of his flesh from my skin a measure of insufficient kindness in a visit that had otherwise afforded a full measure of his condition's cruelty—but I still stayed beneath the spray, enduring its punishment, until I was reddened and raw and able to feel scoured of every part of him.

I crawled into bed and slept, enduring the usual Ethan dreams of my bones twisting into razored shapes inside me.

When I woke, the afternoon light was fading. I got dressed and went downstairs, finding much the same assortment of cousins and aunts and uncles, their positions on the family couches unchanged. I endured the usual questions about anything but Ethan, questions that ranged from whether I was seeing anybody special to whether I'd decided what I was going to do after graduation but somehow never touched on how much I was suffocating. I asked where my mother was, and was informed that she and Dr. Zuvicek were both upstairs with Ethan, who had taken yet another in a long series of turns for the worse and was hardly changing at all, which an elderly aunt who had researched the condition told me was a sign that his remaining lifespan could now be measured in hours.

After that I endured the usual half hour of well-meaning family blather about everything but the crisis at hand; the cousin who had gotten married, the uncle who had moved to another state, the relative of uncertain provenance who had done something even more uninteresting that I was expected to note and file away as vital genetic intelligence. Somebody was doing well in business, somebody else was failing, a third had had fallen out of touch, and a fourth had committed sins that the aunt reporting them considered scandalous enough to impart in shocked whispers. I nodded and pretended to care and then watched as the subject inevitably circled back to Ethan, and how sweet a little boy he had been.

When I finally made my escape I stepped out into the afternoon's fading light and found Jean on the porch swing, smoking a cigarette. I hadn't suspected her of picking up the habit, but she didn't know I had, either, and as I sat down she just handed me the butt without making eye contact. I took a single drag deep enough to make the paper sizzle, then put it out and sat down beside her, watching the sun turn to bright red shrapnel behind the sheltering trees.

"So?" she said, without looking at me. "Ready to leave yet?"

I nudged the porch with my toe to make the seat rock. "Pretty much."

"And you've only been back for a few hours. Try it when it's just you and Mom sitting on opposite ends of the same couch, night after night, trying to find things to talk about in between Ethan noises."

I held up my hands in a gesture of abject surrender. "You win."

She glanced at me out of the corner of her eye, searching for signs of mockery. After a second or two she came to the reluctant decision that I wasn't offering any, and looked away, her anger still burning but unsatisfied by any fit place to put it. "I'm sorry. You offered to stay, too."

That I had; though I'd offered only token resistance when Mom insisted that I had a life to live, that I needed to see to my own future while my poor brother burned through what little was left of his. Give her credit, she hadn't tried to inflict any guilt when I let her win that argument . . . or when I chose a faraway school that would keep me from having to come home and help out on evenings and weekends.

I just hadn't considered the pressure my absence would put on Jean during her own last two years of high school. Two years of always having to rush straight home to help Mom with Ethan. Two years of never being able to spend time with friends, of never being able to go to parties, of never being able to fumble in back seats with boys. Two years until graduation and then two more years of putting her own future on hold, so Mom would not have to deal with our family nightmare alone.

And I had to admit to myself: that was bullshit, too. I mean, that I hadn't considered it. Of course I'd considered it. I'd considered it, taken the offer of freedom from Ethan, and fled while there was still something left of me to flee with.

I wanted to say I was sorry, but that would have been an insult, so I said nothing.

She studied the fading light. "It's not even you I'm mad at. It's them. All those sanctimonious assholes in there. All those covered casseroles and cold cut platters; everybody bringing the same things, every day. Making a big show of being there for Mom, when for all these years it was hell getting any one of them to spare an afternoon or an hour to watch him so I could take her out of the house for a while. When Ethan was just this *thing* that was never going to end, they were all just fine with letting her live like somebody who had to be chained to one spot. They wanted nothing to do with us. But now that's he's almost gone, they're back, wanting back into our lives. It's like . . . Ethan was never anything but a stigma. And once he dies, we'll all be clean again."

"Maybe we will," I said.

I expected anger, but got something worse, a pathetic little half-smile of the sort an adult offers to a child who has not yet learned the ways of the world and who has said something adorable and precocious and sad and naive. "Will we? Is that even possible now? After everything we've seen?"

"Of course it is. I promise you: when this is all over, we'll all go somewhere for a while and figure out how."

A terrible warbling sound erupted from the house. It was less a scream than a chorus of them, all erupting from a throat that now came equipped with a multitude of voices. They all cut off in midhowl, replaced with something bubbling and liquid that invoked the image of a room of bound captives trying to breathe through slit throats.

One of the distant cousins, a stranger to me, burst from the house, fell to his knees, and vomited on our front lawn. It took him several minutes to empty, and even once he did, he remained on hands and knees, trembling, preferring that spot and the view of his own stomach's contents to the prospect of returning to the house inhabited by the family obscenity.

Jean rested her head on my shoulder. "You better keep that promise, bro. I've never even been to Disney World."

It was five hours later. We were back inside, drowning in more premature condolences, when the low hubbub of empty conversation went away all at once. At first I thought it was just one of those awkward conversational lulls endured by all families who have ever endured an extended death watch, but then I registered the gaze of an aunt frozen in the act of dipping a cracker into a bowl of paste, the identical look on the face of her fat husband who'd been napping on and off between forced reminders of her own deep empathy, and the relief on the faces of almost everybody else, as they reacted to something over my shoulder. I turned around and saw Dr. Zuvicek, who had stopped midway down the stairs and now faced us all, looking grim and professorial and older than his years. He had washed up and changed into a new black suit, one unsullied by the various explosive effluents of time spent with Ethan; he had slicked back his hair and resculpted the flared lines of his beard and transformed himself back into the buttoned-down man of medicine, but the ordeal of the last few hours had still taken a lot out of him, and he wore the pain of it on his face and on the shoulders.

He faced us all, and announced, "Ethan's gone."

One of the distant aunts broke the silence with a tremulous, "Are you sure?"

"He is dead now," Zuvicek said, putting a slight emphasis on the word *now*. "There is no respiration, no movement, no reaction to stimulus, no sign of additional transformation. For the last four hours he has done nothing but cool. It is safe, as safe and as decent as it ever could be, to now declare him gone and go on with our lives. We may say good-bye to him."

Our distant aunt valued being part of the drama too much to do the sensible thing and just keep her mouth shut. "But are you *sure*?"

Zuvicek just raised an eyebrow at her and let the silence grow teeth.

I hugged Jean and considered how easy and how terrible it would have been for Ethan's disorder to strike either one of us instead.

"Almost free," she whispered.

"Just a little bit longer," I assured her.

I endured a shoulder squeeze from one of the many cousins jingling car keys and thanked the handful of others who offered spoken condolences. Most couldn't wait to rush outside, to retrieve the funeral urns they had brought. Jean and I were not so lucky. We had to follow Zuvicek upstairs and aid my mother in parceling out Ethan's pieces.

This was the last necessary duty we'd spent so many years dreading. The very nature of Ethan's curse is that he changed. He changed without purpose and he changed without limit and he changed without end. It had taken him years of changing from one foul thing into another to finally change into something without breath, without heart, without voice, without any signs of whatever life meant if you were talking about something like Ethan: something that seemed content to remain what it was and could therefore be considered dead enough for a funeral.

But we couldn't afford to just bury, or even cremate, him. Unlike the more limited shape-changers of the old horror pictures, Ethan had not been granted the dignity of being restored to humanity as he lay dying. He'd remained whatever he was at the moment he stopped moving, and there was no way to know for sure that his corpse was anything but another cruel transformation, one that wouldn't decide, an hour or day or a decade later, that it was just another transition state to be abandoned as soon as it could change back to something alive.

Nor would it have helped to cremate him. After all, so many of the things he'd turned into, over his tormented lifetime, had been on fire. He'd been ashes several times, and had always turned back to living tissue.

There *was* no way to be sure. There never would be.

So his only funeral was a diaspora. His pallbearers all climbed our stairs bearing empty urns and all descended with full ones, each heavier than its mere weight could account for. They piled into their respective cars and made their way back to homes in fourteen states and three foreign countries, burying his pieces in desert sands or sinking them in wetland ooze. They fed pieces of him into raging furnaces and tossed other pieces of him over the railings of cruise ships. They left pieces of him in landfills and in the concrete foundations of office buildings, pieces of him broiling in the world's sun-blasted deserts or forming ice crystals beneath permafrost.

Nobody was going to be half-assed enough to dispose of their pieces of Ethan in any location too close to anybody else's; they'd all heard the terrible sounds from upstairs, and knew that they not want to be responsible for the pieces of Ethan ever finding each other, congealing, and coming back. So notes had been compared, and maps consulted.

Sometime in the hours between midnight and dawn, they were all gone: all except Dr. Zuvicek, who sat with us on the living room, his own piece of Ethan sealed in a little jar beside his chair.

The house seemed emptier than the mere departure of our extended family could account for; it was as if the great family grief that had laid claim to our home for so long, so vast in its scope that the walls had seemed to creak and warp with the strain of containing it, had left only a void. Mom sat holding a teacup in both hands, staring at the tepid drink as if expecting to find some answers there; Jean and I shared the opposite couch, looking anywhere but at the sealed jar containing our own last piece of our doomed little brother.

Zuvicek had just finished saying that he was going to bring his own piece of Ethan back to the old country, where the farmland once owned by our great-grandparents and still likely our property—that being difficult to determine, so many wars and governments later—had grown wild and been reclaimed by forest primeval; he believed he could identify the spot where the old mansion had stood, and bury his piece of Ethan there. "After I'm done," he said, his eyes far away, "I think I'll do a little wandering before my return to these shores. I know I will never again have another patient quite as difficult as this one, but I have still had enough of sickbeds and death vigils for the time being; it is time . . . to regrow myself."

"Good luck with that," Mother said.

Zuvicek must have detected the bitterness in her voice. "You should do the same thing. It is a shame that your dear husband," he hesitated, and looked at us, "your father, did not live to enter this time of healing. And a shame that the rest of the family can only help you so much, that the final step can only be completed by parents and blood siblings. But once you are done with that duty, you should not be afraid to embrace life again. As soon as it is decent, go somewhere fun and do something stupid. Remind yourselves who you are, when you don't have such a terrible thing hanging over you."

Mother covered her eyes. "I'm not sure I remember anymore."

"I understand. But you are still a young woman, with many years of life left to you. And you have two fine healthy children who will help you remember, with their own lives, and someday with the blessing of healthy grandchildren. Remember that." He grabbed his hat and his bag and his piece of Ethan, and stood before us hesitating, searching for the words that would define the moment with as much gravity as it deserved. "You should all move away, when you are done. This has become a bad place for you."

"I know," she said.

Zuvicek bade farewell, accepted our thanks, and departed.

The three remaining members of our immediate family sat in silence for several seconds, neither enjoying nor understanding the sudden emptiness of a home that had until now been driven by the engine of unrelenting pain.

For lack of anything better to do, Jean surveyed the detritus of Ethan's deathwatch: the dirty glasses on their coasters, the plates stained with the remnants of condiments or cake, the extra chairs hauled up from the basement that would need to be folded up and put away. "We'll help you clean up."

"That can wait until morning," Mom said. "We have to say our own good-byes."

I said, "I'm not sure I'm ready for that."

"Neither am I. But he was your brother, my child, our blood. We owe him our strength."

Mom meant that, of course, but we all knew the other thought that had to cower behind the one she could bear to speak out loud. *And besides, this needs to be over. He needs to be gone. This house needs to be quit of him.*

I grabbed the vase. "Right. Might as well get this over with."

The three of us went outside, the screen door slamming behind us. The driveway, all but abandoned by the cars of family members, now only bore my borrowed junker and Jean's secondhand Yaris, each resting part on gravel and part on lawn. The stars above us were few, thanks to light pollution from the new houses that had come to crowd our beleaguered estate, but the few I could see were bright, distant points of fire that still seemed sharp enough to burn.

The moon was just a waning crescent, points curving upward like the grin of the Cheshire cat. It might have been more appropriate full, of course, but if Ethan's life story had any moral at all in the context of our family, it was that nobody can control everything, and that some of us are damned to control less than others.

We went together into the backyard, which was still enclosed by the stone wall and protected by what remaining forest the advancing suburbs had left.

Just before I took the stopper off the urn, its contents shifted with a perverse suddenness that startled me and almost made me drop it. The ceramic rang like a bell, and the grisly contents shifted again: willful, insistent, helpless, defiant, and angry.

My voice cracked. "Oh my God, he's *still moving*—"

Then the jar lurched again. This time I dropped it, enduring the century and a half it took to hit the ground, feeling myself break even as it broke, releasing what was left of Ethan to explode like a balloon of blood. In the moonlight it looked black and shiny, a lot like an afterbirth. Something like an eye floated to the surface and then popped, leaving ripples that smoothed over and became a surface as placid as any mirror.

I said. "He's alive—"

Mom put a hand on my wrist. "Lawrence. Stop putting this off."

"Mom, it's not over, he's moving—"

Her fingernails dug into my flesh, drawing blood.

I gasped and looked her in the face, expecting anger but seeing only an ethereal calm.

"It's over," she said. "

Behind me, Jean said, "Hey."

I turned around and saw that she'd already taken off all her clothes, her breasts hanging pale and white beneath the slivered light. It wasn't just the change. Even before the fur started to sprout from her cheeks, she looked taller than she had in years, more beautiful, more at peace, and more defiantly free.

"Like you said inside," she reminded me, her soft voice turning coarse as her jaw began its transformation to elongated snout. "Let's get this over with."

By then Mom was midway through her own change; not into the common vulpine creature my sister could become, but into the thing that had never borne a name in any human tongue, the thing that had drawn my father to her in the old-country revels. Our extended family has a saying that we each choose our other skins, and what Mom had chosen, in her youth, was broad and powerful and wrapped in a snow-white mantle that glowed with inner fire.

Watching, I could only wonder how many years this self had been lost to her; how many years she'd been condemned to a life of nothing but dull humanity, as she cared for the child whose body had been incapable of making the permanent choice all of our bodies had made.

I decided. Mom and Jean were right. It was time.

I peeled off my shirt, before it could be damaged by the emergence of my girdle of arms. Then we dropped to all fours, lowered ourselves to our departed blood, and began to feed.

I COVET ALL THE WANING HOURS

BY ZAK JARVIS

Zak Jarvis—I kid you not—has never published a story before in his life. I want you to keep that incomprehensible fact in mind as you read the following piece of phenomenally compressed mini-epic fantasy.

Indeed, there's a device at the very beginning of "I Covet All the Waning Hours" that kind of takes my breath away. It instantly sets up a lycanthropic alternate reality so richly realized and thoroughly inhabited that it makes me wish we were all so remarkably evolved.

That, of course, is the power behind this harrowing portrait of an extraordinary woman in a world far better than our own. Past that, I will not say.

Enjoy this remarkable debut.

Lying face down in the salon, Brunhilde smelled her lieutenant through the phone. He was feeling upset, cocky, and a little afraid. She picked up the small glass device and breathed all her annoyance into it; the cedar oil treatment couldn't begin until she was off the phone and Sif had just walked into the room with the bowl.

"We found them," he said, breath and hair bristling over the microphone. "It's a massive camp."

"Have they noticed you?"

"No, Mother. But—" he cut off to shout at someone in the background. "The reverts have a captive. We haven't spotted him yet, but he's beaten down by sickness. There's blood and shit but he's not passing water."

Brunhilde sat up.

"Leave your marker on," she said, projecting maternal calm into the phone. "I'll be there as quickly as I can. Keep sharp and run the perimeter. I want a tally of weapons."

"Just metal edges so far, Mother. I'll keep you posted."

She closed the phone and turned to Sif.

"Postponing again?"

Sif was a good woman, but weak. If she caught any fear she'd spread it to all the base caste.

"Reverts," Brunhilde said, smoothing down her silver hair. "I'll be back in two days, same time."

"Yes, Mother." Sif said, nuzzling Brunhilde's cheek. "Thank you!"

The sun-warmed street smelled of family and other people, workers and herdsmen, children, votary caste. This part of the city belonged to her and Reinmar. It smelled of home.

She sprinted to the barracks, freshened her mark by the door, then took the truck out of the garage. Her horse would be far preferable, but she needed speed. The buzzing ozone stink of the engine hurt her nose. At least it terrified game animals.

Her lieutenant marked a spot three hours north and well west of the Hudson. Out there the villages and towns of the precursors were visible only by the lines their roads had cut, the buildings having long since returned to the earth. She stopped the truck a few miles from her troops and went in on foot, following their scent down deer trails to the outskirts of the camp. Revert stench permeated everything. Burnt meat, standing sewage, the harsh solvent-reek of bodies pushed too far, and something else. Something she hadn't found at any of the other camps.

And she had seen many revert camps. Most were sad and small, a few individuals picking their way through the land and avoiding city outcasts. When they were in larger groups they could be a danger. Some of them had scavenged guns, and guns were a problem for Brunhilde, even at night when the reverts were blind.

She joined her troops below a ridge, then crawled to the top with her lieutenant. Below them all the plants had been stripped from a small village, baring the decaying superstructures of hundred-year-old buildings. Some were patched over with rough timber, some rebuilt, but most were open to the sky. More than a thousand reverts came and went through the ruin, almost as though it were a real city. Their hairless bodies made them look like maggots against the sodden ground. They herded pitiful animals and their own kind with equal disdain, with the same rough collars, with the same spears.

Then she spotted the source of the smell, the most defended structure in the camp. In a twenty by twenty-foot cage they had corralled over a hundred of their females. Many were in some stage of pregnancy, all malnourished. Drifting in rivers from the structure the chlorine-stink of revert sex mixed with effluvia, terror, and drowned hope. Whether intentional or not, it neatly masked the smell of any weapons.

Shifting wind brought her the scent of the captive. He was inside a building on the west side and he was no more than twenty years old.

The youth came from the Lake Erie family. Her borough had a pact to protect them.

She fingered her charm necklace to get Reinmar's scent on her fingers, then climbed back down the hill to prepare her troops.

They waited until after dark to move on the camp. Brunhilde destroyed the guns first, killing the owners and snapping their antique weapons in two.

Then she let the bloodlust take her.

Howling for the sheer joy of hunting, she drove them like game animals. She killed until her claws and teeth hurt, until the smell of blood and marrow drowned everything.

When they'd killed every moving thing outside, she and her troops started going through the buildings.

The captive, when she found him, barely moved. The room had iron hoops set in concrete, though he wasn't restrained. She could see only his back, where hair peeled off in scabrous sheets, his bared skin a mass of sores and knotted lumps. His tail hung limply, broken at the base.

His breath came in wheezing convulsions. Blood and feces pooled beneath him.

Gently, Brunhilde touched his shoulder but the boy did not react. She leaned down to taste his skin, searching for any clue to what had happened. Along with his sick sweat and blood she tasted the bitter oil of revert skin. Had they been pawing him, using him the way they used their own females? There was something disturbingly raw in the taste of him. Head lolling back, his eyes opened.

He had the blue, round eyes of a revert.

Brunhilde stepped backward, growling. It shouldn't be possible. Were the reverts responsible for this? He was becoming one of them. A throwback, one of those hairless, mewling animals—she couldn't bear to be in the room with him. He was beyond saving, his family wouldn't —couldn't want him alive, not like this.

She gave the boy a warrior's funeral, setting fire to the building as she left it.

Outside her troops had been gathering the dead so they could make a proper accounting. Their feet splashed in blood from the pile. One of her teenagers had a camera out to document the victory.

"Over fifteen hundred counted so far, Mother," lieutenant Gavin said. "We haven't cleared out the buildings yet, or that cage."

"Shame to waste so much meat," the documentarian said, sniffing.

"This isn't meat. It's garbage," she said stepping over to the pile. "Their blood is too close to ours; eating them is like cannibalism. And besides, smell them carefully—" she paused to gut a corpse. Coiling and writhing from torn intestines, long white worms spilled out like tiny guts within the guts. "Over half are like this, You want those things in you? "

"But, Mother, you'll take us all to temple when we get back, won't you?"

Gavin growled a little, but stopped when Brunhilde smacked him.

"Yes. Medicine for everyone. Even me."

Especially me, she thought. Her little wisp of fear turned Gavin around, but he said nothing.

On the long drive home she called her mate.

"You smell frightened, Bloodsweet," Reinmar said, his confidence squirting out of the phone. She could smell his deliberation, argument, and the man he'd had sex with. "What happened?"

Brunhilde cradled the phone close. "They had a human captive. From Lake Erie—"

"Oh no."

"I killed him."

Her phone buzzed slightly as it changed mixture; restrained fury, fear, admiration.

"He was changing into one of them."

She could imagine Reinmar, waiting outside the gathering hall with delegates from all the Hudson cities, argent hair pushed down by wind off the lake. Maybe he still had his hand around the waist of that sleek young man from Saratoga. He always narrowed his eyes and looked to the left, like he expected to see a prompter with his thoughts.

Trust came through the phone, but he said nothing.

"I want you back here with me," Brunehilde said. "I tasted the sickness changing him."

She uncoiled the hold she'd kept on her fear and let him smell it, acrid and piercing, like fermenting wood pulp and smoke.

"I'll take the train tonight."

Brunhilde looked up at the facade. She remembered seeing pictures of the early temple and how they'd used recovered taxidermy specimens for the wolves above the archway. Now they were carved into fine stone, quarried nearby under pact from the Potomac cities. She'd been there when her mother negotiated the gold for the fennel stalks, she'd watched it hammered out by the temple crafters. She smiled at Gavin, projecting her pride and sense of duty.

At the threshold Brunhilde had a sudden pang of anxiety. The face of the Lake Erie boy came to her, his eyes, the stink and the taste of his sickness. But that was foolish; she was at temple to get medicine. *Everything would be fine.*

Jade shutters were drawn over the open walls of the narthex, suffusing the room in dim yellow light. At sunset a member of the votary caste would open the screens to let in the western light, but morning was the time for reflection. Members of the base caste lay in piles, cradled by synthetic leaves. The perfumed carpet made each step different, comforting. Fresh meat, musk, pine, mother's milk, clean hair, loving breath. They kept the room warm all year.

Brunhilde passed through a darkened hallway of velvet, the scents becoming more mysterious as she and her procession moved toward the nave. A tongue of light shone from the end of the hall, making the nearest fabric glow gold and blue. Votaries pulled aside the last curtains and flooded everything with sun.

As always, Brunhilde was driven to the ground by the presence of holiness. All her children fell down behind her, all on their bellies, scared to look up.

Father-smell filled everything. Sharp with sweat and teeth and masculinity, softened by fresh kill and downy fur, the smell rolled out of the nave, overwhelming to begin with and growing stronger with each moment. Some of her younger children began to cry. She pressed forward, belly to the earth, until she passed into the shadow of the great statue. Above her the massive holy beast presided. His long head looked down on them in eternal benevolent judgment, atop powerful shoulders cut from sequoia and dressed in coral and steel cable. At the foot of the statue, a decorated priest helped her to her feet while his assistants prepared the needles.

It was midafternoon and the city was cooking. Thousands upon thousands of meals. Game animals, farm animals, every kind of meat that was available. The spices of the Ontario cities dominated—fennel, basil, some rosemary—but she could smell Chicago, too, pine nuts and olive oil, saffron, cannabis. It had been a long time since she'd had any western food. Gavin pretended not to notice that she'd started drooling. They entered the trail of the boat people at the corner of Canal and Broadway.

Buffalo. Fresh killed, seasoned with long-pepper and white turmeric. They were cooking it with blood-stock paste and she could hear the knock of heavy bones in the pot. Her stomach turned over and her knees almost buckled.

"Just a bite before we see Sif."

The smell came from the second floor of a tenement that had been refurnished. Traces of the ancient concrete remained but all the structural beams were carved granite. Aromatic hardwoods darkened the interior and gave the floor a pleasant sag and bounce. Lichen and fresh-planted moss grew in the corners and succulent epiphytes crawled down the walls where sunlight passed. Hallways ended with mortared river stones, kept wet by captured rainwater.

It was a very small family, all direct-blood—a father, mother, and two children. The children worked the kitchen, while Mother embroidered. Father rendered what remained of the buffalo. When Brunhilde drew back the jeweled curtains into their chambers, they all stopped what they were doing and went down on their bellies.

"Can you spare a few bites? I was passing by and could not resist. I've never tried your food."

The father went up on his knees, "I would be honored, and we all welcome you to the Mulga home."

The daughter brought Brunhilde a handful of shredded meat on a cut of banana leaf. Brunhilde closed her eyes, taking it in small bites to savor.

"Some for your child as well?"

Gavin had been pushing too much lately, so she pushed back.

"Yes, he would like some, too."

He hid his irritation very well. The family didn't notice. Brunhilde did.

Sif stood at the doorway with the cedar oil ready. "You won't get away this time, Mother!"

Brunhilde took off her bloodied armor and lay on the table. She always had a difficult time relaxing after a battle. At first the sharpness and warmth of the oil helped, but after a few minutes of patter, Sif's hairless hands began to unnerve her. The cosmetician had always waxed her hands—*otherwise hair tangles up with hair*, she'd said—but now they made Brunhilde think of the boy from Lake Erie.

Fingers wormed through her hair like grubs.

"Just relax, Mother," Sif said. "I'm sure you had a terrible night with those horrible old flat-faces. Let me take care of you. Always so tense."

She let out her breath in a long chuff, just barely holding back the creeping fear that Sif was changing.

"It's okay, Mother. It's okay!" Sif whispered, nuzzling against her ear. "You kept everybody safe, didn't you? Tell me how you did it."

Brunhilde closed her eyes. Sif had taken on some of the fear but she was holding it back far better than anyone would have expected.

She told most of it, playing up the battle and the bloodshed, flexing her claws to punctuate the more daring kills. It helped center her, got her heart pounding and her scent rising. Sif was taken, as she'd hoped. Then she told about the exhausting process of euthanizing the surviving reverts.

"Oh Father's grace!" Sif said, taking Brunhilde's hand. "Your poor claws! Let me get Marcus in here, he'll see to that and get some of that nasty old blood out."

Sif paused for a moment before letting herself sniff, then crunched up her face. "Is that what reverts smell like?"

After the treatment she found her troops gathered in the barracks' garden. She called them over to her tree. Her father had planted the now gnarled oak during the rut of her conception. Now it scented the breeze with whispering shadows.

Surrounded by young men and women, some she'd known since birth, her heart beat faster. Her ears stood up, and she drank their scent like an elixir. The old poets had called the feeling *wolfsliebe*. Only a few ever knew the sensation. Brunhilde basked in it, sleeping with them all gathered around in the shade of the tree. Her tree, in her borough.

If she had known it was the last time she would feel such peace, she could not have savored it more.

Reinmar entered the grove an hour before dawn. She'd sent the videos of the battle. He suppressed his concern and instead lit up when Brunhilde turned to him. He loved her so fiercely in that moment that she could not guess what he would do.

Neither, apparently could he. He watched her from across the clearing, his tail frantically arcing. Finally he leapt over the stone pathway and crashed into her, all closing arms and gentle teeth.

They rolled among the troops until everyone was awake and cheerful, then Brunhilde lead him to the indoor training chamber. She held back everything until he turned to her in the darkness.

"What if I change, too?" she said, her ears flattening down. "I killed the boy because I knew—*knew*—his family would not want him to be one of *them.*"

His tail fallen, Reinmar paced away leaving a trail of plain terror in the air.

"It won't happen."

"What will you do!"

He turned back to face her but couldn't hold her gaze. "Do you want me to end you? I—" he stopped himself, lips pulled back until all his teeth showed. "I could do that."

"I couldn't live like one of them. The things they do to survive —"

"It won't happen," he said, growling low. "It was something inside him. I'm sure of it."

"Reinmar, I tasted it."

He turned to a training dummy and swiped it, tearing open its leather binding. "I don't want you to die," he said, sand pouring out of the dummy behind him. "We'll tell them, at temple. The Father will protect you."

"They'll take the borough from us," she said, stroking his neck. "Then, if I start to change, Ulrich or Aloisia will kill me. I want you to do it."

"It won't come to that," he said. "I won't let it."

He opened his phone and started one of the videos of Brunhilde. The tiny screen showed her bloodied and proud next to her lieutenant, pointing to marks on her armor and talking to someone off screen.

"If you start to change," he said well after the video had stopped. "I promise I'll be the one to tend you."

It took a month for the first signs. At first, nothing more than aching bones. After training she noticed that her sweat smelled faintly of raw meat. *Forty years*, she told herself. *Nothing else.*

Reinmar had to be away, the pact for next year's herd dangled elusively beyond his grasp. Without his negotiations, all the Long Island cities would be without stable food next winter. Hundreds of thousands depended on him.

Although she told herself that the signs were age and nothing else, when he was home she did not let him kiss or taste any part of her.

She avoided close contact with all her troops, even her own blood. To keep her fear from showing, she herself shut down. Subordinates began to question her.

The first tumor appeared on her upper lip. Trivial as a bee sting, but she knew. She couldn't avoid it any longer. The unimaginable future looked back at her from the mirror.

She almost reached for her phone, words ringing in her ears: *It's begun*. But if she spoke them aloud it would be real.

She was not ready to die.

She went to the stables and bridled her horse, smoothing down his hair and whispering encouragement. With her pack loaded she rode out into the sun.

In the garden, Gavin called out to her.

"I'll be back soon," she said. "I want everyone to stay put."

It didn't matter if they could smell the shame and confusion; she'd trained them to obey her orders and they would. She curled her feet under and lightly spurred the horse to a trot.

His hooves sounded hollow against road slats, a pace half the rate of Brunhilde's cowardly heart. She should stay and let Reinmar take her instead of disease.

She imagined him lighting candles. He would put his arms around her, let her breathe in his despair and fury, then he'd slip the knife into the back of her skull. There would be an instant of daylight. And then? Would she run with the Hounds of God, or were the skeptics right?

She fingered her charm necklace, its jade beads binding lengths of Reinmar's hair, a twin to the one he wore. His scent rose up and instead of comfort she felt shame.

Brunhilde did not stop.

She took the Hudson road north. The river smelled bright and clean, peeking between trees and hills, wide as a lake. Old settlements and outposts speckled the verdant hills, some taken over by small families, others left for the earth to dispense with, a task the earth had shown a fine talent for.

She rode for hours, pushing herself and the horse. In the afternoon they found a precursor path that got them west over a long stony bluff, then skirted a dark lake. It ended at an ancient steel bridge bent down to plumb the river below.

Everywhere around her the forest called out, in the vellum caress of leaf against branch, the thousand animal conversations chirped and chittered into the air, in the pads of moss, the filaments aching to become mushrooms within fallen logs, the beetles and the centipedes, the swaying twig insects and the steady white rush of the river.

Everything there a sound and a smell, all of them calling her.

Brunhilde crushed her phone on a rock, spraying a cacophony of smells into the dense forestscape. She commanded the horse to return home and climbed down into the river.

Its current pulled her, but her strength held and she pressed north in waist-deep water. It made her bones ache and her feet kept tangling in submerged obstacles, but she would not let herself rest.

Reinmar would find any trail she left. Part of her wanted to wait for him, but a stronger impulse won. She measured off two excruciating miles, careful always to stay in the deepest water.

Panic stopped her.

Her nose had clogged, as if with a winter cold. She couldn't smell the forest. She climbed half out of the water. She sniffed the ground, she brought her charm necklace to her nose, lifted up rocks.

She could not smell the mud, the grass, the muck under stones, nothing. Not even Reinmar. She dragged herself out of the mud and stumbled north into the woods, running carelessly.

The numb emptiness she'd summoned up vanished like morning fog burned off by the searing daylight of panic.

She groped through the wilderness until she almost walked into a small revert camp. She watched them for a time, trying to see which one led them, but their cues were opaque to her and she moved on.

Over the ridge of a tall hill she spotted a vast pocket of precursor ruins. The tiny hills convolved by ancient roads looked like mossy coral swallowing sparse frames. Vines and weeds covered everything; the ground was a patchwork of clover and crumbling macadam. She found a concrete building still showing windows like eyes, its walls holding strong against encroaching nature.

It was the kind of place reverts would camp. She tentatively stepped inside the stone building, brushing away hanging vines and clinging webs. No, there had been no habitation here. Not reverts at least, not for a very long time. The floor had returned to soil at the entrance, but farther back inside, tiled stone remained. Incomprehensible wooden structures now hosted a profusion of plants and insects.

Marble stairs led to the second floor, dirt and opportunistic plants making it more ramp than steps. Upstairs she found an enclosed room where a crack in the wall had grown a shaft of citrine across the floor, the path of the morning sun painted in moss. She lay down and slept.

The next day she hunted, taking down a deer and hanging it out to dry. She collected useful wood and fortified the ruin. But nothing she did drove out the thoughts of what she'd abandoned, or the fear of what was to come. The absence of people pressed in, magnified by her lost sense of smell.

At night she prayed and thought of Reinmar, of her troops, her city, but the night offered only her tumbling thoughts. What if she had infected Reinmar? What if he found her? She chewed her worries until the room seemed to shake with the pounding of her heart.

The morning brought more tumors.

With nothing else to do she trained, running with stones until her blood etched burning lines through her limbs. She recited poetry to herself. She described books she had read. She told herself how Reinmar had wooed her, about her first pregnancy and nursing her first child.

Every day brought more tumors.

Her teeth began to fall out. So she crushed her food with stones.

Her claws broke off beneath the skin, leaving painful wounds on her fingers. So she used her knife to cut off strips of venison.

Pain woke her more often than not and stayed through the day. Pain turned into agony. Her tail blackened and fell off. She could never go home.

The agony persisted, long after it became intolerable. Until pain itself became a color, pulsing and bright. She imagined Reinmar's face, the strength of his jaws, his powerful arms; they rotted and pulped in her mind. She tried to think of her troops, her children, the city—but anything she could imagine, the pain could destroy.

Her hair came off by the fistful. Every inch of her skin hurt, not the hurt of scratching too much or a healing wound but the abiding hurt of the poisoned hole, a bee sting, a spider bite, an infection.

By the time she wished that she could die, she didn't have the strength to do it herself. She howled until her throat closed. Her eyes crusted shut and her hands hurt too much to pry them open. The pain writhed and flexed and coiled like a snake nailed to a board. Nothing stopped it. It bled into her dreams.

She woke to a world of nauseating color. The forest outside pierced her with its luminous foliage, the same color as the jade beads on her necklace.

She doubled over and vomited, unable to stop herself. Her bowels emptied. Strips of rubbery skin clung inside her throat, flecked dark with old blood. She pulled them out of her mouth and felt it tearing inside her, but she pulled and pulled until her hands were slick with blood. Blood that should have been black roped and clung in sticky gobs of putrid brightness.

Her disgorged stomach-lining smelled of acid and rot, a stink so sharp it penetrated her useless nose.

Brunhilde crawled into the darkest corner of the chamber, closed her eyes tight, and prayed for the return of her life.

Her body finished betraying her by winter. She'd grown swollen milkless breasts and every full moon brought heavy, uncomfortable estrus bleeding. To all outward appearances, she had become a revert. Her reflection nauseated her.

She'd been beautiful once.

With returned strength she took the knife and held its edge against her bare neck. It was the right thing to do. She'd agreed to it, forced the decision on an innocent she'd sworn to protect.

But she could not take her own life.

Furious with herself, she threw the knife away, then had to find it again when it came time to eat. To eat with her new flat teeth.

She began training again. Her body had become too weak. Even revert males were stronger; their females fared poorly. She covered herself in leather and picked up the rocks again. She told herself she'd go back and warn Reinmar once she was strong.

Spying on the nearby reverts became a game she played. How close could she get without being spotted? Foolish, she knew, but while she watched them she could forget there had been another life.

One morning they were there, grunting and squawking, the next they were gone and she was alone in a dead world. She cried herself to sleep, told herself she would go searching for them or others. But every day it became more difficult to leave her ruin.

The reverts came to her. Twenty or so plodded along in a caravan, right past her building. She watched through the cracks but could not see their hierarchy. Who was their leader? His lieutenant? The subordinates? Some clearly lacked standing. But she could not smell them or read their status. Trembling fear threatened to overwhelm her. Would they kill her if she approached the wrong one?

Thinking of Reinmar's promise, she fingered the charm necklace. For the first time in months she smelled it, faint, so very faint. Twenty-five years she'd been paired with him, twenty-five years she'd had his smell nearby, comforting her.

To her revert nose he smelled like a feral animal.

Rank and menacing. She could no longer imagine the length of his jaw or the deep yellow of his eyes.

Brunhilde wiped tears from her flat, hairless face and took the knife out of its sheath. She touched her lips and whispered a prayer, then stepped outside into the path of the caravan.

WHEN SUSSURUS STIRS

BY JEREMY ROBERT JOHNSON

Waaaay out at the deep end of the collective unconscious—where even the bravest of brain cells fear to tread—Jeremy Robert Johnson performs stand-up comedy for the gods. And their laughter is a marvelous, terrible thing.

Like Goodfellow and very few others, he's the kind of post-Lovecraftian genius berserker that makes the Great Old Ones new again. As with Clive Barker, who anticipated them both, there is no glorious mutational eruption that Johnson can't nail directly through your gawping mind's eye.

So run, don't walk—and prepare to swallow hard—as "When Sussurus Stirs" changes the way things are forever, one steadily mounting atrocity at a time.

He tells me their life is the best thing going. He says that I need to imagine what it would be like to crawl into the plushest limousine I can imagine, to flop down into a deep, soft leather chair filled with downy feathers from giant geese, to turn the internal weather controls to "Perfect" and have a constantly changing range of scenery and a nonstop supply of food and fluids.

Then he says, imagine that all you have to do is eat and make babies and watch your life roll by in luxuriant comfort. The American dream, but he's a citizen of everywhere—he's just naturally attained what we're all shooting for. And it doesn't matter how big you get, he says, because when you become too large, part of you just breaks off and becomes another you. No dating or mating required. No awkward social moments, never a viscous string of sticky spit running thick from tooth to tongue while you try to talk a woman of vague sexual persuasion into an allowance of simian grinding.

Never a credit card bill in sight.

And his kids, he says proudly, they all turn out just like him. The emergence of a misplaced chromosome is a nonoption. Every little him is a perfect chip off the ancient block, and has been for eons.

He doesn't speak to me as an individual; I can feel that in his voice as it creeps through my nervous system and vibrates my tympanic membrane from the inside. The idea of "self" is impossible to him. When he speaks to me as "you," I can tell he's addressing our whole species, every last human representing a potential host.

"You are more fun than the elephants," he says, "They didn't drink enough water and always fed us the same things. You feed us the soft pieces, the animal bits. We spread faster now. We are everywhere. We are growing."

I picture Susurrus as a "him" because I don't get along well with women. Always felt more comfortable around men. Can't truck with the idea of a lady crawling around in my intestines, judging me, saying, "Look at how you've treated yourself here. Too much red meat residue in your upper GI, and your colon could become impacted at a second's notice. How about some bran? Some heavy green tea? Something needs to be done. This place is a mess."

I named Susurrus after the analog "SSSSS" that accompanies his voice as it crawls around in my head. There's always this hissing noise that precedes his speaking and hangs on afterwards, like an itch deep in my ear. Sometimes the echo stays with me for hours. Then I play jazz CDs through my headphones and it sounds like I've got old records running under the needle.

Susurrus wasn't always in my brain, but I've been cultivating him, making him more a part of me. When I meditate I imagine the fibers of my spinal cord stretching out toward him, like feelers. They sway and twitch and burrow into my belly and connect to him, linking us. His hiss slides up through my spine and connects with my slow-chanted mantra, my mumbled OMNAMAs, until it's all white noise and for a moment I'm inside him, inside myself, feeling his contentment as his mouths reach out and slurp away at acidy bits of the day's meal, tiny snippets of sausage and soda pop sugars and oil-soaked ciabatta breads.

He is always at peace, a consumptive strand of nirvana.

According to the last X-ray my radiologist took, he's over fifty feet long, and still growing. My doctors have extracted pieces of him from my stool, pulsing egg sacs waiting to find water or flesh and keep the cycle of expansion in motion.

They say he's not a tapeworm, not a guinea worm, not anything they're used to seeing. He doesn't seem to effect my physiology in any negative way, although my grocery bill has ratcheted ever upwards. Still the doctors think I should have him removed. I tell them I'm a pacifist and it's not in my nature to harm a creature, especially if it poses no threat. That gets me worried glances, furrowed brows. But they don't protest much.

I think they're waiting for this thing to kill me so they can take me apart and extract his coiled body. Get a new species, name it after themselves, get published in the right journals, pull grant money.

I'm a cash cow infestation case. On a ticking clock, they imagine. Especially since this thing is spreading. One end is snaking towards my genitals, they say, and the other is coiling its way around my spine, on the way to my brain. There are more mouths showing up, not just the ones that reside in my belly.

"How did it get out of my stomach?" I ask them, not mentioning my meditation, the way Susurrus and I have bonded now. The way I've encouraged him to become part of me.

"Well, we're not exactly sure. It appears to exit through the duodenum as it heads toward your spine. There's a sort of cystic calcification at the point of exit, where it pushed through the stomach tissue. That's what keeps you from becoming toxic via your own acids. Again, this is all speculation. If you'd let us perform a more invasive. . ."

"Nope. No can do, Doc. You say this thing's not hurting me. What're the odds that this procedure would kill it?"

They don't know. These guys really don't know anything. Why should I open up my body, *our* bodies, to guesswork with scalpels?

I think I know where he came from, this new part of my life.

Five months ago I was jogging, a beautiful run at dusk through the sloping, rolling green park near my house. I was sucking down deep lung-loads of air when I ran through a floating mire of gnats. They stuck to me, twitching in my sweat, their tiny bodies suddenly swept up in the forward surge of my run. A few were sucked right into my chest, surely now melting to atoms against my alveoli.

But one of them . . . one of them stuck to the roof of my mouth. There was an itch, so close in sensation to the hiss of Susurrus, and I felt an immediate need to take a nap.

So I did. I collapsed to the ground, mindless of the lactic acidosis that would haunt my muscles, curled there among the duck shit and crawling ants and crushed grass, and I fell into a slumber.

When I awoke there was a tight bubble of tissue on the roof of my mouth, where the gnat had stuck. It hurt when I prodded it with my tongue, so I avoided it.

Later that night the bubble had become even tighter, this small mound of swollen pink tissue with a whitish tip. I stared at it in the mirror, unable to look away from its grotesque new presence.

I could feel my heartbeat inside the bump. There was no way I could sleep with this thing in my mouth. What if it kept expanding until I couldn't breathe?

I rubbed down my tweezers with benzyl alcohol and proceeded to poke and squeeze the bump until it bled. A thin rivulet of blood trickled down from the fleshy stalactite, and the harder I squeezed the more the blood thickened, grew darker. Soon the blood made way for a dense yellow fluid that carried with it the odor of rotten dairy in high heat. I pushed one pointed end of the tweezers directly into the spreading hole at the side of the bump.

Then it ruptured.

The relief of pressure was immediate. My mirror caught the worst of the spray, instantly sheilacked with dead-cell soup in a spray pattern near arterial in its arc.

Then the colors came. A thin drip from the open wound on the roof of my mouth, two drops like oil spilling out, swirling with shades I'd never quite seen before, just outside a spectrum my eyes could comprehend. The drops sat there in the curve of my tongue, merged together like quivering mercury.

I'd never felt so intense a need to swallow something in my entire life.

The sensation of the drops was not fluid. It felt as if they were crawling into me, too impatient for my peristaltic process.

And again, almost immediately, I collapsed into slumber, this time dreaming of a sea of human tissue, all of it shifting and turning and surging, soft and hot and wanting to pull me under.

I hadn't had so explosive a wet dream since I was in junior high.

And when I woke up, curled on the floor of my bathroom with my underwear stuck to me like soaked toilet paper, I was hungry as a newborn.

Four months' time passed like nothing, our perception expanded to a broader sense. The human clock thinks small—within seventy-five-year death limitations.

We laugh at the idea of death. The upside of being We.

And we are larger now. Eighty pounds heavier, abdomen distended, watermelon tight. One poke with a toothpick just below the belly button and we'd tear open like crepe paper. Neck swollen with a circular rash pattern that seeps clear fluids now crusting in the bony pockets of our shoulder blades. White of the eyes yellowing, thickening. Hair falling out in clumps from soft-scalp surface.

Our penis is heavier. Its skin shifts constantly; there are more veins, white beneath the surface. The head has bloomed from mushroom tip to flower; it is open, flayed, in roselike petals, red, pulsing. We bandage it to keep it from seeping down our leg.

We have stopped seeing the doctors. They whispered letters last time.

CDC, they said.

Our I-brain told us this means trouble. We cannot accept "trouble" so close to the next cycle. We force fed the doctors the bits of us they stole from our excretions. So many of us in each segment that even their testing couldn't ruin all the eggs. Our body was shaking then, sweating hands clutching an oily metal tool, eyes crying. It has stopped struggling since. Its feelings are soft echoes now, little more. Things are quiet.

We are hiding. Hiding ends after the next sun-drop.

Our I-brain is remembering passwords, using fat purpled fingers to stroke language keys.

We are feeling better as we see the screen before us change.

Our tickets have been confirmed. The glowing box has thanked us for our purchase.

"You're welcome," we whisper. The rolling chair squeaks under our ever-shifting weight. We stand up with a grunt and feel that the bandages around our meat-sprout are wet again. Cleaning up is no longer important.

We crawl on four bony-stems toward our meditation mat. Light the incense and try to assume the lotus position. Too much of us; our legs can't fold in to the space filled by our twitching belly.

We lay back and stare at the ceiling. Our mantra has been replaced by a new noise. We push our tongue to the front of our teeth and start leaking air, a steady SSSSSS until our I-brain goes soft and quiet and we lie there in the dark room, shaking slightly from our constant eating and squirming. Much of the old us is empty now. Our new muscles, thousands of them, ropy and squeezing against each other, roll us onto our right side.

At some point we insert our thumbs into our mouth and suck the meat clean from the bones.

Anything to feed the new cycle.

The seat in the theater can barely hold us, but we are here and we are ready. It is after the most recent sun-drop, halfway through the dark period. We are wearing leather gloves (they barely fit except for the thumbs, which drape and look sharp) and a trench coat at the suggestion of the remnants of the I-brain.

We sit at the rear of the room. No one sits near us but most of the rows in front of us are full. A bright light appears at the front of the room, large, shimmering.

Our I-brain tells us this is a midnight movie, a Spanish one, one of the best. Hasn't been shown in a while. We knew it would be packed. We see a couple of people have brought their children. There is a pained feeling from the old thoughts, but it fades.

There are thin clouds of sweet white smoke floating in this room. We breathe it in deeply, pulling it with a whistling noise into our one uncollapsed lung.

The show on the screen is strange, like the amusing dreams of our I-brain. The humans aren't acting like humans. They are trapped inside a cave lit by a bonfire. They rub each other with burning metal staffs, men and women screaming, skin bubbling and bursting. They paint their eyes with black ashes. They pull a large creature from a cage at the back of the tunnel, many men struggling and falling as they drag the thing in on chains that run through its skin. Some of the fallen men collapse under it as it is dragged forward and it pulls them up into its fluid mass, absorbing them. The space where their bodies merged and melted in begins to ooze a thick white cream. Women ladle this cream from its skin, drinking it and dancing, circles around the fire, ever faster. The women fall to the ground and their chests open up, ribs turned to spongy soft nothing, hearts missing. Slugs ooze out between spread-wide breasts and crawl toward the creature, still just a shape, still cloaked in dark. The men sit before the fire and sweat black oil. Light glows at the top of their foreheads. The slugs turn their stalks to the lights on the men's heads and shift away from the massive beast quivering in the dark. Then the slugs are on the men, long shining trails on shivering skin.

We are touching ourselves while these images glow before us. We have unbuckled and lowered our pants. The leather on our gloved hands is soaking through with seepage. We do not push aside our jacket, but know that the pulsing rose between our legs is emitting a light-red glow. A hissing noise slips from its center.

We are as quiet as we can be. As expected, the audience uproar in the room buries our birthing sounds. The people in this room are laughing, breathing, smoking, fascinated and excited by a world that is not theirs.

We can taste them on our tongues. Two of our heads have emerged, broken through the belly skin, hissing in the flavor of the room.

We slide down to the swollen meat-sprout at our groin and wrap our long bodies around it. Our fanged mouths find each other and lock up, teeth biting into each other's lower jaws. We are a sheath now, squeezing tight, sliding up and down, pulsing, with the blooming rose at our top, its folds now filling with an oil-slick rainbow of wet color.

There is now a desert on the screen. The cave full of revelers has collapsed. A lone man in a cowboy hat has emerged. He walks on crutches made of elephant ivory. He leaves no print in the sand.

We are ready for the next cycle. Hissing at a higher pitch. Our human head lolls back, its now soft skull squelching against the rear wall of the theater, bits of gray garbage draining out.

Our mouths unlatch from each other and we stop stroking between our legs. We bite into the rose-bloom and taste our old warm blood and the oils of our gestation and we pull back and split the meat-sprout from tip to shaft.

What is left of our I-brain thinks it has gone to a place called Heaven. It feels so good. So alive.

It thinks a word. *Enlightenment.*

Our abdomen muscles contract and push down and a thick, bloody, sausage-shaped sac pushes out of the hole we've torn in our crotch, the old flaps of our meat-sprout shaking and slipping against its emergence.

It is rare and lucky to reach this point in the cycle. We are blessed.

We quickly grasp the tube with our man-hands and bring it to our mouth, licking it clean, the taste stirring an old sense memory of the day we swallowed a bug in the park.

One of our new extensions crawls up through our man-throat and slides over the slick, swollen man-tongue. We bite into the sac, spreading it open.

We smile.

Their wings are already drying.

The film on the screen is so strange that when the man in the desert is suddenly eclipsed by the shadow of thousands of tiny flying gnats, the audience gasps in awe, breathing in deep, smiling with surprise, stunned by spectacle.

We ride in on the waves of their exhalation and find soft purchase.

And the people sleep, and dream, and awake to a subtle hissing sound. It is familiar to them. They hear it in their blood.

We are the waves of an ancient ocean crashing to shore, washing everything clean.

WAR PIG

BY CARLTON MELLICK III

This is by far the biggest, sleaziest, goofiest Monster Smackdown this side of Japan or Adult Swim, courtesy of your friendly neighborhood Carlton Mellick III.

The Bizarro godfather—whose latest books include the terrifying Apeshit *as well as the winsome children's classic* The Faggiest Vampire—*is here deployed at his cheerfully weirdest, dragging us deadpan through a seedy mutant underworld of battling beasts and assorted screwheads. Rest assured that godless mayhem will ensue, and pray for the triumphant, heartwarming conclusion we all so richly deserve.*

The crowd went crazy as the pig-man slammed into the bars of the cage and dropped to the concrete floor. Blood gushed from his gnarled snout, his massive frame twitching as his eyes rolled back into their greasy sockets. The colossal bear-man hovered above him and roared at the audience, beating his furry chest with big black paws. They cheered for him like no other fighter I have ever seen before.

At that moment, I thought it was the end. The War Pig had finally been defeated. This didn't come as much of a shock to me. His opponent, Grizzly Titan, was larger, younger, fiercer. And he was a fucking bear. Even though the old pig had been the longest-running champion in the history of the fights, he had no chance against a grizzly bear. Still, I hoped against reason that he would have found a way to beat him. After all, this is a fight to the death. And he is my father.

War Pig snorted and drooled as Grizzly lifted him by his portly neck and bit into his shoulder. War Pig cried out, a human cry, as the bear growled and thrashed at his flesh. The cry was the only thing I still recognized about my father.

The bell rang before Grizzly Titan could rip my father's throat out. At first, I was relieved. But then I thought it would have been better if he had just finished him off then and there, rather than dragging out the inevitable.

The bear spit War Pig out of his mouth and pushed him back to the ground. Then he stomped at the guard to let him out of the cage. There would be an hour break before the next round, but the old pig spent the first ten minutes of it just lying on the floor, holding the blood in his gaping wounds. Eventually, the doctor's aides scraped him up into a stretcher and carried him out of the cage into the back of the factory.

I wasn't excited to go see the old man. I was done saying good-bye to him a long time ago, and I wasn't willing to do it again just because it was for real this time. But still, if I was going to get any money for lunch today (or any day in the future) I knew I had better get it from him then.

The lower deck of the factory was all standing room. This was where the commoners, the wannabe fighters, and the families of the fighters got to watch the match. The real crowd watched from the upper deck. I had never been allowed up there before.

I pushed my way through the filthy dog shit-smelling mob, knocking a hyena boy off balance. He growled at me, but it only made me laugh. The kid was only fifteen and was already on the serum. Younger and younger people were taking it these days, in the hope that it would get them out of the ghetto. That was what my dad thought when he first took it, but we still lived in squalor. All it did was make him into a hideous creature that killed other creatures for the amusement of the upper class.

They called it the lycanthrope serum, or L serum. For a member of the working class, it cost a month's wages for each shot unless you had a manager to pay for them. Every injection would make you a little less human, and a lot more animal. Which beast you transformed into depended a little on your DNA and a lot on chance. Some fighters became werewolves, some became lions, some became mice. My dad became a wild boar. Once you took the shot, there was no going back. The effect was permanent. It took about six shots before you were strong enough to fight. It took about twelve shots before you lost all of your humanity. My dad was on his eleventh shot.

In the locker room, War Pig was sprawled across a large metal table stained with the blood of a hundred different breeds of lycanthrope. He was getting sewn up by a bald doctor who had two extra pairs of mechanical limbs powered by a rumbling engine strapped to his back. The doctor was tall, about my size, but compared to my father's mass he was a mere toddler operating on a giant. The old pig was conscious now, swatting at the puffs of smoke that issued from the doctor's shoulder pipes.

I locked eyes with my father from the doorway, but I didn't approach. His manager, Mr. Crumbly, was beside him, tapping his metal fingers against the wall and glaring up at his ruined prize fighter.

"You need to take another L-shot," said Mr. Crumbly with curly white lips.

"I'm done," grunted my father. "You told me I didn't have to take any more shots."

As I entered the room, a guard stepped into my path, a soldier who was more machine than human with metal plates for skin, clockwork organs, and a Gatling gun for a left arm. Mr. Crumbly whistled at the guard to let me through, but instead of approaching them I went to a bench on the other side of the room.

"If you don't take another shot, then you have no chance," said Mr. Crumbly. "You will lose. You will die."

"My brain won't be human anymore with another shot," said the old pig.

"Your brain won't be anything anymore when it's ripped out of your skull by that monster out there."

The pig man snorted as the doctor crawled across his chest like a spider. "I'd rather die still thinking like a human."

Mr. Crumbly wiped pig spit from the lapels of his red suit. "I'll cut you a deal. Take the shot and beat this guy. If you win, I'll let you retire. I'll triple your payout and you never have to fight again."

"Bullshit. You've promised that before."

Crumbly lit a cigar and shook his head. "Fine. Have it your way." He walked a few steps away from him, and then turned back. "But with you dead, I'll need to find another fighter. One just like you, but younger and healthier. Know anyone like that?"

Mr. Crumbly glanced over at me, then at the pig man. It took a minute for my father to understand what was meant, but once he did he became furious. He struggled upright and roared at his manager, slapping the doctor off of him and pounding his fist through the back wall. The guard jumped between my father and his manager, ready to turn the crank on his Gatling gun.

"He's eighteen now," said Crumbly. "Perfect fighting age if we can get enough shots in him."

"I'll fucking kill you if you try," screamed the War Pig.

Mr. Crumbly was calm, but backed slightly farther away from the operating table. "Take the shot, win the fight, and I won't need another fighter."

My father looked at me. His eyes red. Snot dripping from his snout.

"I'll take it," he said. "But don't you ever fucking stick that shit in my son or I will rip you limb from limb."

"Fair enough." Mr. Crumbly pulled a vial of blue liquid out of his coat pocket and tossed it to the doctor. "Just make sure you win." Then he left the room.

As the doctor filled a syringe with the blue fluid, my father stared at me. We hadn't had much of a relationship in the past few years, mostly because he was so ashamed of what he had become.

"Take the money out of my locker and buy yourself something to eat," he told me. "Take all of it."

I didn't hesitate.

"Buy a train ticket and get out of town," he said.

I frowned at him.

"Even if I wanted to, where would I go?" I asked.

"As far away from here as you can get," he said.

The doctor held up the shot to my father. The pig man nodded back at him. Then the needle went into his blubbery, hairy arm.

"Tommy . . ." he said, as I was leaving the room. "I don't want you to end up like me."

But I didn't look back.

Through the door, I could hear the sound of his flesh twisting and mutating behind his piglike screams

Through the dark and smoky lower deck of the factory, I made my way to a vendor selling balls of hamburger meat on a stick. After paying, I went to the nearby fire pit to cook the meat, passing a rat woman nibbling on her meat raw. The animal people often preferred the taste of raw meat, though they usually ate it that way because using the fire was an extra cost.

While roasting the hamburger balls, I tried not to imagine what my father was going to be like after the shot. I wasn't sure if he would remember how to tie his shoes, remember who I was, or even remember how to speak. It was rare for a fighter to even live long enough to get to their twelfth shot, so I had never seen the effects firsthand.

I was only eight when my father took his first shot. He used to be a butcher until the economy collapsed and he lost his store. Mom died of tuberculosis years before, so it was just the two of us. Everyone knew there was good money in fighting, but back then it was pretty rare for anyone to agree to sacrifice their human DNA for the sake of a little extra cash. But times were getting tougher and tougher, we were living on the streets, and my father would have done anything to put me in a better life.

In the beginning, my father came crawling to Mr. Crumbly. He knew the man was a ruthless gangster and a flesh peddler, but he thought he had no other choice.

Mr. Crumbly took a deep interest in my father. He said that he'd never seen a man more desperate in his life. Mr. Crumbly was a man who profited from desperation.

The next six months were perhaps the happiest time of my life since Mom died. My father wasn't fighting yet. He was given a shot a month and during that time our well-being was looked out for. We had a roof over our head and food on the table. Mr. Crumbly said my father could make it up to him later, by winning some fights.

But at first, I wasn't happy. I didn't know why my father was changing into a pig at the time. I thought he had some kind of disease. It scared me.

"What's happening to you?" I would cry, curled up in a corner.

He smiled at me. "I'm turning into a piggy!" he would say, as if his changes were cute and fun.

He would get down on all fours and wag his butt at me. "Look at my piggy tail! I can wag it!"

His curly tail would make me laugh a little, but it would make me cry a little more.

"Do you want a piggy ride?" he would ask me.

I would shake my head.

"Come on, I know you would like a piggy ride."

I would shake my head.

"I had all these changes done to me just so that I could give you piggy rides, and now you won't even take them?" Then he would give me a pouting sad face, lowering his pig nose at me.

"Okay," I would tell him, to make him feel better.

I would crawl onto his back, hold onto his floppy ears, and he would run around the house making squealing noises until I started laughing. Eventually, I began to like my dad even better as the pig man. He was able to spend much more time with me than he did while working at the butcher shop and he would give me piggy rides whenever I needed cheering up. The more piglike he got, the more fun he seemed to become.

It went on this way for a few years, until I discovered that he was spending his nights fighting other animal men to the death for money.

"Shots, shots," yelled a dealer passing the fire pit.

I kept my eyes on my food.

"You need an L-shot?" he asked me, peeking through the flames at me. "I got 'em cheap."

"No thanks," I told him.

"Half off," he said.

"No."

He gave me a dirty look and spit on the ground, "Don't you want to be like your old man?" The dealer must have recognized me, but I didn't recognize him.

Even though my meat wasn't fully cooked, I turned and walked away from him, unaware that I was walking into a crowd of dog men. Street gangs commonly hung out in the lower deck of the factory. They came to the fights to buy L and watch the blood fly. Most of them took the serum not to become fighters, but to become stronger more vicious street thugs. If you stayed away from them they usually left you alone, but that dealer had caught me off guard and I wasn't paying attention to where I was going.

A bulldog thug saw me and approached with two of his friends, a Doberman in a trench coat and a Dalmatian with an eyepatch.

"I'll take that," the bulldog said to me with intense dog breath, pulling the food out of my hand and pushing me back. The others laughed as their leader ate one of my meatballs.

As they were about to turn away, I charged at the bulldog and punched him in his slobbery jowls. The stocky punk staggered back in shock. That was probably the first time in a long time that anybody had stood up to him. I tried to retrieve my food, but the Doberman grabbed me from behind. The bulldog punched me in the stomach.

"Do you want to die?" said the bulldog, pulling a knife out of his jacket.

Before he could come at me, the bulldog found a Gatling gun pointed in his face. I turned to see the same metal guard from the locker room. Behind him, stood Mr. Crumbly.

He just whistled at the punks, and they took the hint. They let me go and ran off, taking my food with them. Mr. Crumbly walked over to me and wiped the slobber from my suspenders.

"What was that about?" he asked.

"They took my food."

"And you decided to take on the lot of them?" He laughed. "You've got guts, kid. Just like your old man. Why don't you come to the upper deck and let me buy you some lunch? We can watch the next round from there."

"That's okay," I told him. "I can get some more food myself."

"Nonsense," he said. "Come with me."

The upper deck was a completely different world from the dungeon below. I had never seen anything like it. The lighting was bright. Velvet curtains hung from the walls. Floating steam-powered appetizer trays circled from table to table. All of the people were dressed elegantly, even though most of them were criminals and prostitutes.

As we walked through the upper-class crowd, I noticed that the majority of the people were full of clicking noises. They were all mechanical. An old man puffed on a pipe with a golden mechanical arm. His wife sat next to him with her chest opened up, exposing clockwork gears and steam. I had heard it was possible for the rich to replace their insides with machines, so that they could live much longer lives, but I had no idea that *most* of them did this.

Mr. Crumbly sat me down at a table next to two blue jellyfish girls.

"Tommy, these are the Stinger Twins," he said, introducing me to the women at the table. Then he said to them, "This is Tommy. He's the champ's kid."

"Wow," one of them said, pulling me between them and wrapping her smooth arm around me. "You're the son of the War Pig!"

The other one said, "War Pig has always been my favorite fighter!"

The two of them had nearly translucent skin and not a hair on their entire body. Instead of hair, they had jellyfish tentacles growing down from bell-shaped sacks on their heads, resembling hats. They were obviously prostitutes. It wasn't uncommon for whores to be given the L-serum. Many clients found lycanthrope women to be more exciting than normal women. It was also a way for their pimps to keep them in a life of servitude, because once you started the L injections you could never go back to a respectable way of life.

"Have a drink," Mr. Crumbly told me, pouring me a glass of fine whiskey. "I'll have them bring us some steaks before the fight starts."

One of the jellyfish girls coiled her tentacles around my shoulder and glared at me with her sweet, bulbous eyes.

"Why do they call you the Stinger Twins?" I asked her.

Then a shock entered my neck from her tentacles and she giggled at me.

"That's why," the other one said.

The girl stung me again, flirtatiously.

"They are wild, aren't they?" Mr. Crumbly said, raising his eyebrows.

"Yeah," I said.

The girls rubbed my legs and stung me some more. I was beginning to feel drunk, but I wasn't sure if it was from the whiskey or the jellyfish toxins.

I could see my father entering the cage below. When the crowd saw him standing upright, bigger than he had ever been before, they applauded. They knew he had taken another shot. They knew he was still in this fight.

There wasn't much changed about my father. His muscles were larger and his stamina was increased, but physically he wasn't much different. Mentally, on the other hand, he seemed to be a completely different person. He had a maniacal glare in his eyes. He was hungry for blood. He wasn't my father anymore.

When Grizzly Titan entered the ring, my father didn't even wait for the bell. He just charged his opponent and slammed his fists repeatedly into the beast's snarling jaw. The crowd cheered as War Pig viciously attacked the bear-man. Even though he was still much larger, Grizzly couldn't push the pig away.

The last time my father looked this scary to me was the first time I saw him fight. I was eleven years old, growing more and more curious of where my father was going at night. He said that he was going to work for Mr. Crumbly, but he never told me what he did.

"I make money," he told me. That was all he said.

At first, I thought he meant that he actually printed money for the government, but by eleven I was old enough to know he was keeping his job a secret. So I followed him to work one night, right to this very factory. I snuck into the building through a ventilation duct, emerging into the roaring crowd of the lower deck. I couldn't see what they were all cheering at, so I slipped my way through the mass of people until I got to the front row.

That was when I saw my father in the cage for the first time. Inside of that arena, he was no longer the man who tried to cheer me up with piggy rides. He was the War Pig. With my own eyes, I watched him beat a moose-man to a bloody pulp. After his opponent could no longer move, my father wrapped his arms around the man's antlers and twisted his head off like the cork of a wine bottle. It wasn't just that he killed a man in front of me that I found horrifying. It was that he seemed so thrilled to be doing it, lifting the bloody moose head up in the air, sticking his tongue in and out of his snout at the audience with glee.

My relationship with my father never recovered after that night. I dropped out of school. I started drinking. I beat up on kids smaller than me. I would never hold onto a friendship with anyone for more than a few weeks.

I attended the fights once I was old enough to get in, but I only did that to make sure I got the money if my dad was ever killed. There was a part of me that wanted him to lose, just so that I could be done with him for good.

There was still a part of me that wanted that as I watched the tides change on my father in the cage. The Grizzly Titan had him against the bars, clawing him across the chest. His fresh stitches opened up and drenched his opponent's brown fur, but he continued throwing punches, biting wildly at the air.

"He's the best fighter I've ever had," Mr. Crumbly said to me. "You should be proud."

"I haven't been proud of my father for a long time, Mr. Crumbly."

The old gangster whistled at the jellyfish girl who wasn't paying much attention to me, and she began kissing my ear with slippery blubbery lips.

"Have you ever thought about fighting?" he asked me.

"A little," I said. "But it's not for me. Besides, the old pig would kill me if I even think about taking the serum."

Mr. Crumbly smiled and pulled out a vial of blue liquid. "You can try it right now if you like."

"But my father . . ."

"You're a grown man now," he told me. "You can make your own decisions. Besides, you and I both know that your father can't possibly win this one."

"But he took the shot . . ."

"I wanted him to take the shot so that he could go a few more rounds. All these people came here to see a good show, and I didn't want my prize fighter going out so easily."

I looked into the cage to see War Pig staggering backwards with deep claw marks across his skull.

Then I turned back to Crumbly. "Yeah, I figured he couldn't win this one."

"And after he's dead what are you going to do with yourself? Get a job? Good luck finding anyone hiring a lowlife kid." He saw me looking down at my drink. "No offense."

A jellyfish tentacle coiled across my mouth, as if the girl wanted me to suck on it. I wiped it away, but it just coiled around my ear.

"Fighting pays well," he said. "And who knows, you might be good at it. And if you ask me, you really don't have a lot of options in your current situation."

"I don't know," I said.

"Tell you what . . ." he filled a syringe and placed it on the table in front of me. Then placed a stack of bills next to it. "I'll pay you a thousand dollars to take this one shot."

"I don't want to become some freakish creature," I said.

The jellyfish girls stung me a few times for saying that, but continued rubbing my arms and thighs.

"One shot will hardly do anything to you," he said. "You'll barely notice a difference. But we will get to see what kind of animal you might become. If you're not going to become anything we can use then you can take the money and leave. It will be enough to get you started on a new life somewhere. If you become something that would make a great fighter, well, then I'll see if I can cut you a good enough deal."

I stared good and hard at that stack of money. It was more than I had ever seen in my life. More than my dad would make for winning ten fights.

The jellyfish girl who really seemed to like me said "I want to see what you become. Aren't you curious?"

The other one said, "Maybe you'll become a jellyfish like us. If that happens you wouldn't have to fight."

"And we'd let you spend more time with us," the affectionate one side, caressing my right cheek.

"And you'd be one thousand dollars richer," said Mr. Crumbly.

I looked at the shot and the money, then looked up at the affectionate jellyfish girl. She smiled wide and nodded her head eagerly at me.

"Fine, I'll do it," I said.

And before I had the chance to change my mind, one of the jellyfish girls was already pumping me full of the serum.

By the end of the match, both of the beast men were still standing. My father was in worse shape than Grizzly, but both were badly wounded. Neither one of them exited the cage very quickly.

As the serum raced through my veins, my head began to pound. My flesh started to tickle, then itch, then pulse and twist. The changes were more noticeable than Crumbly had stated. My entire body was changing. My fingernails stretched into claws, my skin grew a thin layer of fur, my teeth sharpened against my tongue. When it was over, I stood up and ripped opened my shirt. My entire chest was coated in golden fur with black spots. A small tail was in my pants.

"Congratulations," Mr. Crumbly said. "You're a jaguar. The first I've ever seen."

"You said it would be hardly noticeable," I said. My voice sounded funny with the longer teeth in my mouth.

Crumbly shrugged. "Some people react better to the serum than others."

The affectionate jellyfish girl rubbed her blue fingers down the spots on my chest. "Preeettty . . ." she said.

I slithered out of her tentacles and grabbed the stack of cash.

"I'll give you another thousand for every shot you take," Mr. Crumbly said to me. "And I'll give you double that if you decide to start fighting. People will pay a ton to see a jaguar in action. What do you say?"

"I'll think about it," I said.

"I'll take that as a yes," he said.

I turned and walked away. As I went through the crowd, I noticed that everyone was staring at me. They seemed thrilled by the sight of me.

"A jaguar, ladies and gentlemen!" Mr. Crumbly shouted at the social elite. "The son of War Pig is a goddamned jaguar!"

They clapped as I went down the stairs to the lower deck.

As soon as I arrived at the lower deck, I noticed a change in the crowd. They were all looking at me with a sense of fear and respect. Even the bulldog punk and his gang of street thugs cowered in my presence.

At that moment, part of me wanted to walk out and take a train out of town just as my father had recommended, another part wanted to break down in tears, and a third part wanted to go right back upstairs and accept Mr. Crumbly's offer. But I found myself doing none of those things. Instead, I went to the back of the factory to find my dad.

Inside the locker room, the doctor was restitching my father's old wounds, and stitching in several new ones. At the first sight of me, his eyes widened.

"What did you do?" he said. His voice was a collection of slurs and snorts.

"I took a shot," I said.

"That motherfucker lied to me again!" He grunted. "I'm going to kill him!"

"It was my choice," I told him.

His eyes became red.

"How many times have I told you that this isn't what I wanted for you? I did all of this so that you'd have a better life than mine."

"What else was I going to do?" I said. My voice was probably just as foreign to him as his was to me. "You're not going to be around forever. Hell, you probably won't even survive another day. I'm going to have to feed myself somehow."

"Not like this," he said. "You need to get out of town. Tonight. Don't take another shot. It's not too late to get out of this."

Even though his words were human, I could tell he was having difficulty forming them. His mind was just barely hanging on.

"I'm sorry," I said. "But I'm pretty sure I want to take Crumbly's deal. He said he'd pay me a thousand dollars for every shot I take. That's more than he ever paid you."

War Pig snarled at me.

"If you make so much money now, then you can give me back the money I gave you."

I held up the small wad of bills he had given me. "This?"

"Give it back," he said.

I threw it at him. "Here." Then I pulled out my large wad of bills, peeled a few off the top and flicked those at him as well. "With interest."

Then I walked toward the door.

"You're no son of mine," he grunted at me.

I looked back. "I am your son. That's the problem."

I left the room and went straight back to the upper deck. I sat down between the jellyfish girls and stared Mr. Crumbly right in the eyes.

"I'll take the deal," I told him.

And the old gangster's smile grew so wide I could see my reflection in his shiny metal teeth.

The match was supposed to have begun already, but my father was nowhere to be seen. If he didn't show up soon, he would be disqualified. This made Mr. Crumbly a bit uneasy, but he tried to keep calm. He whistled at one of the jellyfish girls to sit on his lap. The other girl stayed with me, stroking my jaguar spots.

The crowd was impatient. They didn't want this to be the end of the fight. Nobody would stand for a win without bloodshed.

Then I heard someone chanting my father's name: War Pig. War Pig. War Pig. War Pig.

It was coming from the lower deck. Mr. Crumbly looked down. A large group of people in the lower deck joined in on the chant.

War Pig. War Pig. War Pig. War Pig.

Then the upper class joined in with the chanting. Even Mr. Crumbly and the jellyfish girls.

War Pig. War Pig. War Pig. War Pig.

Standing in the middle of the ring, Grizzly Titan roared at the crowd, pacing in a circle, ready for his opponent. He was the only person not chanting the champion's name. Besides myself.

War Pig. War Pig. War Pig. War Pig.

Suddenly he burst through the doors of the factory, ripping them off their hinges. When the crowd saw him, they fell silent. The War Pig was even larger than before. He was a fifteen-foot-high behemoth, double his mass of moments ago. He now had large tusks growing out of his snout, looking more like a warthog than a wild boar. Most of the crowd couldn't believe it was him. They had never seen such a massive lycanthrope.

I knew what had happened. Using the last of his money, the old pig bought every shot of serum he could get and took them all at once. He didn't want to be human anymore. He just wanted to kill.

He was almost too large to fit through the door of the cage as the guard let him inside. Standing there, dwarfing Grizzly Titan, he roared like a steam engine.

The chanting continued: War Pig. War Pig. War Pig.

He peered down at the bear-man, snot dripping from his tusks.

War Pig. War Pig. War Pig.

When the bell rang, Grizzly charged at my father, growling with claws outstretched.

War Pig. War Pig.

The War Pig threw his fist at Grizzly Titan.

War—

And then it was over. After the massive fist connected, Grizzly's head exploded into a mess of gore and furry bits. The crowd silenced as the headless bear-man staggered across the cage before crumbling to the ground. Then the crowd cheered and hollered for War Pig. The social elite gave him a standing ovation.

War Pig. War Pig. War Pig.

But he wasn't finished yet. War Pig roared and slammed through the door of the cage, crushing the guard beneath it. He climbed the bars until he was face to face with the social elite. Face to face with Mr. Crumbly.

The crowd screamed and scattered as the mammoth leapt to the upper deck. The mechanical guard cranked his Gatling gun at my father, but War Pig just lowered his fist down onto him like he was crushing a tin can. He ripped off the guard's left arm, aimed the gun at the crowd, and opened fire.

Cranking the gun with just two fingers, bullets sprayed through the audience, shattering their metal clockwork hearts. Steam and flames exploded from them as they fell to the ground. Mr. Crumbly used the jellyfish girl on his lap as a human shield. The bullets ripped through her blue flesh until she went limp. Mr. Crumbly calmly wiped her translucent goo from the lapels of his red suit. The other jellyfish girl tried to make it to the stairwell, but her fishy mutation made her less balanced than the humans. She tripped over a corpse and her soft squishy body was quickly trampled to death under the weight of heavy machine people.

When he was out of bullets, War Pig grabbed an old mechanical woman and used her as a hammer against the frenzied mass, clobbering three or four of them at a time, stomping on cowering prostitutes, impaling wealthy gangsters with his blood-soaked tusks. The old woman's head and arms were soon severed, her skin peeled back, until she was just a clicking metal club with which he bludgeoned people.

Mr. Crumbly whistled and three of his fighters came up from the lower deck to protect him. A werewolf, a crocodile man, and a werehorse. But all three were quickly pummeled to death.

The wiry gangster looked back at me. "Your pops sure is something else. A fighter all the way to the end."

Then Mr. Crumbly hit a button on his belt buckle. Steam issued out of his feet and filled the floor around us. His body was lifted off of the ground, into the air above me.

He looked down at me. "I'll be in touch, kid. Remember, we've got a deal."

Then Mr. Crumbly flew away, smoke shooting out of his feet as he crossed to the other side of the deck.

The War Pig saw him getting away and roared. He raised the elderly woman's mechanical corpse and aimed at his manager. Then he launched her through the air, spinning like a giant boomerang. Mr. Crumbly didn't notice the projectile until it connected with his legs, flipping him upside down. He soon found himself rocketing downward.

Mr. Crumbly's neck cracked as his head slammed against the edge of the cage. His steaming rocket shoes spun his lifeless body into a spiral before disappearing into the crowd cowering in the lower decks.

War Pig ignored the small number of surviving audience members, giving them an opening to escape. With his manager dead, there was a look of satisfaction on his face. Now, he was focused on me.

He approached slowly, crushing tables under his massive hooves. The rage was still burning inside his eyes. When he arrived, he towered above me. I was a spotted helpless kitten. As he came down on me, I curled up into a ball and screamed, "Dad, no!"

But he wasn't trying to crush me. He was only kneeling down. He got on all fours and a loud groan rumbled from his fat neck.

Then I noticed his tail was wagging. He looked over at me and I recognized a familiar expression on his face. Although he could no longer speak, in the back of my head I heard him telling me:

"Do you want a piggy ride?"

I cocked my jaguar head at him.

Then he made another facial expression, as if to say, "Come on, I know you would like a piggy ride."

I found myself climbing onto his hairy sweat-drenched back. He squealed and then charged forward. While riding on the back of my mammoth warthog of a father, I couldn't help but laugh. I realized that he had taken all of those extra shots for me. He knew killing Mr. Crumbly was the only chance he had to get me away from this lifestyle.

My father squealed louder and I giggled like a kid again, as he leapt down from the upper deck, galloped through the dark smoky lower deck, and crashed through the factory exit into the bright afternoon sunshine.

DISSERTATION

BY CHUCK PALAHNIUK

It's always wonderful when thousands of years of futile speculation can be laid to rest with a single brilliant unifying theory. And leave it to Chuck Palahniuk to provide precisely the "Eureka!" moment we've been waiting for.

This revelatory stand-alone snippet is from his amazing novel/collection Haunted. *I'd tell you which character tells this tale, but that would ruin everything. So for now, just sit back and enjoy this flawless presentation of his case, and know that you'll never watch* Unsolved Mysteries *on the Discovery Channel the same way again.*

It turns out this wasn't a real date.

Sure, it was beer in a tavern with a pretty-enough girl. A game of pool. Music on the jukebox. A couple hamburgers with fried eggs, French fries. Date food.

It was too soon after Lisa's death, but this felt good. Getting out.

Still, this new girl, she never looks away. Not at the football game on the television above the bar. She misses every pool shot because she can't even watch the cue ball. Her eyes, it's like they're taking dictation. Making shorthand notes. Snapping pictures.

"Did you hear about that little girl getting killed?" she says. "Wasn't she from the reservation?" She says, "Did you ever know her?"

The rough cedar walls of the bar are smoked from years of cigarettes. Sawdust is thick on the floor to soak up the tobacco spit. Christmas lights string back and forth across the black ceiling. Red, blue, and yellow. Green and orange. Some of the lights blinking. Here's the kind of bar where they don't mind you bringing your dog or wearing a gun.

Still, despite appearances, this is less of a date than an interview.

Even when this girl's stating a fact, it comes out as a question:

"Did you know," she says, "that Saint Andrew and Saint Bartholomew tried to convert a giant with a dog's head?" She's not even trying to line up her next shot, saying, "The early Catholic church describes the giant as twelve feet tall with a dog's face, the mane of a lion, and teeth like the tusks of a wild boar."

Of course she misses, but she won't let up. Just: yak, yak, yak.

"Have you ever heard the Italian term *lupa manera*?" she says.

Bent over the pool table, she muffs another easy shot, the two-ball straight in line for a corner pocket. All the time, she's saying, "Have you heard of the French Gandillon family?" Saying, "In 1584, the entire family was burned at the stake. . ."

This girl, Mandy Somebody, she's around campus for the past couple months, since Christmas break maybe. Short skirts and boots with pointed heels sharp as a pencil. Not any sort of clothes a girl could even buy around here. At first, she hung around the anthro office mostly. In "World Peoples 101," she was the graduate TA, and it's there her staring routine really started. Then she's hanging around the English department, asking about the prelaw program. Every day, she's there. Every day, she says hello. Still, even with hamburgers, the Christmas lights, and beer, this is no date.

Now, scratching on the six-ball, she says, "I'm a better anthropologist than I am a pool player." Chalking her cue, she says, "Do you know the word *varulf*? How about a man named Gil Trudeau? He was the guide to General Lafayette during the American Revolution?" Still grinding that little blue chalk cube on the tip of her cue, Mandy Somebody says, "Or have you heard the French term *loup-garou*?"

All the time, her eyes, watching. Measuring. Looking for some answer. A reaction.

It's the anthropology part of her that wants to meet and go out. She moved here from New York City, all that way just to meet guys from the Chewlah Reservation. "Yeah, it's racist," she says. "But it's *good* racist. I just think Chewlah guys are hot. . ."

Over hamburgers, Mandy Somebody leans forward, both elbows on the table, one hand cupped to hold her chin, the other hand fingering an invisible design on the greasy tabletop. She says guys from the Chewlah tribe do all look alike.

"Chewlah men all have a big dick and balls for their face," she says.

What she means is, Chewlah men have square chins that stick a little too far out. They have cleft chins so deep it could be two balls in a sack. Chewlah guys always need a shave, even right after they shave.

That constant dark shadow, Mandy Somebody calls it "Five-Minute Shadow."

Guys from the Chewlah Reservation, they only have one eyebrow, a bush of black thatch, thick as a stand of pubic hair on the bridge of their nose, then trailing away to almost reach their ears on either side.

Between this clump of black curls and their bristly sack of low-hanging chin, there's that Chewlah nose. One long swell of tube, flopped down the middle of their face. A nose so thick and half hard, the fat head of it hides their mouth. A Chewlah nose hangs so long it overlaps their nutsack chin, just a bit.

"Those eyebrows hide their eyes," Mandy says. "The nose hides the mouth."

When you meet a guy from the Chewlah tribe, all you see at first is pubic hair, a big half-hard dick hanging down, and the two balls hanging a little behind it.

"Like Nicolas Cage," she says, "but more so. Like a dick and balls."

She eats a French fry and says, "That's how to tell if any guy's good-looking."

The table is gritty with the salt she's dumped on her French fries. She pays for everything with a color of American Express card the bartender has never seen before. Titanium or uranium.

It's her dissertation that brought her out here. You can only bear to build a case like this, in Manhattan, in the middle of all those anthropology graduate students, giggling, you can only tolerate that so long before your advisers start coaching you to do some fieldwork. In her field, cryptozoology. The study of extinct or legendary animals, like Bigfoot, the Loch Ness Monster, vampires, the Surrey Puma, Mothman, the Jersey Devil. Animals that might or might not exist. It was her adviser's idea she should come here, to visit the Chewlah Reservation, to study the culture and do a little forensic legwork. To build the case for her thesis.

Her eyes jumping up and down, looking for a reaction, some confirmation.

"God," she says, tongue out, fake-gagging, "does that make me come across like some wannabe Margaret Mead?"

Her original plan was to *live* on the Chewlah Reservation. She'd rent a house or something. Her mom and dad are both doctors and want her to follow her dream, not turn out the way they have, no matter how much it costs them. Even talking about herself, Mandy Somebody asked questions. Talking about her parents, she says, "Why don't they change careers? Is that sad or what?"

Her every sentence ending with that question mark.

Her eyes, blue or gray, then silver eyes, still always watching. Her teeth take a bite of her hamburger, even though by now it must be cold. Like eating something dead.

She says, "That girl who died. . ."

Then, "What do you think happened?"

Her dissertation is about how the same giant mysterious creatures occur in all regions around the world. Those giants they call Seeahtiks in the Cascade Mountains around Seattle. They're called Almas in Europe, Yetis in Asia. In California, they're the Oh-man-ah. In Canada, Sasquatch. In Scotland, Fear Liath More, the famous "Gray Men" that roam the mountain Ben Macdhui. In Tibet, the giants are Metoh-kangmi, or Abominable Snowmen.

All of those just different names for hairy giants that wander through the forest, the mountains, sometimes glimpsed by hikers or loggers, sometimes photographed, but never captured.

A cross-cultural phenomenon, she calls it. She says, "I hate the generic term: Bigfoot."

All of these different legends grew up in isolation, but they all describe towering, hairy monsters that stink to high heaven. The monsters are shy, but attack if provoked. In one case, from 1924, a group of miners in the Pacific Northwest shot at what they thought was a gorilla. That night, their cabin on Mount Saint Helens was pounded by a group of these same hairy giants, throwing stones. In 1967, a logger in Oregon watched as another shaggy giant pulled one-ton rocks out of the frozen ground and ate the ground squirrels hibernating under them.

The biggest proof against these monsters is, none have ever been captured. Or found dead. With all the hunters in the wilderness these days, people on motorcycles, it would seem one would bag a Bigfoot.

The bartender comes by the table, asking who wants another round? And Mandy Somebody shuts up talking, like what she's saying is a big state secret. With him standing there, she says, "Run a tab."

When he steps away, she says, "Do you know the Welsh term *gerulfos*?"

She says, "Do you mind?" Twisting herself to one side, putting both hands into her purse on the seat beside her, she takes out a notebook wrapped with a rubber band. "My notes," she says, and rolls off the rubber band, looping it around one wrist for safe keeping.

"Have you heard about the race the ancient Greeks called the *cynocephali*?" she says. With her notebook open, she reads, "How about the *vurvolak*? The *aswang*? The *cadejo*?"

This is the second half of her obsession. "All these names," she says, staking a finger on the open page of her notebook, "people all over the world believe in them, going back thousands of years."

Every language in the world has a word for werewolves. Every culture on earth fears them.

In Haiti, she says, pregnant women are so terrified that a werewolf will eat a newborn, those expectant mothers drink bitter coffee mixed with gasoline. They bathe in a stew of garlic, nutmeg, chives, and coffee. All this to taint the blood of their baby and make it less appetizing to any local werewolf.

That's where Mandy Somebody's thesis comes in.

Bigfoot and werewolves, she says, they're the same phenomenon. The reason science has never found a dead Bigfoot is because it changes back. These monsters are just people, It's only for a few hours or days each year they change. Grow hair. Go *berserk*, the Danish used to call it. They swell up, huge, and need room to roam. In the forest or in the mountains.

"It's kind of like," she says, "their menstrual cycle."

She says, "Even males have these cycles. Male elephants go through their *must* cycle every six months or so. They reek of testosterone. Their ears and genitals change shape, and they're cranky as hell."

Salmon, she says, when they come upstream to spawn, they change shape so much, their jaw deforming, their color, you'd hardly recognize them as the same species of fish. Or grasshoppers becoming locusts. Under these conditions, their entire bodies change size and shape.

"According to my theory," she says, "this Bigfoot gene is related either to hypertrichosis or to the humanoid *Gigantopithecus*, thought to be extinct for a half-million years."

This Ms. Somebody just yak, yak, yaks.

Guys have listened to worse shit, trying to get a piece of ass.

That first big word she says, hypertrichosis, it's some inherited disease where you get fur growing out of every pore on your skin and end up working as a circus side show. Her second big word, *Gigantopithecus*, was a twelve-foot-tall ancestor of humans, discovered in 1934 by some doctor named Koenigwald while he was researching a single huge fossilized tooth.

One finger tapping the open page of her notebook, Mandy Somebody says, "Do you realize why the footprints," and she taps her finger, "photographed by Eric Shipton on Mount Everest in 1951," and she taps her finger, "they look exactly like the footprints photographed on Ben Macdhui in Scotland," and she taps her finger, "and exactly like the footprints found by Bob Gimlin in northern California in 1967?"

Because every lumbering hairy monster, worldwide, is related.

Her theory is, people around the world, isolated groups of people, carry a gene that changes them into these monsters as part of their reproductive cycle. The groups are isolated, they stay alone on tracts of wilderness, because nobody wants to become a towering, shaggy half-animal in the middle of, say, Chicago. Or Disneyland.

"Or," she says, "on that British Airways flight, halfway between Seattle and London. . ."

She's referring to a flight last month. The jet crashed somewhere near the North Pole. The pilot's last communication said something was tearing through the cockpit door. The steel-reinforced, bulletproof, blast-resistant cockpit door. On the flight recorder, the black box, the last sounds include screams, snarls, and the pilot's voice screaming, "What is it? What's going on? What are you?..."

The Federal Aviation Administration says no guns, knives or bombs could possibly have been carried aboard the flight.

The Homeland Security Office says the crash was most likely caused by a single terrorist, high on massive amounts of some designer drug. The drug gave him or her superhuman strength.

Among the dead passengers, Mandy Somebody says, was a thirteen-year-old girl from the Chewlah Reservation.

"This girl was headed for"—she pages through her notes—"Scotland."

Her theory is, the Chewlah tribe was sending her overseas before puberty hit. So she could meet and maybe marry someone from the Ben Macdhui community. Where, tradition holds, giants with gray fur roam the slopes above four thousand feet.

Mandy Somebody, she's full of theories. The New York Public Library has one of the nation's largest collections of books about the occult, she says, because a coven of witches once ran the library.

Mandy Somebody, she says how the Amish keep books of every Amish community on earth. An inventory of every member of their church. So as they travel or immigrate they can always be among, live among, mate among their own kind.

"It's not so outlandish to expect these Bigfoot people keep the same kind of inventory books," she says.

Because the change is always temporary, that's why searchers have never found a dead Bigfoot. And that's why the idea of werewolves occurs in all cultures, over all of human history.

The one piece of movie footage, shot by a man named Roger Patterson in 1967, shows a creature walking upright, covered with fur. A female with a pointed head and enormous breasts and buttocks. Her face and breasts and butt, her entire body covered with shaggy red-brown hair.

That few minutes of film, which some call a fraud, and others call undeniable proof, that's probably just somebody's Aunt Tilly going through her cycle. Running around eating berries and bugs, just trying to steer clear of folks until she changes back.

"That poor woman," Mandy says. "Imagine millions of people seeing a film of you naked on your worst 'bad hair' day?"

Probably, the rest of that woman's family, every time that footage is on television, they probably call her into the living room and tease her.

"What looks like a monster to the world," Mandy says, "it's just home movies to the Chewlah tribe."

And she waits a little window of time, maybe for a reaction. For laughter or a sigh. A nervous twitch.

About the girl on the flight, Mandy Somebody says, imagine how she must have felt. Eating her little in-flight meal, but still hungry. Hungrier than she'd ever felt before. Asking the flight attendant for snacks, leftovers, anything. Then realizing what was about to happen. Until then, she'd only heard the stories how Mon and Dad would hike off into the woods for a few nights, eating deer, skunks, salmon, everything they could catch. Going wild for a few nights, and coming home exhausted and maybe pregnant. Imagine this girl getting up to hide in the airplane bathroom, but it's locked. Occupied. She stands there in the aisle, just outside the bathroom door, getting hungrier and hungrier. When the door at last comes open, the man inside says, "Sorry," but it's too late. What's outside that door isn't human anymore. It's just hunger. It shoves him back into the little plastic bathroom and locks them both inside. Before the man can scream, what had been a thirteen-year-old girl snaps her teeth around his windpipe and rips it out.

She eats and eats. Tearing off his clothes, the way you'd peel an orange, to eat more of the juicy flesh inside.

While the passengers in the main cabin drift off to sleep, this girl eats and eats.

Eats and grows. And maybe then a flight attendant sees the sticky wash of blood coming from underneath the locked bathroom door. Maybe the flight attendant knocks and asks if everything is all right. Or maybe the Chewlah girl eats and eats and is still hungry.

What comes out of that locked bathroom, soaked in blood, it's nowhere near done eating. What bursts out, into the darkened main cabin, grabbing handfuls of face and shoulder, it walks down the cabin aisle the way you'd walk down a buffet, grazing, nibbling. That packed jetliner must've looked like a fat heart-shaped box of chocolates to its hungry yellow eyes.

U-pick human heads on this all-you-can-eat flying smorgasbord.

The captain's last radio transmission, before the cockpit door tore open, he shouted, "Mayday. Mayday. Somebody's eating my flight crew. . ."

Mandy Somebody stops here, her eyes almost full round circles, one hand pressed to her rolling chest as her breathing tries to catch up with all her talk. Her breath, the smell of beer.

From the street, the door opens and a lot of guys walk into the bar, all of them dressed in the same color of bright orange. Their sweatshirts. Vests. Orange coats. A sports team, but really a road crew. On the television above the bar is a commercial to join the navy.

"Can you imagine?" she says.

What will happen if she can prove all this true? If just someone's race will make them a weapon of mass destruction? Will the government order everyone with this secret gene to take drugs to suppress it? Will the United Nations order them all into security quarantine? Concentration camps? Or will they all be tagged with radio transmitters, the way park rangers tag dangerous grizzly bears and track them?

"It's just a matter of time," she says, "don't you think, before the FBI comes to conduct interviews on the reservation?"

Her first week here, she drove out to the reservation and tried to talk to people. The plan was to rent a place and observe everyday life. Soak up the details of Chewlah culture, how people earned their living. Collect an oral account of their legends and history. She drove out there, armed with a tape recorder and five hundred hours of tapes. And no one would sit and talk. There were no houses or apartments or rooms to rent. She wasn't there an hour before the council sheriff told her about some curfew that required she be off the reservation by sunset. What with the length of the drive, he told her she'd best start on her way back right then.

They kicked her out.

"My point is," Mandy Somebody says, "I could've prevented all this."

The girl's feeding frenzy. The crashed jetliner. The FBI only a few days from arriving here. Then the concentration camps. The ethnic cleansing.

Since then, she's hung out at the community college, trying to date a Chewlah guy. Asking questions and waiting. But not waiting for an answer. She's waiting for the applause. Waiting to be right.

That word she said before, *varulf*, it's Swedish for "werewolf." *Loup-garou* is French. That man, Gil Trudeau, the guide to General Lafayette, he was the first werewolf mentioned in American history.

"Tell me I'm right," she says, "and I'll try to help you."

If the FBI gets here, she says, this story will never see the light of day. All the people with the suspected gene will just disappear into government custody. For the public welfare. Or there will be some official accident to resolve the situation. Not genocide, not officially. But there's a good reason why the government went so hard on some tribes, wiping them out with smallpox blankets, or sticking them away on distant reservations. True, not all tribes carried the Bigfoot gene, but a century ago, how could you identify the ones at risk?

"Tell me I'm right," Mandy Somebody says, "and I can get you on the *Today* show in the morning."

Maybe even the A Block. . .

She'll break the story. Create public sympathy. Maybe get Amnesty International involved. This can be the next big civil-rights battle. But global. She's already identified the other communities, tribes, groups around the world most likely to carry her theoretical monster gene. Her breath, the smell of beer, saying "monster" loud enough so the orange road-crew guys look over.

She's got guys all over the world she could be flirting with. Even if this date is a bust, she'll find somebody who'll tell her what she wants to hear.

That werewolves and Bigfoot exist. And that he's both.

Guys have listened to worse shit, trying to get a piece of ass.

Even Chewlah guys with their dicks on their face.

Even me, But I tell her, "That thirteen-year-old, her name was Lisa." I say, "She was my little sister."

"Oral sex," Mandy Somebody says, "is *not* out of the question. . ."

Any guy would be an idiot not to take her home to the reservation. Maybe introduce her to the folks. The whole fam-damnly.

And, standing, I tell her, "You can see the reservation—tonight—but I really need to make a phone call first."

XVIII

THE MOON.

ONLY THE END OF THE WORLD AGAIN

BY NEIL GAIMAN

Here's one thing that Neil Gaiman and I have in common: we're both incredibly happy to see this story published, at long last, between the same set of covers as Lovecraft's "The Shadow over Innsmouth."

So if for some reason you still haven't read the Lovecraft, what's wrong with you? Are you crazy or something? Go do it right now.

The ever-delightful Gaiman brings all of his charm, his cunning pop culture inversions and twists to this existential gothic slapstick noir of vast cosmic shape-shifting proportions.

Incredibly happy, I tell you!

It was a bad day: I woke up naked in the bed with a cramp in my stomach, feeling more or less like hell. Something about the quality of the light, stretched and metallic, like the color of a migraine, told me it was afternoon.

The room was freezing—literally: there was a thin crust of ice on the inside of the windows. The sheets on the bed around me were ripped and clawed, and there was animal hair in the bed. It itched.

I was thinking about staying in bed for the next week—I'm always tired after a change—but a wave of nausea forced me to disentangle myself from the bedding and to stumble, hurriedly, into the apartment's tiny bathroom.

The cramps hit me again as I got to the bathroom door. I held on to the door frame and I started to sweat. Maybe it was a fever; I hoped I wasn't coming down with something.

The cramping was sharp in my guts. My head felt swimmy. I crumpled to the floor, and, before I could manage to raise my head enough to find the toilet bowl, I began to spew.

I vomited a foul-smelling thin yellow liquid; in it was a dog's paw—my guess was a Doberman's, but I'm not really a dog person; a tomato peel; some diced carrots and sweet corn; some lumps of half-chewed meat, raw; and some fingers. They were fairly small pale fingers, obviously a child's.

"Shit."

The cramps eased up, and the nausea subsided. I lay on the floor with stinking drool coming out of my mouth and nose, with the tears you cry when you're being sick drying on my cheeks.

When I felt a little better, I picked up the paw and the fingers from the pool of spew and threw them into the toilet bowl, flushed them away.

I turned on the tap, rinsed out my mouth with the briny Innsmouth water, and spat it into the sink. I mopped up the rest of the sick as best I could with washcloth and toilet paper. Then I turned on the shower and stood in the bathtub like a zombie as the hot water sluiced over me.

I soaped myself down, body and hair. The meager lather turned gray; I must have been filthy. My hair was matted with something that felt like dried blood, and I worked at it with the bar of soap until it was gone. Then I stood under the shower until the water turned icy.

There was a note under the door from my landlady. It said that I owed her for two weeks' rent. It said that all the answers were in the Book of Revelations. It said that I made a lot of noise coming home in the early hours of this morning, and she'd thank me to be quieter in future. It said that when the Elder Gods rose up from the ocean, all the scum of the Earth, all the nonbelievers, all the human garbage and the wastrels and deadbeats would be swept away, and the world would be cleansed by ice and deep water. It said that she felt she ought to remind me that she had assigned me a shelf in the refrigerator when I arrived and she'd thank me if in the future I'd keep to it.

I crumpled the note, dropped it on the floor, where it lay alongside the Big Mac cartons and the empty pizza cartons and the long-dead dried slices of pizza.

It was time to go to work.

I'd been in Innsmouth for two weeks, and I disliked it. It smelled fishy. It was a claustrophobic little town: marshland to the east, cliffs to the west, and, in the center, a harbor that held a few rotting fishing boats and was not even scenic at sunset. The yuppies had come to Innsmouth in the eighties anyway, bought their picturesque fisherman's cottages overlooking the harbor. The yuppies had been gone for some years now, and the cottages by the bay were crumbling, abandoned.

The inhabitants of Innsmouth lived here and there in and around the town and in the trailer parks that ringed it, filled with dank mobile homes that were never going anywhere.

I got dressed, pulled on my boots, put on my coat, and left my room. My landlady was nowhere to be seen. She was a short pop-eyed woman who spoke little, although she left extensive notes for me pinned to doors and placed where I might see them; she kept the house filled with the smell of boiling seafood: huge pots were always simmering on the kitchen stove, filled with things with too many legs and other things with no legs at all.

There were other rooms in the house, but no one else rented them. No one in their right mind would come to Innsmouth in winter.

Outside the house it didn't smell much better. It was colder, though, and my breath steamed in the sea air. The snow on the streets was crusty and filthy; the clouds promised more snow.

A cold salty wind came up off the bay. The gulls were screaming miserably. I felt shitty. My office would be freezing, too. On the corner of Marsh Street and Leng Avenue was a bar, *The Opener*, a squat building with small dark windows that I'd passed two dozen times in the last couple of weeks. I hadn't been in before, but I really needed a drink, and besides, it might be warmer in there. I pushed open the door.

The bar was indeed warm. I stamped the snow off my boots and went inside. It was almost empty and smelled of old ashtrays and stale beer. A couple of elderly men were playing chess by the bar. The barman was reading a battered old gilt-and-green-leather edition of the poetical works of Alfred, Lord Tennyson.

"Hey. How about a Jack Daniel's, straight up?"

"Sure thing. You're new in town," he told me, putting his book face down on the bar, pouring the drink into a glass.

"Does it show?"

He smiled, passed me the Jack Daniel's. The glass was filthy, with a greasy thumbprint on the side, and I shrugged and knocked back the drink anyway. I could barely taste it.

"Hair of the dog?" he said.

"In a manner of speaking."

"There is a belief," said the barman, whose fox-red hair was tightly greased back, "that the *lykanthropoi* can be returned to their natural forms by thanking them, while they're in wolf form, or by calling them by their given names."

"Yeah? Well, thanks."

He poured another shot for me, unasked. He looked a little like Peter Lorre, but then, most of the folk in Innsmouth look a little like Peter Lorre, including my landlady.

I sank the Jack Daniel's, this time felt it burning down into my stomach, the way it should.

"It's what they say. I never said I believed it."

"What *do* you believe?"

"Burn the girdle."

"Pardon?"

"The *lykanthropoi* have girdles of human skin, given to them at their first transformation by their masters in Hell. Burn the girdle."

One of the old chess players turned to me then, his eyes huge and blind and protruding. "If you drink rainwater out of warg-wolf's pawprint, that'll make a wolf of you, when the moon is full," he said. "The only cure is to hunt down the wolf that made the print in the first place and cut off its head with a knife forged of virgin silver."

"Virgin, huh?" I smiled.

His chess partner, bald and wrinkled, shook his head and croaked a single sad sound. Then he moved his queen and croaked again.

There are people like him all over Innsmouth.

I paid for the drinks and left a dollar tip on the bar. The barman was reading his book once more and ignored it.

Outside the bar big wet kissy flakes of snow had begun to fall, settling in my hair and eyelashes. I hate snow. I hate New England. I hate Innsmouth: it's no place to be alone, but if there's a good place to be alone, I've not found it yet. Still, business has kept me on the move for more moons than I like to think about. Business, and other things.

I walked a couple of blocks down Marsh Street—like most of Innsmouth, an unattractive mixture of eighteenth-century American Gothic houses, late-nine-teenth-century stunted brownstones, and late-twentieth prefab gray-brick boxes— until I got to a boarded-up fried chicken joint, and I went up the stone steps next to the store and unlocked the rusting metal security door.

There was a liquor store across the street; a palmist was operating on the second floor.

Someone had scrawled graffiti in black marker on the metal: JUST DIE, it said. Like it was easy.

The stairs were bare wood; the plaster was stained and peeling. My one-room office was at the top of the stairs.

I don't stay anywhere long enough to bother with my name in gilt on glass. It was handwritten in block letters on a piece of ripped cardboard that I'd thumbtacked to the door.

LAWRENCE TALBOT
ADJUSTOR
I unlocked the door to my office and went in.

I inspected my office, while adjectives like *seedy* and *rancid* and *squalid* wandered through my head, then gave up, outclassed. It was fairly unprepossessing—a desk, an office chair, an empty filing cabinet; a window, which gave you a terrific view of the liquor store and the empty palmist's. The smell of old cooking grease permeated from the store below. I wondered how long the fried chicken joint had been boarded up; I imagined a multitude of black cockroaches swarming over every surface in the darkness beneath me.

"That's the shape of the world that you're thinking of there," said a deep dark voice, deep enough that I felt it in the pit of my stomach.

There was an old armchair in one corner of the office. The remains of a pattern showed through the patina of age and grease the years had given it. It was the color of dust.

The fat man sitting in the armchair, his eyes still tightly closed, continued: "We look about in puzzlement at our world, with a sense of unease and disquiet. We think of ourselves as scholars in arcane liturgies, single men trapped in worlds beyond our devising. The truth is far simpler: there are things in the darkness beneath us that wish us harm."

His head was lolled back on the armchair, and the tip of his tongue poked out of the corner of his mouth.

"You read my mind?"

The man in the armchair took a slow deep breath that rattled in the back of his throat. He really was immensely fat, with stubby fingers like discolored sausages. He wore a thick old coat, once black, now an indeterminate gray. The snow on his boots had not entirely melted.

"Perhaps." The end of the world is a strange concept. The world is always ending, and the end is always being averted, by love or foolishness or just plain old dumb luck.

"Ah well. It's too late now: The Elder Gods have chosen their vessels. When the moon rises. . ."

A thin trickle of blood came from one corner of his mouth, oozed down in a thread of silver to his collar. Something scuttled from his collar into the shadows of his coat.

"Yeah? What happens when the moon rises?"

The man in the armchair stirred, opened two little eyes, red and swollen, and blinked them in waking.

"I dreamed I had many mouths," he said, his new voice oddly small and breathy for such a huge man. "I dreamed every mouth was opening and closing independently. Some mouths were talking, some whispering, some eating, some waiting in silence."

He looked around, wiped the spittle from the corner of his mouth, sat back in the chair, blinking puzzledly. "Who are you?"

"I'm the guy who rents this office," I told him.

He belched suddenly, loudly. "I'm sorry," he said in his breathy voice, and lifted himself heavily from the armchair. He was shorter than I was, when he was standing. He looked me up and down blearily. "Silver bullets," he pronounced after a short pause. "Old-fashioned remedy."

"Yeah," I told him. "That's so obvious—must be why I didn't think of it. Gee, I could just kick myself. I really could."

"You're making fun of an old man," he told me.

"Not really. I'm sorry. Now, out of here. Some of us have work to do."

He shambled out. I sat down in the swivel chair at the desk by the window and discovered, after some minutes, through trial and error, that if I swiveled the chair to the left, it fell off its base.

So I sat still and waited for the dusty black telephone on my desk to ring while the light slowly leaked away from the winter sky.

Ring.

A man's voice: *Had I thought about aluminum siding?* I put down the phone.

There was no heating in the office. I wondered how long the fat man had been asleep in the armchair.

Twenty minutes later the phone rang again. A crying woman implored me to help her find her five-year-old daughter, missing since last night, stolen from her bed. The family dog had vanished, too.

I don't do missing children, I told her. *I'm sorry: too many bad memories.* I put down the telephone, feeling sick again.

It was getting dark now, and, for the first time since I had been in Innsmouth, the neon sign across the street flicked on. It told me that MADAME EZEKIEL performed TAROT READINGS AND PALMISTRY.

Red neon stained the falling snow the color of new blood.

Armageddon is averted by small actions. That's the way it was. That's the way it always has to be.

The phone rang a third time. I recognized the voice; it was the aluminum siding man again. "You know," he said chattily, "transformation from man to animal and back being, by definition, impossible, we need to look for other solutions. Depersonalization, obviously, and likewise some form of projection. Brain damage? Perhaps. Pseudoneurotic schizophrenia? Laughably so. Some cases have been treated with intravenous thioridazine hydrochloride."

"Successfully?"

He chuckled. "That's what I like. A man with a sense of humor. I'm sure we can do business."

"I told you already. I don't need aluminum siding."

"Our business is more remarkable than that and of far greater importance. You're new in town, Mr. Talbot. It would be a pity if we found ourselves at, shall we say, loggerheads?"

"You can say whatever you like, pal. In my book you're just another adjustment, waiting to be made."

"We're ending the world, Mr. Talbot. The Deep Ones will rise out of their ocean graves and eat the moon like a ripe plum."

"Then I won't ever have to worry about full moons anymore, will I?"

"Don't try to cross us," he began, but I growled at him, and he fell silent.

Outside my window the snow was still falling.

Across Marsh Street, in the window directly opposite mine, the most beautiful woman I had ever seen stood in the ruby glare of her neon sign, and she stared at me.

She beckoned with one finger.

I put down the phone on the aluminum siding man for the second time that afternoon, and went downstairs, and crossed the street at something close to a run; but I looked both ways before I crossed.

She was dressed in silks. The room was lit only by candles and stank of incense and patchouli oil.

She smiled at me as I walked in, beckoned me over to her seat by the window. She was playing a card game with a tarot deck, some version of solitaire. As I reached her, one elegant hand swept up the cards, wrapped them in a silk scarf, placed them gently in a wooden box.

The scents of the room made my head pound. I hadn't eaten anything today, I realized; perhaps that was what was making me lightheaded. I sat down across the table from her, in the candlelight.

She extended her hand and took my hand in hers.

She stared at my palm, touched it, softly, with her forefinger.

"Hair?" She was puzzled.

"Yeah, well. I'm on my own a lot." I grinned. I had hoped it was a friendly grin, but she raised an eyebrow at me anyway.

"When I look at you," said Madame Ezekiel, "this is what I see. I see the eye of a man. Also I see the eye of a wolf. In the eye of a man I see honesty, decency, innocence. I see an upright man who walks on the square. And in the eye of wolf I see a groaning and a growling, night howls and cries, I see a monster running with blood-flecked spittle in the darkness of the borders of the town."

"How can you see a growl or a cry?"

She smiled. "It is not hard," she said. Her accent was not American. It was Russian, or Maltese, or Egyptian perhaps. "In the eye of the mind we see many things."

Madame Ezekiel closed her green eyes. She had remarkably long eyelashes; her skin was pale, and her black hair was never still—it drifted gently around her head, in the silks, as if it were floating on distant tides.

"There is a traditional way," she told me. "A way to wash off a bad shape. You stand in running water, in clear spring water, while eating white rose petals."

"And then?"

"The shape of darkness will be washed from you."

"It will return," I told her, "with the next full of the moon."

"So," said Madame Ezekiel, "once the shape is washed from you, you open your veins in the running water. It will sting mightily, of course. But the river will carry the blood away."

She was dressed in silks, in scarves and cloths of a hundred different colors, each bright and vivid, even in the muted light of the candles.

Her eyes opened.

"Now," she said, "the tarot." She unwrapped her deck from the black silk scarf that held it, passed me the cards to shuffle. I fanned them, riffed and bridged them.

"Slower, slower," she said. "Let them get to know you. Let them love you, like. . . like a woman would love you."

I held them tightly, then passed them back to her.

She turned over the first card. It was called *The Werewolf*. It showed darkness and amber eyes, a smile in white and red.

Her green eyes showed confusion. They were the green of emeralds. "This is not a card from my deck," she said and turned over the next card. "What did you do to my cards?"

"Nothing, ma'am. I just held them. That's all."

The card she had turned over was *The Deep One*. It showed something green and faintly octopoid. The thing's mouths—if they were indeed mouths and not tentacles—began to writhe on the card as I watched.

She covered it with another card, and then another, and another. The rest of the cards were blank pasteboard.

"Did you do that?" She sounded on the verge of tears.

"No."

"Go now," she said.

"But—"

"*Go.*" She looked down, as if trying to convince herself I no longer existed.

I stood up, in the room that smelled of incense and candlewax, and looked out of her window, across the street. A light flashed briefly in my office window. Two men with flashlights were walking around. They opened the empty filing cabinet, peered around, then took up their positions, one in the armchair, the other behind the door, waiting for me to return. I smiled to myself. It was cold and inhospitable in my office, and with any luck they would wait there for hours until they finally decided I wasn't coming back.

So I left Madame Ezekiel turning over her cards, one by one, staring at them as if that would make the pictures return; and I went downstairs and walked back down Marsh Street until I reached the bar.

The place was empty now; the barman was smoking a cigarette, which he stubbed out as I came in.

"Where are the chess fiends?"

"It's a big night for them tonight. They'll be down at the bay. Let's see. You're a Jack Daniel's? Right?"

"Sounds good."

He poured it for me. I recognized the thumbprint from the last time I had the glass. I picked up the volume of Tennyson poems from the bar top.

"Good book?"

The fox-haired barman took his book from me, opened it, and read:

"Below the thunders of the upper deep;

Far, far beneath in the abysmal sea,

His ancient dreamless, uninvaded sleep

The Kraken sleepeth. . ."

I'd finished my drink. "So? What's your point?"

He walked around the bar, took me over to the window. "See? Out there?"

He pointed toward the west of the town, toward the cliffs. As I stared a bonfire was kindled on the cliff tops; it flared and began to burn with a copper-green flame.

"They're going to wake the Deep Ones," said the barman. "The stars and the planets and the moon are all in the right places. It's time. The dry lands will sink, and the seas shall rise. . ."

"'For the world shall be cleansed with ice and floods, and I'll thank you to keep to your own shelf in the refrigerator,'" I said.

"Sorry?"

"Nothing. What's the quickest way to get up to those cliffs?"

"Back up Marsh Street. Hang a left at the Church of Dagon till you reach

Manuxet Way, then just keep on going." He pulled a coat off the back of the door and put it on. "Cmon. I'll walk you up there. I'd hate to miss any of the fun."

"You sure?"

"No one in town's going to be drinking tonight." We stepped out, and he locked the door to the bar behind us.

It was chilly in the street, and fallen snow blew about the ground like white mists. From street level, I could no longer tell if Madame Ezekiel was in her den above her neon sign or if my guests were still waiting for me in my office.

We put our heads down against the wind, and we walked.

Over the noise of the wind I heard the barman talking to himself:

"Winnow with giant arms the slumbering green," he was saying.

"There hath he lain for ages and will lie

Battening upon huge seaworms in his sleep,

Until the latter fire shall heat the deep;

Then once by men and angels to be seen,

In roaring he shall rise. . ."

He stopped there, and we walked on together in silence with blown snow stinging our faces.

And on the surface die, I thought, but said nothing out loud.

Twenty minutes walking and we were out of Innsmouth. Manuxet Way stopped when we left the town, and it became a narrow dirt path, partly covered with snow and ice, and we slipped and slid our way up it in the darkness.

The moon was not yet up, but the stars had already begun to come out. There were so many of them. They were sprinkled like diamond dust and crushed sapphires across the night sky. You can see so many stars from the seashore, more than you could ever see back in the city.

At the top of the cliff, behind the bonfire, two people were waiting—one huge and fat, one much smaller. The barman left my side and walked over to stand beside them, facing me.

"Behold," he said, "the sacrificial wolf." There was now an oddly familiar quality to his voice.

I didn't say anything. The fire was burning with green flames, and it lit the three of them from below: classic spook lighting.

"Do you know why I brought you up here?" asked the barman, and I knew then why his voice was familiar: it was the voice of the man who had attempted to sell me aluminum siding.

"To stop the world ending?"

He laughed at me then.

The second figure was the fat man I had found asleep in my office chair. "Well, if you're going to get eschatological about it. . ." he murmured in a voice deep enough to rattle walls. His eyes were closed. He was fast asleep.

The third figure was shrouded in dark silks and smelled of patchouli oil. It held a knife. It said nothing.

"This night," said the barman, "the moon is the moon of the Deep Ones. This night are the stars configured in the shapes and patterns of the dark old times. This night, if we call them, they will come. If our sacrifice is worthy. If our cries are heard."

The moon rose, huge and amber and heavy, on the other side of the bay, and a chorus of low croaking rose with it from the ocean far beneath us.

Moonlight on snow and ice is not daylight, but it will do. And my eyes were getting sharper with the moon: in the cold waters men like frogs were surfacing and submerging in a slow water dance. Men like frogs, and women, too: it seemed to me that I could see my landlady down there, writhing and croaking in the bay with the rest of them.

It was too soon for another change; I was still exhausted from the night before; but I felt strange under that amber moon.

"Poor wolf-man," came a whisper from the silks. "All his dreams have come to this: a lonely death upon a distant cliff."

I will dream if I want to, I said, *and my death is my own affair.* But I was unsure if I had said it out loud.

Senses heighten in the moon's light; I heard the roar of the ocean still, but now, overlaid on top of it, I could hear each wave rise and crash; I heard the splash of the frog people; I heard the drowned whispers of the dead in the bay; I heard the creak of green wrecks far beneath the ocean.

Smell improves, too. The aluminum siding man was human, while the fat man had other blood in him.

And the figure in the silks. . .

I had smelled her perfume when I wore man-shape. Now I could smell something else, less heady, beneath it. A smell of decay, of putrefying meat and rotten flesh.

The silks fluttered. She was moving toward me. She held the knife.

"Madame Ezekiel?" My voice was roughening and coarsening. Soon I would lose it all. I didn't understand what was happening, but the moon was rising higher and higher, losing its amber color and filling my mind with its pale light.

"Madame Ezekiel?"

"You deserve to die," she said, her voice cold and low. "If only for what you did to my cards. They were old."

"I don't die," I told her. "'Even a man who is pure in heart, and says his prayers by night.' Remember?"

"It's bullshit," she said. "You know what the oldest way to end the curse of the werewolf is?"

"No."

The bonfire burned brighter now; burned with the green of the world beneath the sea, the green of algae and of slowly drifting weed; burned with the color of emeralds.

"You simply wait till they're in human shape, a whole month away from another change; then you take the sacrificial knife and you kill them. That's all."

I turned to run, but the barman was behind me, pulling my arms, twisting my wrists up into the small of my back. The knife glinted pale silver in the moonlight. Madame Ezekiel smiled.

She sliced across my throat.

Blood began to gush and then to flow. And then it slowed and stopped. . .

—The pounding in the front of my head, the pressure in the back. All a roiling change a how-wow-row-now change a red wall coming toward me from the night

—I tasted stars dissolved in brine, fizzy and distant and salt

—my fingers prickled with pins and my skin was lashed with tongues of flame my eyes were topaz. I could taste the night

My breath steamed and billowed in the icy air.

I growled involuntarily, low in my throat. My forepaws were touching the snow.

I pulled back, tensed, and sprang at her.

There was a sense of corruption that hung in the air, like a mist, surrounding me. High in my leap, I seemed to pause, and something burst like a soap bubble. . .

I was deep, deep in the darkness under the sea, standing on all fours on a slimy rock floor at the entrance of some kind of citadel built of enormous rough-hewn stones. The stones gave off a pale glow-in-the-dark light; a ghostly luminescence, like the hands of a watch.

A cloud of black blood trickled from my neck.

She was standing in the doorway in front of me. She was now six, maybe seven feet high. There was flesh on her skeletal bones, pitted and gnawed, but the silks were weeds, drifting in the cold water, down there in the dreamless deeps. They hid her face like a slow green veil.

There were limpets growing on the upper surfaces of her arms and on the flesh that hung from her ribcage.

I felt like I was being crushed. I couldn't think anymore.

She moved toward me. The weed that surrounded her head shifted. She had a face like the stuff you don't want to eat in a sushi counter, all suckers and spines and drifting anemone fronds; and somewhere in all that I knew she was smiling.

I pushed with my hind legs. We met there, in the deep, and we struggled. It was so cold, so dark. I closed my jaws on her face and felt something rend and tear.

It was almost a kiss, down there in the abysmal deep. . .

I landed softly on the snow, a silk scarf locked between my jaws. The other scarves were fluttering to the ground. Madame Ezekiel was nowhere to be seen.

The silver knife lay on the ground in the snow. I waited on all fours in the moonlight, soaking wet. I shook myself, spraying the brine about. I heard it hiss and spit when it hit the fire.

I was dizzy and weak. I pulled the air deep into my lungs.

Down, far below, in the bay, I could see the frog people hanging on the surface of the sea like dead things; for a handful of seconds, they drifted back and forth on the tide, then they twisted and leapt, and each by each they *plop-plopped* down into the bay and vanished beneath the sea.

There was a scream. It was the fox-haired bartender, the pop-eyed aluminum siding salesman, and he was staring at the night sky, at the clouds that were drifting in, covering the stars, and he was screaming. There was rage and there was frustration in that cry, and it scared me.

He picked up the knife from the ground, wiped the snow from the handle with his fingers, wiped the blood from the blade with his coat. Then he looked across at me. He was crying. "You bastard," he said. "What did you do to her?"

I would have told him I didn't do anything to her, that she was still on guard far beneath the ocean, but I couldn't talk any more, only growl and whine and howl.

He was crying. He stank of insanity and of disappointment. He raised the knife and ran at me, and I moved to one side.

Some people just can't adjust even to tiny changes. The barman stumbled past me, off the cliff, into nothing.

In the moonlight blood is black, not red, and the marks he left on the cliff side as he fell and bounced and fell were smudges of black and dark gray. Then, finally, he lay still on the icy rocks at the base of the cliff until an arm reached out from the sea and dragged him, with a slowness that was almost painful to watch, under the dark water.

A hand scratched the back of my head. It felt good.

"What was she? Just an avatar of the Deep Ones, sir. An eidolon, a manifestation, if you will, sent up to us from the uttermost deeps to bring about the end of the world."

I bristled.

"No, it's over—for now. You disrupted her, sir. And the ritual is most specific. Three of us must stand together and call the sacred names while innocent blood pools and pulses at our feet."

I looked up at the fat man and whined a query. He patted me on the back of the neck sleepily.

"Of course she doesn't love you, boy. She hardly even exists on this plane in any material sense."

The snow began to fall once more. The bonfire was going out.

"Your change tonight incidentally, I would opine, is a direct result of the self-same celestial configurations and lunar forces that made tonight such a perfect night to bring back my old friends from Underneath. . ."

He continued talking in his deep voice, and perhaps he was telling me important things. I'll never know, for the appetite was growing inside me, and his words had lost all but the shadow of any meaning; I had no further interest in the sea or the cliff-top or the fat man.

There were deer running in the woods beyond the meadow: I could smell them on the winter's night's air.

And I was, above all things, hungry.

I was naked when I came to myself again, early the next morning, a half-eaten deer next to me in the snow. A fly crawled across its eye, and its tongue lolled out of its dead mouth, making it look comical and pathetic, like an animal in a newspaper cartoon.

The snow was stained a fluorescent crimson where the deer's belly had been torn out.

My face and chest were sticky and red with the stuff. My throat was scabbed and scarred, and it stung; by the next full moon, it would be whole once more.

The sun was a long way away, small and yellow, but the sky was blue and cloudless, and there was no breeze. I could hear the roar of the sea some distance away.

I was cold and naked and bloody and alone. *Ah well*, I thought, *it happens to all of us in the beginning. I just get it once a month.*

I was painfully exhausted, but I would hold out until I found a deserted barn or a cave; and then I was going to sleep for a couple of weeks.

A hawk flew low over the snow toward me with something dangling from its talons. It hovered above me for a heartbeat, then dropped a small gray squid in the snow at my feet and flew upward. The flaccid thing lay there, still and silent and tentacled in the bloody snow.

I took it as an omen, but whether good or bad I couldn't say and I didn't really care any more; I turned my back to the sea, and on the shadowy town of Innsmouth, and began to make my way toward the city.

SWEETHEART COME

BY ALETHEA KONTIS

And so, at last, we come to the end of our journey, returning to the woods where it all began. And it is here, amongst the beasts and forest-songs, that I leave you in the lush and lovely company of Alethea Kontis's "Sweetheart Come."

This story was originally written for Up Jumped the Devil, *an anthology of original fiction inspired by the works of Nick Cave. It shares with Cave a love of the old tragic ballads that have soothed our poor broken hearts over the long course of humankind.*

I can think of no better, more beautiful way to bring this book to a close.

Sasha was fourteen when the villagers threw her to the wolves.

She was mute: a quirk that eventually unnerved enough people to justify her banishment to the Wild Wood. She surprised them all by emerging from the Wood many months later without a scratch and heavy with child. This time it was the villagers who were struck speechless, but—enchanted or cursed—no one challenged Sasha's right to be there. Upon her daughter's birth, Sasha caught the midwife with her haunting gray eyes and said, "Mara," clear as a bell. The rest of her secrets she kept. By the next full moon, Sasha was gone.

Mara was raised by the midwife, embraced by the villagers, and ended up earning her keep as a huntress. Her tracking skills were unmatched and she had a sixth sense about her prey—virtues which kept the food stores well-stocked through the cold winters. When Fate found the man to tame her wild nature, Mara had one daughter, Rose. Rose "had a nose," and grew to become one of the most sought-after cooks in five counties. The man who sought out her heart instead of her pies was a humble woodcutter, and together they had a daughter named Aurelia, with a voice that could sing the sun down from the sky. When she was of age, Aurelia took up with a band of wandering minstrels, and so was the first since her great-grandmother to leave the village. She and her beloved fiddle player were also the first to bear a son, Bane.

Bane had a shy smile, a quick wit, and a heart of gold. From his grandfather, Bane learned how to cleave a piece of wood in two with one stroke. From his grandmother (and from experience), he learned to tell the difference between good mushrooms and bad. From his father, he learned to play a variety of instruments well enough to coax out a melody for every occasion, but he preferred the fiddle. From his mother, Bane learned how to sing the sun down from the sky. Every evening they would trek to the edge of the village, to the top of the hill that looked down over the Wild Wood, and they would farewell the day. The selections varied with their moods and the seasons, but the last song was always the same lullaby Aurelia had sung to her son every night since his birth.

Have wonderful dreams, love
And dream while you wonder
Of things that are sure as
The sound of the thunder
Love leaves too sudden
And death comes too soon
And wolves they all bay at
The full of the moon

When the sound of his fiddle surpassed that of his voice, Bane played instead while his mother sang. And when his grandmother's apprentice herb-girl returned his shy smile, he asked her to marry him. And when Harvest became pregnant with their child, the nightmares began. For the first three months, one came at every full moon. Bane dreamt of running through the autumn trees at twilight to the top of the hill, hair brushed with dew by the welcome chill of the wind. There, along with his brethren, he turned up his face and howled to the sky. Harvest teased him about his twitching and the soft whimpering noises he made in his sleep.

In the second three months, the dreams increased with both frequency and intensity. Bane imagined himself grooming, hunting, mating, and feeding kits. He awoke angry, amorous, and exhausted in turns—sometimes all three at once. In the daylight hours he found himself resisting the urge to rub his face in the cool spring grass or growl at the rabbit vermin that ran amok in the garden.

In the seventh month of Harvest's pregnancy, Bane's dream-self fought brutally with a wolf from another pack. He awoke on all fours, looming over Harvest and staring at the crescent-shaped marks on her pale white throat. She had slapped him out of his vision; his cheeks stung from the deep scratches her prenatal nails had raked across him. In the midnight silence, a drop of blood fell from his face to her breast.

"Sweetheart," Harvest said calmly, "this has to stop. You have to go to the wolves and ask them for help."

On any other day those words might not have made a lick of sense to him, but right there, bathed in bright moonlight, with the salty taste of his wife's sweat and fear fresh upon his tongue, Bane knew what he had to do. When dawn broke, he packed up his fiddle and a blanket and set out for the hill at the edge of the Wild Wood. Harvest stayed behind at the garden gate, but not before handing him a small bag of food. She had noticed the look in his eye, the look of every man who has left home with no idea of when he might return, or if he should.

"Sweetheart, come back to me," she said as she embraced him. "Come back to me before our baby is born."

Bane kissed his wife hard, with all the love in his golden heart, and promised that he would.

Bane went to the top of the hill that overlooked the Wild Wood and stayed there for three days. He fiddled from twilight into the wee hours of the morning. He played until his throat went hoarse and his fingers bled. He collapsed on the cold, hard ground as the sun rose, breathed in the lingering scent of his wife on the blanket, and slept the day away. He woke in the late afternoon, broke his bread and had a small meal, and waited. He lifted his fiddle and bow in time to farewell the sun, and continued to serenade the waning moon until he could continue no longer. The wolves did not come.

The next day, Bane walked down the hill and into the Wild Wood. He walked through spider webs and sunlit meadows. Every morning he slept, every evening he walked, and every night he lifted his fiddle and bow and sang into the twilight. He slept fitfully on beds of hay and early summer wildflowers that made his golden heart ache for his wife and unborn child. Impatient and frustrated he wandered and played, played and wandered, deeper and deeper into the Wild Wood. Still, the wolves did not come.

After the new moon, after the darkest night in the thickest part of the deep Wood, the dreams returned. Some days he would wake without clothing, his skin covered in angry red scratches. Some days he awoke with blood caked on his lips that was not his own and a full belly. Sometimes he awoke so far from where he fell asleep that he spent the rest of the day following the scent of his blanket back to his fiddle. The smell of his wife was fading; Bane feared that one day he would awake and not be able to find his way back to it. To her.

Still every night he played, the calluses on his fingers growing thick as his limbs grew thin. He played songs of long ago and songs of yesterday. He played songs of adventure and songs of loss. He played teaching songs and drinking songs, songs of life and songs of death, songs for family and enemies. When he had played them all he made up new songs, songs for Harvest and their unborn child, and as he sang he wept tears onto the wood of his fiddle. But he always sang the sun down and up with a variation of that same old tune his mother had taught him.

I dream as I wander
And wandering dream

Through a wild and dark Wood where
I'm not what I seem
I'm lost and I'm lonely
And so with this tune
I call to the wolves
By the light of the moon

At last, on the first night of the full moon, Bane's song was answered by howling. He thought it was his imagination at first—he had imagined many things in his dream-wracked wanderings: the sound of Harvest calling his name, the smell of her skin, the warmth of her breath on the back of his neck. Invigorated, Bane ran up the nearest hill, climbed atop the largest rock there, and started the song again. Beneath his rough beard his smile grew with every howl and his golden heart ached to be so very near the end of his torment, to be so close again to the peaceful life he had before it was rudely interrupted by dreams of a life he didn't want.

The wolves poured down through the trees, their sleek bodies undulating in a neat, dangerous wave. They bound up the hill with predatory speed and encircled the rock on which he stood. Each wolf moved with preternatural grace in a dance as old as the hills themselves, ears perked up, mottled hair bristling, sharp teeth flashing, and for the first time it occurred to Bane to be afraid. He simply poured that fear into his song and used it to fuel his playing as the wolves settled in around him.

In the glow of the moonlight he could hear their breath, taste their scent, smell their fur, feel their hearts beating as one. In the glow of the moonlight his golden heart warred against itself—the half that yearned for freedom and his place in this pack, and the half that yearned for home and the rest of his soul. The circle of wolves parted and, in the glow of the moonlight, the alpha pair stepped forward and became human.

The male grew tall and lean. A thin coating of dark gray hair still covered his body, little enough for Bane to tell that every muscle was tensed and ready to strike if any of his suspicions were confirmed. The female was similarly wiry yet petite. The fuzz that coated her breasts and belly was mottled gray and russet; the rest of the hair that had covered her lupine form now cascaded down her back. There was something not quite right about her face, as if the human mouth she now wore couldn't accommodate all of her tearing, bone crunching teeth. But she pinned him with a yellow stare, and when she spoke, her words were clear.

"Come," she said, "come run with us, cousin."

His blood roared through his veins, pumped wildly through a heart as golden as her eyes in a mad rush of acquiescence. But her invitation had sounded too much like another plea his mind replayed every night when he collapsed in exhaustion and every morning when the sun nudged him awake: *Sweetheart, come back to me. Come back to me before the baby is born.*

"I cannot," he said, and there was far more regret in his voice than he intended. "Please," he implored. "Make the dreams stop."

She stretched out a hand to caress his bare foot, where it dangled down from the rock on which he sat. Her mate growled low in his throat. Her long, narrow palm was warm and rough, the nails that tipped her fingers dark and thick. It would be nothing for her to thrust those nails into his chest, tear out his traitorous golden heart, and replace it with moss and tree sap. "These dreams you dismiss so easily," she said, "they are my dreams."

"I am sorry," he said, and again the words dripped with regret.

"It is not a decision to make lightly," she said. "If I take the dreams from you, any part of you that was ever wolf will be gone forever." No more seeing in the dark. No more singing to the moon. No more smelling his way home. But he could not return to his wife and family-to-be as he was, so dangerous to their well-being and so much less than a man.

"Come run with us, cousin," she asked again. "Be sure that the choice you make is the right one."

He set his fiddle on the rock, hopped down into the swarm of giant, hungry wolves, and slipped his hand into that strange and deadly palm.

Harvest didn't tell her parents about her husband's mad journey for fear they would come and take her away. Her home was the one thing that kept her tethered to sanity. Bane's family was very supportive: During the days, Rose helped her in the garden and her husband built a crib for the nursery. In the evenings, Aurelia and the fiddler played and sang for their supper, lullabying their daughter-in-law and soon-to-be grandchild into bed. For all the well-meaning company, it was the dead of night Harvest lived for most. She would stare out the window, wish on the stars, and blow kisses to the bone-colored moon. She would listen for the creaks and whispers that echoed in the empty corners of the dark world. They had the timbre of Bane's voice and they promised her they would return home before their baby was born. They promised.

The night there was no moon Harvest felt the loneliest she'd ever been in her life. But were it not for the absence of her celestial companion, she never would have noticed the yellow eyes watching her from the far side of the garden. At the same moment there was a kick in her belly—she gasped, and in a flash the wolf was gone.

Harvest looked for the wolf every night, and every night it was there. It never approached the house, simply watched the house from the same spot at the opposite edge of the garden. Harvest felt an irrational kinship with the wolf. She imagined that they were both lonely, both burdened by responsibility, both waiting for something they weren't exactly sure of, and both wanting something they knew they only had a slim chance of obtaining. But the hope was there.

Harvest began leaving food out for the wolf, sometimes not finishing her evening meal on purpose so that there would be scraps left. She walked them as far as she dared, to the near edge of the garden. She never saw the wolf's eyes in the daylight and she never saw it eat, but come dawn the bowl was always empty.

The first night of the full moon, Harvest walked the bowl of scraps out to the garden and saw an old man standing where her wolf had been. Short, dark gray hair covered his skin evenly, barring shocks of pure white on his forehead and temples. He was darkness, but for his sharp teeth and those piercing yellow eyes. Harvest dropped the bowl and squeaked out a tiny shriek, immediately wishing she was a braver woman.

"I liked you better as a wolf," she said.

The wolf-man laughed hoarsely at her statement, baring his mouthful of deadly teeth in the process. Harvest froze, ordering herself to remain calm and show no fear. This was one of the last times her baby would be able to feel her every emotion, and she refused to let cowardice be one of them. *See, baby, your mother is strong. One day, you will grow up and be this strong.*

"You must come with me," said the wolf-man.

"I do not have the dreams," said Harvest. "That is my husband."

"It is for your husband's sake that you must come," said the wolf-man. "I fear for the loss of your husband to the wolves."

Harvest found his phrasing odd—it sounded more like the wolves would steal him away rather than kill him. "He will come back to me," Harvest said defiantly.

"The wolves can be rather persuasive," he said.

"He will come back to me," Harvest repeated. "He promised."

"Yes," said the wolf-man. "But what if he is not capable of keeping that promise? What if he needs your help?"

"Then I would come with you," said Harvest without hesitation. She pulled her kerchief from the pocket of her apron, tied her hair back, and walked across the garden to the wolf-man's side. With a nod and a blur that sparked through the hair on her arms, he quietly transformed back into a wolf and bounded into the darkness, leading Harvest step by trotting step to the heart of the Wild Wood.

She followed him to the top of the hill that overlooked the Wood, recalling the many evenings she had sat with Bane and Aurelia or softly sang along while they serenaded the sunset. Harvest had a small voice, like a chickadee, but her notes still rang true. Aurelia had the voice of a whippoorwill, throaty and loud, with seemingly endless stamina. Bane's voice was a dove's, low and haunting. When he sang of love it made her yearn, and when he sang of loss it made her cry. Harvest placed a hand on the cool, smooth bark of the tree where she had sat to watch him, an invisible silhouette against the moon, and she felt both those things. The wolf huffed to get her attention and she followed him down the hill, into the Wood.

The pair of them made good time, for all that she was so heavily pregnant and he was so terribly impatient. The wolf would growl every time she had to stop to rest, but she knew him for the old man he was and could tell it was all bluster. He growled as well when she paused to look for herbs: greens to keep her strong and flowers to keep her nourished and roots to keep the baby from kicking his way out of the womb before she was ready. Before her beloved sweetheart fulfilled his promise.

They walked in fits and starts until dusk of the next day, or when the trees grew so thick it was hard to tell when day ended and night began. Harvest found a mossy patch on the north side of a large tree that seemed the least rocky and bug-infested. She sat with her back to the tree and crossed her arms over her belly. She wished she had thought to bring a blanket, or a slice of bread, or a chunk of cheese, or her sanity. She wished she had something of Bane's with her, something that might draw him like a lodestone. Something that might speak to him if he could no longer understand her words. The baby flipped over inside her, settling down for the night and reminding her that she did have something of Bane's. The most important thing of all.

She shivered again and the wolf approached her, slinking out of the shadows with his head and tail down to show that he was not a threat. Not knowing the proper way of things, Harvest risked stroking the wolf's muzzle with a gentle hand. The shock of white stared up at her like a third eye seeking deep into her soul. His charcoal fur was thick and rough and smelled of pine and grass and dirt and musk and blood and strength and ferocity. *You have some of that strength in you, baby. One day you will grow up to be this strong.* She sighed. *And one day, I hope your beloved is not chasing* you *into the Wild Wood.*

The wolf knelt down and laid that giant, dark head full of teeth in her lap. Harvest stroked his fur absentmindedly and let his warmth seep down through her legs and up through her belly into her neck and shoulders and arms. Still worried yet safe from harm, Harvest let herself sleep.

It took Harvest and the wolf less than five days to reach Bane's rock, as they were tracking prey and not lost or wandering or falling asleep and waking up somewhere else every other evening. And all the strength and all the stamina Harvest had been absorbing from the moon and the wolf and the Wood suddenly left her. She stretched her arms up until she felt her shoulders pop, pulled her husband's fiddle down from the rock, and collapsed. The tears she shed over the mahogany fell in the same places as the tears he had shed over her before he had transformed into a beast that did not keep promises because he no longer knew what promises were.

Grief and fear and sadness overtook Harvest, seizing her body in violent spasms, and the babe—rightfully so—decided he wanted no part of it. Harvest screamed into the empty daylight. The wolf snapped at the air in frustration. The ground beneath her, already damp with her tears, now muddied with the babe's rushing preamble. "Come back to me," she whispered to no one. "Sweetheart, come back to me."

The old wolf was gone even before she finished speaking, leaving Harvest alone with only the wind and the air and what courage she was able to summon between bouts of racking pain. Her baby was tearing her body apart, her husband had shattered her heart, and she had clearly lost her mind. She wondered how much of her soul had to be torn away before even the gods didn't recognize her anymore. She wondered about the color of the sky, and exactly how much grass she could pull up with one handful. She thought about her own mother, and Bane's. She thought about the tune they played to sing down the sun, the tune that called the wolves. The fiddle reminded her of the melody, but she couldn't remember the words through the pain, so she made up her own.

I'm missing my sweetheart
My sweet heart does miss
The sound of his voice and
The feel of his kiss
The wind it blows colder
The day's light grows dim
But damned if I'm having
This babe without him!

Harvest laughed loud, giddy, hysterical, frantic, and on the next wave that lifted her back off the ground, she saw the wolf pack surrounding her. There was too much love and too much hate and too much of every other emotion warring inside Harvest for her to pick one. As there was only a half moon peeking through the twilight clouds, the female who spoke to her changed only her face so that her words might be understood. She sat neatly, with her long tail wrapped around her paws like a canine sphinx with a mouthful of knives.

For a moment, the pain was so sharp Harvest could not feel her legs. She broke a sweat maintaining a level voice. "Let him go."

"Our cousin runs with us by choice," said the face.

Harvest bit the inside of her lip until she tasted blood. She refused to lose her courage in the face of her adversary. As the pain tore through her in deeper, more frequent bursts, she repeated the only words left to her.

"Come back to me," she asked the sky, for she knew not which wolf in the pack was her husband and that pain dwarfed the babe's like a tear in a rainstorm. The charcoal wolf—her wolf—nudged one beast forward and she saw that its eyes were blue-green, not yet the bile amber-yellow of the rest of the pack.

"Come back to me," she said to him. Her husband recognized her with those still-human eyes—eyes that had traveled just as hard a road as she—but she could tell he did not understand her words.

"Come back to me," she whispered once more. It didn't matter that he had left her. It didn't matter that he now wore a skin of fur and walked on four legs. It didn't matter that she had been forced to walk leagues to track him down. He was here and the babe wasn't born yet; there was still time to keep his promise.

"If he returns to you," said the sphinx, "he will forsake every part of his wolf blood." The bitch had the nerve to preen after her statement. Had she been within arm's reach, Harvest was sure she could have snapped her neck.

Harvest lay back on the rough ground. Invisible thorns pushed their way into the ends of every nerve in her body. She took deep breaths and saw pinpricks of light. Beyond them, a few bright stars sprinkled across the heavens like the rocks under her spine, stars she had wished on since she was old enough to know what wishing was for. "Go then," she said to those stars. "For he has now forsaken me."

A wolf approached her, but it was the charcoal gray. The elder brushed her neck with his muzzle, then leapt over her seizing body to follow the tails of the pack that had already left him behind.

Harvest broke her nails in the dirt and concentrated on the wind and the air and the babe tearing its way out of her. *Courage, little one*, she told it. *It's just you and me, now*. Wind and air and pain. Breathe. Wind and air and pain. Breathe. Wind and air... and a hand on her forehead. She opened her eyes to see Bane standing over her, scrawny and shaggy and smelly. His blessedly furless skin was riddled with angry scratches and bruises as deep and purple as the skin beneath each of his blue-green eyes, and it was the most beautiful sight Harvest had ever seen.

The remnants of his wolf magic fled from his palm into her body, Harvest could taste and feel and smell and live it as it waned, healing her heart and filling her womb before it died completely. As her burdens lifted, the babe escaped her body in a rush of fluids. Bane wrapped his son in the blanket he had left behind and the three of them lay quietly together under the stars.

In addition to a certain amount of strength, stamina, and the ability to see in the dark, Bane lost his voice. He still spoke a little, but his words growled out from low in the back of his throat. There would be no more singing for him. He could still play, though, and when the rest of his memories came back to him, he accompanied his mother to the top of the hill in the evenings to sing down the sun. Harvest made the journey as well, carrying baby Hunter until he was old enough to walk. She sang as well, and though her voice never carried the force of Aurelia's, it grew from that of a chickadee into a lark.

It was spring before any of the wolves dared show their faces. When one did, it was that of the charcoal gray elder. He came to them at the full moon, and it seemed that his coat was sprinkled with far more white than Harvest had noticed previously. She was glad he had returned, so she could properly thank him for fetching her and protecting her. Bane was less happy about the wolf's presence.

"Why are you here?" he snapped. For all that he was pure human now, he acted more like a wolf than before.

"I have come to ask your forgiveness," said the elder. "Our female trapped you, and in doing so, she put you in danger." He looked down at the babe Harvest cradled in her arms. "She put all three of you in danger."

"I want nothing from you," Bane growled.

"The gift is already given," said the elder. "Whether or not you use it is up to you."

"What is it?" asked Harvest.

"The gift is the song," said the wolf. "We took much from you that made you valuable, and for that we must give something in return. Balance must be maintained." He motioned down to the fiddle that hung at Bane's side. "Play the song you know," said the elder, "the song with which you farewell the day. The song with which you called the wolves. If you play the song as you walk through the Wood, no harm will come to you."

"There is no song," said Bane. "I can no longer sing."

"The magic is in the melody," the wolf said to him. And then to Harvest, "The words are yours alone." He placed a palm on Bane's chest. It startled him out of his scowl, but he did not flinch away. "You may not have yellow eyes, cousin, but you still have a golden heart. Perhaps one day you will find forgiveness there." He let his hand fall. "Not today. But one day." He turned to leave, but Harvest stopped him.

"What of our son?" she asked. "Will he experience the same thing when his first child is born?"

"It will not take him as strongly and it may not come at the same time," said the elder, "but he will have to make a choice one day, as all young men do." Harvest mirrored her husband's scowl and the wolf laughed. "Worry not, little mother. Your son has your strength. He will survive. We all will."

Bane and Harvest watched the wolf walk across the garden and into the trees until the shadows swallowed him. Bane lifted his fiddle to play the song once more and Harvest added the words—her own simple words in her clear, simple voice.

> And just as it should, son
> Our happy tale ends with
> Our family three and
> A wolf for a friend
> If life makes you lonely
> And trouble's your boon
> Just sing this wolf song
> By the light of the moon

Bane drew out the last note almost longer than the night itself. When Harvest turned to look at him he stared back at her, his golden heart smiling through his blue-green eyes. She cradled their babe in one arm, and the other hand she held out to him. "Sweetheart, come in to dinner."

Bane lowered his fiddle, slipped his hand into her soft, delicate palm, and followed behind them.

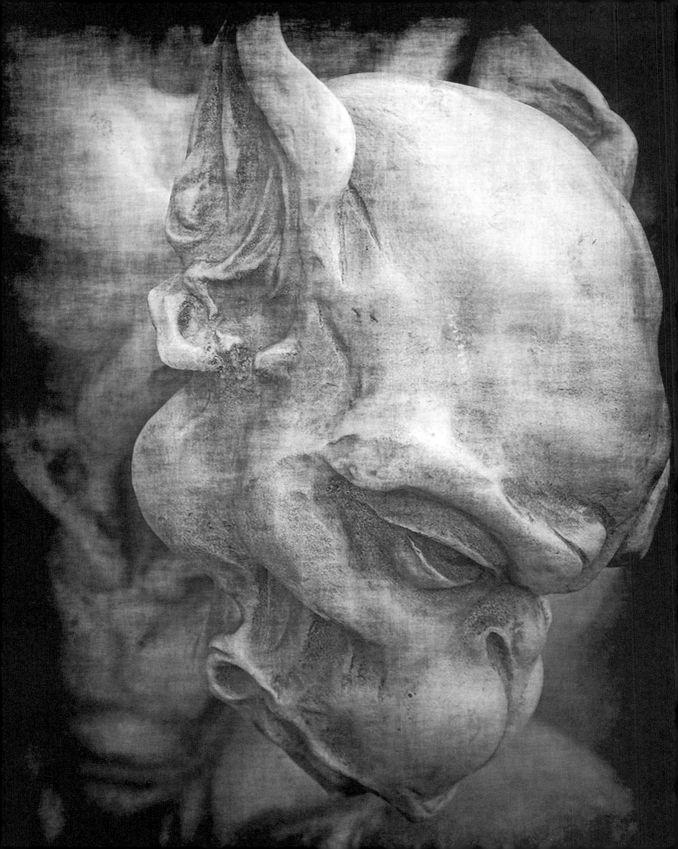

ON WEREWOLVES: HISTORICAL ROOTS

BY CHRISTOPHER KAMPE AND ANTHONY GAMBOL

In approximately 430 BC, Herodotus wrote of the Neuri tribe that "it seems that these people are wizards; for both the Scythians and the Greeks who live in Scythia say that each year every Neurian turns into a wolf for a few days and returns again to his own shape."

Herodotus may here be making the first explicit reference to werewolves in world literature. The region he describes roughly correlates to the border of modern Belarus, Poland, and the Ukraine, its people the progenitors of the modern Slavs, among whom later tales of werewolves have been so prevalent. What's notable is how passing the reference is; it's merely a quirky instance of some local color (he goes on to say how he doesn't believe it).

Herodotus also tells of the youth of Cyrus the Great, first in the line of Achaemenid kings and founder of the Persian Empire. Cyrus was prophesized to overthrow his grandfather Astyages, king of the Medes, on account of which Astyages commanded his steward to dispatch the boy. Through guilt, Cyrus was passed to a lower slave, a herdsman, who was ordered to expose and kill the child.

Cyrus was likewise pitied by the herdsman and his wife, who passed Cyrus off as their own (recently stillborn) child and raised him. The name of the herdsman's wife, likewise a slave to the king, was translated by Herodotus from the Median to *Kuno* in Greek, literally "bitch" or "she-dog."

Eventually Cyrus's noble nature presented itself and he was reunited with his true parents. In further discussion, Herodotus mentions that Cyrus's parents realized the value of the story; it lent depth to their son's nobility to have mythological origins, so they spread that he had literally been raised by a she-wolf. Cyrus went on to found and greatly expand the Persian Empire, one of the most powerful empires in the history of the world, through military conquest.

This simple tale, a royal servant rearing a royal child, gives a plausible foundation to such stories. The Persian Empire is not unique in such a story about its founder. Romulus and Remus, mythical founders of Rome, are likewise purported to have been suckled by a she-wolf.

Herodotus is known for his fanciful stories; this tale of Cyrus's youth is almost certainly not true. However, it hints at a theme that pervades many, most, or all of later werewolf stories. Humans are frail creatures. We gain our strength by the faculties of our mind. Physically, and perhaps instinctually, there is something more powerful about an animal or a person closely attuned to animals. Mythic heroes and, frequently, those that founded dynasties, have been portrayed as reared by animals. The founding kings of Persia and Rome have a bit of that in them, and it places them solidly above their subjects to have both human faculties and the animal's strength, and perhaps lends some form of justification or explanation of the lordship.

These founding stories are not the extent of such human/animal conflation in antiquity. Zeus turned into a bull to seduce Europa, and into a swan for Leda. The Egyptian pantheon is full of gods with animal attributes, and anthropomorphized animals. In Ovid's *Metamorphoses*, the myth of Lycaon bears special attention. Lycaon served Zeus human flesh and Zeus turned him into a wolf for his indiscretion:

> He cut the throat of a . . . hostage . . . and when this flesh was served
> to me . . . I destroyed his dwelling and his worthless household gods, with

vengeful flames. Terrified, he fled, and on the silent fields howling in frustrated attempts to speak; he rages and his greedy jaws, desiring their usual slaughter, turn on the sheep and rejoice in their blood. His face sprouts shaggy hair, his arms change to legs; he became a wolf that walked like his old form. He has the same gray hair, and the same vicious face, and the same shining eyes, and the same ferocious appearance.

One house fell, but not one house deserved to die; evil spread out over all the world and reigned— man has fallen into villainy. May they all more quickly pay the penalties which they deserve to suffer; such my wisdom establishes. (I:199–249)

Here, it is a man's evil that leads to his transformation, although, notably, the language is ambiguous about the exact extent of his transformation. The monster was with him all along. Similar stories are told by Petronius and Pliny the Elder. In these early stories, there is a gravity to consorting with beasts. It is the province of gods and heroes, and gods among men.

Although some of the old stateliness survived, in time, such grand associations relaxed somewhat. Some Norse warriors, known as berserkers, are claimed to have donned the hides of bears and worked themselves into an animalistic, hypnotic frenzy before battle. Medieval Irish texts speak of Cy Roi, an ancient shape-changing king whose name means something like "hound of the battlefield." Despite such pockets of respectability, increasingly the werewolf is associated with mystics and witches, and evil in general.

In Norse mythology, Fenfir was a child of Loki who took the form of a great wolf. He was restrained by the gods (costing Tyr a hand) and subdued. It is said that at Ragnarok he will break his chains and join the giants in their war against the gods; he will take the ultimate prize by killing and consuming Odin, king of the gods.

The Hebrew holy work *Sefer Hasidim*, which was published in Germany in the sixteenth century but written perhaps centuries before, also speaks to the subject. Alukah (more frequently associated with demons or vampires) is represented as a blood-sucking human who can change into a wolf at will. This creature is also attested to in the Old Testament (Prov. 30:15). There, however, it is simply a bloodsucking creature that is never satisfied, compared to other insatiable devourers as a symbol of gluttony and greed. *Sefer Hasidim* seems to conflate the Pentateuch's Alukah (frequently translated as "leach") with more contemporary northern European traditions of monsters. Such conflation is not unique.

Although we now think of the dog as man's best friend, we must remember that, historically, man has not always held the animal in such high regard. Wolves were seen as cunning beasts that slaughtered man's flocks; because of the dog's nature as a scavenger, the creature developed a connection to death and the underworld, whether as the harbingers of Hecate (bride of death and patron of witches) or servants of Anubis (the Egyptian god of the underworld).

As dogs were often found lurking around and scavenging from unburied corpses, the widespread belief developed that they held the restless spirits of those who had died after iniquitous living or met with particularly unsettling ends.

Though not werewolves per se, both Asian and European culture writes of evil spirits who take on dog form. While many cultures were more permissive of shape shifters, Christianity saw them as abominations who operated contrary to the very will of God—the dog or wolf was generally regarded as a servant of the devil, if not the devil himself. In Goethe's *Faust*, the devil first appeared to the protagonist in the form of a black dog before taking on the guise of a man. A roaming wolf is an obvious villain when we are meant to be Christ's flock. If a man had somehow gained the unholy ability to take on the accursed form of a dog, it could only be through some covenant with Satan; any man who formed such a covenant had divorced himself from morality and was seen as an agent of damnation.

Because of the developing connotations of evil, and in large part through the actions of the Church, many mentally ill and particularly violent criminals were increasingly accused or confessed of being werewolves. After eating several children, Gilles Garnier was apprehended, admitted to being a werewolf, and was burned at the stake. Jacques Rollet, the werewolf of Paris, was similarly convicted and burned at the stake after eating children. Such accounts likely derived from and reinforced the more traditional myths.

Medieval folklore held that if you cut a werewolf in human form, fur would emerge from within the wound. In Russian myth, one could tell a werewolf by the hair of its tongue. Serbian werewolves were only active during the warmer months, presumably when there were more travelers roaming; during the winter times they would shed their wolf coats and leave them dangling from the trees—a trait not entirely dissimilar to the Navajo *yee naaldlooshii* (skin-walkers) who, like European witches, would don the pelts of wolves and then assume their forms.

According to Armenian folklore, a woman who had committed a vile sin would become a werewolf for seven years; during the span of this curse a gnawing hunger would overtake her, ultimately driving her to devour her own children. La Bête du Gévaudan, the fabled eighteenth-century beast who was credited with over a hundred murders and twice as many attacks, was widely regarded as a werewolf due to its massive size and uncanny ability to elude capture. Although many put forth a gallant effort to find and exterminate the beast (and many hunters emerged with pelts they claimed belonged to the beast), the killings did not cease until 1767, when a local hunter reportedly killed a giant canine with a silver bullet of his own manufacture—though such a myth probably emerged well after the fact. Many have sought to explain these occurrences through exotic animals or exaggerations of actual wolf attacks, but many people of the time felt that the beast was a punishment from God set upon a sinful world.

A variety of authors and historians have posited that the myth of the werewolf existed to explain murderers and serial killers: specifically their tendencies to prey on children, desecrate the corpses (often through cannibalism), and kill in cycles. In the past (and still) people found it immensely difficult to conceive of any human's doing these horrible things, so they created a beast that was able to hide among them. It is indistinguishable from us and yet, by his actions, distinctively inhuman. The myths explained the unexplainable; how through ritual or possession some external force might turn a man against his own. Perhaps lurking behind the myths, what we'd prefer not to consider, is that there is no external force that drives the beast; rather, some old and bestial component of ourselves. It is free from laws and morals, is violent and rapacious, and is any one of us at any time.

The myth of lycanthropy similarly lends itself to the mundane explanation of outbreaks of rabies or other diseases, when medicine was inadequate to diagnose or treat them. A man is bitten by a feral dog, the wound festers, and the disease sets in. The man becomes feverish; though his body boils he avoids water. Acute pain sets in and his mind is unable to cope. His moods become uncontrollable and his actions violent; he becomes a danger to those around him: at any moment he might lose himself and attack. Whoever gets bitten by him will likewise find themselves infected and they will undergo the same changes before slipping into a coma and dying quietly.

However, this theory might be anachronistic; a disease explains everything to our modern minds for us too neatly: why a man might go bad, turn upon his family, murder his children, and eat their flesh as he might a pig. He might be rationalized and forgiven as the victim of a virus. We, too, look for some outside force to explain why a person would suddenly abandon morality and perform unspeakable acts against his own kith and kin, because the alternative, that man's humanity is precarious, is an unacceptable conclusion.

Furthermore, following the legends, we can't easily describe werewolves as victims only of rabies, porpheria, or hypertrichosis. This is especially true when we consider that such tales are not exclusively European in origin, or that the tales were entirely uniform. In not all cases is the man bitten by a wolf, or is driven from the sun, or is even covered by hair. Myths about werewolves or similar creatures appear throughout all cultures and the range of the creatures' origins, from pacts with the devil, to being bitten by one infected, to the mere donning of a belt or the application of an ointment, and are so disparate in rationale and appearance that it is difficult to tie them to a single phenomenon.

The wolf was a common and feared predator in Europe, and so many of their tales vilify it. For example, in Romania, the *pricolici* is a malevolent undead spirit in the form of a wolf who was said to be the reincarnation of violent men. Other cultures give rise to stories similar in spirit but with distinctly local elements, frequently with the most feared predator in the area.

Leyak of Indonesia steals the entrails of corpses and, sometimes, the sleeping to use in a potion which will transform him into a tiger. *Seua saming* in Thai folklore is another weretiger, which uses guile or seduction to trap and eat its victims. In Korea, *kumiho* is a fox that takes the form of a woman (usually) to seduce or trick its victims and do evil upon them. In Olmec Mesoamerica, the werejaguar was a very common motif, and perhaps a deity. Nigeria and Persia have werehyenas called *bultungin* and *kaftar*, respectively. And not all of such stories are relegated to myths of the misty past.

Such ideas about predatory creatures and such notions of evil inherent to it gradually served to remove most of the humanity from the werewolf. We have refined the creature. Predators are not just strong; they are cunning. Wolves themselves are regarded as tricksters in several traditions (such as the *amaguq* of the Canadian Eskimos, the *kitsune* of Japan, or even the Big Bad Wolf of European folktales), but we have largely removed that capacity from modern werewolves, and perhaps that's why they remain so vivid.

Werewolves frighten us because they *are* us, or at least us as we could be. They represent the willing or unwilling subrogation of our very humanity, casting off our semblances of superiority and putting us into the world with all the other creatures. We would like to think that we could restrain the beast within us, that we could apply those animal strengths to positive ends. However, the application of those capacities must, by necessity, retard the use of our higher faculties and devolve the possessor.

We maintain a romantic fascination with the concept: we'd all like to be imbued with a higher power. But such a power is in its character uncontrollable, and we would truly become the beast; nothing less, nothing more. Until we became civilized, such a spirit was a good thing: it offered us survival. But a beast of this sort has no place in society, even if it still has a place in us. When you release it, as time goes on, it becomes increasingly difficult to recapture it.

Man knows that, in an instant, he can be subsumed by his more primal self. A werewolf is what is left when we strip away the civilized being. At the same time, they also evoke a very real fear of death; a fear of being hunted and killed and eaten by predators, either beast or man. Werewolves embody the full experience of our lives in nature and, as Mark Twain said, "The fear of death follows from the fear of life. A man who lives fully is prepared to die at any time." But we do fear death; and so we fear living fully. We are animals; but we are more than animals. We would like to think that counts for something. We are predators; and we are prey. We are comfortable with neither.

IT'S ONLY NATURAL: WEREWOLVES AND SHAPESHIFTERS IN POPULAR CULTURE

BY JOHN SKIPP AND CODY GOODFELLOW

The lycan and shape-shifter boom is on. There are no two ways about it. We are in the midst of an unprecedented explosion in were-curiosity, riding part and parcel with the boom in supernatural interest in general.

A lot of this, of course, can be attributed to millennial fever: the apocalyptic terror that grips our species every time the calendar zeroes out on another thousand-year cycle. That's just the way we are. Religions split and all manner of esoteric beliefs and suppositions spike in a now-traditional tizzy of End Times panic.

But while some reach for God, some reach for science, some reach for a gun or a bottle or both, many find themselves yearning for a deeper connection to nature, a recapturing of all that's been lost.

And it is there that the were-things can be found. Never more populous, more feared or desired.

The dream—and nightmare—of becoming a beast is almost as old as humanity's realization that we were separated from the animal kingdom. The earliest depictions of gods, from the paleolithic *Le Sorcier* at *Les Trois-Frères* to the polymorphic courtships of Zeus, revered the ability to regress into bestiality as a magical power reserved for gods.

Mortals were forever being demoted into cattle, crickets, spiders, and stags as punishment for offending the gods, but the horror of losing one's civilized self came much later. Although the fear of being devoured by beasts is older than humankind itself, the fear of becoming one did not creep into popular culture until the veneer of civility was something prized, then taken for granted.

Tall tales from every corner of the globe abound with tales of shape-shifting predators walking among us, and few ancient monsters made the leap as easily into the modern age. But when the lurid warnings of folklore were replaced by fictional entertainment, the werewolf became a fearsome reminder of how meaningless our progress and modern security really is.

The werewolf is the totemic face of Western humanity's dark side, but his growth has been stunted in the popular arts. Without an iconic legend like Dracula or Frankenstein's monster, the werewolf story became a rote chain of circumstance that could happen to anyone in wild and unfamiliar surroundings. The complex compulsion that drew us back despite our fears was, for centuries, too terrible to confront.

BOOKS

The earliest fictional appearance of a werewolf was probably *Wagner, the Wehr-Wolf* by G. W. M. Reynolds, in 1846, about ten years after Hans Christian Andersen first published his *Fairy Tales*. This garou-some penny dreadful enjoyed sales rivaling those of Dickens, but it did not appear to be launching a trend.

Sabine Baring-Gould released *The Book of Werewolves* roughly a decade later. This academic treatise/nineteenth-century *Hollywood Babylon* for werethings drew frank parallels between the legends and heinous case studies of cannibals and assorted psychotics, including the noted serial rapist and murderer of children Gilles de Rais.

Two other books showed up at the close of the nineteenth century to bring science center stage in the discussion. The modern age offered many new paths to transformation, but science was even more devious than Satan when it came to granting wishes.

In *The Strange Case of Dr. Jeckyll and Mr. Hyde* (1886), Robert Louis Stevenson's mild-mannered Jeckyll does not so much change as unleash the child-trampling Hyde from deep within his restrained Victorian shell.

Cutting even closer to the bone of the themes of lycanthropy, Hyde did not need to hide behind an animal's mask, but showed a crass, violent beast that could easily pass for human. As such, the Jeckyll trope has spawned its own hosts of reboots, reimaginings, and parodies, from *Mary Reilly* to *The Nutty Professor.*

Here were the first real stirrings of the idea that the beast could offer a desirable alternative to its human host, an alpha predator lost along our evolutionary path.

Fabian Socialist H. G. Wells prefigured *Animal Farm* by decades with 1896's *The Island of Dr. Moreau*, where tortured test animals find the forced ascent to semihumanity to be far more painful than the natural state from which Moreau tries to "save" them. In the Sayer of the Law's flat commandment "not to walk on all fours," we hear the backhanded rebuke of colonial paternalism, and the idea of civilization as a tonic for all humanity's ills.

From there, it's pretty slim pickin's in the novel-length department for round about seventy years. Guy Endore's 1934 classic *The Werewolf of Paris* remains the standout of that span.

Short stories and novellas eagerly filled the gap, with wonderful works by the likes of Saki, A. Merritt, Seabury Quinn, Algernon Blackwood, Ambrose Bierce, Manly Wade Wellman, Robert Bloch, Ray Bradbury, Anthony Boucher, and John Collier periodically poking up to tickle and haunt the possibilities of transformation and otherness.

Three writers in particular were to have a huge effect on nearly everything that followed: two with single, seminal works, and one with an enormous body of transhuman blasphemy.

When traveling salesman Gregor Samsa wakes up as a giant cockroach (or "vermin") in Franz Kafka's "The Metamorphosis," his descent into subhumanity is just getting warmed up. It's not just that he's changed; it's how much everyone's changed toward him, every speck of his value stripped along with his identity, until it's as if he'd never been human at all.

Seeking more paranoia than pathos, "Who Goes There?" by John W. Campbell (as Don A. Stuart) features a chameleonic alien that infiltrates Big Magnet Antarctic outpost and replaces men and sled dogs with alien imposters. Although its native form is blue and worm-haired with three glowing red eyes, the creature perfectly imitates those it eats, forcing the team to separate the men from the beasts with a blood test.

(Screenwriter Charles Lederer dropped the polymorphic nature of the Thing when he adapted the novella into *The Thing from Another World* for Howard Hawks, choosing instead a cheaply realized but effective "intellectual carrot." Bill Lancaster's script for John Carpenter's 1982 *The Thing* definitively realized the original vision of the monstrous mimic, and an upcoming remake of their film promises to realize it even harder and louder.)

But Campbell's, Lederer's and Carpenter's Things all owe their polymorphic natures and icy, interstellar origins to the shapeless shoggoths of H.P. Lovecraft's "At the Mountains of Madness" (1936). Bred as slaves to the alien Old Ones that ruled young earth and created organic life on a lark, the shoggoths were gigantic amoebae capable of producing eyes, limbs and other organs at will from their protoplasmic bodies. Millions of years after they rebelled, the shoggoths still haunt the Antarctic ruins of the Old Ones' cities, speaking with imitations of their masters' weird trumpet-mouths.

Transformation of a more permanent nature preoccupied horror writers of earlier ages, and clearly some racism lay at the back of their fears of subhumans' sporting with monstrous mates. H. P. Lovecraft repeatedly showed remote rural communities devolving into burrowing mole-creatures or piscine hybrids, in "The Lurking Fear" and "The Shadow over Innsmouth," while "The Dunwich Horror" suggested that the countryside abounded with horny abominations looking to drag humanity to the deep end of the gene pool.

In fantasy as well as horror lit, the human form became more mutable than ever before, but the werewolf and its kin were still as far from the spotlight as one could get. One could make a case that Wesstern civilization was not ready for a real werewolf.

Science fiction grandmaster Jack Williamson struck a huge blow for shape-shifters everywhere in 1948 with *Darker Than You Think*, a dreamlike dark fantasy in which werethings turn out to be a forgotten, yet hostile subspecies of humankind.

Defeated and driven underground in ancient history, the Children of Night lurk in the shadows to seduce or kill those on the edge of learning their secret. Outside its influence on pulp culture, Williamson's malign lycanthrope April Bell hijacked the imagination of rocket scientist and Crowley disciple Jack Parsons, who tried to summon the Scarlet Woman in an occult ritual along with fellow self-styled sorcerer L. Ron Hubbard.

Things began to pick up in the late 1970s, when Gary Bradner's *The Howling* and Whitley Strieber's *The Wolfen* caught the attention of Hollywood. Angela Carter's *The Bloody Chamber* and David Morrell's *The Totem* brought the decade to a notable close.

The '80s were the first boom decade, with more than sixty werewolf or shape-shifterly titles emerging on the crest of the horror wave, roughly doubling the output of the previous century. Only a handful of titles stand out, among them Thomas Tessier's *The Nightwalker*; Tanith Lee's *Lycanthia, or The Children of Wolves*; *The Anubis Gates* by Tim Powers; Robert R. McCammon's *The Wolf's Hour*; Melanie Tem's *Wilding*; Clive Barker's multifarious *Books of Blood*; and Stephen King's best-selling proto-YA novel *Cycle of the Werewolf*.

As the horror boom busted in the early '90s, escalation remained in full swing, with a dozen werewolf titles a year the norm, until we were drowning in books that nobody wanted to buy.

Enter R. L. Stine and the *Goosebumps* series of spooky stories for extremely young adults. Picking up where Nancy Drew, the Hardy Boys, and Scooby Doo left off, Stine grabbed the kiddie attention span and ran it up the best-seller charts with a keen insight into the slow, scary metamorphosis of puberty. Grownups may have wearied of mediocre horror stories, but kids knew that even watered-down were-tales like 1995's *Bad Moonlight* were still kind of totally cool.

Fantasy tales were proliferating, as well. Edging slowly but decisively toward the romantic and idealized: the notion that werebeasts were closer to the truth than we were. That they weren't less than us, but *more* than us. That we had much to learn.

Which brings us to the twenty-first century, and the staggering success of paranormal romance fiction, Laurell K. Hamilton's *Lunatic Café* and Kelley Armstrong's *Bitten* paving the way for the Sookie Stackhouse fables of Charlaine Harris, the Kitty Norville tales of Carrie Vaughn, and an onslaught of best sellers far too numerous to mention.

Young adult fiction has been busy as well. The *Wereling* series by Stephen Cole, the *Demonata* series by Darren Shan, and Maggie Stiefvater's *Shiver* being only a few examples.

Bridging the gap between grownup and YA proved the most fertile ground of all, producing both J. K. Rowling's Harry Potter epic saga and the Darkness cycle of Stephanie Meyer, which both offered fierce but goodhearted werewolves. From there, seemingly all things spin off, leaving many naively believing that Rowling and Meyer were where werewolves began.

Which raises the question: Has all of our fictional inquiry into the nature of werebeasts—the human/animal interface at its most direct and confrontational—been funneled down to these popular, yet toothless, trends?

The answer, of course, is no. In the roughly six hundred books about shape-shifting that have been published so far this century, serious kick-ass work has persevered outside the mainstream, as it always does: from the small-press incisive cult horror of Steven Wedel's "Murdered by Human Wolves" to the delirious big-time literary soul-acuity of Michael Chabon's "Werewolves in Their Youth" (which, along with Roald Dahl's "Royal Jelly" and Clive Barker's "Son of Celluloid," Skipp most wishes he could have included in this book.)

But the question cheapens itself, because it suggests that something fascinating and exhilarating isn't happening *within the mainstream itself.* And it most definitely is. Otherwise, people would not be flocking toward it.

As of this writing, the scrupulous online data service SciFi Reader now lists 767 werewolf books, not even counting were-wombats, were-weasels, or were-wolverines. We suspect the number to be nearing twice that, by the time you read these words.

Which is to say that the literature is expanded at an even greater geometric rate than the human race itself. And all of it—from the best to the worst, the most popular to the most esoteric—offers clues to our relationship with each other, the natural world, and the nature-subsuming or obliterating world we have created.

As this book hopes to reflect, there is something for every taste in the fullness of shape-shifting literature.

FILM

With movies came the Renaissance of the werewolf, for not until film was there a story with the werewolf as doomed protagonist: poor old Larry Talbot (Lon Chaney Jr.), the sad-sack tortured hero of 1941's *The Wolf Man*. Sadly, this was just about all movies did with the werewolf, for a very long time.

For many obvious technical reasons, werewolves have been much tougher to portray convincingly onscreen than vampires (fangs) or zombies (shambling). Vampires and sorcerers could morph into bats or wolves in a cloud of smoke and an obvious jump cut, whereas the earliest use of time-lapse photography could add hair and teeth and crude prosthetics to the emerging monster, but anything between a hairy man and a real wolf was simply impossible until special effects makeup fused with mechanics to create eye-popping transformations such as Rob Bottin's work in *The Howling*, or Rick Baker's in *An American Werewolf in London* (both 1981).

Similarly, the modern movie audience was not ready for the werewolf to be anything but a snarling confirmation of their closely held superiority over "primitive" cultures, their painstakingly paved distance from the forest primeval.

In the classic werewolf movie—from *Werewolf Of London* (1935) to *The Wolf Man* to *Curse of the Wolf Man* (1961) and *An American Werewolf in London*—the hero is bitten by a werewolf and is tormented by his changes until he attempts to murder his loved ones, and finally is granted the peace of death . . . until he suffers the curse of a sequel.

Perhaps because it stretches the bounds of plausibility, the werewolf was ripe for parody. In corny potboilers like *I Was a Teenage Werewolf* (1957), *The Shaggy D.A.* (1976) and *Teen Wolf* (1985), the beast is either the epitome of the already out-of-control human victim, or the secret bestial streak that saves an otherwise hopelessly civilized wimp.

It wasn't until *The Howling* that thematic treatments of werewolves caught up to the technical prowess of Hollywood. John Sayles's clever reworking of Brandner's novel takes the amoral self-actualization movements of the '70s to a logical conclusion, as a colony of willing werewolves get in touch with their inner alpha predator, while inhibited, ineffectual humans lie awake in bed, wondering what they're missing. Without dolling them up in puffy shirts or romantic trappings, *The Howling* made werewolves seductive, and offered a bounty of compensation in trade for one's dubiously prized humanity.

The Freudian hothouse of the 1980's spawned a boom of darker, more complex shapeshifters like *The Thing* and Paul Schrader's *Cat People* (1982), which created a fascinating feline shape-shifter clan with its own unique rules, while Neil Jordan's *The Company Of Wolves* (1986) delved into the bloody and sensuous symbolism of fairy tales such as Little Red Riding Hood. At last, we could see lycanthropes at peace with their changeable natures, and the growth of the werewolf into more than just a comment on our inner beast, but on the world of walls we'd built to keep him out.

From there, lycanthropic cinema has been a mixed litter of alphas and runts, from Neil Marshall's savagely underrated *Dog Soldiers* (2002) to the dreamy but declawed *Twilight 2: New Moon* (2010), with plenty of escapist filler like the unfortunate *Van Helsing* (2004). The brief heyday of elaborate and viscerally wrenching mechanical transformations has given way to sleek, rubbery CGI morphing effects that don't seem to occupy space even in the scene itself, let alone in the real world.

In mdern "classic" werewolf flicks like *Wolf* (1994) or *The Wolfman* remake (2010), casting of wolfish alpha loners like Nicholson and Del Toro marks the leads as half-beast before they ever get bit. The affliction allows the aging or inhibited human to shed his human form like a straitjacket. While little is really learned about the borders between men and beasts in these films, Hollywood continues to relish wandering lost in its mystery.

But science always likes to have the last word. And, as usual, it's got answers, just not the kind you were hoping to hear.

Kurt Neumann's 1958 adaptation of George Langelaan's 1957 short story "The Fly" transposed a human scientist's head and hand with that of a housefly, to results that were shocking in their day, but now weirdly the province of comedy gold. Far sillier, but just as rich in creature-feature subtext, cheesy science shockers such as *The Alligator People* (1959), *The Reptile* (1966), and *Sssss!* (1973) proved that human DNA was interchangeable with just about anything.

In David Cronenberg's 1986 reinvention of "The Fly," however, we see a slow, merciless transformation, as an arrogant genius is dismantled by his own creation and remade as a malformed human-insect hybrid. Although a sustained cautionary riff on decay and disease, Jeff Goldblum's wrenching performance is a time capsule of humanity facing the abyss, and losing itself. His Seth Brundle is the new Larry Talbot, with an awful lot more to say.

But no book or film took the shape-shifting scientist further than Paddy Chayevsky's *Altered States* (1980), a loose adaptation (as was *The Day of the Dolphin*) of the real life of renegade cognition researcher John C. Lilly. In Ken Russell's phantasmagoric film version (also 1980), Eddie Jessup (William Hurt) goes spelunking in his own subconscious and unleashes a spree of metamorphoses culled from human ancestral memory. Along the way, he becomes a brutish proto-human and runs amok in a zoo, before devolving into the primordial soup from which all life emerged.

Always learning to expand on its worst mistakes, science has given movies the technological epitome of shape-shifting horror: the T-1000, from James Cameron's *Terminator 2*. Like the monster in Carpenter's *The Thing*, or the digital disease of Agent Smith in *The Matrix* trilogy, the T-1000 effortlessly poses as one of us to mask an unthinkable true form that renders not only humanity, but nature itself, obsolete.

Small wonder that so many of us would like to turn back into wolves.

And science has the answers, there, too. With recent Oscar nominees *District 9* and *Avatar* (both 2009), the xenophobic terror of becoming the other is starkly contrasted with a vision of humankind at last reaching for the power of the gods, and transforming at will into an alien, superbly primal body. While Wikus Van De Merwe is left a hideous outcast by his Lovecraftian transformation, Jake Sully is reborn into a new Eden that has left legions of "Avatards" dreaming of a similar posthuman rebirth with near–Heaven's Gate intensity.

TV + COMICS

The "vast wasteland" of TV is littered with the carcasses of short-lived or aborted shape-shifters such as *Manimal* (1983), but werewolves and other polymorphic antagonists are frequent walk-on staples in any monster-of-the-week show, from *Kolchak* and *Tales from the Crypt* to *The X-Files* and *Buffy the Vampire Slayer*. The tight budgets and schedules of TV shows have generally kept werewolves out of the cathode limelight.

The Wolfman was a regular heavy and frequent cover model of EC and

Warren horror comics, but the stories themselves had little real bite, beyond the surprise of discovering the werewolf was the last person you'd suspect. ("Marie? I think we've trapped the monster! But you're . . . you're . . . AIEEEE!!!")

In the gelded comics of the post-Code era, Marvel tried to inject horror into its spandex-crazy universe with such horror titles as *Tomb of Dracula* and *Werewolf by Night*. Any blood the titular antiheroes shed was scrupulously kept off the page, but it was the medium's commitment to the soap opera serial format that sank any real sense of danger or fear. The only silver bullet that could kill comic book monsters was reader apathy.

The greatest shape-shifter in comics or television is nothing if not a werewolf of science. Bitten by the gamma rays of a nuclear bomb test, meek Bruce Banner originally turned into a raging green behemoth with every nightfall. Creators Stan Lee and Jack Kirby wisely changed the trigger so that Banner became the Hulk whenever he *lost his temper*: which, as a hunted fugitive and brainy purple-pantsed wimp, was bound to happen every few pages.

The original comics incarnation of the Hulk was a tank-tossing ten-foot behemoth; but for television, bodybuilder Lou Ferrigno was the closest they could find, bringing muscle-bound joy to millions. An embodiment of rage itself, the Hulk was yet a pitiful, if not sympathetic creature, with its own identity and a yearning only to find peace. Sadly, whenever he found it, he "died," and again became his hated enemy, Bruce Banner.

This is the heart of the human struggle, at its most garishly colored and emotionally simplified.

But simplicity is the heart of the hunger.

A hunger that—reined in or not—we all share.

WEREWOLVES AND GAMING

Werewolves lurked in the background of horror culture for decades because of technical and creative reasons, playing out the same tired threads, revisiting but seldom reinventing the boy-meets-wolf story arc. It wasn't until 1991 that werewolves got the full mythology treatment, and it didn't come from literature or film.

Mark Rein-Hagen's White Wolf Games, creators of the incredibly popular *World of Darkness* roleplaying milieu, released a Bible of lycanthropy with *Werewolf: The Apocalypse* in 1991. Like its predecessor, *Vampire: The Masquerade*, *Werewolf* cast its players as monsters, and set them loose in a modern-day underworld teeming with hidden monsters.

The Garou lived and fought in packs, and used their shape-shifting powers to defend the natural world (Gaia) and its spirit (Umbra) from the all-consuming forces of the apocalyptic Wyrm. Unlike previous werewolves, the Garou weren't helpless victims or mindless, solitary monsters but unlikely eco-warriors whose primal rage could be channeled as an asset to battle less nature-loving evils.

The development of this mythos may have been influenced by White Wolf's *Vampire* treatment (for which it was successfully sued by Nancy Collins), but Garou and vampires were cast as mortal enemies, and their constant feuding formed the backbone of many *Werewolf* plotlines.

The ripple effect from this deep niche phenomenon spread further than the tie-in novels and anthologies White Wolf put out; the clan structures and blood vendettas between vampires and werewolves formed the basis of the successful *Underworld* (2003) film franchise. *The World of Darkness* game system was retired in 2003, only to rise again with *Werewolf: The Forsaken* (2005).

But the appeal of the beast runs far deeper than the gaming subculture, and its newest expressions are the very public face of stirrings that have run largely unexpressed in all of human culture. The modern primitive and body modification movements spotlighted in the 1990s, and the explosive exposure of Furries in the last decade are but two wild and wooly examples.

Animal cosplay fetishists seem to represent a weird confluence of imprinting on the idealized animal with the totally artificial (furry costumes, like Disneyland characters and sports mascots). Psychology and genetics have barely begun to demystify the cases of people born with the wrong gender, but perhaps it is a predictable symptom of our overcivilized age, that the longng for a reconnection to our lost animal nature would turn the werewolf from a dangerous outsider to the creature we hunger to become.

ACKNOWLEDGEMENTS

Editing this book was a vastly different experience from *Zombies*. For one thing, I hadn't already spent decades spearheading and cheerleading shapeshiftery lit, so it was much more a journey of discovery than a tour I was already prepped to guide.

This time, I also had months to explore the vast range of existing material, and to help provoke tons of original work (as opposed to *Zombies*, which went from deal to delivery in four astoundingly short weeks). So while I had the luxury of time, it came with an embarrassment—make that an avalanche—of riches.

I would like to thank the seriously 100+ people who sent me their stories, or recommended their lists of personal favorites. If you think this book is enormous now, you shoulda seen what MIGHT have been. More fine work than I could possibly fit. And I am enormously grateful.

Once again, my enormous love and thanks to Dinah Dunn and the entire Black Dog and Leventhal team; to Lori Perkins, my ass-busting agent; to Chris Kampe, Anthony Gambole, Scott Bradley, and Doktor Honky for indispensable assistance; to my breathtaking family and friends, without whom I would not be; and to all the writers, estates, and representatives who granted me the right to share these glorious stories.

The opportunity to work with talent of this caliber, and put their work into kaleidoscopic perspective, is one of the great honors and joys of my life. So I'd also like to thank God I lived long enough to have this much unadulterated fun.

Finally, thank you for reading this book. Have a wonderful time.